A NORTON CRITI

TALES OF HE

THE TEXTS OF THE TALES
THE AUTHOR ON HIS CRAFT
CRITICISM

SECOND EDITION

Selected and Edited by

CHRISTOF WEGELIN   HENRY B. WONHAM
              and
UNIVERSITY OF   UNIVERSITY OF
OREGON   OREGON

W • W • NORTON & COMPANY • *New York* • *London*

The text of this book is composed in Fairfield Medium
with the display set in Bernhard Modern.
Composition by PennSet, Inc.
Manufacturing by the Maple-Vail Book Manufacturing Group.
Book design by Antonina Krass.

Library of Congress Cataloging-in-Publication Data

James, Henry, 1843–1916.
    [Short stories. Selections]
    Tales of Henry James : the texts of the tales, the author on his craft, criticism /
        selected and edited by Christof Wegelin and Henry B. Wonham.— 2nd ed.
            p. cm.— (A Norton critical edition)
    Includes bibliographical references (p.).

ISBN 0-393-97710-2

1. United States—Social life and customs—19th century—Fiction. 2. James,
Henry, 1843–1916—Criticism and interpretation. 3. Europe—Social life and
customs—Fiction. 4. Americans—Europe—Fiction. 5. Fiction—Authorship.
6. Short story. I. Wegelin, Christof, 1911–   II. Wonham, Henry B., 1960–
III. Title.

PS2111 .W44 2002
813'.4—dc21   2002026310

W. W. Norton & Company, Inc., 500 Fifth Avenue, New York, N.Y. 10110
www.wwnorton.com

W. W. Norton & Company Ltd., Castle House, 75/76 Wells Street,
London W1T 3QT

3 4 5 6 7 8 9 0

The Editors

CHRISTOF WEGELIN is Professor of English Emeritus at the University of Oregon. He received his Ph.D. from the Johns Hopkins University. He has also taught at Princeton University and at the universities of Göttingen, Zurich, and Regensburg. He is the author of *The Idea of Europe in Henry James* and of articles on Hawthorne, Wharton, Hemingway, and others.

HENRY B. WONHAM is Associate Professor of English at the University of Oregon. He received his Ph.D. from the University of Virginia. He has been a Fulbright Lecturer at the University of Mannheim and at the Charles University in Prague. He is the author of several books on American literature and culture, including a forthcoming study entitled *Playing the Races: Ethnic Caricature and American Literary Realism.*

Contents

Criticism   421

Contents

Criticism 421

Preface to the First Edition

Henry James published his first story in 1864 and in the half-century that followed produced twenty novels and a hundred and twelve shorter narratives that he usually called tales. Although probably best known for his novels, he took his shorter works just as seriously: when he came to represent his life's work in the so-called New York Edition he called it *The Novels and Tales of Henry James*. Some of the novels are short and some of the tales very long, so that the distinction between them may seem arbitrary. Of course length is not the only difference between novels and what today we call short stories. But publishing conditions forced James to be concerned with questions of length, and the nine tales in the present collection illustrate his range in this regard. "Brooksmith," with barely eight thousand words, is one of James's shortest tales; "The Aspern Papers," with almost forty thousand, approaches novel length. The nine tales also exemplify other formal variations. They are told from different points of view, for instance, in the first or third person, by narrators either detached from the action or participating in it to varying degrees. Some of James's favorite subjects and themes are here—the international scene, problems encountered by writers and artists, the human being haunted by visible and invisible ghosts, the exposure of children in the adult world, tyranny in its many guises, among them the willingness to make use of others, which is the closest approach Jamesian characters make to villainy.

The nine stories span most of James's long career. They are reproduced here as they first appeared in books (all but one originally appeared in magazines) and presumably as proofread by the author himself. The texts here presented therefore illustrate the development of his prose style. Occasional inconsistencies in spelling, e.g., *dependant* in "The Middle Years" and *dependent* in "The Beast in the Jungle," have been left standing. But rare typographical errors have been corrected silently, quotation marks have been brought into consistent accord with American usage—double instead of single—and the occasional and now strange printing of contractions—e.g., "had n't" for "hadn't" or "did n't" for "didn't"—normalized.

James was also a practicing critic throughout his career, and his essay "The Art of Fiction" is here offered as an early statement of principles that he never abandoned. Although the essay speaks of novelists and novels, it concerns fiction in general, including short forms. Problems of length and other technical problems of short fiction are discussed in the prefaces that James wrote much later for the New York Edition. There he often "remounts the stream of time" or "the stream of composition" to recall the source of a particular story, the *donnée* or "germ" from which it evolved, and sometimes the thought processes by which it did so. Most of the passages in the prefaces that bear on the tales in this collection, as well as pertinent passages from James's notebooks and letters, are included in the section entitled "The Author on His Craft."

James continues to receive more critical attention than most other American authors. Some general essays on his background and his work, as well as essays on individual stories, are here reproduced. In selecting them my aim has been to enlarge and sharpen the reader's sense of James's mind and artistry. Choosing a few pages out of the enormous mass available has made painful decisions necessary, and readers dismayed by omissions must draw what comfort they can from the editor's fellowship.

The staffs of the University of Oregon Library, of the Department of Rare Books and Special Collections of the Princeton University Library, and of the University of Oregon English Department have been helpful in many ways. Substantial assistance and advice has come from colleagues and students, among them above all Heather Derby, E. G. Moll, Jeffrey Porter, A. K. Weatherhead, and Oliver Willard, and from W. W. Norton's own Barry Wade. To all of them thanks.

C. W.

Preface to the Second Edition

The nearly twenty years that have elapsed since Christof Wegelin's *Tales of Henry James: A Norton Critical Edition* made its debut in 1984 have been eventful ones for James studies. While the canon of American literature has undergone radical change, James has emerged all the more clearly as an indispensable figure, and he continues to receive as much critical attention as any American writer. To be sure, interest in James has evolved with the times, and contemporary debates about his work are more likely to focus on issues of "homosexual panic" or the rise of information technology than on the "international theme." In preparing the second edition of the *Tales of Henry James*, we have tried to offer readers an impression of the richness of James studies, past and present, by selecting texts, background material, and critical excerpts that touch on as many points of interest as possible. This approach has led us to preserve large portions of the first edition intact, but we have also introduced changes to give a new generation of James readers a sense of his uncanny contemporaneity. To this end, we have reluctantly omitted "An International Episode" in order to make room for "In the Cage," a tale that engages James's complex attitudes toward gender, class, and emerging technologies associated with modern communication. The most significant revisions to the first edition appear in the "Criticism" section, which includes ten new selections by writers who have helped to establish the terms of debate about James's tales during the last quarter century. While they are by no means the most recent or the most fashionable examples of James criticism, we hope the selections provided here will expose readers to an exciting variety of critical approaches to his work. The "painful decisions" that produced the first edition of this book have only become more painful with the passage of time and the great outpouring of intelligent commentary on the works of "the master." Readers dismayed by omissions and difficult choices are thus once again invited to draw what comfort they can from the fellowship of the editors.

In addition to the assistance of those institutions and individuals already mentioned in the preface to the first edition, we have received very helpful advice from a variety of scholars, including

Susan Griffin, John Carlos Rowe, Eric Haralson, Michael Anesko, Ross Posnock, and Gary Scharnhorst. Connie Wonham proofread the entire manuscript and thus saved us and Henry James from numerous embarrassing errors. Carol Bemis and Brian Baker of Norton have also provided unstinting guidance and support. We thank them all for their generosity.

C. W., H. W.

The Texts of
THE TALES

Daisy Miller: A Study†

I

At the little town of Vevey, in Switzerland, there is a particularly comfortable hotel. There are, indeed, many hotels; for the entertainment of tourists is the business of the place, which, as many travellers will remember, is seated upon the edge of a remarkably blue lake[1]—a lake that it behoves every tourist to visit. The shore of the lake presents an unbroken array of establishments of this order, of every category, from the "grand hotel" of the newest fashion, with a chalk-white front, a hundred balconies, and a dozen flags flying from its roof, to the little Swiss *pension* of an elder day, with its name inscribed in German-looking lettering upon a pink or yellow wall, and an awkward summer-house in the angle of the garden. One of the hotels at Vevey, however, is famous, even classical, being distinguished from many of its upstart neighbors by an air both of luxury and of maturity. In this region, in the month of June, American travellers are extremely numerous; it may be said, indeed, that Vevey assumes at this period some of the characteristics of an American watering-place. There are sights and sounds which evoke a vision, an echo, of Newport and Saratoga.[2] There is a flitting hither and thither of "stylish" young girls, a rustling of muslin flounces, a rattle of dance-music in the morning hours, a sound of high-pitched voices at all times. You receive an impression of these things at the excellent inn of the "Trois Couronnes,"[3] and are transported in fancy to the Ocean House or to Congress Hall. But at the "Trois Couronnes," it must be added, there are other features that are much at variance with these suggestions: neat German waiters, who look like secretaries of legation; Russian prin-

---

† "Daisy Miller: A Study" first appeared in *Cornhill Magazine*, June–July 1878. Its first appearance in a book was in America in Harper's Half-Hour Series as volume I of *Daisy Miller: A Study/An International Episode/Four Meetings*, published in November 1878. James was in England at the time and did not supervise this edition. The text reprinted here follows the first English Edition published under the same title by Macmillan and Co. in February 1879.
1. Lake Geneva.
2. Newport, Rhode Island, and Saratoga Springs, New York, were resorts.
3. "Three Crowns." The Ocean House and Congress Hall were hotels in Newport and Saratoga, respectively.

cesses sitting in the garden; little Polish boys walking about, held
by the hand, with their governors; a view of the snowy crest of the
Dent du Midi and the picturesque towers of the Castle of Chillon.[4]

I hardly know whether it was the analogies or the differences that
were uppermost in the mind of a young American, who, two or
three years ago, sat in the garden of the "Trois Couronnes," looking
about him, rather idly, at some of the graceful objects I have mentioned. It was a beautiful summer morning, and in whatever fashion
the young American looked at things, they must have seemed to
him charming. He had come from Geneva the day before, by the
little steamer, to see his aunt, who was staying at the hotel—Geneva having been for a long time his place of residence. But his
aunt had a headache—his aunt had almost always a headache—
and now she was shut up in her room, smelling camphor, so that
he was at liberty to wander about. He was some seven-and-twenty
years of age; when his friends spoke of him, they usually said that
he was at Geneva, "studying." When his enemies spoke of him they
said—but, after all, he had no enemies; he was an extremely amiable fellow, and universally liked. What I should say is, simply, that
when certain persons spoke of him they affirmed that the reason
of his spending so much time at Geneva was that he was extremely
devoted to a lady who lived there—a foreign lady—a person older
than himself. Very few Americans—indeed I think none—had ever
seen this lady, about whom there were some singular stories. But
Winterbourne had an old attachment for the little metropolis of
Calvinism;[5] he had been put to school there as a boy, and he had
afterwards gone to college there—circumstances which had led to
his forming a great many youthful friendships. Many of these he
had kept, and they were a source of great satisfaction to him.

After knocking at his aunt's door and learning that she was indisposed, he had taken a walk about the town, and then he had
come in to his breakfast. He had now finished his breakfast; but he
was drinking a small cup of coffee, which had been served to him
on a little table in the garden by one of the waiters who looked like
an *attaché*. At last he finished his coffee and lit a cigarette. Presently
a small boy came walking along the path—an urchin of nine or ten.
The child, who was diminutive for his years, had an aged expression
of countenance, a pale complexion, and sharp little features. He
was dressed in knickerbockers, with red stockings, which displayed
his poor little spindleshanks; he also wore a brilliant red cravat.

---

4. A medieval castle built on a small rocky island in Lake Geneva, made famous among
English speakers by Byron's poem "The Prisoner of Chillon" (1816). The Dent du Midi
is a mountain south of Vevey (hence its name: "tooth of the south").
5. Geneva, where the French reformer Jean Calvin (1509–1564), the founder of the the-
ological system of Calvinism, organized a Protestant republic.

He carried in his hand a long alpenstock, the sharp point of which he thrust into everything that he approached—the flower-beds, the garden-benches, the trains of the ladies' dresses. In front of Winterbourne he paused, looking at him with a pair of bright, penetrating little eyes.

"Will you give me a lump of sugar?" he asked, in a sharp, hard little voice—a voice immature, and yet, somehow, not young.

Winterbourne glanced at the small table near him, on which his coffee-service rested, and saw that several morsels of sugar remained. "Yes, you may take one," he answered; "but I don't think sugar is good for little boys."

This little boy stepped forward and carefully selected three of the coveted fragments, two of which he buried in the pocket of his knickerbockers, depositing the other as promptly in another place. He poked his alpenstock, lance-fashion, into Winterbourne's bench, and tried to crack the lump of sugar with his teeth.

"Oh, blazes; it's har-r-d!" he exclaimed, pronouncing the adjective in a peculiar manner.

Winterbourne had immediately perceived that he might have the honour of claiming him as a fellow-countryman. "Take care you don't hurt your teeth," he said, paternally.

"I haven't got any teeth to hurt. They have all come out. I have only got seven teeth. My mother counted them last night, and one came out right afterwards. She said she'd slap me if any more came out. I can't help it. It's this old Europe. It's the climate that makes them come out. In America they didn't come out. It's these hotels."

Winterbourne was much amused. "If you eat three lumps of sugar, your mother will certainly slap you," he said.

"She's got to give me some candy, then," rejoined his young interlocutor. "I can't get any candy here—any American candy. American candy's the best candy."

"And are American little boys the best little boys?" asked Winterbourne.

"I don't know. I'm an American boy," said the child.

"I see you are one of the best!" laughed Winterbourne.

"Are you an American man?" pursued this vivacious infant. And then, on Winterbourne's affirmative reply—"American men are the best," he declared.

His companion thanked him for the compliment; and the child, who had now got astride of his alpenstock, stood looking about him, while he attacked a second lump of sugar. Winterbourne wondered if he himself had been like this in his infancy, for he had been brought to Europe at about this age.

"Here comes my sister!" cried the child, in a moment. "She's an American girl."

Winterbourne looked along the path and saw a beautiful young lady advancing. "American girls are the best girls," he said, cheerfully, to his young companion.

"My sister ain't the best!" the child declared. "She's always blowing at me."

"I imagine that is your fault, not hers," said Winterbourne. The young lady meanwhile had drawn near. She was dressed in white muslin, with a hundred frills and flounces, and knots of pale-coloured ribbon. She was bare-headed; but she balanced in her hand a large parasol, with a deep border of embroidery; and she was strikingly, admirably pretty. "How pretty they are!" thought Winterbourne, straightening himself in his seat, as if he were prepared to rise.

The young lady paused in front of his bench, near the parapet of the garden, which overlooked the lake. The little boy had now converted his alpenstock into a vaulting-pole, by the aid of which he was springing about in the gravel, and kicking it up not a little.

"Randolph," said the young lady, "what *are* you doing?"

"I'm going up the Alps," replied Randolph. "This is the way!" And he gave another little jump, scattering the pebbles about Winterbourne's ears.

"That's the way they come down," said Winterbourne.

"He's an American man!" cried Randolph, in his little hard voice.

The young lady gave no heed to this announcement, but looked straight at her brother. "Well, I guess you had better be quiet," she simply observed.

It seemed to Winterbourne that he had been in a manner presented. He got up and stepped slowly towards the young girl, throwing away his cigarette. "This little boy and I have made acquaintance," he said, with great civility. In Geneva, as he had been perfectly aware, a young man was not at liberty to speak to a young unmarried lady except under certain rarely-occurring conditions; but here at Vevey, what conditions could be better than these?—a pretty American girl coming and standing in front of you in a garden. This pretty American girl, however, on hearing Winterbourne's observation, simply glanced at him; she then turned her head and looked over the parapet, at the lake and the opposite mountains. He wondered whether he had gone too far; but he decided that he must advance farther, rather than retreat. While he was thinking of something else to say, the young lady turned to the little boy again.

"I should like to know where you got that pole," she said.

"I bought it!" responded Randolph.

"You don't mean to say you're going to take it to Italy."

"Yes, I am going to take it to Italy!" the child declared.

The young girl glanced over the front of her dress, and smoothed out a knot or two of ribbon. Then she rested her eyes upon the prospect again. "Well, I guess you had better leave it somewhere," she said, after a moment.

"Are you going to Italy?" Winterbourne inquired, in a tone of great respect.

The young lady glanced at him again.

"Yes, sir," she replied. And she said nothing more.

"Are you—a—going over the Simplon?" Winterbourne pursued, a little embarrassed.

"I don't know," she said. "I suppose it's some mountain. Randolph, what mountain are we going over?"

"Going where?" the child demanded.

"To Italy," Winterbourne explained.

"I don't know," said Randolph. "I don't want to go to Italy. I want to go to America."

"Oh, Italy is a beautiful place!" rejoined the young man.

"Can you get candy there?" Randolph loudly inquired.

"I hope not," said his sister. "I guess you have had enough candy, and mother thinks so too."

"I haven't had any for ever so long—for a hundred weeks!" cried the boy, still jumping about.

The young lady inspected her flounces and smoothed her ribbons again; and Winterbourne presently risked an observation upon the beauty of the view. He was ceasing to be embarrassed, for he had begun to perceive that she was not in the least embarrassed herself. There had not been the slightest alteration in her charming complexion; she was evidently neither offended nor fluttered. If she looked another way when he spoke to her, and seemed not particularly to hear him, this was simply her habit, her manner. Yet, as he talked a little more, and pointed out some of the objects of interest in the view, with which she appeared quite unacquainted, she gradually gave him more of the benefit of her glance; and then he saw that this glance was perfectly direct and unshrinking. It was not, however, what would have been called an immodest glance, for the young girl's eyes were singularly honest and fresh. They were wonderfully pretty eyes; and, indeed, Winterbourne had not seen for a long time anything prettier than his fair countrywoman's various features—her complexion, her nose, her ears, her teeth. He had a great relish for feminine beauty; he was addicted to observing and analysing it; and as regards this young lady's face he made several observations. It was not at all insipid, but it was not exactly expressive; and though it was eminently delicate Winterbourne mentally accused it—very forgivingly—of a want of finish. He thought it very possible that Master Randolph's sister was a coquette; he was sure she had a spirit of her own; but in her bright, sweet, superficial little visage there was no mockery, no irony. Before long it became obvious that she was much disposed towards conversation. She told him that they were going to Rome for the winter—she and her mother and Randolph. She asked him if he was a "real American"; she wouldn't have taken him for one; he seemed more like a German—this was said after a little hesitation, especially when he spoke. Winterbourne, laughing, answered that he had met Germans who spoke like Americans; but that he had not, so far as he remembered, met an American who spoke like a German. Then he asked her if she would not be more comfortable in sitting upon the bench which he had just quitted. She answered that she liked standing up and walking about; but she presently sat down. She told him she was from New York State—"if you know where that is." Winterbourne learned more about her by catching hold of her small, slippery brother and making him stand a few minutes by his side.

"Tell me your name, my boy," he said.

"Randolph C. Miller," said the boy, sharply. "And I'll tell you her name"; and he levelled his alpenstock at his sister.

"You had better wait till you are asked!" said this young lady, calmly.

"I should like very much to know your name," said Winterbourne.

"Her name is Daisy Miller!" cried the child. "But that isn't her real name; that isn't her name on her cards."

"It's a pity you haven't got one of my cards!" said Miss Miller.

"Her real name is Annie P. Miller," the boy went on.

"Ask him *his* name," said his sister, indicating Winterbourne.

But on this point Randolph seemed perfectly indifferent; he continued to supply information with regard to his own family. "My father's name is Ezra B. Miller," he announced. "My father ain't in Europe; my father's in a better place than Europe."

Winterbourne imagined for a moment that this was the manner in which the child had been taught to intimate that Mr. Miller had been removed to the sphere of celestial rewards. But Randolph immediately added, "My father's in Schenectady. He's got a big business. My father's rich, you bet."

"Well!" ejaculated Miss Miller, lowering her parasol and looking at the embroidered border. Winterbourne presently released the child, who departed, dragging his alpenstock along the path. "He doesn't like Europe," said the young girl. "He wants to go back."

"To Schenectady, you mean?"

"Yes; he wants to go right home. He hasn't got any boys here. There is one boy here, but he always goes round with a teacher; they won't let him play."

"And your brother hasn't any teacher?" Winterbourne inquired.

"Mother thought of getting him one, to travel round with us. There was a lady told her of a very good teacher; an American lady—perhaps you know her—Mrs. Sanders. I think she came from Boston. She told her of this teacher, and we thought of getting him to travel round with us. But Randolph said he didn't want a teacher travelling round with us. He said he wouldn't have lessons when he was in the cars.[6] And we *are* in the cars about half the time. There was an English lady we met in the cars—I think her name was Miss Featherstone; perhaps you know her. She wanted to know why I didn't give Randolph lessons—give him "instruction," she called it. I guess he could give me more instruction than I could give him. He's very smart."

"Yes," said Winterbourne; "he seems very smart."

"Mother's going to get a teacher for him as soon as we get to Italy. Can you get good teachers in Italy?"

"Very good, I should think," said Winterbourne.

"Or else she's going to find some school. He ought to learn some more. He's only nine. He's going to college." And in this way Miss Miller continued to converse upon the affairs of her family, and upon other topics. She sat there with her extremely pretty hands, ornamented with very brilliant rings, folded in her lap, and with her pretty eyes now resting upon those of Winterbourne, now wandering over the garden, the people who passed by, and the beautiful view. She talked to Winterbourne as if she had known him a long time. He found it very pleasant. It was many years since he had heard a young girl talk so much. It might have been said of this unknown young lady, who had come and sat down beside him upon a bench, that she chattered. She was very quiet, she sat in a charming tranquil attitude; but her lips and her eyes were constantly moving. She had a soft, slender, agreeable voice, and her tone was decidedly sociable. She gave Winterbourne a history of her movements and intentions, and those of her mother and brother, in Europe, and enumerated, in particular, the various hotels at which they had stopped. "That English lady in the cars," she said—"Miss Featherstone—asked me if we didn't all live in hotels in America. I told her I had never been in so many hotels in my life as since I came to Europe. I have never seen so many—it's nothing but hotels." But Miss Miller did not make this remark with a querulous accent; she appeared to be in the best humour with everything. She declared that the hotels were very good, when once you got used to their ways, and that Europe was perfectly sweet. She was not disappointed—not a bit. Perhaps it was because she had heard so

6. Railroad cars.

much about it before. She had ever so many intimate friends that had been there ever so many times. And then she had had ever so many dresses and things from Paris. Whenever she put on a Paris dress she felt as if she were in Europe.

"It was a kind of a wishing-cap," said Winterbourne.

"Yes," said Miss Miller, without examining this analogy; "it always made me wish I was here. But I needn't have done that for dresses. I am sure they send all the pretty ones to America; you see the most frightful things here. The only thing I don't like," she proceeded, "is the society. There isn't any society; or, if there is, I don't know where it keeps itself. Do you? I suppose there is some society some-where, but I haven't seen anything of it. I'm very fond of society, and I have always had a great deal of it. I don't mean only in Sche-nectady, but in New York. I used to go to New York every winter. In New York I had lots of society. Last winter I had seventeen dinners given me; and three of them were by gentlemen," added Daisy Miller. "I have more friends in New York than in Sche-nectady—more gentlemen friends; and more young lady friends too," she resumed in a moment. She paused again for an instant; she was looking at Winterbourne with all her prettiness in her lively eyes and in her light, slightly monotonous smile. "I have always had," she said, "a great deal of gentlemen's society."

Poor Winterbourne was amused, perplexed, and decidedly charmed. He had never yet heard a young girl express herself in just this fashion; never, at least, save in cases where to say such things seemed a kind of demonstrative evidence of a certain laxity of deportment. And yet was he to accuse Miss Daisy Miller of actual or potential *inconduite*,[7] as they said at Geneva? He felt that he had lived at Geneva so long that he had lost a good deal; he had become dishabituated to the American tone. Never, indeed, since he had grown old enough to appreciate things, had he encountered a young American girl of so pronounced a type as this. Certainly she was very charming; but how deucedly sociable! Was she simply a pretty girl from New York State—were they all like that, the pretty girls who had a good deal of gentlemen's society? Or was she also a designing, an audacious, an unscrupulous young person? Winter-bourne had lost his instinct in this matter, and his reason could not help him. Miss Daisy Miller looked extremely innocent. Some peo-ple had told him that, after all, American girls were exceedingly innocent; and others had told him that, after all, they were not. He was inclined to think Miss Daisy Miller was a flirt—a pretty Amer-ican flirt. He had never, as yet, had any relations with young ladies of this category. He had known, here in Europe, two or three

7. Misconduct.

women—persons older than Miss Daisy Miller, and provided, for respectability's sake, with husbands—who were great coquettes— dangerous, terrible women, with whom one's relations were liable to take a serious turn. But this young girl was not a coquette in that sense; she was very unsophisticated; she was only a pretty American flirt. Winterbourne was almost grateful for having found the formula that applied to Miss Daisy Miller. He leaned back in his seat; he remarked to himself that she had the most charming nose he had ever seen; he wondered what were the regular conditions and limitations of one's intercourse with a pretty American flirt. It presently became apparent that he was on the way to learn.

"Have you been to that old castle?" asked the young girl, pointing with her parasol to the far-gleaming walls of the Château de Chillon.

"Yes, formerly, more than once," said Winterbourne. "You too, I suppose, have seen it?"

"No; we haven't been there. I want to go there dreadfully. Of course I mean to go there. I wouldn't go away from here without having seen that old castle."

"It's a very pretty excursion," said Winterbourne, "and very easy to make. You can drive, you know, or you can go by the little steamer."

"You can go in the cars," said Miss Miller.

"Yes; you can go in the cars," Winterbourne assented.

"Our courier[8] says they take you right up to the castle," the young girl continued. "We were going last week; but my mother gave out. She suffers dreadfully from dyspepsia. She said she couldn't go. Randolph wouldn't go either; he says he doesn't think much of old castles. But I guess we'll go this week, if we can get Randolph."

"Your brother is not interested in ancient monuments?" Winterbourne inquired, smiling.

"He says he don't care much about old castles. He's only nine. He wants to stay at the hotel. Mother's afraid to leave him alone, and the courier won't stay with him; so we haven't been to many places. But it will be too bad if we don't go up there." And Miss Miller pointed again at the Château de Chillon.

"I should think it might be arranged," said Winterbourne. "Couldn't you get some one to stay—for the afternoon—with Randolph?"

Miss Miller looked at him a moment; and then, very placidly— "I wish *you* would stay with him!" she said.

Winterbourne hesitated a moment. "I would much rather go to Chillon with you."

---

8. Man hired to take charge of travel arrangements.

"With me?" asked the young girl, with the same placidity.

She didn't rise, blushing, as a young girl at Geneva would have done; and yet Winterbourne, conscious that he had been very bold, thought it possible she was offended. "With your mother," he answered very respectfully.

But it seemed that both his audacity and his respect were lost upon Miss Daisy Miller. "I guess my mother won't go, after all," she said. "She don't like to ride round in the afternoon. But did you really mean what you said just now; that you would like to go up there?"

"Most earnestly," Winterbourne declared.

"Then we may arrange it. If mother will stay with Randolph, I guess Eugenio will."

"Eugenio?" the young man inquired.

"Eugenio's our courier. He doesn't like to stay with Randolph; he's the most fastidious man I ever saw. But he's a splendid courier. I guess he'll stay at home with Randolph if mother does, and then we can go to the castle."

Winterbourne reflected for an instant as lucidly as possible— "we" could only mean Miss Daisy Miller and himself. This programme seemed almost too agreeable for credence; he felt as if he ought to kiss the young lady's hand. Possibly he would have done so—and quite spoiled the project; but at this moment another person—presumably Eugenio—appeared. A tall, handsome man, with superb whiskers, wearing a velvet morning-coat and a brilliant watch-chain, approached Miss Miller, looking sharply at her companion. "Oh, Eugenio!" said Miss Miller, with the friendliest accent.

Eugenio had looked at Winterbourne from head to foot; he now bowed gravely to the young lady. "I have the honour to inform mademoiselle that luncheon is upon the table."

Miss Miller slowly rose. "See here, Eugenio," she said. "I'm going to that old castle, any way."

"To the Château de Chillon, mademoiselle?" the courier inquired. "Mademoiselle has made arrangements?" he added, in a tone which struck Winterbourne as very impertinent.

Eugenio's tone apparently threw, even to Miss Miller's own apprehension, a slightly ironical light upon the young girl's situation. She turned to Winterbourne, blushing a little—a very little. "You won't back out?" she said.

"I shall not be happy till we go!" he protested.

"And you are staying in this hotel?" she went on. "And you are really an American?"

The courier stood looking at Winterbourne, offensively. The young man, at least, thought his manner of looking an offence to Miss Miller; it conveyed an imputation that she "picked up" acquaintances. "I shall have the honour of presenting to you a person who will tell you all about me," he said smiling, and referring to his aunt.

"Oh, well, we'll go some day," said Miss Miller. And she gave him a smile and turned away. She put up her parasol and walked back to the inn beside Eugenio. Winterbourne stood looking after her; and as she moved away, drawing her muslin furbelows over the gravel, said to himself that she had the *tournure*[9] of a princess.

II

He had, however, engaged to do more than proved feasible, in promising to present his aunt, Mrs. Costello, to Miss Daisy Miller. As soon as the former lady had got better of her headache he waited upon her in her apartment; and, after the proper inquiries in regard to her health, he asked her if she had observed, in the hotel, an American family—a mamma, a daughter, and a little boy.

"And a courier?" said Mrs. Costello. "Oh, yes, I have observed them. Seen them—heard them—and kept out of their way." Mrs. Costello was a widow with a fortune; a person of much distinction, who frequently intimated that, if she were not so dreadfully liable to sick-headaches, she would probably have left a deeper impress upon her time. She had a long pale face, a high nose, and a great deal of very striking white hair, which she wore in large puffs and *rouleaux*[1] over the top of her head. She had two sons married in New York, and another who was now in Europe. This young man was amusing himself at Homburg,[2] and, though he was on his travels, was rarely perceived to visit any particular city at the moment selected by his mother for her own appearance there. Her nephew, who had come up to Vevey expressly to see her, was therefore more attentive than those who, as she said, were nearer to her. He had imbibed at Geneva the idea that one must always be attentive to one's aunt. Mrs. Costello had not seen him for many years, and she was greatly pleased with him, manifesting her approbation by initiating him into many of the secrets of that social sway which, as she gave him to understand, she exerted in the American capital.[3] She admitted that she was very exclusive; but, if he were acquainted with New York, he would see that one had to be. And her picture of the minutely hierarchical constitution of the society of that city, which she presented to him in many different lights, was, to Winterbourne's imagination, almost oppressively striking.

9. Figure, looks.
1. Coils.
2. A German resort near Frankfurt am Main.
3. The social capital, i.e., New York City.

He immediately perceived, from her tone, that Miss Daisy Miller's place in the social scale was low. "I am afraid you don't approve of them," he said.

"They are very common," Mrs. Costello declared. "They are the sort of Americans that one does one's duty by not—not accepting."

"Ah, you don't accept them?" said the young man.

"I can't, my dear Frederick. I would if I could, but I can't."

"The young girl is very pretty," said Winterbourne, in a moment.

"Of course she's pretty. But she is very common."

"I see what you mean, of course," said Winterbourne, after another pause.

"She has that charming look that they all have," his aunt resumed. "I can't think where they pick it up; and she dresses in perfection—no, you don't know how well she dresses. I can't think where they get their taste."

"But, my dear aunt, she is not, after all, a Comanche savage."

"She is a young lady," said Mrs. Costello, "who has an intimacy with her mamma's courier?"

"An intimacy with the courier?" the young man demanded.

"Oh, the mother is just as bad! They treat the courier like a familiar friend—like a gentleman. I shouldn't wonder if he dines with them. Very likely they have never seen a man with such good manners, such fine clothes, so like a gentleman. He probably corresponds to the young lady's idea of a Count. He sits with them in the garden, in the evening. I think he smokes."

Winterbourne listened with interest to these disclosures; they helped him to make up his mind about Miss Daisy. Evidently she was rather wild. "Well," he said, "I am not a courier, and yet she was very charming to me."

"You had better have said at first," said Mrs. Costello with dignity, "that you had made her acquaintance."

"We simply met in the garden, and we talked a bit."

"*Tout bonnement!*[4] And pray what did you say?"

"I said I should take the liberty of introducing her to my admirable aunt."

"I am much obliged to you."

"It was to guarantee my respectability," said Winterbourne.

"And pray who is to guarantee hers?"

"Ah, you are cruel!" said the young man. "She's a very nice girl."

"You don't say that as if you believed it," Mrs. Costello observed.

"She is completely uncultivated," Winterbourne went on. "But she is wonderfully pretty, and, in short, she is very nice. To prove that I believe it, I am going to take her to the Château de Chillon."

4. Quite simply. Just like that!

"You two are going off there together? I should say it proved just the contrary. How long had you known her, may I ask, when this interesting project was formed? You haven't been twenty-four hours in the house."

"I had known her half-an-hour!" said Winterbourne, smiling.

"Dear me!" cried Mrs. Costello. "What a dreadful girl!"

Her nephew was silent for some moments.

"You really think, then," he began, earnestly, and with a desire for trustworthy information—"you really think that—" But he paused again.

"Think what, sir?" said his aunt.

"That she is the sort of young lady who expects a man—sooner or later—to carry her off?"

"I haven't the least idea what such young ladies expect a man to do. But I really think that you had better not meddle with little American girls that are uncultivated, as you call them. You have lived too long out of the country. You will be sure to make some great mistake. You are too innocent."

"My dear aunt, I am not so innocent," said Winterbourne, smiling and curling his moustache.

"You are too guilty, then!"

Winterbourne continued to curl his moustache, meditatively. "You won't let the poor girl know you then?" he asked at last.

"Is it literally true that she is going to the Château de Chillon with you?"

"I think that she fully intends it."

"Then, my dear Frederick," said Mrs. Costello, "I must decline the honour of her acquaintance. I am an old woman, but I am not too old—thank Heaven—to be shocked!"

"But don't they all do these things—the young girls in America?" Winterbourne inquired.

Mrs. Costello stared a moment. "I should like to see my grand-daughters do them!" she declared, grimly.

This seemed to throw some light upon the matter, for Winterbourne remembered to have heard that his pretty cousins in New York were "tremendous flirts." If, therefore, Miss Daisy Miller exceeded the liberal license allowed to these young ladies, it was probable that anything might be expected of her. Winterbourne was impatient to see her again, and he was vexed with himself that, by instinct, he should not appreciate her justly.

Though he was impatient to see her, he hardly knew what he should say to her about his aunt's refusal to become acquainted with her; but he discovered, promptly enough, that with Miss Daisy Miller there was no great need of walking on tiptoe. He found her that evening in the garden, wandering about in the warm starlight, like an indolent sylph, and swinging to and fro the largest fan he had ever beheld. It was ten o'clock. He had dined with his aunt, had been sitting with her since dinner, and had just taken leave of her till the morrow. Miss Daisy Miller seemed very glad to see him; she declared it was the longest evening she had ever passed.

"Have you been all alone?" he asked.

"I have been walking round with mother. But mother gets tired walking round," she answered.

"Has she gone to bed?"

"No; she doesn't like to go to bed," said the young girl. "She doesn't sleep—not three hours. She says she doesn't know how she lives. She's dreadfully nervous. I guess she sleeps more than she thinks. She's gone somewhere after Randolph; she wants to try to get him to go to bed. He doesn't like to go to bed."

"Let us hope she will persuade him," observed Winterbourne.

"She will talk to him all she can; but she doesn't like her to talk to him," said Miss Daisy, opening her fan. "She's going to try to get Eugenio to talk to him. But he isn't afraid of Eugenio. Eugenio's a splendid courier, but he can't make much impression on Randolph! I don't believe he'll go to bed before eleven." It appeared that Randolph's vigil was in fact triumphantly prolonged, for Winterbourne strolled about with the young girl for some time without meeting her mother. "I have been looking round for that lady you want to introduce me to," his companion resumed. "She's your aunt." Then, on Winterbourne's admitting the fact, and expressing some curiosity as to how she had learned it, she said she had heard all about Mrs. Costello from the chambermaid. She was very quiet and very *comme il faut*;[5] she wore white puffs; she spoke to no one, and she never dined at the *table d'hôte*.[6] Every two days she had a headache. "I think that's a lovely description, headache and all!" said Miss Daisy, chattering along in her thin, gay voice. "I want to know her ever so much. I know just what *your* aunt would be; I know I should like her. She would be very exclusive. I like a lady to be exclusive; I'm dying to be exclusive myself. Well, we *are* exclusive, mother and I. We don't speak to every one—or they don't speak to us. I suppose it's about the same thing. Any way, I shall be ever so glad to know your aunt."

Winterbourne was embarrassed. "She would be most happy," he said; "but I am afraid those headaches will interfere."

The young girl looked at him through the dusk. "But I suppose she doesn't have a headache every day," she said, sympathetically.

5. Proper.
6. A common table in the hotel dining room.

Winterbourne was silent a moment. "She tells me she does," he answered at last—not knowing what to say.

Miss Daisy Miller stopped and stood looking at him. Her prettiness was still visible in the darkness; she was opening and closing her enormous fan. "She doesn't want to know me!" she said, suddenly. "Why don't you say so? You needn't be afraid. I'm not afraid!" And she gave a little laugh.

Winterbourne fancied there was a tremor in her voice; he was touched, shocked, mortified by it. "My dear young lady," he protested, "she knows no one. It's her wretched health."

The young girl walked on a few steps, laughing still. "You needn't be afraid," she repeated. "Why should she want to know me?" Then she paused again; she was close to the parapet of the garden, and in front of her was the starlit lake. There was a vague sheen upon its surface, and in the distance were dimly-seen mountain forms. Daisy Miller looked out upon the mysterious prospect, and then she gave another little laugh. "Gracious! she *is* exclusive!" she said. Winterbourne wondered whether she was seriously wounded; and for a moment almost wished that her sense of injury might be such as to make it becoming in him to attempt to reassure and comfort her. He had a pleasant sense that she would be very approachable for consolatory purposes. He felt then, for the instant, quite ready to sacrifice his aunt, conversationally; to admit that she was a proud, rude woman, and to declare that they needn't mind her. But before he had time to commit himself to this perilous mixture of gallantry and impiety, the young lady, resuming her walk, gave an exclamation in quite another tone. "Well; here's mother! I guess she hasn't got Randolph to go to bed." The figure of a lady appeared, at a distance, very indistinct in the darkness, and advancing with a slow and wavering movement. Suddenly it seemed to pause.

"Are you sure it is your mother? Can you distinguish her in this thick dusk?" Winterbourne asked.

"Well!" cried Miss Daisy Miller, with a laugh, "I guess I know my own mother. And when she has got on my shawl, too! She is always wearing my things."

The lady in question, ceasing to advance, hovered vaguely about the spot at which she had checked her steps.

"I am afraid your mother doesn't see you," said Winterbourne. "Or perhaps," he added—thinking, with Miss Miller, the joke permissible—"perhaps she feels guilty about your shawl."

"Oh, it's a fearful old thing!" the young girl replied, serenely. "I told her she could wear it. She won't come here, because she sees you."

"Ah, then," said Winterbourne, "I had better leave you."

"Oh no; come on!" urged Miss Daisy Miller.

"I'm afraid your mother doesn't approve of my walking with you."

Miss Miller gave him a serious glance. "It isn't for me; it's for you—that is, it's for *her*. Well; I don't know who it's for! But mother doesn't like any of my gentlemen friends. She's right down timid. She always makes a fuss if I introduce a gentleman. But I *do* introduce them—almost always. If I didn't introduce my gentlemen friends to mother," the young girl added, in her little soft, flat monotone, "I shouldn't think I was natural."

"To introduce me," said Winterbourne, "you must know my name." And he proceeded to pronounce it.

"Oh, dear; I can't say all that!" said his companion, with a laugh. But by this time they had come up to Mrs. Miller, who, as they drew near, walked to the parapet of the garden and leaned upon it, looking intently at the lake and turning her back upon them. "Mother!" said the young girl, in a tone of decision. Upon this the elder lady turned round. "Mr. Winterbourne," said Miss Daisy Miller, introducing the young man very frankly and prettily. "Common" she was, as Mrs. Costello had pronounced her; yet it was a wonder to Winterbourne that, with her commonness, she had a singularly delicate grace.

Her mother was a small, spare, light person, with a wandering eye, a very exiguous nose, and a large forehead, decorated with a certain amount of thin, much-frizzled hair. Like her daughter, Mrs. Miller was dressed with extreme elegance; she had enormous diamonds in her ears. So far as Winterbourne could observe, she gave him no greeting—she certainly was not looking at him. Daisy was near her, pulling her shawl straight. "What are you doing, poking round here?" this young lady inquired; but by no means with that harshness of accent which her choice of words may imply.

"I don't know," said her mother, turning towards the lake again.

"I shouldn't think you'd want that shawl!" Daisy exclaimed.

"Well—I do!" her mother answered, with a little laugh.

"Did you get Randolph to go to bed?" asked the young girl.

"No; I couldn't induce him," said Mrs. Miller, very gently. "He wants to talk to the waiter. He likes to talk to that waiter."

"I was telling Mr. Winterbourne," the young girl went on; and to the young man's ear her tone might have indicated that she had been uttering his name all her life.

"Oh, yes!" said Winterbourne; "I have the pleasure of knowing your son."

Randolph's mamma was silent; she turned her attention to the lake. But at last she spoke. "Well, I don't see how he lives!"

"Anyhow, it isn't so bad as it was at Dover," said Daisy Miller.

"And what occurred at Dover?" Winterbourne asked.

"He wouldn't go to bed at all. I guess he sat up all night—in the public parlour. He wasn't in bed at twelve o'clock: I know that."

"It was half-past twelve," declared Mrs. Miller, with mild emphasis.

"Does he sleep much during the day?" Winterbourne demanded.

"I guess he doesn't sleep much," Daisy rejoined.

"I wish he would!" said her mother. "It seems as if he couldn't."

"I think he's real tiresome," Daisy pursued.

Then, for some moments, there was silence. "Well, Daisy Miller," said the elder lady, presently, "I shouldn't think you'd want to talk against your own brother!"

"Well, he *is* tiresome, mother," said Daisy, quite without the asperity of a retort.

"He's only nine," urged Mrs. Miller.

"Well, he wouldn't go to that castle," said the young girl. "I'm going there with Mr. Winterbourne."

To this announcement, very placidly made, Daisy's mamma offered no response. Winterbourne took for granted that she deeply disapproved of the projected excursion; but he said to himself that she was a simple, easily-managed person, and that a few deferential protestations would take the edge from her displeasure. "Yes," he began; "your daughter has kindly allowed me the honour of being her guide."

Mrs. Miller's wandering eyes attached themselves, with a sort of appealing air, to Daisy, who, however, strolled a few steps farther, gently humming to herself. "I presume you will go in the cars," said her mother.

"Yes; or in the boat," said Winterbourne.

"Well, of course, I don't know," Mrs. Miller rejoined. "I have never been to that castle."

"It is a pity you shouldn't go," said Winterbourne, beginning to feel reassured as to her opposition. And yet he was quite prepared to find that, as a matter of course, she meant to accompany her daughter.

"We've been thinking ever so much about going," she pursued; "but it seems as if we couldn't. Of course Daisy—she wants to go round. But there's a lady here—I don't know her name—she says she shouldn't think we'd want to go to see castles *here*; she should think we'd want to wait till we got to Italy. It seems as if there would be so many there," continued Mrs. Miller, with an air of increasing confidence. "Of course, we only want to see the principal ones. We visited several in England," she presently added.

"Ah, yes! in England there are beautiful castles," said Winterbourne. "But Chillon, here, is very well worth seeing."

"Well, if Daisy feels up to it—," said Mrs. Miller, in a tone im-

pregnated with a sense of the magnitude of the enterprise. "It seems
as if there was nothing she wouldn't undertake."

"Oh, I think she'll enjoy it!" Winterbourne declared. And he desired more and more to make it a certainty that he was to have the
privilege of a *tête-à-tête* with the young lady, who was still strolling
along in front of them, softly vocalising. "You are not disposed,
madam," he inquired, "to undertake it yourself?"

Daisy's mother looked at him, an instant, askance, and then
walked forward in silence. Then—"I guess she had better go alone,"
she said, simply.

Winterbourne observed to himself that this was a very different
type of maternity from that of the vigilant matrons who massed
themselves in the forefront of social intercourse in the dark old city
at the other end of the lake. But his meditations were interrupted
by hearing his name very distinctly pronounced by Mrs. Miller's
unprotected daughter.

"Mr. Winterbourne!" murmured Daisy.

"Mademoiselle!" said the young man.

"Don't you want to take me out in a boat?"

"At present?" he asked.

"Of course!" said Daisy.

"Well, Annie Miller!" exclaimed her mother.

"I beg you, madam, to let her go," said Winterbourne, ardently;
for he had never yet enjoyed the sensation of guiding through the
summer starlight a skiff freighted with a fresh and beautiful young
girl.

"I shouldn't think she'd want to," said her mother. "I should think
she'd rather go indoors."

"I'm sure Mr. Winterbourne wants to take me," Daisy declared.
"He's so awfully devoted!"

"I will row you over to Chillon, in the starlight."

"I don't believe it!" said Daisy.

"Well!" ejaculated the elderly lady again.

"You haven't spoken to me for half-an-hour," her daughter went
on.

"I have been having some very pleasant conversation with your
mother," said Winterbourne.

"Well; I want you to take me out in a boat!" Daisy repeated. They
had all stopped, and she had turned round and was looking at Winterbourne. Her face wore a charming smile, her pretty eyes were
gleaming, she was swinging her great fan about. No; it's impossible
to be prettier than that, thought Winterbourne.

"There are half-a-dozen boats moored at that landing-place," he
said, pointing to certain steps which descended from the garden to

the lake. "If you will do me the honour to accept my arm, we will go and select one of them."

Daisy stood there smiling; she threw back her head and gave a little light laugh. "I like a gentleman to be formal!" she declared.

"I assure you it's a formal offer."

"I was bound I would make you say something," Daisy went on.

"You see it's not very difficult," said Winterbourne. "But I am afraid you are chaffing me."

"I think not, sir," remarked Mrs. Miller, very gently.

"Do, then, let me give you a row," he said to the young girl.

"It's quite lovely, the way you say that!" cried Daisy.

"It will be still more lovely to do it."

"Yes, it would be lovely!" said Daisy. But she made no movement to accompany him; she only stood there laughing.

"I should think you had better find out what time it is," interposed her mother.

"It is eleven o'clock, madam," said a voice, with a foreign accent, out of the neighbouring darkness; and Winterbourne, turning, perceived the florid personage who was in attendance upon the two ladies. He had apparently just approached.

"Oh, Eugenio," said Daisy, "I am going out in a boat!"

Eugenio bowed. "At eleven o'clock, mademoiselle?"

"I am going with Mr. Winterbourne. This very minute."

"Do tell her she can't," said Mrs. Miller to the courier.

"I think you had better not go out in a boat, mademoiselle," Eugenio declared.

Winterbourne wished to Heaven this pretty girl were not so familiar with her courier; but he said nothing.

"I suppose you don't think it's proper!" Daisy exclaimed. "Eugenio doesn't think anything's proper."

"I am at your service," said Winterbourne.

"Does mademoiselle propose to go alone?" asked Eugenio of Mrs. Miller.

"Oh, no; with this gentleman!" answered Daisy's mamma.

The courier looked for a moment at Winterbourne—the latter thought he was smiling—and then, solemnly, with a bow, "As mademoiselle pleases!" he said.

"Oh, I hoped you would make a fuss!" said Daisy. "I don't care to go now."

"I myself shall make a fuss if you don't go," said Winterbourne.

"That's all I want—a little fuss!" And the young girl began to laugh again.

"Mr. Randolph has gone to bed!" the courier announced, frigidly.

"Oh, Daisy; now we can go!" said Mrs. Miller.

Daisy turned away from Winterbourne, looking at him, smiling and fanning herself. "Good night," she said; "I hope you are disappointed, or disgusted, or something!"

He looked at her, taking the hand she offered him. "I am puzzled," he answered.

"Well; I hope it won't keep you awake!" she said, very smartly; and, under the escort of the privileged Eugenio, the two ladies passed towards the house.

Winterbourne stood looking after them; he was indeed puzzled. He lingered beside the lake for a quarter of an hour, turning over the mystery of the young girl's sudden familiarities and caprices. But the only very definite conclusion he came to was that he should enjoy deucedly "going off" with her somewhere.

Two days afterwards he went off with her to the Castle of Chillon. He waited for her in the large hall of the hotel, where the couriers, the servants, the foreign tourists were lounging about and staring. It was not the place he would have chosen, but she had appointed it. She came tripping downstairs, buttoning her long gloves, squeezing her folded parasol against her pretty figure, dressed in the perfection of a soberly elegant travelling-costume. Winterbourne was a man of imagination and, as our ancestors used to say, of sensibility; as he looked at her dress and, on the great staircase, her little rapid, confiding step, he felt as if there were something romantic going forward. He could have believed he was going to elope with her. He passed out with her among all the idle people that were assembled there; they were all looking at her very hard; she had begun to chatter as soon as she joined him. Winterbourne's preference had been that they should be conveyed to Chillon in a carriage; but she expressed a lively wish to go in the little steamer; she declared that she had a passion for steamboats. There was always such a lovely breeze upon the water, and you saw such lots of people. The sail was not long, but Winterbourne's companion found time to say a great many things. To the young man himself their little excursion was so much of an escapade—an adventure—that, even allowing for her habitual sense of freedom, he had some expectation of seeing her regard it in the same way. But it must be confessed that, in this particular, he was disappointed. Daisy Miller was extremely animated, she was in charming spirits; but she was apparently not at all excited; she was not fluttered; she avoided neither his eyes nor those of any one else; she blushed neither when she looked at him nor when she saw that people were looking at her. People continued to look at her a great deal, and Winterbourne took much satisfaction in his pretty companion's distinguished air. He had been a little afraid that she would talk loud, laugh overmuch, and even, perhaps, desire to move about the boat a good deal. But he quite forgot his fears; he sat smiling, with his eyes upon her face, while, without moving from her place, she delivered herself of a great number of original reflections. It was the most charming garrulity he had ever heard. He had assented to the idea that she was "common;" but was she so, after all, or was he simply getting used to her commonness? Her conversation was chiefly of what metaphysicians term the objective cast; but every now and then it took a subjective turn.

"What on *earth* are you so grave about?" she suddenly demanded, fixing her agreeable eyes upon Winterbourne's.

"Am I grave?" he asked. "I had an idea I was grinning from ear to ear."

"You look as if you were taking me to a funeral. If that's a grin, your ears are very near together."

"Should you like me to dance a hornpipe on the deck?"

"Pray do, and I'll carry round your hat. It will pay the expenses of our journey."

"I never was better pleased in my life," murmured Winterbourne.

She looked at him a moment, and then burst into a little laugh. "I like to make you say those things! You're a queer mixture!"

In the castle, after they had landed, the subjective element decidedly prevailed. Daisy tripped about the vaulted chambers, rustled her skirts in the corkscrew staircases, flirted back with a pretty little cry and a shudder from the edge of the *oubliettes*,[7] and turned a singularly well-shaped ear to everything Winterbourne told her about the place. But he saw that she cared very little for feudal antiquities, and that the dusky traditions of Chillon made but a slight impression upon her. They had the good fortune to have been able to walk about without other companionship than that of the custodian; and Winterbourne arranged with this functionary that they should not be hurried—that they should linger and pause wherever they chose. The custodian interpreted the bargain generously—Winterbourne, on his side, had been generous—and ended by leaving them quite to themselves. Miss Miller's observations were not remarkable for logical consistency; for anything she wanted to say she was sure to find a pretext. She found a great many pretexts in the rugged embrasures of Chillon for asking Winterbourne sudden questions about himself—his family, his previous history, his tastes, his habits, his intentions—and for supplying information upon corresponding points in her own personality. Of her own tastes, habits and intentions Miss Miller was prepared to give the most definite, and indeed the most favourable, account.

"Well; I hope you know enough!" she said to her companion, after

7. Secret dungeons with trapdoors at the top.

he had told her the history of the unhappy Bonivard.[8] "I never saw a man that knew so much!" The history of Bonivard had evidently, as they say, gone into one ear and out of the other. But Daisy went on to say that she wished Winterbourne would travel with them and "go round" with them; they might know something, in that case. "Don't you want to come and teach Randolph?" she asked. Winterbourne said that nothing could possibly please him so much; but that he had unfortunately other occupations. "Other occupations? I don't believe it!" said Miss Daisy. "What do you mean? You are not in business." The young man admitted that he was not in business; but he had engagements which, even within a day or two, would force him to go back to Geneva. "Oh, bother!" she said, "I don't believe it!" and she began to talk about something else. But a few moments later, when he was pointing out to her the pretty design of an antique fireplace, she broke out irrelevantly, "You don't mean to say you are going back to Geneva?"

"It is a melancholy fact that I shall have to return to Geneva to-morrow."

"Well, Mr. Winterbourne," said Daisy; "I think you're horrid!"

"Oh, don't say such dreadful things!" said Winterbourne—"just at the last."

"The last!" cried the young girl; "I call it the first. I have half a mind to leave you here and go straight back to the hotel alone." And for the next ten minutes she did nothing but call him horrid. Poor Winterbourne was fairly bewildered; no young lady had as yet done him the honour to be so agitated by the announcement of his movements. His companion, after this, ceased to pay any attention to the curiosities of Chillon or the beauties of the lake; she opened fire upon the mysterious charmer in Geneva, whom she appeared to have instantly taken it for granted that he was hurrying back to see. How did Miss Daisy Miller know that there was a charmer in Geneva? Winterbourne, who denied the existence of such a person, was quite unable to discover; and he was divided between amazement at the rapidity of her induction and amusement at the frankness of her *persiflage*. She seemed to him, in all this, an extraordinary mixture of innocence and crudity. "Does she never allow you more than three days at a time?" asked Daisy, ironically. "Doesn't she give you a vacation in summer? There's no one so hard worked but they can get leave to go off somewhere at this season. I suppose, if you stay another day, she'll come after you in the boat. Do wait over till Friday, and I will go down to the landing to see her arrive!" Winterbourne began to think he had been wrong to feel

---

8. Sixteenth-century prisoner in the Castle of Chillon and hero of Byron's poem. Byron scratched his own name into one of the stone pillars of the castle.

disappointed in the temper in which the young lady had embarked. If he had missed the personal accent, the personal accent was now making its appearance. It sounded very distinctly, at last, in her telling him she would stop "teasing" him if he would promise her solemnly to come down to Rome in the winter.

"That's not a difficult promise to make," said Winterbourne. "My aunt has taken an apartment in Rome for the winter, and has already asked me to come and see her."

"I don't want you to come for your aunt," said Daisy; "I want you to come for me." And this was the only allusion that the young man was ever to hear her make to his invidious kinswoman. He declared that, at any rate, he would certainly come. After this Daisy stopped teasing. Winterbourne took a carriage, and they drove back to Vevey in the dusk; the young girl was very quiet.

In the evening Winterbourne mentioned to Mrs. Costello that he had spent the afternoon at Chillon, with Miss Daisy Miller.

"The Americans—of the courier?" asked this lady.

"Ah, happily," said Winterbourne, "the courier stayed at home."

"She went with you all alone?"

"All alone."

Mrs. Costello sniffed a little at her smelling-bottle. "And that," she exclaimed, "is the young person you wanted me to know!"

III

Winterbourne, who had returned to Geneva the day after his excursion to Chillon, went to Rome towards the end of January. His aunt had been established there for several weeks, and he had received a couple of letters from her. "Those people you were so devoted to last summer at Vevey have turned up here, courier and all," she wrote. "They seem to have made several acquaintances, but the courier continues to be the most *intime*.[9] The young lady, however, is also very intimate with some third-rate Italians, with whom she rackets about in a way that makes much talk. Bring me that pretty novel of Cherbuliez's—'Paule Méré'[1]—and don't come later than the 23rd."

In the natural course of events, Winterbourne, on arriving in Rome, would presently have ascertained Mrs. Miller's address at the American banker's and have gone to pay his compliments to

9. Familiar, intimate.
1. Novel (published in 1865) by Victor Cherbuliez (1829–1899) of Geneva. It deals with the love of a weak man for an exceptional woman and reflects the author's accumulated resentments of Genevan self-righteousness. James reviewed Cherbuliez's fiction favorably in *The North American Review*, October 1873. He mentions *Paule Méré* only briefly but refers to the heroine as "a delightfully tender conception" though perhaps "not absolutely natural."

Miss Daisy. "After what happened at Vevey I certainly think I may call upon them," he said to Mrs. Costello.

"If, after what happens—at Vevey and everywhere—you desire to keep up the acquaintance, you are very welcome. Of course a man may know every one. Men are welcome to the privilege!"

"Pray what is it that happens—here, for instance?" Winterbourne demanded.

"The girl goes about alone with her foreigners. As to what happens farther, you must apply elsewhere for information. She has picked up half-a-dozen of the regular Roman fortune-hunters, and she takes them about to people's houses. When she comes to a party she brings with her a gentleman with a good deal of manner and a wonderful moustache."

"And where is the mother?"

"I haven't the least idea. They are very dreadful people."

Winterbourne meditated a moment. "They are very ignorant—very innocent only. Depend upon it they are not bad."

"They are hopelessly vulgar," said Mrs. Costello. "Whether or no being hopelessly vulgar is being 'bad' is a question for the metaphysicians. They are bad enough to dislike, at any rate; and for this short life that is quite enough."

The news that Daisy Miller was surrounded by half-a-dozen wonderful moustaches checked Winterbourne's impulse to go straightway to see her. He had perhaps not definitely flattered himself that he had made an ineffaceable impression upon her heart, but he was annoyed at hearing of a state of affairs so little in harmony with an image that had lately flitted in and out of his own meditations; the image of a very pretty girl looking out of an old Roman window and asking herself urgently when Mr. Winterbourne would arrive. If, however, he determined to wait a little before reminding Miss Miller of his claims to her consideration, he went very soon to call upon two or three other friends. One of these friends was an American lady who had spent several winters at Geneva, where she had placed her children at school. She was a very accomplished woman and she lived in the Via Gregoriana.[2] Winterbourne found her in a little crimson drawing-room, on a third floor; the room was filled with southern sunshine. He had not been there ten minutes when the servant came in, announcing "Madame Mila!" This announcement was presently followed by the entrance of little Randolph Miller, who stopped in the middle of the room and stood staring at Winterbourne. An instant later his pretty sister crossed the threshold; and then, after a considerable interval, Mrs. Miller slowly advanced.

2. A fashionable street near the head of the Spanish Steps.

"I know you!" said Randolph.

"I'm sure you know a great many things," exclaimed Winterbourne, taking him by the hand. "How is your education coming on?"

Daisy was exchanging greetings very prettily with her hostess; but when she heard Winterbourne's voice she quickly turned her head. "Well, I declare!" she said.

"I told you I should come, you know," Winterbourne rejoined smiling.

"Well—I didn't believe it," said Miss Daisy.

"I am much obliged to you," laughed the young man.

"You might have come to see me!" said Daisy.

"I arrived only yesterday."

"I don't believe that!" the young girl declared.

Winterbourne turned with a protesting smile to her mother; but this lady evaded his glance, and seating herself, fixed her eyes upon her son. "We've got a bigger place than this," said Randolph. "It's all gold on the walls."

Mrs. Miller turned uneasily in her chair. "I told you if I were to bring you, you would say something!" she murmured.

"I told *you*!" Randolph exclaimed. "I tell *you*, sir!" he added jocosely, giving Winterbourne a thump on the knee. "It is bigger, too!"

Daisy had entered upon a lively conversation with her hostess; Winterbourne judged it becoming to address a few words to her mother. "I hope you have been well since we parted at Vevey," he said.

Mrs. Miller now certainly looked at him—at his chin. "Not very well, sir," she answered.

"She's got the dyspepsia," said Randolph. "I've got it too. Father's got it. I've got it worst!"

This announcement, instead of embarrassing Mrs. Miller, seemed to relieve her. "I suffer from the liver," she said. "I think it's the climate; it's less bracing than Schenectady, especially in the winter season. I don't know whether you know we reside at Schenectady. I was saying to Daisy that I certainly hadn't found any one like Dr. Davis, and I didn't believe I should. Oh, at Schenectady, he stands first; they think everything of him. He has so much to do, and yet there was nothing he wouldn't do for me. He said he never saw anything like my dyspepsia, but he was bound to cure it. I'm sure there was nothing he wouldn't try. He was just going to try something new when we came off. Mr. Miller wanted Daisy to see Europe for herself. But I wrote to Mr. Miller that it seems as if I couldn't get on without Dr. Davis. At Schenectady he stands at the very top; and there's a great deal of sickness there, too. It affects my sleep."

Winterbourne had a good deal of pathological gossip with Dr. Davis's patient, during which Daisy chattered unremittingly to her own companion. The young man asked Mrs. Miller how she was pleased with Rome. "Well, I must say I am disappointed," she answered. "We had heard so much about it; I suppose we had heard too much. But we couldn't help that. We had been led to expect something different."

"Ah, wait a little, and you will become very fond of it," said Winterbourne.

"I hate it worse and worse every day!" cried Randolph.

"You are like the infant Hannibal,"[3] said Winterbourne.

"No, I ain't!" Randolph declared, at a venture.

"You are not much like an infant," said his mother. "But we have seen places," she resumed, "that I should put a long way before Rome." And in reply to Winterbourne's interrogation, "There's Zurich," she observed; "I think Zurich is lovely; and we hadn't heard half so much about it."

"The best place we've seen is the City of Richmond!" said Randolph.

"He means the ship," his mother explained. "We crossed in that ship. Randolph had a good time on the City of Richmond."

"It's the best place I've seen," the child repeated. "Only it was turned the wrong way."

"Well, we've got to turn the right way some time," said Mrs. Miller, with a little laugh. Winterbourne expressed the hope that her daughter at least found some gratification in Rome, and she declared that Daisy was quite carried away. "It's on account of the society—the society's splendid. She goes round everywhere; she has made a great number of acquaintances. Of course she goes round more than I do. I must say they have been very sociable; they have taken her right in. And then she knows a great many gentlemen. Oh, she thinks there's nothing like Rome. Of course, it's a great deal pleasanter for a young lady if she knows plenty of gentlemen."

By this time Daisy had turned her attention again to Winterbourne. "I've been telling Mrs. Walker how mean you were!" the young girl announced.

"And what is the evidence you have offered?" asked Winterbourne, rather annoyed at Miss Miller's want of appreciation of the zeal of an admirer who on his way down to Rome had stopped neither at Bologna nor at Florence, simply because of a certain

3. Hannibal (247 to 183 or 182 B.C.E.), the Carthaginian general who led his army, including a train of elephants, across the Alps into Italy. Hannibal hated Rome from childhood on, when his father fought the Romans in Sicily and lost.

sentimental impatience. He remembered that a cynical compatriot had once told him that American women—the pretty ones, and this gave a largeness to the axiom—were at once the most exacting in the world and the least endowed with a sense of indebtedness.

"Why, you were awfully mean at Vevey," said Daisy. "You wouldn't do anything. You wouldn't stay there when I asked you."

"My dearest young lady," cried Winterbourne, with eloquence, "have I come all the way to Rome to encounter your reproaches?"

"Just hear him say that!" said Daisy to her hostess, giving a twist to a bow on this lady's dress. "Did you ever hear anything so quaint?"

"So quaint, my dear?" murmured Mrs. Walker, in the tone of a partisan of Winterbourne.

"Well, I don't know," said Daisy, fingering Mrs. Walker's ribbons. "Mrs. Walker, I want to tell you something."

"Motherr," interposed Randolph, with his rough ends to his words, "I tell you you've got to go. Eugenio'll raise something!"

"I'm not afraid of Eugenio," said Daisy, with a toss of her head. "Look here, Mrs. Walker," she went on, "you know I'm coming to your party."

"I am delighted to hear it."

"I've got a lovely dress."

"I am very sure of that."

"But I want to ask a favour—permission to bring a friend."

"I shall be happy to see any of your friends," said Mrs. Walker, turning with a smile to Mrs. Miller.

"Oh, they are not my friends," answered Daisy's mamma, smiling shyly, in her own fashion. "I never spoke to them!"

"It's an intimate friend of mine—Mr. Giovanelli," said Daisy, without a tremor in her clear little voice or a shadow on her brilliant little face.

Mrs. Walker was silent a moment, she gave a rapid glance at Winterbourne. "I shall be glad to see Mr. Giovanelli," she then said.

"He's an Italian," Daisy pursued, with the prettiest serenity. "He's a great friend of mine—he's the handsomest man in the world—except Mr. Winterbourne! He knows plenty of Italians, but he wants to know some Americans. He thinks ever so much of Americans. He's tremendously clever. He's perfectly lovely!"

It was settled that this brilliant personage should be brought to Mrs. Walker's party, and then Mrs. Miller prepared to take her leave. "I guess we'll go back to the hotel," she said.

"You may go back to the hotel, mother, but I'm going to take a walk," said Daisy.

"She's going to walk with Mr. Giovanelli," Randolph proclaimed.

"I am going to the Pincio,"[4] said Daisy, smiling.

"Alone, my dear at this hour?" Mrs. Walker asked. The afternoon was drawing to a close—it was the hour for the throng of carriages and of contemplative pedestrians. "I don't think it's safe, my dear," said Mrs. Walker.

"Neither do I," subjoined Mrs. Miller. "You'll get the fever as sure as you live. Remember what Dr. Davis told you!"

"Give her some medicine before she goes," said Randolph.

The company had risen to its feet; Daisy, still showing her pretty teeth, bent over and kissed her hostess. "Mrs. Walker, you are too perfect," she said. "I'm not going alone; I am going to meet a friend."

"Your friend won't keep you from getting the fever," Mrs. Miller observed.

"Is it Mr. Giovanelli?" asked the hostess.

Winterbourne was watching the young girl; at this question his attention quickened. She stood there smiling and smoothing her bonnet-ribbons; she glanced at Winterbourne. Then, while she glanced and smiled, she answered without a shade of hesitation, "Mr. Giovanelli—the beautiful Giovanelli."

"My dear young friend," said Mrs. Walker, taking her hand, pleadingly, "don't walk off to the Pincio at this hour to meet a beautiful Italian."

"Well, he speaks English," said Mrs. Miller.

"Gracious me!" Daisy exclaimed, "I don't want to do anything improper. There's an easy way to settle it." She continued to glance at Winterbourne. "The Pincio is only a hundred yards distant, and if Mr. Winterbourne were as polite as he pretends he would offer to walk with me!"

Winterbourne's politeness hastened to affirm itself, and the young girl gave him gracious leave to accompany her. They passed downstairs before her mother, and at the door Winterbourne perceived Mrs. Miller's carriage drawn up, with the ornamental courier whose acquaintance he had made at Vevey seated within. "Good-bye, Eugenio!" cried Daisy, "I'm going to take a walk." The distance from the Via Gregoriana to the beautiful garden at the other end of the Pincian Hill is, in fact, rapidly traversed. As the day was splendid, however, and the concourse of vehicles, walkers, and loungers numerous, the young Americans found their progress much delayed. This fact was highly agreeable to Winterbourne, in spite of his consciousness of his singular situation. The slow-moving, idly-gazing Roman crowd bestowed much attention upon the extremely pretty young foreign lady who was passing through it

4. A hill with a fine view of Rome.

upon his arm; and he wondered what on earth had been in Daisy's mind when she proposed to expose herself, unattended, to its appreciation. His own mission, to her sense, apparently, was to consign her to the hands of Mr. Giovanelli; but Winterbourne, at once annoyed and gratified, resolved that he would do no such thing.

"Why haven't you been to see me?" asked Daisy. "You can't get out of that."

"I have had the honour of telling you that I have only just stepped out of the train."

"You must have stayed in the train a good while after it stopped!" cried the young girl, with her little laugh. "I suppose you were asleep. You have had time to go to see Mrs. Walker."

"I knew Mrs. Walker——" Winterbourne began to explain.

"I knew where you knew her. You knew her at Geneva. She told me so. Well, you knew me at Vevey. That's just as good. So you ought to have come." She asked him no other question than this; she began to prattle about her own affairs. "We've got splendid rooms at the hotel; Eugenio says they're the best rooms in Rome. We are going to stay all winter—if we don't die of the fever; and I guess we'll stay then. It's a great deal nicer than I thought; I thought it would be fearfully quiet; I was sure it would be awfully poky. I was sure we should be going round all the time with one of those dreadful old men that explain about the pictures and things. But we only had about a week of that, and now I'm enjoying myself. I know ever so many people, and they are all so charming. The society's extremely select. There are all kinds—English, and Germans, and Italians. I think I like the English best. I like their style of conversation. But there are some lovely Americans. I never saw anything so hospitable. There's something or other every day. There's not much dancing; but I must say I never thought dancing was everything. I was always fond of conversation. I guess I shall have plenty at Mrs. Walker's—her rooms are so small." When they had passed the gate of the Pincian Gardens, Miss Miller began to wonder where Mr. Giovanelli might be. "We had better go straight to that place in front," she said, "where you look at the view."

"I certainly shall not help you to find him," Winterbourne declared.

"Then I shall find him without you," said Miss Daisy.

"You certainly won't leave me!" cried Winterbourne.

She burst into her little laugh. "Are you afraid you'll get lost—or run over? But there's Giovanelli, leaning against that tree. He's staring at the women in the carriages: did you ever see anything so cool?"

Winterbourne perceived at some distance a little man standing with folded arms, nursing his cane. He had a handsome face, an artfully poised hat, a glass in one eye and a nosegay in his button-hole. Winterbourne looked at him a moment and then said, "Do you mean to speak to that man?"

"Do I mean to speak to him? Why, you don't suppose I mean to communicate by signs?"

"Pray understand, then," said Winterbourne, "that I intend to remain with you."

Daisy stopped and looked at him, without a sign of troubled consciousness in her face; with nothing but the presence of her charming eyes and her happy dimples. "Well, she's a cool one!" thought the young man.

"I don't like the way you say that," said Daisy. "It's too imperious."

"I beg your pardon if I say it wrong. The main point is to give you an idea of my meaning."

The young girl looked at him more gravely, but with eyes that were prettier than ever. "I have never allowed a gentleman to dictate to me, or to interfere with anything I do."

"I think you have made a mistake," said Winterbourne. "You should sometimes listen to a gentleman—the right one?"

Daisy began to laugh again. "I do nothing but listen to gentlemen!" she exclaimed. "Tell me if Mr. Giovanelli is the right one."

The gentleman with the nosegay in his bosom had now perceived our two friends, and was approaching the young girl with obsequious rapidity. He bowed to Winterbourne as well as to the latter's companion; he had a brilliant smile, an intelligent eye; Winterbourne thought him not a bad-looking fellow. But he nevertheless said to Daisy—"No, he's not the right one."

Daisy evidently had a natural talent for performing introductions; she mentioned the name of each of her companions to the other. She strolled along with one of them on each side of her; Mr. Giovanelli, who spoke English very cleverly—Winterbourne afterwards learned that he had practised the idiom upon a great many American heiresses—addressed her a great deal of very polite nonsense; he was extremely urbane, and the young American, who said nothing, reflected upon that profundity of Italian cleverness which enables people to appear more gracious in proportion as they are more acutely disappointed. Giovanelli, of course, had counted upon something more intimate; he had not bargained for a party of three. But he kept his temper in a manner which suggested far-stretching intentions. Winterbourne flattered himself that he had taken his measure. "He is not a gentleman," said the young American; "he is only a clever imitation of one. He is a music-master, or a penny-a-liner, or a third-rate artist. Damn his good looks!" Mr. Giovanelli had certainly a very pretty face; but Winterbourne felt a superior indignation at his own lovely fellow-countrywoman's not knowing the difference between a spurious gentleman and a real one. Giovanelli chattered and jested and made himself wonderfully agreeable. It was true that if he was an imitation the imitation was very skillful. "Nevertheless," Winterbourne said to himself, "a nice girl ought to know!" And then he came back to the question whether this was in fact a nice girl. Would a nice girl—even allowing for her being a little American flirt—make a rendezvous with a presumably low-lived foreigner? The rendezvous in this case, indeed, had been in broad daylight, and in the most crowded corner of Rome; but was it not impossible to regard the choice of these circumstances as a proof of extreme cynicism? Singular though it may seem, Winterbourne was vexed that the young girl, in joining her *amoroso*,[5] should not appear more impatient of his own company, and he was vexed because of his inclination. It was impossible to regard her as a perfectly well-conducted young lady; she was wanting in a certain indispensable delicacy. It would therefore simplify matters greatly to be able to treat her as the object of one of those sentiments which are called by romancers "lawless passions." That she should seem to wish to get rid of him would help him to think more lightly of her, and to be able to think more lightly of her would make her much less perplexing. But Daisy, on this occasion, continued to present herself as an inscrutable combination of audacity and innocence.

She had been walking some quarter of an hour, attended by her two cavaliers, and responding in a tone of very childish gaiety, as it seemed to Winterbourne, to the pretty speeches of Mr. Giovanelli, when a carriage that had detached itself from the revolving train drew up beside the path. At the same moment Winterbourne perceived that his friend Mrs. Walker—the lady whose house he had lately left—was seated in the vehicle and was beckoning to him. Leaving Miss Miller's side, he hastened to obey her summons. Mrs. Walker was flushed; she wore an excited air. "It is really too dreadful," she said. "That girl must not do this sort of thing. She must not walk here with you two men. Fifty people have noticed her."

Winterbourne raised his eyebrows. "I think it's a pity to make too much fuss about it."

"It's a pity to let the girl ruin herself!"

"She is very innocent," said Winterbourne.

"She's very crazy!" cried Mrs. Walker. "Did you ever see anything so imbecile as her mother? After you had all left me, just now, I could not sit still for thinking of it. It seemed too pitiful, not even

5. Beau, sweetheart.

to attempt to save her. I ordered the carriage and put on my bonnet, and came here as quickly as possible. Thank heaven I have found you!"

"What do you propose to do with us?" asked Winterbourne, smiling.

"To ask her to get in, to drive her about here for half-an-hour, so that the world may see she is not running absolutely wild, and then to take her safely home."

"I don't think it's a very happy thought," said Winterbourne; "but you can try."

Mrs. Walker tried. The young man went in pursuit of Miss Miller, who had simply nodded and smiled at his interlocutrix in the carriage and had gone her way with her own companion. Daisy, on learning that Mrs. Walker wished to speak to her, retraced her steps with a perfect good grace and with Mr. Giovanelli at her side. She declared that she was delighted to have a chance to present this gentleman to Mrs. Walker. She immediately achieved the introduction, and declared that she had never in her life seen anything so lovely as Mrs. Walker's carriage-rug.

"I am glad you admire it," said this lady, smiling sweetly. "Will you get in and let me put it over you?"

"Oh, no, thank you," said Daisy. "I shall admire it much more as I see you driving round with it."

"Do get in and drive with me," said Mrs. Walker.

"That would be charming, but it's so enchanting just as I am!" and Daisy gave a brilliant glance at the gentlemen on either side of her.

"It may be enchanting, dear child, but it is not the custom here," urged Mrs. Walker, leaning forward in her victoria with her hands devoutly clasped.

"Well, it ought to be, then!" said Daisy. "If I didn't walk I should expire."

"You should walk with your mother, dear," cried the lady from Geneva, losing patience.

"With my mother dear!" exclaimed the young girl. Winterbourne saw that she scented interference. "My mother never walked ten steps in her life. And then, you know," she added with a laugh, "I am more than five years old."

"You are old enough to be more reasonable. You are old enough, dear Miss Miller, to be talked about."

Daisy looked at Mrs. Walker, smiling intensely. "Talked about? What do you mean?"

"Come into my carriage and I will tell you."

Daisy turned her quickened glance again from one of the gentlemen beside her to the other. Mr. Giovanelli was bowing to and fro, rubbing down his gloves and laughing very agreeably; Winterbourne thought it a most unpleasant scene. "I don't think I want to know what you mean," said Daisy presently. "I don't think I should like it."

Winterbourne wished that Mrs. Walker would tuck in her carriage-rug and drive away; but this lady did not enjoy being defied, as she afterwards told him. "Should you prefer being thought a very reckless girl?" she demanded.

"Gracious me!" exclaimed Daisy. She looked again at Mr. Giovanelli, then she turned to Winterbourne. There was a little pink flush in her cheek; she was tremendously pretty. "Does Mr. Winterbourne think," she asked slowly, smiling, throwing back her head and glancing at him from head to foot, "that—to save my reputation—I ought to get into the carriage?"

Winterbourne coloured; for an instant he hesitated greatly. It seemed so strange to hear her speak that way of her "reputation." But he himself, in fact, must speak in accordance with gallantry. The finest gallantry, here, was simply to tell her the truth; and the truth, for Winterbourne, as the few indications I have been able to give have made him known to the reader, was that Daisy Miller should take Mrs. Walker's advice. He looked at her exquisite prettiness; and then he said very gently, "I think you should get into the carriage."

Daisy gave a violent laugh. "I never heard anything so stiff! If this is improper, Mrs. Walker," she pursued, "then I am all improper, and you must give me up. Good-bye; I hope you'll have a lovely ride!" and, with Mr. Giovanelli, who made a triumphantly obsequious salute, she turned away.

Mrs. Walker sat looking after her, and there were tears in Mrs. Walker's eyes. "Get in here, sir," she said to Winterbourne, indicating the place beside her. The young man answered that he felt bound to accompany Miss Miller; whereupon Mrs. Walker declared that if he refused her this favour she would never speak to him again. She was evidently in earnest. Winterbourne overtook Daisy and her companion and, offering the young girl his hand, told her that Mrs. Walker had made an imperious claim upon his society. He expected that in answer she would say something rather free, something to commit herself still farther to that "recklessness" from which Mrs. Walker had so charitably endeavoured to dissuade her. But she only shook his hand, hardly looking at him, while Mr. Giovanelli bade him farewell with a too emphatic flourish of the hat.

Winterbourne was not in the best possible humour as he took his seat in Mrs. Walker's victoria. "That was not clever of you," he said candidly, while the vehicle mingled again with the throng of carriages.

"In such a case," his companion answered, "I don't wish to be clever, I wish to be *earnest!*"

"Well, your earnestness has only offended her and put her off."

"It has happened very well," said Mrs. Walker. "If she is so perfectly determined to compromise herself, the sooner one knows it the better; one can act accordingly."

"I suspect she meant no harm," Winterbourne rejoined.

"So I thought a month ago. But she has been going too far."

"What has she been doing?"

"Everything that is not done here. Flirting with any man she could pick up; sitting in corners with mysterious Italians; dancing all the evening with the same partners; receiving visits at eleven o'clock at night. Her mother goes away when visitors come."

"But her brother," said Winterbourne, laughing, "sits up till midnight."

"He must be edified by what he sees. I'm told that at their hotel every one is talking about her, and that a smile goes round among the servants when a gentleman comes and asks for Miss Miller."

"The servants be hanged!" said Winterbourne angrily. "The poor girl's only fault," he presently added, "is that she is very uncultivated."

"She is naturally indelicate," Mrs. Walker declared. "Take that example this morning. How long had you known her at Vevey?"

"A couple of days."

"Fancy, then, her making it a personal matter that you should have left the place!"

Winterbourne was silent for some moments; then he said, "I suspect, Mrs. Walker, that you and I have lived too long at Geneva!" And he added a request that she should inform him with what particular design she had made him enter her carriage.

"I wished to beg you to cease your relations with Miss Miller—not to flirt with her—to give her no farther opportunity to expose herself—to let her alone, in short."

"I'm afraid I can't do that," said Winterbourne. "I like her extremely."

"All the more reason that you shouldn't help her to make a scandal."

"There shall be nothing scandalous in my attentions to her."

"There certainly will be in the way she takes them. But I have said what I had on my conscience," Mrs. Walker pursued. "If you wish to rejoin the young lady I will put you down. Here, by-the-way, you have a chance."

The carriage was traversing that part of the Pincian Garden which overhangs the wall of Rome and overlooks the beautiful Villa

Borghese.[6] It is bordered by a large parapet, near which there are several seats. One of the seats, at a distance, was occupied by a gentleman and a lady, towards whom Mrs. Walker gave a toss of her head. At the same moment these persons rose and walked towards the parapet. Winterbourne had asked the coachman to stop; he now descended from the carriage. His companion looked at him a moment in silence; then, while he raised his hat, she drove majestically away. Winterbourne stood there; he had turned his eyes towards Daisy and her cavalier. They evidently saw no one; they were too deeply occupied with each other. When they reached the low garden-wall they stood a moment looking off at the great flat-topped pine-clusters of the Villa Borghese; then Giovanelli seated himself familiarly upon the broad ledge of the wall. The western sun in the opposite sky sent out a brilliant shaft through a couple of cloud-bars; whereupon Daisy's companion took her parasol out of her hands and opened it. She came a little nearer and he held the parasol over her; then, still holding it, he let it rest upon her shoulder, so that both of their heads were hidden from Winterbourne. This young man lingered a moment, then he began to walk. But he walked—not towards the couple with the parasol; towards the residence of his aunt, Mrs. Costello.

IV

He flattered himself on the following day that there was no smiling among the servants when he, at least, asked for Mrs. Miller at her hotel. This lady and her daughter, however, were not at home; and on the next day after, repeating his visit, Winterbourne again had the misfortune not to find them. Mrs. Walker's party took place on the evening of the third day, and in spite of the frigidity of his last interview with the hostess Winterbourne was among the guests. Mrs. Walker was one of those American ladies who, while residing abroad, make a point, in their own phrase, of studying European society; and she had on this occasion collected several specimens of her diversely-born fellow-mortals to serve, as it were, as text-books. When Winterbourne arrived Daisy Miller was not there; but in a few moments he saw her mother come in alone, very shyly and ruefully. Mrs. Miller's hair, above her exposed-looking temples, was more frizzled than ever. As she approached Mrs. Walker, Winterbourne also drew near.

"You see I've come all alone," said poor Mrs. Miller. "I'm so frightened; I don't know what to do; it's the first time I've ever been

6. A seventeenth-century palace in a large park.

to a party alone—especially in this country. I wanted to bring Randolph or Eugenio, or some one, but Daisy just pushed me off by myself. I ain't used to going round alone."

"And does not your daughter intend to favour us with her society?" demanded Mrs. Walker, impressively.

"Well, Daisy's all dressed," said Mrs. Miller, with that accent of the dispassionate, if not of the philosophic, historian with which she always recorded the current incidents of her daughter's career. "She got dressed on purpose before dinner. But she's got a friend of hers there; that gentleman—the Italian—that she wanted to bring. They've got going at the piano; it seems as if they couldn't leave off. Mr. Giovanelli sings splendidly. But I guess they'll come before very long," concluded Mrs. Miller hopefully.

"I'm sorry she should come—in that way," said Mrs. Walker.

"Well, I told her that there was no use in her getting dressed before dinner if she was going to wait three hours," responded Daisy's mamma. "I didn't see the use of her putting on such a dress as that to sit round with Mr. Giovanelli."

"This is most horrible!" said Mrs. Walker, turning away and addressing herself to Winterbourne. "*Elle s'affiche.*[7] It's her revenge for my having ventured to remonstrate with her. When she comes I shall not speak to her."

Daisy came after eleven o'clock, but she was not, on such an occasion, a young lady to wait to be spoken to. She rustled forward in radiant loveliness, smiling and chattering, carrying a large bouquet and attended by Mr. Giovanelli. Every one stopped talking, and turned and looked at her. She came straight to Mrs. Walker. "I'm afraid you thought I never was coming, so I sent mother off to tell you. I wanted to make Mr. Giovanelli practise some things before he came; you know he sings beautifully, and I want you to ask him to sing. This is Mr. Giovanelli; you know I introduced him to you; he's got the most lovely voice and he knows the most charming set of songs. I made him go over them this evening, on purpose; we had the greatest time at the hotel." Of all this Daisy delivered herself with the sweetest, brightest audibleness, looking now at her hostess and now round the room, while she gave a series of little pats, round her shoulders, to the edges of her dress. "Is there any one I know?" she asked.

"I think every one knows you!" said Mrs. Walker pregnantly, and she gave a very cursory greeting to Mr. Giovanelli. This gentleman bore himself gallantly. He smiled and bowed and showed his white teeth, he curled his moustaches and rolled his eyes, and performed all the proper functions of a handsome Italian at an evening party.

---

7. She advertises herself (seeks notoriety, makes a show of herself).

He sang, very prettily, half-a-dozen songs, though Mrs. Walker afterwards declared that she had been quite unable to find out who asked him. It was apparently not Daisy who had given him his orders. Daisy sat at a distance from the piano, and though she had publicly, as it were, professed a high admiration for his singing, talked, not inaudibly, while it was going on.

"It's a pity these rooms are so small; we can't dance," she said to Winterbourne, as if she had seen him five minutes before.

"I am not sorry we can't dance," Winterbourne answered, "I don't dance."

"Of course you don't dance; you're too stiff," said Miss Daisy. "I hope you enjoyed your drive with Mrs. Walker."

"No, I didn't enjoy it; I preferred walking with you."

"We paired off, that was much better," said Daisy. "But did you ever hear anything so cool as Mrs. Walker's wanting me to get into her carriage and drop poor Mr. Giovanelli; and under the pretext that it was proper? People have different ideas! It would have been most unkind; he had been talking about that walk for ten days."

"He should not have talked about it at all," said Winterbourne; "he would never have proposed to a young lady of this country to walk about the streets with him."

"About the streets?" cried Daisy, with her pretty stare. "Where then would he have proposed to her to walk? The Pincio is not the streets, either; and I, thank goodness, am not a young lady of this country. The young ladies of this country have a dreadfully pokey time of it, so far as I can learn; I don't see why I should change my habits for *them*."

"I am afraid your habits are those of a flirt," said Winterbourne gravely.

"Of course they are," she cried, giving him her little smiling stare again. "I'm a fearful, frightful flirt! Did you ever hear of a nice girl that was not? But I suppose you will tell me now that I am not a nice girl."

"You're a very nice girl, but I wish you would flirt with me, and me only," said Winterbourne.

"Ah! thank you, thank you very much; you are the last man I should think of flirting with. As I have had the pleasure of informing you, you are too stiff."

"You say that too often," said Winterbourne.

Daisy gave a delighted laugh. "If I could have the sweet hope of making you angry, I would say it again."

"Don't do that; when I am angry I'm stiffer than ever. But if you won't flirt with me, do cease at least to flirt with your friend at the piano; they don't understand that sort of thing here."

"I thought they understood nothing else!" exclaimed Daisy.

"Not in young unmarried women."

"It seems to me much more proper in young unmarried women than in old married ones," Daisy declared.

"Well," said Winterbourne, "when you deal with natives you must go by the custom of the place. Flirting is a purely American custom; it doesn't exist here. So when you show yourself in public with Mr. Giovanelli and without your mother—"

"Gracious! poor mother!" interposed Daisy.

"Though you may be flirting, Mr. Giovanelli is not; he means something else."

"He isn't preaching, at any rate," said Daisy with vivacity. "And if you want very much to know, we are neither of us flirting; we are too good friends for that; we are very intimate friends."

"Ah!" rejoined Winterbourne, "if you are in love with each other it is another affair."

She had allowed him up to this point to talk so frankly that he had no expectation of shocking her by this ejaculation; but she immediately got up, blushing visibly, and leaving him to exclaim mentally that little American flirts were the queerest creatures in the world. "Mr. Giovanelli, at least," she said, giving her interlocutor a single glance, "never says such very disagreeable things to me."

Winterbourne was bewildered; he stood staring. Mr. Giovanelli had finished singing; he left the piano and came over to Daisy. "Won't you come into the other room and have some tea?" he asked, bending before her with his decorative smile.

Daisy turned to Winterbourne, beginning to smile again. He was still more perplexed, for this inconsequent smile made nothing clear, though it seemed to prove, indeed, that she had a sweetness and softness that reverted instinctively to the pardon of offences. "It has never occurred to Mr. Winterbourne to offer me any tea," she said, with her little tormenting manner.

"I have offered you advice," Winterbourne rejoined.

"I prefer weak tea!" cried Daisy, and she went off with the brilliant Giovanelli. She sat with him in the adjoining room, in the embrasure of the window, for the rest of the evening. There was an interesting performance at the piano, but neither of these young people gave heed to it. When Daisy came to take leave of Mrs. Walker, this lady conscientiously repaired the weakness of which she had been guilty at the moment of the young girl's arrival. She turned her back straight upon Miss Miller and left her to depart with what grace she might. Winterbourne was standing near the door; he saw it all. Daisy turned very pale and looked at her mother, but Mrs. Miller was humbly unconscious of any violation of the usual social forms. She appeared, indeed, to have felt an incongruous impulse to draw attention to her own striking observance of them. "Good night, Mrs. Walker," she said; "we've had a beautiful evening. You see if I let Daisy come to parties without me, I don't want her to go away without me." Daisy turned away, looking with a pale, grave face at the circle near the door; Winterbourne saw that, for the first moment, she was too much shocked and puzzled even for indignation. He on his side was greatly touched.

"That was very cruel," he said to Mrs. Walker.

"She never enters my drawing-room again," replied his hostess.

Since Winterbourne was not to meet her in Mrs. Walker's drawing-room, he went as often as possible to Mrs. Miller's hotel. The ladies were rarely at home, but when he found them the devoted Giovanelli was always present. Very often the polished little Roman was in the drawing-room with Daisy alone, Mrs. Miller being apparently constantly of the opinion that discretion is the better part of the surveillance. Winterbourne noted, at first with surprise, that Daisy on these occasions was never embarrassed or annoyed by his own entrance; but he very presently began to feel that she had no more surprises for him; the unexpected in her behaviour was the only thing to expect. She showed no displeasure at her *tête-à-tête* with Giovanelli being interrupted; she could chatter as freshly and freely with two gentlemen as with one; there was always in her conversation, the same odd mixture of audacity and puerility. Winterbourne remarked to himself that if she was seriously interested in Giovanelli it was very singular that she should not take more trouble to preserve the sanctity of their interviews, and he liked her the more for her innocent-looking indifference and her apparently inexhaustible good humour. He could hardly have said why, but she seemed to him a girl who would never be jealous. At the risk of exciting a somewhat derisive smile on the reader's part, I may affirm that with regard to the women who had hitherto interested him it very often seemed to Winterbourne among the possibilities that, given certain contingencies, he should be afraid—literally afraid—of these ladies. He had a pleasant sense that he should never be afraid of Daisy Miller. It must be added that this sentiment was not altogether flattering to Daisy; it was part of his conviction, or rather of his apprehension, that she would prove a very light young person.

But she was evidently very much interested in Giovanelli. She looked at him whenever he spoke; she was perpetually telling him to do this and to do that; she was constantly "chaffing" and abusing him. She appeared completely to have forgotten that Winterbourne had said anything to displease her at Mrs. Walker's little party. One Sunday afternoon, having gone to St. Peter's with his aunt, Winterbourne perceived Daisy strolling about the great church in company with the inevitable Giovanelli. Presently he pointed out the young girl and her cavalier to Mrs. Costello. This lady looked at them a moment through her eyeglass, and then she said:

"That's what makes you so pensive in these days, eh?"

"I had not the least idea I was pensive," said the young man.

"You are very much pre-occupied, you are thinking of something."

"And what is it," he asked, "that you accuse me of thinking of?"

"Of that young lady's—Miss Baker's, Miss Chandler's—what's her name?—Miss Miller's intrigue with that little barber's block."[8]

"Do you call it an intrigue," Winterbourne asked—"an affair that goes on with such peculiar publicity?"

"That's their folly," said Mrs. Costello, "it's not their merit."

"No," rejoined Winterbourne, with something of that pensiveness to which his aunt had alluded. "I don't believe that there is anything to be called an intrigue."

"I have heard a dozen people speak of it; they say she is quite carried away by him."

"They are certainly very intimate," said Winterbourne.

Mrs. Costello inspected the young couple again with her optical instrument. "He is very handsome. One easily sees how it is. She thinks him the most elegant man in the world, the finest gentleman. She has never seen anything like him; he is better even than the courier. It was the courier probably who introduced him, and if he succeeds in marrying the young lady, the courier will come in for a magnificent commission."

"I don't believe she thinks of marrying him," said Winterbourne, "and I don't believe he hopes to marry her."

"You may be very sure she thinks of nothing. She goes on from day to day, from hour to hour, as they did in the Golden Age. I can imagine nothing more vulgar. And at the same time," added Mrs. Costello, "depend upon it that she may tell you any moment that she is 'engaged.'"

"I think that is more than Giovanelli expects," said Winterbourne.

"Who is Giovanelli?"

"The little Italian. I have asked questions about him and learned something. He is apparently a perfectly respectable little man. I believe he is in a small way a *cavaliere avvocato*.[9] But he doesn't move in what are called the first circles. I think it is really not absolutely impossible that the courier introduced him. He is evidently immensely charmed with Miss Miller. If she thinks him the finest gentleman in the world, he, on his side, has never found himself in personal contact with such splendour, such opulence,

8. A wooden head on which wigs are fitted.
9. Gentleman lawyer.

such expensiveness, as this young lady's. And then she must seem to him wonderfully pretty and interesting. I rather doubt whether he dreams of marrying her. That must appear to him too impossible a piece of luck. He has nothing but his handsome face to offer, and there is a substantial Mr. Miller in that mysterious land of dollars. Giovanelli knows that he hasn't a title to offer. If he were only a count or a *marchese*![1] He must wonder at his luck at the way they have taken him up."

"He accounts for it by his handsome face, and thinks Miss Miller a young lady *qui se passe ses fantaisies!*"[2] said Mrs. Costello.

"It is very true," Winterbourne pursued, "that Daisy and her mamma have not yet risen to that stage of—what shall I call it?—of culture, at which the idea of catching a count or a *marchese* begins. I believe that they are intellectually incapable of that conception."

"Ah! but the *cavaliere* can't believe it," said Mrs. Costello.

Of the observation excited by Daisy's "intrigue," Winterbourne gathered that day at St. Peter's sufficient evidence. A dozen of the American colonists in Rome came to talk with Mrs. Costello, who sat on a little portable stool at the base of one of the great pilasters. The vesper-service was going forward in splendid chants and organ-tones in the adjacent choir, and meanwhile, between Mrs. Costello and her friends, there was a great deal said about poor little Miss Miller's going really "too far." Winterbourne was not pleased with what he heard; but when, coming out upon the great steps of the church, he saw Daisy, who had emerged before him, get into an open cab with her accomplice and roll away through the cynical streets of Rome, he could not deny to himself that she was going very far indeed. He felt very sorry for her—not exactly that he believed that she had completely lost her head, but because it was painful to hear so much that was pretty and undefended and natural assigned to a vulgar place among the categories of disorder. He made an attempt after this to give a hint to Mrs. Miller. He met one day in the Corso[3] a friend—a tourist like himself—who had just come out of the Doria Palace, where he had been walking through the beautiful gallery. His friend talked for a moment about the superb portrait of Innocent X. by Velasquez, which hangs in one of the cabinets of the palace, and then said, "And in the same cabinet, by-the-way, I had the pleasure of contemplating a picture of a different kind—that pretty American girl whom you pointed

1. Marquis.
2. Who lives according to her whims.
3. An avenue in the center of Rome. On it is the Doria Palace, an eighteenth-century mansion with a picture gallery containing, among other masterpieces, a portrait of Pope Innocent X by the Spanish painter Velasquez (1599–1660).

out to me last week." In answer to Winterbourne's inquiries, his friend narrated that the pretty American girl—prettier than ever—was seated with a companion in the secluded nook in which the great papal portrait is enshrined.

"Who was her companion?" asked Winterbourne.

"A little Italian with a bouquet in his button-hole. The girl is delightfully pretty, but I thought I understood from you the other day that she was a young lady *du meilleur monde*."[4]

"So she is!" answered Winterbourne; and having assured himself that his informant had seen Daisy and her companion but five minutes before, he jumped into a cab and went to call on Mrs. Miller. She was at home; but she apologised to him for receiving him in Daisy's absence.

"She's gone out somewhere with Mr. Giovanelli," said Mrs. Miller. "She's always going round with Mr. Giovanelli."

"I have noticed that they are very intimate," Winterbourne observed.

"Oh! it seems as if they couldn't live without each other!" said Mrs. Miller. "Well, he's a real gentleman, anyhow. I keep telling Daisy she's engaged!"

"And what does Daisy say?"

"Oh, she says she isn't engaged. But she might as well be!" this impartial parent resumed. "She goes on as if she was. But I've made Mr. Giovanelli promise to tell me, if *she* doesn't. I should want to write to Mr. Miller about it—shouldn't you?"

Winterbourne replied that he certainly should; and the state of mind of Daisy's mamma struck him as so unprecedented in the annals of parental vigilance that he gave up as utterly irrelevant the attempt to place her upon her guard.

After this Daisy was never at home, and Winterbourne ceased to meet her at the houses of their common acquaintance, because, as he perceived, these shrewd people had quite made up their minds that she was going too far. They ceased to invite her, and they intimated that they desired to express to observant Europeans the great truth that, though Miss Daisy Miller was a young American lady, her behaviour was not representative—was regarded by her compatriots as abnormal. Winterbourne wondered how she felt about all the cold shoulders that were turned towards her, and sometimes it annoyed him to suspect that she did not feel at all. He said to himself that she was too light and childish, too uncultivated and unreasoning, too provincial, to have reflected upon her ostracism or even to have perceived it. Then at other moments he believed that she carried about in her elegant and irresponsible little

4. Of the best society.

organism a defiant, passionate, perfectly observant consciousness
of the impression she produced. He asked himself whether Daisy's
defiance came from the consciousness of innocence or from her
being, essentially, a young person of the reckless class. It must be
admitted that holding oneself to a belief in Daisy's "innocence"
came to seem to Winterbourne more and more a matter of fine-
spun gallantry. As I have already had occasion to relate, he was
angry at finding himself reduced to chopping logic about this young
lady; he was vexed at his want of instinctive certitude as to how far
her eccentricities were generic, national, and how far they were
personal. From either view of them he had somehow missed her,
and now it was too late. She was "carried away" by Mr. Giovanelli.

A few days after his brief interview with her mother, he encountered her in that beautiful abode of flowering desolation known as
the Palace of the Cæsars. The early Roman spring had filled the air
with bloom and perfume, and the rugged surface of the Palatine[5]
was muffled with tender verdure. Daisy was strolling along the top
of one of those great mounds of ruin that are embanked with mossy
marble and paved with monumental inscriptions. It seemed to him
that Rome had never been so lovely as just then. He stood looking
off at the enchanting harmony of line and colour that remotely
encircles the city, inhaling the softly humid odours and feeling the
freshness of the year and the antiquity of the place reaffirm themselves in mysterious interfusion. It seemed to him also that Daisy
had never looked so pretty; but this had been an observation of his
whenever he met her. Giovanelli was at her side, and Giovanelli,
too, wore an aspect of even unwonted brilliancy.

"Well," said Daisy, "I should think you would be lonesome!"

"Lonesome?" asked Winterbourne.

"You are always going round by yourself. Can't you get any one
to walk with you?"

"I am not so fortunate," said Winterbourne, "as your companion."

Giovanelli, from the first, had treated Winterbourne with distinguished politeness; he listened with a deferential air to his remarks;
he laughed, punctiliously, at his pleasantries; he seemed disposed
to testify to his belief that Winterbourne was a superior young man.
He carried himself in no degree like a jealous wooer; he had obviously a great deal of tact; he had no objection to your expecting a
little humility of him. It even seemed to Winterbourne at times
that Giovanelli would find a certain mental relief in being able to
have a private understanding with him—to say to him, as an intelligent man, that, bless you, *he* knew how extraordinary was this
young lady, and didn't flatter himself with delusive—or at least *too*

5. A hill park in the center of Rome filled with historical monuments.

delusive—hopes of matrimony and dollars. On this occasion he strolled away from his companion to pluck a sprig of almond blossom, which he carefully arranged in his button-hole.

"I know why you say that," said Daisy, watching Giovanelli. "Because you think I go round too much with *him!*" And she nodded at her attendant.

"Every one thinks so—if you care to know," said Winterbourne.

"Of course I care to know!" Daisy exclaimed seriously. "But I don't believe it. They are only pretending to be shocked. They don't really care a straw what I do. Besides, I don't go round so much."

"I think you will find they do care. They will show it—disagreeably."

Daisy looked at him a moment. "How—disagreeably?"

"Haven't you noticed anything?" Winterbourne asked.

"I have noticed you. But I noticed you were as stiff as an umbrella the first time I saw you."

"You will find I am not so stiff as several others," said Winterbourne, smiling.

"How shall I find it?"

"By going to see the others."

"What will they do to me?"

"They will give you the cold shoulder. Do you know what that means?"

Daisy was looking at him intently; she began to colour. "Do you mean as Mrs. Walker did the other night?"

"Exactly!" said Winterbourne.

She looked away at Giovanelli, who was decorating himself with his almond-blossom. Then looking back at Winterbourne—"I shouldn't think you would let people be so unkind!" she said.

"How can I help it?" he asked.

"I should think you would say something."

"I do say something;" and he paused a moment. "I say that your mother tells me that she believes you are engaged."

"Well, she does," said Daisy very simply.

Winterbourne began to laugh. "And does Randolph believe it?" he asked.

"I guess Randolph doesn't believe anything," said Daisy. Randolph's scepticism excited Winterbourne to farther hilarity, and he observed that Giovanelli was coming back to them. Daisy, observing it too, addressed herself again to her countryman. "Since you have mentioned it," she said, "I *am* engaged." . . . Winterbourne looked at her; he had stopped laughing. "You don't believe it!" she added.

He was silent a moment; and then, "Yes, I believe it!" he said.

"Oh, no, you don't," she answered. "Well, then—I am not!"

The young girl and her cicerone were on their way to the gate of the enclosure, so that Winterbourne, who had but lately entered, presently took leave of them. A week afterwards he went to dine at a beautiful villa on the Cælian Hill,[6] and, on arriving, dismissed his hired vehicle. The evening was charming, and he promised himself the satisfaction of walking home beneath the Arch of Constantine and past the vaguely-lighted monuments of the Forum.[7] There was a waning moon in the sky, and her radiance was not brilliant, but she was veiled in a thin cloud-curtain which seemed to diffuse and equalise it. When, on his return from the villa (it was eleven o'clock), Winterbourne approached the dusky circle of the Colosseum,[8] it occurred to him, as a lover of the picturesque, that the interior, in the pale moonshine, would be well worth a glance. He turned aside and walked to one of the empty arches, near which, as he observed, an open carriage—one of the little Roman street-cabs—was stationed. Then he passed in among the cavernous shadows of the great structure, and emerged upon the clear and silent arena. The place had never seemed to him more impressive. One-half of the gigantic circus was in deep shade; the other was sleeping in the luminous dusk. As he stood there he began to murmur Byron's famous lines, out of "Manfred";[9] but before he had finished his quotation he remembered that if nocturnal meditations in the Colosseum are recommended by the poets, they are deprecated by the doctors. The historic atmosphere was there, certainly; but the historic atmosphere, scientifically considered, was no better than a villanous miasma. Winterbourne walked to the middle of the arena, to take a more general glance, intending thereafter to make a hasty retreat. The great cross in the centre was covered with shadow; it was only as he drew near it that he made it out distinctly. Then he saw that two persons were stationed upon the low steps which formed its base. One of these was a woman, seated; her companion was standing in front of her.

Presently the sound of the woman's voice came to him distinctly in the warm night-air. "Well, he looks at us as one of the old lions or tigers may have looked at the Christian martyrs!" These were the words he heard, in the familiar accent of Miss Daisy Miller.

"Let us hope he is not very hungry," responded the ingenious Giovanelli. "He will have to take me first; you will serve for dessert!"

Winterbourne stopped, with a sort of horror; and, it must be

6. One of the seven hills on which ancient Rome was built.
7. The ruins of the center of pre-Christian Rome. The Arch of Constantine, erected to celebrate the emperor's victory over a rival in 312 C.E., is adorned with bas-reliefs depicting scenes from the lives of Roman emperors.
8. The ancient Roman amphitheater.
9. The lines begin: "I stood within the Coliseum's wall, / Midst the chief relics of almighty Rome; / The trees which grew along the broken arches / Waved dark in the blue midnight. . . ." (III. iv).

added, with a sort of relief. It was as if a sudden illumination had been flashed upon the ambiguity of Daisy's behaviour and the riddle had become easy to read. She was a young lady whom a gentleman need no longer be at pains to respect. He stood there looking at her—looking at her companion, and not reflecting that though he saw them vaguely, he himself must have been more brightly visible. He felt angry with himself that he had bothered so much about the right way of regarding Miss Daisy Miller. Then, as he was going to advance again, he checked himself; not from the fear that he was doing her injustice, but from a sense of the danger of appearing unbecomingly exhilarated by this sudden revulsion from cautious criticism. He turned away towards the entrance of the place; but as he did so he heard Daisy speak again.

"Why, it was Mr. Winterbourne! He saw me—and he cuts me!"

What a clever little reprobate she was, and how smartly she played an injured innocence! But he wouldn't cut her. Winterbourne came forward again, and went towards the great cross. Daisy had got up; Giovanelli lifted his hat. Winterbourne had now begun to think simply of the craziness, from a sanitary point of view, of a delicate young girl lounging away the evening in this nest of malaria. What if she *were* a clever little reprobate? that was no reason for her dying of the *perniciosa*.[1] "How long have you been there?" he asked, almost brutally.

Daisy, lovely in the flattering moonlight, looked at him a moment. Then—"All the evening," she answered gently . . . "I never saw anything so pretty."

"I am afraid," said Winterbourne, "that you will not think Roman fever very pretty. This is the way people catch it. I wonder," he added, turning to Giovanelli, "that you, a native Roman, should countenance such a terrible indiscretion."

"Ah," said the handsome native, "for myself, I am not afraid."

"Neither am I—for you! I am speaking for this young lady."

Giovanelli lifted his well-shaped eyebrows and showed his brilliant teeth. But he took Winterbourne's rebuke with docility. "I told the Signorina it was a grave indiscretion; but when was the Signorina ever prudent?"

"I never was sick, and I don't mean to be!" the Signorina declared. "I don't look like much, but I'm healthy! I was bound to see the Colosseum by moonlight; I shouldn't have wanted to go home without that; and we have had the most beautiful time, haven't we, Mr. Giovanelli? If there has been any danger, Eugenio can give me some pills. He has got some splendid pills."

1. Pernicious fever, i.e., malaria.

"I should advise you," said Winterbourne, "to drive home as fast as possible and take one!"

"What you say is very wise," Giovanelli rejoined. "I will go and make sure the carriage is at hand." And he went forward rapidly.

Daisy followed with Winterbourne. He kept looking at her; she seemed not in the least embarrassed. Winterbourne said nothing; Daisy chattered about the beauty of the place. "Well, I *have* seen the Colosseum by moonlight!" she exclaimed. "That's one good thing." Then, noticing Winterbourne's silence, she asked him why he didn't speak. He made no answer; he only began to laugh. They passed under one of the dark archways; Giovanelli was in front with the carriage. Here Daisy stopped a moment, looking at the young American. "*Did* you believe I was engaged the other day?" she asked.

"It doesn't matter what I believed the other day," said Winterbourne, still laughing.

"Well, what do you believe now?"

"I believe that it makes very little difference whether you are engaged or not!"

He felt the young girl's pretty eyes fixed upon him through the thick gloom of the archway; she was apparently going to answer. But Giovanelli hurried her forward. "Quick, quick," he said; "if we get in by midnight we are quite safe."

Daisy took her seat in the carriage, and the fortunate Italian placed himself beside her. "Don't forget Eugenio's pills!" said Winterbourne, as he lifted his hat.

"I don't care," said Daisy, in a little strange tone, "whether I have Roman fever or not!" Upon this the cab-driver cracked his whip, and they rolled away over the desultory patches of the antique pavement.

Winterbourne—to do him justice, as it were—mentioned to no one that he had encountered Miss Miller, at midnight, in the Colosseum with a gentleman; but nevertheless, a couple of days later, the fact of her having been there under these circumstances was known to every member of the little American circle, and commented accordingly. Winterbourne reflected that they had of course known it at the hotel, and that, after Daisy's return, there had been an exchange of jokes between the porter and the cab-driver. But the young man was conscious at the same moment that it had ceased to be a matter of serious regret to him that the little American flirt should be "talked about" by low-minded menials. These people, a day or two later, had serious information to give: the little American flirt was alarmingly ill. Winterbourne, when the rumour came to him, immediately went to the hotel for more news. He found that two or three charitable friends had preceded him, and that they were being entertained in Mrs. Miller's salon by Randolph.

"It's going round at night," said Randolph—"that's what made her sick. She's always going round at midnight. I shouldn't think she'd want to—it's so plaguey dark. You can't see anything here at night, except when there's a moon. In America there's always a moon!" Mrs. Miller was invisible; she was now, at least, giving her daughter the advantage of her society. It was evident that Daisy was dangerously ill.

Winterbourne went often to ask for news of her, and once he saw Mrs. Miller, who, though deeply alarmed, was—rather to his surprise—perfectly composed, and, as it appeared, a most efficient and judicious nurse. She talked a good deal about Dr. Davis, but Winterbourne paid her the compliment of saying to himself that she was not, after all, such a monstrous goose. "Daisy spoke of you the other day," she said to him. "Half the time she doesn't know what she's saying, but that time I think she did. She gave me a message: she told me to tell you. She told me to tell you that she never was engaged to that handsome Italian. I am sure I am very glad; Mr. Giovanelli hasn't been near us since she was taken ill. I thought he was so much of a gentleman; but I don't call that very polite! A lady told me that he was afraid I was angry with him for taking Daisy round at night. Well, so I am; but I suppose he knows I'm a lady. I would scorn to scold him. Any way, she says she's not engaged. I don't know why she wanted you to know; but she said to me three times—'Mind you tell Mr. Winterbourne.' And then she told me to ask if you remembered the time you went to that castle, in Switzerland. But I said I wouldn't give any such messages as that. Only, if she is not engaged, I'm sure I'm glad to know it."

But, as Winterbourne had said, it mattered very little. A week after this the poor girl died; it had been a terrible case of the fever. Daisy's grave was in the little Protestant cemetery, in an angle of the wall of imperial Rome, beneath the cypresses and the thick spring-flowers. Winterbourne stood there beside it, with a number of other mourners; a number larger than the scandal excited by the young lady's career would have led you to expect. Near him stood Giovanelli, who came nearer still before Winterbourne turned away. Giovanelli was very pale; on this occasion he had no flower in his button-hole; he seemed to wish to say something. At last he said, "She was the most beautiful young lady I ever saw, and the most amiable." And then he added in a moment, "And she was the most innocent."

Winterbourne looked at him, and presently repeated his words, "And the most innocent?"

"The most innocent!"

Winterbourne felt sore and angry. "Why the devil," he asked, "did you take her to that fatal place?"

Mr. Giovanelli's urbanity was apparently imperturbable. He looked on the ground a moment, and then he said, "For myself, I had no fear; and she wanted to go."

"That was no reason!" Winterbourne declared.

The subtle Roman again dropped his eyes. "If she had lived, I should have got nothing. She would never have married me, I am sure."

"She would never have married you?"

"For a moment I hoped so. But no. I am sure."

Winterbourne listened to him; he stood staring at the raw protuberance among the April daisies. When he turned away again Mr. Giovanelli, with his light slow step, had retired.

Winterbourne almost immediately left Rome; but the following summer he again met his aunt, Mrs. Costello, at Vevey. Mrs. Costello was fond of Vevey. In the interval Winterbourne had often thought of Daisy Miller and her mystifying manners. One day he spoke of her to his aunt—said it was on his conscience that he had done her injustice.

"I am sure I don't know," said Mrs. Costello. "How did your injustice affect her?"

"She sent me a message before her death which I didn't understand at the time. But I have understood it since. She would have appreciated one's esteem."

"Is that a modest way," asked Mrs. Costello, "of saying that she would have reciprocated one's affection?"

Winterbourne offered no answer to this question; but he presently said, "You were right in that remark that you made last summer. I was booked to make a mistake. I have lived too long in foreign parts."

Nevertheless, he went back to live at Geneva, whence there continue to come the most contradictory accounts of his motives of sojourn: a report that he is "studying" hard—an intimation that he is much interested in a very clever foreign lady.

The Aspern Papers [†]

I

I had taken Mrs. Prest into my confidence; in truth without her I should have made but little advance, for the fruitful idea in the whole business dropped from her friendly lips. It was she who invented the short cut, who severed the Gordian knot. It is not supposed to be the nature of women to rise as a general thing to the largest and most liberal view—I mean of a practical scheme; but it has struck me that they sometimes throw off a bold conception—such as a man would not have risen to—with singular serenity. "Simply ask them to take you in on the footing of a lodger"—I don't think that unaided I should have risen to that. I was beating about the bush, trying to be ingenious, wondering by what combination of arts I might become an acquaintance, when she offered this happy suggestion that the way to become an acquaintance was first to become an inmate. Her actual knowledge of the Misses Bordereau was scarcely larger than mine, and indeed I had brought with me from England some definite facts which were new to her. Their name had been mixed up ages before with one of the greatest names of the century, and they lived now in Venice in obscurity, on very small means, unvisited, unapproachable, in a dilapidated old palace on an out-of-the-way canal: this was the substance of my friend's impression of them. She herself had been established in Venice for fifteen years and had done a great deal of good there; but the circle of her benevolence did not include the two shy, mysterious, and as it was somehow supposed, scarcely respectable Americans (they were believed to have lost in their long exile all national quality, besides having had, as their name implied, some French strain in their origin), who asked no favours and desired no attention. In the early years of her residence she had made an attempt to see them, but this had been successful only as regards the little one, as Mrs. Prest called the niece; though in reality, as I afterwards learned,

† "The Aspern Papers" first appeared in *The Atlantic Monthly*, March–May 1888. The first edition in a book, reprinted here, was *The Aspern Papers/Louisa Pallant/The Modern Warning* (London and New York: Macmillan and Co., 1888), vol. 1.

she was considerably the bigger of the two. She had heard Miss Bordereau was ill and had a suspicion that she was in want; and she had gone to the house to offer assistance, so that if there were suffering (and American suffering), she should at least not have it on her conscience. The "little one" received her in the great cold, tarnished Venetian sala,[1] the central hall of the house, paved with marble and roofed with dim cross-beams, and did not even ask her to sit down. This was not encouraging for me, who wished to sit so fast, and I remarked as much to Mrs. Prest. She however replied with profundity, "Ah, but there's all the difference: I went to confer a favour and you will go to ask one. If they are proud you will be on the right side." And she offered to show me their house to begin with—to row me thither in her gondola. I let her know that I had already been to look at it half a dozen times; but I accepted her invitation, for it charmed me to hover about the place. I had made my way to it the day after my arrival in Venice (it had been described to me in advance by the friend in England to whom I owed definite information as to their possession of the papers), and I had besieged it with my eyes while I considered my plan of campaign. Jeffrey Aspern had never been in it that I knew of; but some note of his voice seemed to abide there by a roundabout implication, a faint reverberation.

Mrs. Prest knew nothing about the papers, but she was interested in my curiosity, as she was always interested in the joys and sorrows of her friends. As we went, however, in her gondola, gliding there under the sociable hood with the bright Venetian picture framed on either side by the movable window, I could see that she was amused by my infatuation, the way my interest in the papers had become a fixed idea. "One would think you expected to find in them the answer to the riddle of the universe," she said; and I denied the impeachment only by replying that if I had to choose between that precious solution and a bundle of Jeffrey Aspern's letters I knew indeed which would appear to me the greater boon. She pretended to make light of his genius and I took no pains to defend him. One doesn't defend one's god: one's god is in himself a defence. Besides, to-day, after his long comparative obscuration, he hangs high in the heaven of our literature, for all the world to see; he is a part of the light by which we walk. The most I said was that he was no doubt not a woman's poet: to which she rejoined aptly enough that he had been at least Miss Bordereau's. The strange thing had been for me to discover in England that she was still alive: it was as if I had been told Mrs. Siddons was, or Queen Caroline, or the famous Lady

1. Hallway.

Hamilton,[2] for it seemed to me that she belonged to a generation as extinct. "Why, she must be tremendously old—at least a hundred," I had said; but on coming to consider dates I saw that it was not strictly necessary that she should have exceeded by very much the common span. None the less she was very far advanced in life and her relations with Jeffrey Aspern had occurred in her early womanhood. "That is her excuse," said Mrs. Prest, half sententiously and yet also somewhat as if she were ashamed of making a speech so little in the real tone of Venice. As if a woman needed an excuse for having loved the divine poet! He had been not only one of the most brilliant minds of his day (and in those years, when the century was young, there were, as every one knows, many), but one of the most genial men and one of the handsomest.

The niece, according to Mrs. Prest, was not so old, and she risked the conjecture that she was only a grand-niece. This was possible; I had nothing but my share in the very limited knowledge of my English fellow-worshipper John Cumnor, who had never seen the couple. The world, as I say, had recognised Jeffrey Aspern, but Cumnor and I had recognised him most. The multitude, to-day, flocked to his temple, but of that temple he and I regarded ourselves as the ministers. We held, justly, as I think, that we had done more for his memory than any one else, and we had done it by opening lights into his life. He had nothing to fear from us because he had nothing to fear from the truth, which alone at such a distance of time we could be interested in establishing. His early death had been the only dark spot in his life, unless the papers in Miss Bordereau's hands should perversely bring out others. There had been an impression about 1825 that he had "treated her badly," just as there had been an impression that he had "served," as the London populace says, several other ladies in the same way. Each of these cases Cumnor and I had been able to investigate, and we had never failed to acquit him conscientiously of shabby behaviour. I judged him perhaps more indulgently than my friend; certainly, at any rate, it appeared to me that no man could have walked straighter in the given circumstances. These were almost always awkward. Half the women of his time, to speak liberally, had flung themselves at his head, and out of this pernicious fashion many complications, some of them grave, had not failed to arise. He was not a woman's poet, as I had said to Mrs. Prest, in the modern phase of his reputation;

2. Mrs. Sarah Kemble Siddons (1755–1831) was a famous British actress; "Queen Caroline" refers to the queen of either George II (1727–1760) or George IV (1820–1830); Lady Hamilton (1761?–1815) was the mistress of Admiral Nelson, who defeated the French and Spanish fleets in the Battle of Trafalgar in 1815 but was killed in the course of battle.

but the situation had been different when the man's own voice was mingled with his song. That voice, by every testimony, was one of the sweetest ever heard. "Orpheus and the Mænads!"[3] was the exclamation that rose to my lips when I first turned over his correspondence. Almost all the Mænads were unreasonable and many of them insupportable; it struck me in short that he was kinder, more considerate than, in his place (if I could imagine myself in such a place!) I should have been.

It was certainly strange beyond all strangeness, and I shall not take up space with attempting to explain it, that whereas in all these other lines of research we had to deal with phantoms and dust, the mere echoes of echoes, the one living source of information that had lingered on into our time had been unheeded by us. Every one of Aspern's contemporaries had, according to our belief, passed away; we had not been able to look into a single pair of eyes into which his had looked or to feel a transmitted contact in any aged hand that his had touched. Most dead of all did poor Miss Bordereau appear, and yet she alone had survived. We exhausted in the course of months our wonder that we had not found her out sooner, and the substance of our explanation was that she had kept so quiet. The poor lady on the whole had had reason for doing so. But it was a revelation to us that it was possible to keep so quiet as that in the latter half of the nineteenth century—the age of newspapers and telegrams and photographs and interviewers. And she had taken no great trouble about it either: she had not hidden herself away in an undiscoverable hole; she had boldly settled down in a city of exhibition. The only secret of her safety that we could perceive was that Venice contained so many curiosities that were greater than she. And then accident had somehow favoured her, as was shown for example in the fact that Mrs. Prest had never happened to mention her to me, though I had spent three weeks in Venice—under her nose, as it were—five years before. Mrs. Prest had not mentioned this much to any one; she appeared almost to have forgotten she was there. Of course she had the responsibilities of an editor. It was no explanation of the old woman's having eluded us to say that she lived abroad, for our researches had again and again taken us (not only by correspondence but by personal inquiry) to France, to Germany, to Italy, in which countries, not counting his important stay in England, so many of the too few years of Aspern's career were spent. We were glad to think at least that in all our publishings (some people consider I believe that we have overdone them), we had only touched in passing and in the most discreet manner on

3. The legendary Greek poet and musician Orpheus was pursued and ultimately torn to pieces by the Maenads, female worshippers of Dionysus (Bacchus).

Miss Bordereau's connection. Oddly enough, even if we had had the material (and we often wondered what had become of it), it would have been the most difficult episode to handle.

The gondola stopped, the old palace was there; it was a house of the class which in Venice carries even in extreme dilapidation the dignified name. "How charming! It's gray and pink!" my companion exclaimed; and that is the most comprehensive description of it. It was not particularly old, only two or three centuries; and it had an air not so much of decay as of quiet discouragement, as if it had rather missed its career. But its wide front, with a stone balcony from end to end of the *piano nobile* or most important floor, was architectural enough, with the aid of various pilasters and arches; and the stucco with which in the intervals it had long ago been endued was rosy in the April afternoon. It overlooked a clean, melancholy, unfrequented canal, which had a narrow *riva* or convenient footway on either side. "I don't know why—there are no brick gables," said Mrs. Prest, "but this corner has seemed to me before more Dutch than Italian, more like Amsterdam than like Venice. It's perversely clean, for reasons of its own; and though you can pass on foot scarcely any one ever thinks of doing so. It has the air of a Protestant Sunday. Perhaps the people are afraid of the Misses Bordereau. I daresay they have the reputation of witches."

I forget what answer I made to this—I was given up to two other reflections. The first of these was that if the old lady lived in such a big, imposing house she could not be in any sort of misery and therefore would not be tempted by a chance to let a couple of rooms. I expressed this idea to Mrs. Prest, who gave me a very logical reply. "If she didn't live in a big house how could it be a question of her having rooms to spare? If she were not amply lodged herself you would lack ground to approach her. Besides, a big house here, and especially in this *quartier perdu*,[4] proves nothing at all: it is perfectly compatible with a state of penury. Dilapidated old palazzi, if you will go out of the way for them, are to be had for five shillings a year. And as for the people who live in them—no, until you have explored Venice socially as much as I have you can form no idea of their domestic desolation. They live on nothing, for they have nothing to live on." The other idea that had come into my head was connected with a high blank wall which appeared to confine an expanse of ground on one side of the house. Blank I call it, but it was figured over with the patches that please a painter, repaired breaches, crumblings of plaster, extrusions of brick that had turned pink with time; and a few thin trees, with the poles of certain rickety trellises, were visible over the top. The place was a garden

4. Forgotten neighborhood.

and apparently it belonged to the house. It suddenly occurred to me that if it did belong to the house I had my pretext.

I sat looking out on all this with Mrs. Prest (it was covered with the golden glow of Venice) from the shade of our *felze*,[5] and she asked me if I would go in then, while she waited for me, or come back another time. At first I could not decide—it was doubtless very weak of me. I wanted still to think I *might* get a footing, and I was afraid to meet failure, for it would leave me, as I remarked to my companion, without another arrow for my bow. "Why not another?" she inquired, as I sat there hesitating and thinking it over; and she wished to know why even now and before taking the trouble of becoming an inmate (which might be wretchedly uncomfortable after all, even if it succeeded), I had not the resource of simply offering them a sum of money down. In that way I might obtain the documents without bad nights.

"Dearest lady," I exclaimed, "excuse the impatience of my tone when I suggest that you must have forgotten the very fact (surely I communicated it to you) which pushed me to throw myself upon your ingenuity. The old woman won't have the documents spoken of; they are personal, delicate, intimate, and she hasn't modern notions, God bless her! If I should sound that note first I should certainly spoil the game. I can arrive at the papers only by putting her off her guard, and I can put her off her guard only by ingratiating diplomatic practices. Hypocrisy, duplicity are my only chance. I am sorry for it, but for Jeffrey Aspern's sake I would do worse still. First I must take tea with her; then tackle the main job." And I told over what had happened to John Cumnor when he wrote to her. No notice whatever had been taken of his first letter, and the second had been answered very sharply, in six lines, by the niece. "Miss Bordereau requested her to say that she could not imagine what he meant by troubling them. They had none of Mr. Aspern's papers, and if they had should never think of showing them to any one on any account whatever. She didn't know what he was talking about and begged he would let her alone." I certainly did not want to be met that way.

"Well," said Mrs. Prest, after a moment, provokingly, "perhaps after all they haven't any of his things. If they deny it flat how are you sure?"

"John Cumnor is sure, and it would take me long to tell you how his conviction, or his very strong presumption—strong enough to stand against the old lady's not unnatural fib—has built itself up. Besides, he makes much of the internal evidence of the niece's letter."

5. Small cabin of a gondola.

"The internal evidence?"

"Her calling him 'Mr. Aspern.' "

"I don't see what that proves."

"It proves familiarity, and familiarity implies the possession of mementoes, of relics. I can't tell you how that 'Mr.' touches me—how it bridges over the gulf of time and brings our hero near to me—nor what an edge it gives to my desire to see Juliana. You don't say 'Mr.' Shakespeare."

"Would I, any more, if I had a box full of his letters?"

"Yes, if he had been your lover and some one wanted them!" And I added that John Cumnor was so convinced, and so all the more convinced by Miss Bordereau's tone, that he would have come himself to Venice on the business were it not that for him there was the obstacle that it would be difficult to disprove his identity with the person who had written to them, which the old ladies would be sure to suspect in spite of dissimulation and a change of name. If they were to ask him point-blank if he were not their correspondent it would be too awkward for him to lie; whereas I was fortunately not tied in that way. I was a fresh hand and could say no without lying.

"But you will have to change your name," said Mrs. Prest. "Juliana lives out of the world as much as it is possible to live, but none the less she has probably heard of Mr. Aspern's editors; she perhaps possesses what you have published."

"I have thought of that," I returned; and I drew out of my pocketbook a visiting-card, neatly engraved with a name that was not my own.

"You are very extravagant; you might have written it," said my companion.

"This looks more genuine."

"Certainly, you are prepared to go far! But it will be awkward about your letters; they won't come to you in that mask."

"My banker will take them in and I will go every day to fetch them. It will give me a little walk."

"Shall you only depend upon that?" asked Mrs. Prest. "Aren't you coming to see me?"

"Oh, you will have left Venice, for the hot months, long before there are any results. I am prepared to roast all summer—as well as hereafter, perhaps you'll say! Meanwhile, John Cumnor will bombard me with letters addressed, in my feigned name, to the care of the *padrona*."

"She will recognise his hand," my companion suggested.

"On the envelope he can disguise it."

"Well, you're a precious pair! Doesn't it occur to you that even if you are able to say you are not Mr. Cumnor in person they may still suspect you of being his emissary?"

"Certainly, and I see only one way to parry that."

"And what may that be?"

I hesitated a moment. "To make love to the niece."

"Ah," cried Mrs. Prest, "wait till you see her!"

II

"I must work the garden—I must work the garden," I said to myself, five minutes later, as I waited, upstairs, in the long, dusky sala, where the bare scagliola floor gleamed vaguely in a chink of the closed shutters. The place was impressive but it looked cold and cautious. Mrs. Prest had floated away, giving me a rendezvous at the end of half an hour by some neighboring watersteps; and I had been let into the house, after pulling the rusty bell-wire, by a little red-headed, white-faced maid-servant, who was very young and not ugly and wore clicking pattens and a shawl in the fashion of a hood. She had not contented herself with opening the door from above by the usual arrangement of a creaking pulley, though she had looked down at me first from an upper window, dropping the inevitable challenge which in Italy precedes the hospitable act. As a general thing I was irritated by this survival of mediæval manners, though as I liked the old I suppose I ought to have liked it; but I was so determined to be genial that I took my false card out of my pocket and held it up to her, smiling as if it were a magic token. It had the effect of one indeed, for it brought her, as I say, all the way down. I begged her to hand it to her mistress, having first written on it in Italian the words, "Could you very kindly see a gentleman, an American, for a moment?" The little maid was not hostile, and I reflected that even that was perhaps something gained. She coloured, she smiled and looked both frightened and pleased. I could see that my arrival was a great affair, that visits were rare in that house, and that she was a person who would have liked a sociable place. When she pushed forward the heavy door behind me I felt that I had a foot in the citadel. She pattered across the damp, stony lower hall and I followed her up the high staircase—stonier still, as it seemed—without an invitation. I think she had meant I should wait for her below, but such was not my idea, and I took up my station in the sala. She flitted, at the far end of it, into impenetrable regions, and I looked at the place with my heart beating as I had known it to do in the dentist's parlour. It was gloomy and stately, but it owed its character almost entirely to its noble shape and to the fine architectural doors—as high as the doors of houses—which, leading into the various rooms, repeated themselves on either side at intervals. They were surmounted with old faded painted escutcheons, and here and there, in the spaces between them, brown pictures, which I perceived to be bad, in battered frames, were suspended. With the exception of several straw-bottomed chairs with their backs to the wall, the grand obscure vista contained nothing else to minister to effect. It was evidently never used save as a passage, and little even as that. I may add that by the time the door opened again through which the maid-servant had escaped, my eyes had grown used to the want of light.

I had not meant by my private ejaculation that I must myself cultivate the soil of the tangled enclosure which lay beneath the windows, but the lady who came toward me from the distance over the hard, shining floor might have supposed as much from the way in which, as I went rapidly to meet her, I exclaimed, taking care to speak Italian: "The garden, the garden—do me the pleasure to tell me if it's yours!"

She stopped, short, looking at me with wonder; and then, "Nothing here is mine," she answered in English, coldly and sadly.

"Oh, you are English; how delightful!" I remarked, ingenuously. "But surely the garden belongs to the house?"

"Yes, but the house doesn't belong to me." She was a long, lean, pale person, habited apparently in a dull-coloured dressing-gown, and she spoke with a kind of mild literalness. She did not ask me to sit down, any more than years before (if she were the niece) she had asked Mrs. Prest, and we stood face to face in the empty pompous hall.

"Well then, would you kindly tell me to whom I must address myself? I'm afraid you'll think me odiously intrusive, but you know I *must* have a garden—upon my honour I must!"

Her face was not young, but it was simple; it was not fresh, but it was mild. She had large eyes which were not bright, and a great deal of hair which was not "dressed," and long fine hands which were—possibly—not clean. She clasped these members almost convulsively as, with a confused, alarmed look, she broke out, "Oh, don't take it away from us; we like it ourselves!"

"You have the use of it then?"

"Oh yes. If it wasn't for that!" And she gave a shy, melancholy smile.

"Isn't it a luxury, precisely? That's why, intending to be in Venice some weeks, possibly all summer, and having some literary work, some reading and writing to do, so that I must be quiet, and yet if possible a great deal in the open air—that's why I have felt that a garden is really indispensable. I appeal to your own experience," I went on, smiling. "Now can't I look at yours?"

"I don't know, I don't understand," the poor woman murmured, planted there and letting her embarrassed eyes wander all over my strangeness.

"I mean only from one of those windows—such grand ones as you have here—if you will let me open the shutters." And I walked toward the back of the house. When I had advanced half-way I stopped and waited, as if I took it for granted she would accompany me. I had been of necessity very abrupt, but I strove at the same time to give her the impression of extreme courtesy. "I have been looking at furnished rooms all over the place, and it seems impossible to find any with a garden attached. Naturally in a place like Venice gardens are rare. It's absurd if you like, for a man, but I can't live without flowers."

"There are none to speak of down there." She came nearer to me, as if, though she mistrusted me, I had drawn her by an invisible thread. I went on again, and she continued as she followed me: "We have a few, but they are very common. It costs too much to cultivate them; one has to have a man."

"Why shouldn't I be the man?" I asked. "I'll work without wages; or rather I'll put in a gardener. You shall have the sweetest flowers in Venice."

She protested at this, with a queer little sigh which might also have been a gush of rapture at the picture I presented. Then she observed, "We don't know you—we don't know you."

"You know me as much as I know you; that is much more, because you know my name. And if you are English I am almost a countryman."

"We are not English," said my companion, watching me helplessly while I threw open the shutters of one of the divisions of the wide high window.

"You speak the language so beautifully: might I ask what you are?" Seen from above the garden was certainly shabby; but I perceived at a glance that it had great capabilities. She made no rejoinder, she was so lost in staring at me, and I exclaimed, "You don't mean to say you are also by chance American?"

"I don't know; we used to be."

"Used to be? Surely you haven't changed?"

"It's so many years ago—we are nothing."

"So many years that you have been living here? Well, I don't wonder at that; it's a grand old house. I suppose you all use the garden," I went on, "but I assure you I shouldn't be in your way. I would be very quiet and stay in one corner."

"We all use it?" she repeated after me, vaguely, not coming close to the window but looking at my shoes. She appeared to think me capable of throwing her out.

"I mean all your family, as many as you are."

"There is only one other; she is very old—she never goes down."

"Only one other, in all this great house!" I feigned to be not only amazed but almost scandalised. "Dear lady, you must have space then to spare!"

"To spare?" she repeated, in the same dazed way.

"Why, you surely don't live (two quiet women—I see *you* are quiet, at any rate) in fifty rooms!" Then with a burst of hope and cheer I demanded: "Couldn't you let me two or three? That would set me up!"

I had now struck the note that translated my purpose and I need not reproduce the whole of the tune I played. I ended by making my interlocutress believe that I was an honourable person, though of course I did not even attempt to persuade her that I was not an eccentric one. I repeated that I had studies to pursue; that I wanted quiet; that I delighted in a garden and had vainly sought one up and down the city; that I would undertake that before another month was over the dear old house should be smothered in flowers. I think it was the flowers that won my suit, for I afterwards found that Miss Tita (for such the name of this high tremulous spinster proved somewhat incongruously to be) had an insatiable appetite for them. When I speak of my suit as won I mean that before I left her she had promised that she would refer the question to her aunt. I inquired who her aunt might be and she answered, "Why, Miss Bordereau!" with an air of surprise, as if I might have been expected to know. There were contradictions like this in Tita Bordereau which, as I observed later, contributed to make her an odd and affecting person. It was the study of the two ladies to live so that the world should not touch them, and yet they had never altogether accepted the idea that it never heard of them. In Tita at any rate a grateful susceptibility to human contact had not died out, and contact of a limited order there would be if I should come to live in the house.

"We have never done anything of the sort; we have never had a lodger or any kind of inmate." So much as this she made a point of saying to me. "We are very poor, we live very badly. The rooms are very bare—that you might take; they have nothing in them. I don't know how you would sleep, how you would eat."

"With your permission, I could easily put in a bed and a few tables and chairs. *C'est la moindre des choses*[6] and the affair of an hour or two. I know a little man from whom I can hire what I should want for a few months, for a trifle, and my gondolier can bring the things round in his boat. Of course in this great house you must

6. That's the least of things.

have a second kitchen, and my servant, who is a wonderfully handy fellow" (this personage was an evocation of the moment), "can easily cook me a chop there. My tastes and habits are of the simplest; I live on flowers!" And then I ventured to add that if they were very poor it was all the more reason they should let their rooms. They were bad economists—I had never heard of such a waste of material.

I saw in a moment that the good lady had never before been spoken to in that way, with a kind of humorous firmness which did not exclude sympathy but was on the contrary founded on it. She might easily have told me that my sympathy was impertinent, but this by good fortune did not occur to her. I left her with the understanding that she would consider the matter with her aunt and that I might come back the next day for their decision.

"The aunt will refuse; she will think the whole proceeding very *louche*!"[7] Mrs. Prest declared shortly after this, when I had resumed my place in her gondola. She had put the idea into my head and now (so little are women to be counted on) she appeared to take a despondent view of it. Her pessimism provoked me and I pretended to have the best hopes; I went so far as to say that I had a distinct presentiment that I should succeed. Upon this Mrs. Prest broke out, "Oh, I see what's in your head! You fancy you have made such an impression in a quarter of an hour that she is dying for you to come and can be depended upon to bring the old one round. If you do get in you'll count it as a triumph."

I did count it as a triumph, but only for the editor (in the last analysis), not for the man, who had not the tradition of personal conquest. When I went back on the morrow the little maid-servant conducted me straight through the long sala (it opened there as before in perfect perspective and was lighter now, which I thought a good omen) into the apartment from which the recipient of my former visit had emerged on that occasion. It was a large shabby parlour, with a fine old painted ceiling and a strange figure sitting alone at one of the windows. They come back to me now almost with the palpitation they caused, the successive feelings that accompanied my consciousness that as the door of the room closed behind me I was really face to face with the Juliana of some of Aspern's most exquisite and most renowned lyrics. I grew used to her afterwards, though never completely; but as she sat there before me my heart beat as fast as if the miracle of resurrection had taken place for my benefit. Her presence seemed somehow to contain his, and I felt nearer to him at that first moment of seeing her than I ever had been before or ever have been since. Yes, I remember my

7. Suspicious, fishy.

emotions in their order, even including a curious little tremor that took me when I saw that the niece was not there. With her, the day before, I had become sufficiently familiar, but it almost exceeded my courage (much as I had longed for the event) to be left alone with such a terrible relic as the aunt. She was too strange, too literally resurgent. Then came a check, with the perception that we were not really face to face, inasmuch as she had over her eyes a horrible green shade which, for her, served almost as a mask. I believed for the instant that she had put it on expressly, so that from underneath it she might scrutinise me without being scrutinised herself. At the same time it increased the presumption that there was a ghastly death's-head lurking behind it. The divine Juliana as a grinning skull—the vision hung there until it passed. Then it came to me that she *was* tremendously old—so old that death might take her at any moment, before I had time to get what I wanted from her. The next thought was a correction to that; it lighted up the situation. She would die next week, she would die tomorrow—then I could seize her papers. Meanwhile she sat there neither moving nor speaking. She was very small and shrunken, bent forward, with her hands in her lap. She was dressed in black and her head was wrapped in a piece of old black lace which showed no hair.

My emotion keeping me silent she spoke first, and the remark she made was exactly the most unexpected.

III

"Our house is very far from the centre, but the little canal is very *comme il faut.*"

"It's the sweetest corner of Venice and I can imagine nothing more charming," I hastened to reply. The old lady's voice was very thin and weak, but it had an agreeable, cultivated murmur and there was wonder in the thought that that individual note had been in Jeffrey Aspern's ear.

"Please to sit down there. I hear very well," she said quietly, as if perhaps I had been shouting at her; and the chair she pointed to was at a certain distance. I took possession of it, telling her that I was perfectly aware that I had intruded, that I had not been properly introduced and could only throw myself upon her indulgence. Perhaps the other lady, the one I had had the honour of seeing the day before, would have explained to her about the garden. That was literally what had given me courage to take a step so unconventional. I had fallen in love at sight with the whole place (she herself probably was so used to it that she did not know the impression it was capable of making on a stranger), and I had felt it was really a

case to risk something. Was her own kindness in receiving me a
sign that I was not wholly out in my calculation? It would render
me extremely happy to think so. I could give her my word of honour
that I was a most respectable, inoffensive person and that as an
inmate they would be barely conscious of my existence. I would
conform to any regulations, any restrictions if they would only let
me enjoy the garden. Moreover I should be delighted to give her
references; guarantees; they would be of the very best, both in Venice and in England as well as in America.

She listened to me in perfect stillness and I felt that she was
looking at me with great attention, though I could see only the
lower part of her bleached and shrivelled face. Independently of the
refining process of old age it had a delicacy which once must have
been great. She had been very fair, she had had a wonderful complexion. She was silent a little after I had ceased speaking; then she
inquired, "If you are so fond of a garden why don't you go to *terra
firma*,[8] where there are so many far better than this?"

"Oh, it's the combination!" I answered, smiling; and then, with
rather a flight of fancy, "It's the idea of a garden in the middle of
the sea."

"It's not in the middle of the sea; you can't see the water."

I stared a moment, wondering whether she wished to convict me
of fraud. "Can't see the water? Why, dear madam, I can come up
to the very gate in my boat."

She appeared inconsequent, for she said vaguely in reply to this,
"Yes, if you have got a boat. I haven't any; it's many years since I
have been in one of the gondolas." She uttered these words as if
the gondolas were a curious far-away craft which she knew only by
hearsay.

"Let me assure you of the pleasure with which I would put mine
at your service!" I exclaimed. I had scarcely said this however before
I became aware that the speech was in questionable taste and might
also do me the injury of making me appear too eager, too possessed
of a hidden motive. But the old woman remained impenetrable and
her attitude bothered me by suggesting that she had a fuller vision
of me than I had of her. She gave me no thanks for my somewhat
extravagant offer but remarked that the lady I had seen the day
before was her niece; she would presently come in. She had asked
her to stay away a little on purpose, because she herself wished to
see me at first alone. She relapsed into silence and I asked myself
why she had judged this necessary and what was coming yet; also
whether I might venture on some judicious remark in praise of her

8. The mainland: Venice sits on islands some two miles from the mainland.

companion. I went so far as to say that I should be delighted to see her again: she had been so very courteous to me, considering how odd she must have thought me—a declaration which drew from Miss Bordereau another of her whimsical speeches.

"She has very good manners; I bred her up myself!" I was on the point of saying that that accounted for the easy grace of the niece, but I arrested myself in time, and the next moment the old woman went on: "I don't care who you may be—I don't want to know; it signifies very little to-day." This had all the air of being a formula of dismissal, as if her next words would be that I might take myself off now that she had had the amusement of looking on the face of such a monster of indiscretion. Therefore I was all the more surprised when she added, with her soft, venerable quaver, "You may have as many rooms as you like—if you will pay a good deal of money."

I hesitated but for a single instant, long enough to ask myself what she meant in particular by this condition. First it struck me that she must have really a large sum in her mind; then I reasoned quickly that her idea of a large sum would probably not correspond to my own. My deliberation, I think, was not so visible as to diminish the promptitude with which I replied, "I will pay with pleasure and of course in advance whatever you may think it proper to ask me."

"Well then, a thousand francs a month," she rejoined instantly, while her baffling green shade continued to cover her attitude.

The figure, as they say, was startling and my logic had been at fault. The sum she had mentioned was, by the Venetian measure of such matters, exceedingly large; there was many an old palace in an out-of-the-way corner that I might on such terms have enjoyed by the year. But so far as my small means allowed I was prepared to spend money, and my decision was quickly taken. I would pay her with a smiling face what she asked, but in that case I would give myself the compensation of extracting the papers from her for nothing. Moreover if she had asked five times as much I should have risen to the occasion; so odious would it have appeared to me to stand chaffering with Aspern's Juliana. It was queer enough to have a question of money with her at all. I assured her that her views perfectly met my own and that on the morrow I should have the pleasure of putting three months' rent into her hand. She received this announcement with serenity and with no apparent sense that after all it would be becoming of her to say that I ought to see the rooms first. This did not occur to her and indeed her serenity was mainly what I wanted. Our little bargain was just concluded when the door opened and the younger lady appeared on the threshold. As soon as Miss Bordereau saw her niece she cried out almost gaily, "He will give three thousand—three thousand tomorrow!"

Miss Tita stood still, with her patient eyes turning from one of us to the other; then she inquired, scarcely above her breath, "Do you mean francs?"

"Did you mean francs or dollars?"[9] the old woman asked of me at this.

"I think francs were what you said," I answered, smiling.

"That is very good," said Miss Tita, as if she had become conscious that her own question might have looked over-reaching.

"What do *you* know? You are ignorant," Miss Bordereau remarked; not with acerbity but with a strange, soft coldness.

"Yes, of money—certainly of money!" Miss Tita hastened to exclaim.

"I am sure you have your own branches of knowledge," I took the liberty of saying, genially. There was something painful to me, somehow, in the turn the conversation had taken, in the discussion of the rent.

"She had a very good education when she was young. I looked into that myself," said Miss Bordereau. Then she added, "But she has learned nothing since."

"I have always been with you," Miss Tita rejoined very mildly, and evidently with no intention of making an epigram.

"Yes, but for that!" her aunt declared, with more satirical force. She evidently meant that but for this her niece would never have got on at all; the point of the observation however being lost on Miss Tita, though she blushed at hearing her history revealed to a stranger. Miss Bordereau went on, addressing herself to me: "And what time will you come to-morrow with the money?"

"The sooner the better. If it suits you I will come at noon."

"I am always here but I have my hours," said the old woman, as if her convenience were not to be taken for granted.

"You mean the times when you receive?"

"I never receive. But I will see you at noon, when you come with the money."

"Very good, I shall be punctual;" and I added, "May I shake hands with you, on our contract?" I thought there ought to be some little form, it would make me really feel easier, for I foresaw that there would be no other. Besides, though Miss Bordereau could not today

9. In 1890, two years after publication of the story, the official rate of exchange was about five French francs to the dollar. The lira, the currency of the Kingdom of Italy, to which Venice by that time belonged, was not an international trading currency like the franc. But Venice had been involved in international trade for centuries: this may explain why these Americans in Venice think in francs rather than lire.

be called personally attractive and there was something even in her wasted antiquity that bade one stand at one's distance, I felt an irresistible desire to hold in my own for a moment the hand that Jeffrey Aspern had pressed.

For a minute she made no answer and I saw that my proposal failed to meet with her approbation. She indulged in no movement of withdrawal, which I half expected; she only said coldly, "I belong to a time when that was not the custom."

I felt rather snubbed but I exclaimed good-humouredly to Miss Tita, "Oh, you will do as well!" I shook hands with her while she replied, with a small flutter, "Yes, yes, to show it's all arranged!"

"Shall you bring the money in gold?" Miss Bordereau demanded, as I was turning to the door.

I looked at her a moment. "Aren't you a little afraid, after all, of keeping such a sum as that in the house?" It was not that I was annoyed at her avidity but I was really struck with the disparity between such a treasure and such scanty means of guarding it.

"Whom should I be afraid of if I am not afraid of you?" she asked with her shrunken grimness.

"Ah well," said I, laughing, "I shall be in point of fact a protector and I will bring gold if you prefer."

"Thank you," the old woman returned with dignity and with an inclination of her head which evidently signified that I might depart. I passed out of the room, reflecting that it would not be easy to circumvent her. As I stood in the sala again I saw that Miss Tita had followed me and I supposed that as her aunt had neglected to suggest that I should take a look at my quarters it was her purpose to repair the omission. But she made no such suggestion; she only stood there with a dim, though not a languid smile, and with an effect of irresponsible, incompetent youth which was almost comically at variance with the faded facts of her person. She was not infirm, like her aunt, but she struck me as still more helpless, because her inefficiency was spiritual, which was not the case with Miss Bordereau's. I waited to see if she would offer to show me the rest of the house, but I did not precipitate the question, inasmuch as my plan was from this moment to spend as much of my time as possible in her society. I only observed at the end of a minute:

"I have had better fortune than I hoped. It was very kind of her to see me. Perhaps you said a good word for me."

"It was the idea of the money," said Miss Tita.

"And did you suggest that?"

"I told her that you would perhaps give a good deal."

"What made you think that?"

"I told her I thought you were rich."

"And what put that idea into your head?"

"I don't know; the way you talked."

"Dear me, I must talk differently now," I declared. "I'm sorry to say it's not the case."

"Well," said Miss Tita, "I think that in Venice the *forestieri*,[1] in general, often give a great deal for something that after all isn't much." She appeared to make this remark with a comforting intention, to wish to remind me that if I had been extravagant I was not really foolishly singular. We walked together along the sala, and as I took its magnificent measure I said to her that I was afraid it would not form a part of my *quartiere*.[2] Were my rooms by chance to be among those that opened into it? "Not if you go above, on the second floor," she answered with a little startled air, as if she had rather taken for granted I would know my proper place.

"And I infer that that's where your aunt would like me to be."

"She said your apartments ought to be very distinct."

"That certainly would be best." And I listened with respect while she told me that up above I was free to take whatever I liked; that there was another staircase, but only from the floor on which we stood, and that to pass from it to the garden-story or to come up to my lodging I should have in effect to cross the great hall. This was an immense point gained; I foresaw that it would constitute my whole leverage in my relations with the two ladies. When I asked Miss Tita how I was to manage at present to find my way up she replied with an access of that sociable shyness which constantly marked her manner.

"Perhaps you can't. I don't see—unless I should go with you." She evidently had not thought of this before.

We ascended to the upper floor and visited a long succession of empty rooms. The best of them looked over the garden; some of the others had a view of the blue lagoon, above the opposite rough-tiled housetops. They were all dusty and even a little disfigured with long neglect, but I saw that by spending a few hundred francs I should be able to convert three or four of them into a convenient habitation. My experiment was turning out costly, yet now that I had all but taken possession I ceased to allow this to trouble me. I mentioned to my companion a few of the things that I should put in, but she replied rather more precipitately than usual that I might do exactly what I liked; she seemed to wish to notify me that the Misses Bordereau would take no overt interest in my proceedings. I guessed that her aunt had instructed her to adopt this tone, and I may as well say now that I came afterwards to distinguish perfectly (as I believed) between the speeches she made on her own respon-

1. Foreigners.
2. Quarters, lodging.

sibility and those the old lady imposed upon her. She took no notice
of the unswept condition of the rooms and indulged in no explanations nor apologies. I said to myself that this was a sign that
Juliana and her niece (disenchanting idea!) were untidy persons,
with a low Italian standard; but I afterwards recognised that a
lodger who had forced an entrance had no *locus standi*[3] as a critic.
We looked out of a good many windows, for there was nothing
within the rooms to look at, and still I wanted to linger. I asked her
what several different objects in the prospect might be, but in no
case did she appear to know. She was evidently not familiar with
the view—it was as if she had not looked at it for years—and I
presently saw that she was too preoccupied with something else to
pretend to care for it. Suddenly she said—the remark was not suggested:

"I don't know whether it will make any difference to you, but the
money is for me."

"The money?"

"The money you are going to bring."

"Why, you'll make me wish to stay here two or three years." I
spoke as benevolently as possible, though it had begun to act on
my nerves that with these women so associated with Aspern the
pecuniary question should constantly come back.

"That would be very good for me," she replied, smiling.

"You put me on my honour!"

She looked as if she failed to understand this, but went on: "She
wants me to have more. She thinks she is going to die."

"Ah, not soon, I hope!" I exclaimed, with genuine feeling. I had
perfectly considered the possibility that she would destroy her papers on the day she should feel her end really approach. I believed
that she would cling to them till then and I think I had an idea
that she read Aspern's letters over every night or at least pressed
them to her withered lips. I would have given a good deal to have
a glimpse of the latter spectacle. I asked Miss Tita if the old lady
were seriously ill and she replied that she was only very tired—she
had lived so very, very long. That was what she said herself—she
wanted to die for a change. Besides, all her friends were dead long
ago; either they ought to have remained or she ought to have gone.
That was another thing her aunt often said—she was not at all
content.

"But people don't die when they like, do they?" Miss Tita inquired. I took the liberty of asking why, if there was actually enough
money to maintain both of them, there would not be more than
enough in case of her being left alone. She considered this difficult

3. No standing, i.e., no right.

problem a moment and then she said, "Oh, well, you know, she takes care of me. She thinks that when I'm alone I shall be a great fool, I shall not know how to manage."

"I should have supposed rather that you took care of her. I'm afraid she is very proud."

"Why, have you discovered that already?" Miss Tita cried, with the glimmer of an illumination in her face.

"I was shut up with her there for a considerable time, and she struck me, she interested me extremely. It didn't take me long to make my discovery. She won't have much to say to me while I'm here."

"No, I don't think she will," my companion averred.

"Do you suppose she has some suspicion of me?"

Miss Tita's honest eyes gave me no sign that I had touched a mark. "I shouldn't think so—letting you in after all so easily."

"Oh, so easily! she has covered her risk. But where is it that one could take an advantage of her?"

"I oughtn't to tell you if I knew, ought I?" And Miss Tita added, before I had time to reply to this, smiling dolefully, "Do you think we have any weak points?"

"That's exactly what I'm asking. You would only have to mention them for me to respect them religiously."

She looked at me, at this, with that air of timid but candid and even gratified curiosity with which she had confronted me from the first; and then she said, "There is nothing to tell. We are terribly quiet. I don't know how the days pass. We have no life."

"I wish I might think that I should bring you a little."

"Oh, we know what we want," she went on. "It's all right."

There were various things I desired to ask her: how in the world they did live; whether they had any friends or visitors, any relations in America or in other countries. But I judged such an inquiry would be premature; I must leave it to a later chance. "Well, don't *you* be proud," I contented myself with saying. "Don't hide from me altogether."

"Oh, I must stay with my aunt," she returned, without looking at me. And at the same moment, abruptly, without any ceremony of parting, she quitted me and disappeared, leaving me to make my own way downstairs. I remained a while longer, wandering about the bright desert (the sun was pouring in) of the old house, thinking the situation over on the spot. Not even the pattering little *serva*[4] came to look after me and I reflected that after all this treatment showed confidence.

4. Maidservant.

IV

Perhaps it did, but all the same, six weeks later, towards the middle of June, the moment when Mrs. Prest undertook her annual migration, I had made no measurable advance. I was obliged to confess to her that I had no results to speak of. My first step had been unexpectedly rapid, but there was no appearance that it would be followed by a second. I was a thousand miles from taking tea with my hostesses—that privilege of which, as I reminded Mrs. Prest, we both had had a vision. She reproached me with wanting boldness and I answered that even to be bold you must have an opportunity: you may push on through a breach but you can't batter down a dead wall. She answered that the breach I had already made was big enough to admit an army and accused me of wasting precious hours in whimpering in her salon when I ought to have been carrying on the struggle in the field. It is true that I went to see her very often, on the theory that it would console me (I freely expressed my discouragement) for my want of success on my own premises. But I began to perceive that it did not console me to be perpetually chaffed for my scruples, especially when I was really so vigilant; and I was rather glad when my derisive friend closed her house for the summer. She had expected to gather amusement from the drama of my intercourse with the Misses Bordereau and she was disappointed that the intercourse, and consequently the drama, had not come off. "They'll lead you on to your ruin," she said before she left Venice. "They'll get all your money without showing you a scrap." I think I settled down to my business with more concentration after she had gone away.

It was a fact that up to that time I had not, save on a single brief occasion, had even a moment's contact with my queer hostesses. The exception had occurred when I carried them according to my promise the terrible three thousand francs. Then I found Miss Tita waiting for me in the hall, and she took the money from my hand so that I did not see her aunt. The old lady had promised to receive me, but she apparently thought nothing of breaking that vow. The money was contained in a bag of chamois leather, of respectable dimensions, which my banker had given me, and Miss Tita had to make a big fist to receive it. This she did with extreme solemnity, though I tried to treat the affair a little as a joke. It was in no jocular strain, yet it was with simplicity, that she inquired, weighing the money in her two palms: "Don't you think it's too much?" To which I replied that that would depend upon the amount of pleasure I should get for it. Hereupon she turned away from me quickly, as she had done the day before, murmuring in a tone different from any she had used hitherto: "Oh, pleasure, pleasure—there's no pleasure in this house!"

After this, for a long time, I never saw her, and I wondered that the common chances of the day should not have helped us to meet. It could only be evident that she was immensely on her guard against them; and in addition to this the house was so big that for each other we were lost in it. I used to look out for her hopefully as I crossed the sala in my comings and goings, but I was not rewarded with a glimpse of the tail of her dress. It was as if she never peeped out of her aunt's apartment. I used to wonder what she did there week after week and year after year. I had never encountered such a violent *parti pris*[5] of seclusion; it was more than keeping quiet—it was like hunted creatures feigning death. The two ladies appeared to have no visitors whatever and no sort of contact with the world. I judged at least that people could not have come to the house and that Miss Tita could not have gone out without my having some observation of it. I did what I disliked myself for doing (reflecting that it was only once in a way): I questioned my servant about their habits and let him divine that I should be interested in any information he could pick up. But he picked up amazingly little for a knowing Venetian: it must be added that where there is a perpetual fast there are very few crumbs on the floor. His cleverness in other ways was sufficient, if it was not quite all that I had attributed to him on the occasion of my first interview with Miss Tita. He had helped my gondolier to bring me round a boat-load of furniture; and when these articles had been carried to the top of the palace and distributed according to our associated wisdom he organised my household with such promptitude as was consistent with the fact that it was composed exclusively of himself. He made me in short as comfortable as I could be with my indifferent prospects. I should have been glad if he had fallen in love with Miss Bordereau's maid or, failing this, had taken her in aversion; either event might have brought about some kind of catastrophe and a catastrophe might have led to some parley. It was my idea that she would have been sociable, and I myself on various occasions saw her flit to and fro on domestic errands, so that I was sure she was accessible. But I tasted of no gossip from that foundation, and I afterwards learned that Pasquale's affections were fixed upon an object that made him heedless of other women. This was a young lady with a powdered face, a yellow cotton gown and much leisure, who used often to come to see him. She practised, at her convenience, the art of a stringer of beads (these ornaments are made in Venice, in profusion; she had her pocket full of them and I used to

5. Prejudice (in favor of).

find them on the floor of my apartment), and kept an eye on the maiden in the house. It was not for me of course to make the domestics tattle, and I never said a word to Miss Bordereau's cook.

It seemed to me a proof of the old lady's determination to have nothing to do with me that she should never have sent me a receipt for my three months' rent. For some days I looked out for it and then, when I had given it up, I wasted a good deal of time in wondering what her reason had been for neglecting so indispensable and familiar a form. At first I was tempted to send her a reminder, after which I relinquished the idea (against my judgment as to what was right in the particular case), on the general ground of wishing to keep quiet. If Miss Bordereau suspected me of ulterior aims she would suspect me less if I should be businesslike, and yet I consented not to be so. It was possible she intended her omission as an impertinence, a visible irony, to show how she could overreach people who attempted to overreach her. On that hypothesis it was well to let her see that one did not notice her little tricks. The real reading of the matter, I afterwards perceived, was simply the poor old woman's desire to emphasise the fact that I was in the enjoyment of a favour as rigidly limited as it had been liberally bestowed. She had given me part of her house and now she would not give me even a morsel of paper with her name on it. Let me say that even at first this did not make me too miserable, for the whole episode was essentially delightful to me. I foresaw that I should have a summer after my own literary heart, and the sense of holding my opportunity was much greater than the sense of losing it. There could be no Venetian business without patience, and since I adored the place I was much more in the spirit of it for having laid in a large provision. That spirit kept me perpetual company and seemed to look out at me from the revived immortal face—in which all his genius shone—of the great poet who was my prompter. I had invoked him and he had come; he hovered before me half the time; it was as if his bright ghost had returned to earth to tell me that he regarded the affair as his own no less than mine and that we should see it fraternally, cheerfully to a conclusion. It was as if he had said, "Poor dear, be easy with her; she has some natural prejudices; only give her time. Strange as it may appear to you she was very attractive in 1820. Meanwhile are we not in Venice together, and what better place is there for the meeting of dear friends? See how it glows with the advancing summer; how the sky and the sea and the rosy air and the marble of the palaces all shimmer and melt together." My eccentric private errand became a part of the general romance and the general glory—I felt even a mystic companionship, a moral fraternity with all those who in the past had been in the service of art. They had worked for beauty, for a devotion; and what else was I doing? That element was in everything that Jeffrey Aspern had written and I was only bringing it to the light.

I lingered in the sala when I went to and fro; I used to watch— as long as I thought decent—the door that led to Miss Bordereau's part of the house. A person observing me might have supposed I was trying to cast a spell upon it or attempting some odd experiment in hypnotism. But I was only praying it would open or thinking what treasure probably lurked behind it. I hold it singular, as I look back, that I should never have doubted for a moment that the sacred relics were there; never have failed to feel a certain joy at being under the same roof with them. After all they were under my hand—they had not escaped me yet; and they made my life continuous, in a fashion, with the illustrious life they had touched at the other end. I lost myself in this satisfaction to the point of assuming—in my quiet extravagance—that poor Miss Tita also went back, went back as I used to phrase it. She did indeed, the gentle spinster, but not quite so far as Jeffrey Aspern, who was simply heresay to her, quite as he was to me. Only she had lived for years with Juliana, she had seen and handled the papers and (even though she was stupid) some esoteric knowledge had rubbed off on her. That was what the old woman represented—esoteric knowledge; and this was the idea with which my editorial heart used to thrill. It literally beat faster often, of an evening, when I had been out, as I stopped with my candle in the re-echoing hall on my way up to bed. It was as if at such a moment as that, in the stillness, after the long contradiction of the day, Miss Bordereau's secrets were in the air, the wonder of her survival more palpable. These were the acute impressions. I had them in another form, with more of a certain sort of reciprocity, during the hours that I sat in the garden looking up over the top of my book at the closed windows of my hostess. In these windows no sign of life ever appeared; it was as if, for fear of my catching a glimpse of them, the two ladies passed their days in the dark. But this only proved to me that they had something to conceal; which was what I had wished to demonstrate. Their motionless shutters became as expressive as eyes consciously closed, and I took comfort in thinking that at all events though invisible themselves they saw me between the lashes.

I made a point of spending as much time as possible in the garden, to justify the picture I had originally given of my horticultural passion. And I not only spent time, but (hang it! as I said) I spent money. As soon as I had got my rooms arranged and could give the proper thought to the matter I surveyed the place with a clever expert and made terms for having it put in order. I was sorry to do this, for personally I liked it better as it was, with its weeds and its wild, rough tangle, its sweet, characteristic Venetian shabbiness. I had to be consistent, to keep my promise that I would smother the house in flowers. Moreover I formed this graceful project that by flowers I would make my way—I would succeed by big nosegays. I would batter the old women with lilies—I would bombard their citadel with roses. Their door would have to yield to the pressure when a mountain of carnations should be piled up against it. The place in truth had been brutally neglected. The Venetian capacity for dawdling is of the largest, and for a good many days unlimited litter was all my gardener had to show for his ministrations. There was a great digging of holes and carting about of earth, and after a while I grew so impatient that I had thoughts of sending for my bouquets to the nearest stand. But I reflected that the ladies would see through the chinks of their shutters that they must have been bought and might make up their minds from this that I was a humbug. So I composed myself and finally, though the delay was long, perceived some appearances of bloom. This encouraged me and I waited serenely enough till they multiplied. Meanwhile the real summer days arrived and began to pass, and as I look back upon them they seem to me almost the happiest of my life. I took more and more care to be in the garden whenever it was not too hot. I had an arbour arranged and a low table and an armchair put into it; and I carried out books and portfolios (I had always some business of writing in hand), and worked and waited and mused and hoped, while the golden hours elapsed and the plants drank in the light and the inscrutable old palace turned pale and then, as the day waned, began to flush in it and my papers rustled in the wandering breeze of the Adriatic.

Considering how little satisfaction I got from it at first it is remarkable that I should not have grown more tired of wondering what mystic rites of ennui the Misses Bordereau celebrated in their darkened rooms; whether this had always been the tenor of their life and how in previous years they had escaped elbowing their neighbours. It was clear that they must have had other habits and other circumstances; that they must once have been young or at least middle-aged. There was no end to the questions it was possible to ask about them and no end to the answers it was not possible to frame. I had known many of my country-people in Europe and was familiar with the strange ways they were liable to take up there; but the Misses Bordereau formed altogether a new type of the American absentee. Indeed it was plain that the American name had ceased to have any application to them—I had seen this in the ten minutes I spent in the old woman's room. You could never have said whence they came, from the appearance of either of them; wherever it was they had long ago dropped the local accent and fashion. There was nothing in them that one recognised, and putting the question of speech aside they might have been Norwegians or Spaniards. Miss Bordereau, after all, had been in Europe nearly threequarters of a century; it appeared by some verses addressed to her by Aspern on the occasion of his own second absence from America—verses of which Cumnor and I had after infinite conjecture established solidly enough the date—that she was even then, as a girl of twenty, on the foreign side of the sea. There was an implication in the poem (I hope not just for the phrase) that he had come back for her sake. We had no real light upon her circumstances at that moment, any more than we had upon her origin, which we believed to be of the sort usually spoken of as modest. Cumnor had a theory that she had been a governess in some family in which the poet visited and that, in consequence of her position, there was from the first something unavowed, or rather something positively clandestine, in their relations. I on the other hand had hatched a little romance according to which she was the daughter of an artist, a painter or a sculptor, who had left the western world when the century was fresh, to study in the ancient schools. It was essential to my hypothesis that this amiable man should have lost his wife, should have been poor and unsuccessful and should have had a second daughter, of a disposition quite different from Juliana's. It was also indispensable that he should have been accompanied to Europe by these young ladies and should have established himself there for the remainder of a struggling, saddened life. There was a further implication that Miss Bordereau had had in her youth a perverse and adventurous, albeit a generous and fascinating character, and that she had passed through some singular vicissitudes. By what passions had she been ravaged, by what sufferings had she been blanched, what store of memories had she laid away for the monotonous future?

I asked myself these things as I sat spinning theories about her in my arbour and the bees droned in the flowers. It was incontestable that, whether for right or for wrong, most readers of certain of Aspern's poems (poems not as ambiguous as the sonnets—scarcely more divine, I think—of Shakespeare) had taken for granted that Juliana had not always adhered to the steep footway of renunciation. There hovered about her name a perfume of reckless passion, an intimation that she had not been exactly as the respectable young person in general. Was this a sign that her singer had betrayed her, had given her away, as we say nowadays, to posterity? Certain it is that it would have been difficult to put one's finger on the passage in which her fair fame suffered an imputation. Moreover was not any fame fair enough that was so sure of duration and was associated with works immortal through their beauty? It was a part of my idea that the young lady had had a foreign lover (and an unedifying tragical rupture) before her meeting with Jeffrey Aspern.

She had lived with her father and sister in a queer old-fashioned, expatriated, artistic Bohemia, in the days when the æsthetic was only the academic and the painters who knew the best models for a *contadina*[6] and *pifferaro* wore peaked hats and long hair. It was a society less furnished than the coteries of to-day (in its ignorance of the wonderful chances, the opportunities of the early bird, with which its path was strewn), with tatters of old stuff and fragments of old crockery; so that Miss Bordereau appeared not to have picked up or have inherited many objects of importance. There was no enviable *bric-à-brac*, with its provoking legend of cheapness, in the room in which I had seen her. Such a fact as that suggested bareness, but none the less it worked happily into the sentimental interest I had always taken in the early movements of my countrymen as visitors to Europe. When Americans went abroad in 1820 there was something romantic, almost heroic in it, as compared with the perpetual ferryings of the present hour, when photography and other conveniences have annihilated surprise. Miss Bordereau sailed with her family on a tossing brig, in the days of long voyages and sharp differences; she had her emotions on the top of yellow diligences,[7] passed the night at inns where she dreamed of travellers' tales, and was struck, on reaching the eternal city, with the elegance of Roman pearls and scarfs. There was something touching to me in all that and my imagination frequently went back to the period. If Miss Bordereau carried it there of course Jeffrey Aspern at other times had done so a great deal more. It was a much more important fact, if one were looking at his genius critically, that he had lived in the days before the general transfusion. It had happened to me to regret that he had known Europe at all; I should have liked to see what he would have written without that experience, by which he had incontestably been enriched. But as his fate had ordered otherwise I went with him—I tried to judge how the old world would have struck him. It was not only there, however, that I watched him; the relations he had entertained with the new had even a livelier interest. His own country after all had had most of his life, and his muse, as they said at that time, was essentially American. That was originally what I had loved him for: that at a period when our native land was nude and crude and provincial, when the famous "atmosphere" it is supposed to lack was not even missed, when literature was lonely there and art and form almost impossible, he had found means to live and write like one of the first; to be free and general and not at all afraid; to feel, understand and express everything.

6. Country woman; a *pifferaro* is a pipe-player.
7. Stagecoaches.

V

I was seldom at home in the evening, for when I attempted to occupy myself in my apartments the lamplight brought in a swarm of noxious insects, and it was too hot for closed windows. Accordingly I spent the late hours either on the water (the moonlight of Venice is famous), or in the splendid square which serves as a vast forecourt to the strange old basilica of Saint Mark.[8] I sat in front of Florian's *café*, eating ices, listening to music, talking with acquaintances: the traveller will remember how the immense cluster of tables and little chairs stretches like a promontory into the smooth lake of the Piazza. The whole place, of a summer's evening, under the stars and with all the lamps, all the voices and light footsteps on marble (the only sounds of the arcades that enclose it), is like an open-air saloon dedicated to cooling drinks and to a still finer degustation—that of the exquisite impressions received during the day. When I did not prefer to keep mine to myself there was always a stray tourist, disencumbered of his Bädeker,[9] to discuss them with, or some domesticated painter rejoicing in the return of the season of strong effects. The wonderful church, with its low domes and bristling embroideries, the mystery of its mosaic and sculpture, looked ghostly in the tempered gloom, and the sea-breeze passed between the twin columns of the Piazzetta, the lintels of a door no longer guarded, as gently as if a rich curtain were swaying there. I used sometimes on these occasions to think of the Misses Bordereau and of the pity of their being shut up in apartments which in the Venetian July even Venetian vastness did not prevent from being stuffy. Their life seemed miles away from the life of the Piazza, and no doubt it was really too late to make the austere Juliana change her habits. But poor Miss Tita would have enjoyed one of Florian's ices, I was sure; sometimes I even had thoughts of carrying one home to her. Fortunately my patience bore fruit and I was not obliged to do anything so ridiculous.

One evening about the middle of July I came in earlier than usual—I forget what chance had led to this—and instead of going up to my quarters made my way into the garden. The temperature was very high; it was such a night as one would gladly have spent in the open air and I was in no hurry to go to bed. I had floated home in my gondola, listening to the slow splash of the oar in the

8. The Piazza San Marco (Saint Mark's Square) is the centerpiece of Venice, famous for its historical and architectural monuments—for the Basilica, a church which dates back to the eleventh century, for its arcades (or covered galleries), which house famous cafés such as Florian's, and for its pigeons. It opens out onto the Grand Canal through the Piazzetta, which is flanked by the old Doge's Palace and dominated by twin granite columns guarding the entrance from the water.
9. A popular series of guidebooks published in Germany.

narrow dark canals, and now the only thought that solicited me was the vague reflection that it would be pleasant to recline at one's length in the fragrant darkness on a garden bench. The odour of the canal was doubtless at the bottom of that aspiration and the breath of the garden, as I entered it, gave consistency to my purpose. It was delicious—just such an air as must have trembled with Romeo's vows when he stood among the flowers and raised his arms to his mistress's balcony. I looked at the windows of the palace to see if by chance the example of Verona[1] (Verona being not far off) had been followed; but everything was dim, as usual, and everything was still. Juliana, on summer nights in her youth, might have murmured down from open windows at Jeffrey Aspern, but Miss Tita was not a poet's mistress any more than I was a poet. This however did not prevent my gratification from being great as I became aware on reaching the end of the garden that Miss Tita was seated in my little bower. At first I only made out an indistinct figure, not in the least counting on such an overture from one of my hostesses; it even occurred to me that some sentimental maidservant had stolen in to keep a tryst with her sweetheart. I was going to turn away, not to frighten her, when the figure rose to its height and I recognised Miss Bordereau's niece. I must do myself the justice to say that I did not wish to frighten her either, and much as I had longed for some such accident I should have been capable of retreating. It was as if I had laid a trap for her by coming home earlier than usual and adding to that eccentricity by creeping into the garden. As she rose she spoke to me, and then I reflected that perhaps, secure in my almost inveterate absence, it was her nightly practice to take a lonely airing. There was no trap, in truth, because I had had no suspicion. At first I took for granted that the words she uttered expressed discomfiture at my arrival; but as she repeated them—I had not caught them clearly—I had the surprise of hearing her say, "Oh, dear, I'm so very glad you've come!" She and her aunt had in common the property of unexpected speeches. She came out of the arbour almost as if she were going to throw herself into my arms.

I hasten to add that she did nothing of the kind; she did not even shake hands with me. It was a gratification to her to see me and presently she told me why—because she was nervous when she was out-of-doors at night alone. The plants and bushes looked so strange in the dark, and there were all sorts of queer sounds—she could not tell what they were—like the noises of animals. She stood close to me, looking about her with an air of greater security but without any demonstration of interest in me as an individual. Then I guessed that nocturnal prowlings were not in the least her habit,

1. The city where Romeo and Juliet lived.

and I was also reminded (I had been struck with the circumstance in talking with her before I took possession) that it was impossible to over-estimate her simplicity.

"You speak as if you were lost in the backwoods," I said, laughing. "How you manage to keep out of this charming place when you have only three steps to take to get into it, is more than I have yet been able to discover. You hide away mighty well so long as I am on the premises, I know; but I had a hope that you peeped out a little at other times. You and your poor aunt are worse off than Carmelite nuns in their cells. Should you mind telling me how you exist without air, without exercise, without any sort of human contact? I don't see how you carry on the common business of life."

She looked at me as if I were talking some strange tongue and her answer was so little of an answer that I was considerably irritated.

"We go to bed very early—earlier than you would believe." I was on the point of saying that this only deepened the mystery when she gave me some relief by adding, "Before you came we were not so private. But I never have been out at night."

"Never in these fragrant alleys, blooming here under your nose?"

"Ah," said Miss Tita, "they were never nice till now!" There was an unmistakable reference in this and a flattering comparison, so that it seemed to me I had gained a small advantage. As it would help me to follow it up to establish a sort of grievance I asked her why, since she thought my garden nice, she had never thanked me in any way for the flowers I had been sending up in such quantities for the previous three weeks. I had not been discouraged—there had been, as she would have observed, a daily armful; but I had been brought up in the common forms and a word of recognition now and then would have touched me in the right place.

"Why I didn't know they were for me!"

"They were for both of you. Why should I make a difference?"

Miss Tita reflected as if she might be thinking of a reason for that, but she failed to produce one. Instead of this she asked abruptly, "Why in the world do you want to know us?"

"I ought after all to make a difference," I replied. "That question is your aunt's; it isn't yours. You wouldn't ask it if you hadn't been put up to it."

"She didn't tell me to ask you," Miss Tita replied, without confusion; she was the oddest mixture of the shrinking and the direct.

"Well, she has often wondered about it herself and expressed her wonder to you. She has insisted on it, so that she has put the idea into your head that I am unsufferably pushing. Upon my word I think I have been very discreet. And how completely your aunt must have lost every tradition of sociability, to see anything out of the way in the idea that respectable intelligent people, living as we do under the same roof, should occasionally exchange a remark! What could be more natural? We are of the same country and we have at least some of the same tastes, since, like you, I am intensely fond of Venice."

My interlocutress appeared incapable of grasping more than one clause in any proposition, and she declared quickly, eagerly, as if she were answering my whole speech: "I am not in the least fond of Venice. I should like to go far away!"

"Has she always kept you back so?" I went on, to show her that I could be as irrelevant as herself.

"She told me to come out to-night; she has told me very often," said Miss Tita. "It is I who wouldn't come. I don't like to leave her."

"Is she too weak, is she failing?" I demanded, with more emotion, I think, than I intended to show. I judged this by the way her eyes rested upon me in the darkness. It embarrassed me a little, and to turn the matter off I continued genially: "Do let us sit down together comfortably somewhere and you will tell me all about her."

Miss Tita made no resistance to this. We found a bench less secluded, less confidential, as it were, than the one in the arbour; and we were still sitting there when I heard midnight ring out from those clear bells of Venice which vibrate with a solemnity of their own over the lagoon and hold the air so much more than the chimes of other places. We were together more than an hour and our interview gave, as it struck me, a great lift to my undertaking. Miss Tita accepted the situation without a protest; she had avoided me for three months, yet now she treated me almost as if these three months had made me an old friend. If I had chosen I might have inferred from this that though she had avoided me she had given a good deal of consideration to doing so. She paid no attention to the flight of time—never worried at my keeping her so long away from her aunt. She talked freely, answering questions and asking them and not even taking advantage of certain longish pauses with which they inevitably alternated to say she thought she had better go in. It was almost as if she were waiting for something—something I might say to her—and intended to give me my opportunity. I was the more struck by this as she told me that her aunt had been less well for a good many days and in a way that was rather new. She was weaker; at moments it seemed as if she had no strength at all; yet more than ever before she wished to be left alone. That was why she had told her to come out—not even to remain in her own room, which was alongside; she said her niece irritated her, made her nervous. She sat still for hours together, as if she were asleep; she had always done that, musing and dozing; but at such times formerly she gave at intervals some small sign of life, of interest,

liking her companion to be near her with her work. Miss Tita confided to me that at present her aunt was so motionless that she
sometimes feared she was dead; moreover she took hardly any
food—one couldn't see what she lived on. The great thing was that
she still on most days got up; the serious job was to dress her, to
wheel her out of her bedroom. She clung to as many of her old
habits as possible and she had always, little company as they had
received for years, made a point of sitting in the parlour.

I scarcely knew what to think of all this—of Miss Tita's sudden
conversion to sociability and of the strange circumstance that the
more the old lady appeared to decline toward her end the less she
should desire to be looked after. The story did not hang together,
and I even asked myself whether it were not a trap laid for me, the
result of a design to make me show my hand. I could not have told
why my companions (as they could only by courtesy be called)
should have this purpose—why they should try to trip up so lucrative a lodger. At any rate I kept on my guard, so that Miss Tita
should not have occasion again to ask me if I had an *arrière-pensée*.[2]
Poor woman, before we parted for the night my mind was at rest
as to *her* capacity for entertaining one.

She told me more about their affairs than I had hoped; there was
no need to be prying, for it evidently drew her out simply to feel
that I listened, that I cared. She ceased wondering why I cared, and
at last, as she spoke of the brilliant life they had led years before,
she almost chattered. It was Miss Tita who judged it brilliant; she
said that when they first came to live in Venice, years and years
before (I saw that her mind was essentially vague about dates and
the order in which events had occurred), there was scarcely a week
that they had not some visitor or did not make some delightful
passeggio[3] in the city. They had seen all the curiosities; they had
even been to the Lido in a boat (she spoke as if I might think there
was a way on foot); they had had a collation, there, brought in three
baskets and spread out on the grass. I asked her what people they
had known and she said, Oh! very nice ones—the Cavaliere Bom-
bicci and the Contessa Altemura, with whom they had had a great
friendship. Also English people—the Churtons and the Goldies and
Mrs. Stock-Stock, whom they had loved dearly; she was dead and
gone, poor dear. That was the case with most of their pleasant circle
(this expression was Miss Tita's own), though a few were left, which
was a wonder considering how they had neglected them. She mentioned the names of two or three Venetian old women; of a certain

2. Ulterior motive.
3. Outing, trip. Since this is Venice, where canals serve for streets, these outings were
   probably by gondola. The island of the Lido is a fashionable beach resort.

doctor, very clever, who was so kind—he came as a friend, he had really given up practice; of the *avvocato*[4] Pochintesta, who wrote beautiful poems and had addressed one to her aunt. These people came to see them without fail every year, usually at the *capo d'anno*,[5] and of old her aunt used to make them some little present—her aunt and she together: small things that she, Miss Tita, made herself, like paper lamp-shades or mats for the decanters of wine at dinner or those woollen things that in cold weather were worn on the wrists. The last few years there had not been many presents; she could not think what to make and her aunt had lost her interest and never suggested. But the people came all the same; if the Venetians liked you once they liked you for ever.

There was something affecting in the good faith of this sketch of former social glories; the picnic at the Lido had remained vivid through the ages and poor Miss Tita evidently was of the impression that she had had a brilliant youth. She had in fact had a glimpse of the Venetian world in its gossiping, home-keeping, parsimonious, professional walks; for I observed for the first time that she had acquired by contact something of the trick of the familiar, soft-sounding, almost infantile speech of the place. I judged that she had imbibed this invertebrate dialect, from the natural way the names of things and people—mostly purely local—rose to her lips. If she knew little of what they represented she knew still less of anything else. Her aunt had drawn in—her failing interest in the table-mats and lamp-shades was a sign of that—and she had not been able to mingle in society or to entertain it alone; so that the matter of her reminiscences struck one as an old world altogether. If she had not been so decent her references would have seemed to carry one back to the queer rococo Venice of Casanova.[6] I found myself falling into the error of thinking of her too as one of Jeffrey Aspern's contemporaries; this came from her having so little in common with my own. It was possible, I said to myself, that she had not even heard of him; it might very well be that Juliana had not cared to lift even for her the veil that covered the temple of her youth. In this case she perhaps would not know of the existence of the papers, and I welcomed that presumption—it made me feel more safe with her—until I remembered that we had believed the letter of disavowal received by Cumnor to be in the handwriting of the niece. If it had been dictated to her she had of course to know what it was about; yet after all the effect of it was to repudiate the idea of any connection with the poet. I held it probable at all events

4. Lawyer.
5. New Year's Day.
6. A century before the narrative.

that Miss Tita had not read a word of his poetry. Moreover if, with her companion, she had always escaped the interviewer there was little occasion for her having got it into her head that people were "after" the letters. People had not been after them, inasmuch as they had not heard of them; and Cumnor's fruitless feeler would have been a solitary accident.

When midnight sounded Miss Tita got up; but she stopped at the door of the house only after she had wandered two or three times with me round the garden. "When shall I see you again?" I asked, before she went in; to which she replied with promptness that she should like to come out the next night. She added however that she should not come—she was so far from doing everything she liked.

"You might do a few things that *I* like," I said with a sigh.

"Oh, you—I don't believe you!" she murmured, at this, looking at me with her simple solemnity.

"Why don't you believe me?"

"Because I don't understand you."

"That is just the sort of occasion to have faith." I could not say more, though I should have liked to, as I saw that I only mystified her; for I had no wish to have it on my conscience that I might pass for having made love to her. Nothing less should I have seemed to do had I continued to beg a lady to "believe in me" in an Italian garden on a mid-summer night. There was some merit in my scruples, for Miss Tita lingered and lingered: I perceived that she felt that she should not really soon come down again and wished therefore to protract the present. She insisted too on making the talk between us personal to ourselves; and altogether her behaviour was such as would have been possible only to a completely innocent woman.

"I shall like the flowers better now that I know they are also meant for me."

"How could you have doubted it? If you will tell me the kind you like best I will send a double lot of them."

"Oh, I like them all best!" Then she went on, familiarly: "Shall you study—shall you read and write—when you go up to your rooms?"

"I don't do that at night, at this season. The lamplight brings in the animals."

"You might have known that when you came."

"I did know it!"

"And in winter do you work at night?"

"I read a good deal, but I don't often write." She listened as if these details had a rare interest, and suddenly a temptation quite at variance with the prudence I had been teaching myself associated itself with her plain, mild face. Ah yes, she was safe and I could make her safer! It seemed to me from one moment to another that I could not wait longer—that I really must take a sounding. So I went on: "In general before I go to sleep—very often in bed (it's a bad habit, but I confess to it), I read some great poet. In nine cases out of ten it's a volume of Jeffrey Aspern."

I watched her well as I pronounced that name but I saw nothing wonderful. Why should I indeed—was not Jeffrey Aspern the property of the human race?

"Oh, we read him—we *have* read him," she quietly replied.

"He is my poet of poets—I know him almost by heart."

For an instant Miss Tita hesitated; then her sociability was too much for her.

"Oh, by heart—that's nothing!" she murmured, smiling. "My aunt used to know him—to know him"—she paused an instant and I wondered what she was going to say—"to know him as a visitor."

"As a visitor?" I repeated, staring.

"He used to call on her and take her out."

I continued to stare. "My dear lady, he died a hundred years ago!"

"Well," she said, mirthfully, "my aunt is a hundred and fifty."

"Mercy on us!" I exclaimed; "why didn't you tell me before? I should like so to ask her about him."

"She wouldn't care for that—she wouldn't tell you," Miss Tita replied.

"I don't care what she cares for! She *must* tell me—it's not a chance to be lost."

"Oh, you should have come twenty years ago: then she still talked about him."

"And what did she say?" I asked, eagerly.

"I don't know—that he liked her immensely."

"And she—didn't she like him?"

"She said he was a god." Miss Tita gave me this information flatly, without expression; her tone might have made it a piece of trivial gossip. But it stirred me deeply as she dropped the words into the summer night; it seemed such a direct testimony.

"Fancy, fancy!" I murmured. And then, "Tell me this, please—has she got a portrait of him? They are distressingly rare."

"A portrait? I don't know," said Miss Tita; and now there was discomfiture in her face. "Well, good-night!" she added; and she turned into the house.

I accompanied her into the wide, dusky, stone-paved passage which on the ground floor corresponded with our grand sala. It opened at one end into the garden, at the other upon the canal, and was lighted now only by the small lamp that was always left for me to take up as I went to bed. An extinguished candle which Miss

Tita apparently had brought down with her stood on the same table with it. "Good-night, good-night!" I replied, keeping beside her as she went to get her light. "Surely you would know, shouldn't you, if she had one?"

"If she had what?" the poor lady asked, looking at me queerly over the flame of her candle.

"A portrait of the god. I don't know what I wouldn't give to see it."

"I don't know what she has got. She keeps her things locked up." and Miss Tita went away, toward the staircase, with the sense evidently that she had said too much.

I let her go—I wished not to frighten her—and I contented myself with remarking that Miss Bordereau would not have locked up such a glorious possession as that—a thing a person would be proud of and hang up in a prominent place on the parlour-wall. Therefore of course she had not any portrait. Miss Tita made no direct answer to this and candle in hand, with her back to me, ascended two or three stairs. Then she stopped short and turned round looking at me across the dusky space.

"Do you write—do you write?" There was a shake in her voice— she could scarcely bring out what she wanted to ask.

"Do I write? Oh, don't speak of my writing on the same day with Aspern's!"

"Do you write about *him*—do you pry into his life?"

"Ah, that's your aunt's question; it can't be yours!" I said, in a tone of slightly wounded sensibility.

"All the more reason then that you should answer it. Do you, please?"

I thought I had allowed for the falsehoods I should have to tell; but I found that in fact when it came to the point I had not. Besides, now that I had an opening there was a kind of relief in being frank. Lastly (it was perhaps fanciful, even fatuous), I guessed that Miss Tita personally would not in the last resort be less my friend. So after a moment's hesitation I answered, "Yes, I have written about him and I am looking for more material. In heaven's name have you got any?"

"*Santo Dio!*"[7] she exclaimed, without heeding my question; and she hurried upstairs and out of sight. I might count upon her in the last resort, but for the present she was visibly alarmed. The proof of it was that she began to hide again, so that for a fortnight I never beheld her. I found my patience ebbing and after four or five days of this I told the gardener to stop the flowers.

---

7. Good Lord!

VI

One afternoon, as I came down from my quarters to go out, I found Miss Tita in the sala: it was our first encounter on that ground since I had come to the house. She put on no air of being there by accident; there was an ignorance of such arts in her angular, diffident directness. That I might be quite sure she was waiting for me she informed me of the fact and told me that Miss Bordereau wished to see me: she would take me into the room at that moment if I had time. If I had been late for a love-tryst I would have stayed for this, and I quickly signified that I should be delighted to wait upon the old lady. "She wants to talk with you—to know you," Miss Tita said, smiling as if she herself appreciated that idea; and she led me to the door of her aunt's apartment. I stopped her a moment before she had opened it, looking at her with some curiosity. I told her that this was a great satisfaction to me and a great honour; but all the same I should like to ask what had made Miss Bordereau change so suddenly. It was only the other day that she wouldn't suffer me near her. Miss Tita was not embarrassed by my question; she had as many little unexpected serenities as if she told fibs, but the odd part of them was that they had on the contrary their source in her truthfulness. "Oh, my aunt changes," she answered; "it's so terribly dull—I suppose she's tired."

"But you told me that she wanted more and more to be alone."

Poor Miss Tita coloured, as if she found me over-insistent. "Well, if you don't believe she wants to see you—I haven't invented it! I think people often are capricious when they are very old."

"That's perfectly true. I only wanted to be clear as to whether you have repeated to her what I told you the other night."

"What you told me?"

"About Jeffrey Aspern—that I am looking for materials."

"If I had told her do you think she would have sent for you?"

"That's exactly what I want to know. If she wants to keep him to herself she might have sent for me to tell me so."

"She won't speak of him," said Miss Tita. Then as she opened the door she added in a lower tone, "I have told her nothing."

The old woman was sitting in the same place in which I had seen her last, in the same position, with the same mystifying bandage over her eyes. Her welcome was to turn her almost invisible face to me and show me that while she sat silent she saw me clearly. I made no motion to shake hands with her; I felt too well on this occasion that that was out of place for ever. It had been sufficiently enjoined upon me that she was too sacred for that sort of reciprocity—too venerable to touch. There was something so grim in her aspect (it was partly the accident of her green shade), as I stood there to be measured, that I ceased on the spot to feel any doubt as to her knowing my secret, though I did not in the least suspect that Miss Tita had not just spoken the truth. She had not betrayed me, but the old woman's brooding instinct had served her; she had turned me over and over in the long, still hours and she had guessed. The worst of it was that she looked terribly like an old woman who at a pinch would burn her papers. Miss Tita pushed a chair forward, saying to me, "This will be a good place for you to sit." As I took possession of it I asked after Miss Bordereau's health; expressed the hope that in spite of the very hot weather it was satisfactory. She replied that it was good enough—good enough; that it was a great thing to be alive.

"Oh, as to that, it depends upon what you compare it with!" I exclaimed, laughing.

"I don't compare—I don't compare. If I did that I should have given everything up long ago."

I liked to think that this was a subtle allusion to the rapture she had known in the society of Jeffrey Aspern—though it was true that such an allusion would have accorded ill with the wish I imputed to her to keep him buried in her soul. What it accorded with was my constant conviction that no human being had ever had a more delightful social gift than his, and what it seemed to convey was that nothing in the world was worth speaking of if one pretended to speak of that. But one did not! Miss Tita sat down beside her aunt, looking as if she had reason to believe some very remarkable conversation would come off between us.

"It's about the beautiful flowers," said the old lady; "you sent us so many—I ought to have thanked you for them before. But I don't write letters and I receive only at long intervals."

She had not thanked me while the flowers continued to come, but she departed from her custom so far as to send for me as soon as she began to fear that they would not come any more. I noted this; I remembered what an acquisitive propensity she had shown when it was a question of extracting gold from me, and I privately rejoiced at the happy thought I had had in suspending my tribute. She had missed it and she was willing to make a concession to bring it back. At the first sign of this concession I could only go to meet her. "I am afraid you have not had many, of late, but they shall begin again immediately—to-morrow, to-night."

"Oh, do send us some to-night!" Miss Tita cried, as if it were an immense circumstance.

"What else should you do with them? It isn't a manly taste to make a bower of your room," the old woman remarked.

"I don't make a bower of my room, but I am exceedingly fond of growing flowers, of watching their ways. There is nothing unmanly in that: it has been the amusement of philosophers, of statesmen in retirement; even I think of great captains."

"I suppose you know you can sell them—those you don't use," Miss Bordereau went on. "I daresay they wouldn't give you much for them; still, you could make a bargain."

"Oh, I have never made a bargain, as you ought to know. My gardener disposes of them and I ask no questions."

"I would ask a few, I can promise you!" said Miss Bordereau; and it was the first time I had heard her laugh. I could not get used to the idea that this vision of pecuniary profit was what drew out the divine Juliana most.

"Come into the garden yourself and pick them; come as often as you like; come every day. They are for you," I pursued, addressing Miss Tita and carrying off this veracious statement by treating it as an innocent joke. "I can't imagine why she doesn't come down," I added for Miss Bordereau's benefit.

"You must make her come; you must come up and fetch her," said the old woman, to my stupefaction. "That odd thing you have made in the corner would be a capital place for her to sit."

The allusion to my arbour was irreverent; it confirmed the impression I had already received that there was a flicker of impertinence in Miss Bordereau's talk, a strange mocking lambency which must have been a part of her adventurous youth and which had outlived passions and faculties. None the less I asked, "Wouldn't it be possible for you to come down there yourself? Wouldn't it do you good to sit there in the shade, in the sweet air?"

"Oh, sir, when I move out of this it won't be to sit in the air, and I'm afraid that any that may be stirring around me won't be particularly sweet! It will be a very dark shade indeed. But that won't be just yet," Miss Bordereau continued, cannily, as if to correct any hopes that this courageous allusion to the last receptacle of her mortality might lead me to entertain. "I have sat here many a day and I have had enough of arbours in my time. But I'm not afraid to wait till I'm called."

Miss Tita had expected some interesting talk, but perhaps she found it less genial on her aunt's side (considering that I had been sent for with a civil intention) than she had hoped. As if to give the conversation a turn that would put our companion in a light more favourable she said to me, "Didn't I tell you the other night that she had sent me out? You see that I can do what I like!"

"Do you pity her—do you teach her to pity herself?" Miss Bordereau demanded, before I had time to answer this appeal. "She has a much easier life than I had when I was her age."

"You must remember that it has been quite open to me to think you rather inhuman."

"Inhuman? That's what the poets used to call the women a hundred years ago. Don't try that; you won't do as well as they!" Juliana declared. "There is no more poetry in the world—that I know of at least. But I won't bandy words with you," she pursued, and I well remember the old-fashioned, artificial sound she gave to the speech. "You have made me talk, talk! It isn't good for me at all." I got up at this and told her I would take no more of her time; but she detained me to ask, "Do you remember, the day I saw you about the rooms, that you offered us the use of your gondola?" And when I assented, promptly, struck again with her disposition to make a "good thing" of being there and wondering what she now had in her eye, she broke out, "Why don't you take that girl out in it and show her the place?"

"Oh dear aunt, what do you want to do with me?" cried the "girl," with a piteous quaver. "I know all about the place!"

"Well then, go with him as a cicerone!" said Miss Bordereau, with an effect of something like cruelty in her implacable power of retort—an incongruous suggestion that she was a sarcastic, profane, cynical old woman. "Haven't we heard that there have been all sorts of changes in all these years? You ought to see them and at your age (I don't mean because you're so young), you ought to take the chances that come. You're old enough, my dear, and this gentleman won't hurt you. He will show you the famous sunsets, if they still go on—*do* they go on? The sun set for me so long ago. But that's not a reason. Besides, I shall never miss you; you think you are too important. Take her to the Piazza; it used to be very pretty," Miss Bordereau continued, addressing herself to me. "What have they done with the funny old church? I hope it hasn't tumbled down. Let her look at the shops; she may take some money, she may buy what she likes."

Poor Miss Tita had got up, discountenanced and helpless, and as we stood there before her aunt it would certainly have seemed to a spectator of the scene that the old woman was amusing herself at our expense. Miss Tita protested, in a confusion of exclamations and murmurs; but I lost no time in saying that if she would do me the honour to accept the hospitality of my boat I would engage that she should not be bored. Or if she did not want so much of my company the boat itself, with the gondolier, was at her service; he was a capital oar and she might have every confidence. Miss Tita, without definitely answering this speech, looked away from me, out of the window, as if she were going to cry; and I remarked that once we had Miss Bordereau's approval we could easily come to an understanding. We would take an hour, whichever she liked, one of the very next days. As I made my obeisance to the old lady I asked her if she would kindly permit me to see her again.

For a moment she said nothing; then she inquired, "Is it very necessary to your happiness?"

"It diverts me more than I can say."

"You are wonderfully civil. Don't you know it almost kills *me*?"

"How can I believe that when I see you more animated, more brilliant than when I came in?"

"That is very true, aunt," said Miss Tita. "I think it does you good."

"Isn't it touching, the solicitude we each have that the other shall enjoy herself?" sneered Miss Bordereau. "If you think me brilliant to-day you don't know what you are talking about; you have never seen an agreeable woman. Don't try to pay me a compliment; I have been spoiled," she went on. "My door is shut, but you may sometimes knock."

With this she dismissed me and I left the room. The latch closed behind me, but Miss Tita, contrary to my hope, had remained within. I passed slowly across the hall and before taking my way down-stairs I waited a little. My hope was answered; after a minute Miss Tita followed me. "That's a delightful idea about the Piazza," I said. "When will you go—to-night, to-morrow?"

She had been disconcerted, as I have mentioned, but I had already perceived and I was to observe again that when Miss Tita was embarrassed she did not (as most women would have done) turn away from you and try to escape, but came closer, as it were, with a deprecating, clinging appeal to be spared, to be protected. Her attitude was perpetually a sort of prayer for assistance, for explanation; and yet no woman in the world could have been less of a comedian. From the moment you were kind to her she depended on you absolutely; her self-consciousness dropped from her and she took the greatest intimacy, the innocent intimacy which was the only thing she could conceive, for granted. She told me she did not know what had got into her aunt; she had changed so quickly, she had got some idea. I replied that she must find out what the idea was and then let me know; we would go and have an ice together at Florian's and she should tell me while we listened to the band.

"Oh, it will take me a long time to find out!" she said, rather ruefully; and she could promise me this satisfaction neither for that night nor for the next. I was patient now, however, for I felt that I had only to wait; and in fact at the end of the week, one lovely evening after dinner, she stepped into my gondola, to which in honour of the occasion I had attached a second oar.

We swept in the course of five minutes into the Grand Canal; whereupon she uttered a murmur of ecstasy as fresh as if she had been a tourist just arrived. She had forgotten how splendid the great water-way looked on a clear, hot summer evening, and how the sense of floating between marble palaces and reflected lights disposed the mind to sympathetic talk. We floated long and far, and though Miss Tita gave no high-pitched voice to her satisfaction I felt that she surrendered herself. She was more than pleased, she was transported; the whole thing was an immense liberation. The gondola moved with slow strokes, to give her time to enjoy it, and she listened to the plash of the oars, which grew louder and more musically liquid as we passed into narrow canals, as if it were a revelation of Venice. When I asked her how long it was since she had been in a boat she answered, "Oh, I don't know; a long time —not since my aunt began to be ill." This was not the only example she gave me of her extreme vagueness about the previous years and the line which marked off the period when Miss Bordereau flourished. I was not at liberty to keep her out too long, but we took a considerable *giro*[8] before going to the Piazza. I asked her no questions, keeping the conversation on purpose away from her domestic situation and the things I wanted to know; I poured treasures of information about Venice into her ears, described Florence and Rome, discoursed to her on the charms and advantages of travel. She reclined, receptive, on the deep leather cushions, turned her eyes conscientiously to everything I pointed out to her, and never mentioned to me till some time afterwards that she might be supposed to know Florence better than I, as she had lived there for years with Miss Bordereau. At last she asked, with the shy impatience of a child, "Are we not really going to the Piazza? That's what I want to see!" I immediately gave the order that we should go straight; and then we sat silent with the expectation of arrival. As some time still passed, however, she said suddenly, of her own movement, "I have found out what is the matter with my aunt: she is afraid you will go!"

"What has put that into her head?"

"She has had an idea you have not been happy. That is why she is different now."

"You mean she wants to make me happier?"

"Well, she wants you not to go; she wants you to stay."

"I suppose you mean on account of the rent," I remarked candidly.

Miss Tita's candour showed itself a match for my own. "Yes, you know; so that I shall have more."

"How much does she want you to have?" I asked, laughing. "She ought to fix the sum, so that I may stay till it's made up."

8. Stroll.

"Oh, that wouldn't please me," said Miss Tita. "It would be unheard of, your taking that trouble."

"But suppose I should have my own reasons for staying in Venice?"

"Then it would be better for you to stay in some other house."

"And what would your aunt say to that?"

"She wouldn't like it at all. But I should think you would do well to give up your reasons and go away altogether."

"Dear Miss Tita," I said, "it's not so easy to give them up!"

She made no immediate answer to this, but after a moment she broke out: "I think I know what your reasons are!"

"I daresay, because the other night I almost told you how I wish you would help me to make them good."

"I can't do that without being false to my aunt."

"What do you mean, being false to her?"

"Why, she would never consent to what you want. She has been asked, she has been written to. It made her fearfully angry."

"Then she *has* got papers of value?" I demanded, quickly.

"Oh, she has got everything!" sighed Miss Tita, with a curious weariness, a sudden lapse into gloom.

These words caused all my pulses to throb, for I regarded them as precious evidence. For some minutes I was too agitated to speak, and in the interval the gondola approached the Piazzetta. After we had disembarked I asked my companion whether she would rather walk round the square or go and sit at the door of the café; to which she replied that she would do whichever I liked best—I must only remember again how little time she had. I assured her there was plenty to do both, and we made the circuit of the long arcades. Her spirits revived at the sight of the bright shop-windows, and she lingered and stopped, admiring or disapproving of their contents, asking me what I thought of things, theorising about prices. My attention wandered from her; her words of a while before, "Oh, she has got everything!" echoed so in my consciousness. We sat down at last in the crowded circle at Florian's, finding an unoccupied table among those that were ranged in the square. It was a splendid night and all the world was out-of-doors; Miss Tita could not have wished the elements more auspicious for her return to society. I saw that she enjoyed it even more than she told; she was agitated with the multitude of her impressions. She had forgotten what an attractive thing the world is, and it was coming over her that somehow she had for the best years of her life been cheated of it. This did not make her angry; but as she looked all over the charming scene her face had, in spite of its smile of appreciation, the flush of a sort of wounded surprise. She became silent, as if she were thinking with a secret sadness of opportunities, for ever lost, which ought to have been easy; and this gave me a chance to say to her, "Did you mean a while ago that your aunt has a plan of keeping me on by admitting me occasionally to her presence?"

"She thinks it will make a difference with you if you sometimes see her. She wants you so much to stay that she is willing to make that concession."

"And what good does she consider that I think it will do me to see her?"

"I don't know; she thinks it's interesting," said Miss Tita, simply. "You told her you found it so."

"So I did; but every one doesn't think so."

"No, of course not, or more people would try."

"Well, if she is capable of making that reflection she is capable also of making this further one," I went on: "that I must have a particular reason for not doing as others do, in spite of the interest she offers—for not leaving her alone." Miss Tita looked as if she failed to grasp this rather complicated proposition; so I continued, "If you have not told her what I said to you the other night may she not at least have guessed it?"

"I don't know; she is very suspicious."

"But she has not been made so by indiscreet curiosity, by persecution?"

"No, no; it isn't that," said Miss Tita, turning on me a somewhat troubled face. "I don't know how to say it: it's on account of something—ages ago, before I was born—in her life."

"Something? What sort of thing?" I asked, as if I myself could have no idea.

"Oh, she has never told me," Miss Tita answered; and I was sure she was speaking the truth.

Her extreme limpidity was almost provoking, and I felt for the moment that she would have been more satisfactory if she had been less ingenuous. "Do you suppose it's something to which Jeffrey Aspern's letters and papers—I mean the things in her possession —have reference?"

"I daresay it is!" my companion exclaimed, as if this were a very happy suggestion. "I have never looked at any of those things."

"None of them? Then how do you know what they are?"

"I don't," said Miss Tita, placidly. "I have never had them in my hands. But I have seen them when she has had them out."

"Does she have them out often?"

"Not now, but she used to. She is very fond of them."

"In spite of their being compromising?"

"Compromising?" Miss Tita repeated, as if she was ignorant of the meaning of the word. I felt almost as one who corrupts the innocence of youth.

"I mean their containing painful memories."

"Oh, I don't think they are painful."

"You mean you don't think they affect her reputation?"

At this a singular look came into the face of Miss Bordereau's niece—a kind of confession of helplessness, an appeal to me to deal fairly, generously with her. I had brought her to the Piazza, placed her among charming influences, paid her an attention she appreciated, and now I seemed to let her perceive that all this had been a bribe—a bribe to make her turn in some way against her aunt. She was of a yielding nature and capable of doing almost anything to please a person who was kind to her; but the greatest kindness of all would be not to presume too much on this. It was strange enough, as I afterwards thought, that she had not the least air of resenting my want of consideration for her aunt's character, which would have been in the worst possible taste if anything less vital (from my point of view) had been at stake. I don't think she really measured it. "Do you mean that she did something bad?" she asked in a moment.

"Heaven forbid I should say so, and it's none of my business. Besides, if she did," I added, laughing, "it was in other ages, in another world. But why should she not destroy her papers?"

"Oh, she loves them too much."

"Even now, when she may be near her end?"

"Perhaps when she's sure of that she will."

"Well, Miss Tita," I said, "it's just what I should like you to prevent."

"How can I prevent it?"

"Couldn't you get them away from her?"

"And give them to you?"

This put the case very crudely, though I am sure there was no irony in her intention. "Oh, I mean that you might let me see them and look them over. It isn't for myself; there is no personal avidity in my desire. It is simply that they would be of such immense interest to the public, such immeasurable importance as a contribution to Jeffrey Aspern's history."

She listened to me in her usual manner, as if my speech were full of reference to things she had never heard of, and I felt particularly like the reporter of a newspaper who forces his way into a house of mourning. This was especially the case when after a moment she said, "There was a gentleman who some time ago wrote to her in very much those words. He also wanted her papers."

"And did she answer him?" I asked, rather ashamed of myself for not having her rectitude.

"Only when he had written two or three times. He made her very angry."

"And what did she say?"

"She said he was a devil," Miss Tita replied, simply.

"She used that expression in her letter?"

"Oh no; she said it to me. She made me write to him."

"And what did you say?"

"I told him there were no papers at all."

"Ah, poor gentleman!" I exclaimed.

"I knew there were, but I wrote what she bade me."

"Of course you had to do that. But I hope I shall not pass for a devil."

"It will depend upon what you ask me to do for you," said Miss Tita, smiling.

"Oh, if there is a chance of *your* thinking so my affair is in a bad way! I sha'n't ask you to steal for me, nor even to fib—for you can't fib, unless on paper. But the principal thing is this—to prevent her from destroying the papers."

"Why, I have no control of her," said Miss Tita. "It's she who controls me."

"But she doesn't control her own arms and legs, does she? The way she would naturally destroy her letters would be to burn them. Now she can't burn them without fire, and she can't get fire unless you give it to her."

"I have always done everything she has asked," my companion rejoined. "Besides, there's Olimpia."

I was on the point of saying that Olimpia was probably corruptible, but I thought it best not to sound that note. So I simply inquired if that faithful domestic could not be managed.

"Every one can be managed by my aunt," said Miss Tita. And then she observed that her holiday was over; she must go home.

I laid my hand on her arm, across the table, to stay her a moment. "What I want of you is a general promise to help me."

"Oh, how can I—how can I?" she asked, wondering and troubled. She was half surprised, half frightened at my wishing to make her play an active part.

"This is the main thing: to watch her carefully and warn me in time, before she commits that horrible sacrilege."

"I can't watch her when she makes me go out."

"That's very true."

"And when you do too."

"Mercy on us; do you think she will have done anything to-night?"

"I don't know; she is very cunning."

"Are you trying to frighten me?" I asked.

I felt this inquiry sufficiently answered when my companion murmured in a musing, almost envious way, "Oh, but she loves them —she loves them!"

This reflection, repeated with such emphasis, gave me great comfort; but to obtain more of that balm I said, "If she shouldn't intend to destroy the objects we speak of before her death she will probably have made some disposition by will."

"By will?"

"Hasn't she made a will for your benefit?"

"Why, she has so little to leave. That's why she likes money," said Miss Tita.

"Might I ask, since we are really talking things over, what you and she live on?"

"On some money that comes from America, from a lawyer. He sends it every quarter. It isn't much!"

"And won't she have disposed of that?"

My companion hesitated—I saw she was blushing. "I believe it's mine," she said; and the look and tone which accompanied these words betrayed so the absence of the habit of thinking of herself that I almost thought her charming. The next instant she added, "But she had a lawyer once, ever so long ago. And some people came and signed something."

"They were probably witnesses. And you were not asked to sign? Well then," I argued, rapidly and hopefully, "it is because you are the legatee; she has left all her documents to you!"

"If she has it's with very strict conditions," Miss Tita responded, rising quickly, while the movement gave the words a little character of decision. They seemed to imply that the bequest would be accompanied with a command that the articles bequeathed should remain concealed from every inquisitive eye and that I was very much mistaken if I thought she was the person to depart from an injunction so solemn.

"Oh, of course you will have to abide by the terms," I said; and she uttered nothing to mitigate the severity of this conclusion. None the less, later, just before we disembarked at her own door, on our return, which had taken place almost in silence, she said to me abruptly, "I will do what I can to help you." I was grateful for this —it was very well so far as it went; but it did not keep me from remembering that night in a worried waking hour that I now had her word for it to reinforce my own impression that the old woman was very cunning.

VII

The fear of what this side of her character might have led her to do made me nervous for days afterwards. I waited for an intimation from Miss Tita: I almost figured to myself that it was her duty to keep me informed, to let me know definitely whether or no Miss

Bordereau had sacrificed her treasures. But as she gave no sign I lost patience and determined to judge so far as was possible with my own senses. I sent late one afternoon to ask if I might pay the ladies a visit, and my servant came back with surprising news. Miss Bordereau could be approached without the least difficulty; she had been moved out into the sala and was sitting by the window that overlooked the garden. I descended and found this picture correct; the old lady had been wheeled forth into the world and had a certain air, which came mainly perhaps from some brighter element in her dress, of being prepared again to have converse with it. It had not yet, however, begun to flock about her; she was perfectly alone and, though the door leading to her own quarters stood open, I had at first no glimpse of Miss Tita. The window at which she sat had the afternoon shade and, one of the shutters having been pushed back, she could see the pleasant garden, where the summer sun had by this time dried up too many of the plants—she could see the yellow light and the long shadows.

"Have you come to tell me that you will take the rooms for six months more?" she asked, as I approached her, startling me by something coarse in her cupidity almost as much as if she had not already given me a specimen of it. Juliana's desire to make our acquaintance lucrative had been, as I have sufficiently indicated, a false note in my image of the woman who had inspired a great poet with immortal lines; but I may say here definitely that I recognised after all that it behoved me to make a large allowance for her. It was I who had kindled the unholy flame; it was I who had put into her head that she had the means of making money. She appeared never to have thought of that; she had been living wastefully for years, in a house five times too big for her, on a footing that I could explain only by the presumption that, excessive as it was, the space she enjoyed cost her next to nothing and that small as were her revenues they left her, for Venice, an appreciable margin. I had descended on her one day and taught her to calculate, and my almost extravagant comedy on the subject of the garden had presented me irresistibly in the light of a victim. Like all persons who achieve the miracle of changing their point of view when they are old she had been intensely converted; she had seized my hint with a desperate, tremulous clutch.

I invited myself to go and get one of the chairs that stood, at a distance, against the wall (she had given herself no concern as to whether I should sit or stand); and while I placed it near her I began, gaily, "Oh, dear madam, what an imagination you have, what an intellectual sweep! I am a poor devil of a man of letters who lives from day to day. How can I take palaces by the year? My existence is precarious. I don't know whether six months hence I shall have bread to put in my mouth. I have treated myself for once; it has been an immense luxury. But when it comes to going on—!"

"Are your rooms too dear? if they are you can have more for the same money," Juliana responded. "We can arrange, we can *combinare*,[9] as they say here."

"Well yes, since you ask me, they are too dear," I said. "Evidently you suppose me richer than I am."

She looked at me in her barricaded way. "If you write books don't you sell them?"

"Do you mean don't people buy them? A little—not so much as I could wish. Writing books, unless one be a great genius—and even then!—is the last road to fortune. I think there is no more money to be made by literature."

"Perhaps you don't choose good subjects. What do you write about?" Miss Bordereau inquired.

"About the books of other people. I'm a critic, an historian, in a small way." I wondered what she was coming to.

"And what other people, now?"

"Oh, better ones than myself: the great writers mainly—the great philosophers and poets of the past; those who are dead and gone and can't speak for themselves."

"And what do you say about them?"

"I say they sometimes attached themselves to very clever women!" I answered, laughing. I spoke with great deliberation, but as my words fell upon the air they struck me as imprudent. However, I risked them and I was not sorry, for perhaps after all the old woman would be willing to treat. It seemed to be tolerably obvious that she knew my secret: why therefore drag the matter out? But she did not take what I had said as a confession; she only asked:

"Do you think it's right to rake up the past?"

"I don't know that I know what you mean by raking it up; but how can we get at it unless we dig a little? The present has such a rough way of treading it down."

"Oh, I like the past, but I don't like critics," the old woman declared, with her fine tranquillity.

"Neither do I, but I like their discoveries."

"Aren't they mostly lies?"

"The lies are what they sometimes discover," I said, smiling at the quiet impertinence of this. "They often lay bare the truth."

"The truth is God's, it isn't man's; we had better leave it alone. Who can judge of it—who can say?"

"We are terribly in the dark, I know," I admitted; "but if we give up trying what becomes of all the fine things? What becomes of the

9. Arrange things.

work I just mentioned, that of the great philosophers and poets? It is all vain words if there is nothing to measure it by."

"You talk as if you were a tailor," said Miss Bordereau, whimsically; and then she added quickly, in a different manner, "This house is very fine; the proportions are magnificent. Today I wanted to look at this place again. I made them bring me out here. When your man came, just now, to learn if I would see you, I was on the point of sending for you, to ask if you didn't mean to go on. I wanted to judge what I'm letting you have. This sala is very grand," she pursued, like an auctioneer, moving a little, as I guessed, her invisible eyes. "I don't believe you often have lived in such a house, eh?"

"I can't often afford to!" I said.

"Well then, how much will you give for six months?"

I was on the point of exclaiming—and the air of excruciation in my face would have denoted a moral fact—"Don't, Juliana; for *his* sake, don't!" But I controlled myself and asked less passionately: "Why should I remain so long as that?"

"I thought you liked it," said Miss Bordereau, with her shrivelled dignity.

"So I thought I should."

For a moment she said nothing more, and I left my own words to suggest to her what they might. I half expected her to say, coldly enough, that if I had been disappointed we need not continue the discussion, and this in spite of the fact that I believed her now to have in her mind (however it had come there), what would have told her that my disappointment was natural. But to my extreme surprise she ended by observing: "If you don't think we have treated you well enough perhaps we can discover some way of treating you better." This speech was somehow so incongruous that it made me laugh again, and I excused myself by saying that she talked as if I were a sulky boy, pouting in the corner, to be "brought round." I had not a grain of complaint to make; and could anything have exceeded Miss Tita's graciousness in accompanying me a few nights before to the Piazza? At this the old woman went on: "Well, you brought it on yourself!" And then in a different tone, "She is a very nice girl." I assented cordially to this proposition, and she expressed the hope that I did so not merely to be obliging, but that I really liked her. Meanwhile I wondered still more what Miss Bordereau was coming to. "Except for me, to-day," she said, "she has not a relation in the world." Did she by describing her niece as amiable and unencumbered wish to represent her as a *parti*?[1]

It was perfectly true that I could not afford to go on with my rooms at a fancy price and that I had already devoted to my un-

---

1. A match, usually said of a woman with money.

dertaking almost all the hard cash I had set apart for it. My patience and my time were by no means exhausted, but I should be able to draw upon them only on a more usual Venetian basis. I was willing to pay the venerable woman with whom my pecuniary dealings were such a discord twice as much as any other *padrona di casa*,[2] would have asked, but I was not willing to pay her twenty times as much. I told her so plainly, and my plainness appeared to have some success, for she exclaimed, "Very good; you have done what I asked—you have made an offer!"

"Yes, but not for half a year. Only by the month."

"Oh, I must think of that then." She seemed disappointed that I would not tie myself to a period, and I guessed that she wished both to secure me and to discourage me; to say, severely, "Do you dream that you can get off with less than six months? Do you dream that even by the end of that time you will be appreciably nearer your victory?" What was more in my mind was that she had a fancy to play me the trick of making me engage myself when in fact she had annihilated the papers. There was a moment when my suspense on this point was so acute that I all but broke out with the question, and what kept it back was but a kind of instinctive recoil (lest it should be a mistake), from the last violence of self-exposure. She was such a subtle old witch that one could never tell where one stood with her. You may imagine whether it cleared up the puzzle when, just after she had said she would think of my proposal and without any formal transition, she drew out of her pocket with an embarrassed hand a small object wrapped in crumpled white paper. She held it there a moment and then she asked, "Do you know much about curiosities?"

"About curiosities?"

"About antiquities, the old gimcracks that people pay so much for to-day. Do you know the kind of price they bring?"

I thought I saw what was coming, but I said ingenuously, "Do you want to buy something?"

"No, I want to sell. What would an amateur give me for that?" She unfolded the white paper and made a motion for me to take from her a small oval portrait. I possessed myself of it with a hand of which I could only hope that she did not perceive the tremor, and she added, "I would part with it only for a good price."

At the first glance I recognised Jeffrey Aspern, and I was well aware that I flushed with the act. As she was watching me however I had the consistency to exclaim, "What a striking face! Do tell me who it is."

"It's an old friend of mine, a very distinguished man in his day.

2. Landlady.

He gave it to me himself, but I'm afraid to mention his name, lest you never should have heard of him, critic and historian as you are. I know the world goes fast and one generation forgets another. He was all the fashion when I was young."

She was perhaps amazed at my assurance, but I was surprised at hers; at her having the energy, in her state of health and at her time of life, to wish to sport with me that way simply for her private entertainment—the humour to test me and practise on me. This, at least, was the interpretation that I put upon her production of the portrait, for I could not believe that she really desired to sell it or cared for any information I might give her. What she wished was to dangle it before my eyes and put a prohibitive price on it. "The face comes back to me, it torments me," I said, turning the object this way and that and looking at it very critically. It was a careful but not a supreme work of art, larger than the ordinary miniature and representing a young man with a remarkably handsome face, in a high-collared green coat and a buff waistcoat. I judged the picture to have a valuable quality of resemblance and to have been painted when the model was about twenty-five years old. There are, as all the world knows, three other portraits of the poet in existence, but none of them is of so early a date as this elegant production. "I have never seen the original but I have seen other likenesses," I went on. "You expressed doubt of this generation having heard of the gentleman, but he strikes me for all the world as a celebrity. Now who is he? I can't put my finger on him—I can't give him a label. Wasn't he a writer? Surely he's a poet." I was determined that it should be she, not I, who should first pronounce Jeffrey Aspern's name.

My resolution was taken in ignorance of Miss Bordereau's extremely resolute character, and her lips never formed in my hearing the syllables that meant so much for her. She neglected to answer my question but raised her hand to take back the picture, with a gesture which though ineffectual was in a high degree peremptory. "It's only a person who should know for himself that would give me my price," she said with a certain dryness.

"Oh, then, you have a price?" I did not restore the precious thing; not from any vindictive purpose but because I instinctively clung to it. We looked at each other hard while I retained it.

"I know the least I would take. What it occurred to me to ask you about is the most I shall be able to get."

She made a movement, drawing herself together as if, in a spasm of dread at having lost her treasure, she were going to attempt the immense effort of rising to snatch it from me. I instantly placed it in her hand again, saying as I did so, "I should like to have it myself, but with your ideas I could never afford it."

She turned the small oval plate over in her lap, with its face down, and I thought I saw her catch her breath a little, as if she had had a strain or an escape. This however did not prevent her saying in a moment, "You would buy a likeness of a person you don't know, by an artist who has no reputation?"

"The artist may have no reputation, but that thing is wonderfully well painted," I replied, to give myself a reason.

"It's lucky you thought of saying that, because the painter was my father."

"That makes the picture indeed precious!" I exclaimed, laughing; and I may add that a part of my laughter came from my satisfaction in finding that I had been right in my theory of Miss Bordereau's origin. Aspern had of course met the young lady when he went to her father's studio as a sitter. I observed to Miss Bordereau that if she would entrust me with her property for twenty-four hours I should be happy to take advice upon it; but she made no answer to this save to slip it in silence into her pocket. This convinced me still more that she had no sincere intention of selling it during her lifetime, though she may have desired to satisfy herself as to the sum her niece, should she leave it to her, might expect eventually to obtain for it. "Well, at any rate I hope you will not offer it without giving me notice," I said, as she remained irresponsive. "Remember that I am a possible purchaser."

"I should want your money first!" she returned, with unexpected rudeness; and then, as if she bethought herself that I had just cause to complain of such an insinuation and wished to turn the matter off, asked abruptly what I talked about with her niece when I went out with her that way in the evening.

"You speak as if we had set up the habit," I replied. "Certainly I should be very glad if it were to become a habit. But in that case I should feel a still greater scruple at betraying a lady's confidence."

"Her confidence? Has she got confidence?"

"Here she is—she can tell you herself," I said; for Miss Tita now appeared on the threshold of the old woman's parlour. "Have you got confidence, Miss Tita? Your aunt wants very much to know."

"Not in her, not in her!" the younger lady declared, shaking her head with a dolefulness that was neither jocular nor affected. "I don't know what to do with her; she has fits of horrid imprudence. She is so easily tired—and yet she has begun to roam—to drag herself about the house." And she stood looking down at her im- memorial companion with a sort of helpless wonder, as if all their years of familiarity had not made her perversities, on occasion, any more easy to follow.

"I know what I'm about. I'm not losing my mind. I daresay you would like to think so," said Miss Bordereau, with a cynical little sigh.

"I don't suppose you came out here yourself. Miss Tita must have had to lend you a hand," I interposed, with a pacifying intention.

"Oh, she insisted that we should push her; and when she insists!" said Miss Tita, in the same tone of apprehension; as if there were no knowing what service that she disapproved of her aunt might force her next to render.

"I have always got most things done I wanted, thank God! The people I have lived with have humoured me," the old woman continued, speaking out of the gray ashes of her vanity.

"I suppose you mean that they have obeyed you."

"Well, whatever it is, when they like you."

"It's just because I like you that I want to resist," said Miss Tita, with a nervous laugh.

"Oh, I suspect you'll bring Miss Bordereau upstairs next, to pay me a visit," I went on; to which the old lady replied:

"Oh no; I can keep an eye on you from here!"

"You are very tired; you will certainly be ill to-night!" cried Miss Tita.

"Nonsense, my dear; I feel better at this moment than I have done for a month. Tomorrow I shall come out again. I want to be where I can see this clever gentleman."

"Shouldn't you perhaps see me better in your sitting-room?" I inquired.

"Don't you mean shouldn't you have a better chance at me?" she returned, fixing me a moment with her green shade.

"Ah, I haven't that anywhere! I look at you but I don't see you."

"You excite her dreadfully—and that is not good," said Miss Tita, giving me a reproachful, appealing look.

"I want to watch you—I want to watch you!" the old lady went on.

"Well then, let us spend as much of our time together as possible—I don't care where—and that will give you every facility."

"Oh, I've seen you enough for to-day. I'm satisfied. Now I'll go home." Miss Tita laid her hands on the back of her aunt's chair and began to push, but I begged her to let me take her place. "Oh yes, you may move me this way—you sha'n't in any other!" Miss Bordereau exclaimed, as she felt herself propelled firmly and easily over the smooth, hard floor. Before we reached the door of her own apartment she commanded me to stop, and she took a long, last look up and down the noble sala. "Oh, it's a magnificent house!" she murmured; after which I pushed her forward. When we had entered the parlour Miss Tita told me that she should now be able to manage, and at the same moment the little red-haired *donna*³ came to meet her mistress. Miss Tita's idea was evidently to get her aunt immediately back to bed. I confess that in spite of this urgency I was guilty of the indiscretion of lingering; it held me there to think that I was nearer the documents I coveted—that they were probably put away somewhere in the faded, unsociable room. The place had indeed a bareness which did not suggest hidden treasures; there were no dusky nooks nor curtained corners, no massive cabinets nor chests with iron bands. Moreover it was possible, it was perhaps even probable that the old lady had consigned her relics to her bedroom, to some battered box that was shoved under the bed, to the drawer of some lame dressing-table, where they would be in the range of vision by the dim night-lamp. None the less I scrutinised every article of furniture, every conceivable cover for a hoard, and noticed that there were half a dozen things with drawers, and in particular a tall old secretary, with brass ornaments of the style of the Empire—a receptacle somewhat rickety but still capable of keeping a great many secrets. I don't know why this article fascinated me so, inasmuch as I certainly had no definite purpose of breaking into it; but I stared at it so hard that Miss Tita noticed me and changed colour. Her doing this made me think I was right and that wherever they might have been before the Aspern papers at that moment languished behind the peevish little lock of the secretary. It was hard to remove my eyes from the dull mahogany front when I reflected that a simple panel divided me from the goal of my hopes; but I remembered my prudence and with an effort took leave of Miss Bordereau. To make the effort graceful I said to her that I should certainly bring her an opinion about the little picture.

"The little picture?" Miss Tita asked, surprised.

"What do *you* know about it, my dear?" the old woman demanded. "You needn't mind. I have fixed my price."

"And what may that be?"

"A thousand pounds."

"Oh Lord!" cried poor Miss Tita, irrepressibly.

"Is that what she talks to you about?" said Miss Bordereau.

"Imagine your aunt's wanting to know!" I had to separate from Miss Tita with only those words, though I should have liked immensely to add, "For heaven's sake meet me to-night in the garden!"

3. Housemaid.

VIII

As it turned out the precaution had not been needed, for three hours later, just as I had finished my dinner, Miss Bordereau's niece appeared, unannounced, in the open doorway of the room in which my simple repasts were served. I remember well that I felt no surprise at seeing her; which is not a proof that I did not believe in her timidity. It was immense, but in a case in which there was a particular reason for boldness it never would have prevented her from running up to my rooms. I saw that she was now quite full of a particular reason; it threw her forward—made her seize me, as I rose to meet her, by the arm.

"My aunt is very ill; I think she is dying!"

"Never in the world," I answered, bitterly. "Don't you be afraid!"

"Do go for a doctor—do, do! Olimpia is gone for the one we always have, but she doesn't come back; I don't know what has happened to her. I told her that if he was not at home she was to follow him where he had gone; but apparently she is following him all over Venice. I don't know what to do—she looks so as if she were sinking."

"May I see her, may I judge?" I asked. "Of course I shall be delighted to bring some one; but hadn't we better send my man instead, so that I may stay with you?"

Miss Tita assented to this and I despatched my servant for the best doctor in the neighbourhood. I hurried downstairs with her, and on the way she told me that an hour after I quitted them in the afternoon Miss Bordereau had had an attack of "oppression," a terrible difficulty in breathing. This had subsided but had left her so exhausted that she did not come up: she seemed all gone. I repeated that she was not gone, that she would not go yet; whereupon Miss Tita gave me a sharper sidelong glance than she had ever directed at me and said, "Really, what do you mean? I suppose you don't accuse her of making-believe!" I forget what reply I made to this, but I grant that in my heart I thought the old woman capable of any weird manoeuvre. Miss Tita wanted to know what I had done to her; her aunt had told her that I had made her so angry. I declared I had done nothing—I had been exceedingly careful; to which my companion rejoined that Miss Bordereau had assured her she had had a scene with me—a scene that had upset her. I answered with some resentment that it was a scene of her own making—that I couldn't think what she was angry with me for unless for not seeing my way to give a thousand pounds for the portrait of Jeffrey Aspern. "And did she show you that? Oh gracious—oh deary me!" groaned Miss Tita, who appeared to feel that the situation was passing out of her control and that the ele-

ments of her fate were thickening around her. I said that I would
give anything to possess it, yet that I had not a thousand pounds;
but I stopped when we came to the door of Miss Bordereau's room.
I had an immense curiosity to pass it, but I thought it my duty to
represent to Miss Tita that if I made the invalid angry she ought
perhaps to be spared the sight of me. "The sight of you? Do you
think she can *see?*" my companion demanded, almost with indignation. I did think so but forbore to say it, and I softly followed my
conductress.

I remember that what I said to her as I stood for a moment beside
the old woman's bed was, "Does she never show you her eyes then?
Have you never seen them?" Miss Bordereau had been divested of
her green shade, but (it was not my fortune to behold Juliana in
her nightcap) the upper half of her face was covered by the fall of
a piece of dingy lacelike muslin, a sort of extemporised hood which,
wound round her head, descended to the end of her nose, leaving
nothing visible but her white withered cheeks and puckered mouth,
closed tightly and, as it were, consciously. Miss Tita gave me a
glance of surprise, evidently not seeing a reason for my impatience.
"You mean that she always wears something? She does it to preserve
them."

"Because they are so fine?"

"Oh, to-day, to-day!" And Miss Tita shook her head, speaking very
low. "But they used to be magnificent!"

"Yes indeed, we have Aspern's word for that." And as I looked
again at the old woman's wrappings I could imagine that she had
not wished to allow people a reason to say that the great poet had
overdone it. But I did not waste my time in considering Miss Bordereau, in whom the appearance of respiration was so slight as to
suggest that no human attention could ever help her more. I turned
my eyes all over the room, rummaging with them the closets, the
chests of drawers, the tables. Miss Tita met them quickly and read,
I think, what was in them; but she did not answer it, turning away
restlessly, anxiously, so that I felt rebuked, with reason, for a preoccupation that was almost profane in the presence of our dying
companion. All the same I took another look, endeavouring to pick
out mentally the place to try first, for a person who should wish to
put his hand on Miss Bordereau's papers directly after her death.
The room was a dire confusion; it looked like the room of an old
actress. There were clothes hanging over chairs, odd-looking,
shabby bundles here and there, and various paste-board boxes piled
together, battered, bulging and discoloured, which might have been
fifty years old. Miss Tita after a moment noticed the direction of
my eyes again and, as if she guessed how I judged the air of the
place (forgetting I had no business to judge it at all), said, perhaps

to defend herself from the imputation of complicity in such untidiness:

"She likes it this way; we can't move things. There are old bandboxes she has had most of her life." Then she added, half taking pity on my real thought, "Those things were *there*." And she pointed to a small, low trunk which stood under a sofa where there was just room for it. It appeared to be a queer, superannuated coffer, or painted wood, with elaborate handles and shrivelled straps and with the colour (it had last been endued with a coat of light green) much rubbed off. It evidently had travelled with Juliana in the olden time—in the days of her adventures, which it had shared. It would have made a strange figure arriving at a modern hotel.

"*Were* there—they aren't now?" I asked, startled by Miss Tita's implication.

She was going to answer, but at that moment the doctor came in—the doctor whom the little maid had been sent to fetch and whom she had at last overtaken. My servant, going on his own errand, had met her with her companion in tow, and in the sociable Venetian spirit, retracing his steps with them, had also come up to the threshold of Miss Bordereau's room, where I saw him peeping over the doctor's shoulder. I motioned him away the more instantly that the sight of his prying face reminded me that I myself had almost as little to do there—an admonition confirmed by the sharp way the little doctor looked at me, appearing to take me for a rival who had the field before him. He was a short, fat, brisk gentleman who wore the tall hat of his profession and seemed to look at everything but his patient. He looked particularly at me, as if it struck him that I should be better for a dose, so that I bowed to him and left him with the women, going down to smoke a cigar in the garden. I was nervous; I could not go further; I could not leave the place. I don't know exactly what I thought might happen, but it seemed to me important to be there. I wandered about in the alleys—the warm night had come on—smoking cigar after cigar and looking at the light in Miss Bordereau's windows. They were open now, I could see; the situation was different. Sometimes the light moved, but not quickly; it did not suggest the hurry of a crisis. Was the old woman dying or was she already dead? Had the doctor said that there was nothing to be done at her tremendous age but to let her quietly pass away; or had he simply announced with a look a little more conventional that the end of the end had come? Were the other two women moving about to perform the offices that follow in such a case? It made me uneasy not to be nearer, as if I thought the doctor himself might carry away the papers with him. I bit my cigar hard as it came over me again that perhaps there were now no papers to carry!

I wandered about for an hour—for an hour and a half. I looked out for Miss Tita at one of the windows, having a vague idea that she might come there to give me some sign. Would she not see the red tip of my cigar moving about in the dark and feel that I wanted eminently to know what the doctor had said? I am afraid it is a proof my anxieties had made me gross that I should have taken in some degree for granted that at such an hour, in the midst of the greatest change that could take place in her life, they were uppermost also in poor Miss Tita's mind. My servant came down and spoke to me; he knew nothing save that the doctor had gone after a visit of half an hour. If he had stayed half an hour then Miss Bordereau was still alive: it could not have taken so much time as that to enunciate the contrary. I sent the man out of the house; there were moments when the sense of his curiosity annoyed me and this was one of them. *He* had been watching my cigar-tip from an upper window, if Miss Tita had not; he could not know what I was after and I could not tell him, though I was conscious he had fantastic private theories about me which he thought fine and which I, had I known them, should have thought offensive.

I went upstairs at last but I ascended no higher than the sala. The door of Miss Bordereau's apartment was open, showing from the parlour the dimness of a poor candle. I went toward it with a light tread and at the same moment Miss Tita appeared and stood looking at me as I approached. "She's better—she's better," she said, even before I had asked. "The doctor has given her something; she woke up, came back to life while he was there. He says there is no immediate danger."

"No immediate danger? Surely he thinks her condition strange!"

"Yes, because she had been excited. That affects her dreadfully."

"It will do so again then, because she excites herself. She did so this afternoon."

"Yes; she mustn't come out any more," said Miss Tita, with one of her lapses into a deeper placidity.

"What is the use of making such a remark as that if you begin to rattle her about again the first time she bids you?"

"I won't—I won't do it any more."

"You must learn to resist her," I went on.

"Oh, yes, I shall; I shall do so better if you tell me it's right."

"You mustn't do it for me; you must do it for yourself. It all comes back to you, if you are frightened."

"Well, I am not frightened now," said Miss Tita cheerfully. "She is very quiet."

"Is she conscious again—does she speak?"

"No, she doesn't speak, but she takes my hand. She holds it fast."

"Yes," I rejoined, "I can see what force she still has by the way she grabbed that picture this afternoon. But if she holds you fast how comes it that you are here?"

Miss Tita hesitated a moment; though her face was in deep shadow (she had her back to the light in the parlour and I had put down my own candle far off, near the door of the sala), I thought I saw her smile ingenuously. "I came on purpose—I heard your step."

"Why, I came on tiptoe, as inaudibly as possible."

"Well, I heard you," said Miss Tita.

"And is your aunt alone now?"

"Oh no; Olimpia is sitting there."

On my side I hesitated. "Shall we then step in there?" And I nodded at the parlour; I wanted more and more to be on the spot.

"We can't talk there—she will hear us."

I was on the point of replying that in that case we would sit silent, but I was too conscious that this would not do, as there was something I desired immensely to ask her. So I proposed that we should walk a little in the sala, keeping more at the other end, where we should not disturb the old lady. Miss Tita assented unconditionally; the doctor was coming again, she said, and she would be there to meet him at the door. We strolled through the fine superfluous hall, where on the marble floor—particularly as at first we said nothing—our footsteps were more audible than I had expected. When we reached the other end—the wide window, inveterately closed, connecting with the balcony that overhung the canal—I suggested that we should remain there, as she would see the doctor arrive still better. I opened the window and we passed out on the balcony. The air of the canal seemed even heavier, hotter, than that of the sala. The place was hushed and void; the quiet neighbourhood had gone to sleep. A lamp, here and there, over the narrow black water, glimmered in double; the voice of a man going homeward singing, with his jacket on his shoulder and his hat on his ear, came to us from a distance. This did not prevent the scene from being very *comme il faut*, as Miss Bordereau had called it the first time I saw her. Presently a gondola passed along the canal with its slow rhythmical plash, and as we listened we watched it in silence. It did not stop, it did not carry the doctor; and after it had gone on I said to Miss Tita:

"And where are they now—the things that were in the trunk?"

"In the trunk?"

"That green box you pointed out to me in her room. You said her papers had been there; you seemed to imply that she had transferred them."

"Oh, yes; they are not in the trunk," said Miss Tita.

"May I ask if you have looked?"

"Yes, I have looked—for you."

"How for me, dear Miss Tita? Do you mean you would have given them to me if you had found them?" I asked, almost trembling.

She delayed to reply and I waited. Suddenly she broke out, "I don't know what I would do—what I wouldn't!"

"Would you look again—somewhere else?"

She had spoken with a strange, unexpected emotion, and she went on in the same tone: "I can't—I can't—while she lies there. It isn't decent."

"No, it isn't decent," I replied, gravely. "Let the poor lady rest in peace." And the words, on my lips, were not hypocritical, for I felt reprimanded and shamed.

Miss Tita added in a moment, as if she had guessed this and were sorry for me, but at the same time wished to explain that I did drive her on or at least did insist too much: "I can't deceive her that way. I can't deceive her—perhaps on her deathbed."

"Heaven forbid I should ask you, though I have been guilty myself!"

"You have been guilty?"

"I have sailed under false colours." I felt now as if I must tell her that I had given her an invented name, on account of my fear that her aunt would have heard of me and would refuse to take me in. I explained this and also that I had really been a party to the letter written to them by John Cumnor months before.

She listened with great attention, looking at me with parted lips, and when I had made my confession she said, "Then your real name—what is it?" She repeated it over twice when I had told her, accompanying it with the exclamation "Gracious, gracious!" Then she added, "I like your own best."

"So do I," I said, laughing. "Ouf! it's a relief to get rid of the other."

"So it was a regular plot—a kind of conspiracy?"

"Oh, a conspiracy—we were only two," I replied, leaving out Mrs. Prest of course.

She hesitated; I thought she was perhaps going to say that we had been very base. But she remarked after a moment, in a candid, wondering way; "How much you must want them!"

"Oh, I do, passionately!" I conceded, smiling. And this chance made me go on, forgetting my compunction of a moment before. "How can she possibly have changed their place herself? How can she walk? How can she arrive at that sort of muscular exertion? How can she lift and carry things?"

"Oh, when one wants and when one has so much will!" said Miss Tita, as if she had thought over my question already herself and had simply had no choice but that answer—the idea that in the dead of night, or at some moment when the coast was clear, the old woman had been capable of a miraculous effort.

"Have you questioned Olimpia? Hasn't she helped her—hasn't she done it for her?" I asked; to which Miss Tita replied promptly and positively that their servant had had nothing to do with the matter, though without admitting definitely that she had spoken to her. It was as if she were a little shy, a little ashamed now of letting me see how much she had entered into my uneasiness and had me on her mind. Suddenly she said to me, without any immediate relevance:

"I feel as if you were a new person, now that you have got a new name."

"It isn't a new one; it is a very good old one, thank heaven!"

She looked at me a moment. "I do like it better."

"Oh, if you didn't I would almost go on with the other!"

"Would you really?"

I laughed again, but for all answer to this inquiry I said, "Of course if she can rummage about that way she can perfectly have burnt them."

"You must wait—you must wait." Miss Tita moralised mournfully; and her tone ministered little to my patience, for it seemed after all to accept that wretched possibility. I would teach myself to wait; I declared nevertheless; because in the first place I could not do otherwise and in the second I had her promise, given me the other night, that she would help me.

"Of course if the papers are gone that's no use," she said; not as if she wished to recede, but only to be conscientious.

"Naturally. But if you could only find out!" I groaned, quivering again.

"I thought you said you would wait."

"Oh, you mean wait even for that?"

"For what then?"

"Oh, nothing," I replied, rather foolishly, being ashamed to tell her what had been implied in my submission to delay—the idea that she would do more than merely find out. I know not whether she guessed this; at all events she appeared to become aware of the necessity for being a little more rigid.

"I didn't promise to deceive, did I? I don't think I did."

"It doesn't much matter whether you did or not, for you couldn't!"

I don't think Miss Tita would have contested this even had she not been diverted by our seeing the doctor's gondola shoot into the little canal and approach the house. I noted that he came as fast as if he believed that Miss Bordereau was still in danger. We looked down at him while he disembarked and then went back into the sala to meet him. When he came up however I naturally left Miss

Tita to go off with him alone, only asking her leave to come back later for news.

I went out of the house and took a long walk, as far as the Piazza, where my restlessness declined to quit me. I was unable to sit down (it was very late now but there were people still at the little tables in front of the cafés); I could only walk round and round, and I did so half a dozen times. I was uncomfortable, but it gave me a certain pleasure to have told Miss Tita who I really was. At last I took my way home again, slowly getting all but inextricably lost, as I did whenever I went out in Venice: so that it was considerably past midnight when I reached my door. The sala, upstairs, was as dark as usual and my lamp as I crossed it found nothing satisfactory to show me. I was disappointed, for I had notified Miss Tita that I would come back for a report, and I thought she might have left a light there as a sign. The door of the ladies' apartment was closed; which seemed an intimation that my faltering friend had gone to bed, tired of waiting for me. I stood in the middle of the place, considering, hoping she would hear me and perhaps peep out, say- ing to myself too that she would never go to bed with her aunt in a state so critical; she would sit up and watch—she would be in a chair, in her dressing-gown. I went nearer the door; I stopped there and listened. I heard nothing at all and at last I tapped gently. No answer came and after another minute I turned the handle. There was no light in the room; this ought to have prevented me from going in, but it had no such effect. If I have candidly narrated the importunities, the indelicacies, of which my desire to possess myself of Jeffrey Aspern's papers had rendered me capable I need not shrink from confessing this last indiscretion. I think it was the worst thing I did; yet there were extenuating circumstances. I was deeply though doubtless not disinterestedly anxious for more news of the old lady, and Miss Tita had accepted from me, as it were, a ren- dezvous which it might have been a point of honour with me to keep. It may be said that her leaving the place dark was a positive sign that she released me, and to this I can only reply that I desired not to be released.

The door of Miss Bordereau's room was open and I could see beyond it the faintness of a taper. There was no sound—my foot- step caused no one to stir. I came further into the room; I lingered there with my lamp in my hand. I wanted to give Miss Tita a chance to come to me if she were with her aunt, as she must be. I made no noise to call her; I only waited to see if she would not notice my light. She did not, and I explained this (I found afterwards I was right) by the idea that she had fallen asleep. If she had fallen asleep her aunt was not on her mind, and my explanation ought to have led me to go out as I had come. I must repeat again that it did not, for I found myself at the same moment thinking of something else. I had no definite purpose, no bad intention, but I felt myself held to the spot by an acute, though absurd, sense of opportunity. For what I could not have said, inasmuch as it was not in my mind that I might commit a theft. Even if it had been I was confronted with the evident fact that Miss Bordereau did not leave her secretary, her cupboard and the drawers of her tables gaping. I had no keys, no tools and no ambition to smash her furniture. None the less it came to me that I was now, perhaps alone, unmolested, at the hour of temptation and secrecy, nearer to the tormenting treasure than I had ever been. I held up my lamp, let the light play on the different objects as if it could tell me something. Still there came no movement from the other room. If Miss Tita was sleeping she was sleeping sound. Was she doing so—generous creature— on purpose to leave me the field? Did she know I was there and was she just keeping quiet to see what I would do—what I *could* do? But what could I do, when it came to that? She herself knew even better than I how little.

I stopped in front of the secretary, looking at it very idiotically; for what had it to say to me after all? In the first place it was locked, and in the second it almost surely contained nothing in which I was interested. Ten to one the papers had been destroyed; and even if they had not been destroyed the old woman would not have put them in such a place as that after removing them from the green trunk—would not have transferred them, if she had the idea of their safety on her brain, from the better hiding-place to the worse. The secretary was more conspicuous, more accessible in a room in which she could no longer mount guard. It opened with a key, but there was a little brass handle, like a button, as well; I saw this as I played my lamp over it. I did something more than this at that moment: I caught a glimpse of the possibility that Miss Tita wished me really to understand. If she did not wish me to understand, if she wished me to keep away, why had she not locked the door of communication between the sitting-room and the sala? That would have been a definite sign that I was to leave them alone. If I did not leave them alone she meant me to come for a purpose—a purpose now indicated by the quick, fantastic idea that to oblige me she had unlocked the secretary. She had not left the key, but the lid would probably move if I touched the button. This theory fascinated me, and I bent over very close to judge. I did not propose to do anything, not even—not in the least—to let down the lid; I only wanted to test my theory, to see if the cover *would* move. I touched the button with my hand—a mere touch would tell me; and as I did so (it is embarrassing for me to relate it), I looked over my shoulder. It was a chance, an instinct, for I had not heard anything. I almost let my luminary drop and certainly I stepped back, straightening myself up at what I saw. Miss Bordereau stood there in her night-dress, in the doorway of her room, watching me; her hands were raised, she had lifted the everlasting curtain that covered half her face, and for the first, the last, the only time I beheld her extraordinary eyes. They glared at me, they made me horribly ashamed. I never shall forget her strange little bent white tottering figure, with its lifted head, her attitude, her expression; neither shall I forget the tone in which as I turned, looking at her, she hissed out passionately, furiously:

"Ah, you publishing scoundrel!"

I know not what I stammered, to excuse myself to explain; but I went towards her, to tell her I meant no harm. She waved me off with her old hands, retreating before me in horror; and the next thing I knew she had fallen back with a quick spasm, as if death had descended on her, into Miss Tita's arms.

IX

I left Venice the next morning, as soon as I learnt that the old lady had not succumbed, as I feared at the moment, to the shock I had given her—the shock I may also say she had given me. How in the world could I have supposed her capable of getting out of bed by herself? I failed to see Miss Tita before going; I only saw the *donna*, whom I entrusted with a note for her younger mistress. In this note I mentioned that I should be absent but for a few days. I went to Treviso, to Bassano, to Castelfranco;[4] I took walks and drives and looked at musty old churches with ill-lighted pictures and spent hours seated smoking at the doors of cafés, where there were flies and yellow curtains, on the shady side of sleepy little squares. In spite of these pastimes, which were mechanical and perfunctory, I scantily enjoyed my journey: there was too strong a taste of the disagreeable in my life. It had been devilish awkward, as the young men say, to be found by Miss Bordereau in the dead of night examining the attachment of her bureau; and it had not been less so to have to believe for a good many hours afterward that it was highly probable I had killed her. In writing to Miss Tita I attempted to minimise these irregularities; but as she gave me no word of answer I could not know what impression I made upon her. It rankled in my mind that I had been called a publishing scoundrel, for certainly I did publish and certainly I had not been very delicate.

4. Treviso and Bassano del Grappa are medieval cities; Castelfranco Veneto is a medieval stronghold, birthplace of the painter Giorgione (1478?–1511), teacher of Titian (ca. 1477–1576). They are all within about forty miles of Venice, on the mainland.

There was a moment when I stood convinced that the only way to make up for this latter fault was to take myself away altogether on the instant; to sacrifice my hopes and relieve the two poor women for ever of the oppression of my intercourse. Then I reflected that I had better try a short absence first, for I must already have had a sense (unexpressed and dim) that in disappearing completely it would not be merely my own hopes that I should condemn to extinction. It would perhaps be sufficient if I stayed away long enough to give the elder lady time to think she was rid of me. That she would wish to be rid of me after this (if I was not rid of her) was now not to be doubted: that nocturnal scene would have cured her of the disposition to put up with my company for the sake of my dollars. I said to myself that after all I could not abandon Miss Tita, and I continued to say this even while I observed that she quite failed to comply with my earnest request (I had given her two or three addresses, at little towns, *poste restante*) that she would let me know how she was getting on. I would have made my servant write to me but that he was unable to manage a pen. It struck me there was a kind of scorn in Miss Tita's silence (little disdainful as she had ever been), so that I was uncomfortable and sore. I had scruples about going back and yet I had others about not doing so, for I wanted to put myself on a better footing. The end of it was that I did return to Venice on the twelfth day; and as my gondola gently bumped against Miss Bordereau's steps a certain palpitation of suspense told me that I had done myself a violence in holding off so long.

I had faced about so abruptly that I had not telegraphed to my servant. He was therefore not at the station to meet me, but he poked out his head from an upper window when I reached the house. "They have put her into the earth, *la vecchia*,"[5] he said to me in the lower hall, while he shouldered my valise; and he grinned and almost winked, as if he knew I should be pleased at the news.

"She's dead!" I exclaimed, giving him a very different look.

"So it appears, since they have buried her."

"It's all over? When was the funeral?"

"The other yesterday. But a funeral you could scarcely call it, signore; it was a dull little passeggio of two gondolas. Poveretta!"[6] the man continued, referring apparently to Miss Tita. His conception of funerals was apparently that they were mainly to amuse the living.

I wanted to know about Miss Tita—how she was and where she

5. The old woman.
6. Poor woman, poor thing; *passeggio*: promenade.

was—but I asked him no more questions till we had got upstairs. Now that the fact had met me I took a bad view of it, especially of the idea that poor Miss Tita had had to manage by herself after the end. What did she know about arrangements, about the steps to take in such a case? Poveretta indeed! I could only hope that the doctor had given her assistance and that she had not been neglected by the old friends of whom she had told me, the little band of the faithful whose fidelity consisted in coming to the house once a year. I elicited from my servant that two old ladies and an old gentleman had in fact rallied round Miss Tita and had supported her (they had come for her in a gondola of their own) during the journey to the cemetery, the little red-walled island of tombs which lies to the north of the town, on the way to Murano. It appeared from these circumstances that the Misses Bordereau were Catholics, a discovery I had never made, as the old woman could not go to church and her niece, so far as I perceived, either did not or went only to early mass in the parish, before I was stirring. Certainly even the priests respected their seclusion; I had never caught the whisk of the curato's skirt. That evening, an hour later, I sent my servant down with five words written on a card, to ask Miss Tita if she would see me for a few moments. She was not in the house, where he had sought her, he told me when he came back, but in the garden walking about to refresh herself and gathering flowers. He had found her there and she would be very happy to see me.

I went down and passed half an hour with poor Miss Tita. She had always had a look of musty mourning (as if she were wearing out old robes of sorrow that would not come to an end), and in this respect there was no appreciable change in her appearance. But she evidently had been crying, crying a great deal—simply, satisfyingly, refreshingly, with a sort of primitive, retarded sense of loneliness and violence. But she had none of the formalism or the self-consciousness of grief, and I was almost surprised to see her standing there in the first dusk with her hands full of flowers, smiling at me with her reddened eyes. Her white face, in the frame of her mantilla, looked longer, leaner than usual. I had had an idea that she would be a good deal disgusted with me—would consider that I ought to have been on the spot to advise her, to help her; and, though I was sure there was no rancour in her composition and no great conviction of the importance of her affairs, I had prepared myself for a difference in her manner, for some little injured look, half familiar, half estranged, which should say to my conscience, "Well, you are a nice person to have professed things!" But historic truth compels me to declare that Tita Bordereau's countenance expressed unqualified pleasure in seeing her late aunt's lodger. That touched him extremely and he thought it simplified his situation until he found it did not. I was as kind to her that evening as I knew how to be, and I walked about the garden with her for half an hour. There was no explanation of any sort between us; I did not ask her why she had not answered my letter. Still less did I repeat what I had said to her in that communication; if she chose to let me suppose that she had forgotten the position in which Miss Bordereau surprised me that night and the effect of the discovery on the old woman I was quite willing to take it that way: I was grateful to her for not treating me as if I had killed her aunt.

We strolled and strolled and really not much passed between us save the recognition of her bereavement, conveyed in my manner and in a visible air that she had of depending on me now, since I let her see that I took an interest in her. Miss Tita had none of the pride that makes a person wish to preserve the look of independence; she did not in the least pretend that she knew at present what would become of her. I forbore to touch particularly on that however, for I certainly was not prepared to say that I would take charge of her. I was cautious; not ignobly, I think, for I felt that her knowledge of life was so small that in her unsophisticated vision there would be no reason why—since I seemed to pity her—I should not look after her. She told me how her aunt had died, very peacefully at the last, and how everything had been done afterwards by the care of her good friends (fortunately, thanks to me, she said, smiling, there was money in the house; and she repeated that when once the Italians like you they are your friends for life); and when we had gone into this she asked me about my *giro*, my impressions, the places I had seen. I told her what I could, making it up partly, I am afraid, as in my depression I had not seen much; and after she had heard me she exclaimed, quite as if she had forgotten her aunt and her sorrow, "Dear, dear, how much I should like to do such things—to take a little journey!" It came over me for the moment that I ought to propose some tour, say I would take her anywhere she liked; and I remarked at any rate that some excursion —to give her a change—might be managed: we would think of it, talk it over. I said never a word to her about the Aspern documents; asked no questions as to what she had ascertained or what had otherwise happened with regard to them before Miss Bordereau's death. It was not that I was not on pins and needles to know, but that I thought it more decent not to betray my anxiety so soon after the catastrophe. I hoped she herself would say something, but she never glanced that way, and I thought this natural at the time. Later however, that night, it occurred to me that her silence was somewhat strange; for if she had talked of my movements, of anything

so detached as the Giorgione[7] at Castelfranco, she might have alluded to what she could easily remember was in my mind. It was
not to be supposed that the emotion produced by her aunt's death
had blotted out the recollection that I was interested in that lady's
relics, and I fidgeted afterwards as it came to me that her reticence
might very possibly mean simply that nothing had been found. We
separated in the garden (it was she who said she must go in); now
that she was alone in the rooms I felt that (judged, at any rate, by
Venetian ideas) I was on rather a different footing in regard to
visiting her there. As I shook hands with her for good-night I asked
her if she had any general plan—had thought over what she had
better do. "Oh yes, oh yes, but I haven't settled anything yet," she
replied, quite cheerfully. Was her cheerfulness explained by the
impression that I would settle for her?

I was glad the next morning that we had neglected practical questions, for this gave me a pretext for seeing her again immediately.
There was a very practical question to be touched upon. I owed it
to her to let her know formally that of course I did not expect her
to keep me on as a lodger, and also to show some interest in her
own tenure, what she might have on her hands in the way of a
lease. But I was not destined, as it happened, to converse with her
for more than an instant on either of these points. I sent her no
message; I simply went down to the sala and walked to and fro
there. I knew she would come out; she would very soon discover I
was there. Somehow I preferred not to be shut up with her; gardens
and big halls seemed better places to talk. It was a splendid morning, with something in the air that told of the waning of the long
Venetian summer; a freshness from the sea which stirred the flowers in the garden and made a pleasant draught in the house, less
shuttered and darkened now than when the old woman was alive.
It was the beginning of autumn, of the end of the golden months.
With this it was the end of my experiment—or would be in the
course of half an hour, when I should really have learned that the
papers had been reduced to ashes. After that there would be nothing left for me but to go to the station; for seriously (and as it struck
me in the morning light) I could not linger there to act as guardian
to a piece of middle-aged female helplessness. If she had not saved
the papers wherein should I be indebted to her? I think I winced a
little as I asked myself how much, if she *had* saved them, I should
have to recognise and, as it were, to reward such a courtesy. Might
not that circumstance after all saddle me with a guardianship? If

7. The reference is to a particular painting, Giorgione's masterpiece depicting the Madonna
   and Child between Saint Francis and Saint Liberale in the Duomo (cathedral) at
   Castelfranco.

this idea did not make me more uncomfortable as I walked up and down it was because I was convinced I had nothing to look to. If the old woman had not destroyed everything before she pounced upon me in the parlour she had done so afterwards.

It took Miss Tita rather longer than I had expected to guess that I was there; but when at last she came out she looked at me without surprise. I said to her that I had been waiting for her and she asked why I had not let her know. I was glad the next day that I had checked myself before remarking that I had wished to see if a friendly intuition would not tell her: it became a satisfaction to me that I had not indulged in that rather tender joke. What I did say was virtually the truth—that I was too nervous, since I expected her now to settle my fate.

"Your fate?" said Miss Tita, giving me a queer look; and as she spoke I noticed a rare change in her. She was different from what she had been the evening before—less natural, less quiet. She had been crying the day before and she was not crying now, and yet she struck me as less confident. It was as if something had happened to her during the night, or at least as if she had thought of something that troubled her—something in particular that affected her relations with me, made them more embarrassing and complicated. Had she simply perceived that her aunt's not being there now altered my position?

"I mean about our papers. *Are* there any? You must know now."

"Yes, there are a great many; more than I supposed." I was struck with the way her voice trembled as she told me this.

"Do you mean that you have got them in there—and that I may see them?"

"I don't think you can see them," said Miss Tita, with an extraordinary expression of entreaty in her eyes, as if the dearest hope she had in the world now was that I would not take them from her. But how could she expect me to make such a sacrifice as that after all that had passed between us? What had I come back to Venice for but to see them, to take them? My delight at learning they were still in existence was such that if the poor woman had gone down on her knees to beseech me never to mention them again I would have treated the proceeding as a bad joke. "I have got them but I can't show them," she added.

"Not even to me? Ah, Miss Tita!" I groaned, with a voice of infinite remonstrance and reproach.

She coloured and the tears came back to her eyes; I saw that it cost her a kind of anguish to take such a stand but that a dreadful sense of duty had descended upon her. It made me quite sick to find myself confronted with that particular obstacle; all the more that it appeared to me I had been extremely encouraged to leave it out of account. I almost considered that Miss Tita had assured me that if she had no greater hindrance than that—! "You don't mean to say you made her a deathbed promise? It was precisely against your doing anything of that sort that I thought I was safe. Oh, I would rather she had burned the papers outright than that!"

"No, it isn't a promise," said Miss Tita.

"Pray what is it then?"

She hesitated and then she said, "She tried to burn them, but I prevented it. She had hid them in her bed."

"In her bed?"

"Between the mattresses. That's where she put them when she took them out of the trunk. I can't understand how she did it, because Olimpia didn't help her. She tells me so and I believe her. My aunt only told her afterwards so that she shouldn't touch the bed—anything but the sheets. So it was badly made," added Miss Tita, simply.

"I should think so! And how did she try to burn them?"

"She didn't try much; she was too weak, those last days. But she told me—she charged me. Oh, it was terrible! She couldn't speak after that night; she could only make signs."

"And what did you do?"

"I took them away. I locked them up."

"In the secretary?"

"Yes, in the secretary," said Miss Tita, reddening again.

"Did you tell her you would burn them?"

"No, I didn't—on purpose."

"On purpose to gratify me?"

"Yes, only for that."

"And what good will you have done me if after all you won't show them?"

"Oh, none; I know that—I know that."

"And did she believe you had destroyed them?"

"I don't know what she believed at the last. I couldn't tell—she was too far gone."

"Then if there was no promise and no assurance I can't see what ties you."

"Oh, she hated it so—she hated it so! She was so jealous. But here's the portrait—you may have that," Miss Tita announced, taking the little picture, wrapped up in the same manner in which her aunt had wrapped it, out of her pocket.

"I may have it—do you mean you give it to me?" I questioned, staring, as it passed into my hand.

"Oh yes."

"But it's worth money—a large sum."

"Well!" said Miss Tita, still with her strange look.

I did not know what to make of it, for it could scarcely mean that she wanted to bargain like her aunt. She spoke as if she wished to make me a present. "I can't take it from you as a gift," I said, "and yet I can't afford to pay you for it according to the ideas Miss Bordereau had of its value. She rated it at a thousand pounds."

"Couldn't we sell it?" asked Miss Tita.

"God forbid! I prefer the picture to the money."

"Well then keep it."

"You are very generous."

"So are you."

"I don't know why you should think so," I replied; and this was a truthful speech, for the singular creature appeared to have some very fine reference in her mind, which I did not in the least seize.

"Well, you have made a great difference for me," said Miss Tita.

I looked at Jeffrey Aspern's face in the little picture, partly in order not to look at that of my interlocutress, which had begun to trouble me, even to frighten me a little—it was so self-conscious, so unnatural. I made no answer to this last declaration; I only privately consulted Jeffrey Aspern's delightful eyes with my own (they were so young and brilliant, and yet so wise, so full of vision); I asked him what on earth was the matter with Miss Tita. He seemed to smile at me with friendly mockery, as if he were amused at my case. I had got into a pickle for him—as if he needed it! He was unsatisfactory, for the only moment since I had know him. Nevertheless, now that I held the little picture in my hand I felt that it would be a precious possession. "Is this a bribe to make me give up the papers?" I demanded in a moment, perversely. "Much as I value it, if I were to be obliged to choose, the papers are what I should prefer. Ah, but ever so much!"

"How can you choose—how can you choose?" Miss Tita asked, slowly, lamentably.

"I see! Of course there is nothing to be said, if you regard the interdiction that rests upon you as quite insurmountable. In this case it must seem to you that to part with them would be an impiety of the worst kind, a simple sacrilege!"

Miss Tita shook her head, full of her dolefulness. "You would understand if you had known her. I'm afraid," she quavered suddenly—"I'm afraid! She was terrible when she was angry."

"Yes, I saw something of that, that night. She was terrible. Then I saw her eyes. Lord, they were fine!"

"I see them—they stare at me in the dark!" said Miss Tita.

"You are nervous, with all you have been through."

"Oh yes, very—very!"

"You mustn't mind; that will pass away," I said, kindly. Then I added, resignedly, for it really seemed to me that I must accept the situation, "Well, so it is, and it can't be helped. I must renounce." Miss Tita, at this, looking at me, gave a low, soft moan, and I went on: "I only wish to heaven she had destroyed them; then there would be nothing more to say. And I can't understand why, with her ideas, she didn't."

"Oh, she lived on them!" said Miss Tita.

"You can imagine whether that makes me want less to see them," I answered, smiling. "But don't let me stand here as if I had it in my soul to tempt you to do anything base. Naturally you will understand I give up my rooms. I leave Venice immediately." And I took up my hat, which I had placed on a chair. We were still there rather awkwardly, on our feet, in the middle of the sala. She had left the door of the apartments open behind her but she had not led me that way.

A kind of spasm came into her face as she saw me take my hat. "Immediately—do you mean to-day?" The tone of the words was tragical—they were a cry of desolation.

"Oh no; not so long as I can be of the least service to you."

"Well, just a day or two more—just two or three days," she panted. Then controlling herself she added in another manner, "She wanted to say something to me—the last day—something very particular, but she couldn't."

"Something very particular?"

"Something more about the papers."

"And did you guess—have you any idea?"

"No, I have thought—but I don't know. I have thought all kinds of things."

"And for instance?"

"Well, that if you were a relation it would be different."

"If I were a relation?"

"If you were not a stranger. Then it would be the same for you as for me. Anything that is mine—would be yours, and you could do what you like. I couldn't prevent you—and you would have no responsibility."

She brought out this droll explanation with a little nervous rush, as if she were speaking words she had got by heart. They gave me an impression of subtlety and at first I failed to follow. But after a moment her face helped me to see further, and then a light came into my mind. It was embarrassing, and I bent my head over Jeffrey Aspern's portrait. What an odd expression was in his face! "Get out of it as you can, my dear fellow!" I put the picture into the pocket of my coat and said to Miss Tita, "Yes, I'll sell it for you. I sha'n't get a thousand pounds by any means, but I shall get something good."

She looked at me with tears in her eyes, but she seemed to try to smile as she remarked, "We can divide the money."

"No, no, it shall be all yours." Then I went on, "I think I know what your poor aunt wanted to say. She wanted to give directions that her papers should be buried with her."

Miss Tita appeared to consider this suggestion for a moment; after which she declared, with striking decision, "Oh no, she wouldn't have thought that safe!"

"It seems to me nothing could be safer."

"She had an idea that when people want to publish they are capable—" And she paused, blushing.

"Of violating a tomb? Mercy on us, what must she have thought of me!"

"She was not just, she was not generous!" Miss Tita cried with sudden passion.

The light that had come into my mind a moment before increased. "Ah, don't say that, for we *are* a dreadful race." Then I pursued, "If she left a will, that may give you some idea."

"I have found nothing of the sort—she destroyed it. She was very fond of me," Miss Tita added, incongruously. "She wanted me to be happy. And if any person should be kind to me—she wanted to speak of that."

I was almost awestricken at the astuteness with which the good lady found herself inspired, transparent astuteness as it was and sewn, as the phrase is, with white thread. "Depend upon it she didn't want to make any provision that would be agreeable to me."

"No, not to you but to me. She knew I should like it if you could carry out your idea. Not because she cared for you but because she did think of me," Miss Tita went on, with her unexpected, persuasive volubility. "You could see them—you could use them." She stopped, seeing that I perceived the sense of that conditional—stopped long enough for me to give some sign which I did not give. She must have been conscious however that though my face showed the greatest embarrassment that was ever painted on a human countenance it was not set as a stone, it was also full of compassion. It was a comfort to me a long time afterwards to consider that she could not have seen in me the smallest symptom of disrespect. "I don't know what to do; I'm too tormented, I'm too ashamed!" she continued, with vehemence. Then turning away from me and burying her face in her hands she burst into a flood of tears. If she did not know what to do it may be imagined whether I did any better. I stood there dumb, watching her while her sobs resounded in the great empty hall. In a moment she was facing me again, with her streaming eyes. "I would give you everything—and she would understand, where she is—she would forgive me!"

"Ah, Miss Tita—ah, Miss Tita," I stammered, for all reply. I did not know what to do, as I say, but at a venture I made a wild, vague movement, in consequence of which I found myself at the door. I remember standing there and saying, "It wouldn't do—it wouldn't do!" pensively, awkwardly, grotesquely, while I looked away to the opposite end of the sala as if there were a beautiful view there. The next thing I remember is that I was downstairs and out of the house. My gondola was there and my gondolier, reclining on the cushions, sprang up as soon as he saw me. I jumped in and to his usual *"Dove commanda?"*[8] I replied, in a tone that made him stare, "Anywhere, anywhere; out into the lagoon!"

He rowed me away and I sat there prostrate, groaning softly to myself, with my hat pulled over my face. What in the name of the preposterous did she mean if she did not mean to offer me her hand? That was the price—that was the price! And did she think I wanted it, poor deluded, infatuated, extravagant lady? My gondolier, behind me, must have seen my ears red as I wondered, sitting there under the fluttering *tenda*,[9] with my hidden face, noticing nothing as we passed—wondered whether her delusion, her infatuation had been my own reckless work. Did she think I had made love to her, even to get the papers? I had not, I had not; I repeated that over to myself for an hour, for two hours, till I was wearied if not convinced. I don't know where my gondolier took me; we floated aimlessly about on the lagoon, with slow, rare strokes. At last I became conscious that we were near the Lido, far up, on the right hand, as you turn your back to Venice, and I made him put me ashore. I wanted to walk, to move, to shed some of my bewilderment. I crossed the narrow strip and got to the sea-beach—I took my way toward Malamocco.[1] But presently I flung myself down again on the warm sand, in the breeze, on the coarse dry grass. It took it out of me to think I had been so much at fault, that I had unwittingly but none the less deplorably trifled. But I had not given her cause —distinctly I had not. I had said to Mrs. Prest that I would make love to her; but it had been a joke without consequences and I had never said it to Tita Bordereau. I had been as kind as possible, because I really liked her; but since when had that become a crime where a woman of such an age and such an appearance was concerned? I am far from remembering clearly the succession of events and feelings during this long day of confusion, which I spent entirely in wandering about, without going home, until late at night; it only comes back to me that there were moments when I pacified

8. Where do you wish to go?
9. Awning.
1. A fishing village toward the southern end of the Lido.

my conscience and others when I lashed it into pain. I did not laugh all day—that I do recollect; the case, however it might have struck others, seemed to me so little amusing. It would have been better perhaps for me to feel the comic side of it. At any rate, whether I had given cause or not it went without saying that I could not pay the price. I could not accept. I could not, for a bundle of tattered papers, marry a ridiculous, pathetic, provincial old woman. It was a proof that she did not think the idea would come to me, her having determined to suggest it herself in that practical, argumentative, heroic way, in which the timidity however had been so much more striking than the boldness that her reasons appeared to come first and her feelings afterward.

As the day went on I grew to wish that I had never heard of Aspern's relics, and I cursed the extravagant curiosity that had put John Cumnor on the scent of them. We had more than enough material without them and my predicament was the just punishment of that most fatal of human follies, our not having known when to stop. It was very well to say it was no predicament, that the way out was simple, that I had only to leave Venice by the first train in the morning, after writing a note to Miss Tita, to be placed in her hand as soon as I got clear of the house; for it was a strong sign that I was embarrassed that when I tried to make up the note in my mind in advance (I would put it on paper as soon as I got home, before going to bed), I could not think of anything but "How can I thank you for the rare confidence you have placed in me?" That would never do; it sounded exactly as if an acceptance were to follow. Of course I might go away without writing a word, but that would be brutal and my idea was still to exclude brutal solutions. As my confusion cooled I was lost in wonder at the importance I had attached to Miss Bordereau's crumpled scraps; the thought of them became odious to me and I was as vexed with the old witch for the superstition that had prevented her from destroying them as I was with myself for having already spent more money than I could afford in attempting to control their fate. I forget what I did, where I went after leaving the Lido and at what hour or with what recovery of composure I made my way back to my boat. I only know that in the afternoon, when the air was aglow with the sunset, I was standing before the church of Saints John and Paul and looking up at the small square-jawed face of Bartolommeo Colleoni, the terrible *condottiere*[2] who sits so sturdily astride of his huge bronze horse, on the high pedestal on which Venetian gratitude maintains

---

2. The *condottieri* were leaders of mercenary soldiers in fourteenth- and fifteenth-century Italy. Here the reference is to the equestrian statue of one of them, Colleoni (ca. 1400–1475), begun by Verrocchio in 1481 and finished by Leopardi (1488–1496).

him. The statue is incomparable, the finest of all mounted figures, unless that of Marcus Aurelius,[3] who rides benignant before the Roman Capitol, be finer: but I was not thinking of that; I only found myself staring at the triumphant captain as if he had an oracle on his lips. The western light shines into all his grimness at that hour and makes it wonderfully personal. But he continued to look far over my head, at the red immersion of another day—he had seen so many go down into the lagoon through the centuries—and if he were thinking of battles and stratagems they were of a different quality from any I had to tell him of. He could not direct me what to do, gaze up at him as I might. Was it before this or after that I wandered about for an hour in the small canals, to the continued stupefaction of my gondolier, who had never seen me so restless and yet so void of a purpose and could extract from me no order but "Go anywhere—everywhere—all over the place"? He reminded me that I had not lunched and expressed therefore respectfully the hope that I would dine earlier. He had had long periods of leisure during the day, when I had left the boat and rambled, so that I was not obliged to consider him, and I told him that that day, for a change, I would touch no meat. It was an effect of poor Miss Tita's proposal, not altogether auspicious, that I had quite lost my appetite. I don't know why it happened that on this occasion I was more than ever struck with that queer air of sociability, of cousinship and family life, which makes up half the expression of Venice. Without streets and vehicles, the uproar of wheels, the brutality of horses, and with its little winding ways where people crowd together, where voices sound as in the corridors of a house, where the human step circulates as if it skirted the angles of furniture and shoes never wear out, the place has the character of an immense collective apartment, in which Piazza San Marco is the most ornamented corner and palaces and churches, for the rest, play the part of great divans of repose, tables of entertainment, expanses of decoration. And somehow the splendid common domicile, familiar, domestic and resonant, also resembles a theatre, with actors clicking over bridges and, in straggling processions, tripping along fondamentas.[4] As you sit in your gondola the footways that in certain parts edge the canals assume to the eye the importance of a stage, meeting it at the same angle, and the Venetian figures, moving to and fro against the battered scenery of their little houses of comedy, strike you as members of an endless dramatic troupe.

3. Roman emperor, stoic philosopher and writer (121–180).
4. The Italian word *fondamento* (foundation) has the masculine plural *fondamenti* and the feminine plural *fondamenta*, referring to abstract and concrete foundations respectively. In Venice *fondamenta* has a specialized meaning: the quays or pathways between canals and buildings. James seems to have added an English plural *s*.

I went to bed that night very tired, without being able to compose a letter to Miss Tita. Was this failure the reason why I became conscious the next morning as soon as I awoke of a determination to see the poor lady again the first moment she would receive me? That had something to do with it, but what had still more was the fact that during my sleep a very odd revulsion had taken place in my spirit. I found myself aware of this almost as soon as I opened my eyes; it made me jump out of my bed with the movement of a man who remembers that he has left the house-door ajar or a candle burning under a shelf. Was I still in time to save my goods? That question was in my heart; for what had now come to pass was that in the unconscious cerebration of sleep I had swung back to a passionate appreciation of Miss Bordereau's papers. They were now more precious than ever and a kind of ferocity had come into my desire to possess them. The condition Miss Tita had attached to the possession of them no longer appeared an obstacle worth thinking of, and for an hour, that morning, my repentant imagination brushed it aside. It was absurd that I should be able to invent nothing; absurd to renounce so easily and turn away helpless from the idea that the only way to get hold of the papers was to unite myself to her for life. I would not unite myself and yet I would have them. I must add that by the time I sent down to ask if she would see me I had invented no alternative, though to do so I had had all the time that I was dressing. This failure was humiliating, yet what could the alternative be? Miss Tita sent back word that I might come; and as I descended the stairs and crossed the sala to her door—this time she received me in her aunt's forlorn parlour—I hoped she would not think my errand was to tell her I accepted her hand. She certainly would have made the day before the reflection that I declined it.

As soon as I came into the room I saw that she had drawn this inference, but I also saw something which had not been in my forecast. Poor Miss Tita's sense of her failure had produced an extraordinary alteration in her, but I had been too full of my literary concupiscence to think of that. Now I perceived it; I can scarcely tell how it startled me. She stood in the middle of the room with a face of mildness bent upon me, and her look of forgiveness, of absolution made her angelic. It beautified her; she was younger; she was not a ridiculous old woman. This optical trick gave her a sort of phantasmagoric brightness, and while I was still the victim of it I heard a whisper somewhere in the depths of my conscience: "Why not, after all—why not?" It seemed to me I was ready to pay the price. Still more distinctly however than the whisper I heard Miss Tita's own voice. I was so struck with the different effect she made upon me that at first I was not clearly aware of what she was saying; then I perceived she had bade me good-bye—she said something about hoping I should be very happy.

"Good-bye—good-bye?" I repeated, with an inflection interrogative and probably foolish.

I saw she did not feel the interrogation, she only heard the words; she had strung herself up to accepting our separation and they fell upon her ear as a proof. "Are you going today?" she asked. "But it doesn't matter, for whenever you go I shall not see you again. I don't want to." And she smiled strangely, with an infinite gentleness. She had never doubted that I had left her the day before in horror. How could she, since I had not come back before night to contradict, even as a simple form, such an idea? And now she had the force of soul—Miss Tita with force of soul was a new conception—to smile at me in her humiliation.

"What shall you do—where shall you go?" I asked.

"Oh, I don't know. I have done the great thing. I have destroyed the papers."

"Destroyed them?" I faltered.

"Yes; what was I to keep them for? I burnt them last night, one by one, in the kitchen."

"One by one?" I repeated, mechanically.

"It took a long time—there were so many." The room seemed to go round me as she said this and a real darkness for a moment descended upon my eyes. When it passed Miss Tita was there still, but the transfiguration was over and she had changed back to a plain, dingy, elderly person. It was in this character she spoke as she said, "I can't stay with you longer, I can't"; and it was in this character that she turned her back upon me, as I had turned mine upon her twenty-four hours before, and moved to the door of her room. Here she did what I had not done when I quitted her—she paused long enough to give me one look. I have never forgotten it and I sometimes still suffer from it, though it was not resentful. No, there was no resentment, nothing hard or vindictive in poor Miss Tita; for when, later, I sent her in exchange for the portrait of Jeffrey Aspern a larger sum of money than I had hoped to be able to gather for her, writing to her that I had sold the picture, she kept it with thanks; she never sent it back. I wrote to her that I had sold the picture, but I admitted to Mrs. Prest, at the time (I met her in London, in the autumn), that it hangs above my writing-table. When I look at it my chagrin at the loss of the letters becomes almost intolerable.

The Pupil[†]

The poor young man hesitated and procrastinated: it cost him such an effort to broach the subject of terms, to speak of money to a person who spoke only of feelings and, as it were, of the aristocracy. Yet he was unwilling to take leave, treating his engagement as settled, without some more conventional glance in that direction than he could find an opening for in the manner of the large, affable lady who sat there drawing a pair of soiled *gants de Suède*[1] through a fat, jewelled hand and, at once pressing and gliding, repeated over and over everything but the thing he would have liked to hear. He would have liked to hear the figure of his salary; but just as he was nervously about to sound that note the little boy came back—the little boy Mrs. Moreen had sent out of the room to fetch her fan. He came back without the fan, only with the casual observation that he couldn't find it. As he dropped this cynical confession he looked straight and hard at the candidate for the honour of taking his education in hand. This personage reflected, somewhat grimly, that the first thing he should have to teach his little charge would be to appear to address himself to his mother when he spoke to her—especially not to make her such an improper answer as that.

When Mrs. Moreen bethought herself of this pretext for getting rid of their companion, Pemberton supposed it was precisely to approach the delicate subject of his remuneration. But it had been only to say some things about her son which it was better that a boy of eleven shouldn't catch. They were extravagantly to his advantage, save when she lowered her voice to sigh, tapping her left side familiarly: "And all overclouded by *this*, you know—all at the mercy of a weakness—!" Pemberton gathered that the weakness was in the region of the heart. He had known the poor child was not robust: this was the basis on which he had been invited to treat, through an English lady, an Oxford acquaintance, then at Nice,

---

[†] "The Pupil" first appeared in *Longman's Magazine*, March–April 1891. Its first publication in a book was in *The Lesson of the Master* (New York and London: Macmillan and Co., 1892). This text is here reprinted. The American and English issues of this first edition were identical.

1. Suede gloves.

133

who happened to know both his needs and those of the amiable American family looking out for something really superior in the way of a resident tutor.

The young man's impression of his prospective pupil, who had first come into the room, as if to see for himself, as soon as Pemberton was admitted, was not quite the soft solicitation the visitor had taken for granted. Morgan Moreen was, somehow, sickly without being delicate, and that he looked intelligent (it is true Pemberton wouldn't have enjoyed his being stupid), only added to the suggestion that, as with his big mouth and big ears he really couldn't be called pretty, he might be unpleasant. Pemberton was modest—he was even timid; and the chance that his small scholar might prove cleverer than himself had quite figured, to his nervousness, among the dangers of an untried experiment. He reflected, however, that these were risks one had to run when one accepted a position, as it was called, in a private family; when as yet one's University honours had, pecuniarily speaking, remained barren. At any rate, when Mrs. Moreen got up as if to intimate that, since it was understood he would enter upon his duties within the week she would let him off now, he succeeded, in spite of the presence of the child, in squeezing out a phrase about the rate of payment. It was not the fault of the conscious smile which seemed a reference to the lady's expensive identity, if the allusion did not sound rather vulgar. This was exactly because she became still more gracious to reply: "Oh! I can assure you that all that will be quite regular."

Pemberton only wondered, while he took up his hat, what "all that" was to amount to—people had such different ideas. Mrs. Moreen's words, however, seemed to commit the family to a pledge definite enough to elicit from the child a strange little comment, in the shape of the mocking, foreign ejaculation, "Oh, là-là!"

Pemberton, in some confusion, glanced at him as he walked slowly to the window with his back turned, his hands in his pockets and the air in his elderly shoulders of a boy who didn't play. The young man wondered if he could teach him to play, though his mother had said it would never do and that this was why school was impossible. Mrs. Moreen exhibited no discomfiture; she only continued blandly: "Mr. Moreen will be delighted to meet your wishes. As I told you, he has been called to London for a week. As soon as he comes back you shall have it out with him."

This was so frank and friendly that the young man could only reply, laughing as his hostess laughed: "Oh! I don't imagine we shall have much of a battle."

"They'll give you anything you like," the boy remarked unexpectedly, returning from the window. "We don't mind what anything costs—we live awfully well."

"My darling, you're too quaint!" his mother exclaimed, putting out to caress him a practiced but ineffectual hand. He slipped out of it, but looked with intelligent, innocent eyes at Pemberton, who had already had time to notice that from one moment to the other his small satiric face seemed to change its time of life. At this moment it was infantine; yet it appeared also to be under the influence of curious intuitions and knowledges. Pemberton rather disliked precocity, and he was disappointed to find gleams of it in a disciple not yet in his teens. Nevertheless he divined on the spot that Morgan wouldn't prove a bore. He would prove on the contrary a kind of excitement. This idea held the young man, in spite of a certain repulsion.

"You pompous little person! We're not extravagant!" Mrs. Moreen gayly protested, making another unsuccessful attempt to draw the boy to her side. "You must know what to expect," she went on to Pemberton.

"The less you expect the better!" her companion interposed. "But we *are* people of fashion."

"Only so far as *you* make us so!" Mrs. Moreen mocked, tenderly. "Well, then, on Friday—don't tell me you're superstitious—and mind you don't fail us. Then you'll see us all. I'm so sorry the girls are out. I guess you'll like the girls. And, you know, I've another son, quite different from this one."

"He tries to imitate me," said Morgan to Pemberton.

"He tries? Why, he's twenty years old!" cried Mrs. Moreen.

"You're very witty," Pemberton remarked to the child—a proposition that his mother echoed with enthusiasm, declaring that Morgan's sallies were the delight of the house. The boy paid no heed to this; he only inquired abruptly of the visitor, who was surprised afterwards that he hadn't struck him as offensively forward: "Do you *want* very much to come?"

"Can you doubt it, after such a description of what I shall hear?" Pemberton replied. Yet he didn't want to come at all; he was coming because he had to go somewhere, thanks to the collapse of his fortune at the end of a year abroad, spent on the system of putting his tiny patrimony into a single full wave of experience. He had had his full wave, but he couldn't pay his hotel bill. Moreover, he had caught in the boy's eyes the glimpse of a far-off appeal.

"Well, I'll do the best I can for you," said Morgan; with which he turned away again. He passed out of one of the long windows; Pemberton saw him go and lean on the parapet of the terrace. He remained there while the young man took leave of his mother, who, on Pemberton's looking as if he expected a farewell from him, interposed with: "Leave him, leave him; he's so strange!" Pemberton suspected she was afraid of something he might say. "He's a genius—you'll love him," she added. "He's much the most interesting person in the family." And before he could invent some civility to oppose to this, she wound up with: "But we're all good, you know!"

"He's a genius—you'll love him!" were words that recurred to Pemberton before the Friday, suggesting, among other things that geniuses were not invariably lovable. However, it was all the better if there was an element that would make tutorship absorbing: he had perhaps taken too much for granted that it would be dreary. As he left the villa after his interview, he looked up at the balcony and saw the child leaning over it. "We shall have great larks!" he called up.

Morgan hesitated a moment; then he answered, laughing: "By the time you come back I shall have thought of something witty!"

This made Pemberton say to himself: "After all he's rather nice."

II

On the Friday he saw them all, as Mrs. Moreen had promised, for her husband had come back and the girls and the other son were at home. Mr. Moreen had a white moustache, a confiding manner and, in his buttonhole, the ribbon of a foreign order[2]—bestowed, as Pemberton eventually learned, for services. For what services he never clearly ascertained: this was a point—one of a large number—that Mr. Moreen's manner never confided. What it emphatically did confide was that he was a man of the world. Ulick, the firstborn, was in visible training for the same profession—under the disadvantage as yet, however, of a buttonhole only feebly floral and a moustache with no pretensions to type. The girls had hair and figures and manners and small fat feet, but had never been out alone. As for Mrs. Moreen, Pemberton saw on a nearer view that her elegance was intermittent and her parts didn't always match. Her husband, as she had promised, met with enthusiasm Pemberton's ideas in regard to a salary. The young man had endeavoured to make them modest, and Mr. Moreen confided to him that *he* found them positively meagre. He further assured him that he aspired to be intimate with his children, to be their best friend, and

---

2. In the Middle Ages feudal lords in Europe awarded orders of knighthood to their vassals for bravery in war. In recent, less heroic times membership in an order has been gained by services of various kinds, some less meritorious than others, some even of rather hypothetical merit. The ribbon of Mr. Moreen's order seems to be of that kind. Ulick's buttonhole sports only a flower.

that he was always looking out for them. That was what he went off for, to London and other places—to look out; and this vigilance was the theory of life, as well as the real occupation, of the whole family. They all looked out, for they were very frank on the subject of its being necessary. They desired it to be understood that they were earnest people, and also that their fortune, though quite adequate for earnest people, required the most careful administration. Mr. Moreen, as the parent bird, sought sustenance for the nest. Ulick found sustenance mainly at the club, where Pemberton guessed that it was usually served on green cloth.[3] The girls used to do up their hair and their frocks themselves, and our young man felt appealed to be glad, in regard to Morgan's education, that, though it must naturally be of the best, it didn't cost too much. After a little he *was* glad, forgetting at times his own needs in the interest inspired by the child's nature and education and the pleasure of making easy terms for him.

During the first weeks of their acquaintance Morgan had been as puzzling as a page in an unknown language—altogether different from the obvious little Anglo-Saxons who had misrepresented childhood to Pemberton. Indeed the whole mystic volume in which the boy had been bound demanded some practice in translation. To-day, after a considerable interval, there is something phantasmagoric, like a prismatic reflection or a serial novel, in Pemberton's memory of the queerness of the Moreens. If it were not for a few tangible tokens—a lock of Morgan's hair, cut by his own hand, and the half-dozen letters he got from him when they were separated —the whole episode and the figures peopling it would seem too inconsequent for anything but dreamland. The queerest thing about them was their success (as it appeared to him for a while at the time), for he had never seen a family so brilliantly equipped for failure. Wasn't it success to have kept him so hatefully long? Wasn't it success to have drawn him in that first morning at *déjeuner*,[4] the Friday he came—it was enough to *make* one superstitious—so that he utterly committed himself, and this not by calculation or a *mot d' ordre*,[5] but by a happy instinct which made them, like a band of gipsies, work so neatly together? They amused him as much as if they had really been a band of gipsies. He was still young and had not seen much of the world—his English years had been intensely usual; therefore the reversed conventions of the Moreens (for they had their standards), struck him as topsyturvy. He had encountered nothing like them at Oxford; still less had any such note been struck

3. Gambling and billiard tables are usually covered in green.
4. Lunch.
5. Password, secret signal.

to his younger American ear during the four years at Yale in which he had richly supposed himself to be reacting against Puritanism. The reaction of the Moreens, at any rate, went ever so much further. He had thought himself very clever that first day in hitting them all off in his mind with the term "cosmopolite." Later, it seemed feeble and colourless enough—confessedly, helplessly provisional.

However, when he first applied it to them he had a degree of joy—for an instructor he was still empirical—as if from the apprehension that to live with them would really be to see life. Their sociable strangeness was an intimation of that—their chatter of tongues, their gaiety and good humour, their infinite dawdling (they were always getting themselves up, but it took forever, and Pemberton had once found Mr. Moreen shaving in the drawing-room), their French, their Italian and, in the spiced fluency, their cold, tough slices of American. They lived on macaroni and coffee (they had these articles prepared in perfection), but they knew recipes for a hundred other dishes. They overflowed with music and song, were always humming and catching each other up, and had a kind of professional acquaintance with continental cities. They talked of "good places" as if they had been strolling players. They had at Nice a villa, a carriage, a piano and a banjo, and they went to official parties. They were a perfect calendar of the "days"[6] of their friends, which Pemberton knew them, when they were indisposed, to get out of bed to go to, and which made the week larger than life when Mrs. Moreen talked of them with Paula and Amy. Their romantic initiations gave their new inmate at first an almost dazzling sense of culture. Mrs. Moreen had translated something, at some former period—an author whom it made Pemberton feel *borné*[7] never to have heard of. They could imitate Venetian and sing Neapolitan, and when they wanted to say something very particular they communicated with each other in an ingenious dialect of their own— a sort of spoken cipher, which Pemberton at first took for Volapuk,[8] but which he learned to understand as he would not have understood Volapuk.

"It's the family language—Ultramoreen," Morgan explained to him drolly enough; but the boy rarely condescended to use it himself, though he attempted colloquial Latin as if he had been a little prelate.

---

6. Fixed days of the month or week on which people kept open house.
7. Limited, inexperienced.
8. Volapük was an artificial language invented in 1879 and therefore quite new at the time; it has now been superseded by Esperanto. Morgan, able to use Latin—the international language by which the Catholic clergy and sometimes scholars overcome language barriers—had no taste for his family's private language, although it served him as the subject of a pun: Ultramoreen/ultramarine.

Among all the "days" with which Mrs. Moreen's memory was taxed she managed to squeeze in one of her own, which her friends sometimes forgot. But the house derived a frequented air from the number of fine people who were freely named there and from several mysterious men with foreign titles and English clothes whom Morgan called the princes and who, on sofas with the girls, talked French very loud, as if to show they were saying nothing improper. Pemberton wondered how the princes could ever propose in that tone and so publicly: he took for granted cynically that this was what was desired of them. Then he acknowledged that even for the chance of such an advantage Mrs. Moreen would never allow Paula and Amy to receive alone. These young ladies were not at all timid, but it was just the safeguards that made them so graceful. It was a houseful of Bohemians who wanted tremendously to be Philistines.

In one respect, however, certainly, they achieved no rigour—they were wonderfully amiable and ecstatic about Morgan. It was a genuine tenderness, an artless admiration, equally strong in each. They even praised his beauty, which was small, and were rather afraid of him, as if they recognised that he was of a finer clay. They called him a little angel and a little prodigy and pitied his want of health effusively. Pemberton feared at first that their extravagance would make him hate the boy, but before this happened he had become extravagant himself. Later, when he had grown rather to hate the others, it was a bribe to patience for him that they were at any rate nice about Morgan, going on tiptoe if they fancied he was showing symptoms, and even giving up somebody's "day" to procure him a pleasure. But mixed with this was the oddest wish to make him independent, as if they felt that they were not good enough for him. They passed him over to Pemberton very much as if they wished to force a constructive adoption on the obliging bachelor and shirk altogether a responsibility. They were delighted when they perceived that Morgan liked his preceptor, and could think of no higher praise for the young man. It was strange how they contrived to reconcile the appearance, and indeed the essential fact, of adoring the child with their eagerness to wash their hands of him. Did they want to get rid of him before he should find them out? Pemberton was finding them out month by month. At any rate, the boy's relations turned their backs with exaggerated delicacy, as if to escape the charge of interfering. Seeing in time how little he had in common with them (it was by *them* he first observed it—they proclaimed it with complete humility), his preceptor was moved to speculate on the mysteries of transmission, the far jumps of heredity. Where his detachment from most of the things they represented had come from was more than an observer could say—it certainly had burrowed under two or three generations.

As for Pemberton's own estimate of his pupil, it was a good while before he got the point of view, so little had he been prepared for it by the smug young barbarians to whom the tradition of tutorship, as hitherto revealed to him, had been adjusted. Morgan was scrappy and surprising, deficient in many properties supposed common to the *genus* and abounding in others that were the portion only of the supernaturally clever. One day Pemberton made a great stride: it cleared up the question to perceive that Morgan *was* supernaturally clever and that, though the formula was temporarily meagre, this would be the only assumption on which one could successfully deal with him. He had the general quality of a child for whom life had not been simplified by school, a kind of homebred sensibility which might have been bad for himself but was charming for others, and a whole range of refinement and perception—little musical vibrations as taking as picked-up airs—begotten by wandering about Europe at the tail of his migratory tribe. This might not have been an education to recommend in advance, but its results with Morgan were as palpable as a fine texture. At the same time he had in his composition a sharp spice of stoicism, doubtless the fruit of having had to begin early to bear pain, which produced the impression of pluck and made it of less consequence that he might have been thought at school rather a polyglot little beast. Pemberton indeed quickly found himself rejoicing that school was out of the question: in any million of boys it was probably good for all but one, and Morgan was that millionth. It would have made him comparative and superior—it might have made him priggish. Pemberton would try to be school himself—a bigger seminary than five hundred grazing donkeys; so that, winning no prizes, the boy would remain unconscious and irresponsible and amusing—amusing, because, though life was already intense in his childish nature, freshness still made there a strong draught for jokes. It turned out that even in the still air of Morgan's various disabilities jokes flourished greatly. He was a pale, lean, acute, undeveloped little cosmopolite, who liked intellectual gymnastics and who, also, as regards the behaviour of mankind, had noticed more things than you might suppose, but who nevertheless had his proper playroom of superstitions, where he smashed a dozen toys a day.

III

At Nice once, towards evening, as the pair sat resting in the open air after a walk, looking over the sea at the pink western lights, Morgan said suddenly to his companion: "Do you like it—you know, being with us all in this intimate way?"

"My dear fellow, why should I stay if I didn't?"

"How do I know you will stay? I'm almost sure you won't, very long."

"I hope you don't mean to dismiss me," said Pemberton.

Morgan considered a moment, looking at the sunset. "I think if I did right I ought to."

"Well, I know I'm supposed to instruct you in virtue; but in that case don't do right."

"You're very young—fortunately," Morgan went on, turning to him again.

"Oh yes, compared with you!"

"Therefore, it won't matter so much if you do lose a lot of time."

"That's the way to look at it," said Pemberton accommodatingly.

They were silent a minute; after which the boy asked: "Do you like my father and mother very much?"

"Dear me, yes. They're charming people."

Morgan received this with another silence; then, unexpectedly, familiarly, but at the same time affectionately, he remarked: "You're a jolly old humbug!"

For a particular reason the words made Pemberton change colour. The boy noticed in an instant that he had turned red, whereupon he turned red himself and the pupil and the master exchanged a longish glance in which there was a consciousness of many more things than are usually touched upon, even tacitly, in such a relation. It produced for Pemberton an embarrassment; it raised, in a shadowy form, a question (this was the first glimpse of it), which was destined to play as singular and, as he imagined, owing to the altogether peculiar conditions, an unprecedented part in his intercourse with his little companion. Later, when he found himself talking with this small boy in a way in which few small boys could ever have been talked with, he thought of that clumsy moment on the bench at Nice as the dawn of an understanding that had broadened. What had added to the clumsiness then was that he thought it his duty to declare to Morgan that he might abuse him (Pemberton) as much as he liked, but must never abuse his parents. To this Morgan had the easy reply that he hadn't dreamed of abusing them; which appeared to be true: it put Pemberton in the wrong.

"Then why am I a humbug for saying I think them charming?" the young man asked, conscious of a certain rashness.

"Well—they're not *your* parents."

"They love you better than anything in the world—never forget that," said Pemberton.

"Is that why you like them so much?"

"They're very kind to me," Pemberton replied, evasively.

"You *are* a humbug!" laughed Morgan, passing an arm into his tutor's. He leaned against him, looking off at the sea again and swinging his long, thin legs.

"Don't kick my shins," said Pemberton, while he reflected: "Hang it, I can't complain of them to the child!"

"There's another reason, too," Morgan went on, keeping his legs still.

"Another reason for what?"

"Besides their not being your parents."

"I don't understand you," said Pemberton.

"Well, you will before long. All right!"

Pemberton did understand, fully, before long; but he made a fight even with himself before he confessed it. He thought it the oddest thing to have a struggle with the child about. He wondered he didn't detest the child for launching him in such a struggle. But by the time it began the resource of detesting the child was closed to him. Morgan was a special case, but to know him was to accept him on his own odd terms. Pemberton had spent his aversion to special cases before arriving at knowledge. When at last he did arrive he felt that he was in an extreme predicament. Against every interest he had attached himself. They would have to meet things together. Before they went home that evening, at Nice, the boy had said, clinging to his arm:

"Well, at any rate you'll hang on to the last."

"To the last?"

"Till you're fairly beaten."

"*You* ought to be fairly beaten!" cried the young man, drawing him closer.

IV

A year after Pemberton had come to live with them Mr. and Mrs. Moreen suddenly gave up the villa at Nice. Pemberton had got used to suddenness, having seen it practiced on a considerable scale during two jerky little tours—one in Switzerland the first summer, and the other late in the winter, when they all ran down to Florence and then, at the end of ten days, liking it much less than they had intended, straggled back in mysterious depression. They had returned to Nice "for ever," as they said; but this didn't prevent them from squeezing, one rainy, muggy May night, into a second-class railway-carriage—you could never tell by which class they would travel—where Pemberton helped them to stow away a wonderful collection of bundles and bags. The explanation of this manœuvre was that they had determined to spend the summer "in some bracing place;" but in Paris they dropped into a small furnished apartment—a fourth floor in a third-rate avenue, where there was a smell on the staircase and the *portier*[9] was hateful—and passed the next four months in blank indigence.

The better part of this baffled sojourn was for the preceptor and his pupil, who, visiting the Invalides[1] and Notre Dame, the Conciergerie and all the museums, took a hundred remunerative rambles. They learned to know their Paris, which was useful, for they came back another year for a longer stay, the general character of which in Pemberton's memory to-day mixes pitiably and confusedly with that of the first. He sees Morgan's shabby knickerbockers— the everlasting pair that didn't match his blouse and that as he grew longer could only grow faded. He remembers the particular holes in his three or four pair of coloured stockings.

Morgan was dear to his mother, but he never was better dressed than was absolutely necessary—partly, no doubt, by his own fault, for he was as indifferent to his appearance as a German philosopher. "My dear fellow, you *are* coming to pieces," Pemberton would say to him in sceptical remonstrance; to which the child would reply, looking at him serenely up and down: "My dear fellow, so are you! I don't want to cast you in the shade." Pemberton could have no rejoinder for this—the assertion so closely represented the fact. If however the deficiencies of his own wardrobe were a chapter by themselves he didn't like his little charge to look too poor. Later he used to say: "Well, if we are poor, why, after all, shouldn't we look it?" and he consoled himself with thinking there was something rather elderly and gentlemanly in Morgan's seediness—it differed from the untidiness of the urchin who plays and spoils his things. He could trace perfectly the degrees by which, in proportion as her little son confined himself to his tutor for society, Mrs. Moreen shrewdly forbore to renew his garments. She did nothing that didn't show, neglected him because he escaped notice, and then, as he illustrated this clever policy, discouraged at home his public appearances. Her position was logical enough—those members of her family who did show had to be showy.

During this period and several others Pemberton was quite aware of how he and his comrade might strike people; wandering languidly through the Jardin des Plantes[2] as if they had nowhere to go, sitting, on the winter days, in the galleries of the Louvre, so splendidly ironical to the homeless, as if for the advantage of the *calorifère*.[3]

9. Doorkeeper, janitor.
1. A Paris landmark, originally built to house disabled soldiers, and now a military museum; the tomb of Napoleon I is in an adjoining church. Notre Dame is of course the famous Paris cathedral. The Conciergerie is an ancient prison from which many went to the guillotine during the French Revolution.
2. The botanical gardens of Paris, founded in the seventeenth century.
3. Heater.

They joked about it sometimes: it was the sort of joke that was perfectly within the boy's compass. They figured themselves as part of the vast, vague, hand-to-mouth multitude of the enormous city and pretended they were proud of their position in it—it showed them such a lot of life and made them conscious of a sort of democratic brotherhood. If Pemberton could not feel a sympathy in destitution with his small companion (for after all Morgan's fond parents would never have let him really suffer), the boy would at least feel it with him, so it came to the same thing. He used sometimes to wonder what people would think they were—fancy they were looked askance at, as if it might be a suspected case of kidnapping. Morgan wouldn't be taken for a young patrician with a preceptor—he wasn't smart enough; though he might pass for his companion's sickly little brother. Now and then he had a five-franc piece, and except once, when they bought a couple of lovely neckties, one of which he made Pemberton accept, they laid it out scientifically in old books. It was a great day, always spent on the quays, rummaging among the dusty boxes that garnish the parapets.[4] These were occasions that helped them to live, for their books ran low very soon after the beginning of their acquaintance. Pemberton had a good many in England, but he was obliged to write to a friend and ask him kindly to get some fellow to give him something for them.

If the bracing climate was untasted that summer the young man had an idea that at the moment they were about to make a push the cup had been dashed from their lips by a movement of his own. It had been his first blow-out, as he called it, with his patrons; his first successful attempt (though there was little other success about it), to bring them to a consideration of his impossible position. As the ostensible eve of a costly journey the moment struck him as a good one to put in a signal protest—to present an ultimatum. Ridiculous as it sounded he had never yet been able to compass an uninterrupted private interview with the elder pair or with either of them singly. They were always flanked by their elder children, and poor Pemberton usually had his own little charge at his side. He was conscious of its being a house in which the surface of one's delicacy got rather smudged; nevertheless he had kept the bloom of his scruple against announcing to Mr. and Mrs. Moreen with publicity that he couldn't go on longer without a little money. He was still simple enough to suppose Ulick and Paula and Amy might not know that since his arrival he had only had a hundred and forty francs; and he was magnanimous enough to wish not to compro-

4. In the center of Paris dealers in secondhand books and prints of various kinds still display their wares in large boxes mounted on the parapets along the Seine River.

mise their parents in their eyes. Mr. Moreen now listened to him, as he listened to every one and to everything, like a man of the world, and seemed to appeal to him—though not of course too grossly—to try and be a little more of one himself. Pemberton recognised the importance of the character from the advantage it gave Mr. Moreen. He was not even confused, whereas poor Pemberton was more so than there was any reason for. Neither was he surprised—at least any more than a gentleman had to be who freely confessed himself a little shocked, though not, strictly, at Pemberton.

"We must go into this, mustn't we, dear?" he said to his wife. He assured his young friend that the matter should have his very best attention; and he melted into space as elusively as if, at the door, he were taking an inevitable but deprecatory precedence. When, the next moment, Pemberton found himself alone with Mrs. Moreen it was to hear her say: "I see, I see," stroking the roundness of her chin and looking as if she were only hesitating between a dozen easy remedies. If they didn't make their push Mr. Moreen could at least disappear for several days. During his absence his wife took up the subject again spontaneously, but her contribution to it was merely that she had thought all the while they were getting on so beautifully. Pemberton's reply to this revelation was that unless they immediately handed him a substantial sum he would leave them for ever. He knew she would wonder how he would get away, and for a moment expected her to inquire. She didn't, for which he was almost grateful to her, so little was he in a position to tell.

"You won't, you know you won't—you're too interested," she said. "You *are* interested, you know you are, you dear, kind man!" She laughed, with almost condemnatory archness, as if it were a reproach (but she wouldn't insist), while she flirted a soiled pocket-handkerchief at him.

Pemberton's mind was fully made up to quit the house the following week. This would give him time to get an answer to a letter he had despatched to England. If he did nothing of the sort—that is, if he stayed another year and then went away only for three months—it was not merely because before the answer to his letter came (most unsatisfactory when it did arrive), Mr. Moreen generously presented him—again with all the precautions of a man of the world—three hundred francs. He was exasperated to find that Mrs. Moreen was right, that he couldn't bear to leave the child. This stood out clearer for the very reason that, the night of his desperate appeal to his patrons, he had seen fully for the first time where he was. Wasn't it another proof of the success with which those patrons practiced their arts that they had managed to avert for so long the illuminating flash? It descended upon Pemberton

with a luridness which perhaps would have struck a spectator as
comically excessive, after he had returned to his little servile room,
which looked into a close court where a bare, dirty opposite wall
took, with the sound of shrill clatter, the reflection of lighted back-
windows. He had simply given himself away to a band of adventurers. The idea, the word itself, had a sort of romantic horror for
him—he had always lived on such safe lines. Later it assumed a
more interesting, almost a soothing, sense: it pointed a moral, and
Pemberton could enjoy a moral. The Moreens were adventurers not
merely because they didn't pay their debts, because they lived on
society, but because their whole view of life, dim and confused and
instinctive, like that of clever colour-blind animals, was speculative
and rapacious and mean. Oh! they were "respectable," and that only
made them more *immondes*.[5] The young man's analysis of them put
it at last very simply—they were adventurers because they were
abject snobs. That was the completest account of them—it was the
law of their being. Even when this truth became vivid to their ingenious inmate he remained unconscious of how much his mind
had been prepared for it by the extraordinary little boy who had
now become such a complication in his life. Much less could he
then calculate on the information he was still to owe to the extraordinary little boy.

V

But it was during the ensuing time that the real problem came
up—the problem of how far it was excusable to discuss the turpi-
tude of parents with a child of twelve, of thirteen, of fourteen.
Absolutely inexcusable and quite impossible it of course at first appeared; and indeed the question didn't press for a while after Pemberton had received his three hundred francs. They produced a sort
of lull, a relief from the sharpest pressure. Pemberton frugally
amended his wardrobe and even had a few francs in his pocket. He
thought the Moreens looked at him as if he were almost too smart,
as if they ought to take care not to spoil him. If Mr. Moreen hadn't
been such a man of the world he would perhaps have said something to him about his neckties. But Mr. Moreen was always
enough a man of the world to let things pass—he had certainly
shown that. It was singular how Pemberton guessed that Morgan,
though saying nothing about it, knew something had happened. But
three hundred francs, especially when one owed money, couldn't
last for ever; and when they were gone—the boy knew when they
were gone—Morgan did say something. The party had returned to

5. Unclean.

Nice at the beginning of the winter, but not to the charming villa. They went to an hotel, where they stayed three months, and then they went to another hotel, explaining that they had left the first because they had waited and waited and couldn't get the rooms they wanted. These apartments, the rooms they wanted, were generally very splendid; but fortunately they never *could* get them— fortunately, I mean, for Pemberton, who reflected always that if they had got them there would have been still less for educational expenses. What Morgan said at last was said suddenly, irrelevantly, when the moment came, in the middle of a lesson, and consisted of the apparently unfeeling words: "You ought to *filer*,[6] you know —you really ought."

Pemberton stared. He had learnt enough French slang from Morgan to know that to *filer* meant to go away. "Ah, my dear fellow, don't turn me off!"

Morgan pulled a Greek lexicon toward him (he used a Greek-German), to look out a word, instead of asking it of Pemberton. "You can't go on like this, you know."

"Like what, my boy?"

"You know they don't pay you up," said Morgan, blushing and turning his leaves.

"Don't pay me?" Pemberton stared again and feigned amazement. "What on earth put that into your head?"

"It has been there a long time," the boy replied, continuing his search.

Pemberton was silent, then he went on: "I say, what are you hunting for? They pay me beautifully."

"I'm hunting for the Greek for transparent fiction," Morgan dropped.

"Find that rather for gross impertinence, and disabuse your mind. What do I want of money?"

"Oh, that's another question!"

Pemberton hesitated—he was drawn in different ways. The severely correct thing would have been to tell the boy that such a matter was none of his business and bid him go on with his lines.[7] But they were really too intimate for that; it was not the way he was in the habit of treating him; there had been no reason it should be. On the other hand Morgan had quite lighted on the truth—he really shouldn't be able to keep it up much longer; therefore why not let him know one's real motive for forsaking him? At the same time it wasn't decent to abuse to one's pupil the family of one's pupil; it was better to misrepresent than to do that. So in reply to

6. Clear out, scram.
7. Go on translating his text, evidently Greek poetry.

Morgan's last exclamation he just declared, to dismiss the subject, that he had received several payments.

"I say—I say!" the boy ejaculated, laughing.

"That's all right," Pemberton insisted. "Give me your written rendering."

Morgan pushed a copybook across the table, and his companion began to read the page, but with something running in his head that made it no sense. Looking up after a minute or two he found the child's eyes fixed on him, and he saw something strange in them. Then Morgan said: "I'm not afraid of the reality."

"I haven't yet seen the thing that you *are* afraid of—I'll do you that justice!"

This came out with a jump (it was perfectly true), and evidently gave Morgan pleasure. "I've thought of it a long time," he presently resumed.

"Well, don't think of it any more."

The child appeared to comply, and they had a comfortable and even an amusing hour. They had a theory that they were very thorough, and yet they seemed always to be in the amusing part of lessons, the intervals between the tunnels, where there were waysides and views. Yet the morning was brought to a violent end by Morgan's suddenly leaning his arms on the table, burying his head in them and bursting into tears. Pemberton would have been startled at any rate; but he was doubly startled because, as it then occurred to him, it was the first time he had ever seen the boy cry. It was rather awful.

The next day, after much thought, he took a decision and, believing it to be just, immediately acted upon it. He cornered Mr. and Mrs. Moreen again and informed them that if, on the spot, they didn't pay him all they owed him, he would not only leave their house, but would tell Morgan exactly what had brought him to it.

"Oh, you *haven't* told him?" cried Mrs. Moreen, with a pacifying hand on her well-dressed bosom.

"Without warning you? For what do you take me?"

Mr. and Mrs. Moreen looked at each other, and Pemberton could see both that they were relieved and that there was a certain alarm in their relief. "My dear fellow," Mr. Moreen demanded, "what use *can* you have, leading the quiet life we all do, for such a lot of money?"—an inquiry to which Pemberton made no answer, occupied as he was in perceiving that what passed in the mind of his patrons was something like: "Oh, then, if we've felt that the child, dear little angel, has judged us and how he regards us, and we haven't been betrayed, he must have guessed—and, in short, it's *general*!" an idea that rather stirred up Mr. and Mrs. Moreen, as Pemberton had desired that it should. At the same time, if he had thought that his threat would do something towards bringing them round, he was disappointed to find they had taken for granted (how little they appreciated his delicacy!) that he had already given them away to his pupil. There was a mystic uneasiness in their parental breasts, and that was the way they had accounted for it. None the less his threat did touch them; for if they had escaped it was only to meet a new danger. Mr. Moreen appealed to Pemberton, as usual, as a man of the world; but his wife had recourse, for the first time since the arrival of their inmate, to a fine *hauteur*, reminding him that a devoted mother, with her child, had arts that protected her against gross misrepresentation.

"I should misrepresent you grossly if I accused you of common honesty!" the young man replied; but as he closed the door behind him sharply, thinking he had not done himself much good, while Mr. Moreen lighted another cigarette, he heard Mrs. Moreen shout after him, more touchingly:

"Oh, you do, you *do*, put the knife to one's throat!"

The next morning, very early, she came to his room. He recognised her knock, but he had no hope that she brought him money; as to which he was wrong, for she had fifty francs in her hand. She squeezed forward in her dressing-gown and he received her in his own, between his bath-tub and his bed. He had been tolerably schooled by this time to the "foreign ways" of his hosts. Mrs. Moreen was zealous, and when she was zealous she didn't care what she did; so she now sat down on his bed, his clothes being on the chairs, and, in her preoccupation, forgot, as she glanced round, to be ashamed of giving him such a nasty room. What Mrs. Moreen was zealous about on this occasion was to persuade him that in the first place she was very good-natured to bring him fifty francs, and, in the second, if he would only see it, he was really too absurd to expect to be *paid*. Wasn't he paid enough, without perpetual money—wasn't he paid by the comfortable, luxurious home that he enjoyed with them all, without a care, an anxiety, a solitary want? Wasn't he sure of his position, and wasn't that everything to a young man like him, quite unknown, with singularly little to show, the ground of whose exorbitant pretensions it was not easy to discover? Wasn't he paid, above all, by the delightful relation he had established with Morgan—quite ideal, as from master to pupil—and by the simple privilege of knowing and living with so amazingly gifted a child, than whom really—she meant literally what she said—there was no better company in Europe? Mrs. Moreen herself took to appealing to him as a man of the world; she said "Voyons, mon cher," and "My dear sir, look here now;" and urged him to be reasonable, putting it before him that it was really a chance for him. She spoke as if, according as he *should* be reasonable, he would prove himself worthy to be her son's tutor and of the extraordinary confidence they had placed in him.

After all, Pemberton reflected, it was only a difference of theory, and the theory didn't matter much. They had hitherto gone on that of remunerated, as now they would go on that of gratuitous, service; but why should they have so many words about it? Mrs. Moreen, however, continued to be convincing; sitting there with her fifty francs she talked and repeated, as women repeat, and bored and irritated him, while he leaned against the wall with his hands in the pockets of his wrapper, drawing it together round his legs and looking over the head of his visitor at the grey negations of his window. She wound up with saying: "You see I bring you a definite proposal."

"A definite proposal?"

"To make our relations regular, as it were—to put them on a comfortable footing."

"I see—it's a system," said Pemberton. "A kind of blackmail."

Mrs. Moreen bounded up, which was what the young man wanted.

"What do you mean by that?"

"You practice on one's fears—one's fears about the child if one should go away."

"And, pray, what would happen to him in that event?" demanded Mrs. Moreen, with majesty.

"Why, he'd be alone with *you*."

"And pray, with whom *should* a child be but with those whom he loves most?"

"If you think that, why don't you dismiss me?"

"Do you pretend that he loves you more than he loves *us*?" cried Mrs. Moreen.

"I think he ought to. I make sacrifices for him. Though I've heard of those *you* make, I don't see them."

Mrs. Moreen stared a moment; then, with emotion, she grasped Pemberton's hand. "*Will* you make it—the sacrifice?"

Pemberton burst out laughing. "I'll see—I'll do what I can—I'll stay a little longer. Your calculation is just—I *do* hate intensely to give him up; I'm fond of him and he interests me deeply, in spite of the inconvenience I suffer. You know my situation perfectly; I haven't a penny in the world, and, occupied as I am with Morgan, I'm unable to earn money."

Mrs. Moreen tapped her undressed arm with her folded banknote. "Can't you write articles? Can't you translate, as *I* do?"

"I don't know about translating; it's wretchedly paid."

"I am glad to earn what I can," said Mrs. Moreen virtuously, with her head high.

"You ought to tell me who you do it for." Pemberton paused a moment, and she said nothing; so he added: "I've tried to turn off some little sketches, but the magazines won't have them—they're declined with thanks."

"You see then you're not such a phœnix—to have such pretensions," smiled his interlocutress.

"I haven't time to do things properly," Pemberton went on. Then as it came over him that he was almost abjectly good-natured to give these explanations he added: "If I stay on longer it must be on one condition—that Morgan shall know distinctly on what footing I am."

Mrs. Moreen hesitated. "Surely you don't want to show off to a child?"

"To show *you* off, do you mean?"

Again Mrs. Moreen hesitated, but this time it was to produce a still finer flower. "And *you* talk of blackmail!"

"You can easily prevent it," said Pemberton.

"And *you* talk of practicing on fears," Mrs. Moreen continued.

"Yes, there's no doubt I'm a great scoundrel."

His visitor looked at him a moment—it was evident that she was sorely bothered. Then she thrust out her money at him. "Mr. Moreen desired me to give you this on account."

"I'm much obliged to Mr. Moreen; but we have no account."

"You won't take it?"

"That leaves me more free," said Pemberton.

"To poison my darling's mind?" groaned Mrs. Moreen.

"Oh, your darling's mind!" laughed the young man.

She fixed him a moment, and he thought she was going to break out tormentedly, pleadingly. "For God's sake, tell me what *is* in it!" But she checked this impulse—another was stronger. She pocketed the money—the crudity of the alternative was comical—and swept out of the room with the desperate concession: "You may tell him any horror you like!"

VI

A couple of days after this, during which Pemberton had delayed to profit by Mrs. Moreen's permission to tell her son any horror, the two had been for a quarter of an hour walking together in silence when the boy became sociable again with the remark: "I'll tell you how I know it; I know it through Zénobie."

"Zénobie? Who in the world is *she*?"

"A nurse I used to have—ever so many years ago. A charming woman. I liked her awfully, and she liked me."

"There's no accounting for tastes. What is it you know through her?"

"Why, what their idea is. She went away because they didn't pay her. She did like me awfully, and she stayed two years. She told me all about it—that at last she could never get her wages. As soon as they saw how much she liked me they stopped giving her anything. They thought she'd stay for nothing, out of devotion. And she did stay ever so long—as long as she could. She was only a poor girl. She used to send money to her mother. At last she couldn't afford it any longer, and she went away in a fearful rage one night—I mean of course in a rage against *them*. She cried over me tremendously, she hugged me nearly to death. She told me all about it," Morgan repeated. "She told me it was their idea. So I guessed, ever so long ago, that they have had the same idea with you."

"Zénobie was very shrewd," said Pemberton. "And she made you so."

"Oh, that wasn't Zénobie; that was nature. And experience!" Morgan laughed.

"Well, Zénobie was a part of your experience."

"Certainly I was a part of hers, poor dear!" the boy exclaimed. "And I'm a part of yours."

"A very important part. But I don't see how you know that I've been treated like Zénobie."

"Do you take me for an idiot?" Morgan asked. "Haven't I been conscious of what we've been through together?"

"What we've been through?"

"Our privations—our dark days."

"Oh, our days have been bright enough."

Morgan went on in silence for a moment. Then he said: "My dear fellow, you're a hero!"

"Well, you're another!" Pemberton retorted.

"No, I'm not; but I'm not a baby. I won't stand it any longer. You must get some occupation that pays. I'm ashamed, I'm ashamed!" quavered the boy in a little passionate voice that was very touching to Pemberton.

"We ought to go off and live somewhere together," said the young man.

"I'll go like a shot if you'll take me."

"I'd get some work that would keep us both afloat," Pemberton continued.

"So would I. Why shouldn't I work? I ain't such a *crétin*!"[8]

"The difficulty is that your parents wouldn't hear of it," said Pemberton. "They would never part with you; they worship the ground you tread on. Don't you see the proof of it? They don't dislike me;

8. Idiot.

they wish me no harm; they're very amiable people; but they're perfectly ready to treat me badly for your sake."

The silence in which Morgan received this graceful sophistry struck Pemberton somehow as expressive. After a moment Morgan repeated: "You *are* a hero!" Then he added: "They leave me with you altogether. You've all the responsibility. They put me off on you from morning till night. Why, then, should they object to my taking up with you completely? I'd help you."

"They're not particularly keen about my being helped, and they delight in thinking of you as *theirs*. They're tremendously proud of you."

"I'm not proud of them. But you know *that*," Morgan returned.

"Except for the little matter we speak of they're charming people," said Pemberton, not taking up the imputation of lucidity, but wondering greatly at the child's own, and especially at this fresh reminder of something he had been conscious of from the first—the strangest thing in the boy's large little composition, a temper, a sensibility, even a sort of ideal, which made him privately resent the general quality of his kinsfolk. Morgan had in secret a small loftiness which begot an element of reflection, a domestic scorn not imperceptible to his companion (though they never had any talk about it), and absolutely anomalous in a juvenile nature, especially when one noted that it had not made this nature "old-fashioned," as the word is of children—quaint or wizened or offensive. It was as if he had been a little gentleman and had paid the penalty by discovering that he was the only such person in the family. This comparison didn't make him vain; but it could make him melancholy and a trifle austere. When Pemberton guessed at these young dimnesses he saw him serious and gallant, and was partly drawn on and partly checked, as if with a scruple, by the charm of attempting to sound the little cool shallows which were quickly growing deeper. When he tried to figure to himself the morning twilight of childhood, so as to deal with it safely, he perceived that it was never fixed, never arrested, that ignorance, at the instant one touched it, was already flushing faintly into knowledge, that there was nothing that at a given moment you could say a clever child didn't know. It seemed to him that *he* both knew too much to imagine Morgan's simplicity and too little to disembroil his tangle.

The boy paid no heed to his last remark; he only went on: "I should have spoken to them about their idea, as I call it, long ago, if I hadn't been sure what they would say."

"And what would they say?"

"Just what they said about what poor Zénobie told me—that it was a horrid, dreadful story, that they had paid her every penny they owed her."

"Well, perhaps they had," said Pemberton.

"Perhaps they've paid you!"

"Let us pretend they have, and *n'en parlons plus.*"[9]

"They accused her of lying and cheating," Morgan insisted perversely. "That's why I don't want to speak to them."

"Lest they should accuse me, too?"

To this Morgan made no answer, and his companion, looking down at him (the boy turned his eyes, which had filled, away), saw that he couldn't have trusted himself to utter.

"You're right. Don't squeeze them," Pemberton pursued. "Except for that, they *are* charming people."

"Except for *their* lying and *their* cheating?"

"I say—I say!" cried Pemberton, imitating a little tone of the lad's which was itself an imitation.

"We must be frank, at the last; we *must* come to an understanding," said Morgan, with the importance of the small boy who lets himself think he is arranging great affairs—almost playing at shipwreck or at Indians. "I know all about everything," he added.

"I daresay your father has his reasons," Pemberton observed, too vaguely, as he was aware.

"For lying and cheating?"

"For saving and managing and turning his means to the best account. He has plenty to do with his money. You're an expensive family."

"Yes, I'm very expensive," Morgan rejoined, in a manner which made his preceptor burst out laughing.

"He's saving for *you*," said Pemberton. "They think of you in everything they do."

"He might save a little—" The boy paused. Pemberton waited to hear what. Then Morgan brought out oddly: "A little reputation."

"Oh, there's plenty of that. That's all right!"

"Enough of it for the people they know, no doubt. The people they know are awful."

"Do you mean the princes? We mustn't abuse the princes."

"Why not? They haven't married Paula—they haven't married Amy. They only clean out Ulick."

"You *do* know everything!" Pemberton exclaimed.

"No, I don't, after all. I don't know what they live on, or how they live, or *why* they live! What have they got and how did they get it? Are they rich, are they poor, or have they a *modeste aisance?*[1] Why are they always chiveying about—living one year like ambassadors and the next like paupers? Who are they, any way, and what

9. Let's say no more about it.
1. Are they comfortably off?

are they? I've thought of all that—I've thought of a lot of things. They're so beastly worldly. That's what I hate most—oh, I've *seen* it! All they care about is to make an appearance and to pass for something or other. What do they want to pass for? What *do* they, Mr. Pemberton?"

"You pause for a reply," said Pemberton, treating the inquiry as a joke, yet wondering too, and greatly struck with the boy's intense, if imperfect, vision. "I haven't the least idea."

"And what good does it do? Haven't I seen the way people treat them—the 'nice' people, the ones they want to know? They'll take anything from them—they'll lie down and be trampled on. The nice ones hate that—they just sicken them. You're the only really nice person we know."

"Are you sure? They don't lie down for me!"

"Well, you shan't lie down for them. You've got to go—that's what you've got to do." said Morgan.

"And what will become of you?"

"Oh, I'm growing up. I shall get off before long. I'll see you later."

"You had better let me finish you," Pemberton urged, lending himself to the child's extraordinarily competent attitude.

Morgan stopped in their walk, looking up at him. He had to look up much less than a couple of years before—he had grown, in his loose leanness, so long and high. "Finish me?" he echoed.

"There are such a lot of jolly things we can do together yet. I want to turn you out—I want you to do me credit."

Morgan continued to look at him. "To give you credit—do you mean?"

"My dear fellow, you're too clever to live."

"That's just what I'm afraid you think. No, no; it isn't fair—I can't endure it. We'll part next week. The sooner it's over the sooner to sleep."

"If I hear of anything—any other chance, I promise to go," said Pemberton.

Morgan consented to consider this. "But you'll be honest," he demanded; "you won't pretend you haven't heard?"

"I'm much more likely to pretend I have."

"But what can you hear of, this way, stuck in a hole with us? You ought to be on the spot, to go to England—you ought to go to America."

"One would think you were *my* tutor!" said Pemberton.

Morgan walked on, and after a moment he began again: "Well, now that you know that I know and that we look at the facts and keep nothing back—it's much more comfortable, isn't it?"

"My dear boy, it's so amusing, so interesting, that it surely will be quite impossible for me to forego such hours as these."

This made Morgan stop once more. "You *do* keep something back. Oh, you're not straight—*I* am!"

"Why am I not straight?"

"Oh, you've got your idea!"

"My idea?"

"Why, that I probably sha'n't live, and that you can stick it out till I'm removed."

"You *are* too clever to live!" Pemberton repeated.

"I call it a mean idea," Morgan pursued. "But I shall punish you by the way I hang on."

"Look out or I'll poison you!" Pemberton laughed.

"I'm stronger and better every year. Haven't you noticed that there hasn't been a doctor near me since you came?"

"*I'm* your doctor," said the young man, taking his arm and drawing him on again.

Morgan proceeded, and after a few steps he gave a sigh of mingled weariness and relief. "Ah, now that we look at the facts, it's all right!"

VII

They looked at the facts a good deal after this; and one of the first consequences of their doing so was that Pemberton stuck it out, as it were, for the purpose. Morgan made the facts so vivid and so droll, and at the same time so bald and so ugly, that there was fascination in talking them over with him, just as there would have been heartlessness in leaving him alone with them. Now that they had such a number of perceptions in common it was useless for the pair to pretend that they didn't judge such people; but the very judgment, and the exchange of perceptions, created another tie. Morgan had never been so interesting as now that he himself was made plainer by the sidelight of these confidences. What came out in it most was the soreness of his characteristic pride. He had plenty of that, Pemberton felt—so much that it was perhaps well it should have had to take some early bruises. He would have liked his people to be gallant, and he had waked up too soon to the sense that they were perpetually swallowing humble-pie. His mother would consume any amount, and his father would consume even more than his mother. He had a theory that Ulick had wriggled out of an "affair" at Nice: there had once been a flurry at home, a regular panic, after which they all went to bed and took medicine, not to be accounted for on any other supposition. Morgan had a romantic imagination, fed by poetry and history, and he would have liked those who "bore his name" (as he used to say to Pemberton with the humour that made his sensitiveness manly), to have a proper spirit. But their one idea was to get in with people who didn't want them and to take snubs as if they were honourable scars. Why people didn't want them more he didn't know—that was people's own affair; after all they were not superficially repulsive—they were a hundred times cleverer than most of the dreary grandees, the "poor swells" they rushed about Europe to catch up with. "After all, they *are* amusing—they are!" Morgan used to say, with the wisdom of the ages. To which Pemberton always replied: "Amusing—the great Moreen troupe? Why, they're altogether delightful; and if it were not for the hitch that you and I (feeble performers!) make in the *ensemble*, they would carry everything before them."

What the boy couldn't get over was that this particular blight seemed, in a tradition of self-respect, so undeserved and so arbitrary. No doubt people had a right to take the line they liked; but why should *his* people have liked the line of pushing and toadying and lying and cheating? What had their forefathers—all decent folk, so far as he knew—done to them, or what had *he* done to them? Who had poisoned their blood with the fifth-rate social ideal, the fixed idea of making smart acquaintances and getting into the *monde chic*,[2] especially when it was foredoomed to failure and exposure? They showed so what they were after; that was what made the people they wanted not want *them*. And never a movement of dignity, never a throb of shame at looking each other in the face, never any independence or resentment or disgust. If his father or his brother would only knock some one down once or twice a year! Clever as they were they never guessed how they appeared. They were good-natured, yes—as good-natured as Jews at the doors of clothing-shops! But was that the model one wanted one's family to follow? Morgan had dim memories of an old grandfather, the maternal, in New York, whom he had been taken across the ocean to see, at the age of five: a gentleman with a high neckcloth and a good deal of pronunciation, who wore a dress-coat in the morning, which made one wonder what he wore in the evening, and had, or was supposed to have, "property" and something to do with the Bible Society.[3] It couldn't have been but that *he* was a good type. Pemberton himself remembered Mrs. Clancy, a widowed sister of Mr. Moreen's, who was as irritating as a moral tale and had paid a fortnight's visit to the family at Nice shortly after he came to live with them. She was "pure and refined," as Amy said, over the banjo, and had the air of not knowing what they meant and of keeping

2. Fashionable society, smart set.
3. A society for translating and disseminating Bibles, going back to an organization started in early eighteenth-century Germany, from where it spread to England and, in the nineteenth century, to the United States. The Gideons International (founded 1898), which places Bibles in hotel rooms, is an offshoot.

something back. Pemberton judged that what she kept back was an
approval of many of their ways; therefore it was to be supposed that
she too was of a good type, and that Mr. and Mrs. Moreen and
Ulick and Paula and Amy might easily have been better if they
would.

But that they wouldn't was more and more perceptible from day
to day. They continued to "chivey," as Morgan called it, and in due
time became aware of a variety of reasons for proceeding to Venice.
They mentioned a great many of them—they were always strikingly
frank, and had the brightest friendly chatter, at the late foreign
breakfast in especial, before the ladies had made up their faces,
when they leaned their arms on the table, had something to follow
the *demi-tasse*,⁴ and, in the heat of familiar discussion as to what
they "really ought" to do, fell inevitably into the languages in which
they could *tutoyer*.⁵ Even Pemberton liked them, then; he could
endure even Ulick when he heard him give his little flat voice for
the "sweet sea-city." That was what made him have a sneaking kindness for them—that they were so out of the workaday world and
kept him so out of it. The summer had waned when, with cries of
ecstasy, they all passed out on the balcony that overhung the Grand
Canal; the sunsets were splendid—the Dorringtons had arrived.
The Dorringtons were the only reason they had not talked of at
breakfast; but the reasons that they didn't talk of at breakfast always
came out in the end. The Dorringtons, on the other hand, came
out very little; or else, when they did, they stayed—as was natural
—for hours, during which periods Mrs. Moreen and the girls sometimes called at their hotel (to see if they had returned) as many as
three times running. The gondola was for the ladies; for in Venice
too there were "days," which Mrs. Moreen knew in their order an
hour after she arrived. She immediately took one herself, to which
the Dorringtons never came, though on a certain occasion when
Pemberton and his pupil were together at St. Mark's—where, taking the best walks they had ever had and haunting a hundred
churches, they spent a great deal of time—they saw the old lord
turn up with Mr. Moreen and Ulick, who showed him the dim
basilica as if it belonged to them. Pemberton noted how much less,
among its curiosities, Lord Dorrington carried himself as a man of
the world; wondering too whether, for such services, his companions took a fee from him. The autumn, at any rate, waned, the

---

4. Small cup of coffee, usually after dinner, but here at the end of a late breakfast.
5. Use the informal second-person singular *tu* in French. Here it means that the Moreens
   fell to talking French or, since they are polyglot, some other language making a similar
   distinction between formal (polite) and informal (familiar), such as German or Italian.
   The "sweet sea-city," below, refers to Venice.

Dorringtons departed, and Lord Verschoyle, the eldest son, had proposed neither for Amy nor for Paula.

One sad November day, while the wind roared round the old palace and the rain lashed the lagoon, Pemberton, for exercise and even somewhat for warmth (the Moreens were horribly frugal about fires—it was a cause of suffering to their inmate), walked up and down the big bare *sala*[6] with his pupil. The scagliola floor was cold, the high battered casements shook in the storm, and the stately decay of the place was unrelieved by a particle of furniture. Pemberton's spirits were low, and it came over him that the fortune of the Moreens was now even lower. A blast of desolation, a prophecy of disaster and disgrace, seemed to draw through the comfortless hall. Mr. Moreen and Ulick were in the Piazza, looking out for something, strolling drearily, in mackintoshes, under the arcades; but still, in spite of mackintoshes, unmistakable men of the world. Paula and Amy were in bed—it might have been thought they were staying there to keep warm. Pemberton looked askance at the boy at his side, to see to what extent he was conscious of these portents. But Morgan, luckily for him, was now mainly conscious of growing taller and stronger and indeed of being in his fifteenth year. This fact was intensely interesting to him—it was the basis of a private theory (which, however, he had imparted to his tutor) that in a little while he should stand on his own feet. He considered that the situation would change—that, in short, he should be "finished," grown up, producible in the world of affairs and ready to prove himself of sterling ability. Sharply as he was capable, at times, of questioning his circumstances, there were happy hours when he was as superficial as a child; the proof of which was his fundamental assumption that he should presently go to Oxford, to Pemberton's college, and, aided and abetted by Pemberton, do the most wonderful things. It vexed Pemberton to see how little, in such a project, he took account of ways and means: on other matters he was so sceptical about them. Pemberton tried to imagine the Moreens at Oxford, and fortunately failed; yet unless they were to remove there as a family there would be no *modus vivendi* for Morgan. How could he live without an allowance, and where was the allowance to come from? He (Pemberton) might live on Morgan; but how could Morgan live on him? What was to become of him anyhow? Somehow, the fact that he was a big boy now, with better prospects of health, made the question of his future more difficult. So long as he was frail the consideration that he inspired seemed enough of an answer to it. But at the bottom of Pemberton's heart was the

6. Hallway.

recognition of his probably being strong enough to live and not strong enough to thrive. He himself, at any rate, was in a period of natural, boyish rosiness about all this, so that the beating of the tempest seemed to him only the voice of life and the challenge of fate. He had on his shabby little overcoat, with the collar up, but he was enjoying his walk.

It was interrupted at last by the appearance of his mother at the end of the *sala*. She beckoned to Morgan to come to her, and while Pemberton saw him, complacent, pass down the long vista, over the damp false marble, he wondered what was in the air. Mrs. Moreen said a word to the boy and made him go into the room she had quitted. Then, having closed the door after him, she directed her steps swiftly to Pemberton. There *was* something in the air, but his wildest flight of fancy wouldn't have suggested what it proved to be. She signified that she had made a pretext to get Morgan out of the way, and then she inquired—without hesitation—if the young man could lend her sixty francs. While, before bursting into a laugh, he stared at her with surprise, she declared that she was awfully pressed for the money; she was desperate for it—it would save her life.

"Dear lady, *c'est trop fort!*"[7] Pemberton laughed. "Where in the world do you suppose I should get sixty francs, *du train dont vous allez?*"[8]

"I thought you worked—wrote things; don't they pay you?"

"Not a penny."

"Are you such a fool as to work for nothing?"

"You ought surely to know that."

Mrs. Moreen stared an instant, then she coloured a little. Pemberton saw she had quite forgotten the terms—if "terms" they could be called—that he had ended by accepting from herself; they had burdened her memory as little as her conscience. "Oh, yes, I see what you mean—you have been very nice about that; but why go back to it so often?" She had been perfectly urbane with him ever since the rough scene of explanation in his room, the morning he made her accept *his* "terms"—the necessity of his making his case known to Morgan. She had felt no resentment, after seeing that there was no danger of Morgan's taking the matter up with her. Indeed, attributing this immunity to the good taste of his influence with the boy, she had once said to Pemberton: "My dear fellow; it's an immense comfort you're a gentleman." She repeated this, in substance, now. "Of course you're a gentleman—that's a bother the less!" Pemberton reminded her that he had not "gone back" to any-

7. That's really too much!
8. At the rate you go on.

thing; and she also repeated her prayer that, somewhere and some-how, he would find her sixty francs. He took the liberty of declaring that if he could find them it wouldn't be to lend them to *her*—as to which he consciously did himself injustice, knowing that if he had them he would certainly place them in her hand. He accused himself, at bottom and with some truth, of a fantastic, demoralised sympathy with her. If misery made strange bedfellows it also made strange sentiments. It was moreover a part of the demoralisation and of the general bad effect of living with such people that one had to make rough retorts, quite out of the tradition of good man-ners. "Morgan, Morgan, to what pass have I come for you?" he privately exclaimed, while Mrs. Moreen floated voluminously down the *sala* again, to liberate the boy; groaning, as she went, that ev-erything was too odious.

Before the boy was liberated there came a thump at the door communicating with the staircase, followed by the apparition of a dripping youth who poked in his head. Pemberton recognised him as the bearer of a telegram and recognised the telegram as ad-dressed to himself. Morgan came back as, after glancing at the signature (that of a friend in London), he was reading the words: "Found jolly job for you—engagement to coach opulent youth on own terms. Come immediately." The answer, happily, was paid, and the messenger waited. Morgan, who had drawn near, waited too, and looked hard at Pemberton; and Pemberton, after a moment, having met his look, handed him the telegram. It was really by wise looks (they knew each other so well), that, while the telegraph-boy, in his waterproof cape, made a great puddle on the floor, the thing was settled between them. Pemberton wrote the answer with a pen-cil against the frescoed wall, and the messenger departed. When he had gone Pemberton said to Morgan:

"I'll make a tremendous charge; I'll earn a lot of money in a short time, and we'll live on it."

"Well, I hope the opulent youth will be stupid—he probably will—" Morgan parenthesised, "and keep you a long time."

"Of course, the longer he keeps me the more we shall have for our old age."

"But suppose *they* don't pay you!" Morgan awfully suggested.

"Oh, there are not two such—!" Pemberton paused, he was on the point of using an invidious term. Instead of this he said "two such chances."

Morgan flushed—the tears came to his eyes. "*Dites toujours,*[9] two such rascally crews!" Then, in a different tone, he added: "Happy opulent youth!"

9. Go ahead, say it.

"Not if he's stupid!"

"Oh, they're happier then. But you can't have everything, can you?" the boy smiled.

Pemberton held him, his hands on his shoulders. "What will become of *you*, what will you do?" He thought of Mrs. Moreen, desperate for sixty francs.

"I shall turn into a man." And then, as if he recognised all the bearings of Pemberton's allusion: "I shall get on with them better when you're not here."

"Ah, don't say that—it sounds as if I set you against them!"

"You do—the sight of you. It's all right; you know what I mean. I shall be beautiful. I'll take their affairs in hand; I'll marry my sisters."[1]

"You'll marry yourself!" joked Pemberton; as high, rather tense pleasantry would evidently be the right, or the safest, tone for their separation.

It was, however, not purely in this strain that Morgan suddenly asked: "But I say—how will you get to your jolly job? You'll have to telegraph to the opulent youth for money to come on."

Pemberton bethought himself. "They won't like that, will they?"

"Oh, look out for them!"

Then Pemberton brought out his remedy. "I'll go to the American Consul; I'll borrow some money of him—just for the few days, on the strength of the telegram."

Morgan was hilarious. "Show him the telegram—then stay and keep the money!"

Pemberton entered into the joke enough to reply that, for Morgan, he was really capable of that; but the boy, growing more serious, and to prove that he hadn't meant what he said, not only hurried him off to the Consulate (since he was to start that evening, as he had wired to his friend), but insisted on going with him. They splashed through the tortuous perforations[2] and over the humpbacked bridges, and they passed through the Piazza, where they saw Mr. Moreen and Ulick go into a jeweller's shop. The Consul proved accommodating (Pemberton said it wasn't the letter, but Morgan's grand air), and on their way back they went into St. Mark's for a hushed ten minutes. Later they took up and kept up the fun of it to the very end; and it seemed to Pemberton a part of that fun that Mrs. Moreen, who was very angry when he had announced to her his intention, should charge him, grotesquely and vulgarly, and in reference to the loan she had vainly endeavoured to effect, with

1. Marry them off.
2. Pedestrian traffic between Venetian canals often follows winding footpaths, sometimes cut through walls and buildings.

bolting lest they should "get something out" of him. On the other hand he had to do Mr. Moreen and Ulick the justice to recognise that when, on coming in, *they* heard the cruel news, they took it like perfect men of the world.

VIII

When Pemberton got at work with the opulent youth, who was to be taken in hand for Balliol,[3] he found himself unable to say whether he was really an idiot or it was only, on his own part, the long association with an intensely living little mind that made him seem so. From Morgan he heard half-a-dozen times: the boy wrote charming young letters, a patchwork of tongues, with indulgent postscripts in the family Volapuk and, in little squares and rounds and crannies of the text, the drollest illustrations—letters that he was divided between the impulse to show his present disciple, as a kind of wasted incentive, and the sense of something in them that was profanable by publicity. The opulent youth went up,[4] in due course, and failed to pass; but it seemed to add to the presumption that brilliancy was not expected of him all at once that his parents, condoning the lapse, which they good-naturedly treated as little as possible as if it were Pemberton's, should have sounded the rally again, begged the young coach to keep his pupil in hand another year.

The young coach was now in a position to lend Mrs. Moreen sixty francs, and he sent her a post-office order for the amount. In return for his favour he received a frantic, scribbled line from her: "Implore you to come back instantly—Morgan dreadfully ill." They were on the rebound, once more in Paris—often as Pemberton had seen them depressed he had never seen them crushed—and communication was therefore rapid. He wrote to the boy to ascertain the state of his health, but he received no answer to his letter. Accordingly he took an abrupt leave of the opulent youth and, crossing the Channel, alighted at the small hotel, in the quarter of the Champs Elysées, of which Mrs. Moreen had given him the address. A deep if dumb dissatisfaction with this lady and her companions bore him company: they couldn't be vulgarly honest, but they could live at hotels, in velvety *entresols*, amid a smell of burnt pastilles, in the most expensive city in Europe. When he had left them, in Venice, it was with an irrepressible suspicion that something was going to happen; but the only thing that had happened

---

3. Tutored in preparation for the entrance examination to Balliol College (founded before 1268), probably the most distinguished college in Oxford.
4. Went up to Oxford to take the examination.

was that they succeeded in getting away. "How is he? where is he?" he asked of Mrs. Moreen; but before she could speak, these questions were answered by the pressure round his neck of a pair of arms, in shrunken sleeves, which were perfectly capable of an effusive young foreign squeeze.

"Dreadfully ill—I don't see it!" the young man cried. And then, to Morgan: "Why on earth didn't you relieve me? Why didn't you answer my letter?"

Mrs. Moreen declared that when she wrote he was very bad, and Pemberton learned at the same time from the boy that he had answered every letter he had received. This led to the demonstration that Pemberton's note had been intercepted. Mrs. Moreen was prepared to see the fact exposed, as Pemberton perceived, the moment he faced her, that she was prepared for a good many other things. She was prepared above all to maintain that she had acted from a sense of duty, that she was enchanted she had got him over, whatever they might say; and that it was useless of him to pretend that he didn't *know*, in all his bones, that his place at such a time was with Morgan. He had taken the boy away from them, and now he had no right to abandon him. He had created for himself the gravest responsibilities; he must at least abide by what he had done.

"Taken him away from you?" Pemberton exclaimed indignantly.

"Do it—do it, for pity's sake; that's just what I want. I can't stand *this*—and such scenes. They're treacherous!" These words broke from Morgan, who had intermitted his embrace, in a key which made Pemberton turn quickly to him, to see that he suddenly seated himself, was breathing with evident difficulty and was very pale.

"*Now* do you say he's not ill—my precious pet?" shouted his mother, dropping on her knees before him with clasped hands, but touching him no more than if he had been a gilded idol. "It will pass—it's only for an instant; but don't say such dreadful things!"

"I'm all right—all right," Morgan panted to Pemberton, whom he sat looking up at with a strange smile, his hands resting on either side of the sofa.

"Now do you pretend I've been treacherous—that I've deceived?" Mrs. Moreen flashed at Pemberton as she got up.

"It isn't *he* says it, it's I!" the boy returned, apparently easier, but sinking back against the wall; while Pemberton, who had sat down beside him, taking his hand, bent over him.

"Darling child, one does what one can; there are so many things to consider," urged Mrs. Moreen. "It's his *place*—his only place. You see *you* think it is now."

"Take me away—take me away," Morgan went on, smiling to Pemberton from his white face.

"Where shall I take you, and how—oh, *how*, my boy?" the young man stammered, thinking of the rude way in which his friends in London held that, for his convenience, and without a pledge of instantaneous return, he had thrown them over; of the just resentment with which they would already have called in a successor, and of the little help as regarded finding fresh employment that resided for him in the flatness of his having failed to pass his pupil.

"Oh, we'll settle that. You used to talk about it," said Morgan. "If we can only go, all the rest's a detail."

"Talk about it as much as you like, but don't think you can attempt it. Mr. Moreen would never consent—it would be so precarious," Pemberton's hostess explained to him. Then to Morgan she explained: "It would destroy our peace, it would break our hearts. Now that he's back it will be all the same again. You'll have your life, your work and your freedom, and we'll all be happy as we used to be. You'll bloom and grow perfectly well, and we won't have any more silly experiments, will we? They're too absurd. It's Mr. Pemberton's place—every one in his place. You in yours, your papa in his, me in mine—*n'est-ce pas, chéri?*[5] We'll all forget how foolish we've been, and we'll have lovely times."

She continued to talk and to surge vaguely about the little draped, stuffy *salon*, while Pemberton sat with the boy, whose colour gradually came back; and she mixed up her reasons, dropping that there were going to be changes, that the other children might scatter (who knew?—Paula had her ideas), and that then it might be fancied how much the poor old parent-birds would want the little nestling. Morgan looked at Pemberton, who wouldn't let him move; and Pemberton knew exactly how he felt at hearing himself called a little nestling. He admitted that he had had one or two bad days, but he protested afresh against the iniquity of his mother's having made them the ground of an appeal to poor Pemberton. Poor Pemberton could laugh now, apart from the comicality of Mrs. Moreen's producing so much philosophy for her defence (she seemed to shake it out of her agitated petticoats, which knocked over the light gilt chairs), so little did the sick boy strike him as qualified to repudiate any advantage.

He himself was in for it, at any rate. He should have Morgan on his hands again indefinitely; though indeed he saw the lad had a private theory to produce which would be intended to smooth this down. He was obliged to him for it in advance; but the suggested amendment didn't keep his heart from sinking a little, any more than it prevented him from accepting the prospect on the spot, with some confidence moreover that he would do so even better if he could have a little supper. Mrs. Moreen threw out more hints about

5. Isn't that right, darling? Don't you agree?

the changes that were to be looked for, but she was such a mixture of smiles and shudders (she confessed she was very nervous), that he couldn't tell whether she were in high feather or only in hysterics. If the family were really at last going to pieces why shouldn't she recognise the necessity of pitching Morgan into some sort of lifeboat? This presumption was fostered by the fact that they were established in luxurious quarters in the capital of pleasure; that was exactly where they naturally *would* be established in view of going to pieces. Moreover didn't she mention that Mr. Moreen and the others were enjoying themselves at the opera with Mr. Granger, and wasn't *that* also precisely where one would look for them on the eve of a smash? Pemberton gathered that Mr. Granger was a rich, vacant American—a big bill with a flourishy heading and no items; so that one of Paula's "ideas" was probably that this time she had really done it, which was indeed an unprecedented blow to the general cohesion. And if the cohesion was to terminate what was to become of poor Pemberton? He felt quite enough bound up with them to figure, to his alarm, as a floating spar in case of a wreck.

It was Morgan who eventually asked if no supper had been ordered for him; sitting with him below, later, at the dim, delayed meal, in the presence of a great deal of corded green plush, a plate of ornamental biscuit and a languor marked on the part of the waiter. Mrs. Moreen had explained that they had been obliged to secure a room for the visitor out of the house; and Morgan's consolation (he offered it while Pemberton reflected on the nastiness of lukewarm sauces), proved to be, largely, that this circumstance would facilitate their escape. He talked of their escape (recurring to it often afterwards), as if they were making up a "boy's book" together. But he likewise expressed his sense that there was something in the air, that the Moreens couldn't keep it up much longer. In point of fact, as Pemberton was to see, they kept it up for five or six months. All the while, however, Morgan's contention was designed to cheer him. Mr. Moreen and Ulick, whom he had met the day after his return, accepted that return like perfect men of the world. If Paula and Amy treated it even with less formality an allowance was to be made for them, inasmuch as Mr. Granger had not come to the opera after all. He had only placed his box at their service, with a bouquet for each of the party; there was even one apiece, embittering the thought of his profusion, for Mr. Moreen and Ulick. "They're all like that," was Morgan's comment; "at the very last, just when we think we've got them fast, we're chucked!"

Morgan's comments, in these days, were more and more free; they even included a large recognition of the extraordinary tenderness with which he had been treated while Pemberton was away. Oh, yes, they couldn't do enough to be nice to him, to show him

they had him on their mind and make up for his loss. That was just
what made the whole thing so sad, and him so glad, after all, of
Pemberton's return—he had to keep thinking of their affection less,
had less sense of obligation. Pemberton laughed out at this last
reason, and Morgan blushed and said: "You know what I mean."
Pemberton knew perfectly what he meant; but there were a good
many things it didn't make any clearer. This episode of his second
sojourn in Paris stretched itself out wearily, with their resumed
readings and wanderings and maunderings, their potterings on the
quays, their hauntings of the museums, their occasional lingerings
in the Palais Royal,[6] when the first sharp weather came on and
there was a comfort in warm emanations, before Chevet's wonderful
succulent window. Morgan wanted to hear a great deal about the
opulent youth—he took an immense interest in him. Some· of the
details of his opulence—Pemberton could spare him none of
them—evidently intensified the boy's appreciation of all his friend
had given up to come back to him; but in addition to the greater
reciprocity established by such a renunciation he had always his
little brooding theory, in which there was a frivolous gaiety too, that
their long probation was drawing to a close. Morgan's conviction
that the Moreens couldn't go on much longer kept pace with the
unexpended impetus with which, from month to month, they did
go on. Three weeks after Pemberton had rejoined them they went
on to another hotel, a dingier one than the first; but Morgan rejoiced that his tutor had at least still not sacrificed the advantage
of a room outside. He clung to the romantic utility of this when
the day, or rather the night, should arrive for their escape.

   For the first time, in this complicated connection, Pemberton felt
sore and exasperated. It was, as he had said to Mrs. Moreen in
Venice, *trop fort*—everything was *trop fort*. He could neither really
throw off his blighting burden nor find in it the benefit of a pacified
conscience or of a rewarded affection. He had spent all the money
that he had earned in England, and he felt that his youth was going
and that he was getting nothing back for it. It was all very well for
Morgan to seem to consider that he would make up to him for all
inconveniences by settling himself upon him permanently—there
was an irritating flaw in such a view. He saw what the boy had in
his mind; the conception that as his friend had had the generosity
to come back to him he must show his gratitude by giving him his
life. But the poor friend didn't desire the gift—what could he do

6. The Palais Royal, a large complex of buildings and gardens, dates back to the early
   seventeenth century. In the course of its lively history it has housed kings and nobles,
   courtesans and gamblers, a theater, and fashionable shops and restaurants. Chevet's was
   probably a candy or confectioner's store. Today the Palais Royal houses government
   offices and shops with less succulent wares, like antiques and stamp collections.

with Morgan's life? Of course at the same time that Pemberton was irritated he remembered the reason, which was very honourable to Morgan and which consisted simply of the fact that he was perpetually making one forget that he was after all only a child. If one dealt with him on a different basis one's misadventures were one's own fault. So Pemberton waited in a queer confusion of yearning and alarm for the catastrophe which was held to hang over the house of Moreen, of which he certainly at moments felt the symptoms brush his cheek and as to which he wondered much in what form it would come.

Perhaps it would take the form of dispersal—a frightened *sauve qui peut*,[7] a scuttling into selfish corners. Certainly they were less elastic than of yore; they were evidently looking for something they didn't find. The Dorringtons hadn't reappeared, the princes had scattered; wasn't that the beginning of the end? Mrs. Moreen had lost her reckoning of the famous "days"; her social calendar was blurred—it had turned its face to the wall. Pemberton suspected that the great, the cruel, discomfiture had been the extraordinary behaviour of Mr. Granger, who seemed not to know what he wanted, or, what was much worse, what *they* wanted. He kept sending flowers, as if to bestrew the path of his retreat, which was never the path of return. Flowers were all very well, but—Pemberton could complete the proposition. It was now positively conspicuous that in the long run the Moreens were a failure; so that the young man was almost grateful the run had not been short. Mr. Moreen, indeed, was still occasionally able to get away on business, and, what was more surprising, he was also able to get back. Ulick had no club, but you could not have discovered it from his appearance, which was as much as ever that of a person looking at life from the window of such an institution; therefore Pemberton was doubly astonished at an answer he once heard him make to his mother, in the desperate tone of a man familiar with the worst privations. Her question Pemberton had not quite caught; it appeared to be an appeal for a suggestion as to whom they could get to take Amy. "Let the devil take her!" Ulick snapped; so that Pemberton could see that not only they had lost their amiability, but had ceased to believe in themselves. He could also see that if Mrs. Moreen was trying to get people to take her children she might be regarded as closing the hatches for the storm. But Morgan would be the last she would part with.

One winter afternoon—it was a Sunday—he and the boy walked far together in the Bois de Boulogne.[8] The evening was so splendid,

7. Every man for himself.
8. A large park in Paris.

the cold lemon-coloured sunset so clear, the stream of carriages
and pedestrians so amusing and the fascination of Paris so great,
that they stayed out later than usual and became aware that they
would have to hurry home to arrive in time for dinner. They hurried
accordingly, arm-in-arm, good-humoured and hungry, agreeing that
there was nothing like Paris after all and that after all, too, that had
come and gone they were not yet sated with innocent pleasures.
When they reached the hotel they found that, though scandalously
late, they were in time for all the dinner they were likely to sit down
to. Confusion reigned in the apartments of the Moreens (very
shabby ones this time, but the best in the house), and before the
interrupted service of the table (with objects displaced almost as if
there had been a scuffle, and a great wine stain from an overturned
bottle), Pemberton could not blink the fact that there had been a
scene of proprietary mutiny. The storm had come—they were all
seeking refuge. The hatches were down—Paula and Amy were invisible (they had never tried the most casual art upon Pemberton,
but he felt that they had enough of an eye to him not to wish to
meet him as young ladies whose frocks had been confiscated), and
Ulick appeared to have jumped overboard. In a word, the host and
his staff had ceased to "go on" at the pace of their guests, and the
air of embarrassed detention, thanks to a pile of gaping trunks in
the passage, was strangely commingled with the air of indignant
withdrawal.

When Morgan took in all this—and he took it in very quickly—
he blushed to the roots of his hair. He had walked, from his infancy,
among difficulties and dangers, but he had never seen a public
exposure. Pemberton noticed, in a second glance at him, that the
tears had rushed into his eyes and that they were tears of bitter
shame. He wondered for an instant, for the boy's sake, whether he
might successfully pretend not to understand. Not successfully,
he felt, as Mr. and Mrs. Moreen, dinnerless by their extinguished
hearth, rose before him in their little dishonoured *salon*, considering
apparently with much intensity what lively capital would be next on
their list. They were not prostrate, but they were very pale, and
Mrs. Moreen had evidently been crying. Pemberton quickly learned
however that her grief was not for the loss of her dinner, much as
she usually enjoyed it, but on account of a necessity much more
tragic. She lost no time in laying this necessity bare, in telling him
how the change had come, the bolt had fallen, and how they would
all have to turn themselves about. Therefore cruel as it was to them
to part with their darling she must look to him to carry a little
further the influence he had so fortunately acquired with the boy
—to induce his young charge to follow him into some modest retreat. They depended upon him, in a word, to take their delightful

child temporarily under his protection—it would leave Mr. Moreen and herself so much more free to give the proper attention (too little, alas! had been given), to the readjustment of their affairs.

"We trust you—we feel that we can," said Mrs. Moreen, slowly rubbing her plump white hands and looking, with compunction, hard at Morgan, whose chin, not to take liberties, her husband stroked with a tentative paternal forefinger.

"Oh, yes; we feel that we can. We trust Mr. Pemberton fully, Morgan," Mr. Moreen conceded.

Pemberton wondered again if he might pretend not to understand; but the idea was painfully complicated by the immediate perception that Morgan had understood.

"Do you mean that he may take me to live with him—for ever and ever?" cried the boy. "Away, away, anywhere he likes?"

"For ever and ever? *Comme vous-y-allez!*"[9] Mr. Moreen laughed indulgently. "For as long as Mr. Pemberton may be so good."

"We've struggled, we've suffered," his wife went on; "but you've made him so your own that we've already been through the worst of the sacrifice."

Morgan had turned away from his father—he stood looking at Pemberton with a light in his face. His blush had died out, but something had come that was brighter and more vivid. He had a moment of boyish joy, scarcely mitigated by the reflection that, with this unexpected consecration of his hope—too sudden and too violent; the thing was a good deal less like a boy's book—the "escape" was left on their hands. The boyish joy was there for an instant, and Pemberton was almost frightened at the revelation of gratitude and affection that shone through his humiliation. When Morgan stammered "My dear fellow, what do you say to *that*?" he felt that he should say something enthusiastic. But he was still more frightened at something else that immediately followed and that made the lad sit down quickly on the nearest chair. He had turned very white and had raised his hand to his left side. They were all three looking at him, but Mrs. Moreen was the first to bound forward. "Ah, his darling little heart!" she broke out; and this time, on her knees before him and without respect for the idol, she caught him ardently in her arms. "You walked him too far, you hurried him too fast!" she tossed over her shoulder at Pemberton. The boy made no protest, and the next instant his mother, still holding him, sprang up with her face convulsed and with the terrified cry "Help, help! he's going, he's gone!" Pemberton saw, with equal horror, by Morgan's own stricken face, that he *was* gone. He pulled him half out of his mother's hands, and for a moment, while they held him to-

9. How you do go on!

gether, they looked, in their dismay, into each other's eyes. "He couldn't stand it, with his infirmity," said Pemberton—"the shock, the whole scene, the violent emotion."

"But I thought he *wanted* to go to you!" wailed Mrs. Moreen.

"I *told* you he didn't, my dear," argued Mr. Moreen. He was trembling all over, and he was, in his way, as deeply affected as his wife. But, after the first, he took his bereavement like a man of the world.

Brooksmith†

We are scattered now, the friends of the late Mr. Oliver Offord;
but whenever we chance to meet I think we are conscious of a
certain esoteric respect for each other. "Yes, you too have been in
Arcadia,"¹ we seem not too grumpily to allow. When I pass the
house in Mansfield Street I remember that Arcadia was there. I
don't know who has it now, and I don't want to know; it's enough
to be so sure that if I should ring the bell there would be no such
luck for me as that Brooksmith should open the door. Mr. Offord,
the most agreeable, the most lovable of bachelors, was a retired
diplomatist, living on his pension, confined by his infirmities to his
fireside and delighted to be found there any afternoon in the year
by such visitors as Brooksmith allowed to come up. Brooksmith was
his butler and his most intimate friend, to whom we all stood, or I
should say sat, in the same relation in which the subject of the
sovereign finds himself to the prime minister. By having been for
years, in foreign lands, the most delightful Englishman any one had
ever known, Mr. Offord had, in my opinion, rendered signal service
to his country. But I suppose he had been too much liked—liked
even by those who didn't like *it*—so that as people of that sort never
get titles or dotations for the horrid things they have *not* done, his
principal reward was simply that we went to see him.

Oh, we went perpetually, and it was not our fault if he was not
overwhelmed with this particular honour. Any visitor who came
once came again—to come merely once was a slight which nobody,
I am sure, had ever put upon him. His circle, therefore, was essentially composed of *habitués*, who were *habitués* for each other as

† "Brooksmith" first appeared in *Harper's Weekly* and simultaneously in *Black and White*,
May 2, 1891. Its first publication in a book was in *The Lesson of the Master* (New York
and London: Macmillan and Co., 1892). This text is here reprinted. The American and
English issues of this first edition were identical.
1. Arcadia was a rather barren region of central Greece that poets early turned into a Utopia
of rural bliss, an innocent Golden Age, and hence the symbol of an ideal existence. The
phrase "Et in Arcadia ego" ("I am even in Arcadia") first appeared in a picture by Gio-
vanni Francesco Guercino painted in the early seventeenth century, which makes the
point that death is present even in blissful Arcadia. Perhaps because of the slightly later,
more famous French painter Nicolas Poussin, the phrase came to be mistranslated as "I
too have been in Arcadia," and since then many authors, including James, have used or
alluded to it in this sense. See *"Et in Arcadia Ego*: Poussin and the Elegiac Tradition,"
a fascinating essay in *Meaning and the Visual Arts* by Erwin Panofsky.

well as for him, as those of a happy *salon* should be. I remember
vividly every element of the place, down to the intensely Londonish
look of the grey opposite houses, in the gap of the white curtains
of the high windows, and the exact spot where, on a particular
afternoon, I put down my tea-cup for Brooksmith, lingering an instant, to gather it up as if he were plucking a flower. Mr. Offord's
drawing-room was indeed Brooksmith's garden, his pruned and
tended human *parterre*,[2] and if we all flourished there and grew
well in our places it was largely owing to his supervision.

Many persons have heard much, though most have doubtless
seen little, of the famous institution of the *salon*, and many are
born to the depression of knowing that this finest flower of social
life refuses to bloom where the English tongue is spoken. The explanation is usually that our women have not the skill to cultivate
it—the art to direct, between suggestive shores, the course of the
stream of talk. My affectionate, my pious memory of Mr. Offord
contradicts this induction only, I fear, more insidiously to confirm
it. The very sallow and slightly smoked drawing-room in which he
spent so large a portion of the last years of his life certainly deserved
the distinguished name; but on the other hand it could not be said
at all to owe its stamp to the soft pressure of the indispensable sex.
The dear man had indeed been capable of one of those sacrifices
to which women are deemed peculiarly apt; he had recognised (under the influence, in some degree, it is true, of physical infirmity),
that if you wished people to find you at home you must manage
not to be out. He had in short accepted the fact which many dab-
blers in the social art are slow to learn, that you must really, as they
say, take a line and that the only way to be at home is to stay at
home. Finally his own fireside had become a summary of his habits.
Why should he ever have left it?—since this would have been leaving what was notoriously pleasantest in London, the compact
charmed cluster (thinning away indeed into casual couples), round
the fine old last century chimney-piece which, with the exception
of the remarkable collection of miniatures, was the best thing the
place contained. Mr. Offord was not rich; he had nothing but his
pension and the use for life of the somewhat superannuated house.

When I am reminded by some uncomfortable contrast of to-day
how perfectly we were all handled there I ask myself once more
what had been the secret of such perfection. One had taken it for
granted at the time, for anything that is supremely good produces
more acceptance than surprise. I felt we were all happy, but I didn't
consider how our happiness was managed. And yet there were questions to be asked, questions that strike me as singularly obvious

2. Ornamental flower-bed.

now that there is nobody to answer them. Mr. Offord had solved the insoluble; he had, without feminine help (save in the sense that ladies were dying to come to him and he saved the lives of several), established a *salon*; but I might have guessed that there was a method in his madness—a law in his success. He had not hit it off by a mere fluke. There was an art in it all, and how was the art so hidden? Who, indeed, if it came to that, was the occult artist? Launching this inquiry the other day, I had already got hold of the tail of my reply. I was helped by the very wonder of some of the conditions that came back to me—those that used to seem as natural as sunshine in a fine climate.

How was it, for instance, that we never were a crowd, never either too many or too few, always the right people *with* the right people (there must really have been no wrong people at all), always coming and going, never sticking fast nor overstaying, yet never popping in or out with an indecorous familiarity? How was it that we all sat where we wanted and moved when we wanted and met whom we wanted and escaped whom we wanted; joining, according to the accident of inclination, the general circle or falling in with a single talker on a convenient sofa? Why were all the sofas so convenient, the accidents so happy, the talkers so ready, the listeners so willing, the subjects presented to you in a rotation as quickly fore-ordained as the courses at dinner? A dearth of topics would have been as unheard of as a lapse in the service. These speculations couldn't fail to lead me to the fundamental truth that Brooksmith had been somehow at the bottom of the mystery. If he had not established the *salon* at least he had carried it on. Brooksmith, in short, was the artist!

We felt this, covertly, at the time, without formulating it, and were conscious, as an ordered and prosperous community, of his evenhanded justice, untainted with flunkeyism. He had none of that vulgarity—his touch was infinitely fine. The delicacy of it was clear to me on the first occasion my eyes rested, as they were so often to rest again, on the domestic revealed, in the turbid light of the street, by the opening of the house-door. I saw on the spot that though he had plenty of school he carried it without arrogance—he had remained articulate and human. *L'Ecole Anglaise,*[3] Mr. Offord used to call him, laughing, when, later, it happened more than once that we had some conversation about him. But I remember accusing Mr. Offord of not doing him quite ideal justice. That he was not one of the giants of the school, however, my old friend, who really understood him perfectly and was devoted to him, as I shall show, quite admitted; which doubtless poor Brooksmith had

3. The English School.

himself felt, to his cost, when his value in the market was originally determined. The utility of his class in general is estimated by the foot and the inch, and poor Brooksmith had only about five feet two to put into circulation. He acknowledged the inadequacy of this provision, and I am sure was penetrated with the everlasting fitness of the relation between service and stature. If *he* had been Mr. Offord he certainly would have found Brooksmith wanting, and indeed the laxity of his employer on this score was one of many things which he had had to condone and to which he had at last indulgently adapted himself.

I remember the old man's saying to me: "Oh, my servants, if they can live with me a fortnight they can live with me for ever. But it's the first fortnight that tries 'em." It was in the first fortnight, for instance, that Brooksmith had had to learn that he was exposed to being addressed as "my dear fellow" and "my poor child." Strange and deep must such a probation have been to him, and he doubtless emerged from it tempered and purified. This was written to a certain extent in his appearance; in his spare, brisk little person, in his cloistered white face and extraordinarily polished hair, which told of responsibility, looked as if it were kept up to the same high standard as the plate; in his small, clear, anxious eyes, even in the permitted, though not exactly encouraged tuft on his chin. "He thinks me rather mad, but I've broken him in, and now he likes the place, he likes the company," said the old man. I embraced this fully after I had become aware that Brooksmith's main characteristic was a deep and shy refinement, though I remember I was rather puzzled when, on another occasion, Mr. Offord remarked: "What he likes is the talk—mingling in the conversation." I was conscious that I had never seen Brooksmith permit himself this freedom, but I guessed in a moment that what Mr. Offord alluded to was a participation more intense than any speech could have represented—that of being perpetually present on a hundred legitimate pretexts, errands, necessities, and breathing the very atmosphere of criticism, the famous criticism of life. "Quite an education, sir, isn't it, sir?" he said to me one day at the foot of the stairs, when he was letting me out; and I have always remembered the words and the tone as the first sign of the quickening drama of poor Brooksmith's fate. It was indeed an education, but to what was this sensitive young man of thirty-five, of the servile class, being educated?

Practically and inevitably, for the time, to companionship, to the perpetual, the even exaggerated reference and appeal of a person brought to dependence by his time of life and his infirmities and always addicted moreover (this was the exaggeration) to the art of giving you pleasure by letting you do things for him. There were certain things Mr. Offord was capable of pretending he liked you to do, even when he didn't, if he thought *you* liked them. If it happened that you didn't either (this was rare, but it might be), of course there were cross-purposes; but Brooksmith was there to prevent their going very far. This was precisely the way he acted as moderator: he averted misunderstandings or cleared them up. He had been capable, strange as it may appear, of acquiring for this purpose an insight into the French tongue, which was often used at Mr. Offord's; for besides being habitual to most of the foreigners, and they were many, who haunted the place or arrived with letters (letters often requiring a little worried consideration, of which Brooksmith always had cognisance), it had really become the primary language of the master of the house. I don't know if all the *malentendus*[4] were in French, but almost all the explanations were, and this didn't a bit prevent Brooksmith from following them. I know Mr. Offord used to read passages to him from Montaigne and Saint-Simon,[5] for he read perpetually when he was alone—when they were alone, I should say—and Brooksmith was always about. Perhaps you'll say no wonder Mr. Offord's butler regarded him as "rather mad." However, if I'm not sure what he thought about Montaigne I'm convinced he admired Saint-Simon. A certain feeling for letters must have rubbed off on him from the mere handling of his master's books, which he was always carrying to and fro and putting back in their places.

I often noticed that if an anecdote or a quotation, much more a lively discussion, was going forward, he would, if busy with the fire or the curtains, the lamp or the tea, find a pretext for remaining in the room till the point should be reached. If his purpose was to catch it you were not discreet to call him off, and I shall never forget a look, a hard, stony stare (I caught it in its passage), which, one day when there were a good many people in the room, he fastened upon the footman who was helping him in the service and who, in an undertone, had asked him some irrelevant question. It was the only manifestation of harshness that I ever observed on Brooksmith's part, and at first I wondered what was the matter. Then I became conscious that Mr. Offord was relating a very curious anecdote, never before perhaps made so public, and imparted to the narrator by an eye-witness of the fact, bearing upon Lord Byron's life in Italy. Nothing would induce me to reproduce it here;

4. Misunderstandings.
5. Michel Eyquem, Seigneur de Montaigne (1533–1592), French essayist. Saint-Simon refers either to Claude Henri, Comte de Saint-Simon (1760–1825), the influential French socialist; or, more likely, to Louis de Rouvroy, Duc de Saint-Simon (1675–1755), French author famous for his memoirs.

but Brooksmith had been in danger of losing it. If I ever should venture to reproduce it I shall feel how much I lose in not having my fellow-auditor to refer to.

The first day Mr. Offord's door was closed was therefore a dark date in contemporary history. It was raining hard and my umbrella was wet, but Brooksmith took it from me exactly as if this were a preliminary for going upstairs. I observed however that instead of putting it away he held it poised and trickling over the rug, and then I became aware that he was looking at me with deep, acknowledging eyes—his air of universal responsibility. I immediately understood; there was scarcely need of the question and the answer that passed between us. When I did understand that the old man had given up, for the first time, though only for the occasion, I exclaimed dolefully: "What a difference it will make—and to how many people!"

"I shall be one of them, sir!" said Brooksmith; and that was the beginning of the end.

Mr. Offord came down again, but the spell was broken, and the great sign of it was that the conversation was, for the first time, not directed. It wandered and stumbled, a little frightened, like a lost child—it had let go the nurse's hand. "The worst of it is that now we shall talk about my health—*c'est la fin de tout*,"[6] Mr. Offord said, when he reappeared; and then I recognised what a sign of change that would be—for he had never tolerated anything so provincial. The talk became ours, in a word—not his; and as ours, even when *he* talked, it could only be inferior. In this form it was a distress to Brooksmith, whose attention now wandered from it altogether: he had so much closer a vision of his master's intimate conditions than our superficialities represented. There were better hours, and he was more in and out of the room, but I could see that he was conscious that the great institution was falling to pieces. He seemed to wish to take counsel with me about it, to feel responsible for its going on in some form or other. When for the second period—the first had lasted several days—he had to tell me that our old friend didn't receive, I half expected to hear him say after a moment: "Do you think I ought to, sir, in his place?"—as he might have asked me, with the return of autumn, if I thought he had better light the drawing-room fire.

He had a resigned philosophic sense of what his guests—our guests, as I came to regard them in our colloquies—would expect. His feeling was that he wouldn't absolutely have approved of himself as a substitute for the host; but he was so saturated with the religion of habit that he would have made, for our friends, the nec-

6. That's the end of everything.

essary sacrifice to the divinity. He would take them on a little further, till they could look about them. I think I saw him also mentally
confronted with the opportunity to deal—for once in his life—with
some of his own dumb preferences, his limitations of sympathy,
weeding a little, in prospect, and returning to a purer tradition. It
was not unknown to me that he considered that toward the end of
Mr. Offord's career a certain laxity of selection had crept in.

At last it came to be the case that we all found the closed door
more often than the open one; but even when it was closed Brooksmith managed a crack for me to squeeze through; so that practically I never turned away without having paid a visit. The difference
simply came to be that the visit was to Brooksmith. It took place
in the hall, at the familiar foot of the stairs, and we didn't sit
down—at least Brooksmith didn't; moreover it was devoted wholly
to one topic and always had the air of being already over—beginning, as it were, at the end. But it was always interesting—it always
gave me something to think about. It is true that the subject of my
meditation was ever the same—ever "It's all very well, but what *will*
become of Brooksmith?" Even my private answer to this question
left me still unsatisfied. No doubt Mr. Offord would provide for
him, but *what* would he provide? that was the great point. He
couldn't provide society; and society had become a necessity of
Brooksmith's nature. I must add that he never showed a symptom
of what I may call sordid solicitude—anxiety on his own account.
He was rather livid and intensely grave, as befitted a man before
whose eyes the "shade of that which once was great"[7] was passing
away. He had the solemnity of a person winding up, under depressing circumstances, a long established and celebrated business; he
was a kind of social executor or liquidator. But his manner seemed
to testify exclusively to the uncertainty of *our* future. I couldn't in
those days have afforded it—I lived in two rooms in Jermyn Street
and didn't "keep a man"; but even if my income had permitted I
shouldn't have ventured to say to Brooksmith (emulating Mr. Offord), "My dear fellow, I'll take you on." The whole tone of our
intercourse was so much more an implication that it was *I* who
should now want a lift. Indeed there was a tacit assurance in
Brooksmith's whole attitude that he would have me on his mind.

One of the most assiduous members of our circle had been Lady
Kenyon, and I remember his telling me one day that her ladyship
had, in spite of her own infirmities, lately much aggravated, been
in person to inquire. In answer to this I remarked that she would
feel it more than any one. Brooksmith was silent a moment; at the
end of which he said, in a certain tone (there is no reproducing

---

7. A line from Wordsworth's "On the Extinction of the Venetian Republic."

some of his tones), "I'll go and see her." I went to see her myself, and I learned that he had waited upon her; but when I said to her, in the form of a joke but with a core of earnest, that when all was over some of us ought to combine, to club together to set Brooksmith up on his own account, she replied a trifle disappointingly: "Do you mean in a public-house?" I looked at her in a way that I think Brooksmith himself would have approved, and then I answered: "Yes, the Offord Arms." What I had meant, of course, was that, for the love of art itself, we ought to look to it that such a peculiar faculty and so much acquired experience should not be wasted. I really think that if we had caused a few black-edged cards to be struck off and circulated—"Mr. Brooksmith will continue to receive on the old premises from four to seven; business carried on as usual during the alterations"—the majority of us would have rallied.

Several times he took me upstairs—always by his own proposal —and our dear old friend, in bed, in a curious flowered and brocaded *casaque*[8] which made him, especially as his head was tied up in a handkerchief to match, look, to my imagination, like the dying Voltaire, held for ten minutes a sadly shrunken little *salon*. I felt indeed each time, as if I were attending the last *coucher*[9] of some social sovereign. He was royally whimsical about his sufferings and not at all concerned—quite as if the Constitution provided for the case—about his successor. He glided over *our* sufferings charmingly, and none of his jokes—it was a gallant abstention, some of them would have been so easy—were at our expense. Now and again, I confess, there was one at Brooksmith's, but so pathetically sociable as to make the excellent man look at me in a way that seemed to say: "Do exchange a glance with me, or I sha'n't be able to stand it." What he was not able to stand was not what Mr. Offord said about him, but what he wasn't able to say in return. His notion of conversation, for himself, was giving you the convenience of speaking to him; and when he went to "see" Lady Kenyon, for instance, it was to carry her the tribute of his receptive silence. Where would the speech of his betters have been if proper service had been a manifestation of sound? In that case the fundamental difference would have had to be shown by *their* dumbness, and many of them, poor things, were dumb enough without that provision. Brooksmith took an unfailing interest in the preservation of the fundamental difference; it was the thing he had most on his conscience.

What had become of it, however, when Mr. Offord passed away

8. Jacket with wide sleeves.
9. A reception that precedes the going to bed of a king.

like any inferior person—was relegated to eternal stillness like a butler upstairs? His aspect for several days after the expected event may be imagined, and the multiplication by funereal observance of the things he didn't say. When everything was over—it was late the same day—I knocked at the door of the house of mourning as I so often had done before. I could never call on Mr. Offord again, but I had come, literally, to call on Brooksmith. I wanted to ask him if there was anything I could do for him, tainted with vagueness as this inquiry could only be. My wild dream of taking him into my own service had died away: my service was not worth his being taken into. My offer to him could only be to help him to find another place, and yet there was an indelicacy, as it were, in taking for granted that his thoughts would immediately be fixed on another. I had a hope that he would be able to give his life a different form—though certainly not the form, the frequent result of such bereavements, of his setting up a little shop. That would have been dreadful; for I should have wished to further any enterprise that he might embark in, yet how could I have brought myself to go and pay him shillings and take back coppers over a counter? My visit then was simply an intended compliment. He took it as such, gratefully and with all the tact in the world. He knew I really couldn't help him and that I knew he knew I couldn't, but we discussed the situation—with a good deal of elegant generality—at the foot of the stairs, in the hall already dismantled, where I had so often discussed other situations with him. The executors were in possession, as was still more apparent when he made me pass for a few minutes into the dining-room, where various objects were muffled up for removal.

Two definite facts, however, he had to communicate; one being that he was to leave the house for ever that night (servants, for some mysterious reason, seem always to depart by night), and the other—he mentioned it only at the last, with hesitation—that he had already been informed his late master had left him a legacy of eighty pounds. "I'm very glad," I said, and Brooksmith rejoined: "It was so like him to think of me." This was all that passed between us on the subject, and I know nothing of his judgment of Mr. Offord's memento. Eighty pounds are always eighty pounds, and no one has ever left *me* an equal sum; but, all the same, for Brooksmith, I was disappointed. I don't know what I had expected—in short I was disappointed. Eighty pounds might stock a little shop —a *very* little shop; but, I repeat, I couldn't bear to think of that. I asked my friend if he had been able to save a little, and he replied: "No, sir; I have had to do things." I didn't inquire what things he had had to do; they were his own affair, and I took his word for them as assentingly as if he had had the greatness of an ancient house to keep up; especially as there was something in his manner that seemed to convey a prospect of further sacrifice.

"I shall have to turn round a bit, sir—I shall have to look about me," he said; and then he added, indulgently, magnanimously: "If you should happen to hear of anything for me—"

I couldn't let him finish; this was, in its essence, too much in the really grand manner. It would be a help to my getting him off my mind to be able to pretend I *could* find the right place, and that help he wished to give me, for it was doubtless painful to him to see me in so false a position. I interposed with a few words to the effect that I was well aware that wherever he should go, whatever he should do, he would miss our old friend terribly—miss him even more than I should, having been with him so much more. This led him to make the speech that I have always remembered as the very text of the whole episode.

"Oh, sir, it's sad for *you*, very sad, indeed, and for a great many gentlemen and ladies; that it is, sir. But for me, sir, it is, if I may say so, still graver even than that: it's just the loss of something that was everything. For me, sir," he went on, with rising tears, "he was just *all*, if you know what I mean sir. You have others, sir, I daresay—not that I would have you understand me to speak of them as in any way tantamount. But you have the pleasures of society, sir; if it's only in talking about him, sir, as I daresay you do freely—for all his blessed memory has to fear from it—with gentlemen and ladies who have had the same honour. That's not for me, sir, and I have to keep my associations to myself. Mr. Offord was *my* society, and now I have no more. You go back to conversation, sir, after all, and I go back to my place," Brooksmith stammered, without exaggerated irony or dramatic bitterness, but with a flat, unstudied veracity and his hand on the knob of the street-door. He turned it to let me out and then he added: "I just go downstairs, sir, again, and I stay there."

"My poor child," I replied, in my emotion, quite as Mr. Offord used to speak, "my dear fellow, leave it to me; we'll look after you, we'll all do something for you."

"Ah, if you could give me some one *like* him! But there ain't two in the world," said Brooksmith as we parted.

He had given me his address—the place where he would be to be heard of. For a long time I had no occasion to make use of the information; for he proved indeed, on trial, a very difficult case. In a word the people who knew him and had known Mr. Offord, didn't want to take him, and yet I couldn't bear to try to thrust him among people who didn't know him. I spoke to many of our old friends about him, and I found them all governed by the odd mixture of feelings of which I myself was conscious, and disposed, further, to entertain a suspicion that he was "spoiled," with which I then would have nothing to do. In plain terms a certain embarrassment, a sensible awkwardness, when they thought of it, attached to the idea of using him as a menial: they had met him so often in society. Many of them would have asked him, and did ask him, or rather did ask me to ask him, to come and see them; but a mere visiting-list was not what I wanted for him. He was too short for people who were very particular; nevertheless I heard of an opening in a diplomatic household which led me to write him a note, though I was looking much less for something grand than for something human. Five days later I heard from him. The secretary's wife had decided, after keeping him waiting till then, that she couldn't take a servant out of a house in which there had not been a lady. The note had a P.S.: "It's a good job there wasn't sir, such a lady as some."

A week later he came to see me and told me he was "suited"— committed to some highly respectable people (they were something very large in the City), who lived on the Bayswater side of the Park.[1] "I daresay it will be rather poor, sir," he admitted; "but I've seen the fireworks, haven't I, sir?—it can't be fireworks *every* night. After Mansfield Street there ain't much choice." There was a certain amount, however, it seemed; for the following year, going one day to call on a country cousin, a lady of a certain age who was spending a fortnight in town with some friends of her own, a family unknown to me and resident in Chester Square, the door of the house was opened, to my surprise and gratification, by Brooksmith in person. When I came out I had some conversation with him, from which I gathered that he had found the large City people too dull for endurance, and I guessed, though he didn't say it, that he had found them vulgar as well. I don't know what judgment he would have passed on his actual patrons if my relative had not been their friend; but under the circumstances he abstained from comment.

None was necessary, however, for before the lady in question brought her visit to a close they honoured me with an invitation to dinner, which I accepted. There was a largeish party on the occasion, but I confess I thought of Brooksmith rather more than of the seated company. They required no depth of attention—they were all referable to usual, irredeemable, inevitable types. It was the world of cheerful commonplace and conscious gentility and prosperous density, a full-fed, material, insular world, a world of hideous florid plate and ponderous order and thin conversation. There was not a word said about Byron. Nothing would have induced me to look at Brooksmith in the course of the repast, and I felt sure that

1. As a residential district, Bayswater (north of Hyde Park) is socially much inferior to Mansfield Street, where Mr. Offord lived.

not even my overturning the wine would have induced him to meet
my eye. We were in intellectual sympathy—we felt, as regards each
other, a kind of social responsibility. In short we had been in Arcadia together, and we had both come to *this*! No wonder we were
ashamed to be confronted. When he helped on my overcoat, as I
was going away, we parted, for the first time since the earliest days
in Mansfield Street, in silence. I thought he looked lean and wasted,
and I guessed that his new place was not more "human" than his
previous one. There was plenty of beef and beer, but there was no
reciprocity. The question for him to have asked before accepting
the position would have been not "How many footmen are kept?"
but "How much imagination?"

The next time I went to the house—I confess it was not very
soon—I encountered his successor, a personage who evidently enjoyed the good fortune of never having quitted his natural level.
Could any be higher? he seemed to ask—over the heads of three
footmen and even of some visitors. He made me feel as if Brooksmith were dead; but I didn't dare to inquire—I couldn't have borne
his "I haven't the least idea, sir." I despatched a note to the address
Brooksmith had given me after Mr. Offord's death, but I received
no answer. Six months later, however, I was favoured with a visit
from an elderly, dreary, dingy person, who introduced herself to me
as Mr. Brooksmith's aunt and from whom I learned that he was out
of place and out of health and had allowed her to come and say to
me that if I could spare half-an-hour to look in at him he would
take it as a rare honour.

I went the next day—his messenger had given me a new
address—and found my friend lodged in a short sordid street in
Marylebone, one of those corners of London that wear the last
expression of sickly meanness. The room into which I was shown
was above the small establishment of a dyer and cleaner who had
inflated kid gloves and discoloured shawls in his shop-front. There
was a great deal of grimy infant life up and down the place, and
there was a hot, moist smell within, as of the "boiling" of dirty linen.
Brooksmith sat with a blanket over his legs at a clean little window,
where, from behind stiff bluish-white curtains, he could look across
at a huckster's and a tinsmith's and a small greasy public-house.
He had passed through an illness and was convalescent, and his
mother, as well as his aunt, was in attendance on him. I liked the
mother, who was bland and intensely humble, but I didn't much
fancy the aunt, whom I connected, perhaps unjustly, with the opposite public-house (she seemed somehow to be greasy with the
same grease), and whose furtive eye followed every movement of
my hand, as if to see if it were not going into my pocket. It didn't

take this direction—I couldn't, unsolicited, put myself at that sort
of ease with Brooksmith. Several times the door of the room
opened, and mysterious old women peeped in and shuffled back
again. I don't know who they were; poor Brooksmith seemed en-
compassed with vague, prying, beery females.

He was vague himself, and evidently weak, and much embarrassed, and not an allusion was made between us to Mansfield
Street. The vision of the *salon* of which he had been an ornament
hovered before me, however, by contrast, sufficiently. He assured
me that he was really getting better, and his mother remarked that
he would come round if he could only get his spirits up. The aunt
echoed this opinion, and I became more sure that in her own case
she knew where to go for such a purpose. I'm afraid I was rather
weak with my old friend, for I neglected the opportunity, so exceptionally good, to rebuke the levity which had led him to throw
up honourable positions—fine, stiff, steady berths, with morning
prayers, as I knew, attached to one of them—in Bayswater and
Belgravia.[2] Very likely his reasons had been profane and sentimental; he didn't want morning prayers, he wanted to be somebody's
dear fellow; but I couldn't be the person to rebuke him. He shuffled
these episodes out of sight—I saw that he had no wish to discuss
them. I perceived further, strangely enough, that it would probably
be a questionable pleasure for him to see me again: he doubted
now even of my power to condone his aberrations. He didn't wish
to have to explain; and his behaviour, in future, was likely to need
explanation. When I bade him farewell he looked at me a moment
with eyes that said everything: "How can I talk about those exquisite
years in this place, before these people, with the old women poking
their heads in? It was very good of you to come to see me—it wasn't
my idea; *she* brought you. We've said everything; it's over; you'll lose
all patience with me, and I'd rather you shouldn't see the rest." I
sent him some money, in a letter, the next day, but I saw the rest
only in the light of a barren sequel.

A whole year after my visit to him I became aware once, in dining
out, that Brooksmith was one of the several servants who hovered
behind our chairs. He had not opened the door of the house to me,
and I had not recognised him in the cluster of retainers in the hall.
This time I tried to catch his eye, but he never gave me a chance,
and when he handed me a dish I could only be careful to thank
him audibly. Indeed I partook of two *entrées* of which I had my
doubts, subsequently converted into certainties, in order not to
snub him. He looked well enough in health, but much older, and

2. Belgravia is a fashionable section near Buckingham Palace.

wore, in an exceptionally marked degree, the glazed and expressionless mask of the British domestic *de race*.[3] I saw with dismay that if I had not known him I should have taken him, on the showing of his countenance, for an extravagant illustration of irresponsive servile gloom. I said to myself that he had become a reactionary, gone over to the Philistines, thrown himself into religion, the religion of his "place," like a foreign lady *sur le retour*.[4] I divined moreover that he was only engaged for the evening—he had become a mere waiter, had joined the band of the white-waistcoated who "go out." There was something pathetic in this fact, and it was a terrible vulgarisation of Brooksmith. It was the mercenary prose of butlerhood; he had given up the struggle for the poetry. If reciprocity was what he had missed, where was the reciprocity now? Only in the bottoms of the wine-glasses and five shillings (or whatever they get), clapped into his hand by the permanent man. However, I supposed he had taken up a precarious branch of his profession because after all it sent him less downstairs. His relations with London society were more superficial, but they were of course more various. As I went away, on this occasion, I looked out for him eagerly among the four or five attendants whose perpendicular persons, fluting the walls of London passages, are supposed to lubricate the process of departure; but he was not on duty. I asked one of the others if he were not in the house, and received the prompt answer: "Just left, sir. Anything I can do for you, sir?" I wanted to say "Please give him my kind regards;" but I abstained; I didn't want to compromise him, and I never came across him again.

Often and often, in dining out, I looked for him, sometimes accepting invitations on purpose to multiply the chances of my meeting him. But always in vain; so that as I met many other members of the casual class over and over again, I at last adopted the theory that he always procured a list of expected guests beforehand and kept away from the banquets which he thus learned I was to grace. At last I gave up hope, and one day, at the end of three years, I received another visit from his aunt. She was drearier and dingier, almost squalid, and she was in great tribulation and want. Her sister, Mrs. Brooksmith, had been dead a year, and three months later her nephew had disappeared. He had always looked after her a bit—since her troubles; I never knew what her troubles had been—and now she hadn't so much as a petticoat to pawn. She had also a niece, to whom she had been everything, before her troubles, but the niece had treated her most shameful. These were details; the

3. The "thoroughbred" British domestic servant.
4. Past her prime.

great and romantic fact was Brooksmith's final evasion of his fate. He had gone out to wait one evening, as usual, in a white waistcoat she had done up for him with her own hands, being due at a large party up Kensington way. But he had never come home again, and had never arrived at the large party, or at any party that any one could make out. No trace of him had come to light—no gleam of the white waistcoat had pierced the obscurity of his doom. This news was a sharp shock to me, for I had my ideas about his real destination. His aged relative had promptly, as she said, guessed the worst. Somehow and somewhere he had got out of the way altogether, and now I trust that, with characteristic deliberation, he is changing the plates of the immortal gods. As my depressing visitant also said, he never *had* got his spirits up. I was fortunately able to dismiss her with her own somewhat improved. But the dim ghost of poor Brooksmith is one of those that I see. He had indeed been spoiled.

The Real Thing[†]

[†] "The Real Thing" originally appeared in *Black and White*, April 16, 1892. Its first publication in a book was in *The Real Thing and Other Tales* (New York and London: Macmillan and Co., 1893). This text is here reprinted. The American and English issues, published simultaneously, consisted of the same sheets.

I

When the porter's wife (she used to answer the house-bell), announced "A gentleman—with a lady, sir," I had, as I often had in those days, for the wish was father to the thought, an immediate vision of sitters. Sitters my visitors in this case proved to be; but not in the sense I should have preferred. However, there was nothing at first to indicate that they might not have come for a portrait. The gentleman, a man of fifty, very high and very straight, with a moustache slightly grizzled and a dark grey walking-coat admirably fitted, both of which I noted professionally—I don't mean as a barber or yet as a tailor—would have struck me as a celebrity if celebrities often were striking. It was a truth of which I had for some time been conscious that a figure with a good deal of frontage was, as one might say, almost never a public institution. A glance at the lady helped to remind me of this paradoxical law: she also looked too distinguished to be a "personality." Moreover one would scarcely come across two variations together.

Neither of the pair spoke immediately—they only prolonged the preliminary gaze which suggested that each wished to give the other a chance. They were visibly shy; they stood there letting me take them in—which, as I afterwards perceived, was the most practical thing they could have done. In this way their embarrassment served their cause. I had seen people painfully reluctant to mention that they desired anything so gross as to be represented on canvas; but the scruples of my new friends appeared almost insurmountable. Yet the gentleman might have said "I should like a portrait of my wife," and the lady might have said "I should like a portrait of my husband." Perhaps they were not husband and wife—this naturally would make the matter more delicate. Perhaps they wished to be done together—in which case they ought to have brought a third person to break the news.

"We come from Mr. Rivet," the lady said at last, with a dim smile which had the effect of a moist sponge passed over a "sunk"[1] piece of painting, as well as of a vague allusion to vanished beauty. She was as tall and straight, in her degree, as her companion, and with ten years less to carry. She looked as sad as a woman could look whose face was not charged with expression; that is her tinted oval mask showed friction as an exposed surface shows it. The hand of time had played over her freely, but only to simplify. She was slim and stiff, and so well-dressed, in dark blue cloth, with lappets and pockets and buttons, that it was clear she employed the same tailor as her husband. The couple had an indefinable air of prosperous thrift—they evidently got a good deal of luxury for their money. If I was to be one of their luxuries it would behove me to consider my terms.

"Ah, Claude Rivet recommended me?" I inquired; and I added that it was very kind of him, though I could reflect that, as he only painted landscape, this was not a sacrifice.

The lady looked very hard at the gentleman, and the gentleman looked round the room. Then staring at the floor a moment and stroking his moustache, he rested his pleasant eyes on me with the remark: "He said you were the right one."

"I try to be, when people want to sit."

"Yes, we should like to," said the lady anxiously.

"Do you mean together?"

My visitors exchanged a glance. "If you could do anything with *me*, I suppose it would be double," the gentleman stammered.

"Oh yes, there's naturally a higher charge for two figures than for one."

"We should like to make it pay," the husband confessed.

"That's very good of you," I returned, appreciating so unwonted a sympathy—for I supposed he meant pay the artist.

A sense of strangeness seemed to dawn on the lady. "We mean for the illustrations—Mr. Rivet said you might put one in."

"Put one in—an illustration?" I was equally confused.

"Sketch her off, you know," said the gentleman, colouring.

It was only then that I understood the service Claude Rivet had rendered me; he had told them that I worked in black and white, for magazines, for story-books, for sketches of contemporary life, and consequently had frequent employment for models. These

---

1. In painting, certain technical failures, in particular improper preparation of the "ground" (surface), can cause "the 'sinking in' of oil colors" with consequent loss of the original "color effect" (Max Doerner, *The Materials of the Artist and Their Use in Painting with Notes on the Technique of the Old Masters*, translated by Eugen Neuhaus (New York: Harcourt, Brace and Company, 1934), pp. 185–86). The application of moisture to such a painting may create a temporary gloss.

things were true, but it was not less true (I may confess it now—whether because the aspiration was to lead to everything or to nothing I leave the reader to guess), that I couldn't get the honours, to say nothing of the emoluments, of a great painter of portraits out of my head. My "illustrations" were my pot-boilers; I looked to a different branch of art (far and away the most interesting it had always seemed to me), to perpetuate my fame. There was no shame in looking to it also to make my fortune; but that fortune was by so much further from being made from the moment my visitors wished to be "done" for nothing. I was disappointed; for in the pictorial sense I had immediately *seen* them. I had seized their type—I had already settled what I would do with it. Something that wouldn't absolutely have pleased them, I afterwards reflected.

"Ah, you're—you're—a—?" I began, as soon as I had mastered my surprise. I couldn't bring out the dingy word "models"; it seemed to fit the case so little.

"We haven't had much practice," said the lady.

"We've got to *do* something, and we've thought that an artist in your line might perhaps make something of us," her husband threw off. He further mentioned that they didn't know many artists and that they had gone first, on the off-chance (he painted views of course, but sometimes put in figures—perhaps I remembered), to Mr. Rivet, whom they had met a few years before at a place in Norfolk where he was sketching.

"We used to sketch a little ourselves," the lady hinted.

"It's very awkward, but we absolutely *must* do something," her husband went on.

"Of course we're not so *very* young," she admitted, with a wan smile.

With the remark that I might as well know something more about them, the husband had handed me a card extracted from a neat new pocket-book (their appurtenances were all of the freshest) and inscribed with the words "Major Monarch." Impressive as these words were they didn't carry my knowledge much further; but my visitor presently added: "I've left the army, and we've had the misfortune to lose our money. In fact our means are dreadfully small."

"It's an awful bore," said Mrs. Monarch.

They evidently wished to be discreet—to take care not to swagger because they were gentlefolks. I perceived they would have been willing to recognise this as something of a drawback, at the same time that I guessed at an underlying sense—their consolation in adversity—that they *had* their points. They certainly had; but these advantages struck me as preponderantly social; such for instance as would help to make a drawing-room look well. However, a drawing-room was always, or ought to be, a picture.

In consequence of his wife's allusion to their age Major Monarch observed: "Naturally, it's more for the figure that we thought of going in. We can still hold ourselves up." On the instant I saw that the figure was indeed their strong point. His "naturally" didn't sound vain, but it lighted up the question. "*She* has got the best," he continued, nodding at his wife, with a pleasant after-dinner absence of circumlocution. I could only reply, as if we were in fact sitting over our wine, that this didn't prevent his own from being very good; which led him in turn to rejoin: "We thought that if you ever had to do people like us, we might be something like it. *She*, particularly—for a lady in a book, you know."

I was so amused by them that, to get more of it, I did my best to take their point of view; and though it was an embarrassment to find myself appraising physically, as if they were animals on hire or useful blacks, a pair whom I should have expected to meet only in one of the relations in which criticism is tacit, I looked at Mrs. Monarch judicially enough to be able to exclaim, after a moment, with conviction: "Oh yes, a lady in a book!" She was singularly like a bad illustration.

"We'll stand up, if you like," said the Major; and he raised himself before me with a really grand air.

I could take his measure at a glance—he was six feet two and a perfect gentleman. It would have paid any club in process of formation and in want of a stamp to engage him at a salary to stand in the principal window. What struck me immediately was that in coming to me they had rather missed their vocation; they could surely have been turned to better account for advertising purposes. I couldn't of course see the thing in detail, but I could see them make someone's fortune—I don't mean their own. There was something in them for a waistcoat-maker, an hotel-keeper or a soap-vendor. I could imagine "We always use it" pinned on their bosoms with the greatest effect; I had a vision of the promptitude with which they would launch a table d'hôte.

Mrs. Monarch sat still, not from pride but from shyness, and presently her husband said to her: "Get up my dear and show how smart you are." She obeyed, but she had no need to get up to show it. She walked to the end of the studio, and then she came back blushing, with her fluttered eyes on her husband. I was reminded of an incident I had accidentally had a glimpse of in Paris—being with a friend there, a dramatist about to produce a play—when an actress came to him to ask to be intrusted with a part. She went through her paces before him, walked up and down as Mrs. Monarch was doing. Mrs. Monarch did it quite as well, but I asbstained from applauding. It was very odd to see such people apply for such poor pay. She looked as if she had ten thousand a year. Her husband had used the word that described her: she was, in the London current jargon, essentially and typically "smart." Her figure was, in the same order of ideas, conspicuously and irreproachably "good." For a woman of her age her waist was surprisingly small; her elbow moreover had the orthodox crook. She held her head at the conventional angle; but why did she come to *me*? She ought to have tried on jackets at a big shop. I feared my visitors were not only destitute, but "artistic"—which would be a great complication. When she sat down again I thanked her, observing that what a draughtsman most valued in his model was the faculty of keeping quiet.

"Oh, *she* can keep quiet," said Major Monarch. Then he added, jocosely: "I've always kept her quiet."

"I'm not a nasty fidget, am I?" Mrs. Monarch appealed to her husband.

He addressed his answer to me. "Perhaps it isn't out of place to mention—because we ought to be quite business-like, oughtn't we?—that when I married her she was known as the Beautiful Statue."

"Oh dear!" said Mrs. Monarch, ruefully.

"Of course I should want a certain amount of expression," I rejoined.

"Of *course!*" they both exclaimed.

"And then I suppose you know that you'll get awfully tired."

"Oh, we *never* get tired!" they eagerly cried.

"Have you had any kind of practice?"

They hesitated—they looked at each other. "We've been photographed, *immensely*," said Mrs. Monarch.

"She means the fellows have asked us," added the Major.

"I see—because you're so good-looking."

"I don't know what they thought, but they were always after us."

"We always got our photographs for nothing," smiled Mrs. Monarch.

"We might have brought some, my dear," her husband remarked.

"I'm not sure we have any left. We've given quantities away," she explained to me.

"With our autographs and that sort of thing," said the Major.

"Are they to be got in the shops?" I inquired, as a harmless pleasantry.

"Oh, yes; *hers*—they used to be."

"Not now," said Mrs. Monarch, with her eyes on the floor.

II

I could fancy the "sort of thing" they put on the presentation-copies of their photographs, and I was sure they wrote a beautiful hand. It was odd how quickly I was sure of everything that concerned them. If they were now so poor as to have to earn shillings and pence, they never had had much of a margin. Their good looks had been their capital, and they had good-humouredly made the most of the career that this resource marked out for them. It was in their faces, the blankness, the deep intellectual repose of the twenty years of country-house visiting which had given them pleasant intonations. I could see the sunny drawing-rooms, sprinkled with periodicals she didn't read, in which Mrs. Monarch had continuously sat; I could see the wet shrubberies in which she had walked, equipped to admiration for either exercise. I could see the rich covers the Major had helped to shoot and the wonderful garments in which, late at night, he repaired to the smoking-room to talk about them. I could imagine their leggings and waterproofs, their knowing tweeds and rugs, their rolls of sticks and cases of tackle and neat umbrellas; and I could evoke the exact appearance of their servants and the compact variety of their luggage on the platforms of country stations.

They gave small tips, but they were liked; they didn't do anything themselves, but they were welcome. They looked so well everywhere; they gratified the general relish for stature, complexion and "form." They knew it without fatuity or vulgarity, and they respected themselves in consequence. They were not superficial; they were thorough and kept themselves up—it had been their line. People with such a taste for activity had to have some line. I could feel how, even in a dull house, they could have been counted upon for cheerfulness. At present something had happened—it didn't matter what, their little income had grown less, it had grown least—and they had to do something for pocket-money. Their friends liked them, but didn't like to support them. There was something about them that represented credit—their clothes, their manners, their type; but if credit is a large empty pocket in which an occasional chink reverberates, the chink at least must be audible. What they wanted of me was to help to make it so. Fortunately they had no children—I soon divined that. They would also perhaps wish our relations to be kept secret: this was why it was "for the figure"—the reproduction of the face would betray them.

I liked them—they were so simple; and I had no objection to them if they would suit. But, somehow, with all their perfections I didn't easily believe in them. After all they were amateurs, and the ruling passion of my life was the detestation of the amateur. Combined with this was another perversity—an innate preference for the represented subject over the real one: the defect of the real one was so apt to be a lack of representation. I liked things that appeared; then one was sure. Whether they *were* or not was a subordinate and almost always a profitless question. There were other considerations, the first of which was that I already had two or three people in use, notably a young person with big feet, in alpaca, from Kilburn, who for a couple of years had come to me regularly for my illustrations and with whom I was still—perhaps ignobly—satisfied. I frankly explained to my visitors how the case stood; but they had taken more precautions than I supposed. They had reasoned out their opportunity, for Claude Rivet had told them of the projected *édition de luxe* of one of the writers of our day—the rarest of the novelists—who, long neglected by the multitudinous vulgar and dearly prized by the attentive (need I mention Philip Vincent?) had had the happy fortune of seeing, late in life, the dawn and then the full light of a higher criticism—an estimate in which, on the part of the public, there was something really of expiation. The edition in question, planned by a publisher of taste, was practically an act of high reparation; the wood-cuts with which it was to be enriched were the homage of English art to one of the most independent representatives of English letters. Major and Mrs. Monarch confessed to me that they had hoped I might be able to work *them* into my share of the enterprise. They knew I was to do the first of the books, "Rutland Ramsay," but I had to make clear to them that my participation in the rest of the affair—this first book was to be a test—was to depend on the satisfaction I should give. If this should be limited my employers would drop me without a scruple. It was therefore a crisis for me, and naturally I was making special preparations, looking about for new people, if they should be necessary, and securing the best types. I admitted however that I should like to settle down to two or three good models who would do for everything.

"Should we have often to—a—put on special clothes?" Mrs. Monarch timidly demanded.

"Dear, yes—that's half the business."

"And should we be expected to supply our own costumes?"

"Oh, no; I've got a lot of things. A painter's models put on—or put off—anything he likes."

"And do you mean—a—the same?"

"The same?"

Mrs. Monarch looked at her husband again.

"Oh, she was just wondering," he explained, "if the costumes are in *general* use." I had to confess that they were, and I mentioned further that some of them (I had a lot of genuine, greasy last-century things), had served their time, a hundred years ago, on living, world-stained men and women. "We'll put on anything that *fits*," said the Major.

"Oh, I arrange that—they fit in the pictures."

"I'm afraid I should do better for the modern books. I would come as you like," said Mrs. Monarch.

"She has got a lot of clothes at home: they might do for contemporary life," her husband continued.

"Oh, I can fancy scenes in which you'd be quite natur¬l." And indeed I could see the slipshod rearrangements of stale properties —the stories I tried to produce pictures for without the exasperation of reading them—whose sandy tracts the good lady might help to people. But I had to return to the fact that for this sort of work— the daily mechanical grind—I was already equipped; the people I was working with were fully adequate.

"We only thought we might be more like *some* characters," said Mrs. Monarch mildly, getting up.

Her husband also rose; he stood looking at me with a dim wistfulness that was touching in so fine a man. "Wouldn't it be rather a pull sometimes to have—a—to have—?" He hung fire; he wanted me to help him by phrasing what he meant. But I couldn't—I didn't know. So he brought it out, awkwardly: "The *real* thing; a gentleman, you know, or a lady." I was quite ready to give a general assent—I admitted that there was a great deal in that. This encouraged Major Monarch to say, following up his appeal with an unacted gulp: "It's awfully hard—we've tried everything." The gulp was communicative; it proved too much for his wife. Before I knew it Mrs. Monarch had dropped again upon a divan and burst into tears. Her husband sat down beside her, holding one of her hands; whereupon she quickly dried her eyes with the other, while I felt embarrassed as she looked up at me. "There isn't a confounded job I haven't applied for—waited for—prayed for. You can fancy we'd be pretty bad first. Secretaryships and that sort of thing? You might as well ask for a peerage. I'd be *anything*—I'm strong; a messenger or a coalheaver. I'd put on a gold-laced cap and open carriage-doors in front of the haberdasher's; I'd hang about a station, to carry portmanteaus; I'd be a postman. But they won't *look* at you; there are thousands, as good as yourself, already on the ground. *Gentlemen*, poor beggars, who have drunk their wine, who have kept their hunters!"

I was as reassuring as I knew how to be, and my visitors were presently on their feet again while, for the experiment, we agreed on an hour. We were discussing it when the door opened and Miss Churm came in with a wet umbrella. Miss Churm had to take the omnibus to Maida Vale and then walk half-a-mile. She looked a trifle blowsy and slightly splashed. I scarcely ever saw her come in without thinking afresh how odd it was that, being so little in herself, she should yet be so much in others. She was a meagre little Miss Churm, but she was an ample heroine of romance. She was only a freckled cockney, but she could represent everything, from a fine lady to a shepherdess; she had the faculty, as she might have had a fine voice or long hair. She couldn't spell, and she loved beer, but she had two or three "points," and practice, and a knack, and mother-wit, and a kind of whimsical sensibility, and a love of the theatre, and seven sisters, and not an ounce of respect, especially for the *h*. The first thing my visitors saw was that her umbrella was wet, and in their spotless perfection they visibly winced at it. The rain had come on since their arrival.

"I'm all in a soak; there *was* a mess of people in the 'bus. I wish you lived near a stytion," said Miss Churm. I requested her to get ready as quickly as possible, and she passed into the room in which she always changed her dress. But before going out she asked me what she was to get into this time.

"It's the Russian princess, don't you know?" I answered; "the one with the 'golden eyes,' in black velvet, for the long thing in the *Cheapside*."[2]

"Golden eyes? I *say*!" cried Miss Churm, while my companions watched her with intensity as she withdrew. She always arranged herself, when she was late, before I could turn round; and I kept my visitors a little, on purpose, so that they might get an idea, from seeing her, what would be expected of themselves. I mentioned that she was quite my notion of an excellent model—she was really very clever.

"Do you think she looks like a Russian princess?" Major Monarch asked, with lurking alarm.

"When I make her, yes."

"Oh, if you have to *make* her—!" he reasoned, acutely.

"That's the most you can ask. There are so many that are not makeable."

"Well now, *here's* a lady"—and with a persuasive smile he passed his arm into his wife's—"who's already made!"

"Oh, I'm not a Russian princess," Mrs. Monarch protested, a little coldly. I could see that she had known some and didn't like them. There, immediately, was a complication of a kind that I never had to fear with Miss Churm.

This young lady came back in black velvet—the gown was rather rusty and very low on her lean shoulders—and with a Japanese fan in her red hands. I reminded her that in the scene I was doing she

2. A magazine publishing fiction.

had to look over someone's head. "I forget whose it is; but it doesn't matter. Just look over a head."

"I'd rather look over a stove," said Miss Churm; and she took her station near the fire. She fell into position, settled herself into a tall attitude, gave a certain backward inclination to her head and a certain forward droop to her fan, and looked, at least to my prejudiced sense, distinguished and charming, foreign and dangerous. We left her looking so, while I went down-stairs with Major and Mrs. Monarch.

"I think I could come about as near it as that," said Mrs. Monarch.

"Oh, you think she's shabby, but you must allow for the alchemy of art."

However, they went off with an evident increase of comfort, founded on their demonstrable advantage in being the real thing. I could fancy them shuddering over Miss Churm. She was very droll about them when I went back, for I told her what they wanted.

"Well, if *she* can sit I'll tyke to bookkeeping," said my model.

"She's very lady-like," I replied, as an innocent form of aggravation.

"So much the worse for *you*. That means she can't turn round."

"She'll do for the fashionable novels."

"Oh yes, she'll *do* for them!" my model humorously declared. "Ain't they bad enough without her?" I had often sociably denounced them to Miss Churm.

III

It was for the elucidation of a mystery in one of these works that I first tried Mrs. Monarch. Her husband came with her, to be useful if necessary—it was sufficiently clear that as a general thing he would prefer to come with her. At first I wondered if this were for "propriety's" sake—if he were going to be jealous and meddling. The idea was too tiresome, and if it had been confirmed it would speedily have brought our acquaintance to a close. But I soon saw there was nothing in it and that if he accompanied Mrs. Monarch it was (in addition to the chance of being wanted), simply because he had nothing else to do. When she was away from him his occupation was gone—she never *had* been away from him. I judged, rightly, that in their awkward situation their close union was their main comfort and that this union had no weak spot. It was a real marriage, an encouragement to the hesitating, a nut for pessimists to crack. Their address was humble (I remember afterwards thinking it had been the only thing about them that was really professional), and I could fancy the lamentable lodgings in which the

Major would have been left alone. He could bear them with his wife—he couldn't bear them without her.

He had too much tact to try and make himself agreeable when he couldn't be useful; so he simply sat and waited, when I was too absorbed in my work to talk. But I liked to make him talk—it made my work, when it didn't interrupt it, less sordid, less special. To listen to him was to combine the excitement of going out with the economy of staying at home. There was only one hindrance: that I seemed not to know any of the people he and his wife had known. I think he wondered extremely, during the term of our intercourse, whom the deuce I *did* know. He hadn't a stray sixpence of an idea to fumble for; so we didn't spin it very fine—we confined ourselves to questions of leather and even of liquor (saddlers and breeches-makers and how to get good claret cheap), and matters like "good trains" and the habits of small game. His lore on these last subjects was astonishing, he managed to interweave the stationmaster with the ornithologist. When he couldn't talk about greater things he could talk cheerfully about smaller, and since I couldn't accompany him into reminiscences of the fashionable world he could lower the conversation without a visible effort to my level.

So earnest a desire to please was touching in a man who could so easily have knocked one down. He looked after the fire and had an opinion on the draught of the stove, without my asking him, and I could see that he thought many of my arrangements not half clever enough. I remember telling him that if I were only rich I would offer him a salary to come and teach me how to live. Sometimes he gave a random sigh, of which the essence was: "Give me even such a bare old barrack as *this*, and I'd do something with it!" When I wanted to use him he came alone; which was an illustration of the superior courage of women. His wife could bear her solitary second floor, and she was in general more discreet; showing by various small reserves that she was alive to the propriety of keeping our relations markedly professional—not letting them slide into sociability. She wished it to remain clear that she and the Major were employed, not cultivated, and if she approved of me as a superior, who could be kept in his place, she never thought me quite good enough for an equal.

She sat with great intensity, giving the whole of her mind to it, and was capable of remaining for an hour almost as motionless as if she were before a photographer's lens. I could see she had been photographed often, but somehow the very habit that made her good for that purpose unfitted her for mine. At first I was extremely pleased with her lady-like air, and it was a satisfaction, on coming to follow her lines, to see how good they were and how far they could lead the pencil. But after a few times I began to find her too insurmountably stiff; do what I would with it my drawing looked like a photograph or a copy of a photograph. Her figure had no variety of expression—she herself had no sense of variety. You may say that this was my business, was only a question of placing her. I placed her in every conceivable position, but she managed to obliterate their differences. She was always a lady certainly, and into the bargain was always the same lady. She was the real thing, but always the same thing. There were moments when I was oppressed by the serenity of her confidence that she *was* the real thing. All her dealings with me and all her husband's were an implication that this was lucky for *me*. Meanwhile I found myself trying to invent types that approached her own, instead of making her own transform itself—in the clever way that was not impossible, for instance, to poor Miss Churm. Arrange as I would and take the precautions I would, she always, in my pictures, came out too tall—landing me in the dilemma of having represented a fascinating woman as seven feet high, which, out of respect perhaps to my own very much scantier inches, was far from my idea of such a personage.

The case was worse with the Major—nothing I could do would keep *him* down, so that he became useful only for the representation of brawny giants. I adored variety and range, I cherished human accidents, the illustrative note; I wanted to characterise closely, and the thing in the world I most hated was the danger of being ridden by a type. I had quarrelled with some of my friends about it—I had parted company with them for maintaining that one *had* to be, and that if the type was beautiful (witness Raphael and Leonardo), the servitude was only a gain. I was neither Leonardo nor Raphael; I might only be a presumptuous young modern searcher, but I held that everything was to be sacrificed sooner than character. When they averred that the haunting type in question could easily *be* character, I retorted, perhaps superficially: "Whose?" It couldn't be everybody's—it might end in being nobody's.

After I had drawn Mrs. Monarch a dozen times I perceived more clearly than before that the value of such a model as Miss Churm resided precisely in the fact that she had no positive stamp, combined of course with the other fact that what she did have was a curious and inexplicable talent for imitation. Her usual appearance was like a curtain which she could draw up at request for a capital performance. This performance was simply suggestive; but it was a word to the wise—it was vivid and pretty. Sometimes, even, I thought it, though she was plain herself, too insipidly pretty; I made it a reproach to her that the figures drawn from her were monotonously (*bêtement*,[3] as we used to say) graceful. Nothing made her

3. Stupidly.

more angry: it was so much her pride to feel that she could sit for characters that had nothing in common with each other. She would accuse me at such moments of taking away her "reputytion."

It suffered a certain shrinkage, this queer quantity, from the repeated visits of my new friends. Miss Churm was greatly in demand, never in want of employment, so I had no scruple in putting her off occasionally, to try them more at my ease. It was certainly amusing at first to do the real thing—it was amusing to do Major Monarch's trousers. They *were* the real thing, even if he did come out colossal. It was amusing to do his wife's back hair (it was so mathematically neat,) and the particular "smart" tension of her tight stays. She lent herself especially to positions in which the face was somewhat averted or blurred; she abounded in lady-like back views and *profils perdus.*[4] When she stood erect she took naturally one of the attitudes in which court-painters represent queens and princesses; so that I found myself wondering whether, to draw out this accomplishment, I couldn't get the editor of the *Cheapside* to publish a really royal romance, "A Tale of Buckingham Palace." Sometimes, however, the real thing and the make-believe came into contact; by which I mean that Miss Churm, keeping an appointment or coming to make one on days when I had much work in hand, encountered her invidious rivals. The encounter was not on their part, for they noticed her no more than if she had been the housemaid; not from intentional loftiness, but simply because, as yet, professionally, they didn't know how to fraternise, as I could guess that they would have liked—or at least that the Major would. They couldn't talk about the omnibus—they always walked; and they didn't know what else to try—she wasn't interested in good trains or cheap claret. Besides, they must have felt—in the air—that she was amused at them, secretly derisive of their ever knowing how. She was not a person to conceal her scepticism if she had had a chance to show it. On the other hand Mrs. Monarch didn't think her tidy; for why else did she take pains to say to me (it was going out of the way, for Mrs. Monarch), that she didn't like dirty women?

One day when my young lady happened to be present with my other sitters (she even dropped in, when it was convenient, for a chat), I asked her to be so good as to lend a hand in getting tea—a service with which she was familiar and which was one of a class that, living as I did in a small way, with slender domestic resources, I often appealed to my models to render. They liked to lay hands on my property, to break the sitting, and sometimes the china—I made them feel Bohemian. The next time I saw Miss Churm after this incident she surprised me greatly by making a scene about it

4. Literally, lost profiles; that is, views slightly from the back so that the profile is invisible.

—she accused me of having wished to humiliate her. She had not resented the outrage at the time, but had seemed obliging and amused, enjoying the comedy of asking Mrs. Monarch, who sat vague and silent, whether she would have cream and sugar, and putting an exaggerated simper into the question. She had tried intonations—as if she too wished to pass for the real thing; till I was afraid my other visitors would take offence.

Oh, *they* were determined not to do this; and their touching patience was the measure of their great need. They would sit by the hour, uncomplaining, till I was ready to use them; they would come back on the chance of being wanted and would walk away cheerfully if they were not. I used to go to the door with them to see in what magnificent order they retreated. I tried to find other employment for them—I introduced them to several artists. But they didn't "take," for reasons I could appreciate, and I became conscious, rather anxiously, that after such disappointments they fell back upon me with a heavier weight. They did me the honour to think that it was I who was most *their* form. They were not picturesque enough for the painters, and in those days there were not so many serious workers in black and white. Besides, they had an eye to the great job I had mentioned to them—they had secretly set their hearts on supplying the right essence for my pictorial vindication of our fine novelist. They knew that for this undertaking I should want no costume-effects, none of the frippery of past ages—that it was a case in which everything would be contemporary and satirical and, presumably, genteel. If I could work them into it their future would be assured, for the labour would of course be long and the occupation steady.

One day Mrs. Monarch came without her husband—she explained his absence by his having had to go to the City.[5] While she sat there in her usual anxious stiffness there came, at the door, a knock which I immediately recognised as the subdued appeal of a model out of work. It was followed by the entrance of a young man whom I easily perceived to be a foreigner and who proved in fact an Italian acquainted with no English word but my name, which he uttered in a way that made it seem to include all others. I had not then visited his country, nor was I proficient in his tongue; but as he was not so meanly constituted—what Italian is?—as to depend only on that member for expression he conveyed to me, in familiar but graceful mimicry, that he was in search of exactly the employment in which the lady before me was engaged. I was not struck with him at first, and while I continued to draw I emitted rough sounds of discouragement and dismissal. He stood his

5. The banking and commercial district of London.

ground, however, not importunately, but with a dumb, dog-like fidelity in his eyes which amounted to innocent impudence—the manner of a devoted servant (he might have been in the house for years), unjustly suspected. Suddenly I saw that this very attitude and expression made a picture, whereupon I told him to sit down and wait till I should be free. There was another picture in the way he obeyed me, and I observed as I worked that there were others still in the way he looked wonderingly, with his head thrown back, about the high studio. He might have been crossing himself in St. Peter's. Before I finished I said to myself: "The fellow's a bankrupt orange-monger, but he's a treasure."

When Mrs. Monarch withdrew he passed across the room like a flash to open the door for her, standing there with the rapt, pure gaze of the young Dante spellbound by the young Beatrice.[6] As I never insisted, in such situations, on the blankness of the British domestic, I reflected that he had the making of a servant (and I needed one, but couldn't pay him to be only that), as well as of a model; in short I made up my mind to adopt my bright adventurer if he would agree to officiate in the double capacity. He jumped at my offer, and in the event my rashness (for I had known nothing about him), was not brought home to me. He proved a sympathetic though a desultory ministrant, and had in a wonderful degree the *sentiment de la pose*.[7] It was uncultivated, instinctive; a part of the happy instinct which had guided him to my door and helped him to spell out my name on the card nailed to it. He had had no other introduction to me than a guess, from the shape of my high north window, seen outside, that my place was a studio and that as a studio it would contain an artist. He had wandered to England in search of fortune, like other itinerants, and had embarked, with a partner and a small green handcart, on the sale of penny ices. The ices had melted away and the partner had dissolved in their train. My young man wore tight yellow trousers with reddish stripes and his name was Oronte. He was sallow but fair, and when I put him into some old clothes of my own he looked like an Englishman. He was as good as Miss Churm, who could look, when required, like an Italian.

IV

I thought Mrs. Monarch's face slightly convulsed when, on her coming back with her husband, she found Oronte installed. It was

6. Dante Alighieri (1265–1321) was the Italian poet of *The Divine Comedy*. Beatrice is a heavenly figure in that poem (as well as in Dante's *Vita Nuova*), inspired by an earthly love.
7. A real feeling for posing.

strange to have to recognise in a scrap of a lazzarone[8] a competitor
to her magnificent Major. It was she who scented danger first, for
the Major was anecdotically unconscious. But Oronte gave us tea,
with a hundred eager confusions (he had never seen such a queer
process), and I think she thought better of me for having at last an
"establishment." They saw a couple of drawings that I had made of
the establishment, and Mrs. Monarch hinted that it never would
have struck her that he had sat for them. "Now the drawings you
make from *us*, they look exactly like us," she reminded me, smiling
in triumph; and I recognised that this was indeed just their defect.
When I drew the Monarchs I couldn't, somehow, get away from
them—get into the character I wanted to represent; and I had not
the least desire my model should be discoverable in my picture.
Miss Churm never was, and Mrs. Monarch thought I hid her, very
properly, because she was vulgar; whereas if she was lost it was only
as the dead who go to heaven are lost—in the gain of an angel the
more.

By this time I had got a certain start with "Rutland Ramsay," the
first novel in the great projected series; that is I had produced a
dozen drawings, several with the help of the Major and his wife,
and I had sent them in for approval. My understanding with the
publishers, as I have already hinted, had been that I was to be left
to do my work, in this particular case, as I liked, with the whole
book committed to me; but my connection with the rest of the
series was only contingent. There were moments when, frankly, it
was a comfort to have the real thing under one's hand; for there
were characters in "Rutland Ramsay" that were very much like it.
There were people presumably as straight as the Major and women
of as good a fashion as Mrs. Monarch. There was a great deal of
country-house life—treated, it is true, in a fine, fanciful, ironical,
generalised way—and there was a considerable implication of
knickerbockers and kilts. There were certain things I had to settle
at the outset; such things for instance as the exact appearance of
the hero, the particular bloom of the heroine. The author of course
gave me a lead, but there was a margin for interpretation. I took
the Monarchs into my confidence, I told them frankly what I was
about, I mentioned my embarrassments and alternatives. "Oh, take
him!" Mrs. Monarch murmured sweetly, looking at her husband;
and "What could you want better than my wife?" the Major inquired, with the comfortable candour that now prevailed between
us.

I was not obliged to answer these remarks—I was only obliged
to place my sitters. I was not easy in mind, and I postponed, a little

8. Neapolitan rascal.

timidly perhaps, the solution of the question. The book was a large canvas, the other figures were numerous, and I worked off at first some of the episodes in which the hero and the heroine were not concerned. When once I had set *them* up I should have to stick to them—I couldn't make my young man seven feet high in one place and five feet nine in another. I inclined on the whole to the latter measurement, though the Major more than once reminded me that *he* looked about as young as anyone. It was indeed quite possible to arrange him, for the figure, so that it would have been difficult to detect his age. After the spontaneous Oronte had been with me a month, and after I had given him to understand several different times that his native exuberance would presently constitute an insurmountable barrier to our further intercourse, I waked to a sense of his heroic capacity. He was only five feet seven, but the remaining inches were latent. I tried him almost secretly at first, for I was really rather afraid of the judgment my other models would pass on such a choice. If they regarded Miss Churm as little better than a snare, what would they think of the representation by a person so little the real thing as an Italian street-vendor of a protagonist formed by a public school?

If I went a little in fear of them it was not because they bullied me, because they had got an oppressive foothold, but because in their really pathetic decorum and mysteriously permanent newness they counted on me so intensely. I was therefore very glad when Jack Hawley came home: he was always of such good counsel. He painted badly himself, but there was no one like him for putting his finger on the place. He had been absent from England for a year; he had been somewhere—I don't remember where—to get a fresh eye. I was in a good deal of dread of any such organ, but we were old friends; he had been away for months and a sense of emptiness was creeping into my life. I hadn't dodged a missile for a year.

He came back with a fresh eye, but with the same old black velvet blouse, and the first evening he spent in my studio we smoked cigarettes till the small hours. He had done no work himself, he had only got the eye; so the field was clear for the production of my little things. He wanted to see what I had done for the *Cheap-side*, but he was disappointed in the exhibition. That at least seemed the meaning of two or three comprehensive groans which, as he lounged on my big divan, on a folded leg, looking at my latest drawings, issued from his lips with the smoke of the cigarette.

"What's the matter with you?" I asked.

"What's the matter with *you*?"

"Nothing save that I'm mystified."

"You are indeed. You're quite off the hinge. What's the meaning of this new fad?" And he tossed me, with visible irreverence, a drawing in which I happened to have depicted both my majestic models. I asked if he didn't think it good, and he replied that it struck him as execrable, given the sort of thing I had always represented myself to him as wishing to arrive at; but I let that pass, I was so anxious to see exactly what he meant. The two figures in the picture looked colossal, but I supposed this was *not* what he meant, inasmuch as, for aught he knew to the contrary, I might have been trying for that. I maintained that I was working exactly in the same way as when he last had done me the honour to commend me. "Well, there's a big hole somewhere," he answered; "wait a bit and I'll discover it." I depended upon him to do so: where else was the fresh eye? But he produced at last nothing more luminous than "I don't know—I don't like your types." This was lame, for a critic who had never consented to discuss with me anything but the question of execution, the direction of strokes and the mystery of values.

"In the drawings you've been looking at I think my types are very handsome."

"Oh, they won't do!"

"I've had a couple of new models."

"I see you have. *They* won't do."

"Are you very sure of that?"

"Absolutely—they're stupid."

"You mean *I* am—for I ought to get round that."

"You *can't*—with such people. Who are they?"

I told him, as far as was necessary, and he declared, heartlessly: "*Ce sont des gens qu'il faut mettre à la porte.*"[9]

"You've never seen them; they're awfully good," I compassionately objected.

"Not seen them? Why, all this recent work of yours drops to pieces with them. It's all I want to see of them."

"No one else has said anything against it—the *Cheapside* people are pleased."

"Everyone else is an ass, and the *Cheapside* people the biggest asses of all. Come, don't pretend, at this time of day, to have pretty illusions about the public, especially about publishers and editors. It's not for *such* animals you work—it's for those who know, *coloro che sanno*,[1] so keep straight for *me* if you can't keep straight for yourself. There's a certain sort of thing you tried for from the first —and a very good thing it is. But this twaddle isn't *in* it." When I talked with Hawley later about "Rutland Ramsay" and its possible

9. They are people one has to put out the door.
1. In Dante's *Inferno* (IV, 131) Aristotle is referred to as "il maestro di color che sanno," that is, as "the master of those who know." James's *coloro* is the usual form; Dante with poetic license drops the final *o* for the sake of the rhythm.

successors he declared that I must get back into my boat again or I would go to the bottom. His voice in short was the voice of warning.

I noted the warning, but I didn't turn my friends out of doors. They bored me a good deal; but the very fact that they bored me admonished me not to sacrifice them—if there was anything to be done with them—simply to irritation. As I look back at this phase they seem to me to have pervaded my life not a little. I have a vision of them as most of the time in my studio, seated, against the wall, on an old velvet bench to be out of the way, and looking like a pair of patient courtiers in a royal ante-chamber. I am convinced that during the coldest weeks of the winter they held their ground because it saved them fire. Their newness was losing its gloss, and it was impossible not to feel that they were objects of charity. Whenever Miss Churm arrived they went away, and after I was fairly launched in "Rutland Ramsay" Miss Churm arrived pretty often. They managed to express to me tacitly that they supposed I wanted her for the low life of the book, and I let them suppose it, since they had attempted to study the work—it was lying about the studio—without discovering that it dealt only with the highest circles. They had dipped into the most brilliant of our novelists without deciphering many passages. I still took an hour from them, now and again, in spite of Jack Hawley's warning: it would be time enough to dismiss them, if dismissal should be necessary, when the rigour of the season was over. Hawley had made their acquaintance—he had met them at my fireside—and thought them a ridiculous pair. Learning that he was a painter they tried to approach him, to show him too that they were the real thing; but he looked at them, across the big room, as if they were miles away: they were a compendium of everything that he most objected to in the social system of his country. Such people as that, all convention and patent-leather, with ejaculations that stopped conversation, had no business in a studio. A studio was a place to learn to see, and how could you see through a pair of feather beds?

The main inconvenience I suffered at their hands was that, at first, I was shy of letting them discover how my artful little servant had begun to sit to me for "Rutland Ramsay." They knew that I had been odd enough (they were prepared by this time to allow oddity to artists), to pick a foreign vagabond out of the streets, when I might have had a person with whiskers and credentials; but it was some time before they learned how high I rated his accomplishments. They found him in an attitude more than once, but they never doubted I was doing him as an organ-grinder. There were several things they never guessed, and one of them was that for a striking scene in the novel, in which a footman briefly figured, it occurred to me to make use of Major Monarch as the menial. I kept putting this off, I didn't like to ask him to don the livery—besides the difficulty of finding a livery to fit him. At last, one day late in the winter, when I was at work on the despised Oronte (he caught one's idea in an instant), and was in the glow of feeling that I was going very straight, they came in, the Major and his wife, with their society laugh about nothing (there was less and less to laugh at), like country-callers—they always reminded me of that—who have walked across the park after church and are presently persuaded to stay to luncheon. Luncheon was over, but they could stay to tea—I knew they wanted it. The fit was on me, however, and I couldn't let my ardour cool and my work wait, with the fading daylight, while my model prepared it. So I asked Mrs. Monarch if she would mind laying it out—a request which, for an instant, brought all the blood to her face. Her eyes were on her husband's for a second, and some mute telegraphy passed between them. Their folly was over the next instant; his cheerful shrewdness put an end to it. So far from pitying their wounded pride, I must add, I was moved to give it as complete a lesson as I could. They bustled about together and got out the cups and saucers and made the kettle boil. I know they felt as if they were waiting on my servant, and when the tea was prepared I said: "He'll have a cup, please—he's tired." Mrs. Monarch brought him one where he stood, and he took it from her as if he had been a gentleman at a party, squeezing a crush-hat with an elbow.

Then it came over me that she had made a great effort for me—made it with a kind of nobleness—and that I owed her a compensation. Each time I saw her after this I wondered what the compensation could be. I couldn't go on doing the wrong thing to oblige them. Oh, it *was* the wrong thing, the stamp of the work for which they sat—Hawley was not the only person to say it now. I sent in a large number of the drawings I had made for "Rutland Ramsay," and I received a warning that was more to the point than Hawley's. The artistic adviser of the house for which I was working was of opinion that many of my illustrations were not what had been looked for. Most of these illustrations were the subjects in which the Monarchs had figured. Without going into the question of what *had* been looked for, I saw at this rate I shouldn't get the other books to do. I hurled myself in despair upon Miss Churm, I put her through all her paces. I not only adopted Oronte publicly as my hero, but one morning when the Major looked in to see if I didn't require him to finish a figure for the *Cheapside*, for which he had begun to sit the week before, I told him that I had changed my mind—I would do the drawing from my man. At this my visitor turned pale and stood looking at me. "Is *he* your idea of an English gentleman?" he asked.

I was disappointed, I was nervous, I wanted to get on with my work; so I replied with irritation: "Oh, my dear Major—I can't be ruined for *you!*"

He stood another moment; then, without a word, he quitted the studio. I drew a long breath when he was gone, for I said to myself that I shouldn't see him again. I had not told him definitely that I was in danger of having my work rejected, but I was vexed at his not having felt the catastrophe in the air, read with me the moral of our fruitless collaboration, the lesson that, in the deceptive atmosphere of art, even the highest respectability may fail of being plastic.

I didn't owe my friends money, but I did see them again. They re-appeared together, three days later, and under the circumstances there was something tragic in the fact. It was a proof to me that they could find nothing else in life to do. They had threshed the matter out in a dismal conference—they had digested the bad news that they were not in for the series. If they were not useful to me even for the *Cheapside* their function seemed difficult to determine, and I could only judge at first that they had come, forgivingly, decorously, to take a last leave. This made me rejoice in secret that I had little leisure for a scene; for I had placed both my other models in position together and I was pegging away at a drawing from which I hoped to derive glory. It had been suggested by the passage in which Rutland Ramsay, drawing up a chair to Artemisia's piano-stool, says extraordinary things to her while she ostensibly fingers out a difficult piece of music. I had done Miss Churm at the piano before—it was an attitude in which she knew how to take on an absolutely poetic grace. I wished the two figures to "compose" together, intensely, and my little Italian had entered perfectly into my conception. The pair were vividly before me, the piano had been pulled out; it was a charming picture of blended youth and murmured love, which I had only to catch and keep. My visitors stood and looked at it, and I was friendly to them over my shoulder.

They made no response, but I was used to silent company and went on with my work, only a little disconcerted (even though exhilarated by the sense that *this* was at least the ideal thing), at not having got rid of them after all. Presently I heard Mrs. Monarch's sweet voice beside, or rather above me: "I wish her hair was a little better done." I looked up and she was staring with a strange fixedness at Miss Churm, whose back was turned to her. "Do you mind my just touching it?" she went on—a question which made me spring up for an instant, as with the instinctive fear that she might do the young lady a harm. But she quieted me with a glance I shall never forget—I confess I should like to have been able to paint *that*—and went for a moment to my model. She spoke to her softly, laying a hand upon her shoulder and bending over her; and as the girl, understanding, gratefully assented, she disposed her rough curls, with a few quick passes, in such a way as to make Miss Churm's head twice as charming. It was one of the most heroic personal services I have ever seen rendered. Then Mrs. Monarch turned away with a low sigh and, looking about her as if for something to do, stooped to the floor with a noble humility and picked up a dirty rag that had dropped out of my paint-box.

The Major meanwhile had also been looking for something to do and, wandering to the other end of the studio, saw before him my breakfast things, neglected, unremoved. "I say, can't I be useful *here*?" he called out to me with an irrepressible quaver. I assented with a laugh that I fear was awkward and for the next ten minutes, while I worked, I heard the light clatter of china and the tinkle of spoons and glass. Mrs. Monarch assisted her husband—they washed up my crockery, they put it away. They wandered off into my little scullery, and I afterwards found that they had cleaned my knives and that my slender stock of plate had an unprecedented surface. When it came over me, the latent eloquence of what they were doing, I confess that my drawing was blurred for a moment —the picture swam. They had accepted their failure, but they couldn't accept their fate. They had bowed their heads in bewilderment to the perverse and cruel law in virtue of which the real thing could be so much less precious than the unreal; but they didn't want to starve. If my servants were my models, my models might be my servants. They would reverse the parts—the others would sit for the ladies and gentleman, and *they* would do the work. They would still be in the studio—it was an intense dumb appeal to me not to turn them out. "Take us on," they wanted to say— "we'll do *anything*."

When all this hung before me the *afflatus* vanished—my pencil dropped from my hand. My sitting was spoiled and I got rid of my sitters, who were also evidently rather mystified and awestruck. Then, alone with the Major and his wife, I had a most uncomfortable moment. He put their prayer into a single sentence: "I say, you know—just let *us* do for you, can't you?" I couldn't—it was dreadful to see them emptying my slops; but I pretended I could, to oblige them, for about a week. Then I gave them a sum of money to go away; and I never saw them again. I obtained the remaining books, but my friend Hawley repeats that Major and Mrs. Monarch did me a permanent harm, got me into a second-rate trick. If it be true I am content to have paid the price—for the memory.

The Middle Years[†]

The April day was soft and bright, and poor Dencombe, happy in
the conceit of reasserted strength, stood in the garden of the hotel,
comparing, with a deliberation in which, however, there was still
something of languor, the attractions of easy strolls. He liked the
feeling of the south, so far as you could have it in the north, he
liked the sandy cliffs and the clustered pines, he liked even the
colourless sea. "Bournemouth[1] as a health-resort" had sounded like
a mere advertisement, but now he was reconciled to the prosaic.
The sociable country postman, passing through the garden, had just
given him a small parcel, which he took out with him, leaving the
hotel to the right and creeping to a convenient bench that he knew
of, a safe recess in the cliff. It looked to the south, to the tinted
walls of the Island, and was protected behind by the sloping shoulder of the down. He was tired enough when he reached it, and for
a moment he was disappointed; he was better, of course, but better,
after all, than what? He should never again, as at one or two great
moments of the past, be better than himself. The infinite of life
had gone, and what was left of the dose was a small glass engraved
like a thermometer by the apothecary. He sat and stared at the sea,
which appeared all surface and twinkle, far shallower than the spirit
of man. It was the abyss of human illusion that was the real, the
tideless deep. He held his packet, which had come by book-post,
unopened on his knee, liking, in the lapse of so many joys (his
illness had made him feel his age), to know that it was there, but
taking for granted there could be no complete renewal of the pleasure, dear to young experience, of seeing one's self "just out."[2] Dencombe, who had a reputation, had come out too often and knew
too well in advance how he should look.

His postponement associated itself vaguely, after a little, with a

---

† "The Middle Years" first appeared in *Scribner's Magazine*, April 1893. Its first publication
   in a book was in *Terminations* (London: William Heinemann, 1895). This text is here
   reprinted.
1. On the English Channel coast and famous for its pines and clear air. Though Bournemouth is in northern Europe, some of the vegetation in the area resembles that of
   southern Europe. The island with the tinted walls may be the Isle of Wight, though
   almost fifteen miles distant and more east than south.
2. Just published.

group of three persons, two ladies and a young man, whom, beneath him, straggling and seemingly silent, he could see move slowly together along the sands. The gentleman had his head bent over a book and was occasionally brought to a stop by the charm of this volume, which, as Dencombe could perceive even at a distance, had a cover alluringly red. Then his companions, going a little further, waited for him to come up, poking their parasols into the beach, looking around them at the sea and sky and clearly sensible of the beauty of the day. To these things the young man with the book was still more clearly indifferent; lingering, credulous, absorbed, he was an object of envy to an observer from whose connection with literature all such artlessness had faded. One of the ladies was large and mature; the other had the spareness of comparative youth and of a social situation possibly inferior. The large lady carried back Dencombe's imagination to the age of crinoline; she wore a hat of the shape of a mushroom, decorated with a blue veil, and had the air, in her aggressive amplitude, of clinging to a vanished fashion or even a lost cause. Presently her companion produced from under the folds of a mantle a limp, portable chair which she stiffened out and of which the large lady took possession. This act, and something in the movement of either party, instantly characterised the performers—they performed for Dencombe's recreation—as opulent matron and humble dependent. What, moreover, was the use of being an approved novelist if one couldn't establish a relation between such figures; the clever theory, for instance, that the young man was the son of the opulent matron, and that the humble dependant, the daughter of a clergyman or an officer, nourished a secret passion for him? Was that not visible from the way she stole behind her protectress to look back at him?—back to where he had let himself come to a full stop when his mother sat down to rest. His book was a novel; it had the catchpenny cover, and while the romance of life stood neglected at his side he lost himself in that of the circulating library. He moved mechanically to where the sand was softer, and ended by plumping down in it to finish his chapter at his ease. The humble dependant, discouraged by his remoteness, wandered, with a martyred droop of the head, in another direction, and the exorbitant lady, watching the waves, offered a confused resemblance to a flying-machine that had broken down.

When his drama began to fail Dencombe remembered that he had, after all, another pastime. Though such promptitude on the part of the publisher was rare, he was already able to draw from its wrapper his "latest," perhaps his last. The cover of "The Middle Years" was duly meretricious, the smell of the fresh pages the very odour of sanctity; but for the moment he went no further—he had become conscious of a strange alienation. He had forgotten what

his book was about. Had the assault of his old ailment, which he
had so fallaciously come to Bournemouth to ward off, interposed
utter blankness as to what had preceded it? He had finished the
revision of proof before quitting London, but his subsequent fortnight in bed had passed the sponge over colour. He couldn't have
chanted to himself a single sentence, couldn't have turned with
curiosity or confidence to any particular page. His subject had already gone from him, leaving scarcely a superstition behind. He
uttered a low moan as he breathed the chill of this dark void, so
desperately it seemed to represent the completion of a sinister process. The tears filled his mild eyes; something precious had passed
away. This was the pang that had been sharpest during the last few
years—the sense of ebbing time, of shrinking opportunity; and now
he felt not so much that his last chance was going as that it was
gone indeed. He had done all that he should ever do, and yet he
had not done what he wanted. This was the laceration—that practically his career was over: it was as violent as a rough hand at his
throat. He rose from his seat nervously, like a creature hunted by
a dread; then he fell back in his weakness and nervously opened
his book. It was a single volume; he preferred single volumes and
aimed at a rare compression.[3] He began to read, and little by little,
in this occupation, he was pacified and reassured. Everything came
back to him, but came back with a wonder, came back, above all,
with a high and magnificent beauty. He read his own prose, he
turned his own leaves, and had, as he sat there with the spring
sunshine on the page, an emotion peculiar and intense. His career
was over, no doubt, but it was over, after all, with *that*.

He had forgotten during his illness the work of the previous year;
but what he had chiefly forgotten was that it was extraordinarily
good. He lived once more into his story and was drawn down, as
by a siren's hand, to where, in the dim underworld of fiction, the
great glazed tank of art, strange silent subjects float. He recognised
his motive and surrendered to his talent. Never, probably, had that
talent, such as it was, been so fine. His difficulties were still there,
but what was also there, to his perception, though probably, alas!
to nobody's else, was the art that in most cases had surmounted
them. In his surprised enjoyment of this ability he had a glimpse of
a possible reprieve. Surely its force was not spent—there was life
and service in it yet. It had not come to him easily, it had been
backward and roundabout. It was the child of time, the nursling of
delay; he had struggled and suffered for it, making sacrifices not to
be counted, and now that it was really mature was it to cease to

3. In the nineteenth century long novels were usually published in several volumes—often
three. James himself also "aimed" at compression.

yield, to confess itself brutally beaten? There was an infinite charm for Dencombe in feeling as he had never felt before that diligence *vincit omnia*.[4] The result produced in his little book was somehow a result beyond his conscious intention: it was as if he had planted his genius, had trusted his method, and they had grown up and flowered with this sweetness. If the achievement had been real, however, the process had been manful enough. What he saw so intensely to-day, what he felt as a nail driven in, was that only now, at the very last, had he come into possession. His development had been abnormally slow, almost grotesquely gradual. He had been hindered and retarded by experience, and for long periods had only groped his way. It had taken too much of his life to produce too little of his art. The art had come, but it had come after everything else. At such a rate a first existence was too short—long enough only to collect material; so that to fructify, to use the material, one must have a second age, an extension. This extension was what poor Dencombe sighed for. As he turned the last leaves of his volume he murmured: "Ah for another go!—ah for a better chance!"

The three persons he had observed on the sands had vanished and then reappeared; they had now wandered up a path, an artificial and easy ascent, which led to the top of the cliff. Dencombe's bench was half-way down, on a sheltered ledge, and the large lady, a massive, heterogeneous person, with bold black eyes and kind red cheeks, now took a few moments to rest. She wore dirty gauntlets and immense diamond ear-rings; at first she looked vulgar, but she contradicted this announcement in an agreeable off-hand tone. While her companions stood waiting for her she spread her skirts on the end of Dencombe's seat. The young man had gold spectacles, through which, with his finger still in his red-covered book, he glanced at the volume, bound in the same shade of the same colour, lying on the lap of the original occupant of the bench. After an instant Dencombe understood that he was struck with a resemblance, had recognised the gilt stamp on the crimson cloth, was reading "The Middle Years," and now perceived that somebody else had kept pace with him. The stranger was startled, possibly even a little ruffled, to find that he was not the only person who had been favoured with an early copy. The eyes of the two proprietors met for a moment, and Dencombe borrowed amusement from the expression of those of his competitor, those, it might even be inferred, of his admirer. They confessed to some resentment—they seemed to say: "Hang it, has he got it *already*?—Of course he's a brute of

---

4. Conquers all. Cf. *Amor vincit omnia* ("Love conquers all"), a proverbial phrase found in Virgil's *Eclogues* (X, 69) and inscribed on the brooch of Chaucer's Prioress.

a reviewer!" Dencombe shuffled his copy out of sight while the opulent matron, rising from her repose, broke out: "I feel already the good of this air!"

"I can't say I do," said the angular lady. "I find myself quite let down."

"I find myself horribly hungry. At what time did you order lunch?" her protectress pursued.

The young person put the question by. "Doctor Hugh always orders it."

"I ordered nothing to-day—I'm going to make you diet," said their comrade.

"Then I shall go home and sleep. *Qui dort dîne!*"[5]

"Can I trust you to Miss Vernham?" asked Doctor Hugh of his elder companion.

"Don't I trust *you?*" she archly inquired.

"Not too much!" Miss Vernham, with her eyes on the ground, permitted herself to declare. "You must come with us at least to the house," she went on, while the personage on whom they appeared to be in attendance began to mount higher. She had got a little out of ear-shot; nevertheless Miss Vernham became, so far as Dencombe was concerned, less distinctly audible to murmur to the young man: "I don't think you realise all you owe the Countess!"

Absently, a moment, Doctor Hugh caused his gold-rimmed spectacles to shine at her.

"Is that the way I strike you? I see—I see!"

"She's awfully good to us," continued Miss Vernham, compelled by her interlocutor's immovability to stand there in spite of his discussion of private matters. Of what use would it have been that Dencombe should be sensitive to shades had he not detected in that immovability a strange influence from the quiet old convalescent in the great tweed cape? Miss Vernham appeared suddenly to become aware of some such connection, for she added in a moment: "If you want to sun yourself here you can come back after you've seen us home."

Doctor Hugh, at this, hesitated, and Dencombe, in spite of a desire to pass for unconscious, risked a covert glance at him. What his eyes met this time, as it happened, was on the part of the young lady a queer stare, naturally vitreous, which made her aspect remind him of some figure (he couldn't name it) in a play or a novel, some sinister governess or tragic old maid. She seemed to scrutinise him, to challenge him, to say, from general spite: "What have you got to do with us?" At the same instant the rich humour of the Countess

5. Literally, "He who sleeps dines"; i.e., a good sleep is worth a dinner.

reached them from above: "Come, come, my little lambs, you should follow your old *bergère!*"[6] Miss Vernham turned away at this, pursuing the ascent, and Doctor Hugh, after another mute appeal to Dencombe and a moment's evident demur, deposited his book on the bench, as if to keep his place or even as a sign that he would return, and bounded without difficulty up the rougher part of the cliff.

Equally innocent and infinite are the pleasures of observation and the resources engendered by the habit of analysing life. It amused poor Dencombe, as he dawdled in his tepid air-bath, to think that he was waiting for a revelation of something at the back of a fine young mind. He looked hard at the book on the end of the bench, but he wouldn't have touched it for the world. It served his purpose to have a theory which should not be exposed to refutation. He already felt better of his melancholy; he had, according to his old formula, put his head at the window. A passing Countess could draw off the fancy when, like the elder of the ladies who had just retreated, she was as obvious as the giantess of a caravan. It was indeed general views that were terrible; short ones, contrary to an opinion sometimes expressed, were the refuge, were the remedy. Doctor Hugh couldn't possibly be anything but a reviewer who had understandings for early copies with publishers or with newspapers. He reappeared in a quarter of an hour, with visible relief at finding Dencombe on the spot, and the gleam of white teeth in an embarrassed but generous smile. He was perceptibly disappointed at the eclipse of the other copy of the book; it was a pretext the less for speaking to the stranger. But he spoke notwithstanding; he held up his own copy and broke out pleadingly:

"*Do* say, if you have occasion to speak of it, that it's the best thing he has done yet!"

Dencombe responded with a laugh: "Done yet" was so amusing to him, made such a grand avenue of the future. Better still, the young man took *him* for a reviewer. He pulled out "The Middle Years" from under his cape, but instinctively concealed any tell-tale look of fatherhood. This was partly because a person was always a fool for calling attention to his work. "Is that what you're going to say yourself?" he inquired of his visitor.

"I'm not quite sure I shall write anything. I don't, as a regular thing—I enjoy in peace. But it's awfully fine."

Dencombe debated a moment. If his interlocutor had begun to abuse him he would have confessed on the spot to his identity, but there was no harm in drawing him on a little to praise. He drew him on with such success that in a few moments his new acquain-

6. Shepherdess, guardian.

tance, seated by his side, was confessing candidly that Dencombe's novels were the only ones he could read a second time. He had come the day before from London, where a friend of his, a journalist, had lent him his copy of the last—the copy sent to the office of the journal and already the subject of a "notice" which, as was pretended there (but one had to allow for "swagger") it had taken a full quarter of an hour to prepare. He intimated that he was ashamed for his friend, and in the case of a work demanding and repaying study, of such inferior manners; and, with his fresh appreciation and inexplicable wish to express it, he speedily became for poor Dencombe a remarkable, a delightful apparition. Chance had brought the weary man of letters face to face with the greatest admirer in the new generation whom it was supposable he possessed. The admirer, in truth, was mystifying, so rare a case was it to find a bristling young doctor—he looked like a German physiologist—enamoured of literary form. It was an accident, but happier than most accidents, so that Dencombe, exhilarated as well as confounded, spent half an hour in making his visitor talk while he kept himself quiet. He explained his premature possession of "The Middle Years" by an allusion to the friendship of the publisher, who, knowing he was at Bournemouth for his health, had paid him this graceful attention. He admitted that he had been ill, for Doctor Hugh would infallibly have guessed it; he even went so far as to wonder whether he mightn't look for some hygenic "tip" from a personage combining so bright an enthusiasm with a presumable knowledge of the remedies now in vogue. It would shake his faith a little perhaps to have to take a doctor seriously who could take *him* so seriously, but he enjoyed this gushing modern youth and he felt with an acute pang that there would still be work to do in a world in which such odd combinations were presented. It was not true, what he had tried for renunciation's sake to believe, that all the combinations were exhausted. They were not, they were not—they were infinite: the exhaustion was in the miserable artist.

Doctor Hugh was an ardent physiologist, saturated with the spirit of the age—in other words he had just taken his degree; but he was independent and various, he talked like a man who would have preferred to love literature best. He would fain have made fine phrases, but nature had denied him the trick. Some of the finest in "The Middle Years" had struck him inordinately, and he took the liberty of reading them to Dencombe in support of his plea. He grew vivid, in the balmy air, to his companion, for whose deep refreshment he seemed to have been sent; and was particularly ingenuous in describing how recently he had become acquainted, and how instantly infatuated, with the only man who had put flesh between the ribs of an art that was starving on superstitions. He had not yet written to him—he was deterred by a sentiment of respect. Dencombe at this moment felicitated himself more than ever on having never answered the photographers. His visitor's attitude promised him a luxury of intercourse, but he surmised that a certain security in it, for Doctor Hugh, would depend not a little on the Countess. He learned without delay with what variety of Countess they were concerned, as well as the nature of the tie that united the curious trio. The large lady, an Englishwoman by birth and the daughter of a celebrated baritone, whose taste, without his talent, she had inherited, was the widow of a French nobleman and mistress of all that remained of the handsome fortune, the fruit of her father's earnings, that had constituted her dower. Miss Vernham, an odd creature but an accomplished pianist, was attached to her person at a salary. The Countess was generous, independent, eccentric; she travelled with her minstrel and her medical man. Ignorant and passionate, she had nevertheless moments in which she was almost irresistible. Dencombe saw her sit for her portrait in Doctor Hugh's free sketch, and felt the picture of his young friend's relation to her frame itself in his mind. This young friend, for a representative of the new psychology, was himself easily hypnotised, and if he became abnormally communicative it was only a sign of his real subjection. Dencombe did accordingly what he wanted with him, even without being known as Dencombe.

Taken ill on a journey in Switzerland the Countess had picked him up at an hotel, and the accident of his happening to please her had made her offer him, with her imperious liberality, terms that couldn't fail to dazzle a practitioner without patients and whose resources had been drained dry by his studies. It was not the way he would have elected to spend his time, but it was time that would pass quickly, and meanwhile she was wonderfully kind. She exacted perpetual attention, but it was impossible not to like her. He gave details about his queer patient, a "type" if there ever was one, who had in connection with her flushed obesity and in addition to the morbid strain of a violent and aimless will a grave organic disorder; but he came back to his loved novelist, whom he was so good as to pronounce more essentially a poet than many of those who went in for verse, with a zeal excited, as all his indiscretion had been excited, by the happy chance of Dencombe's sympathy and the coincidence of their occupation. Dencombe had confessed to a slight personal acquaintance with the author of "The Middle Years," but had not felt himself as ready as he could have wished when his companion, who had never yet encountered a being so privileged, began to be eager for particulars. He even thought that Doctor Hugh's eye at that moment emitted a glimmer of suspicion. But the young man was too inflamed to be shrewd and repeatedly caught up the book to exclaim: "Did you notice this?" or "Weren't you immensely struck with that?" "There's a beautiful passage toward the end," he broke out; and again he laid his hand upon the volume. As he turned the pages he came upon something else, while Dencombe saw him suddenly change colour. He had taken up, as it lay on the bench, Dencombe's copy instead of his own, and his neighbour immediately guessed the reason of his start. Doctor Hugh looked grave an instant; then he said: "I see you've been altering the text!" Dencombe was a passionate corrector, a fingerer of style; the last thing he ever arrived at was a form final for himself. His ideal would have been to publish secretly, and then, on the published text, treat himself to the terrified revise, sacrificing always a first edition and beginning for posterity and even for the collectors, poor dears, with a second. This morning in "The Middle Years," his pencil had pricked a dozen lights. He was amused at the effect of the young man's reproach; for an instant it made him change colour. He stammered, at any rate, ambiguously; then, through a blur of ebbing consciousness, saw Doctor Hugh's mystified eyes. He only had time to feel he was about to be ill again—that emotion, excitement, fatigue, the heat of the sun, the solicitation of the air, had combined to play him a trick, before, stretching out a hand to his visitor with a plaintive cry, he lost his senses altogether.

Later he knew that he had fainted and that Doctor Hugh had got him home in a bath-chair, the conductor of which, prowling within hail for custom, had happened to remember seeing him in the garden of the hotel. He had recovered his perception in the transit, and had, in bed, that afternoon, a vague recollection of Doctor Hugh's young face, as they went together, bent over him in a comforting laugh and expressive of something more than a suspicion of his identity. That identity was ineffaceable now, and all the more that he was disappointed, disgusted. He had been rash, been stupid, had gone out too soon, stayed out too long. He oughtn't to have exposed himself to strangers, he ought to have taken his servant. He felt as if he had fallen into a hole too deep to descry any little patch of heaven. He was confused about the time that had elapsed —he pieced the fragments together. He had seen his doctor, the real one, the one who had treated him from the first and who had again been very kind. His servant was in and out on tiptoe, looking very wise after the fact. He said more than once something about the sharp young gentleman. The rest was vagueness, in so far as it wasn't despair. The vagueness, however, justified itself by dreams, dozing anxieties from which he finally emerged to the consciousness of a dark room and a shaded candle.

"You'll be all right again—I know all about you now," said a voice near him that he knew to be young. Then his meeting with Doctor

Hugh came back. He was too discouraged to joke about it yet, but he was able to perceive, after a little, that the interest of it was intense for his visitor. "Of course I can't attend you professionally —you've got your own man, with whom I've talked and who's excellent," Doctor Hugh went on. "But you must let me come to see you as a good friend. I've just looked in before going to bed. You're doing beautifully, but it's a good job I was with you on the cliff. I shall come in early to-morrow. I want to do something for you. I want to do everything. You've done a tremendous lot for me." The young man held his hand, hanging over him, and poor Dencombe, weakly aware of this living pressure, simply lay there and accepted his devotion. He couldn't do anything less—he needed help too much.

The idea of the help he needed was very present to him that night, which he spent in a lucid stillness, an intensity of thought that constituted a reaction from his hours of stupor. He was lost, he was lost—he was lost if he couldn't be saved. He was not afraid of suffering, of death; he was not even in love with life; but he had had a deep demonstration of desire. It came over him in the long, quiet hours that only with "The Middle Years" had he taken his flight; only on that day, visited by soundless processions, had he recognised his kingdom. He had had a revelation of his range. What he dreaded was the idea that his reputation should stand on the unfinished. It was not with his past but with his future that it should properly be concerned. Illness and age rose before him like spectres with pitiless eyes: how was he to bribe such fates to give him the second chance? He had had the one chance that all men have—he had had the chance of life. He went to sleep again very late, and when he awoke Doctor Hugh was sitting by his head. There was already, by this time, something beautifully familiar in him.

"Don't think I've turned out your physician," he said; "I'm acting with his consent. He has been here and seen you. Somehow he seems to trust me. I told him how we happened to come together yesterday, and he recognises that I've a peculiar right."

Dencombe looked at him with a calculating earnestness. "How have you squared the Countess?"

The young man blushed a little, but he laughed. "Oh, never mind the Countess!"

"You told me she was very exacting."

Doctor Hugh was silent a moment. "So she is."

"And Miss Vernham's an *intrigante*."[7]

"How do you know that?"

7. Schemer.

"I know everything. One *has* to, to write decently!"

"I think she's mad," said limpid Doctor Hugh.

"Well, don't quarrel with the Countess—she's a present help to you."

"I don't quarrel," Doctor Hugh replied. "But I don't get on with silly women." Presently he added: "You seem very much alone."

"That often happens at my age. I've outlived, I've lost by the way."

Doctor Hugh hesitated; then surmounting a soft scruple: "Whom have you lost?"

"Every one."

"Ah, no," the young man murmured, laying a hand on his arm.

"I once had a wife—I once had a son. My wife died when my child was born, and my boy, at school, was carried off by typhoid."

"I wish I'd been there!" said Doctor Hugh simply.

"Well—if you're here!" Dencombe answered, with a smile that, in spite of dimness, showed how much he liked to be sure of his companion's whereabouts.

"You talk strangely of your age. You're not old."

"Hypocrite—so early!"

"I speak physiologically."

"That's the way I've been speaking for the last five years, and it's exactly what I've been saying to myself. It isn't till we *are* old that we begin to tell ourselves we're not!"

"Yet I know I myself am young," Doctor Hugh declared.

"Not so well as I!" laughed his patient, whose visitor indeed would have established the truth in question by the honesty with which he changed the point of view, remarking that it must be one of the charms of age—at any rate in the case of high distinction—to feel that one has laboured and achieved. Doctor Hugh employed the common phrase about earning one's rest, and it made poor Dencombe, for an instant, almost angry. He recovered himself, however, to explain, lucidly enough, that if he, ungraciously, knew nothing of such a balm, it was doubtless because he had wasted inestimable years. He had followed literature from the first, but he had taken a lifetime to get alongside of her. Only to-day, at last, had he begun to *see*, so that what he had hitherto done was a movement without a direction. He had ripened too late and was so clumsily constituted that he had had to teach himself by mistakes.

"I prefer your flowers, then, to other people's fruit, and your mistakes to other people's successes," said gallant Doctor Hugh. "It's for your mistakes I admire you."

"You're happy—you don't know," Dencombe answered.

Looking at his watch the young man had got up; he named the hour of the afternoon at which he would return. Dencombe warned him against committing himself too deeply, and expressed again all his dread of making him neglect the Countess—perhaps incur her displeasure.

"I want to be like you—I want to learn by mistakes!" Doctor Hugh laughed.

"Take care you don't make too grave a one! But do come back," Dencombe added, with the glimmer of a new idea.

"You should have had more vanity!" Doctor Hugh spoke as if he knew the exact amount required to make a man of letters normal.

"No, no—I only should have had more time. I want another go."

"Another go?"

"I want an extension."

"An extension?" Again Doctor Hugh repeated Dencombe's words, with which he seemed to have been struck.

"Don't you know?—I want to what they call 'live.' "

The young man, for good-bye, had taken his hand, which closed with a certain force. They looked at each other hard a moment. "You *will* live," said Doctor Hugh.

"Don't be superficial. It's too serious!"

"You *shall* live!" Dencombe's visitor declared, turning pale.

"Ah, that's better!" And as he retired the invalid, with a troubled laugh, sank gratefully back.

All that day and all the following night he wondered if it mightn't be arranged. His doctor came again, his servant was attentive, but it was to his confident young friend that he found himself mentally appealing. His collapse on the cliff was plausibly explained, and his liberation, on a better basis, promised for the morrow; meanwhile, however, the intensity of his meditations kept him tranquil and made him indifferent. The idea that occupied him was none the less absorbing because it was a morbid fancy. Here was a clever son of the age, ingenious and ardent, who happened to have set him up for connoisseurs to worship. This servant of his altar had all the new learning in science and all the old reverence in faith; wouldn't he therefore put his knowledge at the disposal of his sympathy, his craft at the disposal of his love? Couldn't he be trusted to invent a remedy for a poor artist to whose art he had paid a tribute? If he couldn't, the alternative was hard: Dencombe would have to surrender to silence, unvindicated and undivined. The rest of the day and all the next he toyed in secret with this sweet futility. Who would work the miracle for him but the young man who could combine such lucidity with such passion? He thought of the fairy-tales of science and charmed himself into forgetting that he looked for a magic that was not of this world. Doctor Hugh was an apparition, and that placed him above the law. He came and went while his patient, who sat up, followed him with supplicating eyes. The interest of knowing the great author had made the young man begin "The Middle Years" afresh, and would help him to find a deeper meaning in its pages. Dencombe had told him what he "tried for;" with all his intelligence, on a first perusal, Doctor Hugh had failed to guess it. The baffled celebrity wondered then who in the world *would* guess it: he was amused once more at the fine, full way with which an intention could be missed. Yet he wouldn't rail at the general mind to-day—consoling as that ever had been: the revelation of his own slowness had seemed to make all stupidity sacred.

Doctor Hugh, after a little, was visibly worried, confessing, on inquiry, to a source of embarrassment at home. "Stick to the Countess—don't mind me," Dencombe said, repeatedly; for his companion was frank enough about the large lady's attitude. She was so jealous that she had fallen ill—she resented such a breach of allegiance. She paid so much for his fidelity that she must have it all: she refused him the right to other sympathies, charged him with scheming to make her die alone, for it was needless to point out how little Miss Vernham was a resource in trouble. When Doctor Hugh mentioned that the Countess would already have left Bournemouth if he hadn't kept her in bed, poor Dencombe held his arm tighter and said with decision: "Take her straight away." They had gone out together, walking back to the sheltered nook in which, the other day, they had met. The young man, who had given his companion a personal support, declared with emphasis that his conscience was clear—he could ride two horses at once. Didn't he dream, for his future, of a time when he should have to ride five hundred? Longing equally for virtue, Dencombe replied that in that golden age no patient would pretend to have contracted with him for his whole attention. On the part of the Countess was not such an avidity lawful? Doctor Hugh denied it, said there was no contract but only a free understanding, and that a sordid servitude was impossible to a generous spirit; he liked moreover to talk about art, and that was the subject on which, this time, as they sat together on the sunny bench, he tried most to engage the author of "The Middle Years." Dencombe, soaring again a little on the weak wings of convalescence and still haunted by that happy notion of an organised rescue, found another strain of eloquence to plead the cause of a certain splendid "last manner," the very citadel, as it would prove, of his reputation, the stronghold into which his real treasure would be gathered. While his listener gave up the morning and the great still sea appeared to wait, he had a wonderful explanatory hour. Even for himself he was inspired as he told of what his treasure would consist—the precious metals he would dig from the mine, the jewels rare, strings of pearls, he would hang between the columns of his temple. He was wonderful for himself, so thick his convictions crowded; but he was still more wonderful for Doctor Hugh, who assured him, none the less, that the very pages he had just published were already encrusted with gems. The young man, however, panted for the combinations to come, and, before the face of the beautiful day, renewed to Dencombe his guarantee that his profession would hold itself responsible for such a life. Then he suddenly clapped his hand upon his watch-pocket and asked leave to absent himself for half an hour. Dencombe waited there for his return, but was at last recalled to the actual by the fall of a shadow across the ground. The shadow darkened into that of Miss Vernham, the young lady in attendance on the Countess; whom Dencombe, recognising her, perceived so clearly to have come to speak to him that he rose from his bench to acknowledge the civility. Miss Vernham indeed proved not particularly civil; she looked strangely agitated, and her type was now unmistakable.

"Excuse me if I inquire," she said, "whether it's too much to hope that you may be induced to leave Doctor Hugh alone." Then, before Dencombe, greatly disconcerted, could protest: "You ought to be informed that you stand in his light; that you may do him a terrible injury."

"Do you mean by causing the Countess to dispense with his services?"

"By causing her to disinherit him." Dencombe stared at this, and Miss Vernham pursued, in the gratification of seeing she could produce an impression: "It has depended on himself to come into something very handsome. He has had a magnificent prospect, but I think you've succeeded in spoiling it."

"Not intentionally, I assure you. Is there no hope the accident may be repaired?" Dencombe asked.

"She was ready to do anything for him. She takes great fancies, she lets herself go—it's her way. She has no relations, she's free to dispose of her money, and she's very ill."

"I'm very sorry to hear it," Dencombe stammered.

"Wouldn't it be possible for you to leave Bournemouth? That's what I've come to ask you."

Poor Dencombe sank down on his bench. "I'm very ill myself, but I'll try!"

Miss Vernham still stood there with her colourless eyes and the brutality of her good conscience. "Before it's too late, please!" she said; and with this she turned her back, in order, quickly, as if it had been a business to which she could spare but a precious moment, to pass out of his sight.

Oh, yes, after this Dencombe was certainly very ill. Miss Vernham had upset him with her rough, fierce news; it was the sharpest shock to him to discover what was at stake for a penniless young man of fine parts. He sat trembling on his bench, staring at the waste of waters, feeling sick with the directness of the blow. He was indeed too weak, too unsteady, too alarmed; but he would make the effort to get away, for he couldn't accept the guilt of interference, and his honour was really involved. He would hobble home, at any rate, and then he would think what was to be done. He made his way back to the hotel and, as he went, had a characteristic vision of Miss Vernham's great motive. The Countess hated women, of course; Dencombe was lucid about that; so the hungry pianist had no personal hopes and could only console herself with the bold conception of helping Doctor Hugh in order either to marry him after he should get his money or to induce him to recognise her title to compensation and buy her off. If she had befriended him at a fruitful crisis he would really, as a man of delicacy, and she knew what to think of that point, have to reckon with her.

At the hotel Dencombe's servant insisted on his going back to bed. The invalid had talked about catching a train and had begun with orders to pack; after which his humming nerves had yielded to a sense of sickness. He consented to see his physician, who immediately was sent for, but he wished it to be understood that his door was irrevocably closed to Doctor Hugh. He had his plan, which was so fine that he rejoiced in it after getting back to bed. Doctor Hugh, suddenly finding himself snubbed without mercy, would, in natural disgust and to the joy of Miss Vernham, renew his allegiance to the Countess. When his physician arrived Dencombe learned that he was feverish and that this was very wrong: he was to cultivate calmness and try, if possible, not to think. For the rest of the day he wooed stupidity; but there was an ache that kept him sentient, the probable sacrifice of his "extension," the limit of his course. His medical adviser was anything but pleased; his successive relapses were ominous. He charged this personage to put out a strong hand and take Doctor Hugh off his mind—it would contribute so much to his being quiet. The agitating name, in his room, was not mentioned again, but his security was a smothered fear, and it was not confirmed by the receipt, at ten o'clock that evening, of a telegram which his servant opened and read for him and to which, with an address in London, the signature of Miss Vernham was attached. "Beseech you to use all influence to make our friend join us here in the morning. Countess much the worse for dreadful journey, but everything may still be saved." The two ladies had gathered themselves up and had been capable in the afternoon of a spiteful revolution. They had started for the capital, and if the elder one, as Miss Vernham had announced, was very ill, she had wished to make it clear that she was proportionately reckless. Poor Dencombe, who was not reckless and who only desired that everything should indeed be "saved," sent this missive straight off to the young man's lodging and had on the morrow the pleasure of knowing that he had quitted Bournemouth by an early train.

Two days later he pressed in with a copy of a literary journal in his hand. He had returned because he was anxious and for the pleasure of flourishing the great review of "The Middle Years." Here at least was something adequate—it rose to the occasion; it was an acclamation, a reparation, a critical attempt to place the author in the niche he had fairly won. Dencombe accepted and submitted; he made neither objection nor inquiry, for old complications had returned and he had had two atrocious days. He was convinced not only that he should never again leave his bed, so that his young friend might pardonably remain, but that the demand he should make on the patience of beholders would be very moderate indeed. Doctor Hugh had been to town, and he tried to find in his eyes some confession that the Countess was pacified and his legacy clinched; but all he could see there was the light of his juvenile joy in two or three of the phrases of the newspaper. Dencombe couldn't read them, but when his visitor had insisted on repeating them more than once he was able to shake an unintoxicated head. "Ah, no; but they would have been true of what I *could* have done!"

"What people 'could have done' is mainly what they've in fact done," Doctor Hugh contended.

"Mainly, yes; but I've been an idiot!" said Dencombe.

Doctor Hugh did remain; the end was coming fast. Two days later Dencombe observed to him, by way of the feeblest of jokes, that there would now be no question whatever of a second chance. At this the young man stared; then he exclaimed: "Why, it has come to pass—it has come to pass! The second chance has been the public's—the chance to find the point of view, to pick up the pearl!"

"Oh, the pearl!" poor Dencombe uneasily sighed. A smile as cold as a winter sunset flickered on his drawn lips as he added: "The pearl is the unwritten—the pearl is the unalloyed, the *rest*, the lost!"

From that moment he was less and less present, heedless to all appearance of what went on around him. His disease was definitely mortal, of an action as relentless, after the short arrest that had enabled him to fall in with Doctor Hugh, as a leak in a great ship. Sinking steadily, though this visitor, a man of rare resources, now cordially approved by his physician, showed endless art in guarding him from pain, poor Dencombe kept no reckoning of favour or neglect, betrayed no symptom of regret or speculation. Yet toward the last he gave a sign of having noticed that for two days Doctor

Hugh had not been in his room, a sign that consisted of his suddenly opening his eyes to ask of him if he had spent the interval with the Countess.

"The Countess is dead," said Doctor Hugh. "I knew that in a particular contingency she wouldn't resist. I went to her grave."

Dencombe's eyes opened wider. "She left you 'something handsome'?"

The young man gave a laugh almost too light for a chamber of woe. "Never a penny. She roundly cursed me."

"Cursed you?" Dencombe murmured.

"For giving her up. I gave her up for *you*. I had to choose," his companion explained.

"You chose to let a fortune go?"

"I chose to accept, whatever they might be, the consequences of my infatuation," smiled Doctor Hugh. Then, as a larger pleasantry: "A fortune be hanged! It's your own fault if I can't get your things out of my head."

The immediate tribute to his humour was a long, bewildered moan; after which, for many hours, many days, Dencombe lay motionless and absent. A response so absolute, such a glimpse of a definite result and such a sense of credit worked together in his mind and, producing a strange commotion, slowly altered and transfigured his despair. The sense of cold submersion left him—he seemed to float without an effort. The incident was extraordinary as evidence, and it shed an intenser light. At the last he signed to Doctor Hugh to listen, and, when he was down on his knees by the pillow, brought him very near.

"You've made me think it all a delusion."

"Not your glory, my dear friend," stammered the young man.

"Not my glory—what there is of it! It *is* glory to have been tested, to have had our little quality and cast our little spell. The thing is to have made somebody care. You happen to be crazy, of course, but that doesn't affect the law."

"You're a great success!" said Doctor Hugh, putting into his young voice the ring of a marriage-bell.

Dencombe lay taking this in; then he gathered strength to speak once more. "A second chance—*that's* the delusion. There never was to be but one. We work in the dark—we do what we can—we give what we have. Our doubt is our passion and our passion is our task. The rest is the madness of art."

"If you've doubted, if you've despaired, you've always 'done' it," his visitor subtly argued.

"We've done something or other," Dencombe conceded.

"Something or other is everything. It's the feasible. It's *you*!"

"Comforter!" poor Dencombe ironically sighed.

"But it's true," insisted his friend.

"It's true. It's frustration that doesn't count."

"Frustration's only life," said Doctor Hugh.

"Yes, it's what passes." Poor Dencombe was barely audible, but he had marked with the words the virtual end of his first and only chance.

In the Cage[†]

It had occurred to her early that in her position—that of a young person spending, in framed and wired confinement, the life of a guinea-pig or a magpie—she should know a great many persons without their recognising the acquaintance. That made it an emotion the more lively—though singularly rare and always, even then, with opportunity still very much smothered—to see any one come in whom she knew, as she called it, outside, and who could add something to the poor identity of her function. Her function was to sit there with two young men—the other telegraphist and the counter-clerk; to mind the "sounder,"[1] which was always going, to dole out stamps and postal-orders, weigh letters, answer stupid questions, give difficult change and, more than anything else, count words as numberless as the sands of the sea, the words of the telegrams thrust, from morning to night, through the gap left in the high lattice, across the encumbered shelf that her forearm ached with rubbing. This transparent screen fenced out or fenced in, according to the side of the narrow counter on which the human lot was cast, the duskiest corner of a shop pervaded not a little, in winter, by the poison of perpetual gas, and at all times by the presence of hams, cheese, dried fish, soap, varnish, paraffin, and other solids and fluids that she came to know perfectly by their smells without consenting to know them by their names.

The barrier that divided the little post-and-telegraph-office from the grocery was a frail structure of wood and wire; but the social, the professional separation was a gulf that fortune, by a stroke quite remarkable, had spared her the necessity of contributing at all publicly to bridge. When Mr. Cocker's young men stepped over from behind the other counter to change a five-pound note—and Mr. Cocker's situation, with the cream of the "Court Guide"[2] and the dearest furnished apartments, Simpkin's, Ladle's, Thrupp's, just round the corner, was so select that his place was quite pervaded

† The first edition of *In the Cage*, published by Duckworth and Co. of London, appeared in August 1898. Herbert S. Stone & Co. released the first American edition in Chicago and New York the following month, and James revised the tale for the New York Edition of his works in 1908. The following text is based on the Duckworth edition.
1. The device through which telegraphic messages are transmitted.
2. A directory of British nobility and high society.

by the crisp rustle of these emblems—she pushed out the sovereigns as if the applicant were no more to her than one of the momentary appearances in the great procession; and this perhaps all the more from the very fact of the connection—only recognised outside indeed—to which she had lent herself with ridiculous inconsequence. She recognised the others the less because she had at last so unreservedly, so irredeemably, recognised Mr. Mudge. But she was a little ashamed, none the less, of having to admit to herself that Mr. Mudge's removal to a higher sphere—to a more commanding position, that is, though to a much lower neighbourhood —would have been described still better as a luxury than as the simplification that she contented herself with calling it. He had, at any rate, ceased to be all day long in her eyes, and this left something a little fresh for them to rest on of a Sunday. During the three months that he had remained at Cocker's after her consent to their engagement, she had often asked herself what it was that marriage would be able to add to a familiarity so final. Opposite there, behind the counter of which his superior stature, his whiter apron, his more clustering curls and more present, too present, h's had been for a couple of years the principal ornament, he had moved to and fro before her as on the small sanded floor of their contracted future. She was conscious now of the improvement of not having to take her present and her future at once. They were about as much as she could manage when taken separate.

She had, none the less, to give her mind steadily to what Mr. Mudge had again written her about, the idea of her applying for a transfer to an office quite similar—she couldn't yet hope for a place in a bigger—under the very roof where he was foreman, so that, dangled before her every minute of the day, he should see her, as he called it, "hourly," and in a part, the far N.W. district, where, with her mother, she would save, on their two rooms alone, nearly three shillings. It would be far from dazzling to exchange Mayfair for Chalk Farm,[3] and it was something of a predicament that he so kept at her; still, it was nothing to the old predicaments, those of the early times of their great misery, her own, her mother's, and her elder sister's—the last of whom had succumbed to all but absolute want when, as conscious, incredulous ladies, suddenly bereaved, betrayed, overwhelmed, they had slipped faster and faster down the steep slope at the bottom of which she alone had rebounded. Her mother had never rebounded any more at the bottom than on the way; had only rumbled and grumbled down and down,

---

3. Mayfair is a district in the west of London. Chalk Farm is a comparatively quiet area north of Regent's Park.

making, in respect of caps and conversation, no effort whatever, and too often, alas! smelling of whisky.

II

It was always rather quiet at Cocker's while the contingent from Ladle's and Thrupp's and all the other great places were at luncheon, or, as the young men used vulgarly to say, while the animals were feeding. She had forty minutes in advance of this to go home for her own dinner; and when she came back, and one of the young men took his turn, there was often half an hour during which she could pull out a bit of work or a book—a book from the place where she borrowed novels, very greasy, in fine print and all about fine folks, at a ha'penny a day. This sacred pause was one of the numerous ways in which the establishment kept its finger on the pulse of fashion and fell into the rhythm of the larger life. It had something to do, one day, with the particular vividness marking the advent of a lady whose meals were apparently irregular, yet whom she was destined, she afterwards found, not to forget. The girl was *blasée*;[4] nothing could belong more, as she perfectly knew, to the intense publicity of her profession; but she had a whimsical mind and wonderful nerves; she was subject, in short, to sudden flickers of antipathy and sympathy, red gleams in the grey, fitful awakings and followings, odd caprices of curiosity. She had a friend who had invented a new career for women—that of being in and out of people's houses to look after the flowers. Mrs. Jordan had a manner of her own of sounding this allusion; "the flowers," on her lips, were, in happy homes, as usual as the coals or the daily papers. She took charge of them, at any rate, in all the rooms, at so much a month, and people were quickly finding out what it was to make over this delicate duty to the widow of a clergyman. The widow, on her side, dilating on the initiations thus opened up to her, had been splendid to her young friend over the way she was made free of the greatest houses—the way, especially when she did the dinner-tables, set out so often for twenty, she felt that a single step more would socially, would absolutely, introduce her. On its being asked of her, then, if she circulated only in a sort of tropical solitude, with the upper servants for picturesque natives, and on her having to assent to this glance at her limitations, she had found a reply to the girl's invidious question. "You've no imagination, my dear!"—that was because the social door might at any moment open so wide.

4. Unremarkable.

Our young lady had not taken up the charge, had dealt with it good-humouredly, just because she knew so well what to think of it. It was at once one of her most cherished complaints and most secret supports that people didn't understand her, and it was accordingly a matter of indifference to her that Mrs. Jordan shouldn't; even though Mrs. Jordan, handed down from their early twilight of gentility and also the victim of reverses, was the only member of her circle in whom she recognised an equal. She was perfectly aware that her imaginative life was the life in which she spent most of her time; and she would have been ready, had it been at all worth while, to contend that, since her outward occupation didn't kill it, it must be strong indeed. Combinations of flowers and green-stuff, forsooth! What *she* could handle freely, she said to herself, was combinations of men and women. The only weakness in her faculty came from the positive abundance of her contact with the human herd; this was so constant, had the effect of becoming so cheap, that there were long stretches in which inspiration, divination and interest, quite dropped. The great thing was the flashes, the quick revivals, absolute accidents all, and neither to be counted on nor to be resisted. Some one had only sometimes to put in a penny for a stamp, and the whole thing was upon her. She was so absurdly constructed that these were literally the moments that made up— made up for the long stiffness of sitting there in the stocks, made up for the cunning hostility of Mr. Buckton and the importunate sympathy of the counter-clerk, made up for the daily, deadly, flourishy letter from Mr. Mudge, made up even for the most haunting of her worries, the rage at moments of not knowing how her mother did "get it."

She had surrendered herself moreover, of late, to a certain expansion of her consciousness; something that seemed perhaps vulgarly accounted for by the fact that, as the blast of the season roared louder and the waves of fashion tossed their spray further over the counter, there were more impressions to be gathered and really— for it came to that—more life to be led. Definite, at any rate, it was that by the time May was well started the kind of company she kept at Cocker's had begun to strike her as a reason—a reason she might almost put forward for a policy of procrastination. It sounded silly, of course, as yet, to plead such a motive, especially as the fascination of the place was, after all, a sort of torment. But she liked her torment; it was a torment she should miss at Chalk Farm. She was ingenious and uncandid, therefore, about leaving the breadth of London a little longer between herself and that austerity. If she had not quite the courage, in short, to say to Mr. Mudge that her actual chance for a play of mind was worth, any week, the three shillings he desired to help her to save, she yet saw something happen in the course of the month that, in her heart of hearts at least, answered the subtle question. This was connected precisely with the appearance of the memorable lady.

III

She pushed in three bescribbled forms which the girl's hand was quick to appropriate, Mr. Buckton having so frequent a perverse instinct for catching first any eye that promised the sort of entertainment with which she had her peculiar affinity. The amusements of captives are full of a desperate contrivance, and one of our young friend's ha'pennyworths had been the charming tale of *Picciola*.[5] It was of course the law of the place that they were never to take no notice, as Mr. Buckton said, whom they served; but this also never prevented, certainly on the same gentleman's own part, what he was fond of describing as the underhand game. Both her companions, for that matter, made no secret of the number of favourites they had among the ladies; sweet familiarities in spite of which she had repeatedly caught each of them in stupidities and mistakes, confusions of identity and lapses of observation that never failed to remind her how the cleverness of men ended where the cleverness of women began. "Marguerite, Regent Street. Try on at six. All Spanish lace. Pearls. The full length." That was the first; it had no signature. "Lady Agnes Orme, Hyde Park Place. Impossible to-night, dining Haddon. Opera to-morrow, promised Fritz, but could do play Wednesday. Will try Haddon for Savoy, and anything in the world you like, if you can get Gussy. Sunday, Montenero. Sit Mason Monday, Tuesday. Marguerite awful. Cissy." That was the second. The third, the girl noted when she took it, was on a foreign form: "Everard, Hôtel Brighton, Paris. Only understand and believe. 22nd to 26th, and certainly 8th and 9th. Perhaps others. Come. Mary."

Mary was very handsome, the handsomest woman, she felt in a moment, she had ever seen—or perhaps it was only Cissy. Perhaps it was both, for she had seen stranger things than that—ladies wiring to different persons under different names. She had seen all sorts of things and pieced together all sorts of mysteries. There had once been one—not long before—who, without winking, sent off five over five different signatures. Perhaps these represented five different friends who had asked her—all women, just as perhaps now Mary and Cissy, or one or other of them, were wiring by deputy. Sometimes she put in too much—too much of her own sense;

5. Xavier Saintine's 1836 story about a prisoner who derives comfort from a plant that he nurtures just outside his cell.

sometimes she put in too little; and in either case this often came round to her afterwards, for she had an extraordinary way of keeping clues. When she noticed, she noticed; that was what it came to. There were days and days, there were weeks sometimes, of vacancy. This arose often from Mr. Buckton's devilish and successful sub-terfuges for keeping her at the sounder whenever it looked as if anything might amuse; the sounder, which it was equally his busi-ness to mind, being the innermost cell of captivity, a cage within the cage, fenced off from the rest by a frame of ground glass. The counter-clerk would have played into her hands; but the counter-clerk was really reduced to idiocy by the effect of his passion for her. She flattered herself moreover, nobly, that with the unpleasant conspicuity of this passion she would never have consented to be obliged to him. The most she would ever do would be always to shove off on him whenever she could the registration of letters, a job she happened particularly to loathe. After the long stupors, at all events, there almost always suddenly would come a sharp taste of something; it was in her mouth before she knew it; it was in her mouth now.

To Cissy, to Mary, whichever it was, she found her curiosity going out with a rush, a mute effusion that floated back to her, like a returning tide, the living colour and splendour of the beautiful head, the light of eyes that seemed to reflect such utterly other things than the mean things actually before them; and, above all, the high, curt consideration of a manner that, even at bad moments, was a magnificent habit and of the very essence of the innumerable things—her beauty, her birth, her father and mother, her cousins, and all her ancestors—that its possessor couldn't have got rid of if she had wished. How did our obscure little public servant know that, for the lady of the telegrams, this was a bad moment? How did she guess all sorts of impossible things, such as, almost on the very spot, the presence of drama, at a critical stage, and the nature of the tie with the gentleman at the Hôtel Brighton? More than ever before it floated to her through the bars of the cage that this at last was the high reality, the bristling truth that she had hitherto only patched up and eked out—one of the creatures, in fine, in whom all the conditions for happiness actually met, and who, in the air they made, bloomed with an unwitting insolence. What came home to the girl was the way the insolence was tempered by something that was equally a part of the distinguished life, the cus-tom of a flowerlike bend to the less fortunate—a dropped fragrance, a mere quick breath, but which in fact pervaded and lingered. The apparition was very young, but certainly married, and our fatigued friend had a sufficient store of mythological comparison to recog-

nise the port of Juno.[6] Marguerite might be "awful," but she knew
how to dress a goddess.

Pearls and Spanish lace—she herself, with assurance, could see
them, and the "full length" too, and also red velvet bows, which,
disposed on the lace in a particular manner (she could have placed
them with the turn of a hand), were of course to adorn the front
of a black brocade that would be like a dress in a picture. However,
neither Marguerite, nor Lady Agnes, nor Haddon, nor Fritz, nor
Gussy was what the wearer of this garment had really come in for.
She had come in for Everard—and that was doubtless not *his* true
name either. If our young lady had never taken such jumps before,
it was simply that she had never before been so affected. She went
all the way. Mary and Cissy had been round together, in their single
superb person, to see him—he must live round the corner; they
had found that, in consequence of something they had come, precisely, to make up for or to have another scene about, he had gone
off—gone off just on purpose to make them feel it; on which they
had come together to Cocker's as to the nearest place; where they
had put in the three forms partly in order not to put in the one
alone. The two others, in a manner, covered it, muffled it, passed
it off. Oh yes, she went all the way, and this was a specimen of
how she often went. She would know the hand again any time. It
was as handsome and as everything else as the woman herself. The
woman herself had, on learning his flight, pushed past Everard's
servant and into his room; she had written her missive at his table
and with his pen. All this, every inch of it, came in the waft that
she blew through and left behind her, the influence that, as I have
said, lingered. And among the things the girl was sure of, happily,
was that she should see her again.

IV

She saw her, in fact, and only ten days later; but this time she
was not alone, and that was exactly a part of the luck of it. Being
clever enough to know through what possibilities it could range,
our young lady had ever since had in her mind a dozen conflicting
theories about Everard's type; as to which, the instant they came
into the place, she felt the point settled with a thump that seemed
somehow addressed straight to her heart. That organ literally beat
faster at the approach of the gentleman who was this time with
Cissy, and who, as seen from within the cage, became on the spot
the happiest of the happy circumstances with which her mind had

<hr/>

6. Wife of Jupiter, queen of heaven, and goddess of light in Roman mythology.

invested the friend of Fritz and Gussy. He was a very happy circumstance indeed as, with his cigarette in his lips and his broken
familiar talk caught by his companion, he put down the half-dozen
telegrams which it would take them together some minutes to des-
patch. And here it occurred, oddly enough, that if, shortly before,
the girl's interest in his companion had sharpened her sense for the
messages then transmitted, her immediate vision of himself had the
effect, while she counted his seventy words, of preventing intelli-
gibility. *His* words were mere numbers, they told her nothing whatever; and after he had gone she was in possession of no name, of
no address, of no meaning, of nothing but a vague, sweet sound
and an immense impression. He had been there but five minutes,
he had smoked in her face, and, busy with his telegrams, with the
tapping pencil and the conscious danger, the odious betrayal that
would come from a mistake, she had had no wandering glances nor
roundabout arts to spare. Yet she had taken him in; she knew everything; she had made up her mind.

He had come back from Paris; everything was re-arranged; the
pair were again shoulder to shoulder in their high encounter with
life, their large and complicated game. The fine, soundless pulse of
this game was in the air for our young woman while they remained
in the shop. While they remained? They remained all day; their
presence continued and abode with her, was in everything she did
till nightfall, in the thousands of other words she counted, she
transmitted, in all the stamps she detached and the letters she
weighed and the change she gave, equally unconscious and unerring in each of these particulars, and not, as the run on the little
office thickened with the afternoon hours, looking up at a single
ugly face in the long sequence, nor really hearing the stupid questions that she patiently and perfectly answered. All patience was
possible now, and all questions stupid after his—all faces ugly. She
had been sure she should see the lady again; and even now she
should perhaps, she should probably, see her often. But for him it
was totally different; she should never, never see him. She wanted
it too much. There was a kind of wanting that helped—she had
arrived, with her rich experience, at that generalisation; and there
was another kind that was fatal. It was this time the fatal kind; it
would prevent.

Well, she saw him the very next day, and on this second occasion
it was quite different; the sense of every syllable he despatched was
fiercely distinct; she indeed felt her progressive pencil, dabbing as
if with a quick caress the marks of his own, put life into every
stroke. He was there a long time—had not brought his forms filled
out, but worked them off in a nook on the counter; and there were

other people as well—a changing, pushing cluster, with every one to mind at once and endless right change to make and information to produce. But she kept hold of him throughout; she continued, for herself, in a relation with him as close as that in which, behind the hated ground glass, Mr. Buckton luckily continued with the sounder. This morning everything changed, but with a kind of dreariness too; she had to swallow the rebuff to her theory about fatal desires, which she did without confusion and indeed with absolute levity; yet if it was now flagrant that he did live close at hand—at Park Chambers—and belonged supremely to the class that wired everything, even their expensive feelings (so that, as he never wrote, his correspondence cost him weekly pounds and pounds, and he might be in and out five times a day), there was, all the same, involved in the prospect, and by reason of its positive excess of light, a perverse melancholy, almost a misery. This was rapidly to give it a place in an order of feelings on which I shall presently touch.

Meanwhile, for a month, he was very constant. Cissy, Mary, never re-appeared with him; he was always either alone or accompanied only by some gentleman who was lost in the blaze of his glory. There was another sense, however—and indeed there was more than one—in which she mostly found herself counting in the splendid creature with whom she had originally connected him. He addressed this correspondent neither as Mary nor as Cissy; but the girl was sure of whom it was, in Eaton Square, that he was perpetually wiring to—and so irreproachably!—as Lady Bradeen. Lady Bradeen was Cissy, Lady Bradeen was Mary, Lady Bradeen was the friend of Fritz and of Gussy, the customer of Marguerite, and the close ally, in short (as was ideally right, only the girl had not yet found a descriptive term that was), of the most magnificent of men. Nothing could equal the frequency and variety of his communications to her ladyship but their extraordinary, their abysmal propriety. It was just the talk—so profuse sometimes that she wondered what was left for their real meetings—of the happiest people in the world. Their real meetings must have been constant, for half of it was appointments and allusions, all swimming in a sea of other allusions still, tangled in a complexity of questions that gave a wondrous image of their life. If Lady Bradeen was Juno, it was all certainly Olympian. If the girl, missing the answers, her ladyship's own outpourings, sometimes wished that Cocker's had only been one of the bigger offices where telegrams arrived as well as departed, there were yet ways in which, on the whole, she pressed the romance closer by reason of the very quantity of imagination that it demanded. The days and hours of this new friend, as she came to account him, were at all events unrolled, and however much more she might have known she would still have wished to go beyond. In fact she did go beyond; she went quite far enough.

But she could none the less, even after a month, scarce have told if the gentlemen who came in with him recurred or changed; and this in spite of the fact that they too were always posting and wiring, smoking in her face and signing or not signing. The gentlemen who came in with him were nothing, at any rate, when he was there. They turned up alone at other times—then only perhaps with a dim richness of reference. He himself, absent as well as present, was all. He was very tall, very fair, and had, in spite of his thick pre-occupations, a good-humour that was exquisite, particularly as it so often had the effect of keeping him on. He could have reached over anybody, and anybody—no matter who—would have let him; but he was so extraordinarily kind that he quite pathetically waited, never waggling things at her out of his turn or saying "Here!" with horrid sharpness. He waited for pottering old ladies, for gaping slaveys, for the perpetual Buttonses from Thrupp's; and the thing in all this that she would have liked most unspeakably to put to the test was the possibility of her having for him a personal identity that might in a particular way appeal. There were moments when he actually struck her as on her side, arranging to help, to support, to spare her.

But such was the singular spirit of our young friend, that she could remind herself with a sort of rage that when people had awfully good manners—people of that class,—you couldn't tell. These manners were for everybody, and it might be drearily unavailing for any poor particular body to be overworked and unusual. What he did take for granted was all sorts of facility; and his high pleasantness, his relighting of cigarettes while he waited, his unconscious bestowal of opportunities, of boons, of blessings, were all a part of his magnificent security, the instinct that told him there was nothing such an existence as his could ever lose by. He was, somehow, at once very bright and very grave, very young and immensely complete; and whatever he was at any moment, it was always as much as all the rest the mere bloom of his beatitude. He was sometimes Everard, as he had been at the Hôtel Brighton, and he was sometimes Captain Everard. He was sometimes Philip with his surname and sometimes Philip without it. In some directions he was merely Phil, in others he was merely Captain. There were relations in which he was none of these things, but a quite different person— "the Count." There were several friends for whom he was William. There were several for whom, in allusion perhaps to his complexion, he was "the Pink 'Un." Once, once only by good luck, he had, coinciding comically, quite miraculously, with another person also

near to her, been "Mudge." Yes, whatever he was, it was a part of
his happiness—whatever he was and probably whatever he wasn't.
And his happiness was a part—it became so little by little—of
something that, almost from the first of her being at Cocker's, had
been deeply with the girl.

v

This was neither more nor less than the queer extension of her
experience, the double life that, in the cage, she grew at last to
lead. As the weeks went on there she lived more and more into the
world of whiffs and glimpses, and found her divinations work faster
and stretch further. It was a prodigious view as the pressure heightened, a panorama fed with facts and figures, flushed with a torrent
of colour and accompanied with wondrous world-music. What it
mainly came to at this period was a picture of how London could
amuse itself; and that, with the running commentary of a witness
so exclusively a witness, turned for the most part to a hardening of
the heart. The nose of this observer was brushed by the bouquet,
yet she could never really pluck even a daisy. What could still remain fresh in her daily grind was the immense disparity, the difference and contrast, from class to class, of every instant and every
motion. There were times when all the wires in the country seemed
to start from the little hole-and-corner where she plied for a livelihood, and where, in the shuffle of feet, the flutter of "forms," the
straying of stamps and the ring of change over the counter, the
people she had fallen into the habit of remembering and fitting
together with others, and of having her theories and interpretations
of, kept up before her their long procession and rotation. What
twisted the knife in her vitals was the way the profligate rich scattered about them, in extravagant chatter over their extravagant
pleasures and sins, an amount of money that would have held the
stricken household of her frightened childhood, her poor pinched
mother and tormented father and lost brother and starved sister,
together for a lifetime. During her first weeks she had often
gasped at the sums people were willing to pay for the stuff they
transmitted—the "much love"s, the "awful" regrets, the compliments and wonderments and vain, vague gestures that cost the price
of a new pair of boots. She had had a way then of glancing at the
people's faces, but she had early learned that if you became a telegraphist you soon ceased to be astonished. Her eye for types
amounted nevertheless to genius, and there were those she liked
and those she hated, her feeling for the latter of which grew to a
positive possession, an instinct of observation and detection. There
were the brazen women, as she called them, of the higher and the

lower fashion, whose squanderings and graspings, whose struggles and secrets and love-affairs and lies, she tracked and stored up against them, till she had at moments, in private, a triumphant, vicious feeling of mastery and power, a sense of having their silly, guilty secrets in her pocket, her small retentive brain, and thereby knowing so much more about them than they suspected or would care to think. There were those she would have liked to betray, to trip up, to bring down with words altered and fatal; and all through a personal hostility provoked by the lightest signs, by their accidents of tone and manner, by the particular kind of relation she always happened instantly to feel.

There were impulses of various kinds, alternately soft and severe, to which she was constitutionally accessible and which were determined by the smallest accidents. She was rigid, in general, on the article of making the public itself affix its stamps, and found a special enjoyment in dealing, to that end, with some of the ladies who were too grand to touch them. She had thus a play of refinement and subtlety greater, she flattered herself, than any of which she could be made the subject; and though most people were too stupid to be conscious of this, it brought her endless little consolations and revenges. She recognised quite as much those of her sex whom she would have liked to help, to warn, to rescue, to see more of; and that alternative as well operated exactly through the hazard of personal sympathy, her vision for silver threads and moonbeams and her gift for keeping the clues and finding her way in the tangle. The moonbeams and silver threads presented at moments all the vision of what poor *she* might have made of happiness. Blurred and blank as the whole thing often inevitably, or mercifully, became, she could still, through crevices and crannies, be stupefied, especially by what, in spite of all seasoning, touched the sorest place in her consciousness, the revelation of the golden shower flying about without a gleam of gold for herself. It remained prodigious to the end, the money her fine friends were able to spend to get still more, or even to complain to fine friends of their own that they were in want. The pleasures they proposed were equalled only by those they declined, and they made their appointments often so expensively that she was left wondering at the nature of the delights to which the mere approaches were so paved with shillings. She quivered on occasion into the perception of this and that one whom she would, at all events, have just simply liked to *be*. Her conceit, her baffled vanity were possibly monstrous; she certainly often threw herself into a defiant conviction that she would have done the whole thing much better. But her greatest comfort, on the whole, was her comparative vision of the men; by whom I mean the unmistakable gentlemen, for she had no interest in the spurious or the shabby, and no mercy at all for the poor. She could have found a sixpence, outside, for an appearance of want; but her fancy, in some directions so alert, had never a throb of response for any sign of the sordid. The men she did follow, moreover, she followed mainly in one relation, the relation as to which the cage convinced her, she believed, more than anything else could have done, that it was quite the most diffused.

She found her ladies, in short, almost always in communication with her gentlemen, and her gentlemen with her ladies, and she read into the immensity of their intercourse stories and meanings without end. Incontestably she grew to think that the men cut the best figure; and in this particular, as in many others, she arrived at a philosophy of her own, all made up of her private notations and cynicisms. It was a striking part of the business, for example, that it was much more the women, on the whole, who were after the men than the men who were after the women: it was literally visible that the general attitude of the one sex was that of the object pursued and defensive, apologetic and attenuating, while the light of her own nature helped her more or less to conclude as to the attitude of the other. Perhaps she herself a little even fell into the custom of pursuit in occasionally deviating only for gentlemen from her high rigour about the stamps. She had early in the day made up her mind, in fine, that they had the best manners; and if there were none of them she noticed when Captain Everard was there, there were plenty she could place and trace and name at other times, plenty who, with their way of being "nice" to her, and of handling, as if their pockets were private tills, loose, mixed masses of silver and gold, were such pleasant appearances that she could envy them without dislike. *They* never had to give change—they only had to get it. They ranged through every suggestion, every shade of fortune, which evidently included indeed lots of bad luck as well as of good, declining even toward Mr. Mudge and his bland, firm thrift, and ascending, in wild signals and rocket-flights, almost to within hail of her highest standard. So, from month to month, she went on with them all, through a thousand ups and downs and a thousand pangs and indifferences. What virtually happened was that in the shuffling herd that passed before her by far the greater part only passed—a proportion but just appreciable stayed. Most of the elements swam straight away, lost themselves in the bottomless common, and by so doing really kept the page clear. On the clearness, therefore, what she did retain stood sharply out; she nipped and caught it, turned it over and interwove it.

VI

She met Mrs. Jordan whenever she could, and learned from her more and more how the great people, under her gentle shake, and after going through everything with the mere shops, were waking up to the gain of putting into the hands of a person of real refinement the question that the shop-people spoke of so vulgarly as that of the floral decorations. The regular dealers in these decorations were all very well; but there was a peculiar magic in the play of taste of a lady who had only to remember, through whatever intervening dusk, all her own little tables, little bowls and little jars and little other arrangements, and the wonderful thing she had made of the garden of the vicarage. This small domain, which her young friend had never seen, bloomed in Mrs. Jordan's discourse like a new Eden, and she converted the past into a bank of violets by the tone in which she said, "Of course you always knew my one passion!" She obviously met now, at any rate, a big contemporary need, measured what it was rapidly becoming for people to feel they could trust her without a tremor. It brought them a peace that—during the quarter of an hour before dinner in especial—was worth more to them than mere payment could express. Mere payment, none the less, was tolerably prompt; she engaged by the month, taking over the whole thing; and there was an evening on which, in respect to our heroine, she at last returned to the charge. "It's growing and growing, and I see that I must really divide the work. One wants an associate—of one's own kind, don't you know? You know the look they want it all to have?—of having come, not from a florist, but from one of themselves. Well, I'm sure *you* could give it—because you *are* one. Then we *should* win. Therefore just come in with me."

"And leave the P.O.?"

"Let the P.O. simply bring you your letters. It would bring you lots, you'd see: orders, after a bit, by the dozen." It was on this, in due course, that the great advantage again came up: "One seems to live again with one's own people." It had taken some little time (after their having parted company in the tempest of their troubles and then, in the glimmering dawn, finally sighted each other again) for each to admit that the other was, in her private circle, her only equal; but the admission came, when it did come, with an honest groan; and since equality *was* named, each found much personal profit in exaggerating the other's original grandeur. Mrs. Jordan was ten years the older, but her young friend was struck with the smaller difference this now made: it had counted otherwise at the time when, much more as a friend of her mother's, the bereaved lady, without a penny of provision, and with stop-gaps, like their own, all

gone, had, across the sordid landing on which the opposite doors
of the pair of scared miseries opened and to which they were be-
wilderedly bolted, borrowed coals and umbrellas that were repaid
in potatoes and postage-stamps. It had been a questionable help,
at that time, to ladies submerged, floundering, panting, swimming
for their lives, that they *were* ladies; but such an advantage could
come up again in proportion as others vanished, and it had grown
very great by the time it was the only ghost of one they possessed.
They had literally watched it take to itself a portion of the substance
of each that had departed; and it became prodigious now, when
they could talk of it together, when they could look back at it across
a desert of accepted derogation, and when, above all, they could
draw from each other a credulity about it that they could draw from
no one else. Nothing was really so marked as that they felt the need
to cultivate this legend much more after having found their feet
and stayed their stomachs in the ultimate obscure than they had
done in the upper air of mere frequent shocks. The thing they could
now oftenest say to each other was that they knew what they meant;
and the sentiment with which, all round, they knew it was known
had been a kind of promise to stick well together again.

Mrs. Jordan was at present fairly dazzling on the subject of the
way that, in the practice of her beautiful art, she more than peeped
in—she penetrated. There was not a house of the great kind—and
it was, of course, only a question of those, real homes of luxury—
in which she was not, at the rate such people now had things, all
over the place. The girl felt before the picture the cold breath of
disinheritance as much as she had ever felt it in the cage; she knew,
moreover, how much she betrayed this, for the experience of poverty had begun, in her life, too early, and her ignorance of the
requirements of homes of luxury had grown, with other active
knowledge, a depth of simplification. She had accordingly at first
often found that in these colloquies she could only pretend she
understood. Educated as she had rapidly been by her chances at
Cocker's, there were still strange gaps in her learning—she could
never, like Mrs. Jordan, have found her way about one of the
"homes." Little by little, however, she had caught on, above all in
the light of what Mrs. Jordan's redemption had materially made of
that lady, giving her, though the years and the struggles had naturally not straightened a feature, an almost super-eminent air.
There were women in and out of Cocker's who were quite nice and
who yet didn't look well; whereas Mrs. Jordan looked well and yet,
with her extraordinarily protrusive teeth, was by no means quite
nice. It would seem, mystifyingly, that it might really come from all
the greatness she could live with. It was fine to hear her talk so
often of dinners of twenty and of her doing, as she said, exactly as

she liked with them. She spoke as if, for that matter, she invited the company. "They simply *give* me the table—all the rest, all the other effects, come afterwards."

VII

"Then you *do* see them?" the girl again asked.

Mrs. Jordan hesitated, and indeed the point had been ambiguous before. "Do you mean the guests?"

Her young friend, cautious about an undue exposure of innocence, was not quite sure. "Well—the people who live there."

"Lady Ventnor? Mrs. Bubb? Lord Rye? Dear, yes. Why, they *like* one."

"But does one personally *know* them?" our young lady went on, since that was the way to speak. "I mean socially, don't you know?—as you know *me*."

"They're not so nice as you!" Mrs. Jordan charmingly cried. "But I *shall* see more and more of them."

Ah, this was the old story. "But how soon?"

"Why, almost any day. Of course," Mrs. Jordan honestly added, "they're nearly always out."

"Then why do they want flowers all over?"

"Oh, that doesn't make any difference." Mrs. Jordan was not philosophic; she was only evidently determined it shouldn't make any. "They're awfully interested in my ideas, and it's inevitable they should meet me over them."

Her interlocutress was sturdy enough. "What do you call your ideas?"

Mrs. Jordan's reply was fine. "If you were to see me some day with a thousand tulips, you'd soon discover."

"A thousand?"—the girl gaped at such a revelation of the scale of it; she felt, for the instant, fairly planted out. "Well, but if in fact they never do meet you?" she none the less pessimistically insisted.

"Never? They *often* do—and evidently quite on purpose. We have grand long talks."

There was something in our young lady that could still stay her from asking for a personal description of these apparitions; that showed too starved a state. But while she considered, she took in afresh the whole of the clergyman's widow. Mrs. Jordan couldn't help her teeth, and her sleeves were a distinct rise in the world. A thousand tulips at a shilling clearly took one further than a thousand words at a penny; and the betrothed of Mr. Mudge, in whom the sense of the race for life was always acute, found herself wondering, with a twinge of her easy jealousy, if it mightn't after all then, for *her* also, be better—better than where she was—to follow some such scent. Where she was was where Mr. Buckton's elbow could freely enter her right side and the counter-clerk's breathing —he had something the matter with his nose—pervade her left ear. It was something to fill an office under Government, and she knew but too well there were places commoner still than Cocker's; but it never required much of a chance to bring back to her the picture of servitude and promiscuity that she must present to the eye of comparative freedom. She was so boxed up with her young men, and anything like a margin so absent, that it needed more art than she should ever possess to pretend in the least to compass, with any one in the nature of an acquaintance—say with Mrs. Jordan herself, flying in, as it might happen, to wire sympathetically to Mrs. Bubb—an approach to a relation of elegant privacy. She remembered the day when Mrs. Jordan *had*, in fact, by the greatest chance, come in with fifty-three words for Lord Rye and a five-pound note to change. This had been the dramatic manner of their reunion— their mutual recognition was so great an event. The girl could at first only see her from the waist up, besides making but little of her long telegram to his lordship. It was a strange whirligig that had converted the clergyman's widow into such a specimen of the class that went beyond the sixpence.

Nothing of the occasion, all the more, had ever become dim; least of all the way that, as her recovered friend looked up from counting, Mrs. Jordan had just blown, in explanation, through her teeth and through the bars of the cage: "I *do* flowers, you know." Our young woman had always, with her little finger crooked out, a pretty movement for counting; and she had not forgotten the small secret advantage, a sharpness of triumph it might even have been called, that fell upon her at this moment and avenged her for the incoherence of the message, an unintelligible enumeration of numbers, colours, days, hours. The correspondence of people she didn't know was one thing; but the correspondence of people she did had an aspect of its own for her, even when she couldn't understand it. The speech in which Mrs. Jordan had defined a position and announced a profession was like a tinkle of bluebells; but, for herself, her one idea about flowers was that people had them at funerals, and her present sole gleam of light was that lords probably had them most. When she watched, a minute later, through the cage, the swing of her visitor's departing petticoats, she saw the sight from the waist down; and when the counter-clerk, after a mere male glance, remarked, with an intention unmistakably low, "Handsome woman!" she had for him the finest of her chills: "She's the widow of a bishop." She always felt, with the counter-clerk, that it was impossible sufficiently to put it on; for what she wished to express to him was the maximum of her contempt, and that element in her nature was confusedly stored. "A bishop" *was* putting it on, but the counter-clerk's approaches were vile. The night, after this, when, in the fullness of time, Mrs. Jordan mentioned the grand long talks, the girl at last brought out: "Should *I* see them?—I mean if I *were* to give up everything for you."

Mrs. Jordan at this became most arch. "I'd send you to all the bachelors!"

Our young lady could be reminded by such a remark that she usually struck her friend as pretty. "Do *they* have their flowers?"

"Oceans. And they're the most particular." Oh, it was a wonderful world. "You should see Lord Rye's."

"His flowers?"

"Yes, and his letters. He writes me pages on pages—with the most adorable little drawings and plans. You should see his diagrams!"

VIII

The girl had in course of time every opportunity to inspect these documents, and they a little disappointed her; but in the meanwhile there had been more talk, and it had led to her saying, as if her friend's guarantee of a life of elegance were not quite definite: "Well, I see every one at *my* place."

"Every one?"

"Lots of swells. They flock. They live, you know, all round, and the place is filled with all the smart people, all the fast people, those whose names are in the papers—mamma has still the *Morning Post*—and who come up for the season."

Mrs. Jordan took this in with complete intelligence. "Yes, and I dare say it's some of your people that *I* do."

Her companion assented, but discriminated. "I doubt if you 'do' them as much as I! Their affairs, their appointments and arrangements, their little games and secrets and vices—those things all pass before me."

This was a picture that could impose on a clergyman's widow a certain strain; it was in intention, moreover, something of a retort to the thousand tulips. "Their vices? Have they got vices?"

Our young critic even more remarkably stared; then with a touch of contempt in her amusement: "Haven't you found *that* out?" The homes of luxury, then, hadn't so much to give. "*I* find out everything," she continued.

Mrs. Jordan, at bottom a very meek person, was visibly struck. "I see. You do 'have' them."

"Oh, I don't care! Much good does it do me!"

Mrs. Jordan, after an instant, recovered her superiority. "No—it doesn't lead to much." Her own initiations so clearly did. Still—after all; and she was not jealous: "There must be a charm."

"In seeing them?" At this the girl suddenly let herself go. "I hate them; there's that charm!"

Mrs. Jordan gaped again. "The *real* 'smarts'?"

"Is that what you call Mrs. Bubb? Yes—it comes to me; I've had Mrs. Bubb. I don't think she has been in herself, but there are things her maid has brought. Well, my dear!"—and the young person from Cocker's, recalling these things and summing them up, seemed suddenly to have much to say. But she didn't say it; she checked it; she only brought out: "Her maid, who's horrid—*she* must have her!" Then she went on with indifference: "They're *too* real! They're selfish brutes."

Mrs. Jordan, turning it over, adopted at last the plan of treating it with a smile. She wished to be liberal. "Well, of course, they do lay it out."

"They bore me to death," her companion pursued with slightly more temperance.

But this was going too far. "Ah, that's because you've no sympathy!"

The girl gave an ironic laugh, only retorting that she wouldn't have any either if she had to count all day all the words in the dictionary; a contention Mrs. Jordan quite granted, the more that she shuddered at the notion of ever failing of the very gift to which she owed the vogue—the rage she might call it—that had caught her up. Without sympathy—or without imagination, for it came back again to that—how should she get, for big dinners, down the middle and toward the far corners at all? It wasn't the combinations, which were easily managed: the strain was over the ineffable simplicities, those that the bachelors above all, and Lord Rye perhaps most of any, threw off—just blew off, like cigarette-puffs—such sketches of. The betrothed of Mr. Mudge at all events accepted the explanation, which had the effect, as almost any turn of their talk was now apt to have, of bringing her round to the terrific question of that gentleman. She was tormented with the desire to get out of Mrs. Jordan, on this subject, what she was sure was at the back of Mrs. Jordan's head; and to get it out of her, queerly enough, if only to vent a certain irritation at it. She knew that what her friend would already have risked if she had not been timid and tortuous was: "Give him up—yes, give him up: you'll see that with your sure chances you'll be able to do much better."

Our young woman had a sense that if that view could only be put before her with a particular sniff for poor Mr. Mudge she should hate it as much as she morally ought. She was conscious of not, as yet, hating it quite so much as that. But she saw that Mrs.

Jordan was conscious of something too, and that there was a sort of assurance she was waiting little by little to gather. The day came when the girl caught a glimpse of what was still wanting to make her friend feel strong; which was nothing less than the prospect of being able to announce the climax of sundry private dreams. The associate of the aristocracy had personal calculations—she pored over them in her lonely lodgings. If she did the flowers for the bachelors, in short, didn't she expect that to have consequences very different from the outlook, at Cocker's, that she had described as leading to nothing? There seemed in very truth something auspicious in the mixture of bachelors and flowers, though, when looked hard in the eye, Mrs. Jordan was not quite prepared to say she had expected a positive proposal from Lord Rye to pop out of it. Our young woman arrived at last, none the less, at a definite vision of what was in her mind. This was a vivid foreknowledge that the betrothed of Mr. Mudge would, unless conciliated in advance by a successful rescue, almost hate her on the day she should break a particular piece of news. How could that unfortunate otherwise endure to hear of what, under the protection of Lady Ventnor, was after all so possible?

IX

Meanwhile, since irritation sometimes relieved her, the betrothed of Mr. Mudge drew straight from that admirer an amount of it that was proportioned to her fidelity. She always walked with him on Sundays, usually in the Regent's Park,[7] and quite often, once or twice a month, he took her, in the Strand[8] or thereabouts, to see a piece that was having a run. The productions he always preferred were the really good ones—Shakespeare, Thompson, or some funny American thing; which, as it also happened that she hated vulgar plays, gave him ground for what was almost the fondest of his approaches, the theory that their tastes were, blissfully, just the same. He was for ever reminding her of that, rejoicing over it, and being affectionate and wise about it. There were times when she wondered how in the world she could bear him, how she could bear any man so smugly unconscious of the immensity of her difference. It was just for this difference that, if she was to be liked at all, she wanted to be liked, and if that was not the source of Mr. Mudge's admiration, she asked herself, what on earth *could* be? She was not different only at one point, she was different all round; unless per-

---

7. A fashionable park in London.
8. London's theater district.

haps indeed in being practically human, which her mind just barely recognised that he also was. She would have made tremendous concessions in other quarters: there was no limit, for instance, to those she would have made to Captain Everard; but what I have named was the most she was prepared to do for Mr. Mudge. It was because *he* was different that, in the oddest way, she liked as well as deplored him; which was after all a proof that the disparity, should they frankly recognise it, wouldn't necessarily be fatal. She felt that, oleaginous[9]—too oleaginous—as he was, he was somehow comparatively primitive: she had once, during the portion of his time at Cocker's that had overlapped her own, seen him collar a drunken soldier, a big, violent man, who, having come in with a mate to get a postal-order cashed, had made a grab at the money before his friend could reach it and had so produced, among the hams and cheeses and the lodgers from Thrupp's, reprisals instantly ensuing a scene of scandal and consternation. Mr. Buckton and the counter-clerk had crouched within the cage, but Mr. Mudge had, with a very quiet but very quick step round the counter, triumphantly interposed in the scrimmage, parted the combatants, and shaken the delinquent in his skin. She had been proud of him at that moment, and had felt that if their affair had not already been settled the neatness of his execution would have left her without resistance.

Their affair had been settled by other things: by the evident sincerity of his passion and by the sense that his high white apron resembled a front of many floors. It had gone a great way with her that he would build up a business to his chin, which he carried quite in the air. This could only be a question of time; he would have all Piccadilly[1] in the pen behind his ear. That was a merit in itself for a girl who had known what she had known. There were hours at which she even found him good-looking, though, frankly, there could be no crown for her effort to imagine, on the part of the tailor or the barber, some such treatment of his appearance as would make him resemble even remotely a gentleman. His very beauty was the beauty of a grocer, and the finest future would offer it none too much room to expand. She had engaged herself, in short, to the perfection of a type, and perfection of anything was much for a person who, out of early troubles, had just escaped with her life. But it contributed hugely at present to carry on the two parallel lines of her contacts in the cage and her contacts out of it. After keeping quiet for some time about this opposition, she

9. Oily.
1. A dense commercial zone in London.

suddenly—one Sunday afternoon on a penny chair in the Regent's Park—broke, for him, capriciously, bewilderingly, into an intimation of what it came to. He naturally pressed more and more on the subject of her again placing herself where he could see her hourly, and for her to recognise that she had as yet given him no sane reason for delay she had no need to hear him say that he couldn't make out what she was up to. As if, with her absurd bad reasons, she knew it herself! Sometimes she thought it would be amusing to let him have them full in the face, for she felt she should die of him unless she once in a while stupefied him; and sometimes she thought it would be disgusting and perhaps even fatal. She liked him, however, to think her silly, for that gave her the margin which, at the best, she would always require; and the only difficulty about this was that he hadn't enough imagination to oblige her. It produced, none the less, something of the desired effect—to leave him simply wondering why, over the matter of their reunion, she didn't yield to his arguments. Then at last, simply as if by accident and out of mere boredom on a day that was rather flat, she preposterously produced her own. "Well, wait a bit. Where I am I still see things." And she talked to him even worse, if possible, than she had talked to Mrs. Jordan.

Little by little, to her own stupefaction, she caught that he was trying to take it as she meant it, and that he was neither astonished nor angry. Oh, the British tradesman—this gave her an idea of his resources! Mr. Mudge would be angry only with a person who, like the drunken soldier in the shop, should have an unfavourable effect upon business. He seemed positively to enter, for the time and without the faintest flash of irony or ripple of laughter, into the whimsical grounds of her enjoyment of Cocker's custom, and instantly to be casting up whatever it might, as Mrs. Jordan had said, lead to. What he had in mind was not, of course, what Mrs. Jordan had had: it was obviously not a source of speculation with him that his sweetheart might pick up a husband. She could see perfectly that this was not, for a moment, even what he supposed she herself dreamed of. What she had done was simply to give his fancy another push into the dim vast of trade. In that direction it was all alert, and she had whisked before it the mild fragrance of a "connection." That was the most he could see in any picture of her keeping in with the gentry; and when, getting to the bottom of this, she quickly proceeded to show him the kind of eye she turned on such people and to give him a sketch of what that eye discovered, she reduced him to the particular confusion in which he could still be amusing to her.

X

"They're the most awful wretches, I assure you—the lot all about there."

"Then why do you want to stay among them?"

"My dear man, just because they *are*. It makes me hate them so."

"Hate them? I thought you liked them."

"Don't be stupid. What I 'like' is just to loathe them. You wouldn't believe what passes before my eyes."

"Then why have you never told me? You didn't mention anything before I left."

"Oh, I hadn't got into it then. It's the sort of thing you don't believe at first; you have to look round you a bit and then you understand. You work into it more and more. Besides," the girl went on, "this is the time of the year when the worst lot come up. They're simply packed together in those smart streets. Talk of the numbers of the poor! What *I* can vouch for is the numbers of the rich! There are new ones every day, and they seem to get richer and richer. Oh, they do come up!" she cried, imitating, for her private recreation— she was sure it wouldn't reach Mr. Mudge—the low intonation of the counter-clerk.

"And where do they come from?" her companion candidly inquired.

She had to think a moment; then she found something. "From the 'spring meetings.' They bet tremendously."

"Well, they bet enough at Chalk Farm, if that's all."

"It *isn't* all. It isn't a millionth part!" she replied with some sharpness. "It's immense fun"—she would tantalise him. Then, as she had heard Mrs. Jordan say, and as the ladies at Cocker's even sometimes wired, "It's quite too dreadful!" She could fully feel how it was Mr. Mudge's propriety, which was extreme—he had a horror of coarseness and attended a Wesleyan chapel—that prevented his asking for details. But she gave him some of the more innocuous in spite of himself, especially putting before him how, at Simpkin's and Ladle's, they all made the money fly. That was indeed what he liked to hear: the connection was not direct, but one was somehow more in the right place where the money was flying than where it was simply and meagrely nesting. It enlivened the air, he had to acknowledge, much less at Chalk Farm than in the district in which his beloved so oddly enjoyed her footing. She gave him, she could see, a restless sense that these might be familiarities not to be sacrificed; germs, possibilities, faint foreshowings—heaven knew what—of the initiation it would prove profitable to have arrived at when, in the fullness of time, he should have his own shop in some such paradise. What really touched him—that was discernible—

was that she could feed him with so much mere vividness of reminder, keep before him, as by the play of a fan, the very wind of
the swift bank-notes and the charm of the existence of a class that
Providence had raised up to be the blessing of grocers. He liked to
think that the class was there, that it was always there, and that
she contributed in her slight but appreciable degree to keep it up
to the mark. He couldn't have formulated his theory of the matter,
but the exuberance of the aristocracy was the advantage of trade,
and everything was knit together in a richness of pattern that it was
good to follow with one's finger-tips. It was a comfort to him to be
thus assured that there were no symptoms of a drop. What did the
sounder, as she called it, nimbly worked, do but keep the ball going?

What it came to, therefore, for Mr. Mudge, was that all enjoy-
ments were, in short, interrelated, and that the more people had
the more they wanted to have. The more flirtations, as he might
roughly express it, the more cheese and pickles. He had even in his
own small way been dimly struck with the concatenation between
the tender passion and cheap champagne. What he would have
liked to say had he been able to work out his thought to the end
was: "I see, I see. Lash them up then, lead them on, keep them
going: some of it can't help, some time, coming *our* way." Yet he
was troubled by the suspicion of subtleties on his companion's part
that spoiled the straight view. He couldn't understand people's hating what they liked or liking what they hated; above all it hurt him
somewhere—for he had his private delicacies—to see anything *but*
money made out of his betters. To be curious at the expense of the
gentry was vaguely wrong; the only thing that was distinctly right
was to be prosperous. Wasn't it just because they were up there
aloft that they were lucrative? He concluded, at any rate, by saying
to his young friend: "If it's improper for you to remain at Cocker's,
then that falls in exactly with the other reasons that I have put
before you for your removal."

"Improper?"—her smile became a long, wide look at him. "My
dear boy, there's no one like you!"

"I dare say," he laughed; "but that doesn't help the question."

"Well," she returned, "I can't give up my friends. I'm making even
more than Mrs. Jordan."

Mr. Mudge considered. "How much is *she* making?"

"Oh, you dear donkey!"—and, regardless of all the Regent's Park,
she patted his cheek. This was the sort of moment at which she
was absolutely tempted to tell him that she liked to be near Park
Chambers. There was a fascination in the idea of seeing if, on a
mention of Captain Everard, he wouldn't do what she thought he
might; wouldn't weigh against the obvious objection the still more
obvious advantage. The advantage, of course, could only strike him

at the best as rather fantastic; but it was always to the good to keep
hold when you *had* hold, and such an attitude would also after all
involve a high tribute to her fidelity. Of one thing she absolutely
never doubted: Mr. Mudge believed in her with a belief——! She
believed in herself too, for that matter: if there was a thing in the
world no one could charge her with, it was being the kind of low
barmaid person who rinsed tumblers and bandied slang. But she
forbore as yet to speak; she had not spoken even to Mrs. Jordan;
and the hush that on her lips surrounded the Captain's name maintained itself as a kind of symbol of the success that, up to this time,
had attended something or other—she couldn't have said what—
that she humoured herself with calling, without words, her relation
with him.

XI

She would have admitted indeed that it consisted of little more
than the fact that his absences, however frequent and however long,
always ended with his turning up again. It was nobody's business
in the world but her own if that fact continued to be enough for
her. It was of course not enough just in itself; what it had taken on
to make it so was the extraordinary possession of the elements of
his life that memory and attention had at last given her. There came
a day when this possession, on the girl's part, actually seemed to
enjoy, between them, while their eyes met, a tacit recognition that
was half a joke and half a deep solemnity. He bade her good morning always now; he often quite raised his hat to her. He passed a
remark when there was time or room, and once she went so far as
to say to him that she had not seen him for "ages." "Ages" was the
word she consciously and carefully, though a trifle tremulously,
used; "ages" was exactly what she meant. To this he replied in terms
doubtless less anxiously selected, but perhaps on that account not
the less remarkable, "Oh yes, hasn't it been awfully wet?" That was
a specimen of their give and take; it fed her fancy that no form of
intercourse so transcendent and distilled had ever been established
on earth. Everything, so far as they chose to consider it so, might
mean almost anything. The want of margin in the cage, when he
peeped through the bars, wholly ceased to be appreciable. It was a
drawback only in superficial commerce. With Captain Everard she
had simply the margin of the universe. It may be imagined, therefore, how their unuttered reference to all she knew about him
could, in this immensity, play at its ease. Every time he handed in
a telegram it was an addition to her knowledge: what did his constant smile mean to mark if it didn't mean to mark that? He never
came into the place without saying to her in this manner: "Oh yes,

you have me by this time so completely at your mercy that it doesn't in the least matter what I give you now. You've become a comfort, I assure you!"

She had only two torments; the greatest of which was that she couldn't, not even once or twice, touch with him on some individual fact. She would have given anything to have been able to allude to one of his friends by name, to one of his engagements by date, to one of his difficulties by the solution. She would have given almost as much for just the right chance—it would have to be tremendously right—to show him in some sharp, sweet way that she had perfectly penetrated the greatest of these last and now lived with it in a kind of heroism of sympathy. He was in love with a woman to whom, and to any view of whom, a lady-telegraphist, and especially one who passed a life among hams and cheeses, was as the sand on the floor; and what her dreams desired was the possibility of its somehow coming to him that her own interest in him could take a pure and noble account of such an infatuation and even of such an impropriety. As yet, however, she could only rub along with the hope that an accident, sooner or later, might give her a lift toward popping out with something that would surprise and perhaps even, some fine day, assist him. What could people mean, moreover— cheaply sarcastic people—by not feeling all that could be got out of the weather? *She* felt it all, and seemed literally to feel it most when she went quite wrong, speaking of the stuffy days as cold, of the cold ones as stuffy, and betraying how little she knew, in her cage, of whether it was foul or fair. It was, for that matter, always stuffy at Cocker's, and she finally settled down to the safe proposition that the outside element was "changeable." Anything seemed true that made him so radiantly assent.

This indeed is a small specimen of her cultivation of insidious ways of making things easy for him—ways to which of course she couldn't be at all sure that he did real justice. Real justice was not of this world: she had had too often to come back to that; yet, strangely, happiness was, and her traps had to be set for it in a manner to keep them unperceived by Mr. Buckton and the counter-clerk. The most she could hope for apart from the question, which constantly flickered up and died down, of the divine chance of his consciously liking her, would be that, without analysing it, he should arrive at a vague sense that Cocker's was—well, attractive; easier, smoother, sociably brighter, slightly more picturesque, in short more propitious in general to his little affairs, than any other establishment just thereabouts. She was quite aware that they couldn't be, in so huddled a hole, particularly quick; but she found her account in the slowness—she certainly could bear it if *he* could. The great pang was that, just thereabouts, post-offices were so awfully thick. She was always seeing him, in imagination, in other places and with other girls. But she would defy any other girl to follow him as she followed. And though they weren't, for so many reasons, quick at Cocker's, she could hurry for him when, through an intimation light as air, she gathered that he was pressed.

When hurry was, better still, impossible, it was because of the pleasantest thing of all, the particular element of their contact— she would have called it their friendship—that consisted of an almost humorous treatment of the look of some of his words. They would never perhaps have grown half so intimate if he had not, by the blessing of heaven, formed some of his letters with a queerness——! It was positive that the queerness could scarce have been greater if he had practised it for the very purpose of bringing their heads together over it as far as was possible to heads on different sides of a cage. It had taken her in reality but once or twice to master these tricks, but, at the cost of striking him perhaps as stupid, she could still challenge them when circumstances favoured. The great circumstance that favoured was that she sometimes actually believed he knew she only feigned perplexity. If he knew it, therefore, he tolerated it; if he tolerated it he came back; and if he came back he liked her. This was her seventh heaven; and she didn't ask much of his liking—she only asked of it to reach the point of his not going away because of her own. He had at times to be away for weeks; he had to lead his life; he had to travel—there were places to which he was constantly wiring for "rooms": all this she granted him, forgave him; in fact, in the long-run, literally blessed and thanked him for. If he had to lead his life, that precisely fostered his leading it so much by telegraph: therefore the benediction was to come in when he could. That was all she asked—that he shouldn't wholly deprive her.

Sometimes she almost felt that he couldn't have done so even had he been minded, on account of the web of revelation that was woven between them. She quite thrilled herself with thinking what, with such a lot of material, a bad girl would do. It would be a scene better than many in her ha'penny novels, this going to him in the dusk of evening at Park Chambers and letting him at last have it. "I know too much about a certain person now not to put it to you —excuse my being so lurid—that it's quite worth your while to buy me off. Come, therefore; buy me!" There was a point indeed at which such flights had to drop again—the point of an unreadiness to name, when it came to that, the purchasing medium. It wouldn't, certainly, be anything so gross as money, and the matter accordingly remained rather vague, all the more that *she* was not a bad girl. It was not for any such reason as might have aggravated a mere minx that she often hoped he would again bring Cissy. The difficulty of this, however, was constantly present to her, for the kind of communion to which Cocker's so richly ministered rested on the fact that Cissy and he were so often in different places. She knew by this time all the places—Suchbury, Monkhouse, Whiteroy, Finches,—and even how the parties, on these occasions, were composed; but her subtlety found ways to make her knowledge fairly protect and promote their keeping, as she had heard Mrs. Jordan say, in touch. So, when he actually sometimes smiled as if he really felt the awkwardness of giving her again one of the same old addresses, all her being went out in the desire—which her face must have expressed—that he should recognise her forbearance to criticise as one of the finest, tenderest sacrifices a woman had ever made for love.

XII

She was occasionally worried, all the same, by the impression that these sacrifices, great as they were, were nothing to those that his own passion had imposed; if indeed it was not rather the passion of his confederate, which had caught him up and was whirling him round like a great steam-wheel. He was at any rate in the strong grip of a dizzy, splendid fate; the wild wind of his life blew him straight before it. Didn't she catch in his face, at times, even through his smile and his happy habit, the gleam of that pale glare with which a bewildered victim appeals, as he passes, to some pair of pitying eyes? He perhaps didn't even himself know how scared he was; but *she* knew. They were in danger, they were in danger, Captain Everard and Lady Bradeen: it beat every novel in the shop. She thought of Mr. Mudge and his safe sentiment; she thought of herself and blushed even more for her tepid response to it. It was a comfort to her at such moments to feel that in another relation —a relation supplying that affinity with her nature that Mr. Mudge, deluded creature, would never supply—she should have been no more tepid than her ladyship. Her deepest soundings were on two or three occasions of finding herself almost sure that, if she dared, her ladyship's lover would have gathered relief from "speaking" to her. She literally fancied once or twice that, projected as he was toward his doom, her own eyes struck him, while the air roared in his ears, as the one pitying pair in the crowd. But how could he speak to her while she sat sandwiched there between the counter-clerk and the sounder?

She had long ago, in her comings and goings, made acquaintance with Park Chambers, and reflected, as she looked up at their luxurious front, that *they*, of course, would supply the ideal setting for the ideal speech. There was not a picture in London that, before the season was over, was more stamped upon her brain. She went round about to pass it, for it was not on the short way; she passed on the opposite side of the street and always looked up, though it had taken her a long time to be sure of the particular set of windows. She had made that out at last by an act of audacity that, at the time, had almost stopped her heart-beats and that, in retrospect, greatly quickened her blushes. One evening, late, she had lingered and watched—watched for some moment when the porter, who was in uniform and often on the steps, had gone in with a visitor. Then she followed boldly, on the calculation that he would have taken the visitor up and that the hall would be free. The hall *was* free, and the electric light played over the gilded and lettered board that showed the names and numbers of the occupants of the different floors. What she wanted looked straight at her—Captain Everard was on the third. It was as if, in the immense intimacy of this, they were, for the instant and the first time, face to face outside the cage. Alas! they were face to face but a second or two: she was whirled out on the wings of a panic fear that he might just then be entering or issuing. This fear was indeed, in her shameless deflections, never very far from her, and was mixed in the oddest way with depressions and disappointments. It was dreadful, as she trembled by, to run the risk of looking to him as if she basely hung about; and yet it was dreadful to be obliged to pass only at such moments as put an encounter out of the question.

At the horrible hour of her first coming to Cocker's he was always—it was to be hoped—snug in bed; and at the hour of her final departure he was of course—she had such things all on her fingers'-ends—dressing for dinner. We may let it pass that if she could not bring herself to hover till he was dressed, this was simply because such a process for such a person could only be terribly prolonged. When she went in the middle of the day to her own dinner she had too little time to do anything but go straight, though it must be added that for a real certainty she would joyously have omitted the repast. She had made up her mind as to there being on the whole no decent pretext to justify her flitting casually past at three o'clock in the morning. That was the hour at which, if the ha'penny novels were not all wrong, he probably came home for the night. She was therefore reduced to merely picturing that miraculous meeting toward which a hundred impossibilities would have to conspire. But if nothing was more impossible than the fact, nothing was more intense than the vision. What may not, we can only moralise, take place in the quickened, muffled perception of a girl of a certain kind of soul? All our young friend's native distinction, her refinement of personal grain, of heredity, of pride, took refuge in this small throbbing spot; for when she was most conscious of the abjection of her vanity and the pitifulness of her little flutters and manœuvres, then the consolation and the redemption were most sure to shine before her in some just discernible sign. He did like her!

XIII

He never brought Cissy back, but Cissy came one day without him, as fresh as before from the hands of Marguerite, or only, at the season's end, a trifle less fresh. She was, however, distinctly less serene. She had brought nothing with her, and looked about with some impatience for the forms and the place to write. The latter convenience, at Cocker's, was obscure and barely adequate, and her clear voice had the light note of disgust which her lover's never showed as she responded with a "There?" of surprise to the gesture made by the counter-clerk in answer to her sharp inquiry. Our young friend was busy with half a dozen people, but she had despatched them in her most business-like manner by the time her ladyship flung through the bars the light of re-appearance. Then the directness with which the girl managed to receive this missive was the result of the concentration that had caused her to make the stamps fly during the few minutes occupied by the production of it. This concentration, in turn, may be described as the effect of the apprehension of imminent relief. It was nineteen days, counted and checked off, since she had seen the object of her homage; and as, had he been in London, she should, with his habits, have been sure to see him often, she was now about to learn what other spot his presence might just then happen to sanctify. For she thought of them, the other spots, as ecstatically conscious of it, expressively happy in it.

But, gracious, how handsome *was* her ladyship, and what an added price it gave him that the air of intimacy he threw out should have flowed originally from such a source! The girl looked straight through the cage at the eyes and lips that must so often have been so near his own—looked at them with a strange passion that, for an instant, had the result of filling out some of the gaps, supplying the missing answers, in his correspondence. Then, as she made out that the features she thus scanned and associated were totally unaware of it, that they glowed only with the colour of quite other and not at all guessable thoughts, this directly added to their splendour, gave the girl the sharpest impression she had yet received of the uplifted, the unattainable plains of heaven, and yet at the same time caused her to thrill with a sense of the high company she did somehow keep. She was with the absent through her ladyship and with her ladyship through the absent. The only pang—but it didn't matter—was the proof in the admirable face, in the sightless pre-occupation of its possessor, that the latter hadn't a notion of her. Her folly had gone to the point of half believing that the other party to the affair must sometimes mention in Eaton Square the extraordinary little person at the place from which he so often wired. Yet the perception of her visitor's blankness actually helped this extraordinary little person, the next instant, to take refuge in a reflection that could be as proud as it liked. "How little she knows, how little she knows!" the girl cried to herself; for what did that show after all but that Captain Everard's telegraphic confidant was Captain Everard's charming secret? Our young friend's perusal of her ladyship's telegram was literally prolonged by a momentary daze: what swam between her and the words, making her see them as through rippled, shallow, sunshot water, was the great, the perpetual flood of "How much *I* know—how much *I* know!" This produced a delay in her catching that, on the face, these words didn't give her what she wanted, though she was prompt enough with her remembrance that her grasp was, half the time, just of what was *not* on the face. "Miss Dolman, Parade Lodge, Parade Terrace, Dover. Let him instantly know right one, Hôtel de France, Ostend.[2] Make it seven nine four nine six one. Wire me alternative Burfield's."

The girl slowly counted. Then he was at Ostend. This hooked on with so sharp a click that, not to feel she was as quickly letting it all slip from her, she had absolutely to hold it a minute longer and to do something to that end. Thus it was that she did on this occasion what she never did—threw off an "Answer paid?" that sounded officious, but that she partly made up for by deliberately affixing the stamps and by waiting till she had done so to give change. She had, for so much coolness, the strength that she considered she knew all about Miss Dolman.

"Yes—paid." She saw all sorts of things in this reply, even to a small, suppressed start of surprise at so correct an assumption; even to an attempt, the next minute, at a fresh air of detachment. "How much, with the answer?" The calculation was not abstruse, but our intense observer required a moment more to make it, and this gave her ladyship time for a second thought. "Oh, just wait!" The white, begemmed hand bared to write rose in sudden nervousness to the side of the wonderful face which, with eyes of anxiety for the paper on the counter, she brought closer to the bars of the cage. "I think I must alter a word!" On this she recovered her telegram and looked over it again; but she had a new, obvious trouble, and studied it without deciding and with much of the effect of making our young woman watch her.

2. Port city in Belgium.

This personage, meanwhile, at the sight of her expression, had decided on the spot. If she had always been sure they were in danger, her ladyship's expression was the best possible sign of it. There was a word wrong, but she had lost the right one, and much, clearly, depended on her finding it again. The girl, therefore, sufficiently estimating the affluence of customers and the distraction of Mr. Buckton and the counter-clerk, took the jump and gave it. "Isn't it Cooper's?"

It was as if she had bodily leaped—cleared the top of the cage and alighted on her interlocutress. "Cooper's?"—the stare was heightened by a blush. Yes, she had made Juno blush.

This was all the more reason for going on. "I mean instead of Burfield's."

Our young friend fairly pitied her; she had made her in an instant so helpless, and yet not a bit haughty nor outraged. She was only mystified and scared. "Oh, you know——?"

"Yes, I know!" Our young friend smiled, meeting the other's eyes, and, having made Juno blush, proceeded to patronise her. "*I'll* do it"—she put out a competent hand. Her ladyship only submitted, confused and bewildered, all presence of mind quite gone; and the next moment the telegram was in the cage again and its author out of the shop. Then quickly, boldly, under all the eyes that might have witnessed her tampering, the extraordinary little person at Cocker's made the proper change. People were really too giddy, and if they *were*, in a certain case, to be caught, it shouldn't be the fault of her own grand memory. Hadn't it been settled weeks before?— for Miss Dolman it was always to be "Cooper's."

XIV

But the summer "holidays" brought a marked difference; they were holidays for almost everyone but the animals in the cage. The August days were flat and dry, and, with so little to feed it, she was conscious of the ebb of her interest in the secrets of the refined. She was in a position to follow the refined to the extent of knowing—they had made so many of their arrangements with her aid—exactly where they were; yet she felt quite as if the panorama had ceased unrolling and the band stopped playing. A stray member of the latter occasionally turned up, but the communications that passed before her bore now largely on rooms at hotels, prices of furnished houses, hours of trains, dates of sailings and arrangements for being "met": she found them for the most part prosaic and coarse. The only thing was that they brought into her stuffy corner as straight a whiff of Alpine meadows and Scotch moors as she might hope ever to inhale; there were moreover, in especial,

fat, hot, dull ladies who had out with her, to exasperation, the terms
for seaside lodgings, which struck her as huge, and the matter of
the number of beds required, which was not less portentous: this
in reference to places of which the names—Eastbourne, Folke-
stone, Cromer, Scarborough, Whitby—tormented her with something of the sound of the plash of water that haunts the traveller
in the desert. She had not been out of London for a dozen years,
and the only thing to give a taste to the present dead weeks was
the spice of a chronic resentment. The sparse customers, the people
she did see, were the people who were "just off"—off on the decks
of fluttered yachts, off to the uttermost point of rocky headlands
where the very breeze was then playing for the want of which she
said to herself that she sickened.

There was accordingly a sense in which, at such a period, the
great differences of the human condition could press upon her
more than ever; a circumstance drawing fresh force, in truth, from
the very fact of the chance that at last, for a change, did squarely
meet her—the chance to be "off," for a bit, almost as far as anybody. They took their turns in the cage as they took them both in
the shop and at Chalk Farm, and she had known these two months
that time was to be allowed in September—no less than eleven
days—for her personal, private holiday. Much of her recent intercourse with Mr. Mudge had consisted of the hopes and fears, expressed mainly by himself, involved in the question of their getting
the same dates—a question that, in proportion as the delight
seemed assured, spread into a sea of speculation over the choice of
where and how. All through July, on the Sunday evenings and at
such other odd times as he could seize, he had flooded their talk
with wild waves of calculation. It was practically settled that, with
her mother, somewhere "on the south coast" (a phrase of which
she liked the sound) they should put in their allowance together;
but she already felt the prospect quite weary and worn with the way
he went round and round on it. It had become his sole topic, the
theme alike of his most solemn prudences and most placid jests, to
which every opening led for return and revision and in which every
little flower of a foretaste was pulled up as soon as planted. He had
announced at the earliest day—characterising the whole business,
from that moment, as their "plans," under which name he handled
it as a syndicate handles a Chinese, or other, Loan—he had
promptly declared that the question must be thoroughly studied,
and he produced, on the whole subject, from day to day, an amount
of information that excited her wonder and even, not a little, as she
frankly let him know, her disdain. When she thought of the danger
in which another pair of lovers rapturously lived, she inquired of
him anew why he could leave nothing to chance. Then she got for

answer that this profundity was just his pride, and he pitted Rams-gate against Bournemouth and even Boulogne against Jersey[3]—for he had great ideas—with all the mastery of detail that was some day, professionally, to carry him far.

The longer the time since she had seen Captain Everard, the more she was booked, as she called it, to pass Park Chambers; and this was the sole amusement that, in the lingering August days and the long, sad twilights, it was left her to cultivate. She had long since learned to know it for a feeble one, though its feebleness was perhaps scarce the reason for her saying to herself each evening as her time for departure approached: "No, no—not to-night." She never failed of that silent remark, any more than she failed of feel-ing, in some deeper place than she had even yet fully sounded, that one's remarks were as weak as straws, and that, however one might indulge in them at eight o'clock, one's fate infallibly declared itself in absolute indifference to them at about eight-fifteen. Remarks were remarks, and very well for that; but fate was fate, and this young lady's was to pass Park Chambers every night in the working week. Out of the immensity of her knowledge of the life of the world there bloomed on these occasions a specific remembrance that it was regarded in that region, in August and September, as rather pleasant just to be caught for something or other in passing through town. Somebody was always passing and somebody might catch somebody else. It was in full cognisance of this subtle law that she adhered to the most ridiculous circuit she could have made to get home. One warm, dull, featureless Friday, when an accident had made her start from Cocker's a little later than usual, she be-came aware that something of which the infinite possibilities had for so long peopled her dreams was at last prodigiously upon her, though the perfection in which the conditions happened to present it was almost rich enough to be but the positive creation of a dream. She saw, straight before her, like a vista painted in a picture, the empty street and the lamps that burned pale in the dusk not yet established. It was into the convenience of this quiet twilight that a gentleman on the doorstep of the Chambers gazed with a vague-ness that our young lady's little figure violently trembled, in the approach, with the measure of its power to dissipate. Everything indeed grew in a flash terrific and distinct; her old uncertainties fell away from her, and, since she was so familiar with fate, she felt as if the very nail that fixed it were driven in by the hard look with which, for a moment, Captain Everard awaited her.

The vestibule was open behind him and the porter as absent as on the day she had peeped in; he had just come out—was in town,

3. Seaside resort towns.

in a tweed suit and a pot hat, but between two journeys—duly bored over his evening and at a loss what to do with it. Then it was that she was glad she had never met him in that way before: she reaped with such ecstasy the benefit of his not being able to think she passed often. She jumped in two seconds to the determination that he should even suppose it to be the first time and the queerest chance: this was while she still wondered if he would identify or notice her. His original attention had not, she instinctively knew, been for the young woman at Cocker's; it had only been for any young woman who might advance with an air of not upholding ugliness. Ah, but then, and just as she had reached the door, came his second observation, a long, light reach with which, visibly and quite amusedly, he recalled and placed her. They were on different sides, but the street, narrow and still, had only made more of a stage for the small momentary drama. It was not over, besides it was far from over, even on his sending across the way, with the pleasantest laugh she had ever heard, a little lift of his hat and an "Oh, good evening!" It was still less over on their meeting, the next minute, though rather indirectly and awkwardly, in the middle of the road—a situation to which three or four steps of her own had unmistakably contributed,—and then passing not again to the side on which she had arrived, but back toward the portal of Park Chambers.

"I didn't know you at first. Are you taking a walk?"

"Oh, I don't take walks at night! I'm going home after my work."

"Oh!"

That was practically what they had meanwhile smiled out, and his exclamation, to which, for a minute, he appeared to have nothing to add, left them face to face and in just such an attitude as, for his part, he might have worn had he been wondering if he could properly ask her to come in. During this interval, in fact, she really felt his question to be just "*How* properly——?" It was simply a question of the degree of properness.

XV

She never knew afterwards quite what she had done to settle it, and at the time she only knew that they presently moved, with vagueness, but with continuity, away from the picture of the lighted vestibule and the quiet stairs and well up the street together. This also must have been in the absence of a definite permission, of anything vulgarly articulate, for that matter, on the part of either; and it was to be, later on, a thing of remembrance and reflection for her that the limit of what, just here, for a longish minute, passed between them was his taking in her thoroughly successful depre-

cation, though conveyed without pride or sound or touch, of the
idea that she might be, out of the cage, the very shopgirl at large
that she hugged the theory she was not. Yes, it was strange, she
afterwards thought, that so much could have come and gone and
yet not troubled the air either with impertinence or with resentment, with any of the horrid notes of that kind of acquaintance.
He had taken no liberty, as she would have called it; and, through
not having to betray the sense of one, she herself had, still more
charmingly, taken none. Yet on the spot, nevertheless, she could
speculate as to what it meant that, if his relation with Lady Bradeen
continued to be what her mind had built it up to, he should feel
free to proceed in any private direction. This was one of the questions he was to leave her to deal with—the question whether people
of his sort still asked girls up to their rooms when they were so
awfully in love with other women. Could people of his sort do that
without what people of *her* sort would call being "false to their
love"? She had already a vision of how the true answer was that
people of her sort didn't, in such cases, matter—didn't count as
infidelity, counted only as something else: she might have been
curious, since it came to that, to see exactly what.

Strolling together slowly in their summer twilight and their empty
corner of Mayfair, they found themselves emerge at last opposite
to one of the smaller gates of the Park; upon which, without any
particular word about it—they were talking so of other things—
they crossed the street and went in and sat down on a bench. She
had gathered by this time one magnificent hope about him—the
hope that he would say nothing vulgar. She knew what she meant
by that; she meant something quite apart from any matter of his
being "false." Their bench was not far within; it was near the Park
Lane paling and the patchy lamplight and the rumbling cabs and
'buses. A strange emotion had come to her, and she felt indeed
excitement within excitement; above all a conscious joy in testing
him with chances he didn't take. She had an intense desire he
should know the type she really was without her doing anything so
low as tell him, and he had surely begun to know it from the moment he didn't seize the opportunities into which a common man
would promptly have blundered. These were on the mere surface,
and *their* relation was behind and below them. She had questioned
so little on the way what they were doing, that as soon as they were
seated she took straight hold of it. Her hours, her confinement, the
many conditions of service in the post-office, had—with a glance
at his own postal resources and alternatives—formed, up to this
stage, the subject of their talk. "Well, here we are, and it may be
right enough; but this isn't the least, you know, where I was going."

"You were going home?"

"Yes, and I was already rather late. I was going to my supper."

"You haven't had it?"

"No, indeed!"

"Then you haven't eaten——?"

He looked, of a sudden, so extravagantly concerned that he laughed out. "All day? Yes, we do feed once. But that was long ago. So I must presently say good-bye."

"Oh, deary *me!*" he exclaimed, with an intonation so droll and yet a touch so light and a distress so marked—a confession of helplessness for such a case, in short, so unrelieved—that she felt sure, on the spot, she had made the great difference plain. He looked at her with the kindest eyes and still without saying what she had known he wouldn't. She had known he wouldn't say, "Then sup with *me!*" but the proof of it made her feel as if she had feasted.

"I'm not a bit hungry," she went on.

"Ah, you *must* be, awfully!" he made answer, but settling himself on the bench as if, after all, that needn't interfere with his spending his evening. "I've always quite wanted the chance to thank you for the trouble you so often take for me."

"Yes, I know," she replied; uttering the words with a sense of the situation far deeper than any pretence of not fitting his allusion. She immediately saw that he was surprised and even a little puzzled at her frank assent; but, for herself, the trouble she had taken could only, in these fleeting minutes—they would probably never come back—be all there like a little hoard of gold in her lap. Certainly he might look at it, handle it, take up the pieces. Yet if he understood anything he must understand all. "I consider you've already immensely thanked me." The horror was back upon her of having seemed to hang about for some reward. "It's awfully odd that you should have been there just the one time——!"

"The one time you've passed my place?"

"Yes; you can fancy I haven't many minutes to waste. There was a place to-night I had to stop at."

"I see, I see"—he knew already so much about her work. "It must be an awful grind—for a lady."

"It is; but I don't think I groan over it any more than my companions—and you've seen *they're* not ladies!" She mildly jested, but with an intention. "One gets used to things, and there are employments I should have hated much more." She had the finest conception of the beauty of not, at least, boring him. To whine, to count up her wrongs, was what a barmaid or a shopgirl would do, and it was quite enough to sit there like one of these.

"If you had had another employment," he remarked after a moment, "we might never have become acquainted."

"It's highly probable—and certainly not in the same way." Then, still with her heap of gold in her lap and something of the pride of it in her manner of holding her head, she continued not to move —she only smiled at him. The evening had thickened now; the scattered lamps were red; the Park, all before them, was full of obscure and ambiguous life; there were other couples on other benches, whom it was impossible not to see, yet at whom it was impossible to look. "But I've walked so much out of my way with you only just to show you that—that"—with this she paused; it was not, after all, so easy to express—"that anything you may have thought is perfectly true."

"Oh, I've thought a tremendous lot!" her companion laughed. "Do you mind my smoking?"

"Why should I? You always smoke *there*."

"At your place? Oh yes, but here it's different."

"No," she said, as he lighted a cigarette, "that's just what it isn't. It's quite the same."

"Well, then, that's because 'there' it's so wonderful!"

"Then you're conscious of how wonderful it is?" she returned.

He jerked his handsome head in literal protest at a doubt. "Why, that's exactly what I mean by my gratitude for all your trouble. It has been just as if you took a particular interest." She only looked at him in answer to this, in such sudden, immediate embarrassment, as she was quite aware, that, while she remained silent, he showed he was at a loss to interpret her expression. "You *have*—haven't you?—taken a particular interest?"

"Oh, a particular interest!" she quavered out, feeling the whole thing—her immediate embarrassment—get terribly the better of her, and wishing, with a sudden scare, all the more to keep her emotion down. She maintained her fixed smile a moment and turned her eyes over the peopled darkness, unconfused now, because there was something much more confusing. This, with a fatal great rush, was simply the fact that they were thus together. They were near, near, and all that she had imagined of that had only become more true, more dreadful and overwhelming. She stared straight away in silence till she felt that she looked like an idiot; then, to say something, to say nothing, she attempted a sound which ended in a flood of tears.

XVI

Her tears helped her really to dissimulate, for she had instantly, in so public a situation, to recover herself. They had come and gone in half a minute, and she immediately explained them. "It's only because I'm tired. It's that—it's that!" Then she added a trifle incoherently: "I shall never see you again."

"Ah, but why not?" The mere tone in which her companion asked this satisfied her once for all as to the amount of imagination for which she could count on him. It was naturally not large: it had exhausted itself in having arrived at what he had already touched upon—the sense of an intention in her poor zeal at Cocker's. But any deficiency of this kind was no fault in him: *he* wasn't obliged to have an inferior cleverness—to have second-rate resources and virtues. It had been as if he almost really believed she had simply cried for fatigue, and he had accordingly put in some kind, confused plea—"You ought really to take something: won't you have something or other *somewhere?*"—to which she had made no response but a headshake of a sharpness that settled it. "Why shan't we all the more keep meeting?"

"I mean meeting this way—only this way. At my place there—*that* I've nothing to do with, and I hope of course you'll turn up, with your correspondence, when it suits you. Whether I stay or not, I mean; for I shall probably not stay."

"You're going somewhere else?"—he put it with positive anxiety.

"Yes; ever so far away—to the other end of London. There are all sorts of reasons I can't tell you; and it's practically settled. It's better for me, much; and I've only kept on at Cocker's for you."

"For me?"

Making out in the dusk that he fairly blushed, she now measured how far he had been from knowing too much. Too much, she called it at present; and that was easy, since it proved so abundantly enough for her that he should simply be where he was. "As we shall never talk this way but tonight—never, never again!—here it all is; I'll say it; I don't care what you think; it doesn't matter; I only want to help you. Besides, you're kind—you're kind. I've been thinking, then, of leaving for ever so long. But you've come so often—at times,—and you've had so much to do, and it has been so pleasant and interesting, that I've remained, I've kept putting off any change. More than once, when I had nearly decided, you've turned up again and I've thought, 'Oh no!' That's the simple fact!" She had by this time got her confusion down so completely that she could laugh. "This is what I meant when I said to you just now that I 'knew.' I've known perfectly that you knew I took trouble for you; and that knowledge has been for me, and I seemed to see it was for you, as if there were something—I don't know what to call it!—between us. I mean something unusual and good—something not a bit horrid or vulgar."

She had by this time, she could see, produced a great effect upon him; but she would have spoken the truth to herself if she had at the same moment declared that she didn't in the least care: all the more that the effect must be one of extreme perplexity. What, in it all, was visibly clear for him, none the less, was that he was tre-mendously glad he had met her. She held him, and he was aston-ished at the force of it; he was intent, immensely considerate. His elbow was on the back of the seat, and his head, with the pot-hat pushed quite back, in a boyish way, so that she really saw almost for the first time his forehead and hair, rested on the hand into which he had crumpled his gloves. "Yes," he assented, "it's not a bit horrid or vulgar."

She just hung fire a moment; then she brought out the whole truth. "I'd do anything for you. I'd do anything for you." Never in her life had she known anything so high and fine as this, just letting him have it and bravely and magnificently leaving it. Didn't the place, the associations and circumstances, perfectly make it sound what it was not? and wasn't that exactly the beauty?

So she bravely and magnificently left it, and little by little she felt him take it up, take it down, as if they had been on a satin sofa in a boudoir. She had never seen a boudoir, but there had been lots of boudoirs in the telegrams. What she had said, at all events, sank into him, so that after a minute he simply made a movement that had the result of placing his hand on her own—presently indeed that of her feeling herself firmly enough grasped. There was no pressure she need return, there was none she need decline; she just sat admirably still, satisfied, for the time, with the surprise and bewilderment of the impression she made on him. His agitation was even greater, on the whole, than she had at first allowed for. "I say, you know, you mustn't think of leaving!" he at last broke out.

"Of leaving Cocker's, you mean?"

"Yes, you must stay on there, whatever happens, and help a fellow."

She was silent a little, partly because it was so strange and ex-quisite to feel him watch her as if it really mattered to him and he were almost in suspense. "Then you *have* quite recognised what I've tried to do?" she asked.

"Why, wasn't that exactly what I dashed over from my door just now to thank you for?"

"Yes; so you said."

"And don't you believe it?"

She looked down a moment at his hand, which continued to cover her own; whereupon he presently drew it back, rather rest-lessly folding his arms. Without answering his question she went on: "Have you ever spoken of me?"

"Spoken of you?"

"Of my being there—of my knowing, and that sort of thing."

"Oh, never to a human creature!" he eagerly declared.

She had a small drop at this, which was expressed in another pause; after which she returned to what he had just asked her.

"Oh yes, I quite believe you like it—my always being there and our taking things up so familiarly and successfully: if not exactly where we left them," she laughed, "almost always, at least, in an interesting place!" He was about to say something in reply to this, but her friendly gaiety was quicker. "You want a great many things in life, a great many comforts and helps and luxuries—you want everything as pleasant as possible. Therefore, so far as it's in the power of any particular person to contribute to all that——" She had turned her face to him smiling, just thinking.

"Oh, see here!" But he was highly amused. "Well, what then?" he inquired, as if to humour her.

"Why, the particular person must never fail. We must manage it for you somehow."

He threw back his head, laughing out; he was really exhilarated. "Oh yes, somehow!"

"Well, I think we each do—don't we?—in one little way and another and according to our limited lights. I'm pleased, at any rate, for myself, that you are; for I assure you I've done my best."

"You do better than any one!" He had struck a match for another cigarette, and the flame lighted an instant his responsive, finished face, magnifying into a pleasant grimace the kindness with which he paid her this tribute. "You're awfully clever, you know; cleverer, cleverer, cleverer——!" He had appeared on the point of making some tremendous statement; then suddenly, puffing his cigarette and shifting almost with violence on his seat, let it altogether fall.

XVII

In spite of this drop, if not just by reason of it, she felt as if Lady Bradeen, all but named out, had popped straight up; and she practically betrayed her consciousness by waiting a little before she rejoined: "Cleverer than who?"

"Well, if I wasn't afraid you'd think I swagger, I should say—than anybody! If you leave your place there, where shall you go?" he more gravely demanded.

"Oh, too far for you ever to find me!"

"I'd find you anywhere."

The tone of this was so still more serious that she had but her one acknowledgment. "I'd do anything for you—I'd do anything for you," she repeated. She had already, she felt, said it all; so what did anything more, anything less, matter? That was the very reason indeed why she could, with a lighter note, ease him generously of any awkwardness produced by solemnity, either his own or hers. "Of course it must be nice for you to be able to think there are people all about who feel in such a way."

In immediate appreciation of this, however, he only smoked without looking at her. "But you don't want to give up your present work?" he at last inquired. "I mean you *will* stay in the post-office?"

"Oh yes; I think I've a genius for that."

"Rather! No one can touch you." With this he turned more to her again. "But you can get, with a move, greater advantages?"

"I can get, in the suburbs, cheaper lodgings. I live with my mother. We need some space; and there's a particular place that has other inducements."

He just hesitated. "Where is it?"

"Oh, quite out of *your* way. You'd never have time."

"But I tell you I'd go anywhere. Don't you believe it?"

"Yes, for once or twice. But you'd soon see it wouldn't do for you."

He smoked and considered; seemed to stretch himself a little and, with his legs out, surrender himself comfortably. "Well, well, well—I believe everything you say. I take it from you—anything you like—in the most extraordinary way." It struck her certainly—and almost without bitterness—that the way in which she was already, as if she had been an old friend, arranging for him and preparing the only magnificence she could muster, was quite the most extraordinary. "Don't, *don't* go!" he presently went on. "I shall miss you too horribly!"

"So that you just put it to me as a definite request?"—oh, how she tried to divest this of all sound of the hardness of bargaining! That ought to have been easy enough, for what was she arranging to get? Before he could answer she had continued: "To be perfectly fair, I should tell you I recognise at Cocker's certain strong attractions. All you people come. I like all the horrors."

"The horrors?"

"Those you all—you know the set I mean, *your* set—show me with as good a conscience as if I had no more feeling than a letter-box."

He looked quite excited at the way she put it. "Oh, they don't know!"

"Don't know I'm not stupid? No, how should they?"

"Yes, how should they?" said the Captain sympathetically. "But isn't 'horrors' rather strong?"

"What you *do* is rather strong!" the girl promptly returned.

"What *I* do?"

"Your extravagance, your selfishness, your immorality, your crimes," she pursued, without heeding his expression.

"I *say*!"—her companion showed the queerest stare.

"I like them, as I tell you—I revel in them. But we needn't go into that," she quietly went on; "for all I get out of it is the harmless pleasure of knowing. I know, I know, I know!"—she breathed it ever so gently.

"Yes; that's what has been between us," he answered much more simply.

She could enjoy his simplicity in silence, and for a moment she did so. "If I do stay because you want it—and I'm rather capable of that—there are two or three things I think you ought to remember. One is, you know, that I'm there sometimes for days and weeks together without your ever coming."

"Oh, I'll come every day!" he exclaimed.

She was on the point, at this, of imitating with her hand his movement of shortly before; but she checked herself, and there was no want of effect in the tranquillising way in which she said: "How can you? How can you?" He had, too manifestly, only to look at it there, in the vulgarly animated gloom, to see that he couldn't; and at this point, by the mere action of his silence, everything they had so definitely not named, the whole presence round which they had been circling became a part of their reference, settled solidly between them. It was as if then, for a minute, they sat and saw it all in each other's eyes, saw so much that there was no need of a transition for sounding it at last. "Your danger, your danger——!" Her voice indeed trembled with it, and she could only, for the moment, again leave it so.

During this moment he leaned back on the bench, meeting her in silence and with a face that grew more strange. It grew so strange that, after a further instant, she got straight up. She stood there as if their talk were now over, and he just sat and watched her. It was as if now—owing to the third person they had brought in—they must be more careful; so that the most he could finally say was: "That's where it is!"

"That's where it is!" the girl as guardedly replied. He sat still, and she added: "I won't abandon you. Good-bye."

"Good-bye?"—he appealed, but without moving.

"I don't quite see my way, but I won't abandon you," she repeated. "There. Good-bye."

It brought him with a jerk to his feet, tossing away his cigarette. His poor face was flushed. "See here—see here!"

"No, I won't; but I must leave you now," she went on as if not hearing him.

"See here—see here!" He tried, from the bench, to take her hand again.

But that definitely settled it for her: this would, after all, be as bad as his asking her to supper. "You mustn't come with me—no, no!"

He sank back, quite blank, as if she had pushed him. "I mayn't see you home?"

"No, no; let me go." He looked almost as if she had struck him, but she didn't care; and the manner in which she spoke—it was literally as if she were angry—had the force of a command. "Stay where you are!"

"See here—see here!" he nevertheless pleaded.

"I won't abandon you!" she cried once more—this time quite with passion; on which she got away from him as fast as she could and left him staring after her.

XVIII

Mr. Mudge had lately been so occupied with their famous "plans" that he had neglected, for a while, the question of her transfer; but down at Bournemouth, which had found itself selected as the field of their recreation by a process consisting, it seemed, exclusively of innumerable pages of the neatest arithmetic in a very greasy but most orderly little pocket-book, the distracting possible melted away—the fleeting irremediable ruled the scene. The plans, hour by hour, were simply superseded, and it was much of a rest to the girl, as she sat on the pier and overlooked the sea and the company, to see them evaporate in rosy fumes and to feel that from moment to moment there was less left to cipher about. The week proved blissfully fine, and her mother, at their lodgings—partly to her embarrassment and partly to her relief—struck up with the landlady an alliance that left the younger couple a great deal of freedom. This relative took her pleasure of a week at Bournemouth in a stuffy back-kitchen and endless talks; to that degree even that Mr. Mudge himself—habitually inclined indeed to a scrutiny of all mysteries and to seeing, as he sometimes admitted, too much in things— made remarks on it as he sat on the cliff with his betrothed, or on the decks of steamers that conveyed them, close-packed items in terrific totals of enjoyment, to the Isle of Wight and the Dorset coast.

He had a lodging in another house, where he had speedily learned the importance of keeping his eyes open, and he made no secret of his suspecting that sinister mutual connivances might spring, under the roof of his companions, from unnatural sociabilities. At the same time he fully recognised that, as a source of anxiety, not to say of expense, his future mother-in-law would have weighted them more in accompanying their steps than in giving her hostess, in the interest of the tendency they considered that they never mentioned, equivalent pledges as to the tea-caddy and the jam-pot. These were the questions—these indeed the familiar commodities—that he had now to put into the scales; and his betrothed had, in consequence, during her holiday, the odd, and yet pleasant and almost languid, sense of an anticlimax. She had become conscious of an extraordinary collapse, a surrender to stillness and to retrospect. She cared neither to walk nor to sail; it was enough for her to sit on benches and wonder at the sea and taste the air and not be at Cocker's and not see the counter-clerk. She still seemed to wait for something—something in the key of the immense discussions that had mapped out their little week of idleness on the scale of a world-atlas. Something came at last, but without perhaps appearing quite adequately to crown the monument.

Preparation and precaution were, however, the natural flowers of Mr. Mudge's mind, and in proportion as these things declined in one quarter they inevitably bloomed elsewhere. He could always, at the worst, have on Tuesday the project of their taking the Swanage boat on Thursday, and on Thursday that of their ordering minced kidneys on Saturday. He had, moreover, a constant gift of inexorable inquiry as to where and what they should have gone and have done if they had not been exactly as they were. He had in short his resources, and his mistress had never been so conscious of them; on the other hand they had never interfered so little with her own. She liked to be as she was—if it could only have lasted. She could accept even without bitterness a rigour of economy so great that the little fee they paid for admission to the pier had to be balanced against other delights. The people at Ladle's and at Thrupp's had *their* ways of amusing themselves, whereas she had to sit and hear Mr. Mudge talk of what he might do if he didn't take a bath, or of the bath he might take if he only hadn't taken something else. He was always with her now, of course, always beside her; she saw him more than "hourly," more than ever yet, more even than he had planned she should do at Chalk Farm. She preferred to sit at the far end, away from the band and the crowd; as to which she had frequent differences with her friend, who reminded her often that they could have only in the thick of it the sense of the money they were getting back. That had little effect on her, for she got back her money by seeing many things, the things of the past year, fall together and connect themselves, undergo the happy relegation that transforms melancholy and misery, passion and effort, into experience and knowledge.

She liked having done with them, as she assured herself she had practically done, and the strange thing was that she neither missed the procession now nor wished to keep her place for it. It had become there, in the sun and the breeze and the sea-smell, a far-away story, a picture of another life. If Mr. Mudge himself liked processions, liked them at Bournemouth and on the pier quite as much as at Chalk Farm or anywhere, she learned after a little not to be worried by his perpetual counting of the figures that made them up. There were dreadful women in particular, usually fat and in men's caps and white shoes, whom he could never let alone—not that *she* cared; it was not the great world, the world of Cocker's and Ladle's and Thrupp's, but it offered an endless field to his faculties of memory, philosophy, and frolic. She had never accepted him so much, never arranged so successfully for making him chatter while she carried on secret conversations. Her talks were with herself; and if they both practised a great thrift, she had quite mastered that of merely spending words enough to keep him imperturbably and continuously going.

He was charmed with the panorama, not knowing—or at any rate not at all showing that he knew—what far other images peopled her mind than the women in the navy caps and the shopboys in the blazers. His observations on these types, his general interpretation of the show, brought home to her the prospect of Chalk Farm. She wondered sometimes that he should have derived so little illumination, during his period, from the society at Cocker's. But one evening, as their holiday cloudlessly waned, he gave her such a proof of his quality as might have made her ashamed of her small reserves. He brought out something that, in all his overflow, he had been able to keep back till other matters were disposed of. It was the announcement that he was at last ready to marry—that he saw his way. A rise at Chalk Farm had been offered him; he was to be taken into the business, bringing with him a capital the estimation of which by other parties constituted the handsomest recognition yet made of the head on his shoulders. Therefore their waiting was over—it could be a question of a near date. They would settle this date before going back, and he meanwhile had his eye on a sweet little home. He would take her to see it on their first Sunday.

XIX

His having kept this great news for the last, having had such a card up his sleeve and not floated it out in the current of his chatter and the luxury of their leisure, was one of those incalculable strokes by which he could still affect her; the kind of thing that reminded her of the latent force that had ejected the drunken soldier—an example of the profundity of which his promotion was the proof. She listened a while in silence, on this occasion, to the wafted strains of the music; she took it in as she had not quite done before that her future was now constituted. Mr. Mudge was distinctly her fate; yet at this moment she turned her face quite away from him, showing him so long a mere quarter of her cheek that she at last again heard his voice. He couldn't see a pair of tears that were partly the reason of her delay to give him the assurance he required; but he expressed at a venture the hope that she had had her fill of Cocker's.

She was finally able to turn back. "Oh, quite. There's nothing going on. No one comes but the Americans at Thrupp's, and *they* don't do much. They don't seem to have a secret in the world."

"Then the extraordinary reason you've been giving me for holding on there has ceased to work?"

She thought a moment. "Yes, that one. I've seen the thing through—I've got them all in my pocket."

"So you're ready to come?"

For a little, again, she made no answer. "No, not yet, all the same. I've still got a reason—a different one."

He looked her all over as if it might have been something she kept in her mouth or her glove or under her jacket—something she was even sitting upon. "Well, I'll have it, please."

"I went out the other night and sat in the Park with a gentleman," she said at last.

Nothing was ever seen like his confidence in her; and she wondered a little now why it didn't irritate her. It only gave her ease and space, as she felt, for telling him the whole truth that no one knew. It had arrived at present at her really wanting to do that, and yet to do it not in the least for Mr. Mudge, but altogether and only for herself. This truth filled out for her there the whole experience she was about to relinquish, suffused and coloured it as a picture that she should keep and that, describe it as she might, no one but herself would ever really see. Moreover she had no desire whatever to make Mr. Mudge jealous; there would be no amusement in it, for the amusement she had lately known had spoiled her for lower pleasures. There were even no materials for it. The odd thing was that she never doubted that, properly handled, his passion was poisonable; what had happened was that he had cannily selected a partner with no poison to distill. She read then and there that she should never interest herself in anybody as to whom some other sentiment, some superior view, wouldn't be sure to interfere, for him, with jealousy. "And what did you get out of that?" he asked with a concern that was not in the least for his honour.

"Nothing but a good chance to promise him I wouldn't forsake him. He's one of my customers."

"Then it's for him not to forsake *you*."

"Well, he won't. It's all right. But I must just keep on as long as he may want me."

"Want you to sit with him in the Park?"

"He may want me for that—but I shan't. I rather liked it, but once, under the circumstances, is enough. I can do better for him in another manner."

"And what manner, pray?"

"Well, elsewhere."

"Elsewhere?—I *say*!"

This was an ejaculation used also by Captain Everard, but, oh, with what a different sound! "You needn't 'say'—there's nothing to be said. And yet you ought perhaps to know."

"Certainly I ought. But *what*—up to now?"

"Why, exactly what I told him. That I would do anything for him."

"What do you mean by 'anything'?"

"Everything."

Mr. Mudge's immediate comment on this statement was to draw from his pocket a crumpled paper containing the remains of half a pound of "sundries." These sundries had figured conspicuously in his prospective sketch of their tour, but it was only at the end of three days that they had defined themselves unmistakably as chocolate-creams. "Have another?—*that* one," he said. She had another, but not the one he indicated, and then he continued: "What took place afterwards?"

"Afterwards?"

"What did you do when you had told him you would do everything?"

"I simply came away."

"Out of the Park?"

"Yes, leaving him there. I didn't let him follow me."

"Then what did you let him do?"

"I didn't let him do anything."

Mr. Mudge considered an instant. "Then what did you go there for?" His tone was even slightly critical.

"I didn't quite know at the time. It was simply to be with him, I suppose—just once. He's in danger, and I wanted him to know I know it. It makes meeting him—at Cocker's, for it's that I want to stay on for—more interesting."

"It makes it mighty interesting for *me*!" Mr. Mudge freely declared. "Yet he didn't follow you?" he asked. "*I* would!"

"Yes, of course. That was the way you began, you know. You're awfully inferior to him."

"Well, my dear, you're not inferior to anybody. You've got a cheek! What is he in danger of?"

"Of being found out. He's in love with a lady—and it isn't right—and *I've* found him out."

"That'll be a look-out for *me!*" Mr. Mudge joked. "You mean she has a husband?"

"Never mind what she has! They're in awful danger, but his is the worst, because he's in danger from her too."

"Like me from you—the woman *I* love? If he's in the same funk as me——"

"He's in a worse one. He's not only afraid of the lady—he's afraid of other things."

Mr. Mudge selected another chocolate-cream. "Well, I'm only afraid of one! But how in the world can you help this party?"

"I don't know—perhaps not at all. But so long as there's a chance——"

"You won't come away?"

"No, you've got to wait for me."

Mr. Mudge enjoyed what was in his mouth. "And what will he give you?"

"Give me?"

"If you do help him."

"Nothing. Nothing in all the wide world."

"Then what will he give *me*?" Mr. Mudge inquired. "I mean for waiting."

The girl thought a moment; then she got up to walk. "He never heard of you," she replied.

"You haven't mentioned me?"

"We never mention anything. What I've told you is just what I've found out."

Mr. Mudge, who had remained on the bench, looked up at her; she often preferred to be quiet when he proposed to walk, but now that he seemed to wish to sit she had a desire to move. "But you haven't told me what *he* has found out."

She considered her lover. "He'd never find *you*, my dear!"

Her lover, still on his seat, appealed to her in something of the attitude in which she had last left Captain Everard, but the impression was not the same. "Then where do I come in?"

"You don't come in at all. That's just the beauty of it!"—and with this she turned to mingle with the multitude collected round the band. Mr. Mudge presently overtook her and drew her arm into his own with a quiet force that expressed the serenity of possession; in consonance with which it was only when they parted for the night at her door that he referred again to what she had told him.

"Have you seen him since?"

"Since the night in the Park? No, not once."

"Oh, what a cad!" said Mr. Mudge.

XX

It was not till the end of October that she saw Captain Everard again, and on that occasion—the only one of all the series on which hindrance had been so utter—no communication with him proved possible. She had made out, even from the cage, that it was a charming golden day: a patch of hazy autumn sunlight lay across the sanded floor and also, higher up, quickened into brightness a row of ruddy bottled syrups. Work was slack and the place in general empty; the town, as they said in the cage, had not waked up, and the feeling of the day likened itself to something that in happier conditions she would have thought of romantically as St. Martin's summer.[4] The counter-clerk had gone to his dinner; she herself was busy with arrears of postal jobs, in the midst of which she became aware that Captain Everard had apparently been in the shop a minute and that Mr. Buckton had already seized him.

He had, as usual, half a dozen telegrams; and when he saw that she saw him and their eyes met, he gave, on bowing to her, an exaggerated laugh in which she read a new consciousness. It was a confession of awkwardness; it seemed to tell her that of course he knew he ought better to have kept his head, ought to have been clever enough to wait, on some pretext, till he should have found her free. Mr. Buckton was a long time with him, and her attention was soon demanded by other visitors; so that nothing passed between them but the fulness of their silence. The look she took from him was his greeting, and the other one a simple sign of the eyes sent her before going out. The only token they exchanged, therefore, was his tacit assent to her wish that, since they couldn't attempt a certain frankness, they should attempt nothing at all. This was her intense preference; she could be as still and cold as any one when that was the sole solution.

Yet, more than any contact hitherto achieved, these counted instants struck her as marking a step: they were built so—just in the mere flash—on the recognition of his now definitely knowing what it was she would do for him. The "anything, anything" she had uttered in the Park went to and fro between them and under the poked-out chins that interposed. It had all at last even put on the air of their not needing now clumsily to manœuvre to converse: their former little postal make-believes, the intense implications of questions and answers and change, had become in the light of the personal fact, of their having had their moment, a possibility comparatively poor. It was as if they had met for all time—it exerted on their being in presence again an influence so prodigious. When

4. Equivalent to "Indian summer."

she watched herself, in the memory of that night, walk away from him as if she were making an end, she found something too pitiful in the primness of such a gait. Hadn't she precisely established on the part of each a consciousness that could end only with death?

It must be admitted that, in spite of this brave margin, an irritation, after he had gone, remained with her; a sense that presently became one with a still sharper hatred of Mr. Buckton, who, on her friend's withdrawal, had retired with the telegrams to the sounder and left her the other work. She knew indeed she should have a chance to see them, when she would, on file; and she was divided, as the day went on, between the two impressions of all that was lost and all that was re-asserted. What beset her above all, and as she had almost never known it before, was the desire to bound straight out, to overtake the autumn afternoon before it passed away for ever and hurry off to the Park and perhaps be with him there again on a bench. It became, for an hour, a fantastic vision with her that he might just have gone to sit and wait for her. She could almost hear him, through the tick of the sounder, scatter with his stick, in his impatience, the fallen leaves of October. Why should such a vision seize her at this particular moment with such a shake? There was a time—from four to five—when she could have cried with happiness and rage.

Business quickened, it seemed, toward five, as if the town did wake up; she had therefore more to do, and she went through it with little sharp stampings and jerkings: she made the crisp postal-orders fairly snap while she breathed to herself: "It's the last day—the last day!" The last day of what? She couldn't have told. All she knew now was that if she *were* out of the cage she wouldn't in the least have minded, this time, its not yet being dark. She would have gone straight toward Park Chambers and have hung about there till no matter when. She would have waited, stayed, rung, asked, have gone in, sat on the stairs. What the day was the last of was probably, to her strained inner sense, the group of golden ones, of any occasion for seeing the hazy sunshine slant at that angle into the smelly shop, of any range of chances for his wishing still to repeat to her the two words that, in the Park, she had scarcely let him bring out. "See here—see here!"—the sound of these two words had been with her perpetually; but it was in her ears to-day without mercy, with a loudness that grew and grew. What was it they then expressed? what was it he had wanted her to see? She seemed, whatever it was, perfectly to see it now—to see that if she should just chuck the whole thing, should have a great and beautiful courage, he would somehow make everything up to her. When the clock struck five she was on the very point of saying to Mr. Buckton that she was deadly ill and rapidly getting worse. This announcement was on her lips, and she had quite composed the pale, hard face she would offer him: "I can't stop—I must go home. If I feel better, later on, I'll come back. I'm very sorry, but I *must* go." At that instant Captain Everard once more stood there, producing in her agitated spirit, by his real presence, the strangest, quickest revolution. He stopped her off without knowing it, and by the time he had been a minute in the shop she felt that she was saved.

That was from the first minute what she called it to herself. There were again other persons with whom she was occupied, and again the situation could only be expressed by their silence. It was expressed, in fact, in a larger phrase than ever yet, for her eyes now spoke to him with a kind of supplication. "Be quiet, be quiet!" they pleaded; and they saw his own reply: "I'll do whatever you say; I won't even look at you—see, see!" They kept conveying thus, with the friendliest liberality, that they wouldn't look, quite positively wouldn't. What she was to see was that he hovered at the other end of the counter, Mr. Buckton's end, surrendered himself again to that frustration. It quickly proved so great indeed that what she was to see further was how he turned away before he was attended to, and hung off, waiting, smoking, looking about the shop; how he went over to Mr. Cocker's own counter and appeared to price things, gave in fact presently two or three orders and put down money, stood there a long time with his back to her, considerately abstaining from any glance round to see if she were free. It at last came to pass in this way that he had remained in the shop longer than she had ever yet known him to do, and that, nevertheless, when he did turn about she could see him time himself—she was freshly taken up—and cross straight to her postal subordinate, whom some one else had released. He had in his hand all this while neither letters nor telegrams, and now that he was close to her— for she was close to the counter-clerk—it brought her heart into her mouth merely to see him look at her neighbour and open his lips. She was too nervous to bear it. He asked for a Post-Office Guide, and the young man whipped out a new one; whereupon he said that he wished not to purchase, but only to consult one a moment; with which, the copy kept on loan being produced, he once more wandered off.

What was he doing to her? What did he want of her? Well, it was just the aggravation of his "See here!" She felt at this moment strangely and portentously afraid of him—had in her ears the hum of a sense that, should it come to that kind of tension, she must fly on the spot to Chalk Farm. Mixed with her dread and with her reflection was the idea that, if he wanted her so much as he seemed to show, it might be after all simply to do for him the "anything" she had promised, the "everything" she had thought it so fine to

bring out to Mr. Mudge. He might want her to help him, might
have some particular appeal; though, of a truth, his manner didn't
denote that—denoted, on the contrary, an embarrassment, an in-
decision, something of a desire not so much to be helped as to be
treated rather more nicely than she had treated him the other time.
Yes, he considered quite probably that he had help rather to offer
than to ask for. Still, none the less, when he again saw her free he
continued to keep away from her; when he came back with his
Guide it was Mr. Buckton he caught—it was from Mr. Buckton he
obtained half-a-crown's-worth of stamps.

After asking for the stamps he asked, quite as a second thought,
for a postal-order for ten shillings. What did he want with so many
stamps when he wrote so few letters? How could he enclose a
postal-order in a telegram? She expected him, the next thing, to go
into the corner and make up one of his telegrams—half a dozen of
them—on purpose to prolong his presence. She had so completely
stopped looking at him that she could only guess his movements—
guess even where his eyes rested. Finally she saw him make a dash
that might have been towards the nook where the forms were hung;
and at this she suddenly felt that she couldn't keep it up. The
counter-clerk had just taken a telegram from a slavey, and, to give
herself something to cover her, she snatched it out of his hand. The
gesture was so violent that he gave her an odd look, and she also
perceived that Mr. Buckton noticed it. The latter personage, with
a quick stare at her, appeared for an instant to wonder whether his
snatching it in *his* turn mightn't be the thing she would least like,
and she anticipated this practical criticism by the frankest glare she
had ever given him. It sufficed: this time it paralysed him; and she
sought with her trophy the refuge of the sounder.

XXI

It was repeated the next day; it went on for three days; and at
the end of that time she knew what to think. When, at the beginning, she had emerged from her temporary shelter Captain Everard
had quitted the shop; and he had not come again that evening, as
it had struck her he possibly might—might all the more easily that
there were numberless persons who came, morning and afternoon,
numberless times, so that he wouldn't necessarily have attracted
attention. The second day it was different and yet on the whole
worse. His access to her had become possible—she felt herself even
reaping the fruit of her yesterday's glare at Mr. Buckton; but trans-
acting his business with him didn't simplify—it could, in spite of
the rigour of circumstance, feed so her new conviction. The rigour
was tremendous, and his telegrams—not, now, mere pretexts for

getting at her—were apparently genuine; yet the conviction had taken but a night to develop. It could be simply enough expressed; she had had the glimmer of it the day before in her idea that he needed no more help than she had already given; that it was help he himself was prepared to render. He had come up to town but for three or four days; he had been absolutely obliged to be absent after the other time; yet he would, now that he was face to face with her, stay on as much longer as she liked. Little by little it was thus clarified, though from the first flash of his re-appearance she had read into it the real essence.

That was what the night before, at eight o'clock, her hour to go, had made her hang back and dawdle. She did last things or pretended to do them; to be in the cage had suddenly become her safety, and she was literally afraid of the alternate self who might be waiting outside. *He* might be waiting; it was he who was her alternate self, and of him she was afraid. The most extraordinary change had taken place in her from the moment of her catching the impression he seemed to have returned on purpose to give her. Just before she had done so, on that bewitched afternoon, she had seen herself approach, without a scruple, the porter at Park Chambers; then, as the effect of the rush of a consciousness quite altered, she had, on at last quitting Cocker's, gone straight home for the first time since her return from Bournemouth. She had passed his door every night for weeks, but nothing would have induced her to pass it now. This change was the tribute of her fear—the result of a change in himself as to which she needed no more explanation than his mere face vividly gave her; strange though it was to find an element of deterrence in the object that she regarded as the most beautiful in the world. He had taken it from her in the Park that night that she wanted him not to propose to her to sup; but he had put away the lesson by this time—he practically proposed supper every time he looked at her. This was what, for that matter, mainly filled the three days. He came in twice on each of these, and it was as if he came in to give her a chance to relent. That was, after all, she said to herself in the intervals, the most that he did. There were ways, she fully recognised, in which he spared her, and other particular ways as to which she meant that her silence should be full, to him, of exquisite pleading. The most particular of all was his not being outside, at the corner, when she quitted the place for the night. This he might so easily have been—so easily if he hadn't been so nice. She continued to recognise in his forbearance the fruit of her dumb supplication, and the only compensation he found for it was the harmless freedom of being able to appear to say: "Yes, I'm in town only for three or four days, but, you know, I *would* stay on." He struck her as calling attention each day, each hour, to the rapid ebb of time; he exaggerated to the point of putting it that there were only two days more, that there was at last, dreadfully, only one.

There were other things still that he struck her as doing with a special intention; as to the most marked of which—unless indeed it were the most obscure—she might well have marvelled that it didn't seem to her more horrid. It was either the frenzy of her imagination or the disorder of his baffled passion that gave her once or twice the vision of his putting down redundant money—sovereigns not concerned with the little payments he was perpetually making—so that she might give him some sign of helping him to slip them over to her. What was most extraordinary in this impression was the amount of excuse that, with some incoherence, she found for him. He wanted to pay her because there was nothing to pay her for. He wanted to offer her things that he knew she wouldn't take. He wanted to show her how much he respected her by giving her the supreme chance to show *him* she was respectable. Over the driest transactions, at any rate, their eyes had out these questions. On the third day he put in a telegram that had evidently something of the same point as the stray sovereigns—a message that was, in the first place, concocted, and that, on a second thought, he took back from her before she had stamped it. He had given her time to read it, and had only then bethought himself that he had better not send it. If it was not to Lady Bradeen at Twindle— where she knew her ladyship then to be—this was because an address to Doctor Buzzard at Brickwood was just as good, with the added merit of its not giving away quite so much a person whom he had still, after all, in a manner to consider. It was of course most complicated, only half lighted; but there was, discernibly enough, a scheme of communication in which Lady Bradeen at Twindle and Dr. Buzzard at Brickwood were, within limits, one and the same person. The words he had shown her and then taken back consisted, at all events, of the brief but vivid phrase: "Absolutely impossible." The point was not that she should transmit it; the point was just that she should see it. What was absolutely impossible was that before he had settled something at Cocker's he should go either to Twindle or to Brickwood.

The logic of this, in turn, for herself, was that she could lend herself to no settlement so long as she so intensely knew. What she knew was that he was, almost under peril of life, clenched in a situation: therefore how could she also know where a poor girl in the P.O. might really stand? It was more and more between them that if he might convey to her that he was free, that everything she had seen so deep into was a closed chapter, her own case might become different for her, she might understand and meet him and listen. But he could convey nothing of the sort, and he only fidgeted and floundered in his want of power. The chapter wasn't in the least closed, not for the other party; and the other party had a pull, somehow and somewhere: this his whole attitude and expression confessed, at the same time that they entreated her not to remember and not to mind. So long as she did remember and did mind he could only circle about and go and come, doing futile things of which he was ashamed. He was ashamed of his two words to Dr. Buzzard, and went out of the shop as soon as he had crumpled up the paper again and thrust it into his pocket. It had been an abject little exposure of dreadful, impossible passion. He appeared in fact to be too ashamed to come back. He had left town again, and a first week elapsed, and a second. He had had naturally to return to the real mistress of his fate; she had insisted—she knew how, and he couldn't put in another hour. There was always a day when she called time. It was known to our young friend moreover that he had now been despatching telegrams from other offices. She knew at last so much, that she had quite lost her earlier sense of merely guessing. There were no shades of distinctness—it all bounced out.

XXII

Eighteen days elapsed, and she had begun to think it probable she should never see him again. He too then understood now: he had made out that she had secrets and reasons and impediments, that even a poor girl at the P.O. might have her complications. With the charm she had cast on him lightened by distance he had suffered a final delicacy to speak to him, had made up his mind that it would be only decent to let her alone. Never so much as during these latter days had she felt the precariousness of their relation— the happy, beautiful, untroubled original one, if it could only have been restored,—in which the public servant and the casual public only were concerned. It hung at the best by the merest silken thread, which was at the mercy of any accident and might snap at any minute. She arrived by the end of the fortnight at the highest sense of actual fitness, never doubting that her decision was now complete. She would just give him a few days more to come back to her on a proper impersonal basis—for even to an embarrassing representative of the casual public a public servant with a conscience did owe something,—and then would signify to Mr. Mudge that she was ready for the little home. It had been visited, in the further talk she had had with him at Bournemouth, from garret to cellar, and they had especially lingered, with their respectively darkened brows, before the niche into which it was to be broached to her mother that she was to find means to fit.

He had put it to her more definitely than before that his calculations had allowed for that dingy presence, and he had thereby marked the greatest impression he had ever made on her. It was a stroke superior even again to his handling of the drunken soldier. What she considered that, in the face of it, she hung on at Cocker's for, was something that she could only have described as the common fairness of a last word. Her actual last word had been, till it should be superseded, that she wouldn't abandon her other friend, and it stuck to her, through thick and thin, that she was still at her post and on her honour. This other friend had shown so much beauty of conduct already that he would surely, after all, just reappear long enough to relieve her, to give her something she could take away. She saw it, caught it, at times, his parting present; and there were moments when she felt herself sitting like a beggar with a hand held out to an almsgiver who only fumbled. She hadn't taken the sovereigns, but she *would* take the penny. She heard, in imagination, on the counter, the ring of the copper. "Don't put yourself out any longer," he would say, "for so bad a case. You've done all there is to be done. I thank and acquit and release you. Our lives take us. I don't know much—though I have really been interested —about yours; but I suppose you've got one. Mine, at any rate, will take *me*—and where it will. Heigh-ho! Good-bye." And then once more, for the sweetest, faintest flower of all: "Only, I say—see here!" She had framed the whole picture with a squareness that included also the image of how again she would decline to "see there," decline, as she might say, to see anywhere or anything. Yet it befell that just in the fury of this escape she saw more than ever.

He came back one night with a rush, near the moment of their closing, and showed her a face so different and new, so upset and anxious, that almost anything seemed to look out of it but clear recognition. He poked in a telegram very much as if the simple sense of pressure, the distress of extreme haste, had blurred the remembrance of where in particular he was. But as she met his eyes a light came; it broke indeed on the spot into a positive, conscious glare. That made up for everything, for it was an instant proclamation of the celebrated "danger"; it seemed to pour things out in a flood. "Oh yes, here it is—it's upon me at last! Forget, for God's sake, my having worried or bored you, and just help me, just *save* me, by getting this off without the loss of a second!" Something grave had clearly occurred, a crisis declared itself. She recognised immediately the person to whom the telegram was addressed—the Miss Dolman, of Parade Lodge, to whom Lady Bradeen had wired, at Dover, on the last occasion, and whom she had then, with her recollection of previous arrangements, fitted into a particular setting. Miss Dolman had figured before and not figured since, but she was now the subject of an imperative appeal. "Absolutely necessary to see you. Take last train Victoria if you can catch it. If not, earliest morning, and answer me direct either way."

"Reply paid?" said the girl. Mr. Buckton had just departed, and the counter-clerk was at the sounder. There was no other representative of the public, and she had never yet, as it seemed to her, not even in the street or in the Park, been so alone with him.

"Oh yes, reply paid, and as sharp as possible, please."

She affixed the stamps in a flash. "She'll catch the train!" she then declared to him breathlessly, as if she could absolutely guarantee it.

"I don't know—I hope so. It's awfully important. So kind of you. Awfully sharp, please." It was wonderfully innocent now, his oblivion of all but his danger. Anything else that had ever passed between them was utterly out of it. Well, she had wanted him to be impersonal!

There was less of the same need therefore, happily, for herself; yet she only took time, before she flew to the sounder, to gasp at him: "You're in trouble?"

"Horrid, horrid—there's a row!" But they parted, on it, in the next breath; and as she dashed at the sounder, almost pushing, in her violence, the counter-clerk off the stool, she caught the bang with which, at Cocker's door, in his further precipitation, he closed the apron of the cab into which he had leaped. As he rushed off to some other precaution suggested by his alarm, his appeal to Miss Dolman flashed straight away.

But she had not, on the morrow, been in the place five minutes before he was with her again, still more discomposed and quite, now, as she said to herself, like a frightened child coming to its mother. Her companions were there, and she felt it to be remarkable how, in the presence of his agitation, his mere scared, exposed nature, she suddenly ceased to mind. It came to her as it had never come to her before that with absolute directness and assurance they might carry almost anything off. He had nothing to send—she was sure he had been wiring all over,—and yet his business was evidently huge. There was nothing but that in his eyes—not a glimmer of reference or memory. He was almost haggard with anxiety, and had clearly not slept a wink. Her pity for him would have given her any courage, and she seemed to know at last why she had been such a fool. "She didn't come?" she panted.

"Oh yes, she came; but there has been some mistake. We want a telegram."

"A telegram?"

"One that was sent from here ever so long ago. There was something in it that has to be recovered. Something very, *very* important, please—we want it immediately."

He really spoke to her as if she had been some strange young woman at Knightsbridge or Paddington;[5] but it had no other effect on her than to give her the measure of his tremendous flurry. Then it was that, above all, she felt how much she had missed in the gaps and blanks and absent answers—how much she had had to dispense with: it was black darkness now, save for this little wild red flare. So much as that she saw and possessed. One of the lovers was quaking somewhere out of town, and the other was quaking just where he stood. This was vivid enough, and after an instant she knew it was all she wanted. She wanted no detail, no fact—she wanted no nearer vision of discovery or shame. "When was your telegram? Do you mean you sent it from here?" She tried to do the young woman at Knightsbridge.

"Oh yes, from here—several weeks ago. Five, six, seven"—he was confused and impatient,—"don't you remember?"

"Remember?" she could scarcely keep out of her face, at the word, the strangest of smiles.

But the way he didn't catch what it meant was perhaps even stranger still. "I mean, don't you keep the old ones?"

"For a certain time."

"But how long?"

She thought; she *must* do the young woman, and she knew exactly what the young woman would say and, still more, wouldn't. "Can you give me the date?"

"Oh God, no! It was some time or other in August—toward the end. It was to the same address as the one I gave you last night."

"Oh!" said the girl, knowing at this the deepest thrill she had ever felt. It came to her there, with her eyes on his face, that she held the whole thing in her hand, held it as she held her pencil, which might have broken at that instant in her tightened grip. This made her feel like the very fountain of fate, but the emotion was such a flood that she had to press it back with all her force. That was positively the reason, again, of her flute-like Paddington tone. "You can't give us anything a little nearer?" Her "little" and her "us" came straight from Paddington. These things were no false note for him —his difficulty absorbed them all. The eyes with which he pressed her, and in the depths of which she read terror and rage and literal tears, were just the same he would have shown any other prim person.

"I don't know the date. I only know the thing went from here,

5. I.e., as if she were a mere telegraph operator, rather than an intimate acquaintance.

and just about the time I speak of. It wasn't delivered, you see. We've got to recover it."

XXIII

She was as struck with the beauty of his plural pronoun as she had judged he might be with that of her own; but she knew now so well what she was about that she could almost play with him and with her new-born joy. "You say 'about the time you speak of.' But I don't think you speak of an exact time—*do* you?"

He looked splendidly helpless. "That's just what I want to find out. Don't you keep the old ones?—can't you look it up?"

Our young lady—still at Paddington—turned the question over. "It wasn't delivered?"

"Yes, it *was*; yet, at the same time, don't you know? it wasn't." He just hung back, but he brought it out. "I mean it was intercepted, don't you know? and there was something in it." He paused again and, as if to further his quest and woo and supplicate success and recovery, even smiled with an effort at the agreeable that was almost ghastly and that turned the knife in her tenderness. What must be the pain of it all, of the open gulf and the throbbing fever, when this was the mere hot breath? "We want to get what was in it—to know what it was."

"I see—I see." She managed just the accent they had at Paddington when they stared like dead fish. "And you have no clue?"

"Not at all—I've the clue I've just given you."

"Oh, the last of August?" If she kept it up long enough she would make him really angry.

"Yes, and the address, as I've said."

"Oh, the same as last night?"

He visibly quivered, as if with a gleam of hope; but it only poured oil on her quietude, and she was still deliberate. She ranged some papers. "Won't you look?" he went on.

"I remember your coming," she replied.

He blinked with a new uneasiness; it might have begun to come to him, through her difference, that he was somehow different himself. "You were much quicker then, you know!"

"So were you—you must do me that justice," she answered with a smile. "But let me see. Wasn't it Dover?"

"Yes, Miss Dolman——"

"Parade Lodge, Parade Terrace?"

"Exactly—thank you so awfully much!" He began to hope again. "Then you *have* it—the other one?"

She hesitated afresh; she quite dangled him. "It was brought by a lady?"

"Yes; and she put in by mistake something wrong. That's what we've got to get hold of!"

Heavens! what was he going to say?—flooding poor Paddington with wild betrayals! She couldn't too much, for her joy, dangle him, yet she couldn't either, for his dignity, warn or control or check him. What she found herself doing was just to treat herself to the middle way. "It was intercepted?"

"It fell into the wrong hands. But there's something in it," he continued to blurt out, "that *may* be all right. That is, if it's wrong, don't you know? It's all right if it's wrong," he remarkably explained.

What *was* he, on earth, going to say? Mr. Buckton and the counter-clerk were already interested; no one *would* have the decency to come in; and she was divided between her particular terror for him and her general curiosity. Yet she already saw with what brilliancy she could add, to carry the thing off, a little false knowledge to all her real. "I quite understand," she said with benevolent, with almost patronising quickness. "The lady has forgotten what she did put."

"Forgotten most wretchedly, and it's an immense inconvenience. It has only just been found that it didn't get there; so that if we could immediately have it——"

"Immediately?"

"Every minute counts. You *have*," he pleaded, "surely got them on file?"

"So that you can see it on the spot?"

"Yes, please—this very minute." The counter rang with his knuckles, with the knob of his stick, with his panic of alarm. "Do, *do* hunt it up!" he repeated.

"I dare say we could get it for you," the girl sweetly returned.

"Get it?"—he looked aghast. "When?"

"Probably by to-morrow."

"Then it isn't here?"—his face was pitiful.

She caught only the uncovered gleams that peeped out of the blackness, and she wondered what complication, even among the most supposable, the very worst, could be bad enough to account for the degree of his terror. There were twists and turns, there were places where the screw drew blood, that she couldn't guess. She was more and more glad she didn't want to. "It has been sent on."

"But how do you know if you don't look?"

She gave him a smile that was meant to be, in the absolute irony of its propriety, quite divine. "It was August 23rd, and we have nothing later here than August 27th."

Something leaped into his face. "27th—23rd? Then you're sure? You know?"

She felt she scarce knew what—as if she might soon be pounced upon for some lurid connection with a scandal. It was the queerest of all sensations, for she had heard, she had read, of these things, and the wealth of her intimacy with them at Cocker's might be supposed to have schooled and seasoned her. This particular one that she had really quite lived with was, after all, an old story; yet what it had been before was dim and distant beside the touch under which she now winced. Scandal?—it had never been but a silly word. Now it was a great palpable surface, and the surface was, somehow, Captain Everard's wonderful face. Deep down in his eyes was a picture, the vision of a great place like a chamber of justice, where, before a watching crowd, a poor girl, exposed but heroic, swore with a quavering voice to a document, proved an *alibi*, supplied a link. In this picture she bravely took her place. "It was the 23rd."

"Then can't you get it this morning—or some time to-day?"

She considered, still holding him with her look, which she then turned on her two companions, who were by this time unreservedly enlisted. She didn't care—not a scrap, and she glanced about for a piece of paper. With this she had to recognise the rigour of official thrift—a morsel of blackened blotter was the only loose paper to be seen. "Have you got a card?" she said to her visitor. He was quite away from Paddington now, and the next instant, with a pocket-book in his hand, he had whipped a card out. She gave no glance at the name on it—only turned it to the other side. She continued to hold him, she felt at present, as she had never held him; and her command of her colleagues was, for the moment, not less marked. She wrote something on the back of the card and pushed it across to him.

He fairly glared at it. "Seven, nine, four——"

"Nine, six, one"—she obligingly completed the number. "Is it right?" she smiled.

He took the whole thing in with a flushed intensity; then there broke out in him a visibility of relief that was simply a tremendous exposure. He shone at them all like a tall lighthouse, embracing even, for sympathy, the blinking young men. "By all the powers—it's wrong!" And without another look, without a word of thanks, without time for anything or anybody, he turned on them the broad back of his great stature, straightened his triumphant shoulders, and strode out of the place.

She was left confronted with her habitual critics. " 'If it's wrong it's all right!' " she extravagantly quoted to them.

The counter-clerk was really awe-stricken. "But how did you know, dear?"

"I remembered, love!"

Mr. Buckton, on the contrary, was rude. "And what game is that, miss?"

No happiness she had ever known came within miles of it, and some minutes elapsed before she could recall herself sufficiently to reply that it was none of his business.

XXIV

If life at Cocker's, with the dreadful drop of August, had lost something of its savour, she had not been slow to infer that a heavier blight had fallen on the graceful industry of Mrs. Jordan. With Lord Rye and Lady Ventnor and Mrs. Bubb all out of town, with the blinds down on all the homes of luxury, this ingenious woman might well have found her wonderful taste left quite on her hands. She bore up, however, in a way that began by exciting much of her young friend's esteem; they perhaps even more frequently met as the wine of life flowed less free from other sources, and each, in the lack of better diversion, carried on with more mystification for the other an intercourse that consisted not a little of peeping out and drawing back. Each waited for the other to commit herself, each profusely curtained for the other the limits of low horizons. Mrs. Jordan was indeed probably the more reckless skirmisher; nothing could exceed her frequent incoherence unless it was indeed her occasional bursts of confidence. Her account of her private affairs rose and fell like a flame in the wind—sometimes the bravest bonfire and sometimes a handful of ashes. This our young woman took to be an effect of the position, at one moment and another, of the famous door of the great world. She had been struck in one of her ha'penny volumes with the translation of a French proverb according to which a door had to be either open or shut; and it seemed a part of the precariousness of Mrs. Jordan's life that hers mostly managed to be neither. There had been occasions when it appeared to gape wide—fairly to woo her across its threshold; there had been others, of an order distinctly disconcerting, when it was all but banged in her face. On the whole, however, she had evidently not lost heart; these still belonged to the class of things in spite of which she looked well. She intimated that the profits of her trade had swollen so as to float her through any state of the tide, and she had, besides this, a hundred profundities and explanations.

She rose superior, above all, on the happy fact that there were always gentlemen in town and that gentlemen were her greatest admirers; gentlemen from the City in especial—as to whom she was full of information about the passion and pride excited in such breasts by the objects of her charming commerce. The City men *did*, in short, go in for flowers. There was a certain type of awfully smart stockbroker—Lord Rye called them Jews and "bounders," but she didn't care—whose extravagance, she more than once threw out, had really, if one had any conscience, to be forcibly restrained. It was not perhaps a pure love of beauty: it was a matter of vanity and a sign of business; they wished to crush their rivals, and that was one of their weapons. Mrs. Jordan's shrewdness was extreme; she knew, in any case, her customer—she dealt, as she said, with all sorts; and it was, at the worst, a race for her—a race even in the dull months—from one set of chambers to another. And then, after all, there were also still the ladies; the ladies of stockbroking circles were perpetually up and down. They were not quite perhaps Mrs. Bubb or Lady Ventnor; but you couldn't tell the difference unless you quarrelled with them, and then you knew it only by their making-up sooner. These ladies formed the branch of her subject on which she most swayed in the breeze; to that degree that her confidant had ended with an inference or two tending to banish regret for opportunities not embraced. There were indeed tea-gowns that Mrs. Jordan described—but tea-gowns were not the whole of respectability, and it was odd that a clergyman's widow should sometimes speak as if she almost thought so. She came back, it was true, unfailingly, to Lord Rye, never, evidently, quite losing sight of him even on the longest excursions. That he was kindness itself had become in fact the very moral it all pointed—pointed in strange flashes of the poor woman's nearsighted eyes. She launched at her young friend many portentous looks, solemn heralds of some extraordinary communication. The communication itself, from week to week, hung fire; but it was to the facts over which it hovered that she owed her power of going on. "They *are*, in one way *and* another," she often emphasised, "a tower of strength"; and as the allusion was to the aristocracy, the girl could quite wonder why, if they were so in "one" way, they should require to be so in two. She thoroughly knew, however, how many ways Mrs. Jordan counted in. It all meant simply that her fate was pressing her close. If that fate was to be sealed at the matrimonial altar it was perhaps not remarkable that she shouldn't come all at once to the scratch of overwhelming a mere telegraphist. It would necessarily present to such a person a prospect of regretful sacrifice. Lord Rye—if it *was* Lord Rye—wouldn't be "kind" to a nonentity of that sort, even though people quite as good had been.

One Sunday afternoon in November they went, by arrangement, to church together; after which—on the inspiration of the moment; the arrangement had not included it—they proceeded to Mrs. Jordan's lodging in the region of Maida Vale. She had raved to her friend about her service of predilection; she was excessively "high," and had more than once wished to introduce the girl to the same comfort and privilege. There was a thick brown fog, and Maida Vale tasted of acrid smoke; but they had been sitting among chants and incense and wonderful music, during which, though the effect of such things on her mind was great, our young lady had indulged in a series of reflections but indirectly related to them. One of these was the result of Mrs. Jordan's having said to her on the way, and with a certain fine significance, that Lord Rye had been for some time in town. She had spoken as if it were a circumstance to which little required to be added—as if the bearing of such an item on her life might easily be grasped. Perhaps it was the wonder of whether Lord Rye wished to marry her that made her guest, with thoughts straying to that quarter, quite determine that some other nuptials also should take place at St. Julian's. Mr. Mudge was still an attendant at his Wesleyan chapel, but this was the least of her worries—it had never even vexed her enough for her to so much as name it to Mrs. Jordan. Mr. Mudge's form of worship was one of several things—they made up in superiority and beauty for what they wanted in number—that she had long ago settled he should take from her, and she had now moreover for the first time definitely established her own. Its principal feature was that it was to be the same as that of Mrs. Jordan and Lord Rye; which was indeed very much what she said to her hostess as they sat together later on. The brown fog was in this hostess's little parlour, where it acted as a postponement of the question of there being, besides, anything else than the teacups and a pewter pot, and a very black little fire, and a paraffin lamp without a shade. There was at any rate no sign of a flower; it was not for herself Mrs. Jordan gathered sweets. The girl waited till they had had a cup of tea—waited for the announcement that she fairly believed her friend had, this time, possessed herself of her formally at last to make; but nothing came, after the interval, save a little poke at the fire, which was like the clearing of a throat for a speech.

XXV

"I think you must have heard me speak of Mr. Drake?" Mrs. Jordan had never looked so queer, nor her smile so suggestive of a large benevolent bite.

"Mr. Drake? Oh yes; isn't he a friend of Lord Rye?"

"A great and trusted friend. Almost—I may say—a loved friend."

Mrs. Jordan's "almost" had such an oddity that her companion was moved, rather flippantly perhaps, to take it up. "Don't people as good as love their friends when they 'trust' them?"

It pulled up a little the eulogist of Mr. Drake. "Well, my dear, I love *you*——"

"But you don't trust me?" the girl unmercifully asked.

Again Mrs. Jordan paused—still she looked queer. "Yes," she replied with a certain austerity; "that's exactly what I'm about to give you rather a remarkable proof of." The sense of its being remarkable was already so strong that, while she bridled a little, this held her auditor in a momentary muteness of submission. "Mr. Drake has rendered his lordship, for several years, services that his lordship has highly appreciated and that make it all the more—a—unexpected that they should, perhaps a little suddenly, separate."

"Separate?" Our young lady was mystified, but she tried to be interested; and she already saw that she had put the saddle on the wrong horse. She had heard something of Mr. Drake, who was a member of his lordship's circle—the member with whom, apparently, Mrs. Jordan's avocations had most happened to throw her. She was only a little puzzled at the "separation." "Well, at any rate," she smiled, "if they separate as friends——!"

"Oh, his lordship takes the greatest interest in Mr. Drake's future. He'll do anything for him; he has in fact just done a great deal. There *must*, you know, be changes——!"

"No one knows it better than I," the girl said. She wished to draw her interlocutress out. "There will be changes enough for me."

"You're leaving Cocker's?"

The ornament of that establishment waited a moment to answer, and then it was indirect. "Tell me what *you're* doing."

"Well, what will you think of it?"

"Why, that you've found the opening you were always so sure of."

Mrs. Jordan, on this, appeared to muse with embarrassed intensity. "I was always sure, yes—and yet I often wasn't!"

"Well, I hope you're sure now. Sure. I mean, of Mr. Drake."

"Yes, my dear, I think I may say I *am*. I kept him going till I was."

"Then he's yours?"

"My very own."

"How nice! And awfully rich?" our young woman went on.

Mrs. Jordan showed promptly enough that she loved for higher things. "Awfully handsome—six foot two. And he *has* put by."

"Quite like Mr. Mudge, then!" that gentleman's friend rather desperately exclaimed.

"Oh, not *quite*!" Mr. Drake's was ambiguous about it, but the name of Mr. Mudge had evidently given her some sort of stimulus. "He'll have more opportunity now, at any rate. He's going to Lady Bradeen."

"To Lady Bradeen?" This was bewilderment. " 'Going—'?"

The girl had seen, from the way Mrs. Jordan looked at her, that the effect of the name had been to make her let something out. "Do you know her?"

She hesitated; then she found her feet. "Well, you'll remember I've often told you that if you have grand clients, I have them too."

"Yes," said Mrs. Jordan; "but the great difference is that you hate yours, whereas I really love mine. *Do* you know Lady Bradeen?" she pursued.

"Down to the ground! She's always in and out."

Mrs. Jordan's foolish eyes confessed, in fixing themselves on this sketch, to a degree of wonder and even of envy. But she bore up and, with a certain gaiety, "Do you hate *her?*" she demanded.

Her visitor's reply was prompt. "Dear no!—not nearly so much as some of them. She's too outrageously beautiful."

Mrs. Jordan continued to gaze. "Outrageously?"

"Well, yes; deliciously." What was really delicious was Mrs. Jordan's vagueness. "You don't know her—you've not seen her?" her guest lightly continued.

"No, but I've heard a great deal about her."

"So have I!" our young lady exclaimed.

Mrs. Jordan looked an instant as if she suspected her good faith, or at least her seriousness. "You know some friend——?"

"Of Lady Bradeen's? Oh yes—I know one."

"Only one?"

The girl laughed out. "Only one—but he's so intimate."

Mrs. Jordan just hesitated. "He's a gentleman?"

"Yes, he's not a lady."

Her interlocutress appeared to muse. "She's immensely surrounded."

"She *will* be—with Mr. Drake!"

Mrs. Jordan's gaze became strangely fixed. "Is she *very* good-looking?"

"The handsomest person I know."

Mrs. Jordan continued to contemplate. "Well, *I* know some beauties." Then, with her odd jerkiness, "Do you think she looks *good?*" she inquired.

"Because that's not always the case with the good-looking?"—the other took it up. "No, indeed, it isn't: that's one thing Cocker's has taught me. Still, there are some people who have everything. Lady Bradeen, at any rate, has enough: eyes and a nose and a mouth, a complexion, a figure——"

"A figure?" Mrs. Jordan almost broke in.

"A figure, a head of hair!" The girl made a little conscious motion that seemed to let the hair all down, and her companion watched the wonderful show. "But Mr. Drake *is* another——?"

"Another?"—Mrs. Jordan's thoughts had to come back from a distance.

"Of her ladyship's admirers. He's 'going,' you say, to her?"

At this Mrs. Jordan really faltered. "She has engaged him."

"Engaged him?"—our young woman was quite at sea.

"In the same capacity as Lord Rye."

"And was Lord Rye engaged?"

XXVI

Mrs. Jordan looked away from her now—looked, she thought, rather injured and, as if trifled with, even a little angry. The mention of Lady Bradeen had frustrated for a while the convergence of our heroine's thoughts; but with this impression of her old friend's combined impatience and diffidence they began again to whirl round her, and continued it till one of them appeared to dart at her, out of the dance, as if with a sharp peck. It came to her with a lively shock, with a positive sting, that Mr. Drake was—could it be possible? With the idea she found herself afresh on the edge of laughter, of a sudden and strange perversity of mirth. Mr. Drake loomed, in a swift image, before her; such a figure as she had seen in open doorways of houses in Cocker's quarter—majestic, middle-aged, erect, flanked on either side by a footman and taking the name of a visitor. Mr. Drake then verily *was* a person who opened the door! Before she had time; however, to recover from the effect of her evocation, she was offered a vision which quite engulphed it. It was communicated to her somehow that the face with which she had seen it rise prompted Mrs. Jordan to dash, at a venture, at something that might attenuate criticism. "Lady Bradeen is rearranging—she's going to be married."

"Married?" The girl echoed it ever so softly, but there it was at last.

"Didn't you know it?"

She summoned all her sturdiness. "No, she hasn't told me."

"And her friends—haven't they?"

"I haven't seen any of them lately. I'm not so fortunate as *you*."

Mrs. Jordan gathered herself. "Then you haven't even heard of Lord Bradeen's death?"

Her comrade, unable for a moment to speak, gave a slow headshake. "You know it from Mr. Drake?" It was better surely not to learn things at all than to learn them by the butler.

"She tells him everything."

"And he tells *you*—I see." Our young lady got up; recovering her muff and her gloves, she smiled. "Well, I haven't, unfortunately, any Mr. Drake. I congratulate you with all my heart. Even without your sort of assistance, however, there's a trifle here and there that I do pick up. I gather that if she's to marry any one, it must quite necessarily be my friend."

Mrs. Jordan was now also on her feet. "Is Captain Everard your friend?"

The girl considered, drawing on a glove. "I saw, at one time, an immense deal of him."

Mrs. Jordan looked hard at the glove, but she had not, after all, waited for that to be sorry it was not cleaner. "What time was that?"

"It must have been the time you were seeing so much of Mr. Drake." She had now fairly taken it in: the distinguished person Mrs. Jordan was to marry would answer bells and put on coals and superintend, at least, the cleaning of boots for the other distinguished person whom *she* might—well, whom she might have had, if she had wished, so much more to say to. "Good-bye," she added; "good-bye."

Mrs. Jordan, however, again taking her muff from her, turned it over, brushed it off, and thoughtfully peeped into it. "Tell me this before you go. You spoke just now of your own changes. Do you mean that Mr. Mudge——?"

"Mr. Mudge has had great patience with me—he has brought me at last to the point. We're to be married next month and have a nice little home. But he's only a grocer, you know"—the girl met her friend's intent eyes—"so that I'm afraid that, with the set you've got into, you won't see your way to keep up our friendship."

Mrs. Jordan for a moment made no answer to this; she only held the muff up to her face, after which she gave it back. "You don't like it. I see, I see."

To her guest's astonishment there were tears now in her eyes. "I don't like what?" the girl asked.

"Why, my engagement. Only, with your great cleverness," the poor lady quavered out, "you put it in your own way. I mean that you'll cool off. You already *have*——!" And on this, the next instant, her tears began to flow. She succumbed to them and collapsed; she sank down again, burying her face and trying to smother her sobs.

Her young friend stood there, still in some rigour, but taken much by surprise even if not yet fully moved to pity. "I don't put anything in any 'way,' and I'm very glad you're suited. Only, you know, you did put to *me* so splendidly what, even for me, if I had listened to you, it might lead to."

Mrs. Jordan kept up a mild, thin, weak wail; then, drying her eyes, as feebly considered this reminder. "It has led to my not starving!" she faintly gasped.

Our young lady, at this, dropped into the place beside her, and now, in a rush, the small, silly misery was clear. She took her hand as a sign of pitying it, then, after another instant, confirmed this expression with a consoling kiss. They sat there together; they looked out, hand in hand, into the damp, dusky, shabby little room and into the future, of no such very different suggestion, at last accepted by each. There was no definite utterance, on either side, of Mr. Drake's position in the great world, but the temporary collapse of his prospective bride threw all further necessary light; and what our heroine saw and felt for in the whole business was the vivid reflection of her own dreams and delusions and her own return to reality. Reality, for the poor things they both were, could only be ugliness and obscurity, could never be the escape, the rise. She pressed her friend—she had tact enough for that—with no other personal question, brought on no need of further revelations, only just continued to hold and comfort her and to acknowledge by stiff little forbearances the common element in their fate. She felt indeed magnanimous in such matters; for if it was very well, for condolence or re-assurance, to suppress just then invidious shrinkings, she yet by no means saw herself sitting down, as she might say, to the same table with Mr. Drake. There would luckily, to all appearance, be little question of tables; and the circumstance that, on their peculiar lines, her friend's interests would still attach themselves to Mayfair flung over Chalk Farm the first radiance it had shown. Where was one's pride and one's passion when the real way to judge of one's luck was by making not the wrong, but the right, comparison? Before she had again gathered herself to go she felt very small and cautious and thankful. "We shall have our own house," she said, "and you must come very soon and let me show it you."

"*We* shall have our own too," Mrs. Jordan replied; "for, don't you know, he makes it a condition that he sleeps out?"

"A condition?"—the girl felt out of it.

"For any new position. It was on that he parted with Lord Rye. His lordship can't meet it; so Mr. Drake has given him up."

"And all for you?"—our young woman put it as cheerfully as possible.

"For me and Lady Bradeen. Her ladyship's too glad to get him at any price. Lord Rye, out of interest in us, has in fact quite *made* her take him. So, as I tell you, he will have his own establishment."

Mrs. Jordan, in the elation of it, had begun to revive; but there was nevertheless between them rather a conscious pause—a pause in which neither visitor nor hostess brought out a hope or an invitation. It expressed in the last resort that, in spite of submission and sympathy, they could now, after all, only look at each other across the social gulf. They remained together as if it would be indeed their last chance, still sitting, though awkwardly, quite close, and feeling also—and this most unmistakably—that there was one thing more to go into. By the time it came to the surface, moreover, our young friend had recognised the whole of the main truth, from which she even drew again a slight irritation. It was not the main truth perhaps that most signified; but after her momentary effort, her embarrassment and her tears, Mrs. Jordan had begun to sound afresh—and even without speaking—the note of a social connection. She hadn't really let go of it that she was marrying into society. Well, it was a harmless compensation, and it was all that the prospective bride of Mr. Mudge had to leave with her.

XXVII

This young lady at last rose again, but she lingered before going. "And has Captain Everard nothing to say to it?"

"To what, dear?"

"Why, to such questions—the domestic arrangements, things in the house."

"How *can* he, with any authority, when nothing in the house is his?"

"Not his?" The girl wondered, perfectly conscious of the appearance she thus conferred on Mrs. Jordan of knowing, in comparison with herself, so tremendously much about it. Well, there were things she wanted so to get at that she was willing at last, though it hurt her, to pay for them with humiliation. "Why are they not his?"

"Don't you know, dear, that he has nothing?"

"Nothing?" It was hard to see him in such a light, but Mrs. Jordan's power to answer for it had a superiority that began, on the spot, to grow. "Isn't he rich?"

Mrs. Jordan looked immensely, looked both generally and particularly, informed. "It depends upon what you call——! Not, at any rate, in the least as *she* is. What does he bring? Think what she has. And then, my love, his debts."

"His debts?" His young friend was fairly betrayed into helpless innocence. She could struggle a little, but she had to let herself go; and if she had spoken frankly she would have said: "Do tell me, for I don't know so much about him as *that!*" As she didn't speak frankly she only said: "His debts are nothing—when she so adores him."

Mrs. Jordan began to fix her again, and now she saw that she could only take it all. That was what it had come to: his having sat with her there, on the bench and under the trees, in the summer darkness, and put his hand on her, making her know what he would have said if permitted; his having returned to her afterwards, repeatedly, with supplicating eyes and a fever in his blood; and her having, on her side, hard and pedantic, helped by some miracle and with her impossible condition, only answered him, yet supplicating back, through the bars of the cage,—all simply that she might hear of him, now for ever lost, only through Mrs. Jordan, who touched him through Mr. Drake, who reached him through Lady Bradeen. "She adores him—but of course that wasn't all there was about it."

The girl met her eyes a minute, then quite surrendered. "What was there else about it?"

"Why, don't you know?"—Mrs. Jordan was almost compassionate.

Her interlocutress had, in the cage, sounded depths, but there was a suggestion here somehow of an abyss quite measureless. "Of course I know that she would never let him alone."

"How *could* she—fancy!—when he had so compromised her?"

The most artless cry they had ever uttered broke, at this, from the younger pair of lips. "*Had* he so——?"

"Why, don't you know the scandal?"

Our heroine thought, recollected; there was something, whatever it was, that she knew, after all, much more of than Mrs. Jordan. She saw him again as she had seen him come that morning to recover the telegram—she saw him as she had seen him leave the shop. She perched herself a moment on this. "Oh, there was nothing public."

"Not exactly public—no. But there was an awful scare and an awful row. It was all on the very point of coming out. Something was lost—something was found."

"Ah yes," the girl replied, smiling as if with the revival of a blurred memory; "something was found."

"It all got about—and there was a point at which Lord Bradeen had to act."

"Had to—yes. But he didn't."

Mrs. Jordan was obliged to admit it. "No, he didn't. And then, luckily for them, he died."

"I didn't know about his death," her companion said.

"It was nine weeks ago, and most sudden. It has given them a prompt chance."

"To get married"—this was a wonder—"within nine weeks?"

"Oh, not immediately, but—in all the circumstances—very quietly and, I assure you, very soon. Every preparation's made. Above all, she holds him."

"Oh yes, she holds him!" our young friend threw off. She had this before her again a minute; then she continued: "You mean through his having made her talked about?"

"Yes, but not only that. She has still another pull."

"Another?"

Mrs. Jordan hesitated. "Why, he was *in* something."

Her comrade wondered. "In what?"

"I don't know. Something bad. As I tell you, something was found."

The girl stared. "Well?"

"It would have been very bad for him. But she helped him some way—she recovered it, got hold of it. It's even said she stole it!"

Our young woman considered afresh. "Why, it was what was found that precisely saved him."

Mrs. Jordan, however, was positive. "I beg your pardon. I happen to know."

Her disciple faltered but an instant. "Do you mean through Mr. Drake? Do they tell *him* these things?"

"A good servant," said Mrs. Jordan, now thoroughly superior and proportionately sententious, "doesn't need to be told! Her ladyship saved—as a woman so often saves!—the man she loves."

This time our heroine took longer to recover herself, but she found a voice at last. "Ah well—of course I don't know! The great thing was that he got off. They seem then, in a manner," she added, "to have done a great deal for each other."

"Well, it's she that has done most. She has him tight."

"I see, I see. Good-bye." The women had already embraced, and this was not repeated; but Mrs. Jordan went down with her guest to the door of the house. Here again the younger lingered, reverting, though three or four other remarks had on the way passed between them, to Captain Everard and Lady Bradeen. "Did you mean just now that if she hadn't saved him, as you call it, she wouldn't hold him so tight?"

"Well, I daresay." Mrs. Jordan, on the doorstep, smiled with a reflection that had come to her; she took one of her big bites of the brown gloom. "Men always dislike one when they have done one an injury."

"But what injury had he done her?"

"The one I've mentioned. He *must* marry her, you know."

"And didn't he want to?"

"Not before."

"Not before she recovered the telegram?"

Mrs. Jordan was pulled up a little. "Was it a telegram?"

The girl hesitated. "I thought you said so. I mean whatever it was."

"Yes, whatever it was, I don't think she saw *that*."

"So she just nailed him?"

"She just nailed him." The departing friend was now at the bottom of the little flight of steps; the other was at the top, with a certain thickness of fog. "And when am I to think of you in your little home?—next month?" asked the voice from the top.

"At the very latest. And when am I to think of you in yours?"

"Oh, even sooner. I feel, after so much talk with you about it, as if I were already there!" Then "*Good*-bye!" came out of the fog.

"Good-*bye!*" went into it. Our young lady went into it also, in the opposed quarter, and presently, after a few sightless turns, came out on the Paddington canal. Distinguishing vaguely what the low parapet enclosed, she stopped close to it and stood a while, very intently, but perhaps still sightlessly, looking down on it. A policeman, while she remained, strolled past her; then, going his way a little further and half lost in the atmosphere, paused and watched her. But she was quite unaware—she was full of her thoughts. They were too numerous to find a place just here, but two of the number may at least be mentioned. One of these was that, decidedly, her little home must be not for next month, but for next week; the other, which came indeed as she resumed her walk and went her way, was that it was strange such a matter should be at last settled for her by Mr. Drake.

The Beast in the Jungle[†]

I

What determined the speech that startled him in the course of their encounter scarcely matters, being probably but some words spoken by himself quite without intention—spoken as they lingered and slowly moved together after their renewal of acquaintance. He had been conveyed by friends, an hour or two before, to the house at which she was staying; the party of visitors at the other house, of whom he was one, and thanks to whom it was his theory, as always, that he was lost in the crowd, had been invited over to luncheon. There had been after luncheon much dispersal, all in the interest of the original motive, a view of Weatherend itself and the fine things, intrinsic features, pictures, heirlooms, treasures of all the arts, that made the place almost famous; and the great rooms were so numerous that guests could wander at their will, hang back from the principal group, and, in cases where they took such matters with the last seriousness, give themselves up to mysterious appreciations and measurements. There were persons to be observed, singly or in couples, bending toward objects in out-of-the-way corners with their hands on their knees and their heads nodding quite as with the emphasis of an excited sense of smell. When they were two they either mingled their sounds of ecstasy or melted into silences of even deeper import, so that there were aspects of the occasion that gave it for Marcher much the air of the "look round," previous to a sale highly advertised, that excites or quenches, as may be, the dream of acquisition. The dream of acquisition at Weatherend would have had to be wild indeed, and John Marcher found himself, among such suggestions, disconcerted almost equally by the presence of those who knew too much and by that of those who knew nothing. The great rooms caused so much poetry and history to press upon him that he needed to wander apart to feel in a proper relation with them, though his doing so was not, as happened, like the gloating of some of his companions, to be compared to the movements of a dog sniffing a cupboard. It had

[†] "The Beast in the Jungle" had no magazine appearance before it first was published in *The Better Sort* (London: Methuen & Co., 1903). This text is here reprinted.

an issue promptly enough in a direction that was not to have been calculated.

It led, in short, in the course of the October afternoon, to his closer meeting with May Bartram, whose face, a reminder, yet not quite a remembrance, as they sat, much separated, at a very long table, had begun merely by troubling him rather pleasantly. It affected him as the sequel of something of which he had lost the beginning. He knew it, and for the time quite welcomed it, as a continuation, but didn't know what it continued, which was an interest, or an amusement, the greater as he was also somehow aware—yet without a direct sign from her—that the young woman herself had not lost the thread. She had not lost it, but she wouldn't give it back to him, he saw, without some putting forth of his hand for it; and he not only saw that, but saw several things more, things odd enough in the light of the fact that at the moment some accident of grouping brought them face to face he was still merely fumbling with the idea that any contact between them in the past would have had no importance. If it had had no importance he scarcely knew why his actual impression of her should so seem to have so much; the answer to which, however, was that in such a life as they all appeared to be leading for the moment one could but take things as they came. He was satisfied, without in the least being able to say why, that this young lady might roughly have ranked in the house as a poor relation; satisfied also that she was not there on a brief visit, but was more or less a part of the establishment—almost a working, a remunerated part. Didn't she enjoy at periods a protection that she paid for by helping, among other services, to show the place and explain it, deal with the tiresome people, answer questions about the dates of the buildings, the styles of the furniture, the authorship of the pictures, the favourite haunts of the ghost? It wasn't that she looked as if you could have given her shillings—it was impossible to look less so. Yet when she finally drifted toward him, distinctly handsome, though ever so much older—older than when he had seen her before—it might have been as an effect of her guessing that he had, within the couple of hours, devoted more imagination to her than to all the others put together, and had thereby penetrated to a kind of truth that the others were too stupid for. She *was* there on harder terms than anyone; she was there as a consequence of things suffered, in one way and another, in the interval of years; and she remembered him very much as she was remembered—only a good deal better.

By the time they at last thus came to speech they were alone in one of the rooms—remarkable for a fine portrait over the chimney-place—out of which their friends had passed, and the charm of it was that even before they had spoken they had practically arranged with each other to stay behind for talk. The charm, happily, was in other things too; it was partly in there being scarce a spot at Weatherend without something to stay behind for. It was in the way the autumn day looked into the high windows as it waned; in the way the red light, breaking at the close from under a low, sombre sky, reached out in a long shaft and played over old wainscots, old tapestry, old gold, old colour. It was most of all perhaps in the way she came to him as if, since she had been turned on to deal with the simpler sort, he might, should he choose to keep the whole thing down, just take her mild attention for a part of her general business. As soon as he heard her voice, however, the gap was filled up and the missing link supplied; the slight irony he divined in her attitude lost its advantage. He almost jumped at it to get there before her. "I met you years and years ago in Rome. I remember all about it." She confessed to disappointment—she had been so sure he didn't; and to prove how well he did he began to pour forth the particular recollections that popped up as he called for them. Her face and her voice, all at his service now, worked the miracle—the impression, operating like the torch of a lamplighter who touches into flame, one by one, a long row of gas jets. Marcher flattered himself that the illumination was brilliant, yet he was really still more pleased on her showing him, with amusement, that in his haste to make everything right he had got most things rather wrong. It hadn't been at Rome—it had been at Naples; and it hadn't been seven years before—it had been more nearly ten. She hadn't been either with her uncle and aunt, but with her mother and her brother; in addition to which it was not with the Pembles that *he* had been, but with the Boyers, coming down in their company from Rome—a point on which she insisted, a little to his confusion, and as to which she had her evidence in hand. The Boyers she had known, but she didn't know the Pembles, though she had heard of them, and it was the people he was with who had made them acquainted. The incident of the thunderstorm that had raged round them with such violence as to drive them for refuge into an excavation—this incident had not occurred at the Palace of the Cæsars, but at Pompeii, on an occasion when they had been present there at an important find.

He accepted her amendments, he enjoyed her corrections, though the moral of them was, she pointed out, that he *really* didn't remember the least thing about her; and he only felt it as a drawback that when all was made conformable to the truth there didn't appear much of anything left. They lingered together still, she neglecting her office—for from the moment he was so clever she had no proper right to him—and both neglecting the house, just waiting as to see if a memory or two more wouldn't again breathe upon them. It had not taken them many minutes, after all, to put down on the table, like the cards of a pack, those that constituted their respective hands; only what came out was that the pack was unfortunately not perfect—that the past, invoked, invited, encouraged, could give them, naturally, no more than it had. It had made them meet—her at twenty, him at twenty-five; but nothing was so strange, they seemed to say to each other, as that, while so occupied, it hadn't done a little more for them. They looked at each other as with the feeling of an occasion missed; the present one would have been so much better if the other, in the far distance, in the foreign land, hadn't been so stupidly meagre. There weren't, apparently, all counted, more than a dozen little old things that had succeeded in coming to pass between them; trivialities of youth, simplicities of freshness, stupidities of ignorance, small possible germs, but too deeply buried—too deeply (didn't it seem?) to sprout after so many years. Marcher said to himself that he ought to have rendered her some service—saved her from a capsized boat in the Bay, or at least recovered her dressing-bag, filched from her cab, in the streets of Naples, by a lazzarone[1] with a stiletto. Or it would have been nice if he could have been taken with fever, alone, at his hotel, and she could have come to look after him, to write to his people, to drive him out in convalescence. *Then* they would be in possession of the something or other that their actual show seemed to lack. It yet somehow presented itself, this show, as too good to be spoiled; so that they were reduced for a few minutes more to wondering a little helplessly why—since they seemed to know a certain number of the same people—their reunion had been so long averted. They didn't use that name for it, but their delay from minute to minute to join the others was a kind of confession that they didn't quite want it to be a failure. Their attempted supposition of reasons for their not having met but showed how little they knew of each other. There came in fact a moment when Marcher felt a positive pang. It was vain to pretend she was an old friend, for all the communities were wanting, in spite of which it was as an old friend that he saw she would have suited him. He had new ones enough—was surrounded with them, for instance, at that hour at the other house; as a new one he probably wouldn't have so much as noticed her. He would have liked to invent something, get her to make-believe with him that some passage of a romantic or critical kind *had* originally occurred. He was really almost reaching out in imagination—as against time—for something that would do, and saying to himself that if it didn't come this new incident would

1. A slacker.

simply and rather awkwardly close. They would separate, and now for no second or for no third chance. They would have tried and not succeeded. Then it was, just at the turn, as he afterwards made it out to himself, that, everything else failing, she herself decided to take up the case and, as it were, save the situation. He felt as soon as she spoke that she had been consciously keeping back what she said and hoping to get on without it; a scruple in her that immensely touched him when, by the end of three or four minutes more, he was able to measure it. What she brought out, at any rate, quite cleared the air and supplied the link—the link it was such a mystery he should frivolously have managed to lose.

"You know you told me something that I've never forgotten and that again and again has made me think of you since; it was that tremendously hot day when we went to Sorrento, across the bay, for the breeze. What I allude to was what you said to me, on the way back, as we sat, under the awning of the boat, enjoying the cool. Have you forgotten?"

He had forgotten, and he was even more surprised than ashamed. But the great thing was that he saw it was no vulgar reminder of any "sweet" speech. The vanity of women had long memories, but she was making no claim on him of a compliment or a mistake. With another woman, a totally different one, he might have feared the recall possibly even some imbecile "offer." So, in having to say that he had indeed forgotten, he was conscious rather of a loss than of a gain; he already saw an interest in the matter of her reference. "I try to think—but I give it up. Yet I remember the Sorrento day."

"I'm not very sure you do," May Bartram after a moment said; "and I'm not very sure I ought to want you to. It's dreadful to bring a person back, at any time, to what he was ten years before. If you've lived away from it," she smiled, "so much the better."

"Ah, if *you* haven't why should I?" he asked.

"Lived away, you mean, from what I myself was?"

"From what *I* was. I was of course an ass," Marcher went on; "but I would rather know from you just the sort of ass I was than —from the moment you have something in your mind—not know anything."

Still, however, she hesitated. "But if you've completely ceased to be that sort—?"

"Why, I can then just so all the more bear to know. Besides, perhaps I haven't."

"Perhaps. Yet if you haven't," she added. "I should suppose you would remember. Not indeed that *I* in the least connect with my impression the invidious name you use. If I had only thought you foolish," she explained, "the thing I speak of wouldn't so have remained with me. It was about yourself." She waited, as if it might come to him; but as, only meeting her eyes in wonder, he gave no sign, she burnt her ships. "Has it ever happened?"

Then it was that, while he continued to stare, a light broke for him and the blood slowly came to his face, which began to burn with recognition. "Do you mean I told you—?" But he faltered, lest what came to him shouldn't be right, lest he should only give himself away.

"It was something about yourself that it was natural one shouldn't forget—that is if one remembered you at all. That's why I ask you," she smiled, "if the thing you then spoke of has ever come to pass?"

Oh, then he saw, but he was lost in wonder and found himself embarrassed. This, he also saw, made her sorry for him, as if her allusion had been a mistake. It took him but a moment, however, to feel that it had not been, much as it had been a surprise. After the first little shock of it her knowledge on the contrary began, even if rather strangely, to taste sweet to him. She was the only other person in the world then who would have it, and she had had it all these years, while the fact of his having so breathed his secret had unaccountably faded from him. No wonder they couldn't have met as if nothing had happened. "I judge," he finally said, "that I know what you mean. Only I had strangely enough lost the consciousness of having taken you so far into my confidence."

"Is it because you've taken so many others as well?"

"I've taken nobody. Not a creature since then."

"So that I'm the only person who knows?"

"The only person in the world.

"Well," she quickly replied, "I myself have never spoken. I've never, never repeated of you what you told me." She looked at him so that he perfectly believed her. Their eyes met over it in such a way that he was without a doubt. "And I never will."

She spoke with an earnestness that, as if almost excessive, put him at ease about her possible derision. Somehow the whole question was a new luxury to him—that is, from the moment she was in possession. If she didn't take the ironic view she clearly took the sympathetic, and that was what he had had, in all the long time, from no one whomsoever. What he felt was that he couldn't at present have begun to tell her and yet could profit perhaps exquisitely by the accident of having done so of old. "Please don't then. We're just right as it is."

"Oh, I am," she laughed, "if you are!" To which she added: "Then you do still feel in the same way?"

It was impossible to him not to take to himself that she was really interested, and it all kept coming as a sort of revelation. He had thought of himself so long as abominably alone, and, lo, he wasn't alone a bit. He hadn't been, it appeared, for an hour—since those moments on the Sorrento boat. It was *she* who had been, he seemed to see as he looked at her—she who had been made so by the graceless fact of his lapse of fidelity. To tell her what he had told her—what had it been but to ask something of her? something that she had given, in her charity, without his having, by a remembrance, by a return of the spirit, failing another encounter, so much as thanked her. What he had asked of her had been simply at first not to laugh at him. She had beautifully not done so for ten years, and she was not doing so now. So he had endless gratitude to make up. Only for that he must see just how he had figured to her. "What, exactly, was the account I gave—?"

"Of the way you did feel? Well, it was very simple. You said you had had from your earliest time, as the deepest thing within you, the sense of being kept for something rare and strange, possibly prodigious and terrible, that was sooner or later to happen to you, that you had in your bones the foreboding and the conviction of, and that would perhaps overwhelm you."

"Do you call that very simple?" John Marcher asked.

She thought a moment. "It was perhaps because I seemed, as you spoke, to understand it."

"You do understand it?" he eagerly asked.

Again she kept her kind eyes on him. "You still have the belief?"

"Oh!" he exclaimed helplessly. There was too much to say.

"Whatever it is to be," she clearly made out, "it hasn't yet come."

He shook his head in complete surrender now. "It hasn't yet come. Only, you know, it isn't anything I'm to *do*, to achieve in the world, to be distinguished or admired for. I'm not such an ass as *that*. It would be much better, no doubt, if I were."

"It's to be something you're merely to suffer?"

"Well, say to wait for—to have to meet, to face, to see suddenly break out in my life; possibly destroying all further consciousness, possibly annihilating me; possibly, on the other hand, only altering everything, striking at the root of all my world and leaving me to the consequences, however they shape themselves."

She took this in, but the light in her eyes continued for him not to be that of mockery. "Isn't what you describe perhaps but the expectation—or, at any rate, the sense of danger, familiar to so many people—of falling in love?"

John Marcher thought. "Did you ask me that before?"

"No—I wasn't so free-and-easy then. But it's what strikes me now."

"Of course," he said after a moment, "it strikes you. Of course it strikes *me*. Of course what's in store for me may be no more than that. The only thing is," he went on, "that I think that if it had been that, I should by this time know."

"Do you mean because you've *been* in love?" And then as he but looked at her in silence: "You've been in love, and it hasn't meant such a cataclysm, hasn't proved the great affair?"

"Here I am, you see. It hasn't been overwhelming."

"Then it hasn't been love," said May Bartram.

"Well, I at least thought it was. I took it for that—I've taken it till now. It was agreeable, it was delightful, it was miserable," he explained. "But it wasn't strange. It wasn't what *my* affair's to be."

"You want something all to yourself—something that nobody else knows or *has* known?"

"It isn't a question of what I 'want'—God knows I don't want anything. It's only a question of the apprehension that haunts me —that I live with day by day."

He said this so lucidly and consistently that, visibly, it further imposed itself. If she had not been interested before she would have been interested now. "Is it a sense of coming violence?"

Evidently now too, again, he liked to talk of it. "I don't think of it as—when it does come—necessarily violent. I only think of it as natural and as of course, above all, unmistakeable. I think of it simply as *the* thing. *The* thing will of itself appear natural."

"Then how will it appear strange?"

Marcher bethought himself. "It won't—to *me*."

"To whom then?"

"Well," he replied, smiling at last, "say to you."

"Oh then, I'm to be present?"

"Why, you *are* present—since you know."

"I see." She turned it over. "But I mean at the catastrophe."[2]

At this, for a minute, their lightness gave way to their gravity; it was as if the long look they exchanged held them together. "It will only depend on yourself—if you'll watch with me."

"Are you afraid?" she asked.

"Don't leave me *now*," he went on.

"Are you afraid?" she repeated.

"Do you think me simply out of my mind?" he pursued instead of answering. "Do I merely strike you as a harmless lunatic?"

"No," said May Bartram. "I understand you. I believe you."

"You mean you feel how my obsession—poor old thing!—may correspond to some possible reality?"

"To some possible reality."

2. The final event, not necessarily disastrous.

"Then you *will* watch with me?"

She hesitated, then for the third time put her question. "Are you afraid?"

"Did I tell you I was—at Naples?"

"No, you said nothing about it."

"Then I don't know. And I should *like* to know," said John Marcher. "You'll tell me yourself whether you think so. If you'll watch with me you'll see."

"Very good then." They had been moving by this time across the room, and at the door, before passing out, they paused as if for the full wind-up of their understanding. "I'll watch with you," said May Bartram.

II

The fact that she "knew"—knew and yet neither chaffed him nor betrayed him—had in a short time begun to constitute between them a sensible bond, which became more marked when, within the year that followed their afternoon at Weatherend, the opportunities for meeting multiplied. The event that thus promoted these occasions was the death of the ancient lady, her great-aunt, under whose wing, since losing her mother, she had to such an extent found shelter, and who, though but the widowed mother of the new successor to the property, had succeeded—thanks to a high tone and a high temper—in not forfeiting the supreme position at the great house. The deposition of this personage arrived but with her death, which, followed by many changes, made in particular a difference for the young woman in whom Marcher's expert attention had recognised from the first a dependent with a pride that might ache though it didn't bristle. Nothing for a long time had made him easier than the thought that the aching must have been much soothed by Miss Bartram's now finding herself able to set up a small home in London. She had acquired property, to an amount that made that luxury just possible, under her aunt's extremely complicated will, and when the whole matter began to be straightened out, which indeed took time, she let him know that the happy issue was at last in view. He had seen her again before that day, both because she had more than once accompanied the ancient lady to town and because he had paid another visit to the friends who so conveniently made of Weatherend one of the charms of their own hospitality. These friends had taken him back there; he had achieved there again with Miss Bartram some quiet detachment; and he had in London succeeded in persuading her to more than one brief absence from her aunt. They went together, on these latter occasions, to the National Gallery and the South Kensington Museum,[3] where, among vivid reminders, they talked of Italy at large—not now attempting to recover, as at first, the taste of their youth and their ignorance. That recovery, the first day at Weath-erend, had served its purpose well, had given them quite enough; so that they were, to Marcher's sense, no longer hovering about the head-waters of their stream, but had felt their boat pushed sharply off and down the current.

They were literally afloat together; for our gentleman this was marked, quite as marked as that the fortunate cause of it was just the buried treasure of her knowledge. He had with his own hands dug up this little hoard, brought to light—that is to within reach of the dim day constituted by their discretions and privacies—the object of value the hiding-place of which he had, after putting it into the ground himself, so strangely, so long forgotten. The ex-quisite luck of having again just stumbled on the spot made him indifferent to any other question; he would doubtless have devoted more time to the odd accident of his lapse of memory if he had not been moved to devote so much to the sweetness, the comfort, as he felt, for the future, that this accident itself had helped to keep fresh. It had never entered into his plan that anyone should "know," and mainly for the reason that it was not in him to tell anyone. That would have been impossible, since nothing but the amusement of a cold world would have waited on it. Since, however, a myste-rious fate had opened his mouth in youth, in spite of him, he would count that a compensation and profit by it to the utmost. That the right person *should* know tempered the asperity of his secret more even than his shyness had permitted him to imagine; and May Bar-tram was clearly right, because—well, because there she was. Her knowledge simply settled it; he would have been sure enough by this time had she been wrong. There was that in his situation, no doubt, that disposed him too much to see her as a mere confidant, taking all her light for him from the fact—the fact only—of her interest in his predicament, from her mercy, sympathy, seriousness, her consent not to regard him as the funniest of the funny. Aware, in fine, that her price for him was just in her giving him this con-stant sense of his being admirably spared, he was careful to remem-ber that she had, after all, also a life of her own, with things that might happen to *her*, things that in friendship one should likewise take account of. Something fairly remarkable came to pass with him, for that matter, in this connection—something represented by

---

3. The National Gallery is the most famous art museum in London; the South Kensington Museum, now usually called the Victoria and Albert Museum, is another art museum, devoted to architecture and sculpture as well as to painting.

a certain passage of his consciousness, in the suddenest way, from one extreme to the other.

He had thought himself, so long as nobody knew, the most disinterested person in the world, carrying his concentrated burden, his perpetual suspense, ever so quietly, holding his tongue about it, giving others no glimpse of it nor of its effect upon his life, asking of them no allowance and only making on his side all those that were asked. He had disturbed nobody with the queerness of having to know a haunted man, though he had had moments of rather special temptation on hearing people say that they were "unsettled." If they were as unsettled as he was—he who had never been settled for an hour in his life—they would know what it meant. Yet it wasn't, all the same, for him to make them, and he listened to them civilly enough. This was why he had such good—though possibly such rather colourless—manners; this was why, above all, he could regard himself, in a greedy world, as decently—as, in fact, perhaps even a little sublimely—unselfish. Our point is accordingly that he valued this character quite sufficiently to measure his present danger of letting it lapse, against which he promised himself to be much on his guard. He was quite ready, none the less, to be selfish just a little, since, surely, no more charming occasion for it had come to him. "Just a little," in a word, was just as much as Miss Bartram, taking one day with another, would let him. He never would be in the least coercive, and he would keep well before him the lines on which consideration for her—the very highest—ought to proceed. He would thoroughly establish the heads under which her affairs, her requirements, her peculiarities—he went so far as to give them the latitude of that name—would come into their intercourse. All this naturally was a sign of how much he took the intercourse itself for granted. There was nothing more to be done about *that*. It simply existed; had sprung into being with her first penetrating question to him in the autumn light there at Weatherend. The real form it should have taken on the basis that stood out large was the form of their marrying. But the devil in this was that the very basis itself put marrying out of the question. His conviction, his apprehension, his obsession, in short, was not a condition he could invite a woman to share; and that consequence of it was precisely what was the matter with him. Something or other lay in wait for him, amid the twists and the turns of the months and the years, like a crouching beast in the jungle. It signified little whether the crouching beast were destined to slay him or to be slain. The definite point was the ·inevitable spring of the creature; and the definite lesson from that was that a man of feeling didn't cause himself to be accompanied by a lady on a tiger-hunt. Such was the image under which he had ended by figuring his life.

They had at first, none the less, in the scattered hours spent together, made no allusion to that view of it; which was a sign he was handsomely ready to give that he didn't expect, that he in fact didn't care always to be talking about it. Such a feature in one's outlook was really like a hump on one's back. The difference it made every minute of the day existed quite independently of discussion. One discussed, of course, *like* a hunchback, for there was always, if nothing else, the hunchback face. That remained, and she was watching him; but people watched best, as a general thing, in silence, so that such would be predominantly the manner of their vigil. Yet he didn't want, at the same time, to be solemn; solemn was what he imagined he too much tended to be with other people. The thing to be, with the one person who knew, was easy and natural—to make the reference rather than be seeming to avoid it, to avoid it rather than be seeming to make it, and to keep it, in any case, familiar, facetious even, rather than pedantic and portentous. Some such consideration as the latter was doubtless in his mind, for instance, when he wrote pleasantly to Miss Bartram that perhaps the great thing he had so long felt as in the lap of the gods was no more than this circumstance, which touched him so nearly, of her acquiring a house in London. It was the first allusion they had yet again made, needing any other hitherto so little; but when she replied, after having given him the news, that she was by no means satisfied with such a trifle, as the climax to so special a suspense, she almost set him wondering if she hadn't even a larger conception of singularity for him than he had for himself. He was at all events destined to become aware little by little, as time went by, that she was all the while looking at his life, judging it, measuring it, in the light of the thing she knew, which grew to be at last, with the consecration of the years, never mentioned between them save as "the real truth" about him. That had always been his own form of reference to it, but she adopted the form so quietly that, looking back at the end of a period, he knew there was no moment at which it was traceable that she had, as he might say, got inside his condition, or exchanged the attitude of beautifully indulging for that of still more beautifully believing him.

It was always open to him to accuse her of seeing him but as the most harmless of maniacs, and this, in the long run—since it covered so much ground—was his easiest description of their friendship. He had a screw loose for her, but she liked him in spite of it, and was practically, against the rest of the world, his kind, wise keeper, unremunerated, but fairly amused and, in the absence of other near ties, not disreputably occupied. The rest of the world of course thought him queer, but she, she only, knew how, and above all why, queer; which was precisely what enabled her to dispose the concealing veil in the right folds. She took his gaiety from him—since it had to pass with them for gaiety—as she took everything else; but she certainly so far justified by her unerring touch his finer sense of the degree to which he had ended by convincing her. *She* at least never spoke of the secret of his life except as "the real truth about you," and she had in fact a wonderful way of making it seem, as such, the secret of her own life too. That was in fine how he so constantly felt her as allowing for him; he couldn't on the whole call it anything else. He allowed for himself, but she, exactly, allowed still more; partly because, better placed for a sight of the matter, she traced his unhappy perversion through portions of its course into which he could scarce follow it. He knew how he felt, but, besides knowing that, she knew how he *looked* as well; he knew each of the things of importance he was insidiously kept from doing, but she could add up the amount they made, understand how much, with a lighter weight on his spirit, he might have done, and thereby establish how, clever as he was, he fell short. Above all she was in the secret of the difference between the forms he went through—those of his little office under Government, those of caring for his modest patrimony, for his library, for his garden in the country, for the people in London whose invitations he accepted and repaid—and the detachment that reigned beneath them and that made of all behaviour, all that could in the least be called behaviour, a long act of dissimulation. What it had come to was that he wore a mask painted with the social simper, out of the eyeholes of which there looked eyes of an expression not in the least matching the other features. This the stupid world, even after years, had never more than half discovered. It was only May Bartram who had, and she achieved, by an art indescribable, the feat of at once —or perhaps it was only alternately—meeting the eyes from in front and mingling her own vision, as from over his shoulder, with their peep through the apertures.

So, while they grew older together, she did watch with him, and so she let this association give shape and colour to her own existence. Beneath *her* forms as well detachment had learned to sit, and behaviour had become for her, in the social sense, a false account of herself. There was but one account of her that would have been true all the while, and that she could give, directly, to nobody, least of all to John Marcher. Her whole attitude was a virtual statement, but the perception of that only seemed destined to take its place for him as one of the many things necessarily crowded out of his consciousness. If she had, moreover, like himself, to make sacrifices to their real truth, it was to be granted that her compensation might have affected her as more prompt and more natural. They had long periods, in this London time, during which, when they were together, a stranger might have listened to them without in the least pricking up his ears; on the other hand, the real truth was equally liable at any moment to rise to the surface, and the auditor would then have wondered indeed what they were talking about. They had from an early time made up their mind that society was, luckily, unintelligent, and the margin that this gave them had fairly become one of their commonplaces. Yet there were still moments when the situation turned almost fresh—usually under the effect of some expression drawn from herself. Her expressions doubtless repeated themselves, but her intervals were generous. "What saves us, you know, is that we answer so completely to so usual an appearance: that of the man and woman whose friendship has become such a daily habit, or almost, as to be at least indispensable." That, for instance, was a remark she had frequently enough had occasion to make, though she had given it at different times different developments. What we are especially concerned with is the turn it happened to take from her one afternoon when he had come to see her in honour of her birthday. This anniversary had fallen on a Sunday, at a season of thick fog and general outward gloom; but he had brought her his customary offering, having known her now long enough to have established a hundred little customs. It was one of his proofs to himself, the present he made her on her birthday, that he had not sunk into real selfishness. It was mostly nothing more than a small trinket, but it was always fine of its kind, and he was regularly careful to pay for it more than he thought he could afford. "Our habit saves you, at least, don't you see? because it makes you, after all, for the vulgar, indistinguishable from other men. What's the most inveterate mark of men in general? Why, the capacity to spend endless time with dull women—to spend it, I won't say without being bored, but without minding that they are, without being driven off at a tangent by it; which comes to the same thing. I'm your dull woman, a part of the daily bread for which you pray at church. That covers your tracks more than anything."

"And what covers yours?" asked Marcher, whom his dull woman could mostly to this extent amuse. "I see of course what you mean by your saving me, in one way and another, so far as other people are concerned—I've seen it all along. Only, what is it that saves *you*? I often think, you know, of that."

She looked as if she sometimes thought of that too, but in rather a different way. "Where other people, you mean, are concerned?"

"Well, you're really so in with me, you know—as a sort of result of my being so in with yourself. I mean of my having such an immense regard for you, being so tremendously grateful for all you've done for me. I sometimes ask myself if it's quite fair. Fair I mean to have so involved and—since one may say it—interested you. I almost feel as if you hadn't really had time to do anything else."

"Anything else but be interested?" she asked. "Ah, what else does one ever want to be? If I've been 'watching' with you, as we long ago agreed that I was to do, watching is always in itself an absorption."

"Oh, certainly," John Marcher said, "if you hadn't had your curiousity—! Only, doesn't it sometimes come to you, as time goes on, that your curiosity is not being particularly repaid?"

May Bartram had a pause. "Do you ask that, by any chance, because you feel at all that yours isn't? I mean because you have to wait so long."

Oh, he understood what she meant. "For the thing to happen that never does happen? For the beast to jump out? No, I'm just where I was about it. It isn't a matter as to which I can *choose*, I can decide for a change. It isn't one as to which there *can* be a change. It's in the lap of the gods. One's in the hands of one's law—there one is. As to the form the law will take, the way it will operate, that's its own affair."

"Yes," Miss Bartram replied; "of course one's fate is coming, of course it *has* come, in its own form and its own way, all the while. Only, you know, the form and the way in your case were to have been—well, something so exceptional and, as one may say, so particularly *your* own."

Something in this made him look at her with suspicion. "You say 'were to *have* been,' as if in your heart you had begun to doubt."

"Oh!" she vaguely protested.

"As if you believed," he went on, "that nothing will now take place."

She shook her head slowly, but rather inscrutably. "You're far from my thought."

He continued to look at her. "What then is the matter with you?"

"Well," she said after another wait, "the matter with me is simply that I'm more sure than ever my curiosity, as you call it, will be but too well repaid."

They were frankly grave now; he had got up from his seat, had turned once more about the little drawing-room to which, year after year, he brought his inevitable topic; in which he had, as he might have said, tasted their intimate community with every sauce, where every object was as familiar to him as the things of his own house and the very carpets were worn with his fitful walk very much as the desks in old counting-houses are worn by the elbows of generations of clerks. The generations of his nervous moods had been at work there, and the place was the written history of his whole middle life. Under the impression of what his friend had just said he knew himself, for some reason, more aware of these things, which made him, after a moment, stop again before her. "Is it, possibly, that you've grown afraid?"

"Afraid?" He thought, as she repeated the word, that his question had made her, a little, change colour; so that, lest he should have touched on a truth, he explained very kindly, "You remember that that was what you asked *me* long ago—that first day at Weatherend."

"Oh yes, and you told me you didn't know—that I was to see for myself. We've said little about it since, even in so long a time."

"Precisely," Marcher interposed—"quite as if it were too delicate a matter for us to make free with. Quite as if we might find, on pressure, that I *am* afraid. For then," he said, "we shouldn't, should we? quite know what to do."

She had for the time no answer to this question. "There have been days when I thought you were. Only, of course," she added, "there have been days when we have thought almost anything."

"Everything. Oh!" Marcher softly groaned as with a gasp, half spent, at the face, more uncovered just then than it had been for a long while, of the imagination always with them. It had always had its incalculable moments of glaring out, quite as with the very eyes of the very Beast, and, used as he was to them, they could still draw from him the tribute of a sigh that rose from the depths of his being. All that they had thought, first and last, rolled over him; the past seemed to have been reduced to mere barren speculation. This in fact was what the place had just struck him as so full of—the simplification of everything but the state of suspense. That remained only by seeming to hang in the void surrounding it. Even his original fear, if fear it had been, had lost itself in the desert. "I judge, however," he continued, "that you see I'm not afraid now."

"What I see is, as I make it out, that you've achieved something almost unprecedented in the way of getting used to danger. Living with it so long and so closely, you've lost your sense of it; you know it's there, but you're indifferent, and you cease even, as of old, to have to whistle in the dark. Considering what the danger is," May Bartram wound up, "I'm bound to say that I don't think your attitude could well be surpassed."

John Marcher faintly smiled. "It's heroic?"

"Certainly—call it that."

He considered. "I *am*, then, a man of courage?"

"That's what you were to show me."

He still, however, wondered. "But doesn't the man of courage know what he's afraid of—or *not* afraid of? I don't know *that*, you see. I don't focus it. I can't name it. I only know I'm exposed."

"Yes, but exposed—how shall I say?—so directly. So intimately. That's surely enough."

"Enough to make you feel, then—at what we may call the end of our watch—that I'm not afraid?"

"You're not afraid. But it isn't," she said, "the end of our watch. That is it isn't the end of yours. You've everything still to see."

"Then why haven't *you?*" he asked. He had had, all along, to-day, the sense of her keeping something back, and he still had it. As this was his first impression of that, it made a kind of date. The case was the more marked as she didn't at first answer; which in turn made him go on. "You know something I don't." Then his voice, for that of a man of courage, trembled a little. "You know what's to happen." Her silence, with the face she showed, was almost a confession—it made him sure. "You know; and you're afraid to tell me. It's so bad that you're afraid I'll find out."

All this might be true, for she did look as if, unexpectedly to her, he had crossed some mystic line that she had secretly drawn round her. Yet she might, after all, not have worried; and the real upshot was that he himself, at all events, needn't. "You'll never find out."

III

It was all to have made, none the less, as I have said, a date; as came out in the fact that again and again, even after long intervals, other things that passed between them wore, in relation to this hour, but the character of recalls and results. Its immediate effect had been indeed rather to lighten insistence—almost to provoke a reaction; as if their topic had dropped by its own weight and as if moreover, for that matter, Marcher had been visited by one of his occasional warnings against egotism. He had kept up, he felt, and very decently on the whole, his consciousness of the importance of not being selfish, and it was true that he had never sinned in that direction without promptly enough trying to press the scales the other way. He often repaired his fault, the season permitting, by inviting his friend to accompany him to the opera; and it not infrequently thus happened that, to show he didn't wish her to have but one sort of food for her mind, he was the cause of her appearing there with him a dozen nights in the month. It even happened that, seeing her home at such times, he occasionally went in with her to finish, as he called it, the evening, and, the better to make his point, sat down to the frugal but always careful little supper that awaited his pleasure. His point was made, he thought, by his not eternally insisting with her on himself; made for instance, at such hours, when it befell that, her piano at hand and each of them familiar with it, they went over passages of the opera together. It chanced to be on one of these occasions, however, that he reminded her of her not having answered a certain question he had put to her during the talk that had taken place between them on her last birthday. "What is it that saves *you*?"—saved her, he meant, from that appearance of variation from the usual human type. If he had practically escaped remark, as she pretended, by doing, in the most important particular, what most men do—find the answer to life in patching up an alliance of a sort with a woman no better than himself—how had she escaped it, and how could the alliance, such as it was, since they must suppose it had been more or less noticed, have failed to make her rather positively talked about?

"I never said," May Bartram replied, "that it hadn't made me talked about."

"Ah well then, you're not 'saved.' "

"It has not been a question for me. If you've had your woman, I've had," she said, "my man."

"And you mean that makes you all right?"

She hesitated. "I don't know why it shouldn't make me—humanly, which is what we're speaking of—as right as it makes you."

"I see," Marcher returned. " 'Humanly,' no doubt, as showing that you're living for something. Not, that is, just for me and my secret."

May Bartram smiled. "I don't pretend it exactly shows that I'm not living for you. It's my intimacy with you that's in question."

He laughed as he saw what she meant. "Yes, but since, as you say, I'm only, so far as people make out, ordinary, you're—aren't you—no more than ordinary either. You help me to pass for a man like another. So if I *am*, as I understand you, you're not compromised. Is that it?"

She had another hesitation, but she spoke clearly enough. "That's it. It's all that concerns me—to help you to pass for a man like another."

He was careful to acknowledge the remark handsomely. "How kind, how beautiful, you are to me! How shall I ever repay you?"

She had her last grave pause, as if there might be a choice of ways. But she chose. "By going on as you are."

It was into this going on as he was that they relapsed, and really for so long a time that the day inevitably came for a further sounding of their depths. It was as if these depths, constantly bridged over by a structure that was firm enough in spite of its lightness and of its occasional oscillation in the somewhat vertiginous air, invited on occasion, in the interest of their nerves, a dropping of the plummet and a measurement of the abyss. A difference had been made moreover, once for all, by the fact that she had, all the while, not appeared to feel the need of rebutting his charge of an idea within her that she didn't dare to express, uttered just before one of the fullest of their later discussions ended. It had come up for him then that she "knew" something and that what she knew was bad—too bad to tell him. When he had spoken of it as visibly so bad that she was afraid he might find it out, her reply had left the matter too equivocal to be let alone and yet, for Marcher's special sensibility, almost too formidable again to touch. He circled about it at a distance that alternately narrowed and widened and that yet was not much affected by the consciousness in him that there was nothing she could "know," after all, better than he did. She had no source of knowledge that he hadn't equally—except of course that she might have finer nerves. That was what women had where they were interested; they made out things, where people were concerned, that the people often couldn't have made out for themselves. Their nerves, their sensibility, their imagination, were conductors and revealers, and the beauty of May Bartram was in particular that she had given herself so to his case. He felt in these days what, oddly enough, he had never felt before, the growth of a dread of losing her by some catastrophe—some catastrophe that yet wouldn't at all be *the* catastrophe: partly because she had, almost of a sudden, begun to strike him as useful to him as never yet, and partly by reason of an appearance of uncertainty in her health, coincident and equally new. It was characteristic of the inner detachment he had hitherto so successfully cultivated and to which our whole account of him is a reference, it was characteristic that his complications, such as they were, had never yet seemed so as at this crisis to thicken about him, even to the point of making him ask himself if he were, by any chance, of a truth, within sight or sound, within touch or reach, within the immediate jurisdiction of the thing that waited.

When the day came, as come it had to, that his friend confessed to him her fear of a deep disorder in her blood, he felt somehow the shadow of a change and the chill of a shock. He immediately began to imagine aggravations and disasters, and above all to think of her peril as the direct menace for himself of personal privation. This indeed gave him one of those partial recoveries of equanimity that were agreeable to him—it showed him that what was still first in his mind was the loss she herself might suffer. "What if she should have to die before knowing, before seeing—?" It would have been brutal, in the early stages of her trouble, to put that question to her; but it had immediately sounded for him to his own concern, and the possibility was what most made him sorry for her. If she did "know," moreover, in the sense of her having had some—what should he think?—mystical, irresistible light, this would make the matter not better, but worse, inasmuch as her original adoption of his own curiosity had quite become the basis of her life. She had been living to see what would *be* to be seen, and it would be cruel to her to have to give up before the accomplishment of the vision.

These reflections, as I say, refreshed his generosity; yet, make them as he might, he saw himself, with the lapse of the period, more and more disconcerted. It lapsed for him with a strange, steady sweep, and the oddest oddity was that it gave him, independently of the threat of much inconvenience, almost the only positive surprise his career, if career it could be called, had yet offered him. She kept the house as she had never done; he had to go to her to see her—she could meet him nowhere now, though there was scarce a corner of their loved old London in which she had not in the past, at one time or another, done so; and he found her always seated by her fire in the deep, old-fashioned chair she was less and less able to leave. He had been struck one day, after an absence exceeding his usual measure, with her suddenly looking much older to him than he had ever thought of her being; then he recognised that the suddenness was all on his side—he had just been suddenly struck. She looked older because inevitably, after so many years, she *was* old, or almost; which was of course true in still greater measure of her companion. If she was old, or almost, John Marcher assuredly was, and yet it was her showing of the lesson, not his own, that brought the truth home to him. His surprises began here; when once they had begun they multiplied; they came rather with a rush: it was as if, in the oddest way in the world, they had all been kept back, sown in a thick cluster, for the late afternoon of life, the time at which, for people in general, the unexpected has died out.

One of them was that he should have caught himself—for he *had* so done—*really* wondering if the great accident would take form now as nothing more than his being condemned to see this charming woman, this admirable friend, pass away from him. He had never so unreservedly qualified her as while confronted in thought with such a possibility; in spite of which there was small doubt for him that as an answer to his long riddle the mere effacement of even so fine a feature of his situation would be an abject anticlimax. It would represent, as connected with his past attitude, a drop of dignity under the shadow of which his existence could only become the most grotesque of failures. He had been far from holding it a failure—long as he had waited for the appearance that was to make it a success. He had waited for a quite other thing, not for such a one as that. The breath of his good faith came short, however, as he recognised how long he had waited, or how long, at least, his companion had. That she, at all events, might be recorded as having waited in vain—this affected him sharply, and all the more because of his at first having done little more than amuse himself with the idea. It grew more grave as the gravity of her condition grew, and the state of mind it produced in him, which he ended by watching, himself, as if it had been some definite disfigurement of his outer person, may pass for another of his surprises. This conjoined itself still with another, the really stupefying consciousness of a question that he would have allowed to shape itself had he dared. What did everything mean—what, that is, did *she* mean, she and her vain waiting and her probable death and the soundless admonition of it all—unless that, at this time of day, it was simply, it was overwhelmingly too late? He had never, at any stage of his queer consciousness, admitted the whisper of such a correction; he had never, till within these last few months, been so false to his conviction as not to hold that what was to come to him had time, whether *he* struck himself as having it or not. That at last, at last, he certainly hadn't it, to speak of, or had it but in the scantiest measure—such, soon enough, as things went with him, became the inference with which his old obsession had to reckon: and this it was not helped to do by the more and more confirmed appearance that the great vagueness casting the long shadow in which he had lived had, to attest itself, almost no margin left. Since it was in Time that he was to have met his fate, so it was in Time that his fate was to have acted; and as he waked up to the sense of no longer being young, which was exactly the sense of being stale, just as that, in turn, was the sense of being weak, he waked up to another matter beside. It all hung together; they were subject, he and the great vagueness, to an equal and indivisible law. When the possibilities themselves had, accordingly, turned stale, when the secret of the gods had grown faint, had perhaps even quite evaporated, that, and that only, was failure. It wouldn't have been failure to be bankrupt, dishonoured, pilloried, hanged; it was failure not to be anything. And so, in the dark valley into which his path had taken its unlooked-for twist, he wondered not a little as he groped. He didn't care what awful crash might overtake him, with what ignominy or what monstrosity he might yet be associated—since he wasn't, after all, too utterly old to suffer—if it would only be decently proportionate to the posture he had kept, all his life, in the promised presence of it. He had but one desire left—that he shouldn't have been "sold."

IV

Then it was that one afternoon, while the spring of the year was young and new, she met, all in her own way, his frankest betrayal of these alarms. He had gone in late to see her, but evening had not settled, and she was presented to him in that long, fresh light of waning April days which affects us often with a sadness sharper than the greyest hours of autumn. The week had been warm, the spring was supposed to have begun early, and May Bartram sat, for

the first time in the year, without a fire, a fact that, to Marcher's
sense, gave the scene of which she formed part a smooth and ultimate look, an air of knowing, in its immaculate order and its cold,
meaningless cheer, that it would never see a fire again. Her own
aspect—he could scarce have said why—intensified this note. Almost as white as wax, with the marks and signs in her face as
numerous and as fine as if they had been etched by a needle, with
soft white draperies relieved by a faded green scarf, the delicate
tone of which had been consecrated by the years, she was the picture of a serene, exquisite, but impenetrable sphinx, whose head,
or indeed all whose person, might have been powdered with silver.
She was a sphinx, yet with her white petals and green fronds she
might have been a lily too—only an artificial lily, wonderfully imi-
tated and constantly kept, without dust or stain, though not exempt
from a slight droop and a complexity of faint creases, under some
clear glass bell. The perfection of household care, of high polish
and finish, always reigned in her rooms, but they especially looked
to Marcher at present as if everything had been wound up, tucked
in, put away, so that she might sit with folded hands and with
nothing more to do. She was "out of it," to his vision; her work was
over; she communicated with him as across some gulf, or from
some island of rest that she had already reached, and it made him
feel strangely abandoned. Was it—or, rather, wasn't it—that if for
so long she had been watching with him the answer to their question had swum into her ken and taken on its name, so that her
occupation was verily gone? He had as much as charged her with
this in saying to her, many months before, that she even then knew
something she was keeping from him. It was a point he had never
since ventured to press, vaguely fearing, as he did, that it might
become a difference, perhaps a disagreement, between them. He
had in short, in this later time, turned nervous, which was what, in
all the other years, he had never been; and the oddity was that his
nervousness should have waited till he had begun to doubt, should
have held off so long as he was sure. There was something, it
seemed to him, that the wrong word would bring down on his head,
something that would so at least put an end to his suspense. But
he wanted not to speak the wrong word; that would make everything
ugly. He wanted the knowledge he lacked to drop on him, if drop
it could, by its own august weight. If she was to forsake him it was
surely for her to take leave. This was why he didn't ask her again,
directly, what she knew; but it was also why, approaching the matter
from another side, he said to her in the course of his visit: "What
do you regard as the very worst that, at this time of day, *can* happen
to me?"

He had asked her that in the past often enough; they had, with the odd, irregular rhythm of their intensities and avoidances, exchanged ideas about it and then had seen the ideas washed away by cool intervals, washed like figures traced in sea-sand. It had ever been the mark of their talk that the oldest allusions in it required but a little dismissal and reaction to come out again, sounding for the hour as new. She could thus at present meet his inquiry quite freshly and patiently. "Oh yes, I've repeatedly thought, only it always seemed to me of old that I couldn't quite make up my mind. I thought of dreadful things, between which it was difficult to choose; and so must you have done."

"Rather! I feel now as if I had scarce done anything else. I appear to myself to have spent my life in thinking of nothing *but* dreadful things. A great many of them I've at different times named to you, but there were others I couldn't name."

"They were too, too dreadful?"

"Too, too dreadful—some of them."

She looked at him a minute, and there came to him as he met it an inconsequent sense that her eyes, when one got their full clearness, were still as beautiful as they had been in youth, only beautiful with a strange, cold light—a light that somehow was a part of the effect, if it wasn't rather a part of the cause, of the pale, hard sweetness of the season and the hour. "And yet," she said at last, "there are horrors we have mentioned."

It deepened the strangeness to see her, as such a figure in such a picture, talk of "horrors," but she was to do, in a few minutes, something stranger yet—though even of this he was to take the full measure but afterwards—and the note of it was already in the air. It was, for the matter of that, one of the signs that her eyes were having again such a high flicker of their prime. He had to admit, however, what she said. "Oh yes, there were times when we did go far." He caught himself in the act of speaking as if it all were over. Well, he wished it were; and the consummation depended, for him, clearly, more and more on his companion.

But she had now a soft smile. "Oh, far—!

It was oddly ironic. "Do you mean you're prepared to go further?"

She was frail and ancient and charming as she continued to look at him, yet it was rather as if she had lost the thread. "Do you consider that we went so far?"

"Why, I thought it the point you were just making—that we *had* looked most things in the face."

"Including each other?" She still smiled. "But you're quite right. We've had together great imaginations, often great fears; but some of them have been unspoken."

"Then the worst—we haven't faced that. I *could* face it, I believe, if I knew what you think it. I feel," he explained, "as if I had lost my power to conceive such things." And he wondered if he looked as blank as he sounded. "It's spent."

"Then why do you assume," she asked, "that mine isn't?"

"Because you've given me signs to the contrary. It isn't a question for you of conceiving, imagining, comparing. It isn't a question now of choosing." At last he came out with it. "You know something that I don't. You've shown me that before."

These last words affected her, he could see in a moment, re-markably, and she spoke with firmness. "I've shown you, my dear, nothing."

He shook his head. "You can't hide it."

"Oh, oh!" May Bartram murmured over what she couldn't hide. It was almost a smothered groan.

"You admitted it months ago, when I spoke of it to you as of something you were afraid I would find out. Your answer was that I couldn't, that I wouldn't, and I don't pretend I have. But you had something therefore in mind, and I see now that it must have been, that it still is, the possibility that, of all possibilities, has settled itself for you as the worst. This," he went on, "is why I appeal to you. I'm only afraid of ignorance now—I'm not afraid of knowl-edge." And then as for a while she said nothing: "What makes me sure is that I see in your face and feel here, in this air and amid these appearances, that you're out of it. You've done. You've had your experience. You leave me to my fate."

Well, she listened, motionless and white in her chair, as if she had in fact a decision to make, so that her whole manner was a virtual confession, though still with a small, fine, inner stiffness, an imperfect surrender. "It *would* be the worst," she finally let herself say. "I mean the thing that I've never said."

It hushed him a moment. "More monstrous than all the mon-strosities we've named?"

"More monstrous. Isn't that what you sufficiently express," she asked, "in calling it the worst?"

Marcher thought. "Assuredly—if you mean, as I do, something that includes all the loss and all the shame that are thinkable."

"It would if it *should* happen," said May Bartram. "What we're speaking of, remember, is only my idea."

"It's your belief," Marcher returned. "That's enough for me. I feel your beliefs are right. Therefore if, having this one, you give me no more light on it, you abandon me."

"No, no!" she repeated. "I'm with you—don't you see?—still." And as if to make it more vivid to him she rose from her chair—a move-ment she seldom made in these days—and showed herself, all draped and all soft, in her fairness and slimness. "I haven't forsaken you."

It was really, in its effort against weakness, a generous assurance, and had the success of the impulse not, happily, been great, it would have touched him to pain more than to pleasure. But the cold charm in her eyes had spread, as she hovered before him, to all the rest of her person, so that it was, for the minute, almost like a recovery of youth. He couldn't pity her for that; he could only take her as she showed—as capable still of helping him. It was as if, at the same time, her light might at any instant go out; wherefore he must make the most of it. There passed before him with intensity the three or four things he wanted most to know; but the question that came of itself to his lips really covered the others. "Then tell me if I shall consciously suffer."

She promptly shook her head. "Never!"

It confirmed the authority he imputed to her, and it produced on him an extraordinary effect. "Well, what's better than that? Do you call that the worst?"

"You think nothing is better?" she asked.

She seemed to mean something so special that he again sharply wondered, though still with the dawn of a prospect of relief. "Why not, if one doesn't *know*?" After which, as their eyes, over his question, met in a silence, the dawn deepened and something to his purpose came, prodigiously, out of her very face. His own, as he took it in, suddenly flushed to the forehead; and he gasped with the force of a perception to which, on the instant, everything fitted. The sound of his gasp filled the air; then he became articulate. "I see—if I don't suffer!"

In her own look, however, was doubt. "You see what?"

"Why, what you mean—what you've always meant."

She again shook her head. "What I mean isn't what I've always meant. It's different."

"It's something new?"

She hesitated. "Something new. It's not what you think. I see what you think."

His divination drew breath then; only her correction might be wrong. "It isn't that I *am* a donkey?" he asked between faintness and grimness. "It isn't that it's all a mistake?"

"A mistake?" she pityingly echoed. *That* possibility, for her, he saw, would be monstrous; and if she guaranteed him the immunity from pain it would accordingly not be what she had in mind. "Oh, no," she declared; "it's nothing of that sort. You've been right."

Yet he couldn't help asking himself if she weren't, thus pressed, speaking but to save him. It seemed to him he should be most lost if his history should prove all a platitude. "Are you telling me the truth, so that I sha'n't have been a bigger idiot than I can bear to know? I *haven't* lived with a vain imagination, in the most besotted illusion? I haven't waited but to see the door shut in my face?"

She shook her head again. "However the case stands *that* isn't the truth. Whatever the reality, it *is* a reality. The door isn't shut. The door's open," said May Bartram.

"Then something's to come?"

She waited once again, always with her cold, sweet eyes on him. "It's never too late." She had, with her gliding step, diminished the distance between them, and she stood nearer to him, close to him, a minute, as if still full of the unspoken. Her movement might have been for some finer emphasis of what she was at once hesitating and deciding to say. He had been standing by the chimney-piece, fireless and sparely adorned, a small, perfect old French clock and two morsels of rosy Dresden constituting all its furniture; and her hand grasped the shelf while she kept him waiting, grasped it a little as for support and encouragement. She only kept him waiting, however; that is he only waited. It had become suddenly, from her movement and attitude, beautiful and vivid to him that she had something more to give him; her wasted face delicately shone with it, and it glittered, almost as with the white lustre of silver, in her expression. She was right, incontestably, for what he saw in her face was the truth, and strangely, without consequence, while their talk of it as dreadful was still in the air, she appeared to present it as inordinately soft. This, prompting bewilderment, made him but gape the more gratefully for her revelation, so that they continued for some minutes silent, her face shining at him, her contact imponderably pressing, and his stare all kind, but all expectant. The end, none the less, was that what he had expected failed to sound. Something else took place instead, which seemed to consist at first in the mere closing of her eyes. She gave way at the same instant to a slow, fine shudder, and though he remained staring—though he stared, in fact, but the harder—she turned off and regained her chair. It was the end of what she had been intending, but it left him thinking only of that.

"Well, you don't say—?"

She had touched in her passage a bell near the chimney and had sunk back, strangely pale. "I'm afraid I'm too ill."

"Too ill to tell me?" It sprang up sharp to him, and almost to his lips, the fear that she would die without giving him light. He checked himself in time from so expressing his question, but she answered as if she had heard the words.

"Don't you know—now?"

" 'Now'—?" She had spoken as if something that had made a difference had come up within the moment. But her maid, quickly obedient to her bell, was already with them. "I know nothing." And he was afterwards to say to himself that he must have spoken with odious impatience, such an impatience as to show that, supremely disconcerted, he washed his hands of the whole question.

"Oh!" said May Bartram.

"Are you in pain?" he asked, as the woman went to her.

"No," said May Bartram.

Her maid, who had put an arm round her as if to take her to her room, fixed on him eyes that appealingly contradicted her; in spite of which, however, he showed once more his mystification. "What then has happened?"

She was once more, with her companion's help, on her feet, and, feeling withdrawal imposed on him, he had found, blankly, his hat and gloves and had reached the door. Yet he waited for her answer. "What *was* to," she said.

v

He came back the next day, but she was then unable to see him, and as it was literally the first time this had occurred in the long stretch of their acquaintance he turned away, defeated and sore, almost angry—or feeling at least that such a break in their custom was really the beginning of the end—and wandered alone with his thoughts, especially with one of them that he was unable to keep down. She was dying, and he would lose her; she was dying, and his life would end. He stopped in the park, into which he had passed, and stared before him at his recurrent doubt. Away from her the doubt pressed again; in her presence he had believed her, but as he felt his forlornness he threw himself into the explanation that, nearest at hand, had most of a miserable warmth for him and least of a cold torment. She had deceived him to save him—to put him off with something in which he should be able to rest. What could the thing that was to happen to him be, after all, but just this thing that had begun to happen? Her dying, her death, his consequent solitude—*that* was what he had figured as the beast in the jungle, that was what had been in the lap of the gods. He had had her word for it as he left her; for what else, on earth, could she have meant? It wasn't a thing of a monstrous order; not a fate rare and distinguished; not a stroke of fortune that overwhelmed and immortalized; it had only the stamp of the common doom. But poor Marcher, at this hour, judged the common doom sufficient. It would serve his turn, and even as the consummation of infinite waiting he would bend his pride to accept it. He sat down on a bench in the twilight. He hadn't been a fool. Something had *been*, as she had said, to come. Before he rose indeed it had quite struck him that the final fact really matched with the long avenue through which he had had to reach it. As sharing his suspense, and as giving herself all, giving her life, to bring it to an end, she had come with him every step of the way. He had lived by her aid, and to leave her behind would be cruelly, damnably to miss her. What could be more overwhelming than that?

Well, he was to know within the week, for though she kept him a while at bay, left him restless and wretched during a series of days on each of which he asked about her only again to have to turn away, she ended his trial by receiving him where she had always received him. Yet she had been brought out at some hazard into the presence of so many of the things that were consciously, vainly, half their past, and there was scant service left in the gentleness of her mere desire, all too visible, to check his obsession and wind up his long trouble. That was clearly what she wanted; the one thing more, for her own peace, while she could still put out her hand. He was so affected by her state that, once seated by her chair, he was moved to let everything go; it was she herself therefore who brought him back, took up again, before she dismissed him, her last word of the other time. She showed how she wished to leave their affair in order. "I'm not sure you understood. You've nothing to wait for more. It *has* come."

Oh, how he looked at her! "Really?"

"Really."

"The thing that, as you said, *was* to?"

"The thing that we began in our youth to watch for."

Face to face with her once more he believed her; it was a claim to which he had so abjectly little to oppose. "You mean that it has come as a positive, definite occurrence, with a name and a date?"

"Positive. Definite. I don't know about the 'name,' but, oh, with a date!"

He found himself again too helplessly at sea. "But come in the night—come and passed me by?"

May Bartram had her strange, faint smile. "Oh no, it hasn't passed you by!"

"But if I haven't been aware of it, and it hasn't touched me—?"

"Ah, your not being aware of it," and she seemed to hesitate an instant to deal with this—"your not being aware of it is the strangeness *in* the strangeness. It's the wonder *of* the wonder." She spoke as with the softness almost of a sick child, yet now at last, at the end of all, with the perfect straightness of a sibyl. She visibly knew that she knew, and the effect on him was of something co-ordinate, in its high character, with the law that had ruled him. It was the true voice of the law; so on her lips would the law itself have sounded. "It *has* touched you," she went on. "It has done its office. It has made you all its own."

"So utterly without my knowing it?"

"So utterly without your knowing it." His hand as he leaned to her, was on the arm of her chair, and, dimly smiling always now, she placed her own on it. "It's enough if *I* know it."

"Oh!" he confusedly sounded, as she herself of late so often had done.

"What I long ago said is true. You'll never know now, and I think you ought to be content. You've *had* it," said May Bartram.

"But had what?"

"Why, what was to have marked you out. The proof of your law. It has acted. I'm too glad," she then bravely added, "to have been able to see what it's *not*."

He continued to attach his eyes to her, and with the sense that it was all beyond him, and that *she* was too, he would still have sharply challenged her, had he not felt it an abuse of her weakness to do more than take devoutly what she gave him, take it as hushed as to a revelation. If he did speak, it was out of the foreknowledge of his loneliness to come. "If you're glad of what it's 'not,' it might then have been worse?"

She turned her eyes away, she looked straight before her with which, after a moment: "Well, you know our fears."

He wondered. "It's something then we never feared?"

On this, slowly, she turned to him. "Did we ever dream, with all our dreams, that we should sit and talk of it thus?"

He tried for a little to make out if they had; but it was as if their dreams, numberless enough, were in solution in some thick, cold mist, in which thought lost itself. "It might have been that we couldn't talk?"

"Well"—she did her best for him—"not from this side. This, you see," she said, "is the *other* side."

"I think," poor Marcher returned, "that all sides are the same to me." Then, however, as she softly shook her head in correction: "We mightn't, as it were, have got across—?"

"To where we are—no. We're *here*"—she made her weak emphasis.

"And much good does it do us!" was her friend's frank comment.

"It does us the good it can. It does us the good that *it* isn't here. It's past. It's behind," said May Bartram. "Before—" but her voice dropped.

He had got up, not to tire her, but it was hard to combat his yearning. She after all told him nothing but that his light had failed—which he knew well enough without her. "Before—?" he blankly echoed.

"Before, you see, it was always to *come*. That kept it present."

"Oh, I don't care what comes now! Besides," Marcher added, "it seems to me I liked it better present, as you say, than I can like it absent with *your* absence."

"Oh, mine!"—and her pale hands made light of it.

"With the absence of everything." He had a dreadful sense of standing there before her for—so far as anything but this proved, this bottomless drop was concerned—the last time of their life. It rested on him with a weight he felt he could scarce bear, and this weight it apparently was that still pressed out what remained in him of speakable protest. "I believe you; but I can't begin to pretend I understand. *Nothing*, for me, is past; nothing *will* pass until I pass myself, which I pray my stars may be as soon as possible. Say, however," he added, "that I've eaten my cake, as you contend, to the last crumb—how can the thing I've never felt at all be the thing I was marked out to feel?"

She met him, perhaps, less directly, but she met him unperturbed. "You take your 'feelings' for granted. You were to suffer your fate. That was not necessarily to know it."

"How in the world—when what is such knowledge but suffering?"

She looked up at him a while, in silence. "No—you don't understand."

"I suffer,' said John Marcher.

"Don't, don't!"

"How can I help at least *that*?"

"*Don't!*" May Bartram repeated.

She spoke it in a tone so special, in spite of her weakness, that he stared an instant—stared as if some light, hitherto hidden, had shimmered across his vision. Darkness again closed over it, but the gleam had already become for him an idea. "Because I haven't the right—?"

"Don't *know*—when you needn't," she mercifully urged. "You needn't—for we shouldn't."

"Shouldn't?" If he could but know what she meant!

"No—it's too much."

"Too much?" he still asked—but with a mystification that was the next moment, of a sudden, to give way. Her words, if they meant something, affected him in this light—the light also of her wasted face—as meaning *all*, and the sense of what knowledge had been for herself came over him with a rush which broke through into a question. "Is it of that, then, you're dying?"

She but watched him, gravely at first, as if to see, with this, where he was, and she might have seen something, or feared something, that moved her sympathy. "I would live for you still—if I could." Her eyes closed for a little, as if, withdrawn into herself, she were, for a last time, trying. "But I can't!" she said as she raised them again to take leave of him.

She couldn't indeed, as but too promptly and sharply appeared, and he had no vision of her after this that was anything but darkness and doom. They had parted forever in that strange talk; access to her chamber of pain, rigidly guarded, was almost wholly forbidden him; he was feeling now moreover, in the face of doctors, nurses, the two or three relatives attracted doubtless by the presumption of what she had to "leave," how few were the rights, as they were called in such cases, that he had to put forward, and how odd it might even seem that their intimacy shouldn't have given him more of them. The stupidest fourth cousin had more, even though she had been nothing in such a person's life. She had been a feature of features in *his*, for what else was it to have been so indispensable? Strange beyond saying were the ways of existence, baffling for him the anomaly of his lack, as he felt it to be, of producible claim. A woman might have been, as it were, everything to him, and it might yet present him in no connection that anyone appeared obliged to recognise. If this was the case in these closing weeks it was the case more sharply on the occasion of the last offices rendered, in the great grey London cemetery, to what had been mortal, to what had been precious, in his friend. The concourse at her grave was not numerous, but he saw himself treated as scarce more nearly concerned with it than if there had been a thousand others. He was in short from this moment face to face with the fact that he was to profit extraordinarily little by the interest May Bartram had taken in him. He couldn't quite have said what he expected, but he had somehow not expected this approach to a double privation. Not only had her interest failed him, but he seemed to feel himself unattended—and for a reason he couldn't sound—by the distinction, the dignity, the propriety, if nothing else, of the man markedly bereaved. It was as if, in the view of society, he had not *been* markedly bereaved, as if there still failed some sign or proof of it, and as if, none the less, his character could never be affirmed, nor the deficiency ever made up. There were moments, as the weeks went by, when he would have liked, by some almost aggressive act, to take his stand on the intimacy of his loss, in order that it *might* be questioned and his retort, to the relief of his spirit, so recorded; but the moments of an irritation more helpless followed fast on these, the moments during which, turning things over with a good conscience but with a bare horizon, he found himself wondering if he oughtn't to have begun, so to speak, further back.

He found himself wondering indeed at many things, and this last speculation had others to keep it comany. What could he have done, after all, in her lifetime, without giving them both, as it were, away? He couldn't have made it known she was watching him, for that would have published the superstition of the Beast. This was what closed his mouth now—now that the Jungle had been threshed to vacancy and that the Beast had stolen away. It sounded too foolish and too flat; the difference for him in this particular, the extinction in his life of the element of suspense, was such in fact as to surprise him. He could scarce have said what the effect resembled; the abrupt cessation, the positive prohibition, of music perhaps, more than anything else, in some place all adjusted and all accustomed to sonority and to attention. If he could at any rate have conceived lifting the veil from his image at some moment of the past (what had he done, after all, if not lift it to *her*?), so to do this to-day, to talk to people at large of the jungle cleared and confide to them that he now felt it as safe, would have been not only to see them listen as to a goodwife's tale, but really to hear himself tell one. What it presently came to in truth was that poor Marcher waded through his beaten grass, where no life stirred, where no breath sounded, where no evil eye seemed to gleam from a possible lair, very much as if vaguely looking for the Beast, and still more as if missing it. He walked about in an existence that had grown strangely more spacious, and, stopping fitfully in places where the undergrowth of life struck him as closer, asked himself yearningly, wondered secretly and sorely, if it would have lurked here or there. It would have at all events *sprung*; what was at least complete was his belief in the truth itself of the assurance given him. The change from his old sense to his new was absolute and final: what was to happen *had* so absolutely and finally happened that he was as little able to know a fear for his future as to know a hope; so absent in short was any question of anything still to come. He was to live entirely with the other question, that of his unidentified past, that of his having to see his fortune impenetrably muffled and masked.

The torment of this vision became then his occupation; he couldn't perhaps have consented to live but for the possibility of guessing. She had told him, his friend, not to guess; she had forbidden him, so far as he might, to know, and she had even in a sort denied the power in him to learn: which were so many things, precisely, to deprive him of rest. It wasn't that he wanted, he argued for fairness, that anything that had happened to him should happen over again; it was only that he shouldn't, as an anticlimax, have been taken sleeping so sound as not to be able to win back by an effort of thought the lost stuff of consciousness. He declared to himself at moments that he would either win it back or have done with consciousness for ever; he made this idea his one motive, in

fine, made it so much his passion that none other, to compare with
it, seemed ever to have touched him. The lost stuff of consciousness
became thus for him as a strayed or stolen child to an unappeasable
father; he hunted it up and down very much as if he were knocking
at doors and inquiring of the police. This was the spirit in which,
inevitably, he set himself to travel; he started on a journey that was
to be as long as he could make it; it danced before him that, as the
other side of the globe couldn't possibly have less to say to him, it
might, by a possibility of suggestion, have more. Before he quitted
London, however, he made a pilgrimage to May Bartram's grave,
took his way to it through the endless avenues of the grim suburban
necropolis, sought it out in the wilderness of tombs, and, though
he had come but for the renewal of the act of farewell, found himself, when he had at last stood by it, beguiled into long intensities.
He stood for an hour, powerless to turn away and yet powerless to
penetrate the darkness of death; fixing with his eyes her inscribed
name and date, beating his forehead against the fact of the secret
they kept, drawing his breath, while he waited as if, in pity of him,
some sense would rise from the stones. He kneeled on the stones,
however, in vain; they kept what they concealed; and if the face of
the tomb did become a face for him it was because her two names
were like a pair of eyes that didn't know him. He gave them a last
long look, but no palest light broke.

VI

He stayed away, after this, for a year; he visited the depths of
Asia, spending himself on scenes of romantic interest, of superlative
sanctity; but what was present to him everywhere was that for a
man who had known what *he* had known the world was vulgar and
vain. The state of mind in which he had lived for so many years
shone out to him, in reflection, as a light that coloured and refined,
a light beside which the glow of the East was garish, cheap and
thin. The terrible truth was that he had lost—with everything else—
a distinction as well; the things he saw couldn't help being common
when he had become common to look at them. He was simply now
one of them himself—he was in the dust, without a peg for the
sense of difference; and there were hours when, before the temples
of gods and the sepulchres of kings, his spirit turned, for nobleness
of association, to the barely discriminated slab in the London suburb. That had become for him, and more intensely with time and
distance, his one witness of a past glory. It was all that was left to
him for proof or pride, yet the past glories of Pharaohs were nothing
to him as he thought of it. Small wonder then that he came back
to it on the morrow of his return. He was drawn there this time as

irresistibly as the other, yet with a confidence, almost, that was doubtless the effect of the many months that had elapsed. He had lived, in spite of himself, into his change of feeling, and in wandering over the earth had wandered, as might be said, from the circumference to the centre of his desert. He had settled to his safety and accepted perforce his extinction; figuring to himself, with some colour, in the likeness of certain little old men he remembered to have seen, of whom, all meagre and wizened as they might look, it was related that they had in their time fought twenty duels or been loved by ten princesses. They indeed had been wondrous for others, while he was but wondrous for himself; which, however, was exactly the cause of his haste to renew the wonder by getting back, as he might put it, into his own presence. That had quickened his steps and checked his delay. If his visit was prompt it was because he had been separated so long from the part of himself that alone he now valued.

It is accordingly not false to say that he reached his goal with a certain elation and stood there again with a certain assurance. The creature beneath the sod *knew* of his rare experience, so that, strangely now, the place had lost for him its mere blankness of expression. It met him in mildness—not, as before, in mockery; it wore for him the air of conscious greeting that we find, after absence, in things that have closely belonged to us and which seem to confess of themselves to the connection. The plot of ground, the graven tablet, the tended flowers affected him so as belonging to him that he quite felt for the hour like a contented landlord reviewing a piece of property. Whatever had happened—well, had happened. He had not come back this time with the vanity of that question, his former worrying, "What, *what*?" now practically so spent. Yet he would, none the less, never again so cut himself off from the spot; he would come back to it every month, for if he did nothing else by its aid he at least held up his head. It thus grew for him, in the oddest way, a positive resource; he carried out his idea of periodical returns, which took their place at last among the most inveterate of his habits. What it all amounted to, oddly enough, was that, in his now so simplified world, this garden of death gave him the few square feet of earth on which he could still most live. It was as if, being nothing anywhere else for anyone, nothing even for himself, he were just everything here, and if not for a crowd of witnesses, or indeed for any witness but John Marcher, then by clear right of the register that he could scan like an open page. The open page was the tomb of his friend, and *there* were the facts of the past, there the truth of his life, there the backward reaches in which he could lose himself. He did this, from time to time, with such effect that he seemed to wander through the old years with his hand in the arm of a companion who was, in the most extraordinary manner, his other, his younger self; and to wander, which was more extraordinary yet, round and round a third presence—not wandering she, but stationary, still, whose eyes, turning with his revolution, never ceased to follow him, and whose seat was his point, so to speak, of orientation. Thus in short he settled to live—feeding only on the sense that he once *had* lived, and dependent on it not only for a support but for an identity.

It sufficed him, in its way, for months, and the year elapsed; it would doubtless even have carried him further but for an accident, superficially slight, which moved him, in a quite other direction, with a force beyond any of his impressions of Egypt or of India. It was a thing of the merest chance—the turn, as he afterwards felt, of a hair, though he was indeed to live to believe that if light hadn't come to him in this particular fashion it would still have come in another. He was to live to believe this, I say, though he was not to live, I may not less definitely mention, to do much else. We allow him at any rate the benefit of the conviction, struggling up for him at the end, that, whatever might have happened or not happened, he would have come round of himself to the light. The incident of an autumn day had put the match to the train laid from of old by his misery. With the light before him he knew that even of late his ache had only been smothered. It was strangely drugged, but it throbbed; at the touch it began to bleed. And the touch, in the event, was the face of a fellow-mortal. This face, one grey afternoon when the leaves were thick in the alleys, looked into Marcher's own, at the cemetery, with an expression like the cut of a blade. He felt it, that is, so deep down that he winced at the steady thrust. The person who so mutely assaulted him was a figure he had noticed, on reaching his own goal, absorbed by a grave a short distance away, a grave apparently fresh, so that the emotion of the visitor would probably match it for frankness. This fact alone forbade further attention, though during the time he stayed he remained vaguely conscious of his neighbour, a middle-aged man apparently, in mourning, whose bowed back, among the clustered monuments and mortuary yews, was constantly presented. Marcher's theory that these were elements in contact with which he himself revived, had suffered, on this occasion, it may be granted, a sensible though inscrutable check. The autumn day was dire for him as none had recently been, and he rested with a heaviness he had not yet known on the low stone table that bore May Bartram's name. He rested without power to move, as if some spring in him, some spell vouchsafed, had suddenly been broken forever. If he could have done that moment as he wanted he would simply have stretched himself on the slab that was ready to take him, treating it as a place prepared to receive his last sleep. What in all the wide world had he now to keep awake for? He stared before him with the question, and it was then that, as one of the cemetery walks passed near him, he caught the shock of the face.

His neighbour at the other grave had withdrawn, as he himself, with force in him to move, would have done by now, and was advancing along the path on his way to one of the gates. This brought him near, and his pace was slow, so that—and all the more as there was a kind of hunger in his look—the two men were for a minute directly confronted. Marcher felt him on the spot as one of the deeply stricken—a perception so sharp that nothing else in the picture lived for it, neither his dress, his age, nor his presumable character and class; nothing lived but the deep ravage of the features that he showed. He *showed* them—that was the point; he was moved, as he passed, by some impulse that was either a signal for sympathy or, more possibly, a challenge to another sorrow. He might already have been aware of our friend, might, at some previous hour, have noticed in him the smooth habit of the scene, with which the state of his own senses so scantly consorted, and might thereby have been stirred as by a kind of overt discord. What Marcher was at all events conscious of was, in the first place, that the image of scarred passion presented to him was conscious too —of something that profaned the air; and, in the second, that, roused, startled, shocked, he was yet the next moment looking after it, as it went, with envy. The most extraordinary thing that had happened to him—though he had given that name to other matters as well—took place, after his immediate vague stare, as a consequence of this impression. The stranger passed, but the raw glare of his grief remained, making our friend wonder in pity what wrong, what wound it expressed, what injury not to be healed. What had the man *had* to make him, by the loss of it, so bleed and yet live?

Something—and this reached him with a pang—that *he*, John Marcher, hadn't; the proof of which was precisely John Marcher's arid end. No passion had ever touched him, for this was what passion meant; he had survived and maundered and pined, but where had been *his* deep ravage? The extraordinary thing we speak of was the sudden rush of the result of this question. The sight that had just met his eyes named to him, as in letters of quick flame, something he had utterly, insanely missed, and what he had missed made these things a train of fire, made them mark themselves in an anguish of inward throbs. He had seen *outside* of his life, not learned it within, the way a woman was mourned when she had been loved for herself; such was the force of his conviction of the meaning of the stranger's face, which still flared for him like a smoky torch. It had not come to him, the knowledge, on the wings of experience;

it had brushed him, jostled him, upset him, with the disrespect of chance, the insolence of an accident. Now that the illumination had begun, however, it blazed to the zenith, and what he presently stood there gazing at was the sounded void of his life. He gazed, he drew breath, in pain; he turned in his dismay, and, turning, he had before him in sharper incision than ever the open page of his story. The name on the table smote him as the passage of his neighbour had done, and what it said to him, full in the face, was that *she* was what he had missed. This was the awful thought, the answer to all the past, the vision at the dread clearness of which he turned as cold as the stone beneath him. Everything fell together, confessed, explained, overwhelmed; leaving him most of all stupefied at the blindness he had cherished. The fate he had been marked for he had met with a vengeance—he had emptied the cup to the lees; he had been the man of his time, *the* man, to whom nothing on earth was to have happened. That was the rare stroke—that was his visitation. So he saw it, as we say, in pale horror, while the pieces fitted and fitted. So *she* had seen it, while he didn't, and so she served at this hour to drive the truth home. It was the truth, vivid and monstrous, that all the while he had waited the wait was itself his portion. This the companion of his vigil had a given moment perceived, and she had then offered him the chance to baffle his doom. One's doom, however, was never baffled, and on the day she had told him that his own had come down she had seen him but stupidly stare at the escape she offered him.

The escape would have been to love her; then, *then* he would have lived. *She* had lived—who could say now with what passion?—since she had loved him for himself; whereas he had never thought of her (ah, how it hugely glared at him!) but in the chill of his egotism and the light of her use. Her spoken words came back to him, and the chain stretched and stretched. The beast had lurked indeed, and the beast, at its hour, had sprung; it had sprung in that twilight of the cold April when, pale, ill, wasted, but all beautiful, and perhaps even then recoverable, she had risen from her chair to stand before him and let him imaginably guess. It had sprung as he didn't guess; it had sprung as she hopelessly turned from him, and the mark, by the time he left her, had fallen where it *was* to fall. He had justified his fear and achieved his fate; he had failed, with the last exactitude, of all he was to fail of; and a moan now rose to his lips as he remembered she had prayed he mightn't know. This horror of waking—*this* was knowledge, knowledge under the breath of which the very tears in his eyes seemed to freeze. Through them, none the less, he tried to fix it and hold it; he kept it there before him so that he might feel the pain. That at least, belated and bitter, had something of the taste of life. But the bitterness suddenly sickened him, and it was as if, horribly, he saw, in the truth, in the cruelty of his image, what had been appointed and done. He saw the Jungle of his life and saw the lurking Beast; then, while he looked, perceived it, as by a stir of the air, rise, huge and hideous, for the leap that was to settle him. His eyes darkened—it was close; and, instinctively turning, in his hallucination, to avoid it, he flung himself, on his face, on the tomb.

The Jolly Corner[†]

"Every one asks me what I 'think' of everything," said Spencer
Brydon; "and I make answer as I can—begging or dodging the question, putting them off with any nonsense. It wouldn't matter to any
of them really," he went on, "for, even were it possible to meet in
that stand-and-deliver way so silly a demand on so big a subject,
my 'thoughts' would still be almost altogether about something that
concerns only myself." He was talking to Miss Staverton, with
whom for a couple of months now he had availed himself of every
possible occasion to talk; this disposition and this resource, this
comfort and support, as the situation in fact presented itself, having
promptly enough taken the first place in the considerable array of
rather unattenuated surprises attending his so strangely belated return to America. Everything was somehow a surprise; and that
might be natural when one had so long and so consistently neglected everything, taken pains to give surprises so much margin
for play. He had given them more than thirty years—thirty-three,
to be exact; and they now seemed to him to have organised their
performance quite on the scale of that licence. He had been twenty-
three on leaving New York—he was fifty-six to-day: unless indeed
he were to reckon as he had sometimes, since his repatriation,
found himself feeling; in which case he would have lived longer
than is often allotted to man. It would have taken a century, he
repeatedly said to himself, and said also to Alice Staverton, it would
have taken a longer absence and a more averted mind than those
even of which he had been guilty, to pile up the differences, the
newnesses, the queernesses, above all the bignesses, for the better
or the worse, that at present assaulted his vision wherever he
looked.

The great fact all the while however had been the incalculability;
since he *had* supposed himself, from decade to decade, to be allow-

---

† "The Jolly Corner" first appeared in Ford Madox Ford's *English Review*, December 1908,
and had its first appearance in a book in vol. 17 of *The Novels and Tales of Henry James*
(New York: Charles Scribner's Sons, 1909)—the so-called New York Edition. This text
is here reprinted.

ing, and in the most liberal and intelligent manner, for brilliancy of change. He actually saw that he had allowed for nothing; he missed what he would have been sure of finding, he found what he would never have imagined. Proportions and values were upside-down; the ugly things he had expected, the ugly things of his far-away youth, when he had too promptly waked up to a sense of the ugly—these uncanny phenomena placed him rather, as it happened, under the charm; whereas the "swagger" things, the modern, the monstrous, the famous things, those he had more particularly, like thousands of ingenuous enquirers every year, come over to see, were exactly his sources of dismay. They were as so many set traps for displeasure, above all for reaction, of which his restless tread was constantly pressing the spring. It was interesting, doubtless, the whole show, but it would have been too disconcerting hadn't a certain finer truth saved the situation. He had distinctly not, in this steadier light, come over *all* for the monstrosities; he had come, not only in the last analysis but quite on the face of the act, under an impulse with which they had nothing to do. He had come—putting the thing pompously—to look at his "property," which he had thus for a third of a century not been within four thousand miles of; or, expressing it less sordidly, he had yielded to the humour of seeing again his house on the jolly corner, as he usually, and quite fondly, described it—the one in which he had first seen the light, in which various members of his family had lived and had died, in which the holidays of his overschooled boyhood had been passed and the few social flowers of his chilled adolescence gathered, and which, alienated then for so long a period, had, through the successive deaths of his two brothers and the termination of old arrangements, come wholly into his hands. He was the owner of another, not quite so "good" —the jolly corner having been, from far back, superlatively extended and consecrated; and the value of the pair represented his main capital, with an income consisting, in these later years, of their respective rents which (thanks precisely to their original excellent type) had never been depressingly low. He could live in "Europe," as he had been in the habit of living, on the product of these flourishing New York leases, and all the better since, that of the second structure, the mere number in its long row, having within a twelvemonth fallen in, renovation at a high advance had proved beautifully possible.

These were items of property indeed, but he had found himself since his arrival distinguishing more than ever between them. The house within the street, two bristling blocks westward, was already in course of reconstruction as a tall mass of flats; he had acceded, some time before, to overtures for this conversion—in which, now that it was going forward, it had been not the least of his astonish-

ments to find himself able, on the spot, and though without a previous ounce of such experience, to participate with a certain
intelligence, almost with a certain authority. He had lived his life
with his back so turned to such concerns and his face addressed to
those of so different an order that he scarce knew what to make of
this lively stir, in a compartment of his mind never yet penetrated,
of a capacity for business and a sense for construction. These virtues, so common all round him now, had been dormant in his own
organism—where it might be said of them perhaps that they had
slept the sleep of the just. At present, in the splendid autumn
weather—the autumn at least was a pure boon in the terrible
place—he loafed about his "work" undeterred, secretly agitated; not
in the least "minding" that the whole proposition, as they said, was
vulgar and sordid, and ready to climb ladders, to walk the plank, to
handle materials and look wise about them, to ask questions, in
fine, and challenge explanations and really "go into" figures.

It amused, it verily quite charmed him; and, by the same stroke,
it amused, and even more, Alice Staverton, though perhaps charming her perceptibly less. She wasn't however going to be better-off
for it, as *he* was—and so astonishingly much: nothing was now
likely, he knew, ever to make her better-off than she found herself,
in the afternoon of life, as the delicately frugal possessor and tenant
of the small house in Irving Place[1] to which she had subtly managed
to cling through her almost unbroken New York career. If he knew
the way to it now better than to any other address among the dreadful multiplied numberings which seemed to him to reduce the
whole place to some vast ledger-page, overgrown, fantastic, of ruled
and criss-crossed lines and figures—if he had formed, for his consolation, that habit, it was really not a little because of the charm
of his having encountered and recognised, in the vast wilderness of
the wholesale, breaking through the mere gross generalisation of
wealth and force and success, a small still scene where items and
shades, all delicate things, kept the sharpness of the notes of a high
voice perfectly trained, and where economy hung about like the
scent of a garden. His old friend lived with one maid and herself
dusted her relics and trimmed her lamps and polished her silver;
she stood off, in the awful modern crush, when she could, but she
sallied forth and did battle when the challenge was really to "spirit,"
the spirit she after all confessed to, proudly and a little shyly, as to
that of the better time, that of *their* common, their quite far-away

---

1. A short street between Fourteenth and Twentieth Streets one block east of Union Square
and Park Avenue South. The whole action takes place in the general section of New
York City where James lived as a child (1847–48 at 11 Fifth Avenue, 1848–55 at
58 West Fourteenth Street). Except for Irving Place the story does not identify streets
by name, though the "conservative avenue" mentioned later may be Fifth Avenue.

and antediluvian social period and order. She made use of the street-cars when need be, the terrible things that people scrambled for as the panic-stricken at sea scramble for the boats; she affronted, inscrutably, under stress, all the public concussions and ordeals; and yet, with that slim mystifying grace of her appearance, which defied you to say if she were a fair young woman who looked older through trouble, or a fine smooth older one who looked young through successful indifference; with her precious reference, above all, to memories and histories into which he could enter, she was as exquisite for him as some pale pressed flower (a rarity to begin with), and, failing other sweetnesses, she was a sufficient reward of his effort. They had communities of knowledge, "their" knowledge (this discriminating possessive was always on her lips) of presences of the other age, presences all overlaid, in his case, by the experience of a man and the freedom of a wanderer, overlaid by pleasure, by infidelity, by passages of life that were strange and dim to her, just by "Europe" in short, but still unobscured, still exposed and cherished, under that pious visitation of the spirit from which she had never been diverted.

She had come with him one day to see how his "apartment-house" was rising; he had helped her over gaps and explained to her plans, and while they were there had happened to have, before her, a brief but lively discussion with the man in charge, the representative of the building-firm that had undertaken his work. He had found himself quite "standing-up" to this personage over a failure on the latter's part to observe some detail of one of their noted conditions, and had so lucidly argued his case that, besides ever so prettily flushing, at the time, for sympathy in his triumph, she had afterwards said to him (though to a slightly greater effect of irony) that he had clearly for too many years neglected a real gift. If he had but stayed at home he would have anticipated the inventor of the sky-scraper. If he had but stayed at home he would have discovered his genius in time really to start some new variety of awful architectural hare and run it till it burrowed in a gold-mine. He was to remember these words, while the weeks elapsed, for the small silver ring they had sounded over the queerest and deepest of his own lately most disguised and most muffled vibrations.

It had begun to be present to him after the first fortnight, it had broken out with the oddest abruptness, this particular wanton wonderment: it met him there—and this was the image under which he himself judged the matter, or at least, not a little, thrilled and flushed with it—very much as he might have been met by some strange figure, some unexpected occupant, at a turn of one of the dim passages of an empty house. The quaint analogy quite hauntingly remained with him, when he didn't indeed rather improve it

by a still intenser form: that of his opening a door behind which he
would have made sure of finding nothing, a door into a room shuttered and void, and yet so coming, with a great suppressed start,
on some quite erect confronting presence, something planted in the
middle of the place and facing him through the dusk. After that
visit to the house in construction he walked with his companion to
see the other and always so much the better one, which in the
eastward direction formed one of the corners, the "jolly" one precisely, of the street now so generally dishonoured and disfigured in
its westward reaches, and of the comparatively conservative Avenue.
The Avenue still had pretensions, as Miss Staverton said, to decency; the old people had mostly gone, the old names were unknown, and here and there an old association seemed to stray, all
vaguely, like some very aged person, out too late, whom you might
meet and feel the impulse to watch or follow, in kindness, for safe
restoration to shelter.

They went in together, our friends; he admitted himself with his
key, as he kept no one there, he explained, preferring, for his reasons, to leave the place empty, under a simple arrangement with a
good woman living in the neighbourhood and who came for a daily
hour to open windows and dust and sweep. Spencer Brydon had
his reasons and was growingly aware of them; they seemed to him
better each time he was there, though he didn't name them all to
his companion, any more than he told her as yet how often, how
quite absurdly often, he himself came. He only let her see for the
present, while they walked through the great blank rooms, that absolute vacancy reigned and that, from top to bottom, there was
nothing but Mrs. Muldoon's broomstick, in a corner, to tempt the
burglar. Mrs. Muldoon was then on the premises, and she loqua-
ciously attended the visitors, preceding them from room to room
and pushing back shutters and throwing up sashes—all to show
them, as she remarked, how little there was to see. There was little
indeed to see in the great gaunt shell where the main dispositions
and the general apportionment of space, the style of an age of am-
pler allowances, had nevertheless for its master their honest pleading message, affecting him as some good old servant's, some lifelong
retainer's appeal for a character,[2] or even for a retiring-pension; yet
it was also a remark of Mrs. Muldoon's that, glad as she was to
oblige him by her noonday round, there was a request she greatly
hoped he would never make of her. If he should wish her for any
reason to come in after dark she would just tell him, if he "plased,"
that he must ask it of somebody else.

The fact that there was nothing to see didn't militate for the

2. A character reference.

worthy woman against what one *might* see, and she put it frankly
to Miss Staverton that no lady could be expected to like, could she?
"craping up to thim top storeys in the ayvil hours." The gas and the
electric light were off the house, and she fairly evoked a gruesome
vision of her march through the great grey rooms—so many of them
as there were too!—with her glimmering taper. Miss Staverton met
her honest glare with a smile and the profession that she herself
certainly would recoil from such an adventure. Spencer Brydon
meanwhile held his peace—for the moment; the question of the
"evil" hours in his old home had already become too grave for him.
He had begun some time since to "crape," and he knew just why a
packet of candles addressed to that pursuit had been stowed by his
own hand, three weeks before, at the back of a drawer of the fine
old sideboard that occupied, as a "fixture," the deep recess in the
dining-room. Just now he laughed at his companions—quickly however changing the subject; for the reason that, in the first place, his
laugh struck him even at that moment as starting the odd echo, the
conscious human resonance (he scarce knew how to qualify it) that
sounds made while he was there alone sent back to his ear or his
fancy; and that, in the second, he imagined Alice Staverton for the
instant on the point of asking him, with a divination, if he ever so
prowled. There were divinations he was unprepared for, and he had
at all events averted enquiry by the time Mrs. Muldoon had left
them, passing on to other parts.

There was happily enough to say, on so consecrated a spot, that
could be said freely and fairly; so that a whole train of declarations was precipitated by his friend's having herself broken out, after
a yearning look round: "But I hope you don't mean they want you
to pull *this* to pieces!" His answer came, promptly, with his re-
awakened wrath: it was of course exactly what they wanted, and
what they were "at" him for, daily, with the iteration of people who
couldn't for their life understand a man's liability to decent feelings.
He had found the place, just as it stood and beyond what he could
express, an interest and a joy. There were values other than the
beastly rent-values, and in short, in short—! But it was thus Miss
Staverton took him up. "In short you're to make so good a thing of
your sky-scraper that, living in luxury on *those* ill-gotten gains, you
can afford for a while to be sentimental here!" Her smile had for
him, with the words, the particular mild irony with which he found
half her talk suffused; an irony without bitterness and that came,
exactly, from her having so much imagination—not, like the cheap
sarcasms with which one heard most people, about the world of
"society," bid for the reputation of cleverness, from nobody's really
having any. It was agreeable to him at this very moment to be sure
that when he had answered, after a brief demur, "Well yes: so,

precisely, you may put it!" her imagination would still do him justice. He explained that even if never a dollar were to come to him from the other house he would nevertheless cherish this one; and he dwelt, further, while they lingered and wandered, on the fact of the stupefaction he was already exciting, the positive mystification he felt himself create.

He spoke of the value of all he read into it, into the mere sight of the walls, mere shapes of the rooms, mere sound of the floors, mere feel, in his hand, of the old silver-plated knobs of the several mahogany doors, which suggested the pressure of the palms of the dead; the seventy years of the past in fine that these things represented, the annals of nearly three generations, counting his grandfather's, the one that had ended there, and the impalpable ashes of his long-extinct youth, afloat in the very air like microscopic motes. She listened to everything; she was a woman who answered intimately but who utterly didn't chatter. She scattered abroad therefore no cloud of words; she could assent, she could agree, above all she could encourage, without doing that. Only at the last she went a little further than he had done himself. "And then how do you know? You may still, after all, want to live here." It rather indeed pulled him up, for it wasn't what he had been thinking, at least in her sense of the words. "You mean I may decide to stay on for the sake of it?"

"Well, *with* such a home—!" But, quite beautifully, she had too much tact to dot so monstrous an *i*, and it was precisely an illustration of the way she didn't rattle. How could any one—of any wit—insist on any one else's "wanting" to live in New York?

"Oh," he said, "I *might* have lived here (since I had my opportunity early in life); I might have put in here all these years. Then everything would have been different enough—and, I dare say, 'funny' enough. But that's another matter. And then the beauty of it—I mean of my perversity, of my refusal to agree to a 'deal'—is just in the total absence of a reason. Don't you see that if I had a reason about the matter at all it would *have* to be the other way, and would then be inevitably a reason of dollars? There are no reasons here *but* of dollars. Let us therefore have none whatever—not the ghost of one."

They were back in the hall then for departure, but from where they stood the vista was large, through an open door, into the great square main saloon, with its almost antique felicity of brave spaces between windows. Her eyes came back from that reach and met his own a moment. "Are you very sure the 'ghost' of one doesn't, much rather, serve—?"

He had a positive sense of turning pale. But it was as near as they were then to come. For he made answer, he believed, between a glare and a grin: "Oh ghosts—of course the place must swarm with them! I should be ashamed of it if it didn't. Poor Mrs. Muldoon's right, and it's why I haven't asked her to do more than look in."

Miss Staverton's gaze again lost itself, and things she didn't utter, it was clear, came and went in her mind. She might even for the minute, off there in the fine room, have imagined some element dimly gathering. Simplified like the death-mask of a handsome face, it perhaps produced for her just then an effect akin to the stir of an expression in the "set" commemorative plaster. Yet whatever her impression may have been she produced instead a vague platitude. "Well, if it were only furnished and lived in—!"

She appeared to imply that in case of its being still furnished he might have been a little less opposed to the idea of a return. But she passed straight into the vestibule, as if to leave her words behind her, and the next moment he had opened the house-door and was standing with her on the steps. He closed the door and, while he re-pocketed his key, looking up and down, they took in the comparatively harsh actuality of the Avenue, which reminded him of the assault of the outer light of the Desert on the traveller emerging from an Egyptian tomb. But he risked before they stepped into the street his gathered answer to her speech. "For me it *is* lived in. For me it *is* furnished." At which it was easy for her to sigh "Ah yes—!" all vaguely and discreetly; since his parents and his favourite sister, to say nothing of other kin, in numbers, had run their course and met their end there. That represented, within the walls, ineffaceable life.

It was a few days after this that, during an hour passed with her again, he had expressed his impatience of the too flattering curiosity—among the people he met—about his appreciation of New York. He had arrived at none at all that was socially producible, and as for that matter of his "thinking" (thinking the better or the worse of anything there) he was wholly taken up with one subject of thought. It was mere vain egoism, and it was moreover, if she liked, a morbid obsession. He found all things come back to the question of what he personally might have been, how he might have led his life and "turned out," if he had not so, at the outset, given it up. And confessing for the first time to the intensity within him of this absurd speculation—which but proved also, no doubt, the habit of too selfishly thinking—he affirmed the impotence there of any other source of interest, any other native appeal. "What would it have made of me, what would it have made of me? I keep for ever wondering, all idiotically; as if I could possibly know! I see what it has made of dozens of others, those I meet, and it positively aches within me, to the point of exasperation, that it would have made something of me as well. Only I can't make out *what*, and the worry of it, the small rage of curiosity never to be satisfied, brings back what I remember to have felt, once or twice, after judging best, for reasons, to burn some important letter unopened. I've been sorry, I've hated it—I've never known what was in the letter. You may of course say it's a trifle—!"

"I don't say it's a trifle," Miss Staverton gravely interrupted.

She was seated by her fire, and before her, on his feet and restless, he turned to and fro between this intensity of his idea and a fitful and unseeing inspection, through his single eye-glass, of the dear little old objects on her chimney-piece. Her interruption made him for an instant look at her harder. "I shouldn't care if you did!" he laughed, however; "and it's only a figure, at any rate, for the way I now feel. *Not* to have followed my perverse young course—and almost in the teeth of my father's curse, as I may say; not to have kept it up, so, 'over there,' from that day to this, without a doubt or a pang; not, above all, to have liked it, to have loved it, so much, loved it, no doubt, with such an abysmal conceit of my own preference: some variation from *that*, I say, must have produced some different effect for my life and for my 'form.' I should have stuck here—if it had been possible; and I was too young, at twenty-three, to judge, *pour deux sous,*[3] whether it *were* possible. If I had waited I might have seen it was, and then I might have been, by staying here, something nearer to one of these types who have been hammered so hard and made so keen by their conditions. It isn't that I admire them so much—the question of any charm in them, or of any charm, beyond that of the rank money-passion, exerted by their conditions *for* them, has nothing to do with the matter: it's only a question of what fantastic, yet perfectly possible, development of my own nature I mayn't have missed. It comes over me that I had then a strange *alter ego* deep down somewhere within me, as the full-blown flower is in the small tight bud, and that I just took the course, I just transferred him to the climate, that blighted him for once and for ever."

"And you wonder about the flower," Miss Staverton said. "So do I, if you want to know; and so I've been wondering these several weeks. I believe in the flower," she continued, "I feel it would have been quite splendid, quite huge and monstrous."

"Monstrous above all!" her visitor echoed; "and I imagine, by the same stroke, quite hideous and offensive."

"You don't believe that," she returned; "if you did you wouldn't wonder. You'd know, and that would be enough for you. What you feel—and what I feel *for* you—is that you'd have had power."

3. "For two cents." I wasn't capable of even the most cursory or hasty judgment.

"You'd have liked me that way?" he asked.

She barely hung fire. "How should I not have liked you?"

"I see. You'd have liked me, have preferred me, a billionaire!"

"How should I not have liked you?" she simply again asked.

He stood before her still—her question kept him motionless. He took it in, so much there was of it; and indeed his not otherwise meeting it testified to that. "I know at least what I am," he simply went on; "the other side of the medal's clear enough. I've not been edifying—I believe I'm thought in a hundred quarters, to have been barely decent. I've followed strange paths and worshipped strange gods; it must have come to you again and again—in fact, you've admitted to me as much—that I was leading, at any time these thirty years, a selfish frivolous scandalous life. And you see what it has made of me."

She just waited, smiling at him. "You see what it has made of *me*."

"Oh you're a person whom nothing can have altered. You were born to be what you are, anywhere, anyway: you've the perfection nothing else could have blighted. And don't you see how, without my exile, I shouldn't have been waiting till now—?" But he pulled up for the strange pang.

"The great thing to see," she presently said, "seems to me to be that it has spoiled nothing. It hasn't spoiled your being here at last. It hasn't spoiled this. It hasn't spoiled your speaking—" She also however faltered.

He wondered at everything her controlled emotion might mean. "Do you believe then—too dreadfully!—that I *am* as good as I might ever have been?"

"Oh no! Far from it!" With which she got up from her chair and was nearer to him. "But I don't care," she smiled.

"You mean I'm good enough?"

She considered a little. "Will you believe it if I say so? I mean will you let that settle your question for you?" And then as if making out in his face that he drew back from this, that he had some idea which, however absurd, he couldn't yet bargain away: "Oh you don't care either—but very differently: you don't care for anything but yourself."

Spencer Brydon recognised it—it was in fact what he had absolutely professed. Yet he importantly qualified. "*He* isn't myself. He's the just so totally other person. But I do want to see him," he added. "And I can. And I shall."

Their eyes met for a minute while he guessed from something in hers that she divined his strange sense. But neither of them otherwise expressed it, and her apparent understanding, with no protesting shock, no easy derision, touched him more deeply than anything yet, constituting for his stifled perversity, on the spot, an element that was like breatheable air. What she said however was unexpected. "Well, *I've* seen him."

"You—?"

"I've seen him in a dream."

"Oh a 'dream'—!" It let him down.

"But twice over," she continued. "I saw him as I see you now."

"You've dreamed the same dream—?"

"Twice over," she repeated. "The very same."

This did somehow a little speak to him, as it also gratified him. "You dream about me at that rate?"

"Ah about *him!*" she smiled.

His eyes again sounded her. "Then you know all about him." And as she said nothing more: "What's the wretch like?"

She hesitated, and it was as if he were pressing her so hard that, resisting for reasons of her own, she had to turn away. "I'll tell you some other time!"

II

It was after this that there was most of a virtue for him, most of a cultivated charm, most of a preposterous secret thrill, in the particular form of surrender to his obsession and of address to what he more and more believed to be his privilege. It was what in these weeks he was living for—since he really felt life to begin but after Mrs. Muldoon had retired from the scene and, visiting the ample house from attic to cellar, making sure he was alone, he knew himself in safe possession and, as he tacitly expressed it, let himself go. He sometimes came twice in the twenty-four hours; the moments he liked best were those of gathering dusk, of the short autumn twilight; this was the time of which, again and again, he found himself hoping most. Then he could, as seemed to him, most intimately wander and wait, linger and listen, feel his fine attention, never in his life before so fine, on the pulse of the great vague place: he preferred the lampless hour and only wished he might have prolonged each day the deep crepuscular spell. Later—rarely much before midnight, but then for a considerable vigil—he watched with his glimmering light; moving slowly, holding it high, playing it far, rejoicing above all, as much as he might, in open vistas, reaches of communication between rooms and by passages; the long straight chance or show, as he would have called it, for the revelation he pretended to invite. It was a practice he found he could perfectly "work" without exciting remark; no one was in the least the wiser for it; even Alice Staverton, who was moreover a well of discretion, didn't quite fully imagine.

He let himself in and let himself out with the assurance of calm proprietorship; and accident so far favoured him that, if a fat Avenue "officer" had happened on occasion to see him entering at eleven-thirty, he had never yet, to the best of his belief, been noticed as emerging at two. He walked there on the crisp November nights, arrived regularly at the evening's end; it was as easy to do this after dining out as to take his way to a club or to his hotel. When he left his club, if he hadn't been dining out, it was ostensibly to go to his hotel; and when he left his hotel, if he had spent a part of the evening there, it was ostensibly to go to his club. Everything was easy in fine; everything conspired and promoted: there was truly even in the strain of his experience something that glossed over, something that salved and simplified, all the rest of consciousness. He circulated, talked, renewed, loosely and pleasantly, old relations—met indeed, so far as he could, new expectations and seemed to make out on the whole that in spite of the career, of such different contacts, which he had spoken of to Miss Staverton as ministering so little, for those who might have watched it, to edification, he was positively rather liked than not. He was a dim secondary social success—and all with people who had truly not an idea of him. It was all mere surface sound, this murmur of their welcome, this popping of their corks—just as his gestures of response were the extravagant shadows, emphatic in proportion as they meant little, of some game of *ombres chinoises*.[4] He projected himself all day, in thought, straight over the bristling line of hard unconscious heads and into the other, the real, the waiting life; the life that, as soon as he had heard behind him the click of his great house-door, began for him, on the jolly corner, as beguilingly as the slow opening bars of some rich music follow the tap of the conductor's wand.

He always caught the first effect of the steel point of his stick on the old marble of the hall pavement, large black-and-white squares that he remembered as the admiration of his childhood and that had then made in him, as he now saw, for the growth of an early conception of style. This effect was the dim reverberating tinkle as of some far-off bell hung who should say where?—in the depths of the house, of the past, of that mystical other world that might have flourished for him had he not, for weal or woe, abandoned it. On this impression he did ever the same thing; he put his stick noiselessly away in a corner—feeling the place once more in the likeness of some great glass bowl, all precious concave crystal, set delicately humming by the play of a moist finger round its edge. The concave crystal held, as it were, this mystical other world, and the indescrib-

4. Shadow theater.

ably fine murmur of its rim was the sigh there, the scarce audible pathetic wail to his strained ear, of all the old baffled forsworn possibilities. What he did therefore by this appeal of his hushed presence was to wake them into such measure of ghostly life as they might still enjoy. They were shy, all but unappeasably shy, but they weren't really sinister; at least they weren't as he had hitherto felt them—before they had taken the Form he so yearned to make them take, the Form he at moments saw himself in the light of fairly hunting on tiptoe, the points of his evening-shoes, from room to room and from storey to storey.

That was the essence of his vision—which was all rank folly, if one would, while he was out of the house and otherwise occupied, but which took on the last verisimilitude as soon as he was placed and posted. He knew what he meant and what he wanted; it was as clear as the figure on a cheque presented in demand for cash. His *alter ego* "walked"—that was the note of his image of him, while his image of his motive for his own odd pastime was the desire to waylay him and meet him. He roamed, slowly, warily, but all rest-lessly, he himself did—Mrs. Muldoon had been right, absolutely, with her figure of their "craping"; and the presence he watched for would roam restlessly too. But it would be as cautious and as shifty; the conviction of its probable, in fact its already quite sensible, quite audible evasion of pursuit grew for him from night to night, laying on him finally a rigour to which nothing in his life had been com-parable. It had been the theory of many superficially-judging per-sons, he knew, that he was wasting that life in a surrender to sensations, but he had tasted of no pleasure so fine as his actual tension, had been introduced to no sport that demanded at once the patience and the nerve of this stalking of a creature more subtle, yet at bay perhaps more formidable, than any beast of the forest. The terms, the comparisons, the very practices of the chase posi-tively came again into play; there were even moments when pas-sages of his occasional experience as a sportsman, stirred memories, from his younger time, of moor and mountain and desert, revived for him—and to the increase of his keenness—by the tremendous force of analogy. He found himself at moments—once he had placed his single light on some mantel-shelf or in some recess—stepping back into shelter or shade, effacing himself behind a door or in an embrasure, as he had sought of old the vantage of rock and tree; he found himself holding his breath and living in the joy of the instant, the supreme suspense created by big game alone.

He wasn't afraid (though putting himself the question as he be-lieved gentlemen on Bengal tiger-shoots or in close quarters with the great bear of the Rockies had been known to confess to having put it); and this indeed—since here at least he might be frank!—

because of the impression, so intimate and so strange, that he himself produced as yet a dread, produced certainly a strain, beyond
the liveliest he was likely to feel. They fell for him into categories,
they fairly became familiar, the signs, for his own perception, of
the alarm his presence and his vigilance created; though leaving
him always to remark, portentously, on his probably having formed
a relation, his probably enjoying a consciousness, unique in the
experience of man. People enough, first and last, had been in terror
of apparitions, but who had ever before so turned the tables and
become himself, in the apparitional world, an incalculable terror?
He might have found this sublime had he quite dared to think of
it; but he didn't too much insist, truly, on that side of his privilege.
With habit and repetition he gained to an extraordinary degree the
power to penetrate the dusk of distances and the darkness of corners, to resolve back into their innocence the treacheries of uncertain light, the evil-looking forms taken in the gloom by mere
shadows, by accidents of the air, by shifting effects of perspective;
putting down his dim luminary he could still wander on without it,
pass into other rooms and, only knowing it was there behind him
in case of need, see his way about, visually project for his purpose
a comparative clearness. It made him feel, this acquired faculty,
like some monstrous stealthy cat; he wondered if he would have
glared at these moments with large shining yellow eyes, and what
it mightn't verily be, for the poor hard-pressed *alter ego,* to be confronted with such a type.

He liked however the open shutters; he opened everywhere those
Mrs. Muldoon had closed, closing them as carefully afterwards, so
that she shouldn't notice: he liked—oh this he did like, and above
all in the upper rooms!—the sense of the hard silver of the autumn
stars through the window-panes, and scarcely less the flare of the
street-lamps below, the white electric lustre which it would have
taken curtains to keep out. This was human actual social; this was
of the world he had lived in, and he was more at his ease certainly
for the countenance, coldly general and impersonal, that all the
while and in spite of his detachment it seemed to give him. He had
support of course mostly in the rooms at the wide front and the
prolonged side; it failed him considerably in the central shades and
the parts at the back. But if he sometimes, on his rounds, was glad
of his optical reach, so none the less often the rear of the house
affected him as the very jungle of his prey. The place was there
more subdivided; a large "extension" in particular, where small
rooms for servants had been multiplied, abounded in nooks and
corners, in closets and passages, in the ramifications especially of
an ample back staircase over which he leaned, many a time, to look
far down—not deterred from his gravity even while aware that he

might, for a spectator, have figured some solemn simpleton playing at hide-and-seek. Outside in fact he might himself make that ironic *rapprochement*,[5] but within the walls, and in spite of the clear windows, his consistency was proof against the cynical light of New York.

It had belonged to that idea of the exasperated consciousness of his victim to become a real test for him; since he had quite put it to himself from the first that, oh distinctly! he could "cultivate" his whole perception. He had felt it as above all open to cultivation— which indeed was but another name for his manner of spending his time. He was bringing it on, bringing it to perfection, by practice; in consequence of which it had grown so fine that he was now aware of impressions, attestations of his general postulate, that couldn't have broken upon him at once. This was the case more specifically with a phenomenon at last quite frequent for him in the upper rooms, the recognition—absolutely unmistakeable, and by a turn dating from a particular hour, his resumption of his campaign after a diplomatic drop, a calculated absence of three nights—of his being definitely followed, tracked at a distance carefully taken and to the express end that he should the less confidently, less arrogantly, appear to himself merely to pursue. It worried, it finally quite broke him up, for it proved, of all the conceivable impressions, the one least suited to his book. He was kept in sight while remaining himself—as regards the essence of his position—sightless, and his only recourse then was in abrupt turns, rapid recoveries of ground. He wheeled about, retracing his steps, as if he might so catch in his face at least the stirred air of some other quick revolution. It was indeed true that his fully dislocalised thought of these manoeuvres recalled to him Pantaloon, at the Christmas farce, buffeted and tricked from behind by ubiquitous Harlequin;[6] but if left intact the influence of the conditions themselves each time he was re-exposed to them, so that in fact this association, had he suffered it to become constant, would on a certain side have but ministered to his intenser gravity. He had made, as I have said, to create on the premises the baseless sense of a reprieve, his three absences; and the result of the third was to confirm the after-effect of the second.

On his return, that night—the night succeeding his last intermission—he stood in the hall and looked up the staircase with a certainty more intimate than any he had yet known. "He's *there*,

5. Comparison.
6. Pantaloon and Harlequin are characters derived from the Commedia dell'arte, a popular form of early Italian comedy (sixteenth to eighteenth centuries), and surviving in the English Pantomime, a theatrical spectacle, traditionally performed during the Christmas season.

at the top, and waiting—not, as in general, falling back for disappearance. He's holding his ground, and it's the first time—which is
a proof, isn't it? that something has happened for him." So Brydon
argued with his hand on the banister and his foot on the lowest
stair; in which position he felt as never before the air chilled by his
logic. He himself turned cold in it, for he seemed of a sudden to
know what now was involved. "Harder pressed?—yes, he takes it
in, with its thus making clear to him that I've come, as they say, 'to
stay.' He finally doesn't like and can't bear it, in the sense, I mean,
that his wrath, his menaced interest, now balances with his dread.
I've hunted him till he has 'turned': that, up there, is what has
happened—he's the fanged or the antlered animal brought at last
to bay." There came to him, as I say—but determined by an influence beyond my notation!—the acuteness of this certainty; under
which however the next moment he had broken into a sweat that
he would as little have consented to attribute to fear as he would
have dared immediately to act upon it for enterprise. It marked
none the less a prodigious thrill, a thrill that represented sudden
dismay, no doubt, but also represented, and with the selfsame
throb, the strangest, the most joyous, possibly the next minute almost the proudest, duplication of consciousness.

"He has been dodging, retreating, hiding, but now, worked up to
anger, he'll fight!"—this intense impression made a single mouth-
ful, as it were, of terror and applause. But what was wondrous was
that the applause, for the felt fact, was so eager, since, if it was his
other self he was running to earth, this ineffable identity was thus
in the last resort not unworthy of him. It bristled there—somewhere
near at hand, however unseen still—as the hunted thing, even as
the trodden worm of the adage *must* at last bristle; and Brydon at
this instant tasted probably of a sensation more complex than had
ever before found itself consistent with sanity. It was as if it would
have shamed him that a character so associated with his own should
triumphantly succeed in just skulking, should to the end not risk
the open; so that the drop of this danger was, on the spot, a great
lift of the whole situation. Yet with another rare shift of the same
subtlety he was already trying to measure by how much more he
himself might now be in peril of fear; so rejoicing that he could, in
another form, actively inspire that fear, and simultaneously quaking
for the form in which he might passively know it.

The apprehension of knowing it must after a little have grown in
him, and the strangest moment of his adventure perhaps, the most
memorable or really most interesting, afterwards, of his crisis, was
the lapse of certain instants of concentrated conscious *combat*, the
sense of a need to hold on to something, even after the manner of
a man slipping and slipping on some awful incline; the vivid im-

pulse, above all, to move, to act, to charge, somehow and upon something—to show himself, in a word, that he wasn't afraid. The state of "holding-on" was thus the state to which he was momentarily reduced; if there had been anything, in the great vacancy, to seize, he would presently have been aware of having clutched it as he might under a shock at home have clutched the nearest chairback. He had been surprised at any rate—of this he *was* aware—into something unprecedented since his original appropriation of the place; he had closed his eyes, held them tight, for a long minute, as with that instinct of dismay and that terror of vision. When he opened them the room, the other contiguous rooms, extraordinarily, seemed lighter—so light, almost, that at first he took the change for day. He stood firm, however that might be, just where he had paused; his resistance had helped him—it was as if there were something he had tided over. He knew after a little what this was —it had been in the imminent danger of flight. He had stiffened his will against going; without this he would have made for the stairs, and it seemed to him that, still with his eyes closed, he would have descended them, would have known how, straight and swiftly, to the bottom.

Well, as he had held out, here he was—still at the top, among the more intricate upper rooms and with the gauntlet of the others, of all the rest of the house, still to run when it should be his time to go. He would go at his time—only at his time: didn't he go every night very much at the same hour? He took out his watch—there was light for that: it was scarcely a quarter past one, and he had never withdrawn so soon. He reached his lodgings for the most part at two—with his walk of a quarter of an hour. He would wait for the last quarter—he wouldn't stir till then; and he kept his watch there with his eyes on it, reflecting while he held it that this deliberate wait, a wait with an effort, which he recognised, would serve perfectly for the attestation he desired to make. It would prove his courage—unless indeed the latter might most be proved by his budging at last from his place. What he mainly felt now was that, since he hadn't originally scuttled, he had his dignities—which had never in his life seemed so many—all to preserve and to carry aloft. This was before him in truth as a physical image, an image almost worthy of an age of greater romance. That remark indeed glimmered for him only to glow the next instant with a finer light; since what age of romance, after all, could have matched either the state of his mind or, "objectively," as they said, the wonder of his situation? The only difference would have been that, brandishing his dignities over his head as in a parchment scroll, he might then—that is in the heroic time—have proceeded downstairs with a drawn sword in his other grasp.

At present, really, the light he had set down on the mantel of the next room would have to figure his sword; which utensil, in the course of a minute, he had taken the requisite number of steps to possess himself of. The door between the rooms was open, and from the second another door opened to a third. These rooms, as he remembered, gave all three upon a common corridor as well, but there was a fourth, beyond them, without issue save through the preceding. To have moved, to have heard his step again, was appreciably a help; though even in recognising this he lingered once more a little by the chimney-piece on which his light had rested. When he next moved, just hesitating where to turn, he found himself considering a circumstance that, after his first and comparatively vague apprehension of it, produced in him the start that often attends some pang of recollection, the violent shock of having ceased happily to forget. He had come into sight of the door in which the brief chain of communication ended and which he now surveyed from the nearer threshold, the one not directly facing it. Placed at some distance to the left of this point, it would have admitted him to the last room of the four, the room without other approach or egress, had it not, to his intimate conviction, been closed *since* his former visitation, the matter probably of a quarter of an hour before. He stared with all his eyes at the wonder of the fact, arrested again where he stood and again holding his breath while he sounded its sense. Surely it had been *subsequently* closed—that is it had been on his previous passage indubitably open!

He took it full in the face that something had happened between—that he couldn't not have noticed before (by which he meant on his original tour of all the rooms that evening) that such a barrier had exceptionally presented itself. He had indeed since that moment undergone an agitation so extraordinary that it might have muddled for him any earlier view; and he tried to convince himself that he might perhaps then have gone into the room and, inadvertently, automatically, on coming out, have drawn the door after him. The difficulty was that this exactly was what he never did; it was against his whole policy, as he might have said, the essence of which was to keep vistas clear. He had them from the first, as he was well aware, quite on the brain: the strange apparition, at the far end of one of them, of his baffled "prey" (which had become by so sharp an irony so little the term now to apply!) was the form of success his imagination had most cherished, projecting into it always a refinement of beauty. He had known fifty times the start of perception that had afterwards dropped; had fifty times gasped to himself "There!" under some fond brief hallucination. The house, as the case stood, admirably lent itself; he might wonder at the taste, the native architecture of the particular time, which could rejoice so in the multiplication of doors—the opposite extreme to the modern, the actual almost complete proscription of them; but it had fairly contributed to provoke this obsession of the presence encountered telescopically, as he might say, focussed and studied in diminishing perspective and as by a rest for the elbow.

It was with these considerations that his present attention was charged—they perfectly availed to make what he saw portentous. He *couldn't*, by any lapse, have blocked that aperture; and if he hadn't, if it was unthinkable, why what else was clear but that there had been another agent? Another agent?—he had been catching, as he felt, a moment back, the very breath of him; but when had he been so close as in this simple, this logical, this completely personal act? It was so logical, that is, that one might have *taken* it for personal; yet for what did Brydon take it, he asked himself, while, softly panting, he felt his eyes almost leave their sockets. Ah this time at last they *were*, the two, the opposed projections of him, in presence; and this time, as much as one would, the question of danger loomed. With it rose, as not before, the question of courage—for what he knew the blank face of the door to say to him was "Show us how much you have!" It stared, it glared back at him with that challenge; it put to him the two alternatives: should he just push it open or not? Oh to have this consciousness was to *think*—and to think, Brydon knew, as he stood there, was, with the lapsing moments, not to have acted! Not to have acted—that was the misery and the pang—was even still not to act; was in fact *all* to feel the thing in another, in a new and terrible way. How long did he pause and how long did he debate? There was presently nothing to measure it; for his vibration had already changed—as just by the effect of its intensity. Shut up there, at bay, defiant, and with the prodigy of the thing palpably proveably *done*, thus giving notice like some stark signboard—under that accession of accent the situation itself had turned; and Brydon at last remarkably made up his mind on what it had turned to.

It had turned altogether to a different admonition; to a supreme hint, for him, of the value of Discretion! This slowly dawned, no doubt—for it could take its time; so perfectly, on his threshold, had he been stayed, so little as yet had he either advanced or retreated. It was the strangest of all things that now when, by his taking ten steps and applying his hand to a latch, or even his shoulder and his knee, if necessary, to a panel, all the hunger of his prime need might have been met, his high curiosity crowned, his unrest assuaged—it was amazing, but it was also exquisite and rare, that insistence should have, at a touch, quite dropped from him. Discretion—he jumped at that; and yet not, verily, at such a pitch, because it saved his nerves or his skin, but because, much more valuably, it saved the situation. When I say he "jumped" at it I feel the consonance of this term with the fact that—at the end indeed of I know not how long—he did move again, he crossed straight to the door. He wouldn't touch it—it seemed now that he might *if* he would: he would only just wait there a little, to show, to prove, that he wouldn't. He had thus another station, close to the thin partition by which revelation was denied him; but with his eyes bent and his hands held off in a mere intensity of stillness. He listened as if there had been something to hear, but this attitude, while it lasted, was his own communication. "If you won't then—good: I spare you and I give up. You affect me as by the appeal positively for pity: you convince me that for reasons rigid and sublime—what do I know?—we both of us should have suffered. I respect them then, and, though moved and privileged as, I believe, it has never been given to man, I retire, I renounce—never, on my honour, to try again. So rest for ever—and let *me*!"

That, for Brydon was the deep sense of this last demonstration —solemn, measured, directed, as he felt it to be. He brought it to a close, he turned away; and now verily he knew how deeply he had been stirred. He retraced his steps, taking up his candle, burnt, he observed, well-nigh to the socket, and marking again, lighten it as he would, the distinctness of his footfall; after which, in a moment, he knew himself at the other side of the house. He did here what he had not yet done at these hours—he opened half a casement, one of those in the front, and let in the air of the night; a thing he would have taken at any time previous for a sharp rupture of his spell. His spell was broken now, and it didn't matter—broken by his concession and his surrender, which made it idle henceforth that he should ever come back. The empty street—its other life so marked even by the great lamplit vacancy—was within call, within touch; he stayed there as to be in it again, high above it though he was still perched; he watched as for some comforting common fact, some vulgar human note, the passage of a scavenger or a thief, some night-bird however base. He would have blessed that sign of life; he would have welcomed positively the slow approach of his friend the policeman, whom he had hitherto only sought to avoid, and was not sure that if the patrol had come into sight he mightn't have felt the impulse to get into relation with it, to hail it, on some pretext, from his fourth floor.

The pretext that wouldn't have been too silly or too compromis- ing, the explanation that would have saved his dignity and kept his name, in such a case, out of the papers, was not definite to him: he was so occupied with the thought of recording his Discretion— as an effect of the vow he had just uttered to his intimate adversary—that the importance of this loomed large and something had overtaken all ironically his sense of proportion. If there had been a ladder applied to the front of the house, even one of the vertiginous perpendiculars employed by painters and roofers and sometimes left standing overnight, he would have managed somehow, astride of the window-sill, to compass by outstretched leg and arm that mode of descent. If there had been some such uncanny thing as he had found in his room at hotels, a workable fire-escape in the form of notched cable or a canvas shoot, he would have availed himself of it as a proof—well, of his present delicacy. He nursed that sentiment, as the question stood, a little in vain, and even—at the end of he scarce knew, once more, how long—found it, as by the action on his mind of the failure of response of the outer world, sinking back to vague anguish. It seemed to him he had waited an age for some stir of the great grim hush; the life of the town was itself under a spell—so unnaturally, up and down the whole prospect of known and rather ugly objects, the blankness and the silence lasted. Had they ever, he asked himself, the hard-faced houses, which had begun to look livid in the dim dawn, had they ever spoken so little to any need of his spirit? Great builded voids, great crowded stillnesses put on, often, in the heart of cities, for the small hours, a sort of sinister mask, and it was of this large collective negation that Brydon presently became conscious—all the more that the break of day was, almost incredibly, now at hand, proving to him what a night he had made of it.

He looked again at his watch, saw what had become of his time-values (he had taken hours for minutes—not, as in other tense situations, minutes for hours) and the strange air of the streets was but the weak, the sullen flush of a dawn in which everything was still locked up. His choked appeal from his own open window had been the sole note of life, and he could but break off at last as for a worse despair. Yet while so deeply demoralised he was capable again of an impulse denoting—at least by his present measure—extraordinary resolution; of retracing his steps to the spot where he had turned cold with the extinction of his last pulse of doubt as to there being in the place another presence than his own. This required an effort strong enough to sicken him; but he had his reason, which overmastered for the moment everything else. There was the whole of the rest of the house to traverse, and how should he screw himself to that if the door he had seen closed were at present open? He could hold to the idea that the closing had practically been for him an act of mercy, a chance offered him to descend, depart, get off the ground and never again profane it. This conception held together, it worked; but what it meant for him depended now clearly on the amount of forbearance his recent action, or rather his recent inaction, had engendered. The image of the "presence," whatever it was, waiting there for him to go—this image had not yet been so concrete for his nerves as when he stopped short of the point at which certainty would have come to him. For, with all his resolution, or more exactly with all his dread, he did stop short—he hung back from really seeing. The risk was too great and his fear too definite: it took at this moment an awful specific form.

He knew—yes, as he had never known anything—that, *should* he see the door open, it would all too abjectly be the end of him. It would mean that the agent of his shame—for his shame was the deep abjection—was once more at large and in general possession; and what glared him thus in the face was the act that this would determine for him. It would send him straight about to the window he had left open, and by that window, be long ladder and dangling rope as absent as they would, he saw himself uncontrollably insanely fatally take his way to the street. The hideous chance of this he at least could avert; but he could only avert it by recoiling in time from assurance. He had the whole house to deal with, this fact was still there; only he now knew that uncertainty alone could start him. He stole back from where he had checked himself—merely to do so was suddenly like safety—and, making blindly for the greater staircase, left gaping rooms and sounding passages behind. Here was the top of the stairs, with a fine large dim descent and three spacious landings to mark off. His instinct was all for mildness, but his feet were harsh on the floors, and, strangely, when he had in a couple of minutes become aware of this, it counted somehow for help. He couldn't have spoken, the tone of his voice would have scared him, and the common conceit or resource of "whistling in the dark" (whether literally or figuratively) have appeared basely vulgar; yet he liked none the less to hear himself go, and when he had reached his first landing—taking it all with no rush, but quite steadily—that stage of success drew from him a gasp of relief.

The house, withal, seemed immense, the scale of space again inordinate; the open rooms, to no one of which his eyes deflected, gloomed in their shuttered state like mouths of caverns; only the high skylight that formed the crown of the deep well created for him a medium in which he could advance, but which might have been, for queerness of colour, some watery under-world. He tried to think of something noble, as that his property was really grand, a splendid possession; but this nobleness took the form too of the clear delight with which he was finally to sacrifice it. They might come in now, the builders, the destroyers—they might come as soon as they would. At the end of two flights he had dropped to another zone, and from the middle of the third, with only one more left, he recognised the influence of the lower windows, of half-drawn blinds, of the occasional gleam of street-lamps, of the glazed spaces of the vestibule. This was the bottom of the sea, which showed an illumination of its own and which he even saw paved—when at a given moment he drew up to sink a long look over the banisters—with the marble squares of his childhood. By that time indubitably he felt, as he might have said in a commoner cause, better; it had allowed him to stop and draw breath, and the ease increased with the sight of the old black-and-white slabs. But what he most felt was that now surely, with the element of impunity pulling him as by hard firm hands, the case was settled for what he might have seen above had he dared that last look. The closed door, blessedly remote now, was still closed—and he had only in short to reach that of the house.

He came down further, he crossed the passage forming the access to the last flight; and if here again he stopped an instant it was almost for the sharpness of the thrill of assured escape. It made him shut his eyes—which opened again to the straight slope of the remainder of the stairs. Here was impunity still, but impunity almost excessive; inasmuch as the sidelights and the high fan-tracery of the entrance were glimmering straight into the hall; an appearance produced, he the next instant saw, by the fact that the vestibule gaped wide, that the hinged halves of the inner door had been thrown far back. Out of that again the *question* sprang at him, making his eyes, as he felt, half-start from his head, as they had done, at the top of the house, before the sign of the other door. If he had left that one open, hadn't he left this one closed, and wasn't he now in *most* immediate presence of some inconceivable occult activity? It was as sharp, the question, as a knife in his side, but the answer hung fire still and seemed to lose itself in the vague darkness to which the thin admitted dawn, glimmering archwise over the whole outer door, made a semicircular margin, a cold silvery nimbus that seemed to play a little as he looked—to shift and expand and contract.

It was as if there had been something within it, protected by indistinctness and corresponding in extent with the opaque surface behind, the painted panels of the last barrier to his escape, of which the key was in his pocket. The indistinctness mocked him even while he stared, affected him as somehow shrouding or challenging certitude, so that after faltering an instant on his step he let himself go with the sense that here *was* at last something to meet, to touch, to take, to know—something all unnatural and dreadful, but to advance upon which was the condition for him either of liberation or of supreme defeat. The penumbra, dense and dark, was the virtual screen of a figure which stood in it as still as some image erect in a niche or as some black-vizored sentinel guarding a treasure. Brydon was to know afterwards, was to recall and make out, the particular thing he had believed during the rest of his descent. He saw, in its great grey glimmering margin, the central vagueness diminish, and he felt it to be taking the very form toward which, for so many days, the passion of his curiosity had yearned. It gloomed, it loomed, it was something, it was somebody, the prodigy of a personal presence.

Rigid and conscious, spectral yet human, a man of his own substance and stature waited there to measure himself with his power to dismay. This only could it be—this only till he recognised, with his advance, that what made the face dim was the pair of raised hands that covered it and in which, so far from being offered in defiance, it was buried as for dark deprecation. So Brydon, before him, took him in; with every fact of him now, in the higher light, hard and acute—his planted stillness, his vivid truth, his grizzled bent head and white masking hands, his queer actuality of evening-dress, of dangling double eye-glass, of gleaming silk lappet and white linen, of pearl button and gold watch-guard and polished shoe. No portrait by a great modern master could have presented him with more intensity, thrust him out of his frame with more art, as if there had been "treatment," of the consummate sort, in his every shade and salience. The revulsion, for our friend, had become, before he knew it, immense—this drop, in the act of apprehension, to the sense of his adversary's inscrutable manœuvre. That meaning at least, while he gaped, it offered him; for he could but gape at his other self in this other anguish, gape as a proof that *he*, standing there for the achieved, the enjoyed, the triumphant life, couldn't be faced in his triumph. Wasn't the proof in the splendid covering hands, strong and completely spread?—so spread and so intentional that, in spite of a special verity that surpassed every other, the fact that one of these hands had lost two fingers, which were reduced to stumps, as if accidentally shot away, the face was effectually guarded and saved.

"Saved," though, *would* it be?—Brydon breathed his wonder till the very impunity of his attitude and the very insistence of his eyes produced, as he felt, a sudden stir which showed the next instant as a deeper portent, while the head raised itself, the betrayal of a braver purpose. The hands, as he looked, began to move, to open; then, as if deciding in a flash, dropped from the face and left it uncovered and presented. Horror, with the sight, had leaped into Brydon's throat, gasping there in a sound he couldn't utter; for the bared identity was too hideous as *his*, and his glare was the passion of his protest. The face, *that* face, Spencer Brydon's?—he searched it still, but looking away from it in dismay and denial, falling straight from his height of sublimity. It was unknown, inconceivable, awful, disconnected from any possibility—! He had been "sold," he inwardly moaned, stalking such game as this: the presence before him was a presence, the horror within him a horror, but the waste of his nights had been only grotesque and the success of his adventure an irony. Such an identity fitted his at *no* point, made its alternative monstrous. A thousand times yes, as it came upon him nearer now—the face was the face of a stranger. It came upon him nearer now, quite as one of those expanding fantastic images projected by the magic lantern of childhood; for the stranger, whoever he might be, evil, odious, blatant, vulgar, had advanced as for aggression, and he knew himself give ground. Then harder pressed still, sick with the force of his shock, and falling back as under the hot breath and the roused passion of a life larger than his own, a rage of personality before which his own collapsed, he felt the whole vision turn to darkness and his very feet give way. His head went round; he was going; he had gone.

III

What had next brought him back, clearly—though after how long?—was Mrs. Muldoon's voice, coming to him from quite near, from so near that he seemed presently to see her as kneeling on the ground before him while he lay looking up at her; himself not wholly on the ground, but half-raised and upheld—conscious, yes, of tenderness of support and, more particularly, of a head pillowed in extraordinary softness and faintly refreshing fragrance. He considered, he wondered, his wit but half at his service; then another face intervened, bending more directly over him, and he finally knew that Alice Staverton had made her lap an ample and perfect cushion to him, and that she had to this end seated herself on the lowest degree of the staircase, the rest of his long person remaining stretched on his old black-and-white slabs. They were cold, these marble squares of his youth; but *he* somehow was not, in this rich return of consciousness—the most wonderful hour, little by little, that he had ever known, leaving him, as it did, so gratefully, so abysmally passive, and yet as with a treasure of intelligence waiting all round him for quiet appropriation; dissolved, he might call it, in the air of the place and producing the golden glow of a late autumn afternoon. He had come back, yes—come back from further away than any man but himself had ever travelled; but it was strange how with this sense of what he had come back *to* seemed really the great thing, and as if his prodigious journey had been all for the sake of it. Slowly but surely his consciousness grew, his vision of his state thus completing itself: he had been miraculously *carried* back—

lifted and carefully borne as from where he had been picked up, the uttermost end of an interminable grey passage. Even with this he was suffered to rest, and what had now brought him to knowledge was the break in the long mild motion.

It had brought him to knowledge, to knowledge—yes, this was the beauty of his state; which came to resemble more and more that of a man who has gone to sleep on some news of a great inheritance, and then, after dreaming it away, after profaning it with matters strange to it, has waked up again to serenity of certitude and has only to lie and watch it grow. This was the drift of his patience—that he had only to let it shine on him. He must moreover, with intermissions, still have been lifted and borne; since why and how else should he have known himself, later on, with the afternoon glow intenser, no longer at the foot of his stairs—situated as these now seemed at that dark other end of his tunnel—but on a deep window-bench of his high saloon, over which had been spread, couch-fashion, a mantle of soft stuff lined with grey fur that was familiar to his eyes and that one of his hands kept fondly feeling as for its pledge of truth. Mrs. Muldoon's face had gone, but the other, the second he had recognised, hung over him in a way that showed how he was still propped and pillowed. He took it all in, and the more he took it the more it seemed to suffice: he was as much at peace as if he had had food and drink. It was the two women who had found him, on Mrs. Muldoon's having plied, at her usual hour, her latch-key—and on her having above all arrived while Miss Staverton still lingered near the house. She had been turning away, all anxiety, from worrying the vain bell-handle—her calculation having been of the hour of the good woman's visit; but the latter, blessedly, had come up while she was still there, and they had entered together. He had then lain, beyond the vestibule, very much as he was lying now—quite, that is, as he appeared to have fallen, but all so wondrously without bruise or gash; only in a depth of stupor. What he most took in, however, at present, with the steadier clearance, was that Alice Staverton had for a long unspeakable moment not doubted he was dead.

"It must have been that I *was*." He made it out as she held him. "Yes—I can only have died. You brought me literally to life. Only," he wondered, his eyes rising to her, "only, in the name of all the benedictions, how?"

It took her but an instant to bend her face and kiss him, and something in the manner of it, and in the way her hands clasped and locked his head while he felt the cool charity and virtue of her lips, something in all this beatitude somehow answered everything. "And now I keep you," she said.

"Oh keep me, keep me!" he pleaded while her face still hung over him: in response to which it dropped again and stayed close, clingingly close. It was the seal of their situation—of which he tasted the impress for a long blissful moment in silence. But he came back. "Yet how did you know—?"

"I was uneasy. You were to have come, you remember—and you had sent no word."

"Yes, I remember—I was to have gone to you at one to-day." It caught on to their "old" life and relation—which were so near and so far. "I was still out there in my strange darkness—where was it, what was it? I must have stayed there so long." He could but wonder at the depth and the duration of his swoon.

"Since last night?" she asked with a shade of fear for her possible indiscretion.

"Since this morning—it must have been: the cold dim dawn of to-day. Where have I been," he vaguely wailed, "where have I been?" He felt her hold him close, and it was as if this helped him now to make in all security his mild moan. "What a long dark day!"

All in her tenderness she had waited a moment. "In the cold dim dawn?" she quavered.

But he had already gone on piecing together the parts of the whole prodigy. "As I didn't turn up you came straight—?"

She barely cast about. "I went first to your hotel—where they told me of your absence. You had dined out last evening and hadn't been back since. But they appeared to know you had been at your club."

"So you had the idea of *this*—?"

"Of what?" she asked in a moment.

"Well—of what has happened."

"I believed at least you'd have been here. I've known, all along," she said, "that you've been coming."

" 'Known' it—?"

"Well, I've believed it. I said nothing to you after that talk we had a month ago—but I felt sure. I knew you *would*," she declared.

"That I'd persist, you mean?"

"That you'd see him."

"Ah but I didn't!" cried Brydon with his long wail. "There's somebody—an awful beast; whom I brought, too horribly, to bay. But it's not me."

At this she bent over him again, and her eyes were in his eyes. "No—it's not you." And it was as if, while her face hovered, he might have made out in it, hadn't it been so near, some particular meaning blurred by a smile. "No, thank heaven," she repeated—"it's not you! Of course it wasn't to have been."

"Ah but it *was*," he gently insisted. And he stared before him now as he had been staring for so many weeks. "I was to have known myself."

"You couldn't!" she returned consolingly. And then reverting, and as if to account further for what she had herself done, "But it wasn't only *that*, that you hadn't been at home," she went on. "I waited till the hour at which we had found Mrs. Muldoon that day of my going with you; and she arrived, as I've told you, while, failing to bring any one to the door, I lingered in my despair on the steps. After a little, if she hadn't come, by such a mercy, I should have found means to hunt her up. But it wasn't," said Alice Staverton, as if once more with her fine intention—"it wasn't only that."

His eyes, as he lay, turned back to her. "What more then?"

She met it, the wonder she had stirred. "In the cold dim dawn, you say? Well, in the cold dim dawn of this morning I too saw you."

"Saw *me*—?"

"Saw *him*," said Alice Staverton. "It must have been at the same moment."

He lay an instant taking it in—as if he wished to be quite reasonable. "At the same moment?"

"Yes—in my dream again, the same one I've named to you. He came back to me. Then I knew it for a sign. He had come to you."

At this Brydon raised himself; he had to see her better. She helped him when she understood his movement, and he sat up, steadying himself beside her there on the window-bench and with his right hand grasping her left. "*He* didn't come to me."

"You came to yourself," she beautifully smiled.

"Ah I've come to myself now—thanks to you, dearest. But this brute, with his awful face—this brute's a black stranger. He's none of *me*, even as I *might* have been," Brydon sturdily declared.

But she kept the clearness that was like the breath of infallibility. "Isn't the whole point that you'd have been different?"

He almost scowled for it. "As different as *that*—?"

Her look again was more beautiful to him than the things of this world. "Haven't you exactly wanted to know *how* different? So this morning," she said, "you appeared to me."

"Like *him*?"

"A black stranger!"

"Then how did you know it was I?"

"Because, as I told you weeks ago, my mind, my imagination, had worked so over what you might, what you mightn't have been—to show you, you see, how I've thought of you. In the midst of that you came to me—that my wonder might be answered. So I knew," she went on; "and believed that, since the question held you too so fast, as you told me that day, you too would see for yourself. And when this morning I again saw I knew it would be because you had—and also then, from the first moment, because you somehow wanted me. *He* seemed to tell me of that. So why," she strangely smiled, "shouldn't I like him?"

It brought Spencer Brydon to his feet. "You 'like' that horror—?"

"I *could* have liked him. And to me," she said, "he was no horror. I had accepted him."

" 'Accepted'—?" Brydon oddly sounded.

"Before, for the interest of his difference—yes. And as *I* didn't disown him, as *I* knew him—which you at last, confronted with him in his difference, so cruelly didn't, my dear—well, he must have been, you see, less dreadful to me. And it may have pleased him that I pitied him."

She was beside him on her feet, but still holding his hand—still with her arm supporting him. But though it all brought for him thus a dim light, "You 'pitied' him?" he grudgingly, resentfully asked.

"He has been unhappy, he has been ravaged," she said.

"And haven't I been unhappy? Am not I—you've only to look at me!—ravaged?"

"Ah I don't say I like him *better*," she granted after a thought. "But he's grim, he's worn—and things have happened to him. He doesn't make shift, for sight, with your charming monocle."

"No"—it struck Brydon: "I couldn't have sported mine 'downtown.' They'd have guyed me there."

"His great convex pince-nez—I saw it, I recognised the kind—is for his poor ruined sight. And his poor right hand—!"

"Ah!" Brydon winced—whether for his proved identity or for his lost fingers. Then, "He has a million a year," he lucidly added. "But he hasn't you."

"And he isn't—no, he isn't—*you!*" she murmured as he drew her to his breast.

THE AUTHOR
ON HIS CRAFT

Editors' Commentary

James's critical vocabulary derived in part from the criticism of painting, as his seminal essay on "The Art of Fiction" (1884) demonstrates. In childhood he had been exposed to the great monuments of European art, and he studied painting before he took up writing. As a young man he explored the museums and churches of the Old World, reporting the results in a series of articles, and these exercises in the description of visual art in part account for his critical vocabulary. Since the English language lacked an established terminology for the formal criticism of fiction, James was free to draw some of the terms of his literary theory from art criticism. The "analogy between the art of the novelist and the art of the painter," he wrote in "The Art of Fiction," is complete. "They may learn from each other, they may explain and sustain each other." Throughout his life painting terms served him as metaphors for his own art.[1]

One of the traps one must avoid in speaking of James's critical principles is to make him out to have been more consistent than he was. In the essays he wrote over a stretch of decades and even in the prefaces to the New York Edition his aesthetic is not very systematic. Some of his terms are informal. The word *story* usually meant narrative to him and might cover anything from a long novel such as *The Ambassadors* to a very short piece such as "Brooksmith." The new term *short story* (in the *Oxford English Dictionary* first noted for 1898) he used with equal informality when he used it at all. But he did theorize about short fiction, and his theory is reflected in the passages here reprinted from his prefaces. It turns upon two central and related distinctions: of length, between shorter and longer, and of method, between "scenic" and "pictorial."

Length. Editorial rules prevailing in James's time specified that a short story should extend from six to eight thousand words, and James found these limits constricting. His ideal was "the beautiful and blest *nouvelle*,"[2] whose elasticity better fitted his inclinations. It allowed room for growth, for change of character, for interaction

---

1. These and related matters have been treated authoritatively by Viola Hopkins Winner in *Henry James and the Visual Arts* (Charlottesville: University Press of Virginia, 1970).
2. *The Art of the Novel* (New York and London: Charles Scribner's Sons, 1948), p. 220.

between characters, for plot reversal—in a word, for development, as in "Daisy Miller," which he declared "pre-eminently a *nouvelle*" (see p. 401 below). The shorter form he usually termed "anecdote."

Method. The writer of fiction, James maintained, has the choice of treating a subject as picture or as scene.[3] Scene is dramatic, picture is descriptive and internal. Scene shows characters involved in action and speech; picture tells what they experience, what they feel and think, what they remember. If we are surprised to find a character's reflections denoted as picture, the explanation is that the portrayal has affinity with painting, as James's concept of fore-shortening or perspective underlines. *Foreshortening* is a key word in his aesthetic; it too shows the influence of painting. In painting it refers to the method of achieving depth by shortening the outlines of distant objects. James knew that the grammar of fiction contains no such exact techniques: "the grammar of painting is . . . much more definite," he says in "The Art of Fiction" (see p. 381 below). Still—as he pointed out some twenty years later in the preface to "Daisy Miller"—in fiction, too, foreshortening achieves perspective. It consists in narrative summary that bridges time and distance and hence is an "economic device." It allows the author to contain the complexities of his subject within a compact treatment.

James's distinction between the scenic method and the pictorial is related to the matter of length and therefore to the distinction between anecdote and *nouvelle.* A picture, an impression, may present a "foreshortened" form of a complex subject that involves progression and development, in other words, the kind of subject James thought appropriate to the *nouvelle.* But in James's own practice the distinction between the scenic and the pictorial method operates in fact everywhere. "The Middle Years," one of his short pieces on a subject "demanding 'developments,' " is poured into the form of the "concise anecdote" (see p. 413 below), though not as concise as he thought, and the nouvelle "Daisy Miller" contains both scenic and pictorial passages. So, we may add, do all of James's short stories. "The Beast in the Jungle," for instance, alternates dramatic scenes with long internalized passages that picture the hero's self-absorbed creation of what he believes to be his fate. The alternation of narrative perspective and dramatic scenes (partly because a memory may include specific scenes) is a hallmark of James's practice from his shortest stories to his longest novels.

James's definition of picture, finally, leads to another formal characteristic of his fiction, his concern with narrative point of view. One of his means of organizing his material was to present char-

3. Ibid., p. 300.

acters and action as they are perceived by a participant. The analogy with painting applies to these functional figures—reflectors, registers, central intelligences, centers of consciousness, as James variously called them. Their function is comparable to the painter's frame. What the painter achieves by framing or limiting the field of his vision James achieves by the limited focus of his centers. He explains in his preface to "The Pupil," for instance, that presenting his material, the family of the Moreens, indirectly through the "troubled vision" of their son Morgan and his tutor, was to give it "proportion and perspective" (see p. 411 below). James's formal concerns, in sum, are closely related to his preoccupations as a psychological novelist. He was interested in psychological manifestations of all kinds, and the interest in the varieties of consciousness is reflected in his technical experiments with limited narrative points of view. At first this method of presenting and organizing his subjects served him primarily as a compositional device to achieve focus and thereby clarity and intensity. In time consciousness became his very subject.

HENRY JAMES

The Art of Fiction†

I should not have affixed so comprehensive a title to these few remarks, necessarily wanting in any completeness upon a subject the full consideration of which would carry us far, did I not seem to discover a pretext for my temerity in the interesting pamphlet lately published under this name by Mr. Walter Besant.[1] Mr. Besant's lecture at the Royal Institution—the original form of his pamphlet—appears to indicate that many persons are interested in the art of fiction, and are not indifferent to such remarks, as those who practise it may attempt to make about it. I am therefore anxious not to lose the benefit of this favourable association, and to edge in a few words under cover of the attention which Mr. Besant

---

† From Henry James, *Partial Portraits* (London: Macmillan and Co., Limited, 1905), pp. 375–408. (First edition 1888. Reprinted 1894, 1899, 1905.) The essay was originally published in *Longman's Magazine* of September 1884. The text here reprinted was revised by the author. It may bear repeating that although the essay speaks of novels and novelists, its subject—as the title indicates—is fiction, regardless of length. The footnotes for this selection are by the editors of this Norton Critical Edition.
1. British novelist (1836–1901). On April 25, 1884, Besant had lectured on "The Art of Fiction" at the Royal Institution (founded in 1799 to promote research in connection with the experimental sciences). The lecture was published as a pamphlet, and this in turn gave James the impulse and opportunity for his essay.

is sure to have excited. There is something very encouraging in his
having put into form certain of his ideas on the mystery of story-
telling.

It is a proof of life and curiosity—curiosity on the part of the
brotherhood of novelists as well as on the part of their readers. Only
a short time ago it might have been supposed that the English novel
was not what the French call *discutable*.[2] It had no air of having a
theory, a conviction, a consciousness of itself behind it—of being
the expression of an artistic faith, the result of choice and comparison. I do not say it was necessarily the worse for that: it would take
much more courage than I possess to intimate that the form of the
novel as Dickens and Thackeray (for instance) saw it had any taint
of incompleteness. It was, however, *naïf*[3] (if I may help myself out
with another French word); and evidently if it be destined to suffer
in any way for having lost its *naïveté* it has now an idea of making
sure of the corresponding advantages. During the period I have
alluded to there was a comfortable, good-humoured feeling abroad
that a novel is a novel, as a pudding is a pudding, and that our only
business with it could be to swallow it. But within a year or two,
for some reason or other, there have been signs of returning
animation—the era of discussion would appear to have been to a
certain extent opened. Art lives upon discussion, upon experiment,
upon curiosity, upon variety of attempt, upon the exchange of views
and the comparison of standpoints; and there is a presumption that
those times when no one has anything particular to say about it,
and has no reason to give for practice or preference, though they
may be times of honour, are not times of development—are times,
possibly even, a little of dullness. The successful application of any
art is a delightful spectacle, but the theory too is interesting; and
though there is a great deal of the latter without the former I suspect there has never been a genuine success that has not had a
latent core of conviction. Discussion, suggestion, formulation, these
things are fertilising when they are frank and sincere. Mr. Besant
has set an excellent example in saying what he thinks, for his part,
about the way in which fiction should be written, as well as about
the way in which it should be published; for his view of the "art,"
carried on into an appendix, covers that too. Other labourers in the
same field will doubtless take up the argument, they will give it the
light of their experience, and the effect will surely be to make our
interest in the novel a little more what it had for some time threatened to fail to be—a serious, active, inquiring interest, under pro-

2. Debatable, a subject for serious discussion.
3. Unsophisticated, unselfconscious.

tection of which this delightful study may, in moments of confidence, venture to say a little more what it thinks of itself.

It must take itself seriously for the public to take it so. The old superstition about fiction being "wicked" has doubtless died out in England; but the spirit of it lingers in a certain oblique regard directed toward any story which does not more or less admit that it is only a joke. Even the most jocular novel feels in some degree the weight of the proscription that was formerly directed against literary levity: the jocularity does not always succeed in passing for orthodoxy. It is still expected, though perhaps people are ashamed to say it, that a production which is after all only a "make-believe" (for what else is a "story"?) shall be in some degree apologetic—shall renounce the pretension of attempting really to represent life. This, of course, any sensible, wide-awake story declines to do, for it quickly perceives that the tolerance granted to it on such a condition is only an attempt to stifle it disguised in the form of generosity. The old evangelical hostility to the novel, which was as explicit as it was narrow, and which regarded it as little less favourable to our immortal part than a stage-play, was in reality far less insulting. The only reason for the existence of a novel is that it does attempt to represent life. When it relinquishes this attempt, the same attempt that we see on the canvas of the painter, it will have arrived at a very strange pass. It is not expected of the picture that it will make itself humble in order to be forgiven; and the analogy between the art of the painter and the art of the novelist is, so far as I am able to see, complete. Their inspiration is the same, their process (allowing for the different quality of the vehicle), is the same, their success is the same. They may learn from each other, they may explain and sustain each other. Their cause is the same, and the honour of one is the honour of another. The Mahometans[4] think a picture an unholy thing, but it is a long time since any Christian did, and it is therefore the more odd that in the Christian mind the traces (dissimulated though they may be) of a suspicion of the sister art should linger to this day. The only effectual way to lay it to rest is to emphasise the analogy to which I just alluded—to insist on the fact that as the picture is reality, so the novel is history. That is the only general description (which does it justice) that we may give of the novel. But history also is allowed to represent life; it is not, any more than painting, expected to apologise. The subject-matter of fiction is stored up likewise in documents and records, and if it will not give itself away, as they say in California, it must speak with assurance, with the tone of the historian. Certain ac-

---

4. Mohammedans; i.e., Muslims.

complished novelists have a habit of giving themselves away which
must often bring tears to the eyes of people who take their fiction
seriously. I was lately struck, in reading over many pages of Anthony
Trollope,[5] with his want of discretion in this particular. In a di-
gression, a parenthesis or an aside, he concedes to the reader that
he and this trusting friend are only "making believe." He admits
that the events he narrates have not really happened, and that he
can give his narrative any turn the reader may like best. Such a
betrayal of a sacred office seems to me, I confess, a terrible crime;
it is what I mean by the attitude of apology, and it shocks me every
whit as much in Trollope as it would have shocked me in Gibbon
or Macaulay.[6] It implies that the novelist is less occupied in looking for the truth (the truth, of course I mean, that he assumes, the
premises that we must grant him, whatever they may be), than the
historian, and in doing so it deprives him at a stroke of all his
standing-room. To represent and illustrate the past, the actions of
men, is the task of either writer, and the only difference that I can
see is, in proportion as he succeeds, to the honour of the novelist,
consisting as it does in his having more difficulty in collecting his
evidence, which is so far from being purely literary. It seems to me
to give him a great character, the fact that he has at once so much
in common with the philosopher and the painter; this double analogy is a magnificent heritage.

It is of all this evidently that Mr. Besant is full when he insists
upon the fact that fiction is one of the *fine* arts, deserving in its
turn of all the honours and emoluments that have hitherto been
reserved for the successful profession of music, poetry, painting,
architecture. It is impossible to insist too much on so important a
truth, and the place that Mr. Besant demands for the work of the
novelist may be represented, a trifle less abstractly, by saying that
he demands not only that it shall be reputed artistic, but that it
shall be reputed very artistic indeed. It is excellent that he should
have struck this note, for his doing so indicates that there was need
of it, that his proposition may be to many people a novelty. One
rubs one's eyes at the thought; but the rest of Mr. Besant's essay
confirms the revelation. I suspect in truth that it would be possible
to confirm it still further, and that one would not be far wrong in
saying that in addition to the people to whom it has never occurred
that a novel ought to be artistic, there are a great many others who,
if this principle were urged upon them, would be filled with an
indefinable mistrust. They would find it difficult to explain their

5. British novelist (1815–1882).
6. Edward Gibbon (1737–1794) and Thomas Babington Macaulay (1800–1859) were eminent British historians, respectively authors of *The Decline and Fall of the Roman
   Empire* and *Macaulay's History of England from the Accession of James II.*

repugnance, but it would operate strongly to put them on their guard. "Art," in our Protestant communities, where so many things have got so strangely twisted about, is supposed in certain circles to have some vaguely injurious effect upon those who make it an important consideration, who let it weigh in the balance. It is assumed to be opposed in some mysterious manner to morality, to amusement, to instruction. When it is embodied in the work of the painter (the sculptor is another affair!) you know what it is: it stands there before you, in the honesty of pink and green and a gilt frame; you can see the worst of it at a glance, and you can be on your guard. But when it is introduced into literature it becomes more insidious—there is danger of its hurting you before you know it. Literature should be either instructive or amusing, and there is in many minds an impression that these artistic preoccupations, the search for form, contribute to neither end, interfere indeed with both. They are too frivolous to be edifying, and too serious to be diverting; and they are moreover priggish and paradoxical and superfluous. That, I think, represents the manner in which the latent thought of many people who read novels as an exercise in skipping would explain itself if it were to become articulate. They would argue, of course, that a novel ought to be "good," but they would interpret this term in a fashion of their own, which indeed would vary considerably from one critic to another. One would say that being good means representing virtuous and aspiring characters, placed in prominent positions; another would say that it depends on a "happy ending," on a distribution at the last of prizes, pensions, husbands, wives, babies, millions, appended paragraphs, and cheerful remarks. Another still would say that it means being full of incident and movement, so that we shall wish to jump ahead, to see who was the mysterious stranger, and if the stolen will was ever found, and shall not be distracted from this pleasure by any tiresome analysis or "description." But they would all agree that the "artistic" idea would spoil some of their fun. One would hold it accountable for all the description, another would see it revealed in the absence of sympathy. Its hostility to a happy ending would be evident, and it might even in some cases render any ending at all impossible. The "ending" of a novel is, for many persons, like that of a good dinner, a course of dessert and ices, and the artist in fiction is regarded as a sort of meddlesome doctor who forbids agreeable aftertastes. It is therefore true that this conception of Mr. Besant's of the novel as a superior form encounters not only a negative but a positive indifference. It matters little that as a work of art it should really be as little or as much of its essence to supply happy endings, sympathetic characters, and an objective tone, as if it were a work of mechanics: the association of ideas, however incongruous, might easily be too much for it if an eloquent voice were not sometimes raised to call attention to the fact that it is at once as free and as serious a branch of literature as any other.

Certainly this might sometimes be doubted in presence of the enormous number of works of fiction that appeal to the credulity of our generation, for it might easily seem that there could be no great character in a commodity so quickly and easily produced. It must be admitted that good novels are much compromised by bad ones, and that the field at large suffers discredit from overcrowding. I think, however, that this injury is only superficial, and that the superabundance of written fiction proves nothing against the principle itself. It has been vulgarised, like all other kinds of literature, like everything else to-day, and it has proved more than some kinds accessible to vulgarisation. But there is as much difference as there ever was between a good novel and a bad one: the bad is swept with all the daubed canvases and spoiled marble into some unvisited limbo, or infinite rubbish-yard beneath the back-windows of the world, and the good subsists and emits its light and stimulates our desire for perfection. As I shall take the liberty of making but a single criticism of Mr. Besant, whose tone is so full of the love of his art, I may as well have done with it at once. He seems to me to mistake in attempting to say so definitely beforehand what sort of an affair the good novel will be. To indicate the danger of such an error as that has been the purpose of these few pages; to suggest that certain traditions on the subject, applied *a priori,* have already had much to answer for, and that the good health of an art which undertakes so immediately to reproduce life must demand that it be perfectly free. It lives upon exercise, and the very meaning of exercise is freedom. The only obligation to which in advance we may hold a novel, without incurring the accusation of being arbitrary, is that it be interesting. That general responsibility rests upon it, but it is the only one I can think of. The ways in which it is at liberty to accomplish this result (of interesting us) strike me as innumerable, and such as can only suffer from being marked out or fenced in by prescription. They are as various as the temperament of man, and they are successful in proportion as they reveal a particular mind, different from others. A novel is in its broadest definition a personal, a direct impression of life: that, to begin with, constitutes its value, which is greater or less according to the intensity of the impression. But there will be no intensity at all, and therefore no value, unless there is freedom to feel and say. The tracing of a line to be followed, of a tone to be taken, of a form to be filled out, is a limitation of that freedom and a suppression of the very thing that we are most curious about. The form, it seems to me, is to be appreciated after the fact: then the author's choice has been made, his standard has been indicated; then we can follow lines and directions and compare tones and resemblances. Then in a word we can enjoy one of the most charming of pleasures, we can estimate quality, we can apply the test of execution. The execution belongs to the author alone; it is what is most personal to him, and we measure him by that. The advantage, the luxury, as well as the torment and responsibility of the novelist, is that there is no limit to what he may attempt as an executant—no limit to his possible experiments, efforts, discoveries, successes. Here it is especially that he works, step by step, like his brother of the brush, of whom we may always say that he has painted his picture in a manner best known to himself. His manner is his secret, not necessarily a jealous one. He cannot disclose it as a general thing if he would; he would be at a loss to teach it to others. I say this with a due recollection of having insisted on the community of method of the artist who paints a picture and the artist who writes a novel. The painter *is* able to teach the rudiments of his practice, and it is possible, from the study of good work (granted the aptitude), both to learn how to paint and to learn how to write. Yet it remains true, without injury to the *rapprochement*,[7] that the literary artist would be obliged to say to his pupil much more than the other, "Ah, well, you must do it as you can!" It is a question of degree, a matter of delicacy. If there are exact sciences, there are also exact arts, and the grammar of painting is so much more definite that it makes the difference.

I ought to add, however, that if Mr. Besant says at the beginning of his essay that the "laws of fiction may be laid down and taught with as much precision and exactness as the laws of harmony, perspective, and proportion," he mitigates what might appear to be an extravagance by applying his remark to "general" laws, and by expressing most of these rules in a manner with which it would certainly be unaccommodating to disagree. That the novelist must write from his experience, that his "characters must be real and such as might be met with in actual life"; that "a young lady brought up in a quiet country village should avoid descriptions of garrison life," and "a writer whose friends and personal experiences belong to the lower middle-class should carefully avoid introducing his characters into society"; that one should enter one's notes in a common-place book;[8] that one's figures should be clear in outline; that making them clear by some trick of speech or of carriage is a bad method, and "describing them at length" is a worse one; that

7. Comparison.
8. A notebook in which one collects ideas, observations, and noteworthy passages from other writers.

English Fiction should have a "conscious moral purpose"; that "it is almost impossible to estimate too highly the value of careful workmanship—that is, of style"; that "the most important point of all is the story," that "the story is everything": these are principles with most of which it is surely impossible not to sympathise. That remark about the lower middle-class writer and his knowing his place is perhaps rather chilling; but for the rest I should find it difficult to dissent from any one of these recommendations. At the same time, I should find it difficult positively to assent to them, with the exception, perhaps, of the injunction as to entering one's notes in a common-place book. They scarcely seem to me to have the quality that Mr. Besant attributes to the rules of the novelist— the "precision and exactness" of "the laws of harmony, perspective, and proportion." They are suggestive, they are even inspiring, but they are not exact, though they are doubtless as much so as the case admits of: which is a proof of that liberty of interpretation for which I just contended. For the value of these different injunctions—so beautiful and so vague—is wholly in the meaning one attaches to them. The characters, the situation, which strike one as real will be those that touch and interest one most, but the measure of reality is very difficult to fix. The reality of Don Quixote or of Mr. Micawber[9] is a very delicate shade; it is a reality so col- oured by the author's vision that, vivid as it may be, one would hesitate to propose it as a model: one would expose one's self to some very embarrassing questions on the part of a pupil. It goes without saying that you will not write a good novel unless you pos- sess the sense of reality; but it will be difficult to give you a recipe for calling that sense into being. Humanity is immense, and reality has a myriad forms; the most one can affirm is that some of the flowers of fiction have the odour of it, and others have not; as for telling you in advance how your nosegay should be composed, that is another affair. It is equally excellent and inconclusive to say that one must write from experience; to our supposititious aspirant such a declaration might savour of mockery. What kind of experience is intended, and where does it begin and end? Experience is never limited, and it is never complete; it is an immense sensibility, a kind of huge spider-web of the finest silken threads suspended in the chamber of consciousness, and catching every airborne particle in its tissue. It is the very atmosphere of the mind; and when the mind is imaginative—much more when it happens to be that of a man of genius—it takes to itself the faintest hints of life, it converts the very pulses of the air into revelations. The young lady living in a

---

9. Character in *David Copperfield* by Charles Dickens (1812–1870). Don Quixote is of course the title hero of the novel by Miguel de Cervantes (1547–1616).

village has only to be a damsel upon whom nothing is lost to make it quite unfair (as it seems to me) to declare to her that she shall have nothing to say about the military. Greater miracles have been seen than that, imagination assisting, she should speak the truth about some of these gentlemen. I remember an English novelist, a woman of genius, telling me that she was much commended for the impression she had managed to give in one of her tales of the nature and way of life of the French Protestant youth. She had been asked where she learned so much about this recondite being, she had been congratulated on her peculiar opportunities. These opportunities consisted in her having once, in Paris, as she ascended a staircase, passed an open door where, in the household of a *pasteur*,[1] some of the young Protestants were seated at table round a finished meal. The glimpse made a picture; it lasted only a moment, but that moment was experience. She had got her direct personal impression, and she turned out her type. She knew what youth was, and what Protestantism; she also had the advantage of having seen what it was to be French, so that she converted these ideas into a concrete image and produced a reality. Above all, however, she was blessed with the faculty which when you give it an inch takes an ell, and which for the artist is a much greater source of strength than any accident of residence or of place in the social scale. The power to guess the unseen from the seen, to trace the implication of things, to judge the whole piece by the pattern, the condition of feeling life in general so completely that you are well on your way to knowing any particular corner of it—this cluster of gifts may almost be said to constitute experience, and they occur in country and in town, and in the most differing stages of education. If experience consists of impressions, it may be said that impressions *are* experience, just as (have we not seen it?) they are the very air we breathe. Therefore, if I should certainly say to a novice, "Write from experience and experience only," I should feel that this was rather a tantalising monition if I were not careful immediately to add, "Try to be one of the people on whom nothing is lost!"

I am far from intending by this to minimise the importance of exactness—of truth of detail. One can speak best from one's own taste, and I may therefore venture to say that the air of reality (solidity of specification) seems to me to be the supreme virtue of a novel—the merit on which all its other merits (including that conscious moral purpose of which Mr. Besant speaks) helplessly and submissively depend. If it be not there they are all as nothing, and if these be there, they owe their effect to the success with which the author has produced the illusion of life. The cultivation

1. Clergyman.

of this success, the study of this exquisite process, form, to my taste, the beginning and the end of the art of the novelist. They are his inspiration, his despair, his reward, his torment, his delight. It is here in very truth that he competes with life; it is here that he competes with his brother the painter in *his* attempt to render the look of things, the look that conveys their meaning, to catch the colour, the relief, the expression, the surface, the substance of the human spectacle. It is in regard to this that Mr. Besant is well inspired when he bids him take notes. He cannot possibly take too many, he cannot possibly take enough. All life solicits him, and to "render" the simplest surface, to produce the most momentary illusion, is a very complicated business. His case would be easier, and the rule would be more exact, if Mr. Besant had been able to tell him what notes to take. But this, I fear, he can never learn in any manual; it is the business of his life. He has to take a great many in order to select a few, he has to work them up as he can, and even the guides and philosophers who might have most to say to him must leave him alone when it comes to the application of precepts, as we leave the painter in communion with his palette. That his characters "must be clear in outline," as Mr. Besant says —he feels that down to his boots; but how he shall make them so is a secret between his good angel and himself. It would be absurdly simple if he could be taught that a great deal of "description" would make them so, or that on the contrary the absence of description and the cultivation of dialogue, or the absence of dialogue and the multiplication of "incident," would rescue him from his difficulties. Nothing, for instance, is more possible than that he be of a turn of mind for which this odd, literal opposition of description and dialogue, incident and description, has little meaning and light. People often talk of these things as if they had a kind of internecine distinctness, instead of melting into each other at every breath, and being intimately associated parts of one general effort of expression. I cannot imagine composition existing in a series of blocks, nor conceive, in any novel worth discussing at all, of a passage of description that is not in its intention narrative, a passage of dialogue that is not in its intention descriptive, a touch of truth of any sort that does not partake of the nature of incident, or an incident that derives its interest from any other source than the general and only source of the success of a work of art—that of being illustrative. A novel is a living thing, all one and continuous, like any other organism, and in proportion as it lives will it be found, I think, that in each of the parts there is something of each of the other parts. The critic who over the close texture of a finished work shall pretend to trace a geography of items will mark some frontiers as artificial, I fear, as any that have been known to history. There is an

old-fashioned distinction between the novel of characters and the
novel of incident which must have cost many a smile to the intending fabulist who was keen about his work. It appears to me as
little to the point as the equally celebrated distinction between the
novel and the romance—to answer as little to any reality. There are
bad novels and good novels, as there are bad pictures and good
pictures; but that is the only distinction in which I see any meaning,
and I can as little imagine speaking of a novel of character as I can
imagine speaking of a picture of character. When one says picture
one says of character, when one says novel one says of incident,
and the terms may be transposed at will. What is character but the
determination of incident? What is incident but the illustration of
character? What is either a picture or a novel that is *not* of character? What else do we seek in it and find in it? It is an incident
for a woman to stand up with her hand resting on a table and look
out at you in a certain way; or if it be not an incident I think it will
be hard to say what it is. At the same time it is an expression of
character. If you say you don't see it (character in *that—allons
donc!*[2]), this is exactly what the artist who has reasons of his own
for thinking he *does* see it undertakes to show you. When a young
man makes up his mind that he has not faith enough after all to
enter the church as he intended, that is an incident, though you
may not hurry to the end of the chapter to see whether perhaps he
doesn't change once more. I do not say that these are extraordinary
or startling incidents. I do not pretend to estimate the degree of
interest proceeding from them, for this will depend upon the skill
of the painter. It sounds almost puerile to say that some incidents
are intrinsically much more important than others, and I need not
take this precaution after having professed my sympathy for the
major ones in remarking that the only classification of the novel
that I can understand is into that which has life and that which
has it not.

The novel and the romance, the novel of incident and that of
character—these clumsy separations appear to me to have been
made by critics and readers for their own convenience, and to help
them out of some of their occasional queer predicaments, but to
have little reality or interest for the producer, from whose point of
view it is of course that we are attempting to consider the art of
fiction. The case is the same with another shadowy category which
Mr. Besant apparently is disposed to set up—that of the "modern
English novel"; unless indeed it be that in this matter he has fallen
into an accidental confusion of standpoints. It is not quite clear
whether he intends the remarks in which he alludes to it to be

2. Come on now! Surely not!

didactic or historical. It is as difficult to suppose a person intending to write a modern English as to suppose him writing an ancient English novel: that is a label which begs the question. One writes the novel, one paints the picture, of one's language and of one's time, and calling it modern English will not, alas! make the difficult task any easier. No more, unfortunately, will calling this or that work of one's fellow-artist a romance—unless it be, of course, simply for the pleasantness of the thing, as for instance when Hawthorne gave this heading to his story of *Blithedale*. The French, who have brought the theory of fiction to remarkable completeness, have but one name for the novel, and have not attempted smaller things in it, that I can see, for that. I can think of no obligation to which the "romancer" would not be held equally with the novelist; the standard of execution is equally high for each. Of course it is of execution that we are talking—that being the only point of a novel that is open to contention. This is perhaps too often lost sight of, only to produce interminable confusions and cross-purposes. We must grant the artist his subject, his idea, his *donnée*:[3] our criticism is applied only to what he makes of it. Naturally I do not mean that we are bound to like it or find it interesting: in case we do not our course is perfectly simple—to let it alone. We may believe that of a certain idea even the most sincere novelist can make nothing at all, and the event may perfectly justify our belief; but the failure will have been a failure to execute, and it is in the execution that the fatal weakness is recorded. If we pretend to respect the artist at all, we must allow him his freedom of choice, in the face, in particular cases, of innumerable presumptions that the choice will not fructify. Art derives a considerable part of its beneficial exercise from flying in the face of presumptions, and some of the most interesting experiments of which it is capable are hidden in the bosom of common things. Gustave Flaubert[4] has written a story about the devotion of a servant-girl to a parrot, and the production, highly finished as it is, cannot on the whole be called a success. We are perfectly free to find it flat, but I think it might have been interesting; and I, for my part, am extremely glad he should have written it; it is a contribution to our knowledge of what can be done—or what cannot. Ivan Turgénieff[5] has written a tale about a deaf and dumb serf and a lap-dog, and the thing is touching, loving, a little masterpiece. He struck the note of life where Gustave Flaubert missed it—he flew in the face of a presumption and achieved a victory.

3. A favorite expression of James's, meaning the starting point, the original notion, the germ from which he develops his narrative.
4. French novelist (1821–1880).
5. Russian novelist (1818–1883). Also spelled Turgenev.

Nothing, of course, will ever take the place of the good old fashion of "liking" a work of art or not liking it: the most improved criticism will not abolish that primitive, that ultimate test. I mention this to guard myself from the accusation of intimating that the idea, the subject, of a novel or a picture, does not matter. It matters, to my sense, in the highest degree, and if I might put up a prayer it would be that artists should select none but the richest. Some, as I have already hastened to admit, are much more remunerative than others, and it would be a world happily arranged in which persons intending to treat them should be exempt from confusions and mistakes. This fortunate condition will arrive only, I fear, on the same day that critics become purged from error. Meanwhile, I repeat, we do not judge the artist with fairness unless we say to him, "Oh, I grant you your starting-point, because if I did not I should seem to prescribe to you, and heaven forbid I should take that responsibility. If I pretend to tell you what you must not take, you will call upon me to tell you then what you must take; in which case I shall be prettily caught. Moreover, it isn't till I have accepted your data that I can begin to measure you. I have the standard, the pitch; I have no right to tamper with your flute and then criticise your music. Of course I may not care for your idea at all; I may think it silly, or stale, or unclean; in which case I wash my hands of you altogether. I may content myself with believing that you will not have succeeded in being interesting, but I shall, of course, not attempt to demonstrate it, and you will be as indifferent to me as I am to you. I needn't remind you that there are all sorts of tastes: who can know it better? Some people, for excellent reasons, don't like to read about carpenters; others, for reasons even better, don't like to read about courtesans. Many object to Americans. Others (I believe they are mainly editors and publishers) won't look at Italians. Some readers don't like quiet subjects; others don't like bustling ones. Some enjoy a complete illusion, others the consciousness of large concessions. They choose their novels accordingly, and if they don't care about your idea they won't, *a fortiori*,[6] care about your treatment."

So that it comes back very quickly, as I have said, to the liking: in spite of M. Zola,[7] who reasons less powerfully than he represents, and who will not reconcile himself to this absoluteness of taste, thinking that there are certain things that people ought to like, and that they can be made to like. I am quite at a loss to imagine anything (at any rate in this matter of fiction) that people *ought* to like or to dislike. Selection will be sure to take care of itself, for it

6. Even more certainly.
7. Emile Zola (1840–1902), French novelist.

has a constant motive behind it. That motive is simply experience. As people feel life, so they will feel the art that is most closely related to it. This closeness of relation is what we should never forget in talking of the effort of the novel. Many people speak of it as a factitious, artificial form, a product of ingenuity, the business of which is to alter and arrange the things that surround us, to translate them into conventional, traditional moulds. This, however, is a view of the matter which carries us but a very short way, condemns the art to an eternal repetition of a few familiar *clichés* cuts short its development, and leads us straight up to a dead wall. Catching the very note and trick, the strange irregular rhythm of life, that is the attempt whose strenuous force keeps Fiction upon her feet. In proportion as in what she offers us we see life *without* rearrangement do we feel that we are touching the truth; in proportion as we see it *with* rearrangement do we feel that we are being put off with a substitute, a compromise and convention. It is not uncommon to hear an extraordinary assurance of remark in regard to this matter of rearranging, which is often spoken of as if it were the last word of art. Mr. Besant seems to me in danger of falling into the great error with his rather unguarded talk about "selection." Art is essentially selection, but it is a selection whose main care is to be typical, to be inclusive. For many people art means rose-coloured window-panes, and selection means picking a bouquet for Mrs. Grundy.[8] They will tell you glibly that artistic considerations have nothing to do with the disagreeable, with the ugly; they will rattle off shallow commonplaces about the province of art and the limits of art till you are moved to some wonder in return as to the province and the limits of ignorance. It appears to me that no one can ever have made a seriously artistic attempt without becoming conscious of an immense increase—a kind of revelation—of freedom. One perceives in that case—by the light of a heavenly ray—that the province of art is all life, all feeling, all observation, all vision. As Mr. Besant so justly intimates, it is all experience. That is a sufficient answer to those who maintain that it must not touch the sad things of life, who stick into its divine unconscious bosom little prohibitory inscriptions on the end of sticks, such as we see in public gardens—"It is forbidden to walk on the grass; it is forbidden to touch the flowers; it is not allowed to introduce dogs or to remain after dark; it is requested to keep to the right." The young aspirant in the line of fiction whom we continue to imagine will do nothing without taste, for in that case his freedom would be of little use to him; but the first advantage of his taste will be to reveal to

---

8. A character—and a symbol of conventional propriety—in *Speed the Plough* (1798), a play by Thomas Morton.

him the absurdity of the little sticks and tickets. If he have taste, I must add, of course he will have ingenuity, and my disrespectful reference to that quality just now was not meant to imply that it is useless in fiction. But it is only a secondary aid; the first is a capacity for receiving straight impressions.

Mr. Besant has some remarks on the question of "the story" which I shall not attempt to criticise, though they seem to me to contain a singular ambiguity, because I do not think I understand them. I cannot see what is meant by talking as if there were a part of a novel which is the story and part of it which for mystical reasons is not—unless indeed the distinction be made in a sense in which it is difficult to suppose that any one should attempt to convey anything. "The story," if it represents anything, represents the subject, the idea, the *donnée* of the novel; and there is surely no "school"—Mr. Besant speaks of a school—which urges that a novel should be all treatment and no subject. There must assuredly be something to treat; every school is intimately conscious of that. This sense of the story being the idea, the starting-point, of the novel, is the only one that I see in which it can be spoken of as something different from its organic whole; and since in proportion as the work is successful the idea permeates and penetrates it, informs and animates it, so that every word and every punctuation-point contribute directly to the expression, in that proportion do we lose our sense of the story being a blade which may be drawn more or less out of its sheath. The story and the novel, the idea and the form, are the needle and thread, and I never heard of a guild of tailors who recommended the use of the thread without the needle, or the needle without the thread. Mr. Besant is not the only critic who may be observed to have spoken as if there were certain things in life which constitute stories, and certain others which do not. I find the same odd implication in an entertaining article in the *Pall Mall Gazette,* devoted, as it happens, to Mr. Besant's lecture. "The story is the thing!" says this graceful writer, as if with a tone of opposition to some other idea. I should think it was, as every painter who, as the time for "sending in" his picture looms in the distance, finds himself still in quest of a subject—as every belated artist not fixed about his theme will heartily agree. There are some subjects which speak to us and others which do not, but he would be a clever man who should undertake to give a rule—an index expurgatorius[9]—by which the story and the no-story should be known apart. It is impossible (to me at least) to imagine any such rule which shall not be altogether arbitrary. The writer in the *Pall Mall* opposes the

9. The *Index Expurgatorius* is a list of books that the Roman Catholic Church allows its members to read only when expurgated or corrected.

delightful (as I suppose) novel of *Margot la Balafrée* to certain tales in which "Bostonian nymphs" appear to have "rejected English dukes for psychological reasons."[1] I am not acquainted with the romance just designated, and can scarcely forgive the *Pall Mall* critic for not mentioning the name of the author, but the title appears to refer to a lady who may have received a scar in some heroic adventure. I am inconsolable at not being acquainted with this episode, but am utterly at a loss to see why it is a story when the rejection (or acceptance) of a duke is not, and why a reason, psychological or other, is not a subject when a cicatrix is. They are all particles of the multitudinous life with which the novel deals, and surely no dogma which pretends to make it lawful to touch the one and unlawful to touch the other will stand for a moment on its feet. It is the special picture that must stand or fall, according as it seem to possess truth or to lack it. Mr. Besant does not, to my sense, light up the subject by intimating that a story must, under penalty of not being a story, consist of "adventures." Why of adventures more than of green spectacles? He mentions a category of impossible things, and among them he places "fiction without adventure." Why without adventure, more than without matrimony, or celibacy, or parturition, or cholera, or hydropathy, or Jansenism?[2] This seems to me to bring the novel back to the hapless little *rôle* of being an artificial, ingenious thing—bring it down from its large, free character of an immense and exquisite correspondence with life. And what *is* adventure, when it comes to that, and by what sign is the listening pupil to recognise it? It is an adventure—an immense one—for me to write this little article; and for a Bostonian nymph to reject an English duke is an adventure only less stirring, I should say, than for an English duke to be rejected by a Bostonian nymph. I see dramas within dramas in that, and innumerable points of view. A psychological reason is, to my imagination, an object adorably pictorial; to catch the tint of its complexion—I feel as if that idea might inspire one to Titianesque[3] efforts. There are few things more exciting to me, in short, than a psychological reason, and yet, I protest, the novel seems to me the most magnificent form of art. I have just been reading, at the same time, the delightful story of *Treasure Island*, by Mr. Robert Louis Stevenson[4] and, in a manner

1. This may refer either to James's own *Portrait of a Lady* (1881), in which Isabel Archer rejects an offer of marriage from Lord Warburton, or to his earlier "An International Episode."
2. The doctrine of Cornelius Jansen, a seventeenth-century Roman Catholic bishop in France.
3. In the (grand) manner of Titian (ca. 1477–1576), the Italian painter.
4. British novelist and poet (1850–1894). Also, incidentally, the author of "A Humble Remonstrance," an essay answering James. The result was an exchange of letters and a warm friendship between the two writers.

less consecutive, the last tale from M. Edmond de Goncourt,[5] which is entitled *Chérie*. One of these works treats of murders, mysteries, islands of dreadful renown, hairbreadth escapes, miraculous coincidences and buried doubloons. The other treats of a little French girl who lived in a fine house in Paris, and died of wounded sensibility because no one would marry her. I call *Treasure Island* delightful, because it appears to me to have succeeded wonderfully in what it attempts; and I venture to bestow no epithet upon *Chérie*, which strikes me as having failed deplorably in what it attempts—that is in tracing the development of the moral consciousness of a child. But one of these productions strikes me as exactly as much of a novel as the other, and as having a "story" quite as much. The moral consciousness of a child is as much a part of life as the islands of the Spanish Main, and the one sort of geography seems to me to have those "surprises" of which Mr. Besant speaks quite as much as the other. For myself (since it comes back in the last resort, as I say, to the preference of the individual), the picture of the child's experience has the advantage that I can at successive steps (an immense luxury, near to the "sensual pleasure" of which Mr. Besant's critic in the *Pall Mall* speaks) say Yes or No, as it may be, to what the artist puts before me. I have been a child in fact, but I have been on a quest for a buried treasure only in supposition, and it is a simple accident that with M. de Goncourt I should have for the most part to say No. With George Eliot,[6] when she painted that country with a far other intelligence, I always said Yes.

The most interesting part of Mr. Besant's lecture is unfortunately the briefest passage—his very cursory allusion to the "conscious moral purpose" of the novel. Here again it is not very clear whether he be recording a fact or laying down a principle; it is a great pity that in the latter case he should not have developed his idea. This branch of the subject is of immense importance, and Mr. Besant's few words point to considerations of the widest reach, not to be lightly disposed of. He will have treated the art of fiction but superficially who is not prepared to go every inch of the way that these considerations will carry him. It is for this reason that at the beginning of these remarks I was careful to notify the reader that my reflections on so large a theme have no pretension to be exhaustive. Like Mr. Besant, I have left the question of the morality of the novel till the last, and at the last I find I have used up my space. It is a question surrounded with difficulties, as witness the very first that meets us, in the form of a definite question, on the threshold.

5. French novelist and critic (1822–1896).
6. Pseudonym of Mary Ann Evans (1819–1880), British novelist.

Vagueness, in such a discussion, is fatal, and what is the meaning of your morality and your conscious moral purpose? Will you not define your terms and explain how (a novel being a picture) a picture can be either moral or immoral? You wish to paint a moral picture or carve a moral statue: will you not tell us how you would set about it? We are discussing the Art of Fiction; questions of art are questions (in the widest sense) of execution; questions of morality are quite another affair, and will you not let us see how it is that you find it so easy to mix them up? These things are so clear to Mr. Besant that he has deduced from them a law which he sees embodied in English Fiction, and which is "a truly admirable thing and a great cause for congratulation." It is a great cause for congratulation indeed when such thorny problems become as smooth as silk. I may add that in so far as Mr. Besant perceives that in point of fact English Fiction has addressed itself preponderantly to these delicate questions he will appear to many people to have made a vain discovery. They will have been positively struck, on the contrary, with the moral timidity of the usual English novelist; with his (or with her) aversion to face the difficulties with which on every side the treatment of reality bristles. He is apt to be extremely shy (whereas the picture that Mr. Besant draws is a picture of boldness), and the sign of his work, for the most part, is a cautious silence on certain subjects. In the English novel (by which of course I mean the American as well), more than in any other, there is a traditional difference between that which people know and that which they agree to admit that they know, that which they see and that which they speak of, that which they feel to be a part of life and that which they allow to enter into literature. There is the great difference, in short, between what they talk of in conversation and what they talk of in print. The essence of moral energy is to survey the whole field, and I should directly reverse Mr. Besant's remark and say not that the English novel has a purpose, but that it has a diffidence. To what degree a purpose in a work of art is a source of corruption I shall not attempt to inquire; the one that seems to me least dangerous is the purpose of making a perfect work. As for our novel, I may say lastly on this score that as we find it in England to-day it strikes me as addressed in a large degree to "young people," and that this in itself constitutes a presumption that it will be rather shy. There are certain things which it is generally agreed not to discuss, not even to mention, before young people. That is very well, but the absence of discussion is not a symptom of the moral passion. The purpose of the English novel—"a truly admirable thing, and a great cause for congratulation"—strikes me therefore as rather negative.

There is one point at which the moral sense and the artistic sense lie very near together; that is in the light of the very obvious truth that the deepest quality of a work of art will always be the quality of the mind of the producer. In proportion as that intelligence is fine will the novel, the picture, the statue partake of the substance of beauty and truth. To be constituted of such elements is, to my vision, to have purpose enough. No good novel will ever proceed from a superficial mind; that seems to me an axiom which, for the artist in fiction, will cover all needful moral ground: if the youthful aspirant take it to heart it will illuminate for him many of the mysteries of "purpose." There are many other useful things that might be said to him, but I have come to the end of my article, and can only touch them as I pass. The critic in the *Pall Mall Gazette,* whom I have already quoted, draws attention to the danger, in speaking of the art of fiction, of generalising. The danger that he has in mind is rather, I imagine, that of particularising, for there are some comprehensive remarks which, in addition to those embodied in Mr. Besant's suggestive lecture, might without fear of misleading him be addressed to the ingenuous student. I should remind him first of the magnificence of the form that is open to him, which offers to sight so few restrictions and such innumerable opportunities. The other arts, in comparison, appear confined and hampered; the various conditions under which they are exercised are so rigid and definite. But the only condition that I can think of attaching to the composition of the novel is, as I have already said, that it be sincere. This freedom is a splendid privilege, and the first lesson of the young novelist is to learn to be worthy of it. "Enjoy it as it deserves," I should say to him; "take possession of it, explore it to its utmost extent, publish it, rejoice in it. All life belongs to you, and do not listen either to those who would shut you up into corners of it and tell you that it is only here and there that art inhabits, or to those who would persuade you that this heavenly messenger wings her way outside of life altogether, breathing a superfine air, and turning away her head from the truth of things. There is no impression of life, no manner of seeing it and feeling it, to which the plan of the novelist may not offer a place; you have only to remember that talents so dissimilar as those of Alexandre Dumas and Jane Austen,[7] Charles Dickens and Gustave Flaubert have worked in this field with equal glory. Do not think too much about optimism and pessimism; try and catch the colour of life itself. In France to-day we see a prodigious effort (that of Emile Zola, to whose solid and serious work no explorer of the capacity of the novel can allude with-

---

7. Austen (1775–1815), the British novelist, and Dumas (1802–1870), the French novelist and dramatist. For the contrast James is less likely to have thought of the son, Alexandre Dumas (1824–1895) known as "Dumas *fils.*"

out respect), we see an extraordinary effort vitiated by a spirit of pessimism on a narrow basis. M. Zola is magnificent, but he strikes an English reader as ignorant; he has an air of working in the dark; if he had as much light as energy, his results would be of the highest value. As for the aberrations of a shallow optimism, the ground (of English fiction especially) is strewn with their brittle particles as with broken glass. If you must indulge in conclusions, let them have the taste of a wide knowledge. Remember that your first duty is to be as complete as possible—to make as perfect a work. Be generous and delicate and pursue the prize."

From His Notebooks†

[*On the origin of "Brooksmith"*]

[LONDON, JUNE 19, 1884]

Another little thing was told me the other day by Mrs. R. about D<uncan> S<tewart>'s little maid (lady's maid), Past, who was with her for years before her death, and whom I often saw there. She had to find a new place of course, on Mrs. S.'s death, to relapse into ordinary service. Her sorrow, the way she felt the change, and the way she expressed it to Mrs. R. "Ah yes, ma'am, you have lost your mother, and it's a great grief, but what is your loss to mine?" (She was devoted to Mrs. D.S.) "You continue to see good society, to live with clever, cultivated people: but I fall again into my own class, I shall never see such company—hear such talk—again. She was so good to me that I lived *with* her, as it were; and nothing will ever make up to me again for the loss of her conversation. Common, vulgar people now: that's my lot for the future!" Represent this —the refined nature of the little plain, quiet woman—her appreciation—and the way her new conditions sicken her, with a denouement if possible. Represent first, of course, her life with the old lady—figure of old Mrs. D. S. (modified)—her interior—her talk. Mrs. R.'s relations with her servants. "My child—my dear child."

† From *The Notebooks of Henry James*, ed. F. O. Matthiessen and Kenneth Murdock (New York: Oxford University Press, 1947), pp. 64, 71–72, 102–4, 121–22, 311, 367–68. Copyright © Oxford University Press, Inc. Used by permission of Oxford University Press, Inc. Except as noted, the footnotes for these selections are by the editors of this Norton Critical Edition.

[On the origin of "The Aspern Papers"]

[FLORENCE, JANUARY 12, 1887]

Hamilton (V.L.'s brother) told me a curious thing of Capt. Silsbee—the Boston art-critic and Shelley-worshipper; that is of a curious adventure of his. Miss Claremont,[1] Bryon's *ci-devant* mistress[2] (the mother of Allegra) was living, until lately, here in Florence, at a great age, 80 or thereabouts, and with her lived her niece, a younger Miss Claremont—of about 50. Silsbee knew that they had interesting papers—letters of Shelley's and Byron's—he had known it for a long time and cherished the idea of getting hold of them. To this end he laid the plan of going to lodge with the Misses Claremont—hoping that the old lady in view of her great age and failing condition would die while he was there, so that he might then put his hand upon the documents, which she hugged close in life. He carried out this scheme—and things *se passèrent*[3] as he had expected. The old woman *did* die—and then he approached the younger one—the old maid of 50—on the subject of his desires. Her answer was—'I will give you all the letters if you marry me!' H. says that Silsbee *court encore!*[4] Certainly there is a little subject there: the picture of the two faded, queer, poor and discredited old English women—living on into a strange generation, in their musty corner of a foreign town—with these illustrious letters their most precious possession. Then the plot of the Shelley fanatic—his watchings and waitings—the way he *couvers*[5] the treasure. The denouement needn't be the one related of poor Silsbee; and at any rate the general situation is in itself a subject and a picture. It strikes me much. The interest would be in some price that the man has to pay—that the old woman—or the survivor—sets upon the papers. His hesitations—his struggle—for he really would give almost anything.—The Countess Gamba came in while I was there: her husband is a nephew of the Guiccioli—and it was *à propos* of their having a lot of Byron's letters of which they are rather illiberal and dangerous guardians, that H. told me the above. They won't show them or publish any of them—and the Countess was very angry once on H.'s representing to her that it was her duty—especially to the English public!—to let them at least be seen. *Elle se fiche bien*[6] of the English public. She says the letters—addressed

1. Clairmont is the usual form of the name, and the one used by James in his preface to *The Aspern Papers* [Note by Matthiessen and Myrdock].
2. Ex-mistress.
3. Happened, took place.
4. Is still running.
5. Here James uses the infinitive of a French verb—*couver* ["to brood over"—*Editor*] and adds an English termination [*Note by Matthiessen and Murdock*].
6. She doesn't give a hoot. (She couldn't care less.)

in Italian to the Guiccioli—are discreditable to Byron; and H. elicited from her that she had *burned* one of them!

[*On the origin of "The Real Thing"*]

PARIS, HOTEL WESTMINSTER, FEBRUARY 22, 1891

In pursuance of my plan of writing some very short tales—things of from 7000 to 10,000 words, the easiest length to "place," I began yesterday the little story that was suggested to me some time ago by an incident related to me by George du Maurier[7]—the lady and gentleman who called upon him with a word from Frith, an oldish, faded, ruined pair—he an officer in the army—who unable to turn a penny in any other way, were trying to find employment as models. I was struck with the pathos, the oddity and typicalness of the situation—the little tragedy of good-looking gentlefolk, who had been all their life stupid and well-dressed, living, on a fixed income, at country-houses, watering places and clubs, like so many others of their class in England, and were now utterly unable to *do* anything, had no cleverness, no art nor craft to make use of as a *gagne-pain*[8]—could only *show* themselves, clumsily, for the fine, clean, well-groomed animals that they were, only hope to make a little money by—in this manner—just simply *being*. I thought I saw a subject for very brief treatment in this *donnée*[9]—and I think I do still; but to do anything worth while with it I must (as always, great Heavens!) be very clear as to what is in it and what I wish to get out of it. I tried a beginning yesterday, but I instantly became conscious that I must straighten out the little idea. It must be an idea—it can't be a "story" in the vulgar sense of the word. It must be a picture; it must illustrate something. God knows that's enough—if the thing *does* illustrate. To make little anecdotes of this kind real *morceaux de vie*[1] is a plan quite inspiring enough. *Voyons un peu,*[2] therefore, what one can put into this one—I mean how much of life. One must put a little action—not a stupid, mechanical, arbitrary action, but something that is of the real essence of the subject. I thought of representing the husband as jealous of the wife—that is, jealous of the artist employing her, from the moment that, in point of fact, she begins to sit. But this is vulgar and obvious—worth nothing. What I wish to represent is the baffled, ineffectual, incompetent character of their attempt, and how it illustrates once again the everlasting English amateurishness—the way superficial,

7. British novelist and illustrator (1834–1896).
8. Livelihood.
9. Notion, idea.
1. Slices of life.
2. Let's see now.

untrained, unprofessional effort goes to the wall when confronted with trained, competitive, intelligent, *qualified* art—in whatever line it may be a question of. It is out of *that* element that my little action and movement must come; and now I begin to see just how—as one always *does*—Glory be to the Highest—when one begins to look at a thing hard and straight and seriously—to fix it—as I am so sadly lax and desultory about doing. What subjects I should find—for *everything*—if I could only achieve this more as a habit! Let my contrast and complication here come from the opposition —to my melancholy Major and his wife—of a couple of little vulgar professional people *who know,* with the consequent bewilderment, vagueness, depression of the former—their failure to understand how such people can be better than *they*—their failure, disappointment, disappearance—going forth into the vague again. *Il y a bien quelque chose à tirer de ça.*[3] They have no pictorial sense. They are only clean and stiff and stupid. The others are dirty, even—the melancholy Major and his wife remark on it, wondering. The artist is beginning a big illustrated book, a new edition of a famous novel—say *Tom Jones*; and he is willing to try to work them in— for he takes an interest in their predicament, and feels—sceptically, but, with his flexible artistic sympathy—the appeal of their type. He is willing to give them a trial. Make it out that *he* himself is on trial—he is young and "rising," but he has still his golden spurs to win. He can't afford, *en somme,*[4] to make many mistakes. He has regular work in drawing every week for a serial novel in an illustrated paper; but the great project—that of a big house—of issuing an illustrated Fielding[5] promises him a big lift. He has been intrusted with (say) *Joseph Andrews,* experimentally; he will have to do this brilliantly in order to have the engagement for the rest confirmed. He has already 2 models in his service—the "complication" must come from *them.* One is a common clever, London girl, of the smallest origin and without conventional beauty, but of aptitude, of perceptions—knowing thoroughly *how.* She says "lydy" and "plice,"[6] but she has the pictorial sense; and can look like anything he wants her to look like. She poses, in short, in perfection. So does her colleague, a professional Italian, a little fellow—ill dressed, smelling of garlic, but admirably serviceable, quite universal. They must be contrasted, confronted, *juxtaposed* with the others; whom they take for people who *pay,* themselves, till they learn the truth when they are overwhelmed with derisive amazement. The denouement simply that the melancholy Major and his wife won't do—

3. Something can certainly be made of this.
4. In short.
5. Henry Fielding (1707–1764), British novelist, author of *Tom Jones* and *Joseph Andrews.*
6. Cockney pronunciations of *lady* and *place.*

they're not "in it." Their surprise—their helpless, proud assent—
without other prospects: yet at the same time *their* degree of more
silent amazement at the success of the two inferior people—who
are so much less nice-looking than themselves. Frankly, however,
is this contrast enough of a *story*, by itself? It seems to me Yes—
for it's an IDEA—and how the deuce should I get *more* into 7000
words? It must be simply 50 pp. of my manuscript. The little tale
of *The Servant* (*Brooksmith*) which I did the other day for *Black
and White* and which I thought of at the same time as this, proved
a very tight squeeze into the same tiny number of words, and I
probably shall find that there is much more to be done with this
than the compass will admit of. Make it tremendously succinct—
with a very short pulse or rhythm—and the closest selection of
detail—in other words *summarize* intensely and keep down the lat-
eral development. It *should* be a little gem of bright, quick, vivid
form. I shall get every grain of "action" that the space admits of if
I make something, for the artist, hang in the balance—depend on
the way he does this particular work. It's when he finds that he
shall lose his great opportunity if he keeps on with them, that he
has to tell the gentlemanly couple, that, frankly, they won't serve
his turn—and make them wander forth into the cold world again.
I must keep them the age I've made them—50 and 40—because
it's more touching; but I must bring up the age of the 2 real models
to almost the same thing. That increases the incomprehensibility
(to the amateurs) of their usefulness. Picture the immanence, in
the latter, of the idle, provided-for, country-house habit—the blankness of their *manière d'être*.[7] But in how tremendously few words I
must do it. This is a lesson—a *magnificent* lesson—if I'm to do a
good many. Something as admirably compact and selected as
Maupassant.[8]

[*On the origin of "The Middle Years"*]

[LONDON, DE VERE GARDENS, MAY 12, 1892]

The idea of the old artist, or man of letters, who, at the end, feels
a kind of anguish of desire for a respite, a prolongation—another
period of life to do the *real* thing that he has in him—the things
for which all the others have been but a slow preparation. He is
the man who has developed late, obstructedly, with difficulty, has
needed all life to learn, to see his way, to collect material, and now
feels that if he can only have another life to make use of this clear
start, he can show what he is really capable of. Some incident, then,

7. Way of life.
8. Guy de Maupassant (1850–1893), French short story writer and novelist.

to show that what he *has* done *is* that of which he is capable—that he has done all he can, that he has put into his things the love of perfection and that they will live by that. Or else an incident acting just the other way—showing him what he might do, just when he must give up forever. The 1st idea the best. A young doctor, a young pilgrim who admires him. A deep sleep in which he dreams he *has* had his respite. Then his waking to find that what he has dreamed of is only what he has *done*.

[*On the origin of "The Beast in the Jungle"*]

[RYE, LAMB HOUSE, AUGUST 27, 1901]

Meanwhile there is something else—a very tiny *fantaisie*[9] probably—in small notion that comes to me of a man haunted by the fear, more and more, throughout life, that *something will happen to him*: he doesn't quite know what. His life *seems* safe and ordered, his liabilities and exposures (as a *result* of the fear) a good deal curtailed and cut down, so that the years go by and the stroke doesn't fall. Yet "It *will* come, it will still come," he finds himself believing—and indeed saying to some one, some second-consciousness in the anecdote. "It will come before death; I shan't die without it." Finally I think it must be *he* who sees—not the 2d consciousness. Mustn't indeed the "2nd consciousness" be some woman, and it be she who *helps* him to see? She has always loved him—yes, *that*, for the story, "pretty," and he, saying, protecting, exempting his life (always, really, with and *for* the fear), has never known it. He likes her, talks to her, confides in her, sees her often—*la côtoie*, as to her hidden passion, but never guesses.[1] She meanwhile, all the time, sees his life as it is. It is to her that he tells his fear—yes, she is the "2nd consciousness." At first she *feels*, herself, for him, his feeling of his fear, and is tender, reassuring, protective. Then she reads, as I say, his real case, and is, though unexpressedly, *lucid*. The years go by and *she sees the thing not happen*. At last one day they are somehow, some day, face to face over it, and then she speaks. "It *has*, the great thing you've always lived in dread of, had the foreboding of—it *has* happened to you." He wonders—when, how, what? "What is it?—why, it is that *nothing* has happened!" Then, later on, I think, to keep up the prettiness, it must be that HE sees, that he understands. She has loved him always—and *that* might have happened. But it's too late—she's dead. That, I think, at least, he comes to later on, after an interval, after her death. She is dying, or ill, when she says it. He *then* DOESN'T understand,

9. Odd fancy.
1. "Keeps coming close" to the question of her secret passion without ever catching on.

doesn't see—or so far, only as to agree with her, ruefully, that that
very well *may* be it: that nothing has happened. He goes back; she
is gone; she is dead. *What* she has said to him has in a way, by its
truth, created the need for her, made him want her, *positively* want
her, more. But she is gone, he has lost her, and *then* he sees all
she has meant. She has loved him. (*It must come for the* READER
thus, at this moment.) With his base safety and shrinkage he never
knew. *That* was what might have happened, and what *has* happened
is that it didn't.

[*Regarding "The Jolly Corner" in retrospect*]

[LONDON, 1914]

The most intimate idea of *that*[2] is that my hero's adventure there
takes the form so to speak of his turning the tables, as I think I
called it, on a "ghost" or whatever, a visiting or haunting apparition
otherwise qualified to appal *him*; and thereby winning a sort of
victory by the appearance, and the evidence, that this personage or
presence was more overwhelmingly affected by him than he by *it*.

From His Prefaces

[*On "Daisy Miller"*]†

It was in Rome during the autumn of 1877; a friend then living
there but settled now in a South less weighted with appeals and
memories happened to mention . . . some simple and uninformed
American lady of the previous winter, whose young daughter, a
child of nature and of freedom, accompanying her from hotel to
hotel, had "picked up" by the wayside, with the best conscience in
the world, a good-looking Roman, of vague identity, astonished at
his luck, yet . . . all innocently, all serenely exhibited and introduced: this at least till the occurrence of some small social check,
some interrupting incident, of no great gravity or dignity, and which
I forget. I had never heard, save on this showing, of the amiable
but not otherwise eminent ladies, who weren't in fact named, I
think, and whose case had merely served to point a familiar moral;
and it must have been just their want of salience that left a margin
for the small pencil-mark inveterately signifying, in such connexions, "Dramatise, dramatise!" The result of my recognising a few

---

2. "The Jolly Corner."
† From *The Novels and Tales of Henry James*, vol. 18 (New York: Charles Scribner's Sons,
   1909), pp. v–viii. All notes to the prefaces are by the editors of this Norton Critical
   Edition.

months later the sense of my pencil-mark was the short chronicle of "Daisy Miller," which I indited in London the following spring and then addressed, with no conditions attached, as I remember, to the editor of a magazine[1] that had its seat of publication at Philadelphia and had lately appeared to appreciate my contributions. That gentleman however (an historian of some repute) promptly returned me my missive, and with an absence of comment that struck me at the time as rather grim—as, given the circumstances, requiring indeed some explanation: till a friend to whom I appealed for light, giving him the thing to read, declared it could only have passed with the Philadelphian critic for "an outrage on American girlhood." This was verily a light, and of bewildering intensity; though I was presently to read into the matter a further helpful inference. To the fault of being outrageous this little composition added that of being essentially and pre-eminently a *nouvelle*; a signal example in fact of that type, foredoomed at the best, in more cases than not, to editorial disfavour. If accordingly I was afterwards to be cradled, almost blissfully, in the conception that "Daisy" at least, among my productions, might approach "success," such success for example, on her eventual appearance, as the state of being promptly pirated in Boston—a sweet tribute I hadn't yet received and was never again to know—the irony of things yet claimed its rights, I couldn't but long continue to feel, in the circumstance that quite a special reprobation had waited on the first appearance in the world of the ultimately most prosperous child of my invention. So doubly discredited, at all events, this bantling met indulgence, with no great delay, in the eyes of my admirable friend the late Leslie Stephen[2] and was published in two numbers of *The Cornhill Magazine* (1878).

It qualified itself in that publication and afterwards as "a Study"; for reasons which I confess I fail to recapture unless they may have taken account simply of a certain flatness in my poor little heroine's literal denomination. Flatness indeed, one must have felt, was the very sum of her story; so that perhaps after all the attached epithet was meant but as a deprecation, addressed to the reader, of any great critical hope of stirring scenes. It provided for mere concentration, and on an object scant and superficially vulgar—from which, however, a sufficiently brooding tenderness might eventually extract a shy incongruous charm. I suppress at all events here the appended qualification—in view of the simple truth, which ought from the first to have been apparent to me, that my little exhibition

---

1. *Lippincott's Magazine.*
2. British man of letters (1832–1904)—philosopher, critic, biographer, editor of the *Dictionary of National Biography*, father of Virginia Woolf.

is made to no degree whatever in critical but, quite inordinately and extravagantly, in poetical terms. It comes back to me that I was at a certain hour long afterwards to have reflected, in this connexion, on the characteristic free play of the whirligig of time. It was in Italy again—in Venice and in the prized society of an interesting friend, now dead, with whom I happened to wait, on the Grand Canal, at the animated water-steps of one of the hotels. The considerable little terrace there was so disposed as to make a salient stage for certain demonstrations on the part of two young girls, children *they*, if ever, of nature and of freedom, whose use of those resources, in the general public eye, and under our own as we sat in the gondola, drew from the lips of a second companion, sociably afloat with us, the remark that there before us, with no sign absent, were a couple of attesting Daisy Millers. Then it was that, in my charming hostess's prompt protest, the whirligig, as I have called it, at once betrayed itself. "How can you liken *those* creatures to a figure of which the only fault is touchingly to have transmuted so sorry a type and to have, by a poetic artifice, not only led our judgement of it astray, but made *any* judgement quite impossible?" With which this gentle lady and admirable critic turned on the author himself. "You *know* you quite falsified, by the turn you gave it, the thing you had begun with having in mind, the thing you had had, to satiety, the chance of 'observing': your pretty perversion of it, or your unprincipled mystification of our sense of it, does it really too much honour—in spite of which, none the less, as anything charming or touching always to that extent justifies itself, we after a fashion forgive and understand you. But why *waste* your romance? There are cases, too many, in which you've done it again; in which, provoked by a spirit of observation at first no doubt sufficiently sincere, and with the measured and felt truth fairly twitching your sleeve, you have yielded to your incurable prejudice in favour of grace—to whatever it is in you that makes so inordinately for form and prettiness and pathos; not to say sometimes for misplaced drolling. Is it that you've after all too much imagination? Those awful young women capering at the hotel-door, *they* are the real little Daisy Millers that were; whereas yours in the tale is such a one, more's the pity, as—for pitch of the ingenuous, for quality of the artless—couldn't possibly have been at all." My answer to all which bristled of course with more professions that I can or need report here; the chief of them inevitably to the effect that my supposedly typical little figure was of course pure poetry, and had never been anything else; since this is what helpful imagination, in however slight a dose, ever directly makes for.

[On "The Aspern Papers"]†

I not only recover with ease, but I delight to recall, the first impulse given to the idea of "The Aspern Papers." It is at the same
time true that my present mention of it may perhaps too effectually
dispose of any complacent claim to my having "found" the situation.
Not that I quite know indeed what situations the seeking fabulist
does "find"; he seeks them enough assuredly, but his discoveries
are, like those of the navigator, the chemist, the biologist, scarce
more than alert recognitions. He *comes upon* the interesting thing
as Columbus came upon the isle of San Salvador, because he had
moved in the right direction for it—also because he knew, with the
encounter, what "making land" then and there represented. Nature
had so placed it, to profit—if as profit we may measure the
matter!—by his fine unrest, just as history, "literary history" we in
this connexion call it, had in an out-of-the-way corner of the great
garden of life thrown off a curious flower that I was to feel worth
gathering as soon as I saw it. I got wind of my positive fact, I
followed the scent. It was in Florence years ago; which is precisely,
of the whole matter, what I like most to remember. The air of the
old-time Italy invests it, a mixture that on the faintest invitation I
rejoice again to inhale—and this in spite of the mere cold renewal,
ever, of the infirm side of that felicity, the sense, in the whole
element, of things too numerous, too deep, too obscure, too strange,
or even simply too beautiful, for any ease of intellectual relation.
One must pay one's self largely with words, I think, one must induce almost any "Italian subject" *to make believe* it gives up its
secret, in order to keep at all on working—or call them perhaps
rather playing—terms with the general impression. We entertain it
thus, the impression, by the aid of a merciful convention which
resembles the fashion of our intercourse with Iberians or Orientals
whose form of courtesy places everything they have at our disposal.
We thank them and call upon them, but without acting on their
professions. The offer has been too large and our assurance is too
small; we peep at most into two or three of the chambers of their
hospitality, with the rest of the case stretching beyond our ken and
escaping our penetration. The pious fiction suffices; we have entered, we have seen, we are charmed. So, right and left, in Italy—
before the great historic complexity at least—penetration fails; we
scratch at the extensive surface, we meet the perfunctory smile, we
hang about in the golden air. But we exaggerate our gathered values
only if we are eminently witless. It is fortunately the exhibition in

† From *The Novels and Tales of Henry James*, vol. 12 (New York: Charles Scribner's Sons,
1908), pp. v–xiv.

all the world before which, as admirers, we can most remain superficial without feeling silly.

All of which I note, however, perhaps with too scant relevance
to the inexhaustible charm of Roman and Florentine memories. Off
the ground, at a distance, our fond indifference to being "silly"
grows fonder still; the working convention, as I have called it—the
convention of the real revelations and surrenders on one side and
the real immersions and appreciations on the other—has not only
nothing to keep it down, but every glimpse of contrast, every pang
of exile and every nostalgic twinge to keep it up. These latter haunting presences in fact, let me note, almost reduce at first to a mere
blurred, sad, scarcely consolable vision this present revisiting, re-
appropriating impulse. There are parts of one's past, evidently, that
bask consentingly and serenely enough in the light of other days—
which is but the intensity of thought; and there are other parts that
take it as with agitation and pain, a troubled consciousness that
heaves as with the disorder of drinking it deeply in. So it is at any
rate, fairly in too thick and rich a retrospect, that I see my old
Venice of "The Aspern Papers," that I see the still earlier one of
Jeffrey Aspern himself, and that I see even the comparatively recent
Florence that was to drop into my ear the solicitation of these
things. I would fain "lay it on" thick for the very love of them—
that at least I may profess; and, with the ground of this desire
frankly admitted, something that somehow makes, in the whole
story, for a romantic harmony. * * * I shall presently say why this
small case so ranges itself, but must first refer more exactly to the
thrill of appreciation it was immediately to excite in me. I saw it
somehow at the very first blush as romantic—for the use, of course
I mean, I should certainly have had to make of it—that Jane Clairmont, the half-sister of Mary Godwin, Shelley's second wife and for
a while the intimate friend of Byron and the mother of his daughter
Allegra, should have been living on in Florence, where she had long
lived, up to our own day, and that in fact, had I happened to hear
of her but a little sooner, I might have seen her in the flesh. The
question of whether I should have wished to do so was another
matter—the question of whether I shouldn't have preferred to keep
her preciously unseen, to run no risk, in other words, by too rude
a choice, of depreciating that romance-value which, as I say, it was
instantly inevitable to attach (through association above all, with
another signal circumstance) to her long survival.

I had luckily not had to deal with the difficult option; difficult in
such a case by reason of that odd law which somehow always makes
the minimum of valid suggestion serve the man of imagination better than the maximum. The historian, essentially, wants more documents than he can really use; the dramatist only wants more

liberties than he can really take. Nothing, fortunately, however, had,
as the case stood, depended on my delicacy; I might have "looked
up" Miss Clairmont in previous years had I been earlier informed
—the silence about her seemed full of the "irony of fate"; but I felt
myself more concerned with the mere strong fact of her having
testified for the reality and the closeness of our relation to the past
than with any question of the particular sort of person I might have
flattered myself I "found." I had certainly at the very least been
saved the undue simplicity of pretending to read meanings into
things absolutely sealed and beyond test or proof—to tap a fount
of waters that couldn't possibly not have run dry. The thrill of learning that she had "overlapped," and by so much, and the wonder of
my having doubtless at several earlier seasons passed again and
again, all unknowing, the door of her house, where she sat above,
within call and in her habit as she lived, these things gave me all I
wanted; I seem to remember in fact that my more or less immediately recognising that I positively oughtn't—"for anything to come
of it"—to have wanted more. I saw, quickly, how something might
come of it *thus*: whereas a fine instinct told me that the effect of a
nearer view of the case (the case of the overlapping) would probably
have had to be quite differently calculable. It was really with another item of knowledge, however, that I measured the mistake I
should have made in waking up sooner to the question of opportunity. That item consisted of the action taken on the premises by
a person who *had* waked up in time, and the legend of whose consequent adventure, as a few spoken words put it before me, at once
kindled a flame. This gentleman, an American of long ago, an ardent Shelleyite, a singularly marked figure and himself in the highest degree a subject for a free sketch—I had known him a little,
but there is not a reflected glint of him in "The Aspern Papers"—
was named to me as having made interest with Miss Clairmont to
be accepted as a lodger on the calculation that she would have
Shelley documents for which, in the possibly not remote event of
her death, he would thus enjoy priority of chance to treat with her
representatives. He had at any rate, according to the legend, become, on earnest Shelley grounds, her yearning, though also her
highly diplomatic, *pensionnaire*[3]—but without gathering, as was to
befall, the fruit of his design.

Legend here dropped to another key; it remained in a manner
interesting, but became to my ear a trifle coarse, or at least rather
vague and obscure. It mentioned a younger female relative of the
ancient woman as a person who, for a queer climax, had had to be
dealt with; it flickered so for a moment and then, as a light, to my

3. Lodger, boarder.

great relief, quite went out. It had flickered indeed but at the best
—yet had flickered enough to give me my "facts," bare facts of
intimation; which, scant handful though they were, were more distinct and more numerous than I mostly *like* facts: like them, that
is, as we say of an etcher's progressive subject, in an early "state."
Nine tenths of the artist's interest in them is that of what he shall
add to them and how he shall turn them. Mine, however, in the
connexion I speak of, had fortunately got away from me, and quite
of their own movement, in time not to crush me. So it was, at all
events, that my imagination preserved power to react under the
mere essential charm—that, I mean, of a final scene of the rich
dim Shelley drama played out in the very theatre of our own "modernity." This was the beauty that appealed to me; there had been,
so to speak, a forward continuity, from the actual man, the divine
poet, on; and the curious, the ingenious, the admirable thing would
be to throw it backward again, to compress—squeezing it hard!—
the connexion that had drawn itself out, and convert so the
stretched relation into a value of nearness on our own part. In short
I saw my chance as admirable, and one reason, when the direction
is right, may serve as well as fifty; but if I "took over," as I say,
everything that was of the essence, I stayed my hand for the rest.
The Italian side of the legend closely clung; if only because the so
possible terms of my Juliana's life in the Italy of other days could
make conceivable for her the fortunate privacy, the long uninvaded
and uninterviewed state on which I represent her situation as
founded. Yes, a surviving unexploited unparagraphed Juliana was
up to a quarter of a century since still supposeable—as much so as
any such buried treasure, any such grave unprofaned, would defy
probability now. And then the case had the air of the past just in
the degree in which that air, I confess, most appeals to me—when
the region over which it hangs is far enough away without being
too far.

I delight in a palpable imaginable *visitable* past—in the nearer
distances and the clearer mysteries, the marks and signs of a world
we may reach over to as by making a long arm we grasp an object
at the other end of our own table. The table is the one, the common
expanse, and where we lean, so stretching, we find it firm and continuous. That, to my imagination, is the past fragrant of all, or
of almost all, the poetry of the thing outlived and lost and gone,
and yet in which the precious element of closeness, telling so of
connexions but tasting so of differences, remains appreciable. * * * We are divided of course between liking to feel the past
strange and liking to feel it familiar; the difficulty is, for intensity,
to catch it at the moment when the scales of the balance hang with
the right evenness. I say for intensity, for we may profit by them in

other aspects enough if we are content to measure or to feel loosely. It would take me too far, however, to tell why the particular afternoon light that I thus call intense rests clearer to my sense on the Byronic age, as I conveniently name it, than on periods more protected by the "dignity" of history. With the times beyond, intrinsically more "strange," the tender grace, for the backward vision, has faded, the afternoon darkened; for any time nearer to us the special effect hasn't begun. So there, to put the matter crudely, is the appeal I fondly recognise, an appeal residing doubtless more in the "special effect," in some deep associational force, than in a virtue more intrinsic. I am afraid I must add, since I allow myself so much to fantasticate, that the impulse had more than once taken me to project the Byronic age and the afternoon light across the great sea, to see in short whether association would carry so far and what the young century might pass for on that side of the modern world where it was not only itself so irremediably youngest, but was bound up with youth in everything else. There was a refinement of curiosity in this imputation of a golden strangeness to American social facts—though I cannot pretend, I fear, that there was any greater wisdom.

Since what it had come to then was, harmlessly enough, cultivating a sense of the past under that close protection, it was natural, it was fond and filial, to wonder if a few of the distilled drops mightn't be gathered from some vision of, say, "old" New York. Would that human congeries, to aid obligingly in the production of a fable, be conceivable as "taking" the afternoon light with the right happy slant?—or could a recogniseable reflexion of the Byronic age, in other words, be picked up on the banks of the Hudson? (Only just there, beyond the great sea, if anywhere: in no other connexion would the question so much as raise its head. I admit that Jeffrey Aspern isn't even feebly localised, but I *thought* New York as I projected him.) It was "amusing," in any case, always, to try experiments; and the experiment for the right *transposition* of my Juliana would be to fit her out with an immortalising poet as transposed as herself. Delicacy had demanded, I felt, that my appropriation of the Florentine legend should purge it, first of all, of references too obvious; so that, to begin with, I shifted the scene of the adventure. Juliana, as I saw her, was thinkable only in Byronic and more or less immediately post-Byronic Italy; but there were conditions in which she was ideally arrangeable, as happened, especially in respect to the later time and the long undetected survival; there being absolutely no refinement of the mouldy rococo, in human or whatever other form, that you may not disembark at the dislocated water-steps of almost any decayed monument of Venetian greatness in auspicious quest of. It was a question, in fine, of covering one's tracks—though with no great elaboration I am bound to admit; and I felt I couldn't cover mine more than in postulating a comparative American Byron to match an American Miss Clairmont—she as absolute as she would. I scarce know whether best to say for this device to-day that it cost me little or that it cost me much; it was "cheap" or expensive according to the degree of verisimilitude artfully obtained. If that degree appears *nil* the "art," such as it was, is wasted, and my rememberance of the contention, on the part of a highly critical friend who at that time and later on often had my ear, that it had been simply foredoomed to be wasted, puts before me the passage in the private history of "The Aspern Papers," that I now find, I confess, most interesting.   *   *   *

My friend's argument bore then—at the time and afterward—on my vicious practice, as he maintained, of postulating for the purpose of my fable celebrities who not only *hadn't* existed in the conditions I imputed to them, but who for the most part (and in no case more markedly than in that of Jeffrey Aspern) couldn't possibly have done so.   *   *   *

The charge being that I foist upon our early American annals a distinguished presence for which they yield me absolutely no warrant—"Where, within them, gracious heaven, were we to look for so much as an approach to the social elements of habitat and climate of birds of that note and plumage?"—I find his link with reality then just in the tone of the picture wrought round him. What was that tone but exactly, but exquisitely, calculated, the harmless hocus-pocus under cover of which we might suppose him to have existed? This tone is the tone, artistically speaking, of "amusement," the current floating that precious influence home quite as one of those high tides watched by the smugglers of old might, in case of their boat's being boarded, be trusted to wash far up the strand the cask of foreign liquor expertly committed to it. If through our lean prime Western period no dim and charming ghost of an adventurous lyric genius might by a stretch of fancy flit, if the time was really too hard to "take," in the light form proposed, the elegant reflexion, then so much the worse for the time—it was all one could say! The retort to that of course was that such a plea represented no "link" with reality—which was what was under discussion—but only a link, and flimsy enough too, with the deepest depths of the artificial: the restrictive truth exactly contended for, which may embody my critic's last word rather of course than my own. My own, so far as I shall pretend in that especial connexion to report it, was that one's warrant, in such a case, hangs essentially on the question of whether or no the false element imputed would have borne that test of further development which so exposes the wrong and so consecrates the right. My last word was, heaven forgive me, that, occasion favouring, I could have perfectly "worked out" Jeffrey Aspern.

[On "The Pupil"]†

My urchin of "The Pupil" (1891) has sensibility in abundance, it would seem—and yet preserves in spite of it, I judge, his strong little male quality. But there are fifty things to say here; which indeed rush upon me within my present close limits in such a cloud as to demand much clearance. This is perhaps indeed but the aftersense of the assault made on my mind, as I perfectly recall, by every aspect of the original vision, which struck me as abounding in aspects. It lives again for me, this vision, as it first alighted; though the inimitable prime flutter, the air as of an ineffable sign made by the immediate beat of the wings of the poised figure of fancy that has just settled, is one of those guarantees of value that can never be recaptured. The sign has been made to the seer only —it is *his* queer affair; of which any report to others, not as yet involved, has but the same effect of flatness as attends, amid a group gathered under the canopy of night, any stray allusion to a shooting star. The miracle, since miracle it seems, is all for the candid exclaimer. The miracle for the author of "The Pupil," at any rate, was when, years ago, one summer day, in a very hot Italian railway-carriage, which stopped and dawdled everywhere, favouring conversation, a friend with whom I shared it, a doctor of medicine who had come from a far country to settle in Florence, happened to speak to me of a wonderful American family, an odd adventurous, extravagant band, of high but rather unauthenticated pretensions, the most interesting member of which was a small boy, acute and precocious, afflicted with a heart of weak action, but beautifully intelligent, who saw their prowling precarious life exactly as it was, and measured and judged it, and measured and judged *them*, all round, ever so quaintly; presenting himself in short as an extraordinary little person. Here was more than enough for a summer's day even in old Italy—here was a thumping windfall. No process and no steps intervened: I *saw* on the spot, little Morgan Moreen, I saw all the rest of the Moreens; I felt, to the last delicacy, the nature of my young friend's relation with them (he had become at once my young friend) and, by the same stroke, to its uttermost fine throb, the subjection to *him* of the beguiled, bewildered, defrauded, unremunerated, yet after all richly repaid youth who would

† From *The Novels and Tales of Henry James*, vol. 11 (New York: Charles Scribner's Sons, 1908), pp. xiv–xviii.

to a certainty, under stress of compassion, embark with the tribe on tutorship, and whose edifying connexion with it would be my leading document.

This must serve as my account of the origin of "The Pupil": it will commend itself, I feel, to all imaginative and projective persons who have had—and what imaginative and projective person hasn't?—any like experience of the suddenly-determined *absolute* of perception. The whole cluster of items forming the image is on these occasions born at once; the parts are not pieced together, they conspire and interdepend; but what it really comes to, no doubt, is that at a simple touch an old latent and dormant impression, a buried germ, implanted by experience and then forgotten, flashes to the surface as a fish, with a single "squirm," rises to the baited hook, and there meets instantly the vivifying ray. I remember at all events having no doubt of anything or anyone here; the vision kept to the end its ease and its charm; it worked itself out with confidence. These are minor matters when the question is of minor results; yet almost any assured and downright imaginative act is— granted the sort of record in which I here indulge—worth fondly commemorating. One cherishes, after the fact, any proved case of the independent life of the imagination; above all if by that faculty one has been appointed mainly to live. We are then *never* detached from the question of what it may out of simple charity do for us. Besides which, in relation to the poor Moreens, innumerable notes, as I have intimated, all equally urging their relevance, press here to the front. The general adventure of the little composition itself— for singular things were to happen to it, though among such importunities not the most worth noting now—would be, occasion favouring, a thing to live over; moving as one did, roundabout it, in I scarce know what thick and coloured air of slightly tarnished anecdote, of dim association, of casual confused romance; a compound defying analysis, but truly, for the social chronicler, any student in especial of the copious "cosmopolite" legend, a boundless and tangled, but highly explorable, garden. Why, somehow— these were the intensifying questions—did one see the Moreens, whom I place at Nice, at Venice, in Paris, as of the special essence of the little old miscellaneous cosmopolite Florence, the Florence of other, of irrecoverable years, the restless yet withal so convenient scene of a society that has passed away for ever with all its faded ghosts and fragile relics; immaterial presences that have quite ceased to revisit (trust an old romancer's, an old pious observer's fine sense to have made sure of it!) walks and prospects once sacred and shaded, but now laid bare, gaping wide, despoiled of their past and unfriendly to any appreciation of it?—through which the unconscious Barbarians troop with the regularity and passivity of "supplies," or other promiscuous goods, prepaid and forwarded.

They had nothing to do, the dear Moreens, with this dreadful period, any more than I, as occupied and charmed with them, was humiliatingly subject to it; we were, all together, of a better romantic age and faith; we referred ourselves, with our highest complacency, to the classic years of the great Americano-European legend; the years of limited communication, of monstrous and unattenuated contrast, of prodigious and unrecorded adventure. The comparatively brief but infinitely rich "cycle" of romance embedded in the earlier, the very early American reactions and returns (mediaeval in the sense of being, at most, of the mid-century), what does it resemble today but a gold-mine overgrown and smothered, dislocated, and no longer workable?—all for want of the right indications for sounding, the right implements for digging, doubtless even of the right workmen, those with the right tradition and "feeling" for the job. The most extraordinary things appear to have happened, during that golden age, in the "old" countries—in Asia and Africa as well as in Europe—to the candid children of the West, things admirably incongruous and incredible; but no story of all the list was to find its just interpreter, and nothing is now more probable than that every key to interpretation has been lost. The modern reporter's big brushes, attached to broom-handles that match the height of his sky-scrapers, would sadly besmear the fine parchment of our missing record. We were to lose, clearly, at any rate, a vast body of precious anecdotes, a long gallery of wonderful portraits, an array of the oddest possible figures in the oddest possible attitudes. The Moreens were of the family then of the great unstudied precursors—poor and shabby members, no doubt; dim and superseded types. I must add indeed that, such as they were, or as they may at present incoherently appear, I don't pretend really to have "done" them; all I have given in "The Pupil" is little Morgan's troubled vision of them as reflected in the vision, also troubled enough, of his devoted friend. The manner of the thing may thus illustrate the author's incorrigible taste for gradations and superpositions of effect; his love, when it is a question of a picture, of anything that makes for proportion and perspective, that contributes to a view of *all* the dimensions. Addicted to seeing "through"—one thing through another, accordingly, and still other things through *that*— he takes, too greedily perhaps, on any errand, as many things as possible by the way. It is after this fashion that he incurs the stigma of labouring uncannily for a certain fulness of truth—truth diffused, distributed and, as it were, atmospheric.

[On "Brooksmith" and "The Real Thing"]†

As to the "The Real Thing" (1890) and "Brooksmith" (1891) my recollection is sharp; the subject of each of these tales was suggested to me by a briefly-reported case. To begin with the second-named of them, the appreciative daughter of a friend some time dead had mentioned to me a visit received by her from a servant of the late distinguished lady, a devoted maid whom I remembered well to have repeatedly seen at the latter's side and who had come to discharge herself so far as she might of a sorry burden. She had lived in her mistress's delightful society and in that of the many so interesting friends of the house; she had been formed by nature, as unluckily happened, to enjoy this privilege to the utmost, and the deprivation of everything was now bitterness in her cup. She had had her choice, and had made her trial, of common situations or of a return to her own people, and had found these ordeals alike too cruel. She had in her years of service tasted of conversation and been spoiled for life; she had, in recall of Stendhal's[4] inveterate motto, caught at glimpse, all untimely, of "la beauté parfaite," and should never find again what she had lost—so that nothing was left her but to languish to her end. *There* was a touched spring, of course, to make "Dramatise, dramatise!" ring out; only my little derived drama, in the event, seemed to require, to be ample enough, a hero rather than a heroine. I desired for my poor lost spirit the measured maximum of the fatal experience: the thing became, in a word, to my imagination, the obscure tragedy of the "intelligent" butler present at rare table-talk, rather than that of the more effaced tirewoman,[5] with which of course was involved a corresponding change from mistress to master.

In like manner my much-loved friend George du Maurier[6] had spoken to me of a call from a strange and striking couple desirous to propose themselves as artist's models for his weekly "social" illustrations to *Punch*,[7] and the acceptance of whose services would have entailed the dismissal of an undistinguished but highly expert pair, also husband and wife, who had come to him from far back on the irregular day and whom, thanks to a happy, and to that extent lucrative, appearance of "type" on the part of each, he had reproduced, to the best effect, in a thousand drawing-room attitudes and combinations. Exceedingly modest members of society,

---

† From *The Novels and Tales of Henry James*, vol. 18 (New York: Charles Scribner's Sons, 1909), pp. xix–xxi.
4. Stendhal is the pseudonym of the French novelist Marie Henri Beyle (1783–1842); his motto "la beauté parfaite," means "perfect (or absolute) beauty."
5. Lady's maid (who "attires" her mistress).
6. British illustrator and novelist (1834–1896).
7. Illustrated comic weekly, founded in 1841.

they earned their bread by looking and, with the aid of supplied toggery, dressing, greater favourites of fortune to the life; or, otherwise expressed, by skilfully feigning a virtue not in the least native to them. Here meanwhile were their so handsome proposed, so anxious, so almost haggard competitors, originally, by every sign, of the best condition and estate, but overtaken by reverses even while conforming impeccably to the standard of superficial "smartness" and pleading with well-bred ease and the right light tone, not to say with feverish gaiety, that (as in the interest of art itself) *they* at least shouldn't have to "make believe." The question thus thrown up by the two friendly critics of the rather lurid little passage was of whether their not having to make believe *would* in fact serve them, and above all serve their interpreter as well as the borrowed graces of the comparatively sordid professionals who had had, for dear life, to *know how* (which was to have learnt how) to do something. The question, I recall, struck me as exquisite, and out of a momentary fond consideration of it "The Real Thing" sprang at a bound.

[On "The Middle Years"]†

What I had lately and most particularly to say of "The Coxon Fund" is no less true of "The Middle Years," first published in *Scribner's Magazine* (1893)—that recollection mainly and most promptly associates with it the number of times I had to do it over to make sure of it. To get it right was to squeeze my subject into the five or six thousand words I had been invited to make it consist of—it consists, in fact, should the curious care to know, of some 5550[8] —and I scarce perhaps recall another case, with the exception I shall presently name, in which my struggle to keep compression rich, if not, better still, to keep accretions compressed, betrayed for me such community with the anxious effort of some warden of the insane engaged at a critical moment in making fast a victim's straitjacket. The form of "The Middle Years" is not that of the *nouvelle*, but that of the concise anecdote; whereas the subject treated would perhaps seem one comparatively demanding "developments"—if indeed, amid these mysteries, distinctions were so absolute. (There is of course neither close nor fixed measure of the reach of a development, which in some connexions seems almost superfluous and then in others to represent the whole sense of the matter; and we should doubtless speak more thoroughly by book had we some secret for exactly tracing deflexions and returns.) However this may

---

† From *The Novels and Tales of Henry James*, vol. 16 (New York: Charles Scribner's Sons, 1909), pp. v–vi.
8. If the curious care enough to count they find that it is almost 8,000.

be, it was as an anecdote, an anecdote only, that I was determined my little situation here should figure; to which end my effort was of course to follow it as much as possible from its outer edge in, rather than from its centre outward. That fond formula, I had alas already discovered, may set as many traps in the garden as its opposite may set in the wood; so that after boilings and reboilings of the contents of my small cauldron, after added pounds of salutary sugar, as numerous as those prescribed in the choicest recipe for the thickest jam, I well remember finding the whole process and act (which, to the exclusion of everything else, dragged itself out for a month) one of the most expensive of its sort in which I had ever engaged.

But I recall, by good luck, no less vividly how much finer a sweetness than any mere spooned-out saccharine dwelt in the fascination of the questions involved. Treating a theme that "gave" much in a form that, at the best, would give little, might indeed represent a peck of troubles; yet who, none the less, beforehand, was to pronounce with authority such and such an idea anecdotic and such and such another developmental?

[On "In the Cage"]†

* * *

The second in order of these fictions speaks for itself, I think, so frankly as scarce to suffer further expatiation. Its origin is written upon it large, and the idea it puts into play so abides in one of the commonest and most taken-for-granted of London impressions that some such experimentally-figured situation as that of "In the Cage" must again and again have flowered (granted the grain of observation) in generous minds. It had become for me, at any rate, an old story by the time (1898) I cast it into this particular form. The postal-telegraph office in general, and above all the small local office of one's immediate neighbourhood, scene of the transaction of so much of one's daily business, haunt of one's needs and one's duties, of one's labours and one's patiences, almost of one's rewards and one's disappointments, one's joys and one's sorrows, had ever had, to my sense, so much of London to give out, so much of its huge perpetual story to tell, that any momentary wait there seemed to take place in a strong social draught, the stiffest possible breeze of the human comedy. One had of course in these connexions one's especial resort, the office nearest one's own door, where one had come to enjoy in a manner the fruits of frequentation and the amenities of intercourse. So had grown up, for speculation—prone

† From *The Novels and Tales of Henry James*, vol. 11 (New York: Charles Scribner's Sons, 1908), pp. xviii–xxii.

as one's mind had ever been to that form of waste—the question
of what it might "mean," wherever the admirable service was installed, for confined and cramped and yet considerably tutored
young officials of either sex to be made so free, intellectually, of a
range of experience otherwise quite closed to them. This wonderment, once the spark was kindled, became an amusement, or an
obsession, like another; though falling indeed, at the best, no doubt,
but into that deepest abyss of all the wonderments that break out
for the student of great cities. From the moment that he *is* a student, this most beset of critics, his danger is inevitably of imputing
to too many others, right and left, the critical impulse and the
acuter vision—so very long may it take him to learn that the mass
of mankind are banded, probably by the sanest of instincts, to defend themselves to the death against any such vitiation of their
simplicity. To criticise is to appreciate, to appropriate, to take intellectual possession, to establish in fine a relation with the criti-
cised thing and make it one's own. The large intellectual appetite
projects itself thus on many things, while the small—not better
advised, but unconscious of need for advice—projects itself on few.

Admirable thus its economic instinct; it is curious of nothing that
it hasn't vital use for. You may starve in London, it is clear, without
discovering a use for any theory of the more equal division of
victuals—which is moreover exactly what it would appear that
thousands of the non-speculative annually do. Their example is
much to the point, in the light of all the barren trouble they are
saved; but somehow, after all, it gives no pause to the "artist," to
the morbid, imagination. That rash, that idle faculty continues to
abound in questions, and to supply answers to as many of them as
possible; all of which makes a great occupation for idleness. To the
fantastic scale on which this last-named state may, in favoring conditions, organise itself, to the activities it may practise when the
favouring conditions happen to crop up in Mayfair or in Kensington, our portrayal of the caged telegraphist may well appear a proper
little monument. The composition before us tells in fact clearly
enough, it seems to me, the story of its growth; and relevance will
probably be found in any moral it may pluck—by which I mean any
moral the impulse to have framed it may pluck—from the vice of
reading rank subtleties into simple souls and reckless expenditure
into thrifty ones. The matter comes back again, I fear, but to the
author's irrepressible and insatiable, his extravagant and immoral,
interest in personal character and in the "nature" of a mind, of
almost any mind the heaving little sea of his subject may cast up
—as to which these remarks have already, in other connexions,
recorded his apology: all without prejudice to such shrines and stations of penance as still shall enliven our way. The range of won-

derment attributed in our tale to the young woman employed at Cocker's differs little in essence from the speculative thread on which the pearls of Maisie's experience, in this same volume— pearls of so strange an iridescence—are mostly strung. She won- ders, putting it simply, very much as Morgan Moreen wonders; and they all wonder, for that matter, very much after the fashion of our portentous little Hyacinth of "The Princess Casamassima," tainted to the core, as we have seen him, with the trick of mental reaction on the things about him and fairly staggering under the appropri- ations, as I have called them, that he owes to the critical spirit. He collapses, poor Hyacinth, like a thief at night, overcharged with treasures of reflexion and spoils of passion of which he can give, in his poverty and obscurity, no honest account.

It is much in this manner, we see on analysis, that Morgan Mo- reen breaks down—his burden indeed not so heavy, but his strength so much less formed. The two little spirits of maidens, in the group, bear up, oddly enough, beyond those of their brothers; but the just remark for each of these small exhibited lives is of course that, in the longer or the shorter piece, they are actively, are luxuriously, lived. The luxury is that of the number of their moral vibrations, well-nigh unrestricted—not that of an account at the grocer's: whatever it be, at any rate, it makes them, as examples and "cases," rare. My brooding telegraphist may be in fact, on her ground of ingenuity, scarcely more thinkable than desirable; yet if I have made her but a libel, up and down the city, on an estimable class, I feel it still something to have admonished that class, even though ob- scurely enough, of neglected interests and undivined occasions. My central spirit, in the anecdote, is, for verisimilitude, I grant, too ardent a focus of divination; but without this excess the phenomena detailed would have lacked their principle of cohesion. The action of the drama is simply the girl's "subjective" adventure—that of her quite definitely winged intelligence; just as the catastrophe, just as the solution, depends on her winged wit. Why, however, should I explain further—for a case that, modestly as it would seem to pre- sent itself, has yet already whirled us so far? A course of incident complicated by the intervention of winged wit—which is here, as I say, confessed to—would be generally expected, I judge, to commit me to the explanation of everything. But from that undertaking I shrink, and take refuge instead, for an instant, in a much looser privilege.

If I speak, as just above, of the *action* embodied, each time, in these so "quiet" recitals, it is under renewed recognition of the inveterate instinct with which they keep conforming to the "scenic" law. They demean themselves for all the world—they quite insist on it, that is, whenever they have a chance—as little constituted dramas, little exhibitions founded on the logic of the "scene," the unit of the scene, the general scenic consistency, and knowing little more than that. To read them over has been to find them on this ground never at fault. The process repeats and renews itself, moving in the light it has once for all adopted. These finer idiosyncracies of a literary form seem to be regarded as outside the scope of criticism—small reference to them do I remember ever to have met; such surprises of re-perusal, such recoveries of old fundamental intention, such moments of almost ruefully independent discrimination, would doubtless in that case not have waylaid my steps. Going over the pages here placed together has been for me, at all events, quite to watch the scenic system at play. The treatment by "scene," regularly, quite rhythmically recurs; the intervals between, the massing of the elements to a different effect and by a quite other law, remain, in this fashion, all preparative, just as the scenic occasions in themselves become, at a given moment, illustrative, each of the agents, true to its function, taking up the theme from the other very much as the fiddles, in an orchestra, may take it up from the cornets and flutes, or the wind-instruments take it up from the violins. The point, however, is that the scenic passages are *wholly* and logically scenic, having for their rule of beauty the principle of the "conduct," the organic development, of a scene—the entire succession of values that flower and bear fruit on ground solidly laid for them. The great advantage for the total effect is that we feel, with the definite alternation, how the theme *is* being treated. That is we feel it when, in such tangled connexions, we happen to care. I shouldn't really go on as if this were the case with many readers.

[On "The Beast in the Jungle"]†

* * * The subject of this elaborated fantasy—which, I must add, I hold a successful thing only as its motive may seem to the reader to stand out sharp—can't quite have belonged to the immemorial company of such solicitations; though in spite of this I meet it, in ten lines of an old note-book, but as a recorded conceit and an accomplished fact. Another poor sensitive gentleman, fit indeed to mate with Stransom of "The Altar"—my attested predilection for poor sensitive gentlemen almost embarrasses me as I march!—was to have been, after a strange fashion and from the threshold of his career, condemned to keep counting with the unreasoned prevision of some extraordinary fate; the conviction, lodged in his brain, part and parcel of his imagination from far back,

† From *The Novels and Tales of Henry James*, vol. 17 (New York: Charles Scribner's Sons, 1909), pp. ix–xi.

that experience would be marked for him, and whether for good or for ill, by some rare distinction, some incalculable violence or unprecedented stroke. So I seemed to see him start in life—under the so mixed star of the extreme of apprehension and the extreme of confidence; all to the logical, the quite inevitable effect of the complication aforesaid: his having to wait and wait for the right recognition; none of the mere usual and normal human adventures, whether delights or disconcertments, appearing to conform to the great type of his fortune. So it is that he's depicted. No gathering appearance, no descried or interpreted promise or portent, affects his superstitious soul either as a damnation deep enough (if damnation be in question) for his appointed *quality* of consciousness, or as a translation into bliss sublime enough (on *that* hypothesis) to fill, in vulgar parlance, the bill. Therefore as each item of experience comes, with its possibilities, into view, he can but dismiss it under this sterilising habit of the failure to find it good enough and thence to appropriate it.

His one desire remains of course to meet his fate, or at least to divine it, to see it as intelligible, to learn it, in a word; but none of its harbingers, pretended or supposed, speak his ear in the true voice; they wait their moment at his door only to pass on unheeded, and the years ebb while he holds his breath and stays his hand and—from the dread not less of imputed pride than of imputed pusillanimity—stifles his distinguished secret. He perforce lets everything go—leaving all the while his general presumption disguised and his general abstention unexplained; since he's ridden by the idea of what things may lead to, since they mostly always lead to human communities, wider or intenser, of experience, and since, above all, in his uncertainty, he mustn't compromise others. Like the blinded seeker in the old-fashioned game he "burns," on occasion, as with the sense of the hidden thing near—only to deviate again however into the chill; the chill that indeed settles on him as the striking of his hour is deferred. His career thus resolves itself into a great negative adventure, my report of which presents, for its centre, the fine case that has caused him most tormentedly to "burn," and then most unprofitably to stray. He is afraid to recognise what he incidentally misses, since what his high belief amounts to is not that he shall have felt and vibrated less than any one else, but that he shall have felt and vibrated more; which no acknowledgement of the minor loss must conflict with. Such a course of existence naturally involves a climax—the final flash of the light under which he reads his lifelong riddle and sees his conviction proved. He has indeed been marked and indeed suffered his fortune—which is precisely to have been the man in the world to whom nothing whatever was to happen. My picture leaves him overwhelmed—at last he has understood; though in thus disengaging my treated theme for the reader's benefit I seem to acknowledge that this more detached witness may not successfully have done so. I certainly grant that any felt merit in the thing must all depend on the clearness and charm with which the subject just noted expresses itself.

[On "The Jolly Corner"]†

* * * odd though it may sound to pretend that one feels on safer ground in tracing such an adventure as that of the hero of "The Jolly Corner" than in pursuing a bright career among pirates or detectives, I allow that composition to pass as the measure or limit, on my own part, of any achievable comfort in the "adventure-story"; and this not because I may "render"—well, what my poor gentleman attempted and suffered in the New York house—better than I may render detectives or pirates or other splendid desperadoes, though even here too there would be something to say; but because the spirit engaged with the forces of violence interests me most when I can think of it as engaged most deeply, most finely and most "subtly" (precious term!). For then it is that, as with the longest and firmest prongs of consciousness, I grasp and hold the throbbing subject; *there* it is above all that I find the steady light of the picture.

† From *The Novels and Tales of Henry James*, vol. 17 (New York: Charles Scribner's Sons, 1909), pp. xx–xxi.

CRITICISM

RICHARD A. HOCKS

James and the Art of Short Fiction†

Although Henry James is routinely called the "novelist's novelist," his short fiction comprises twelve volumes, attesting to his productivity in the writing of tales and to their importance in his overall canon. Indeed, the New York Edition of his works, which bears his selection and careful revision of texts, is entitled, aptly, *The Novels and Tales of Henry James*. James was, of course, a prolific writer of novels and shorter fiction as well as the author of literary criticism, autobiographical volumes, travel literature, and even cultural analyses after the manner of Matthew Arnold, John Ruskin, and his friend Henry Adams. What should be stressed about his short fiction is that, like his work in general, it exhibits both high quantity and consistent quality. This sets him apart from the plight of the premodern American writer, voiced in the famous lament of Ernest Hemingway that our classic authors fail to exhibit a "third act" in their literary careers. Even cursory reflection on the work of Poe, Melville, Twain, Crane, and even Hawthorne will reveal that, although the absence of an extended proliferation of fine tales occurs for different reasons in their respective careers, each failed to produce short fiction with that combination of quantity, quality, and artistic development which marks James's and earns him the appellation of "master," although many feel that designation is now suspect for its disguise of James's artistic, personal, and professional economic anxieties. Poe pioneered the form, but his distinguished corpus remains small; Melville mastered it in a brief spurt in the early 1850s, but then left "Billy Budd" unfinished at his death almost forty years later; Twain, to be sure, wrote "shorter works" all his life, but the perennial question he poses is just how many of these qualify as short stories: if Melville, as Nina Baym once expressed it, had a "quarrel with fiction," Twain did not seem especially to like fiction, at least if judged by his own reading. Stephen Crane and Kate Chopin, in a sense like Poe at a later stage, perfected, refined, and advanced the short story as a work of art, but owing to early death and other factors their canons were somewhat stinted. And Howells, the author of "Editha" and the ally of James in the new post–Civil War realism, remained predominantly a nov-

† From Richard A. Hocks, *Henry James: A Study of the Short Fiction* (Boston: Twayne, 1990), pp. 3–11.

elist, critic, journalist, editor, and author of travel volumes rather than a writer of tales.

Only Hawthorne among James's predecessors and early contemporaries compares with or surpasses Poe as a significant composer of fine tales. Yet even Hawthorne, from whom James learned the "deeper psychology," cannot strictly be thought of as one whose work *evolved* artistically in any sense resembling James's: for example, the tale most consider his masterpiece, "My Kinsman Major Molineux," was written very early in Hawthorne's career; still, he did not deem it worthy of inclusion in either edition of *Twice-told Tales* or in *Mosses from an Old Manse*. One cannot imagine a similar occurrence in James's career, that he would have written his most profound tale so early; or, if he had, would then have overlooked it in putting together an important collection. Readers and critics, to be sure, are frequently discovering how strong a heretofore unanthologized story by James in fact is, but one never finds an opposing tendency to devalue stories that have been admired for some time. The early "Daisy Miller," the middle "Aspern Papers," and the late "Jolly Corner" remain as widely read as ever, regardless of the increasing interest in "The Great Good Place," "Glasses," "In the Cage," "The Tree of Knowledge," or "Maud-Evelyn." What this suggests is that James's contribution to both the canon and development of the American short story remains immense, perhaps the most important contribution of any American writer before the modern period. Historically speaking, he is our first poetic realist of prose.

Internationalism and the Quasi-Supernatural Realm

While James is most often celebrated for inventing "the international novel," the subject of which treats the conflict or confrontation of American characters with the labyrinth of European culture, his short stories exhibit a wider range of subject matter while by no means ignoring the so-called international theme, as evidenced by such early tales as "A Passionate Pilgrim," "Four Meetings," "Daisy Miller," "A Bundle of Letters," "Madame de Mauve," and "An International Episode." James's international fiction can be thought of as the "second frontier" in our literary history: at the time it sensed the completion of the westward settlement, the American psyche instinctively began to gravitate back toward its European "memory." The international theme—or, more accurately in James, the international subject—is prominent in his early period, tends to disappear in the middle period, and reappears with great complexity in his late period or major phase. That pattern, however, is somewhat truer for the novels than the tales, which follow the first two stages more closely than the third: those of the late period duplicate the complexity of the late novels but do not as a group exhibit the corresponding emphasis on internationalism, although both "A Round of Visits" and "The Jolly Corner" would qualify as "reverse international" (Americans returning home after long stays in Europe). In general, however, I believe James's international subject transposes imaginatively into the deep and archetypal paradigms of innocence and experience, nature and art, the ethical and aesthetic consciousness, freedom and determinism. James's international fiction, in short, often recapitulates the deep structure of universal polar or dialectical themes.

Some of his finest stories, however, are set in Europe, frequently England, and may just as often not even include American characters. Among the best that do not are "The Marriages," "The Bench of Desolation," and one of the most explicated tales in the language, "The Beast in the Jungle." Furthermore, his canon includes a very significant group of parable stories of artists and writers; these most frequently come from the 1890s and include such strong works as "The Lesson of the Master," "Greville Fane," "The Real Thing," and "The Figure in the Carpet."

Still another category of stories—in certain respects the most important—are James's "ghostly" or "quasi-supernatural" tales, the imaginative outgrowth of his preoccupation with the psychology of character. James's profound and abiding literary interest in normal psychology, so to speak, just kept deepening until eventually he began to probe the caverns and weirs of abnormal psychology, especially the condition of obsession. The best known of these tales is, of course, "The Turn of the Screw," the meaning of which has caused more debate than even Melville's "Billy Budd," yet unlike Melville's classic work, it does not derive its ambiguity primarily from its being unfinished and reconstructed from working manuscripts. But there are other ghostly tales in James's prolific canon, including "The Altar of the Dead," "The Friends of the Friends," "The Great Good Place," "The Real Right Thing," and the masterful "Jolly Corner," a work that at once reinvents the very genre of "double" literature and simultaneously condenses rich and multitudinous levels of meaning into an economy of form comparable to one of T. S. Eliot's *Four Quartets*, with which it also has thematic affinities. "The Beast in the Jungle," among its inexhaustible dimensions, is also one of James's ghostly tales. James's quasi-supernaturalism actually culminated in his 1910 essay "Is There a Life After Death?," the only spiritual document he ever wrote and the distillation of his preoccupation with abnormal psychology and the ghostly realm—a document, moreover, that corresponds closely to William James's psychological exploration of religious experience.[1]

Furthermore, there are tales that focus and depict the comedy or the tragedy of society, a thematic thread that also runs through the overwhelming majority of James's novels and is present in all three periods of his career independent of the international theme. In these, especially the tragedies, one often finds his abiding moral interest in human "cannibalism" or exploitation of one character by another. Although several tales are admixtures and classify uneasily, among the comedies are "An International Episode," "The Point of View," "The Liar," "Lady Barbarina," "Greville Fane," "Miss Gunton of Poughkeepsie," and "The Birthplace"; among the tragedies are "The Pupil," "Julia Bride," "Europe," "The Beast in the Jungle," "The Bench of Desolation," and "A Round of Visits." The well-executed "Aspern Papers," primarily a comedy, could, I suspect, also be grouped with most of the Jamesian classifications discussed hitherto, with the exception, perhaps, of the "ghostly" category—although Miss Tina's transformation at the end has for the unscrupulous narrator at least the effect of an "apparition," if not the tenor of it.

Jamesian Technique

In addition to James's wide range of subjects, his tales exhibit the distinctively Jamesian development of fiction as art and technical mastery for which the novels are famous. He was the first major critic and theoretician of fiction after Edgar Allan Poe, the author of innumerable essays on the writers of his time, and the composer of the definitive *Prefaces* to the New York Edition between 1907 and 1909, written with the same care and creativity he put into his best late fiction. Although he infrequently speaks there generically of the short story—far more often addressing the issue or challenge of a specific given tale—he does compare the short story to the "hard, shining sonnet, one of the most indestructible forms of composition," and acknowledges that "Great for me from far back had been the interest of the whole 'question' of the short story."[2] This view is greatly confirmed and amplified by his *Notebooks*.

In general, his experimentation in fiction makes one feel that,

1. For a discussion of James's "Is There a Life after Death?" and its relationship to William James's *The Varieties of Religious Experience*, see my *Henry James and Pragmatistic Thought: A Study in the Relationship between the Philosophy of William James and the Literary Art of Henry James* (Chapel Hill: University of North Carolina Press, 1974), 208–25.
2. *The Art of the Novel: Critical Prefaces*, ed. R. P. Blackmur (New York: Charles Scribner's Sons, 1934), 240, 178; hereafter cited in the text as *AN*.

were it not demeaning to the genuine accomplishment of his great predecessors, we might say James delivers to us our native genre's "coming of age" in his mastery of the form and the articulation of its poetics. He is most conventionally associated with the development of "narrator point of view," or what he liked to call more fluidly and dramatically his various "registers" or "deputies"; chief among these is his creation of "the unreliable narrator" or, just as frequently, the specious third-person narrative "register." He is also associated with the doctrine of the author's originating "germ," which expands through the creative process into a living whole, often (but not always) endowing the finished work with a neo-Coleridgean unity or Goethean metamorphosis, though shorn of those writers' spiritual cosmology. Finally, James is associated with the brilliant alternation of what Percy Lubbock in one of the earliest and most important studies of prose fiction labeled "the panoramic" and "the dramatic."[3] James's own terms for these alternating structural elements in his fiction are "picture" (the rendering of interior thought) and "scene" (characters in action and speech)—the latter he also sometimes called "discriminated occasions." All such subtle narrative strategy, however, eventually conspires to intensify the condition of ambiguity and deception in a world where the simpler Cartesian division between mind and external phenomena no longer quite prevails, or at least provides us that consistent line of demarcation we might have wished.

Beyond "the Rise of Realism"

As already indicated, James's short fiction reflects his career phases, from the early, sharply delineated critiques of society to the late, rich, convoluted poetic prose, which conveys reality in its affective flux. Indeed, it is sometimes hard to decide which issue pertains to the development of James himself and which to the morphology of the American short story. James began his long career as an exponent of psychological realism. He collaborated with the other realists—William Dean Howells, Sarah Orne Jewett, Mary Wilkins Freeman, Hamlin Garland, Kate Chopin, and others—in formulating and practicing what is academically designated "the Rise of Realism," or what Vernon Louis Parrington called "the Beginnings of Critical Realism," a school of fiction that put a premium on the close notation of ordinary life, the rendition of a specific geographical region, the dramatization and criticism of social taboos, and the delineation of individual character. This post–Civil War movement flourished in the last three decades of the century and was greatly

3. See Percy Lubbock, *The Craft of Fiction* (1921; New York: Viking Press, 1957), 156–202 and passim.

influenced by continental rather than English masters—especially
Balzac, Flaubert, Turgenev, Maupassant, and, in the case of Howells, at least, Tolstoy. Also for later James, as for one of his successors, James Joyce, the name of Henrik Ibsen must be added, for the
Danish writer's combination of poetic drama, social consciousness,
technical innovation, and the study of individual psychology made
his work consonant with James's fiction beginning in the 1890s and
continuing through the first decade of the twentieth century.

James's special province within "the Rise of Realism" is increasingly the psychology of individual character. His early stories, to be
sure, like Howells's fiction generally, exhibit social realism and what
Howells liked to call a "scientific decorum," or what James called
the "direct impression of life": they tend to subordinate the study
of an individual's psyche to a conflict or misunderstanding that
arises from social and cultural conditioning, as in "An International
Episode," "A Bundle of Letters," "The Point of View," and "Daisy
Miller." On the other hand, James's mature tales take their point
of departure from the aspirations best voiced in his most famous
critical essay, "The Art of Fiction" (1884), one of the most widely
read and reprinted essays on prose fiction ever written by a practicing author. In the essay James not only establishes fiction as a
fine art but continues to insist that its purpose is to "represent life,"
that all questions really come back to "execution," that fiction has
a double heritage and analogy with both painting and history (thus
fusing the realist program with high artistic composition), and finally, that the moral quality of a work of art resides not in any
conscious moral purpose but rather in "the quality of the mind of
the producer," that is, the aspiring author, who should "Try to be
one of the people on whom nothing is lost."

In the same essay, however, he also makes a statement about the
writer's experience that more than any other captures the heart of
his doctrine and anticipates the ruling feature of his own short
fiction from the late 1880s onward, well beyond his practice of
anything like documentary realism. "Experience," he writes,

> is never limited and it is never complete; it is an immense
> sensibility, a kind of huge spider web of the finest silken
> threads suspended in the chamber of consciousness, and
> catching every air-borne particle in its tissue. It is the very
> atmosphere of the mind; and when the mind is imaginative—
> much more when it happens to be that of a man of genius—
> it takes to itself the faintest hints of life, it converts the very
> pulses of the air into revelations. . . . The power to guess the
> unseen from the seen, to trace the implication of things, to
> judge the whole piece by the pattern, the condition of feeling
> life in general so completely that you are well on your way to

knowing any particular corner of it—this cluster of gifts may almost be said to constitute experience, and they occur in country and in town and in the most differing stages of education. If experience consists of impressions, it may be said that impressions *are* experience, just as (have we not seen it?) they are the very air we breathe.[4]

This famous statement promises us, among other things, that later the psychology of Jame's best and most mature work will render the drama of consciousness and convey for his characters and readers alike the moment-to-moment sense of human experience as bewilderment and discovery. Consciousness he conceives of as a field, in philosophical language what his brother William James, anticipating modern phenomenology, calls a "function" rather than an "entity," or, to adopt for a moment the terminology of contemporary thinker Owen Barfield, a "participating" rather than an isolated and onlooking faculty; that is to say, a mechanism not dichotomized from the phenomena of which it is conscious. James's late fiction suggests that reality itself is an affective flux corresponding to something like field theory. For this reason he came more and more to present subtle shades of human perception and intellectual nuance, to diminish physical action—or rather to present physical action as a living extension of consciousness—and to invent a prose style of elliptical syntax, periodic sentence, and capacious extended metaphor. His genius for linguistic experimentation began to simulate reality as a field even while he otherwise allied himself, precariously, to the assumptions of mimesis, his "direct impression of life." It is no accident therefore that his momentous influence on modern literature has become as strong on poetry as on fiction itself. It is also not surprising that scholars and critics of James's work today focus far less on his realism and more on his transcendence of the limitations of realism. Indeed, Sergio Perosa considers him the "great uncle of postmodernism," and John Carlos Rowe nothing less than the refracting prism for every major school of contemporary critical theory.[5] James has been regarded, then, for quite a long time as craftsman extraordinaire and innovator of fictive technique, but by now I believe more and more readers and scholars alike recognize that all such technique, at least in his later work, is but the avenue into the broader epistemological issues just sketched.

4. "The Art of Fiction," in *Partial Portraits* (London: Macmillan, 1888), 388–89. The passage appears on pages 382–83 of this Norton Critical Edition.
5. Sergio Perosa, *Henry James and the Experimental Novel* (Charlottesville: University Press of Virginia, 1978); John Carlos Rowe, *The Theoretical Dimensions of Henry James* (Madison: University of Wisconsin Press, 1984); another strong argument that James transcends realism, though not as proto-modernist, is Daniel M. Fogel, *Henry James and the Structure of the Romantic Imagination* (Baton Rouge: Louisiana State University Press, 1981).

Female Consciousness

Finally, James is justly celebrated for the creation of great women characters in the novels. One thinks of them as a veritable gallery —Isabel Archer, Olive Chancellor, Fleda Vetch, Maisie Farange, Christina Light, Milly Theale, Kate Croy, Charlotte Stant, Maggie Verver. In his tales James does not, I believe, exhibit quite the comparable achievement. Inasmuch as his tales are obviously full of women, such a judgment is inevitably a matter of personal taste and interpretation, even perhaps of definition. I am thinking from the novels primarily of female protagonists and narrative "registers" along the lines of Isabel, Maisie, Fleda, Milly, and Maggie. The Governess in "The Turn of the Screw" is a great creation, to be sure, although a disturbing individual; the unnamed telegraphist of "In the Cage" is certainly an important figure * * *. Yet even Daisy Miller, among the most unforgettable of James's women characters, is not the "register" of her tale. It is not that James fails to provide vivid female figures such as Caroline Spencer, Miranda Hope, Tina Bordereau, Lily Gunton, Mora Montravers, or Kate Cookham; it is only that male "registers" seem to predominate in the tales. It makes one wonder whether or not the more ample development possible in the novel better suited James's rendering of the internal working of female consciousness. At the very beginning of his *Prefaces* James defines the novel as "a long fiction with a 'complicated' subject" (*AN*, 4). Possibly he felt that, other things being equal, the "registering" of interior female consciousness was a "complicated subject" better suited to the novel.

One might counterclaim, however, that James's own narrative consciousness *within* the text of his fiction is as much female as male. I believe a glimpse at his "enabling androgyny"—to use a phrase from *Theoretical Dimensions* (Rowe, 91)—may be had in these reflections from his Preface to *The Princess Casamassima*:

> My report of people's experience—my report as a 'story teller' —is essentially my appreciation of it, and there is no 'interest' for me in what my hero, my heroine or any one else does save through that admirable process. As soon as I begin to appreciate simplification is imperilled: the sharply distinguished parts of any adventure, any case of endurance and performance, melt together as an appeal. . . . I can't be intimate without that sense and taste, and I can't appreciate save by intimacy, any more than I can report save by a projected light. (*AN*, 65–66)

However we decide this question of James's "engendered" text, his best tales, whatever their length and the specific gender of their viewpoint characters, are inevitably marked by an imaginative concision not unlike the genius of Emily Dickinson and suggesting perhaps the aptness of James's comparison of the genre to the sonnet. From the period of his artistic maturity in the late 1880s and 1890s through his major phase after 1900, the tales exhibit increasingly subtle layers of meaning, stratification of irony and theme, integration of complex imagery, and, as always, psychology of character.

MILLICENT BELL

["Daisy Miller"]†

Despite its compact shapeliness and the narrative tone which seems to emanate from a fixed elevation of authorial detachment, this early work nonetheless focuses on a central consciousness, whose inability to arrive at certainty is the source of so much Jamesian drama. It is Daisy Miller, and not the bemused and sluggish Winterbourne, whose name figures in James's title, but she is the subject of Winterbourne's inquiry rather than ours. Whether we like it or not, we are compelled to occupy ourselves with his unengaging personality rather than with Daisy's. This is again the result of a shift of narrative focus—from observed to observer—similar to that made in *Roderick Hudson*, published three years before. Despite that novel's title, James later realized, the "centre of interest" hadn't so much been Roderick as it had been the consciousness of his witnessing friend, Rowland Mallet.[1]

In "Daisy Miller," as in *Roderick Hudson*, James makes use of a third-person narrator who depends upon the perceptions of a character whose interest is directed upon someone to whom we have no other access. We can never arrive except by guesswork at the truth about Daisy; she can only be seen from the outside through the lens of Winterbourne's special viewpoint. We are never allowed to know her unspoken thoughts but only the reflections about her uttered to him by others, and only his surmises. Unlike the situation in *Roderick Hudson*, in which Rowland Mallet maintains a claim to some trust, skepticism must slowly emerge as we find ourselves

† From *Meaning in Henry James* by Millicent Bell, 54–65, Cambridge, MA: Harvard University Press. Copyright © 1991 by the President and Fellows of Harvard College. Reprinted by permission of the publisher. References to this Norton Critical Edition appear in brackets following the author's original citations, which refer to the New York Edition of *The Novels and Tales of Henry James*, vol. 18 (New York: Scribner & Sons, 1907–1910).
1. "The drama is the very drama of that consciousness," James admitted in *Literary Criticism: Essays on Literature, American Writers, English Writers* (New York: Library of America, 1984), p. 1750.

studying Winterbourne even more closely than we do Daisy, and, in the end, we become convinced of the inadequacy of his insight in a way that looks forward to the "autobiographic" form[2] of "The Aspern Papers," in which the observer-narrator himself loses our confidence.

Winterbourne, rather than Rowland Mallet, is the first of those Jamesian witnesses whose efforts to truly know the Other, to understand the Other's story, are representations of the writer's—and the reader's—bemused efforts to solve the mystery of character and plot. His unease about his young countrywoman's propriety is quaint today; and we are unlikely to share the prejudices of the contemporary reader who was shocked by her as much as was Winterbourne himself. But if we jump to the conclusion that the story "dates" and so has only historical interest, we miss the truth that Winterbourne's *process* of observation and placement is not at all foreign to us. We are no less likely than the nineteenth-century reader to strive to place others in ready-made categories and to interpret their fates conventionally; only the categories and conventions have changed.

Among the categories and conventions still relevant are those that confine the female subject—and if "Daisy Miller" is not about Daisy exactly, it is certainly about recognizably *masculine* ways of looking at women. Winterbourne, the girl-watcher who idly sits on his hotel terrace waiting for a particularly arresting feminine figure to come into his purview, is prototypically poised for the encounter, equipped with preconceptions and, one may imagine, practiced ploys of approach. As soon as we realize that *he* is what *we* are watching, we can put aside the charge by some feminist readers that James is simply showing his own attachment to female stereotypes.[3]

2. James used this expression to designate first-person narrative in the preface to *The Ambassadors*. See Henry James, *Literary Criticism: French Writers, Other European Writers, The Prefaces to the New York Edition* (New York: Library of America, 1984), p. 1316.

3. The case of Daisy Miller is the first among several of James's female portraits * * * which seem to invite criticism of his own categorical thinking. One school of feminist criticism has accused James of creating sexist stereotypes. Judith Fryer argues that James's women "are not women at all, but reflections of the prevailing images of women in the 19th century" (*The Faces of Eve: Women in the Nineteenth Century American Novel*, Oxford, Oxford University Press, 1976, p. 23). Nan Bauer Maglin believes that James's attitude "toward independent women, the women's movement, and women in general" is one of "disgust and mockery (perhaps with the exception of women in their 'proper place')"; "Fictional Feminists in *The Bostonians* and *The Odd Women*," in *Images of Women in Fiction: Feminist Perspectives*, ed. Susan Koppelman Cormillion (Bowling Green, Ohio, Bowling Green University Popular Press, 1972). See also Wendy Martin, "Seduced and Abandoned in the New World: The Image of Woman in American Fiction," in *Women in Sexist Society: Studies in Power and Powerlessness*, ed. Vivian Gornick and Barbara K. Moran (New York, Basic Books New American Library, 1971), pp. 329–346. But James gives us in Winterbourne a detached, ultimately critical image of the masculine representative of such views, and he may be assumed to have had some sympathy with Daisy's unideological and primitive will to independent being. * * *

James must have been aware of his complicity with Winterbourne, nonetheless. In writing this very story was he not himself assisting the development of a popular stereotype? If he aimed to expose the fallacies of stereotypical thinking, the further life of his Daisy Miller in the popular imagination must have afterward shown him that he, too, could be held responsible for creating a concept as limiting as any that had gone before. His intention to criticize such thinking was—and still is—seldom understood. Just the same, however, he was himself a young man, and could not have helped sharing Winterbourne's masculine perspective. In any case * * * he was a young writer for whom the whole question of typological definition had a special importance; how else but by means of types could character be understood? The process of art itself is represented in Winterbourne's encounters with Daisy; Winterbourne's way of making her comprehensible to himself, his reduction of her to a "character" for whom he anticipates a certain story, is a literary effort.

It is interesting, therefore, to notice the signs of James's identification with this imaginary young American observer. To begin with, the narrative voice reveals a mind close to Winterbourne's, for Winterbourne is exactly the sort of sophisticated traveler who would understand the narrator's discriminations among the various hotels at Vevey and also be able to compare and contrast them with scenes at Saratoga, as the narrative persona, that of a traveled American, does. This anonymous personality may become personal and erupt into an "I" from time to time in self-conscious separation from his subject: "I hardly know whether it was the analogies or the differences that were uppermost in the mind of a young American, who two or three years ago, sat in the garden of the 'Trois Couronnes,' looking about him rather idly at some of the graceful objects I have mentioned" (4) [4]. But the habit of mind we have just seen illustrated—of making cultural comparisons of scene and personal type—is one which narrator and character share.

They also share this habit with the novelist and writer of charming travel essays for American magazines. But there is a further mark of Winterbourne's affiliation with Henry James. We are told that Winterbourne had gone "on trial" to the old "Academy on the steep and stony hillside" in Geneva. Winterbourne has an affection, consequently, for the "little capital of Calvinism" (5) [4] and some continuing friendships there—a prehistory drawn so precisely from James's own youthful experience as to seem the writer's sly reminder (perhaps only to himself) of this identity with his character. In 1860, the James family had been in Geneva, where the seventeen-year-old Henry was enrolled at the Academy as a special student.[4] The wording of the 1909 text increases this autobiographical element; his first version in the *Cornhill Magazine*[5] said simply that Winterbourne had "gone to College" in Geneva. But in his essay "Swiss Notes," published in *Transatlantic Sketches* three years before "Daisy Miller," James expressed a feeling of "old-time kindness for Geneva, to which I was introduced years ago, in my schooldays, when I was as good an idler as the best."[6] He paraphrases this thought in "Daisy Miller" as "Winterbourne had an old attachment for the little capital of Calvinism; he had been put to school there as a boy" (5) [4].

The process of composing fictions about others is not limited to author, narrator, and Winterbourne. Everyone plays at the same game. To remind us of this, Winterbourne's friends speak of his "studying" in Geneva; his enemies ("but after all he had no enemies," the narrator interjects when his own pointed style has betrayed him into an antithesis) say that he spent time there because "he was extremely devoted to a lady who lived there—a foreign lady, a person older than himself" (4–5) [4]. As though anticipating the way James's tale will enforce upon us the realization of the unreliability of *any* narrative, no choice is made among these theories; we will be returned at the end to the same alternatives by the gossip which reports that he is either studying hard in Geneva or much interested in a very clever foreign lady. This return to the beginning, announcing that for Winterbourne there has been no significant change, should also have the function of reminding us that Winterbourne has always had a sexual liaison with a European, but that since he is a man of discretion and not, like Daisy, a rash young woman, there can be no real "story in it" after all.

Winterbourne's own observations exhibit from start to finish the categorical judgment which is the object of major scrutiny in "Daisy Miller." Comically, he shares it first with Randolph, Daisy's small brother, who already has the habit of cultural comparison when it comes to candy, and says, "American candy's the best candy." To this, Winterbourne responds, "Are American boys the best little boys?" and is told, "American men are the best." So, Daisy is welcomed upon the scene by Winterbourne with the same comparative tribute: "American girls are the best girls" (7) [6]. He still sees only a category rather than an individual when he looks at her for the

4. Letter to Thomas S. Perry, May 13, 1860, in Edel, ed., *Letters* [Cambridge: Harvard University Press, 1987], 1:19.
5. "Daisy Miller: A Study," *Cornhill Magazine* 37 (June 1878), reprinted in *James's Daisy Miller: The Story, the Play, the Critics*, ed. William T. Stafford (New York, Charles Scribner's Sons, 1963), p. 8. James's revisions for the first book edition of his story (New York, Harper & Brothers, 1878), do not appreciably alter the text in the direction I am observing. Further references to the 1878 text will be to the Stafford reprint.
6. Henry James, *Transatlantic Sketches* (Boston, James R. Osgood and Co., 1875), p. 58.

first time and exclaims to himself, "How pretty they are!" (8) [6].

For a moment, Winterbourne finds himself a little adrift from the familiar boundaries which, particularly in sexual relations, standardize not only persons but behavior, and forecast expectable stories: "In Geneva, as he had been perfectly aware, a young man wasn't at liberty to speak to a young unmarried lady save under certain rarely-occurring conditions; but here at Vevey what conditions could be better than these?" (8–9) [6]. But his generalizing soon puts him at ease:

> She might be cold, she might be austere, she might even be prim; for that was apparently—he had already so generalized —what the most "distant" American girls did: they came and planted themselves straight in front of you to show how rigidly unapproachable they were. There hadn't been the slightest flush in her fresh fairness however; so that she was clearly neither offended nor fluttered. Only she was composed—he had seen that before too—of charming little parts that didn't match and that made no *ensemble*; and if she looked another way when he spoke to her, and seemed not particularly to hear him, this was simply her habit, her manner, the result of her having no idea whatever of "form."   (10–11) [7–8]

As he listens to Daisy's chatter in this opening scene, Winterbourne is amused and perplexed, for his frames of reference—his collection of "cases" and "types"—don't satisfactorily collect her "little parts." They particularly fail to accommodate her stories of "gentlemen friends": "He had never yet heard a young girl express herself in just this fashion; never at least save in cases where to say such things was to have at the same time some rather complicated consciousness about them"—and he decides that he has "lost the right sense for the young American tone. Never indeed since he had grown old enough to appreciate things had he encountered a young compatriot of so 'strong' a type as this." He is at sea, unable to choose the appropriate formula for the "type" confronting him. "Were they all like that, the pretty girls who had had a good deal of gentlemen's society? Or was she also a designing, an audacious, in short an expert young person? . . . Some people had told him that after all American girls *were* exceedingly innocent, and others had told him that after all they weren't" (16–17) [10]. Is she what the Europeans would call a coquette?

It is significant that Winterbourne resorts to a foreign concept, the "coquette," in his desperate need of a category for Daisy. This and other foreign terms he seizes upon suggest not merely his cosmopolitanism but his need to make imprisoning divisions which have no labels in English or can be more comfortably referred to by a foreign word than by an embarrassing native one. He will wonder if he can accuse her of all that is implied by " 'inconduite,' as they say in Geneva." He will try, unsuccessfully, to assert that Daisy belongs to the "meilleur monde," but also characterize her meeting with her Italian friend as a "rendezvous," which, in the English mouth, suggests a secret or even illicit romantic meeting; even her earlier "têtes-à-têtes" with Giovanelli sound more covert in French. Finally, when he is convinced of Daisy's depravity he speaks of her Italian friend as her "amoroso"—evading the explicitness of the English "lover."

But nothing is more abhorrent to the classifying mind than doubt, and the dynamics of James's narrative consist exactly of Winterbourne's efforts to secure himself from uncertainty by means of a fixed system of generalities. The reader is compelled to share his anxious effort, to consider seriously whether or not each hypothesis will not eventually provide a closure to the inquiry upon which he is jointly launched with this man—to expect a further unfolding of plot which will make one conclusion absolute and kill off all alternatives glimpsed along the way. Winterbourne is relieved to "discover" at this point that there is a class, after all, to which Daisy can be assigned: "He must on the whole take Miss Daisy Miller for a flirt—a pretty American flirt. He had never as yet had relations with representatives of that class." And having established her membership in the class, he is at his ease. "Winterbourne was almost grateful for having found the formula that applied to Miss Daisy Miller. He leaned back in his seat . . . he wondered what were the regular conditions and limitations of one's intercourse with a pretty American flirt" (17) [11].

This is not the last time that we will observe the way the need for "formula" preys upon Winterbourne and the relief with which he arrives at one that appears to fit the instance. One may want to analyze this compulsion psychologically, and ask, as one would ask if he were a real person, what fear of Daisy's sexual attractiveness is at the root of his desire to reduce her to an intellectual concept. A feminist reading of the story can certainly assert confidently that Daisy's nature is being read by a masculine mind nervously in need of those imprisoning definitions which assure its dominance. However motivated, psychologically or sociologically, James's categorizer exhibits the desperation underlying the need of category generally. But if the writer wondered whether it was possible for fiction to dispense with such means for recognizing and identifying human personality—whether characters in fiction could be "natural" or "free"—the problem had an acute form when it came to female character. These words, we shall see, are to be associated very soon with Catherine Sloper and even more with James's greater American heroine, Isabel Archer, whose explicit desire it is to resist the traps of definition. But even the crude, inarticulate Daisy seems engaged in the defense of her own indeterminacy.

Winterbourne's aunt, Mrs. Costello, has a categorical dismissal ready for the whole Miller family—"They're the *sort* of Americans that one does one's duty by just ignoring" (23) [14] (my emphasis). Confused by her calling Daisy "a horror," Winterbourne resorts to another trite conception in the place of his "pretty American flirt," and asks his aunt if Daisy is "the sort of young lady who expects a man sooner or later to—well, we'll call it carry her off ?" (25) [15]. The exchange between nephew and aunt is high comedy. Mrs. Costello has an unshakable attachment to her generalizing view of Daisy—she does not need to verify it by meeting her, and when she hears further news of the young woman she calls her simply "an abomination" (both this word and "horror" (25) [15] are additions in the New York Edition text of Mrs. Costello's remarks; she is less categorically dismissive in the 1878 text). Winterbourne, on the other hand, is driven to surrender first one and then another of his "sorts," each time replacing his idea by one as banal as the previous. His uneasy journey from one concept to another is the story's profoundest plot and at the same time a dramatization of our reading experience.

Of course, Winterbourne is charmed by Daisy—this is one of the sources of his difficulty while it gives zest to the inquiry. " 'Common' she might be, as Mrs. Costello had pronounced her; yet what provision was made by that epithet for her queer little native grace?" (31) [18]. The epither, the abstraction, may be inadequate to contain this specimen after all. At the conclusion of the discussion with her mother and the courier, Eugenio, about a jaunt to the Chateau de Chillon with Winterbourne, Daisy seems merely whimsical as she teases him with a demand for some judgment: "Good-night—I hope you're disappointed or disgusted or something!" But Winterbourne can only offer, "I'm puzzled, if you want to know!" (38) [22]. Two days later he is off across the lake on the little steamer, his companion making "many characteristic remarks" while he ponders the "character" of which they give evidence: "If he had assented to the idea that she was 'common,' at any rate, *was* she proving so, after all, or was he simply getting used to her commonness?" (39, 40) [22, 23].

Just as he watches Daisy for the "characteristic" behavior she exhibits to him, so for Winterbourne the occasion has distinctly a conventional character; it is something to be identified by that term for a certain commonplace narrative, an "adventure"—a word which has a suggestion of the unprincipled (as when we call someone a "mere" adventurer) or, at least, the improper. He is somewhat disappointed to notice that his companion does not seem to have his own sense of the delightfully illicit. When she challenges him familiarly about his reasons for returning the next day to Geneva, he can only conclude that she is "an extraordinary mixture of innocence and crudity" (43) [24].

In Rome, he hears more about the "dreadful" behavior of the Millers, and tries to reassure his aunt: "They're very ignorant—very innocent only, and utterly uncivilised. Depend on it they're not 'bad,' " the last word used with self-conscious quotation-marks. The slippery relativity of language is acknowledged by Mrs. Costello, who remarks, "Whether or no being hopelessly vulgar is being 'bad' is a question for the metaphysicians. They're bad enough to blush for, at any rate; and for this short life that's quite enough" (46) [26]. For Winterbourne, however, mere vulgarity is not an adequate synonym for badness, and in the case of Daisy herself, it is clear that female "badness" has for him its traditional sense of sexual irregularity—and it is of this that he wants to exempt her. Then, to fill the gap of his doubt, he hears her announce, at the house of his American friend, Mrs. Walker, that she is going for an evening walk on the Pincio with a "Mr. Giovanelli." Winterbourne escorts her to this dubious rendezvous, and one glance is enough to convince him that "the beautiful Giovanelli" isn't "the right gentleman" for a nice young lady. His quick perception of "types" enables him to "take his measure" unhesitatingly: "He's anything but a gentleman . . . He's a music-master or a penny-a-liner or a third rate artist"—regretting that Miss Miller hasn't "instinctively discriminated against such a type" (58). The word "type" is an addition of the New York Edition; in 1878 James had written, "Winterbourne felt a superior indignation at his own lovely fellow-countrywoman's not knowing the difference between a spurious gentleman and a real one" [32–33], but in revising he wanted, clearly, to stress Winterbourne's typological compulsion.

Not to understand types is a mark against one's own membership in the right type. "Would a nice girl—even allowing for her being a little American flirt—make a rendezvous with a presumably low-lived foreigner?" (58) [33]. He swings to the conviction that she is not merely vulgar; she is not even "nice"—the word suggesting sexual laxness at the same time that it retains the sense of an inability to make discriminations. And, again, we notice that his devotion to the absolute category is so determined that it makes him impatient of discrepancy. He is positively annoyed that her assignation occurs in a crowded public place in broad daylight instead of some dark corner. He is "vexed that the girl, in joining her *amoroso* shouldn't appear impatient of his own company . . . It was impossible to regard her as a wholly unspotted flower—she lacked a certain indispensable fineness; and it would therefore much simplify the situation to be able to treat her as the subject of one of the visitations known to romancers as 'lawless passions' " (59) [33].

That James is parodying common ideas of virtue and vice as well as trite literature is obvious from the language which his free indirect style employs in representing Winterbourne's thinking. "Unspotted flower" is a sentimental cliché heightening the literary self-consciousness of the passage, and it should have the same quotation-marks about it as "lawless passions." (It is an addition of the New York Edition text. The 1878 text has in its place "a perfectly well-conducted young lady" [33].) The tale Winterbourne's imagination "writes" for Daisy is vulgar romance. James's reference to literary or sub-literary tradition is, of course, an explicit reflexiveness by the writer who understood the uses of such language in the popular literature of the day. "Daisy Miller" may have been suggested to James, in fact, not only by his own observation but by a forgotten novel by a Swiss writer, Victor Cherbuliez, whose *Paule Méré* (1864) James summarized as "a tale expressly to prove that frank nature is out of favor (in Geneva), and his heroine dies of a broken heart because her spontaneity passes for impropriety.[7] Translated into English, Cherbuliez's novel had attained the kind of popularity that James might have envied for himself, while his own ironic version of it distanced itself from the model and its sentimental typology.[8]

At Mrs. Walker's party Winterbourne tries to fit his concepts of "flirt" and "nice girl" to Daisy, who conflates them; "I'm a fearful frightful flirt! Did you ever hear of a nice girl that wasn't?" In the face of this cynicism he collapses into a more cynical gallantry, "You're a very nice girl, but I wish you'd flirt with me, and me only," only to be told, "You're the last man I should think of flirting with" (71) [39]. Winterbourne decides that "she was nothing every way if not light" (75) [41], this word implying the sexual sense of a wanton, a "light woman" along with its overt meaning simply of "unserious."

His interest reaches a new stage of ease, quite free of tension despite the constant presence of the Italian admirer who turns out to be "a perfectly respectable little man" (77) [42], a *cavaliere avvocato*—not really, at all, the "type" Winterbourne had earlier identified. Daisy has quite ruined her reputation with the Anglo-

---

7. Ibid., p. 58.
8. That this more obscure intention may have lingered in James's mind may be indicated by his casual insertion in *Daisy Miller* of a reference to *Paule Méré*, when Winterbourne, in Geneva, receives his aunt's report of the arrival of the Millers in Rome. She concludes her letter, seemingly without point: "Bring me that pretty novel of Cherbuliez's—Paule Méré" (45) [25].

American colony; Mrs. Walker has turned her back on her, and all the others close their doors. Winterbourne still insists that she is "du meilleur monde" (79) [44], and holds on, with forced gallantry, to the idea of her "innocence." He alternates between thinking her childishly oblivious of the effect she is producing and, insisting on a category, thinking her "a young person of the reckless class," whatever that is. The narrator, obtruding once more, remarks, "As I have already had occasion to relate, he was reduced without pleasure to this chopping of logic and vexed at his poor fallibility, his want of instinctive certitude as to how far her extravagance was generic and national and how far it was crudely personal" (81) [45].

Daisy, however, gives him little help. When he meets her one day with Giovanelli in the Palace of the Caesars, he tries to make her understand how people regard her and mentions that her mother thinks she is engaged. Her response is perversely teasing. She is— but if he really believes it—she isn't! And then, a week later, he finds her taking the night air with her companion in the Colosseum. His struggles of definition are over; his relief is total.

> Winterbourne felt himself pulled up with final horror now— and, it must be added, with final relief. It was as if a sudden clearance had taken place in the ambiguity of the poor girl's appearances and the whole riddle of her contradictions had grown easy to read. She was a young lady about the *shades* of whose perversity a foolish puzzled gentleman need no longer trouble his head or his heart. That once questionable quantity *had* no shades—it was a mere black little blot. He stood looking at her, looking at her companion too, and not reflecting that though he saw them vaguely he himself must have been more brightly presented. He felt angry at all his shiftings of view—he felt ashamed of all his tender little scruples and all his witless little mercies. He was about to advance again, and then again checked himself; not from the fear of doing her injustice, but from the sense of the danger of showing undue exhilaration for this disburdenment of cautious criticism.   (86) [47–48]

The passage is remarkable for its exposure of the meaning of Winterbourne's enterprise—the establishment of that certainty which Daisy has so far managed to resist. And it is he who is "more brightly presented" by the episode than is Daisy. She calls him "stiff," as she has already done several times before—"it had always been her great word." He *is* stiff as the sides of a pigeonhole are stiff, stiff as the inflexible categories which govern his thinking. The third sentence of the passage just quoted, with its emphasis, again, upon Winterbourne's compulsion to define and classify, is the alteration of the New York Edition from the earlier, "She was a young lady whom a gentleman need no longer be at pains to respect" [48]. Having placed her, all secondary questions are futile: it makes very little difference, he tells her, whether or not she is engaged. Dying, she will send him the message that she had never been engaged to Giovanelli "but as Winterbourne had originally judged, the truth on this question had small actual relevance" (91) [50].

At the Colosseum, he decides not to "cut her dead" but instead threatens her with literal death—the Roman fever which she imprudently risks. Daisy's response suggests either that she is a silly fool or that her romantic desire to "see the Colosseum by moonlight" (or as it is described in the famous passage from *Manfred* which Winterbourne had been murmuring to himself just a few moments earlier) is a better thing than his prudence. That she may feel for Winterbourne himself, despite his stiffness, a romantic emotion suitable to the context of the moonlight and Byron, one that he wounds by his own harshness, is suggested by the suicidal (or is it merely petulant?) quality of her last remark, "I don't care whether I have Roman fever or not!" (89) [49]. If this is so, she is one of those feminine characters—who appear early and late in James—whose capacity for love is unperceived or unvalued by a colder (a "winter-born") man; she is, then, cousin to Tina Bordereau of "The Aspern Papers" and May Bartram of "The Beast in the Jungle." Her own death-defying extravagance is itself a romantic expression of the passion of a character who desires, at whatever cost, to preserve the potentiality of her own being, something denied by Winterbourne's compulsion to "read . . . the riddle of her contradictions."

That Daisy dies so romantically as to be a martyr to her own faith in an unconfined selfhood seems too large a claim—and James undermines our readiness to give her such grand proportions by making her literally the victim of imprudence, of a disease still not understood to be conveyed by a nocturnal insect but correctly associated with the dangerous air of summer nights in nineteenth-century Rome. Yet her posture in the arena where Christian martyrs had died before her is not entirely an ironic touch. Her individuality, such as it is, is doomed by Winterbourne's decision to "cut her dead" and the stiff box into which his categorical mind has thrust her is in effect a coffin.

But the interpretive contest that has seemingly come to rest at last is not really over. There is Giovanelli's declaration at Daisy's grave, "She was the most beautiful young lady I ever saw, and the most amiable . . . Also . . . the most innocent" (92) [50]. So she lingers in Winterbourne's mind—if not in his heart: he "often thought of the most interesting member of that [Miller family] trio—of her mystifying manner and her queer adventure," and even confesses to his aunt that he may have done her an injustice—"she would have appreciated one's esteem." Mrs. Costello, taking the measure of his erotic regret, says that this means merely that "she would have reciprocated one's affection" (93) [51], but Winterbourne's view of Daisy may not be so simple any longer, and it is on no certain closure of conviction that the story ends. Few readers notice the slippage that has taken place in his final observation to his aunt, "You were right in that remark you made to me last summer. I was booked to make a mistake. I've lived too long in foreign parts" (93) [51]. But the mistake she had predicted was quite the opposite of the one he may be admitting now. When, at the outset, she warned, "You've lived too long out of the country. You'll be sure to make some great mistake" (25–26) [15], it was because he seemed, then, to be inclined to think too well of Daisy rather than too ill. But James does not make this explicit, preferring the ambiguity of his close. He wrote a reviewer of "Daisy Miller," "Nothing is my *last* word about anything—I am interminably super-subtle and analytic."[9]

WILLIAM VEEDER

["The Aspern Papers"]†

* * *

The early chapters of "The Aspern Papers" reveal the polymorphous nature of desire by dramatizing the editor's sexual dysfunction. His ineptitude with women is obvious enough; what requires study is the way he associates eros and sight. Watching the maid move from the sala into the Misses Bordereau's rooms, he imagines her disappearing "into impenetrable regions"[1] [60]; seeing Juliana's eyeshade still in place at their second meeting, he feels "the old woman remained impenetrable" (62) [66]. What resists the editor is not the eyeshade, of course, but Juliana's indomitable will, as we see when

> Miss Bordereau had been divested of her green shade [at a subsequent meeting] . . . the upper half of her face was covered

9. Letter to Mrs. F. H. Hill, March 21, 1879, in Edel, ed., *Letters*, 2:221.
† From "The Aspern Portrait," *The Henry James Review* 20:1 (1999), 22–42. © The Johns Hopkins University Press. Reprinted by permission of The Johns Hopkins University Press.
1. Henry James, "The Aspern Papers," in *Great Short Works of Henry James* (New York: Harper and Row, 1966), 55. Hereafter cited parenthetically within the text. References to corresponding passages in this Norton Critical Edition appear in brackets following the author's original citations. In instances where the author refers specifically to the 1888 edition, only the bracketed citation appears.

by the fall of a piece of dingy, lace-like muslin . . . descended to the end of her nose, leaving nothing visible but her white withered cheeks and puckered mouth. . . . "You mean she always wears something [over her eyes]? She does it to preserve them." [109]

The editor's ocular anxiety is two-fold. Not only can he not penetrate women, but they *can* penetrate him. That Juliana from behind her eyeshade "might take me all in without my getting at herself. . . . had a fuller vision of me than I had of her" (60, 62) [65, 66] establishes the *fact* of his vulnerability, but the *extent* of it, the fear and anguish he experiences, is revealed most graphically when he looks toward her "impenetrable regions. . . . I looked at the place with my heart beating as I had known it to do in dentists' parlours." Tooth extraction is what occurred in Victorian dentist parlors, so the editor's analogy here—and his subsequent image of Juliana "extracting gold from me" (92) [90]—reveal how archaic his fears are, how real for him is the fantasy of the phallic mother who can penetrate and castrate.

Against his fears the editor erects two defenses. Projection and affiliation. He attempts, on the one hand, to control women by projection. At his second meeting with Juliana he calls her horrifying green eyeshade "the same mystifying bandage" (91) [89]. How can an eyeshade be a *bandage*? By the logic of reaction formation. What bandages cover are wounds. And "wound" is how woman's genitals are traditionally characterized—as cut and scar, as absence. Thus the editor "castrates" the phallic mother by projecting onto her the visual emasculation that excises her penetrating gaze and thus reassures his anxious masculinity. (He does the same thing when he describes Juliana with images of detumescence—"shriveled" (61, 107) [66, 102], "shrunken" (60, 65) [65, 69], "withered" (68, 115) [71, 109], "impotent" (109) [105], "she didn't come up. . . . she seemed all spent" (114) [108]. How phantasmic the editor's ocular fears are is indicated when Tina responds to his fatuous statement that "if I made the invalid angry she ought perhaps to be spared the sight of me. 'The sight of you? Do you think she can *see?*'" (115) [109].

Obviously the editor's wish fulfillments cannot solve his very real psychological problems—especially since the bandage projection constitutes his *second* attempt to castrate Juliana visually. Recall his initial terror at the eyeshade: "she might take me all in without my getting at herself. At the same time it [the eyeshade] increased a presumption of some ghastly death's-head lurking behind it. The divine Juliana as a grinning skull . . ." (60) [65]. Person glosses "this startling hallucination" as "an exaggerated male fear of women. . . . Juliana is an embodiment of mortality."[2] I agree, but I believe the image is overdetermined. The very conventionality of the equation of women and death suggests to me a defense. If Juliana can be converted into a skull, then she cannot see into the editor—skulls have no eyes. She's thus "castrated" (again), her penetrating gaze replaced not only by an icon replete with multiple orifices but also by a patriarchal stereotype. Woman = death. Death is again projected reassuringly when Juliana's eyeshade comes off and the editor still cannot see her eyes. "I looked again at the old woman's wrappings" [109]. Wrappings suggest cerements, the accoutrements of the grave that the editor imagined when he first encountered Juliana's "horrible green shade. . . . death might take her at any moment. . . . then I could pounce on her possessions. . . . She was dressed in black and her head was wrapped in a piece of old black lace" (60) [65]. Woman = death means woman = absent-for-good, in both senses.

At a level less archaic than the fantasy of the phallic mother, Juliana also poses a threat, and here what the editor projects defensively are scenarios. He admits quite candidly that he's "hatched a little romance" (76) [78] in speculating about her past, but readers have proven surprisingly gullible (proposing, for instance, that Tina might be the daughter of Juliana's sister—when in fact there is *no* evidence that Juliana had a sister). The editor's scenario is as "interested" as his images. He again projects the Juliana he needs. One of these needs Church unmasks forcefully:

> This romance [that Juliana's mother was dead before Aspern appeared in her husband's studio] constitutes a scene of generation of narrativity (letters) in which the male artist can begin his work of representation only when the woman is absent. . . . the narrator's wording makes it sound as if it [the daughter's existence] were an act of parthenogenesis: the father "had [a] daughter."[3]

Unquestionably the editor needs to exclude women from creativity, but once again his projection functions overdeterminedly. "Aspern had of course met the young lady on his going to her father's studio as a sitter" [105]. What attracts Jeffrey is thus not Juliana but her father, not eros but narcissism and the bond of fellow creators. Of course. This attempt to undermine Juliana's attractiveness reinforces the editor's earlier deployment of one of the traditional ways to discredit women. "By what passions had she been ravaged?"

2. Leland S. Person, Jr., "Eroticism and Creativity in *The Aspern Papers*," *Literature and Psychology* 32 (1986): 24, 25.

3. Joseph Church, "Writing and the Dispossession of Woman in *The Aspern Papers*," *American Imago* 47 (1990): 32. (Final bracket Church's.)

(76) [78]. Rather than a virgin whose love for Aspern had flowered in a grand, if doomed, affair, Juliana is portrayed as promiscuous and thus justly punished. "It was part of my idea that the young lady had had a foreign lover—and say an unedifying tragical rupture—before her meeting with Jeffrey Aspern" (77) [78]. No man so fine as Aspern could have taken seriously any woman so available and expendable; Juliana was one of the poet's many adventures rather than the love of his life. Of course. The editor can muster not a scintilla of evidence for this scenario because compulsion, not data, is what drives his projections. "It was essential to my hypotheses that . . . It was also indispensable that . . ." (76) [78]. So relentless a need to discredit Juliana derives from a comparably desperate need to keep Aspern free of women—and thus free for himself.

Rivalry with Juliana brings us to the editor's second defense against woman. In addition to projecting scenarios and images, he affiliates himself aggressively with Jeffrey Aspern: "I took no pains to defend him. One doesn't defend one's god: one's god is himself a defence" (46) [54]. Aspern's role as defense is as overdetermined as the editor's desires.

He hangs high in the heaven of our literature. (46) [54]

The vision [of the death's-head behind Juliana's eyeshade] hung there until it passed. (60) [65]

In the wish-fulfilling logic of the editor's fearful fantasizing, Juliana-as-specter passes *because* Jeffrey-as-god endures. "Passed" connotes "dead" here because patriarchy's fundamental binary—woman = absence *vs* man = presence—is being projected onto recalcitrant reality. In point of fact, Jeffrey is dead and Juliana is alive. But since great poems outlive their muses, Aspern's enduring reputation constitutes the editor's warrant for seeing him as a god and her as a skull.

Aspern's function goes beyond defending the editor against a rival: "The sacred relics . . . made my life continuous, in a fashion, with the illustrious life they had touched" (73) [76].[4] Discontinuity is the editor's paramount danger. Fragmentation. Seen from the perspective of this archaic fear, women are *occasions* of trouble rather than its root cause. The editor has never achieved that self-cohesion which constitutes the precondition for intimacy. (His weak sense of self is evident in his pride in his family name: " 'It isn't a new one; it's a very good old one, thank fortune!' " (121) [114].

4. In the 1888 version of the novella, James ended this sentence with "thank heavens!" "Heavens" here, echoing the "heaven" where the editor's god hangs high, indicates that family gives the editor a sense of social continuity analogous to the professional continuity provided by Aspern's relics.

In his affiliations with both his family name and his favorite poet, the editor experiences a sense of self that comes from the outside as a blessing bestowed, rather than from within as something inherent. Value *is* continuity—being a member of a long-established family line that's part of a long-established community and being the editor of a world-renowned poet who's firmly established in the lyric tradition.) In turn, the defense that Jeffrey Aspern offers against fragmentation is not what post-Freudian psychoanalysts such as Winnicott and Kohut would prescribe, not the holding and mirroring that might heal narcissistic injuries and integrate the self. Fantasizing about being "continuous . . . with the [poet's] illustrious life . . . I lost myself in this satisfaction" (73, 74) [76, 76]. Loss of self, not integration of the self, is what satisfies the editor. Fusion is his fantasy solution to fragmentation.

He thus joins one of James's saddest confraternities.

> . . . I asked after Miss Bordereau's health. . . . She answered that it was good enough—good enough; that it was a great thing to be alive.
>
> "Oh as to that, it depends upon what you compare it with!" I returned with a laugh.
>
> "I don't compare—I don't compare. If I did that I should have given everything up long ago." (91) [90]

To live comparatively is to have no life at all, no self. James's fiction repeatedly features characters who exist only through others. And these characters are not only noxiously parasitic like Selah Tarrant and Matthias Pardon in *The Bostonians* or abjectly accommodating like Mitchy in *The Awkward Age*. Even the gifted telegraphist in "In the Cage" is shaky enough to ask "where was one's pride and one's passion when the real way to judge of one's luck was by making not the wrong but the right comparison?"[5] When the editor tries to defend his biographical excavations of authors' lives by arguing that "it's all vain words if there's nothing to measure it by,' " Juliana belittles his comparative penchant again, " 'You talk as if you were a tailor' " [102].[6] Juliana, splendid in her refusal to live comparatively, displays the resiliency of self that enabled her to risk a passionate affair with Jeffrey Aspern at the height of his sexual and poetic powers. The editor, in turn, reveals why he seeks fusional continuity with a corpse: he experiences his options as merger or disintegration.

---

5. Henry James, *In the Cage: Eight Tales from the Major Phase*, ed. Morton Dauwen Zabel (New York: Norton, 1958), 261 [298].
6. Likewise the editor feels as if he were a mannequin "as I stood there to be measured" by Juliana's relentless gaze (96).

How overdetermined his affiliation is with Aspern is indicated by his most protracted fantasy in the opening chapters.

> That spirit [of patience] kept me perpetual company and seemed to look out at me from the revived immortal face—in which all his genius shone—of the great poet who was my prompter. I had invoked him and he had come . . . it was as if his bright ghost had returned to earth to assure me he regarded the affair as his own no less than as mine. . . . It was as if he had said: "Poor dear, be easy with her. . . . Strange as it may appear to you she was very attractive in 1820. Meanwhile, aren't we in Venice together. . . . See . . . how the sky and the sea and the rosy air and the marble of their palaces all shimmer and melt together." My eccentric private errand became a part of the general romance and the general glory—I felt even a mystic companionship, a moral fraternity with all those who in the past had been in the service of art. (73) [75]

Affiliation with Aspern here is effected at various levels of the psyche. Most archaically, there is merger: with Jeffrey himself, through their exclusive tête-à-tête; with men like him ("fraternity" excludes women) who have served art; and with his world, both city and nature, through the impressionistic shimmer that melts all things together in fusional oneness. At a less archaic level, the homoerotic strain that marks the editor's relationship with Aspern and that fuels his rivalry with Juliana surfaces here as well. " 'Poor dear' " seems initially like direct address. Preceded by "as if he had said," and followed by the imperative " 'be easy,' " and consonant with the commiserative tone already set, " 'poor dear' " seems to tenderly establish the editor as Jeffrey's object of affection. In turn, the fact that the " 'poor dear' " is actually Juliana indicates how the editor relates to her throughout the novel. As in a Girardian triangle, woman functions for him not as an object of desire in her own right but as a conduit of desire between two men. "I felt an irresistible desire to hold in my own for a moment the hand Jeffrey Aspern had pressed. . . . we [he and Cumnor] had not been able to look into a single pair of eyes into which his had looked" (65, 48) [69, 56]. Moreover, both the suggestive diction of the Venice fantasy (keep company . . . made him come . . . in Venice together . . . romance) and the misogyny (strange to say she was attractive once) resonate with homoerotic moments throughout the novella. Finally, there is the heterosexual level. Here the editor figures himself as a man having an "affair," and Jeffrey is assigned the role of "prompter."

Heterosexual, homosexual, and fusional fantasies all in play in one scene . . . "The Aspern Papers" is indeed a tale of polymorphous desire. While critics have done strong work with one or another aspect of the editor's psyche,[7] what remains unexamined is how these aspects interact—how his desires are structured and how terrors from different levels of the unconscious jeopardize their realization. First, his desires. It is always precarious to think in terms of structure when addressing something so volatile as the psyche: "stages" and "levels" suggest a tidy uni-directional development and a cleanly demarcated form to what is obviously a ceaselessly reciprocal process. We all also know, however, that Freud's paramount insight was not that the unconscious exists but that it has a structure, and that Lacan's core revision of Freud was his claim that the unconscious is structured like a language. I believe the opening chapters of "The Aspern Papers" set forth a structure of desires that increase in intensity as they become more archaic and less conscious.

Structure of Desires in "The Aspern Papers"

Desire	Stage	Jeffrey Aspern	Woman	Language	Image
heterosexual	latent and oedipal	role: self-object; editor's desire: to be phallic like JA	role: to be controlled; violence against: "ransack her drawers"	JA as "prompter": his poems are models to live by	JA's face
homosexual	Negative Oedipal	role: obj. of desire; editor's desire: to receive the phallus from JA	role: to be replaced by editor as rival; violence against: matricide	professional as screen for tabooed personal desire: letters as fetish	JA as "light" we walk by
fusional archaic		role: merger site; editor's desire: to be continuous with JA	absent	at first, projected onto JA; then, silence	JA's face becomes editor's in frame

7. In addition to the Church, Rowe, and Person work already cited, see recent essays and chapters by Carton, Graham, Person ("James's Homo-Aesthetics"), Reesman, Rivkin, and Tanner.

Rather than belabor each element here, I will single out those that add to what I've said about the editor's desires. His fantasy of having a heterosexual "affair" in Venice is largely a screen, but his investment in normative sexuality is real (He feels true shame when confessing to Mrs. Prest his un-Aspern-like failure with women.) Even this quite conscious fantasy indicates the editor's polymorphousness, however, since the "affair" contains elements of both latency and the oedipus. There is no murderous rivalry with Jeffrey Aspern who, as "prompter," enacts the role that Freud assigns to the father during latency: he is a guide and a model. Oedipal elements persist, however, since the imagined "affair" is with the father-figure's beloved, a woman old enough—literally—to be the editor's mother.

That the oedipal conflict remains unresolved is confirmed by the fact that the editor is sexually attracted to the father-figure as well as to the mother. The Negative Oedipus constitutes a fixation early in the process of oedipal resolution. The son not only gives up mother as the object of desire but also imagines himself replacing her in the father's affections. "He accepts in fantasy castration by the father, gives it a libidinal significance, and takes the father as a love object."[8] Understanding the editor's attraction to Aspern in terms of the Negative Oedipus is helpful in at least two ways. On the one hand, the fantasy of castration by the father can soothe the anxiety of a son unsuccessful with women. Sexuality is not lost; *hetero*sexuality is simply sacrificed to the higher goal of homosexual union with the father. The editor's (necessarily sanitized) version of this tabooed fantasy projects him as the (surely celibate) acolyte devoted to serving a god well-hung in heaven.

On the other hand, the Negative Oedipus also helps explain the editor's murderous rage against Juliana. Reversing the object of oedipal desire reverses the object of oedipal antagonism. I thus agree with Church that Juliana's "death signifies a matricide."[9] And I believe the Negative Oedipus clarifies the dynamic here. Church, positing correctly that the editor's invasion of Juliana's parlor and his subsequent movements toward her put into action the violence inherent in his fantasy of "ransack[ing] her drawers," argues that "the man's desire to recover the phallus has the markings of necrophilia. . . . In oedipal terms, the imaginary necrophilia enables the son to take possession of 'his' puissance without actually having to transgress and thereby incur terrors of mutilation (from mother or father)."[1] Invading the woman's bedroom is oedipal in so far as

8. Ruth Mack Brunswick, "The Preoedipal Phase of Libidinal Development," in *The Psychoanalytic Reader*, ed. Robert Fliess, Vol. 1 (New York: International University Press, 1948), 266.
9. Church, "Writing and the Dispossession," 34.
1. Ibid., 33.

Juliana is the father-figure's beloved. But since the principle purpose of the invasion is not to copulate with Juliana but to kill her —not *petit* but *gros mort*—the editor's matricidal rage is *negative* oedipal. His intention is dual: to extirpate the rival Juliana and to connect with the desired Jeffrey through contact with his safely professionalized papers-as-fetish. Puissance comes *through* the father rather than at his expense.

That the editor's rage here is also *pre*-oedipal takes us to the most archaic of his desires. To elide fantasies of homoerotic union and of fusion is a mistake. "The homoerotic (as well as narcissistic) aspect of the narrator's idolatry is evident in several scenes, but most especially when through prosopopeia the editor brings the poet back to life and the two 'melt together' in a gush of decadent imagery."[2] Rather than a single "aspect," the homoerotic and the fusional are, I believe, different desires in play in an overdetermined fantasy sequence. Melting together does indeed occur in the Venice fantasy, but what melts together are not "the two" men. James specifies that what "all shimmer and melt together" are "the sky and the sea and the rosy air and the marble." The editor—*at this moment* in the fantasized scene—projects not the union of two men but the merger of "all" in a oneness archaic rather than decadent, a grandiose wholeness that recreates infantine fusion with the All-Mother. Church's "gush" makes ejaculatory what I believe is pregenital at this moment in the fantasy. To confuse the Negative Oedipal and the pre-oedipal is to elide two desires that seek realization in two different articulations of Jeffrey Aspern. The papers and the portrait.

Before studying these two modes of articulation, we need to account more fully for the pre-oedipal terrors that jeopardize the realization of polymorphous desires. The editor feels such terrific fear of the phallic mother because he experiences *both* of the forms in which she haunts the psyche. Not only the woman-who-wields-the-penis but also the woman-who-contains-the-penis. In addition to the Juliana whom we've already seen terrify the editor, the evidently phallic figure who "I felt . . . look at me with great penetration" [66], another Juliana also threatens his continuity with Jeffrey. "Her presence seemed somehow to contain and express his own" (59) [64]. The editor participates here in an incorporative fantasy more archaic than the evidently phallic woman of Freud and Brunswick. Unlike these analysts who see the imago as "a fantasy of regressive, compensatory nature . . . a hypothesis made to insure the mother's possession of the penis"[3] at the developmentally rather late moment

2. Ibid., 37.
3. Brunswick, "Libidinal Development," 270.

when the child refuses to accept sexual difference and maternal castration, Melanie Klein believes the fantasy is

> a sexual theory, formed at a very early stage of development, to the effect that the mother incorporates the father's penis in the act of coitus. . . . she thus became an object of anxiety for the boy [under analysis], because she now carried his father's terrifying penis (= his father) inside herself. . . . the sexual theory that the mother has a penis of her own is, I think, the result of a modification by displacement of more deeply seated fears of her body as a place which is filled with a number of dangerous penises. . . . "The woman with a penis" always means, I should say, the woman with the father's penis.[4]

This fantasy of the woman-who-contains-the-penis is mobilized by Charlotte Brontë in a novel that James knew well. When Jane Eyre is exiled to Mrs. Reed's terrifying "red room," she finds "a certain secret drawer in the wardrobe, where were stored diverse parchments, her jewel-casket, and a miniature of her dead husband."[5] Like Mrs. Reed's wardrobe, Juliana's secretary beckons James's editor with comparably fetishistic relics of Jeffrey Aspern. Brontë's protagonist is not, however, obsessed with the woman-who-contains-the-penis, as James's editor is.

His speculations about Aspern's relics focus repeatedly on their placement. " 'She had hid them in her bed.' 'In her bed?' 'Between the mattresses. . . . I can't understand how she did it' " [123]. Did what? How she could incorporate the father's penis is terrifyingly evident to the fantasizing male. Sex castrates. Woman's acquisition of the phallus obsesses the editor because he fears the consequences for the father-figure (and thus for himself). Two consequences in particular—violation and incorporation. On the one hand, "that individual note [of Juliana's voice] had been in Jeffrey Aspern's ear" (61) [65]. Church entertains "the possibility that his [the editor's] anxiety of being violated by the 'phallic mother' disguises a fear of being violated by a man."[6] Anything so taboo as homosexuality in the Victorian period would unquestionably generate fear in the editor, and thus denial and disguise, at the Negative Oedipal level, but would he defend by activating a still more threatening imago from the archaic unconscious? Especially since he desires sexual union with the "violating" man? I believe the ed-

---

4. Melanie Klein, *The Psycho-Analysis of Children*, trans. Alix Strachey (New York: Free Press, 1975), 65, 23, 245. This quotation appeared originally in Klein's important early paper, "Early Stages of the Oedipus Conflict." Klein repeats the quotation verbatim in Chapter 4 of *The Psycho-Analysis of Children* (65) and amplifies it throughout the volume.
5. Charlotte Brontë, *Jane Eyre*, ed. Michael Mason (London: Penguin, 1996), chapter 2.
6. Church, "Writing and the Dispossession," 36.

itor fears that the man himself may be violated by the woman who's appropriated his penis. How vulnerable to penetration—and thus to effeminating role-reversal—is the god who's supposed to be the editor's "defence" against the feminine figure who's repeatedly penetrated him! Rape by the phallic mother is not the disguise but the thing feared.

On the other hand, the editor fears Juliana's incorporative capacity. He speculates that " 'she wanted to give directions that her papers should be buried with her' " [125]. The fear that womb is tomb surfaces early in the novella ("buried in her soul") and is heightened when the editor confronts the likeliest site of the relics' interment. "A queer superannuated coffer" (116) [110]. The word "coffer" evokes "coffin," as "trunk" and "box" do not. "Superannuated," rather than "decrepit" or "antiquated" or just plain "old," suggests a broad sweep of time ("beyond the years") that reinforces the archaic nature of the fear here (as "queer" confirms the Negative Oedipal union that's threatened).[7] Still more archaic and thus more horrifying is the possibility that Juliana's incorporative relation to the relics—and thus her murder of the father—may be oral. " 'Oh she lived on them!' " (135) [124]. That the editor too can be incorporated is what he's fearing when he believes "for the instant that she had put it [the eyeshade] on expressly, so that from underneath it she might take me all in" (60) [65]. To "take in" is a pun that indicates the editor's overdetermined vulnerabilities. At the manifest level, Juliana will take him in professionally, will deceive him about the papers; at the archaic, Juliana will incorporate "all" of him. How primitive her interiority seems to him at this level is evident when he says "she looked at me as from the mouth of her cave" (105) [100].

Incorporation and violation . . . scary indeed. Since rage is a reaction formation against fear, the matricidal rage loosed on Juliana by the editor is overdetermined—fueled both by his Negative Oedipal desire to extirpate the rival for Jeffrey Aspern's affections and by his multiple fears of the woman-who-wields-and-contains-the-penis. These fears and rages also help explain an apparently eccentric feature of the editor's desire for fusion. Since merger is his most archaic fantasy, why doesn't he, like virtually all of us, fantasize re-fusing with the original object? Normally the self-obliterating nature of such fusion is masked by regressive nostalgia for the all-providing mother. But the editor knows better. For whatever reason (Brunswick speculates that "undue aggression toward

---

7. Although the *OED* does not acknowledge "queer" meaning "gay" until the 1920s, I agree with Sedgwick and others that the word recurs too frequently in homoerotic moments in James's fiction to be inadvertent, especially given his manifold associations with the gay subculture in London.

the mother" is experienced when developmental activity is im-
paired[8]), he feels the menace of the incorporative mother so intensely that fear overshadows her potential beneficence for him. "I
preferred not to be shut up with her" [121]. He's too damaged,
however, too fragmented, to simply outgrow the dream of fusion.
So, he substitutes father for mother.

To merge with Jeffrey Aspern, to be loved by him, to be like him.
On all three levels of desire—fusional, homosexual, heterosexual—
the editor's fantasizing gives him pleasure. What it gives us readers
is cause for concern. Boundary formation and reality testing are
indices of maturity, but boundaries and reality are just what tend
to shimmer away when the editor fantasizes. Though "psychotic" is
too strong a term, at least this early in the story, the editor does
display a tendency to "borderline" behavior that's troubling. For me,
the chief drama from this point on in "The Aspern Papers" is not
whether the editor will possess the letters but whether he can develop enough self-possession, a strong enough sense of self, to resist
his obliterative desire for merger. And thereby escape death-in-life.

* * *

MICHAEL MOON

["The Pupil"]†

* * *

One of the most pervasive of the fantasies informing the "perverse" initiation rituals I'm discussing and the uncanny, sexually
disorienting effects they produce is that of a person's being able to
ravish and hold captive another person by the unaided agency of a
powerful gaze, and the attendant danger of this gaze's making its
director more rather than less highly susceptible to other people's
gazes * * *. The fantasy of the pupil of the eye as the focal point
of visual and erotic capture is at the core of Henry James's tale
"The Pupil," which treats of a series of visual and erotic captures
and struggles to escape both into and away from a "perverse" circle
constituted by a brilliant little boy, his loving and beloved tutor, and
the boy's mother, who is attractive and socially ambitious but perpetually financially embarrassed. The precincts of James's fiction

8. Brunswick, "Libidinal Development," 282.
† From "A Small Boy and Others: Sexual Disorientation in Henry James, Kenneth Anger,
and David Lynch," *Comparative American Identities: Race, Sex and Nationality in the
Modern Text*, edited by Hortense Spillers. Copyright © 1991. Reproduced by permission
of Routledge, Inc., part of The Taylor & Francis Group. Page numbers in brackets refer
to this Norton Critical Edition.

may seem remote from those of a recent and flagrantly "perverse" film like *Blue-Velvet*,[1] but they are not as far apart as they may at first appear. Despite James's own announced distaste for the project of some of his contemporaries of representing "perversion" relatively openly and sensationally—Wilde's *Dorian Grey*, for example— James's own literary explorations of the circulation of "perverse" desires are elaborate and searching, and remarkably unconstrained by contemporary standards of gentility and prudery. "The Pupil" was summarily rejected by the editor of the *Atlantic Monthly*, one of the very few times one of James's fictions was declined by the journals to which he regularly contributed. James professed to be unable to understand why, but it may well have been because it produced the same kinds of discomfort in the editor that an anonymous critic writing in the *Independent* expressed a few years later in response to *The Turn of the Screw*. "How Mr. James could . . . choose to make such a study of infernal human debauchery . . . is unaccountable," the reviewer writes, going on to say, "The study . . . affects the reader with a disgust that is not to be expressed. The feeling after perusal of the horrible story is that one has been assisting in an outrage upon . . . human innocence, and helping to debauch—at least by standing helplessly by—the pure and trusting nature of children. Human imagination can go no further into infamy, literary art could not be used with more refined subtlety of spiritual defilement."[2] In other words, James's work looked to some of his contemporaries—and may look to us, if we allow it to—the way *Blue Velvet* looks to us: shocking and disturbing. Or to put it another way, if James were writing today, his work would look more like *Blue Velvet* than it would like Merchant and Ivory's ponderously reverent period "recreations" of his novels.

One thing James's work registers continuously that Merchant and Ivory's betrays little feeling for is the investment of "sexiness" in, the fetish-character of, a given epoch's favored fashions in dress and styles of interior decoration. The Paris of the Second Empire was the most formative setting of James's childhood according to his own testimony, and it is a principal setting of "The Pupil." The bourgeois culture of this period may be said to have had its own intense velvet fetish. According to Walter Benjamin in his study of Baudelaire, bourgeois domestic interiors at the latter end of the period had become velvet- and plush-lined carapaces for a social

---

1. Part of Moon's essay not reprinted here deals with David Lynch's 1986 film [Editors].
2. *The Independent* (January 5, 1899), 73; rpt. in Robert Kimbrough, ed., *Henry James: The Turn of the Screw* (New York: Norton, 1966), p. 175. Shoshana Felman discusses this review in *Writing and Madness: Literature/Philosophy/Psychoanalysis*, trans. Martha Noel Evans and the author with the assistance of Brian Massumi (Ithaca, N.Y.: Cornell Univ. Press, 1985), pp. 143–144.

class that seemed to want to insulate itself from the world from which it derived its wealth and power behind a grotesque barrier of such luxury fabrics—in clothing for ordinary and ceremonial occasions, in upholstery and wallcoverings, and, perhaps most significantly, in linings for instrument cases, jewelry boxes, and coffins.[3]

"Velvet" is everywhere in James, once one becomes aware of it, and it is there unsurprisingly, given the characteristic settings and concerns of his fiction—freedom and domination, glamor and stigma, during what he calls in the preface to "The Pupil" "the classic years of the great Americano-European legend" [411]. When the tutor Pemberton in "The Pupil" wonders resentfully how his penurious employers can manage to keep installing themselves in what the narrator calls the "velvety *entresols*" of the best hotels in Paris, "the most expensive city in Europe," "velvet" still bears the unambiguously positive charge it had carried forty years before in Thackeray's *Vanity Fair*, the repository of so many of James's basic props for signaling fine degrees of upward and downward social mobility, as when Becky Sharp finds herself at one of the peaks of her success being waited on by a "velvetfooted butler" [163].[4] There is a striking detail in the opening lines of "The Pupil," however, that suggests the more ambiguous charge a luxury fabric could bear as sign late in the nineteenth century. When the characters of Pemberton the tutor and Mrs. Moreen are first introduced, he is called simply "[t]he poor young man" and his new employer, Mrs. Moreen, is "the large, affable lady who sat there drawing a pair of soiled *gants de Suède* through a fat, jewelled hand. . . ." [133] This description occurs in the second sentence of the story and it is easy enough for one to overlook it as a gratuitous "realistic" detail, but on reflection one can see in what rich detail these images signify "trouble ahead" for Pemberton and even the ambiguous nature of that "trouble." Mrs. Moreen's gesture of drawing her soiled suede gloves through her "fat, jewelled hand" mimes an unspoken desire —not necessarily her own—for her son, who is both the only other person present at this conversation and the most mixed quantity in the story, the figure in it who is neither entirely innocent of the shabbiness or willful moral abjectness of the rest of the Moreen family, nor entirely guilty of it, but rather only tainted or "soiled" with it by unavoidable association. Pemberton squirms with discomfort during this initial (and initiatory) interview because Mrs. Moreen is performing this curious mime of displaying a bit of her dirty laundry to him instead of settling the matter of his salary, which

---

3. Benjamin, *Charles Baudelaire: A Lyric Poet in the Era of High Capitalism*, trans. Harry Zohn (London: Verso, 1983), pp. 46–47.
4. *Vanity Fair* (New York: New American Library, 1962), p. 257.

the narrator refers to as "the question of terms." What Pemberton does not see at the beginning of the story is that while his salary is not being discussed, his real compensation for his work—an invitation to desire Morgan—is being repeatedly issued in mime by Mrs. Moreen. His intense but unnamed relationship to her little son—here is the real "question of terms" that is in contest in the story and beyond it—will partake of the mixed character of her "soiled" gloves. Rather than being something that sets them apart from the rest of the Moreen household, the "scandal" of the intimacy between tutor and pupil is perfectly "at home" with the more inclusive "scandal" of the kind of mixed clean-and-dirty surface Mrs. Moreen and the rest of the family show to the world. I shall return to the detail of the soiled gloves a little later on.

When Morgan dies at the story's climax, his body doesn't end up simply in his tutor's arms, as it might if the story were just a pederastic idyll, as I would argue it is not, nor does his body end up in his mother's arms, in the kind of vignette that would anticipate the similar death of little Miles in the arms of his governess at the climax of *The Turn of the Screw*. Rather, the body of the dead boy ends up suspended between his tutor and his mother. When Pemberton sees that Morgan is dead, the narrator says, "[h]e pulled him half out of his mother's hands, and for a moment, while they held him together, they looked, in their dismay, into each other's eyes" [170]. The resemblance of this last image in the tale to its first one is striking: young Morgan's dead body occupies precisely the place of the dirty suede gloves, but this time instead of merely noticing them unreflectively while Mrs. Moreen pulls them through her hands, Pemberton actively intervenes to draw Morgan's body "half out of [her] hands." Suspended between childhood and manhood (he has grown from age eleven to fifteen in the course of the story) and between mother and tutor, Morgan's body at the moment of death becomes a kind of uncanny puppet, a "soiled" handpuppet like a "soiled" glove. Although Pemberton and Mrs. Moreen have repeatedly quarreled over which of them has made the greater "sacrifice" for Morgan, the boy himself ends up, perhaps not entirely unwillingly, the sacrificial victim of the rituals the three practice, leaving tutor and mother in the utterly abject position of members of a collapsed cult.

I want to consider a little further the possible significance of "soiled" suede as a figure for relations in "The Pupil." Like those of "velvet," the erotic and class associations of "suede" have shifted and mutated considerably over the past century and more. The possible erotic association that makes soiled "suede" rather than velvet the appropriate figure for whatever unnameable bond unites Mrs. Moreen and her little son at the beginning of the story, a bond into which they admit, and with which they secure Pemberton, is primarily a verbal one: English-language guides to proper dress from mid-century forward inform the reader that the newly fashionable fabric "*Suède*" is "undressed kid." Those who would argue that "undressed kid" could not have meant, even subliminally, "undressed child" to James and his readers because "kid" did not then in that place and time commonly mean "child," need only look in the *OED* to see that it was precisely in the decade or two before "The Pupil" was written that "kid" as a term for "child" ceased to be "low slang" as it long had been and entered into common use among the English upper class as a term of familiar affection for a child or children of one's own: William Morris writes of the health of his "kid" in a personal letter of the 1860s, and Lord Shaftesbury makes a notation of several happy days spent with his "wife and kids" in a passage from his journal published in the 1880s. If my translations of the phrase "drawing a pair of soiled *gants de Suède* through a fat, jewelled hand" into "handling dirty undressed-kid gloves" and, possibly, into other permutations of that phrase, including "handling a dirty undressed kid," seem farfetched, it is only because the erotic wish encrypted, mimed but unspoken, in the text of "The Pupil" is precisely the kind of meaning that requires just such high-intensity translation or decoding—not only because James may have been to some degree unconscious of this meaning but also because of our own resistance to recognizing the access to "perverse" energies that his writing frequently affords us.

* * *

PHILIP HORNE

[The Master and the 'Queer Affair' of 'The Pupil']†

* * *

At this juncture I'd like to put forward what might be called a methodological misgiving about perhaps the most impressive, certainly the most influential, of 'Queer' readers of James. My misgiving concerns Eve Sedgwick's powerful and imaginative argument about 'The Beast in the Jungle' in *The Epistemology of the Closet* (1990), and that in the essay 'Is the Rectum Straight?: Identification and Identity in *The Wings of the Dove*' in *Tendencies* (1994). The point requires a remark about the history of James criticism. Read-

---

† From "Henry James: The Master and the 'Queer Affair' of 'The Pupil' " in *Henry James: The Short Fiction: Reassessments*, edited by N. H. Reeve (New York: St. Martin's Press, 1997), pp. 114–37. Reprinted by permission of Macmillan Ltd. References to this Norton Critical Edition appear in brackets.

ers of James are familiar with the late Jamesian practice of abstaining from specification of significant facts, names and events,
creating epistemological abysses round which one warily treads—
gaps one may imagine filling in a multiplicity of ways, temptations
to the over-confident guesser: in *The Ambassadors* what the New-
somes manufacture in Woollett; in 'The Turn of the Screw' what
Miles says at school that is so bad; in 'The Figure in the Carpet',
especially, what is the clue to the works of Hugh Vereker. Mysteries
of reference are James's stock in trade.

Critics confronted by these abysses have tended to divide into the
bravely or foolishly literal guessers, diving in after condoms or
'homoerotic sexual adventures' or 'love'; and more resignedly or
elaborately sophisticated refrainers who remain peering down from
the brink, trying to find a meaning for the fact of ambiguity without
dissolving it. Eve Sedgwick, an ingenious reader understandably reluctant to forfeit the flexibility that comes with her hermeneutic
initiations and yet seeking 'historical specificity'[1] for Queer Theory
wherever possible, does her best to keep one foot on the edge of
the abyss while with the other, and most of her weight, she steps
decisively into the darkness. Performing this manoeuvre in her
'Beast in the Jungle' discussion, glossing John Marcher's fate of
being '*the* man, to whom nothing on earth was to have happened',[2]
she makes brilliant use of a sophisticated turn on that 'nothing':

> A more frankly 'full' meaning for that unspeakable fate might
> come from the centuries-long historical chain of substantive
> uses of space-clearing negatives to void and at the same time
> to underline the possibility of male same-sex genitality. The
> rhetorical name for this figure is preterition. Unspeakable, Un-
> mentionable, . . . 'the love that dare not speak its name'—such
> *were* the speakable nonmedical terms in Christian tradition, for
> the homosexual possibility for men.[3]

She starts by calling the link she thus asserts between Marcher's
fate and 'the love that dare not speak its name' 'an *oblique* relation'
[504], 'highly equivocal' [505], and disavows a wish 'to pretend to
say one thing' [505]; then for the last six pages of the essay she
puts forward her 'hypothesis' about Marcher's 'male homosexual

---

1. Eve Kosofsky Sedgwick, *Tendencies* (London, 1994), p. 13.
2. Henry James, 'The Beast in the Jungle', *The Better Sort* (London, 1903), 139–178,
   p. 178.
3. Sedgwick, *The Epistemology of the Closet* (Berkeley & Los Angeles, 1990), [504]. She
   has built on this in her discussion of *The Wings of the Dove* in *Tendencies*, where she
   claims that 'Lionel Croy's homosexuality is spelled out in a simple code with deep historical roots: the code of *illum crimen horribile quod non nominandum est*, of "the crime
   not to be named among Christian men" and "the love that dare not speak its name" ';
   James's locutions 'specify the homosexual secret by failing to specify anything, speak by
   refusing to utter' (*Tendencies*, p. 75).

panic' and the damage it does May Bartram (the concept *The Epistemology of the Closet* as a whole advances). The hypotheticalness is at first signalled formally at the head of each paragraph or the start of each new stage: 'In my hypothesis', 'In this reading', and 'I hypothesize that . . . ' [508]. 'In this reading' makes one further brief appearance, and the essay takes off into the hypothesis, which is where it resoundingly ends.

I'll quickly state my difficulties here. First on the 'preterition' move. No one would deny the ingenuity of the connection. But as *argument* we obviously can't accept the syllogism that citing it might seem to imply:

1. James writes about the unnamable;
2. Homosexuality has often been spoken of as unnamable;
3. James *therefore* means homosexuality when he refers to something unnamable.

Sedgwick wisely doesn't attempt to draw more than an innuendo out of this. Only a few of the things unnamble in the public world are homosexual, after all. Many other unnamable things, unnamable because of different taboos and interests, creep in under the same umbrella. And unnamability may be an effect of a particular situation or of an individual psychology.

There is a comparable question about the enlistment of 'queer' in James, one of his repertory company of terms, a matter which needs an informed, dispassionate and intelligent discussion. Partridge's *Dictionary of Historical Slang* may not be the last word but it gives a rich variety of senses for 'queer'—criminal, drunk, giddy, inauspicious, dishonest, eccentric—without specific mention of homosexuality. Of course homosexual people would have been called 'queer'—but along with many other kinds of people. I mention this because Sedgwick follows the 'preterition' argument with 'some "fuller", though still highly equivocal, lexical pointers to a homosexual meaning', in the form of quotations:

'The rest of the world of course thought him *queer* . . . '
'She took his *gaiety* from him . . . '
'She traced his unhappy *perversion* . . . '

[505]

For all her sophistication, and the hedgings about 'highly equivocal', Sedgwick, like Kaplan and others, is always quoting occurrences of 'queer' in James. The sense of 'queer' in James and much other late-nineteenth-century writing is surely extremely powerful *because* it is multiple and ambiguous. I make this point partly because my title picks up James's reference to his inspiration for 'The Pupil' as his own 'queer affair', just the sort of phrase taken as a green light by much gender discourse. As evidence for the purposes of gender discourse, I would argue, the light shed by 'queer' is amber at most.

I've already hinted at a second reservation, one which is far from applying only to gender discourse. This might be called the abuse of speculation. A crux is summarized and a hypothetical interpretation presented, explicitly as hypothetical. Building on this hypothesis, the critic reaches a second crux, another fork in the road. We get a second hypothesis, then a third and a fourth. Obviously there is nothing intrinsically wrong about hypotheses. The reader is at liberty to find the hypotheses not convincing or not useful. What can be disturbing or frustrating is when the acknowledgment of hypotheticalness functions as scaffolding, which has been put up in order to produce the argument, and then is silently removed, so that its origins in speculation disappear and it becomes more like fact. Sedgwick does this with great verve, but there remains the question of what the sceptical reader is supposed to do with these chains of hypotheses if not convinced, how they escape arbitrariness.

The appeal of much of Sedgwick's work evidently lies in her address to 'a collective sexual identity smaller than "all [of] the people" ', but she is nimble-witted enough to have a great deal to offer, if not 'all the people', then much of the critical community at large. One of the areas of interest she is stimulatingly helping to open up, or refresh, is shame. Shame can be one obverse of Gay Pride, of course, and we could connect her new project with the recent move in homosexual politics from 'gay' to 'queer', a move which actively goes from a euphemistic label to one which takes over what has become a term of abuse, a term of shame, and revalues it as a point of pride. At any rate, in her essay 'Queer Performativity: Henry James's *The Art of the Novel*', she dwells on the 'terrifying powerlessness of gender-dissonant or otherwise stigmatized childhood', and thinks about shame as 'a form of communication' (through blushes, etc.), as making identity, and as contagious.[4]

Sedgwick has a paragraph in her discussion of 'The Beast in the Jungle', alleging that most James criticism (including, presumably, that of F. O. Matthiessen) has shown 'active incuriosity' and 'repressive blankness' on the subject of 'different erotic paths'. She offers some possible sympathetic (as against homophobic) reasons, considerations controlling the critical expression of a sense of James as in some way 'queer' (a word she broadens to take in many inflections of perversity): that critics have wanted to protect James

---

4. Sedgwick, 'Queer Performativity: Henry James's *The Art of the Novel*', *GLQ: A Journal of Lesbian and Gay Studies*, 1.1 (1993), 1–16, pp. 4, 5, 14.

from homophobic misreadings in a homophobic world; that they want to protect James from 'what they imagine as anachronistically gay readings'; that they fear discussion of homosexual desires in James will result in a marginalization of him, or themselves, *as* homosexual; that they read James as 'translating lived homosexual desires . . . into written heterosexual ones . . . so successfully that . . . the transmutation leaves no residue' (*Epistemology*, 197); that they agree with Sedgwick that James often incompletely transmutes homosexual desires into heterosexual forms, leaving residues, but do not want to accuse him of therefore lacking candour, or of artistic failure.

This is a helpful list, and doubtless these motives have played their part in keeping silent those who believe James to have been 'queer'. Other motives, though, may have kept other, non-homophobic, critics silent: not thinking 'male-male desire' identifiably— or discussably—present in James's work; or not thinking it a centrally interesting topic, compared with many others, in appreciating James's works; or thinking the 'possibilities' interesting, but feeling the lack of firm evidence would confine discussion to ramifications of highly speculative ingenuity. Critical discussion of the matter, also, requires some reflection on, and usually some degree of subscription to, the current notions about sexuality and gender-identity, an area in which, as I've already noted, Eve Sedgwick herself identifies a persistent disagreement between 'essentialist' and 'constructed' accounts of homosexuality. There's a good deal of confusion about what it means to be 'homosexual', what 'homoerotic' involves, and so on; and thus about how stable or wobbly a foundation theories of homosexuality offer for readings of literary works, particularly those in which there is no explicit reference to homosexuality.

*   *   *

When Edward Wagenknecht declared in 1984 that 'In days gone by, some readers were given to sniffing out homosexuality in the relations between Pemberton and his charge; this nonsense seems now to have been abandoned . . . ',[5] he seriously overplayed his hand. The story is for instance the first item in Edmund White's 1991 *Faber Anthology of Gay Short Fiction*;[6] and figures centrally, alongside two films, *Blue Velvet* and *Scorpio Rising*, in Michael Moon's spectacular essay of the same year, 'A Small Boy and

---

5. Quoted in Helen Hoy, 'Homotextual Duplicity in Henry James's "The Pupil" ', *The Henry James Review*, 14.1 (Winter 1993), 34–42, p. 35.
6. Disappointingly, White's Introduction makes no specific reference to the story, and thus offers no justification for its inclusion.

Others: Sexual Disorientation in Henry James, Kenneth Anger, and David Lynch'. Moon claims 'The Pupil' as 'representing heavily rit- ualized performances of some substantial part of the whole round of "perverse" desires and fantasies, autoerotic, homoerotic, voyeur- istic, exhibitionistic, incestuous, fetishistic, and sadomasochistic'.[7] Moon establishes the relevance of 'sadomasochistic desire and prac- tices between males[8] to *Blue Velvet* (where Dennis Hopper's char- acter kisses then beats up Kyle Maclachlan's) more convincingly than he does to 'The Pupil', which, he announces, 'treats of a series of visual and erotic captures and struggles to escape both into and away from a "perverse" circle constituted by a brilliant little boy, his loving and beloved tutor, and the boy's mother' [453].[9] At the climax, in this reading, 'the boy himself ends up, perhaps not en- tirely unwillingly, the sacrificial victim of the rituals the three prac- tise' [456]. The chief detail, bizarrely, on which Moon leans for support is the 'pair of soiled *gants de Suède* Mrs Moreen is 'drawing through a fat, jewelled hand' in the opening scene. Moon finds *Suède* glossed during the period as 'undressed kid', cites OED oc- currences of 'kid' for 'child' from the 1860s and after, and comes up with ' "handling a dirty undressed kid" ' as what Mrs Moreen is gesturally proposing. 'If my translations . . . seem far-fetched,' he says hopefully, 'it is only because the erotic wish encrypted, mimed but unspoken, in the text of "The Pupil" is precisely the kind of meaning that requires just such high-intensity translation or decod- ing' [457].

Fred Kaplan's 1992 biography makes out a case of lower inten- sity, not unlike Terence Martin's of 1958, for the homoerotic aspect of the story; and he is interesting about the ending, which is even for James strikingly ambiguous. Kaplan's claim is that 'the problem- atic relationship between an older man and a young boy has both autoerotic and homoerotic resonances'; meaning by 'autoerotic' that Pemberton and Morgan both represent aspects of James himself, past and present. Kaplan produces a phrase he often applies in the biography to James's feelings about men, to evoke the 'homoerotic': Pemberton 'falls in love with' Morgan—an expression not used in the story.

'The Pupil' is a tale in which, perhaps because of its compression —James wrote that he had 'boiled it down repeatedly'—it is difficult to give due weight to all the elements, even if one grasps the de-

7. Michael Moon, 'A Small Boy and Others: Sexual Disorientation in Henry James, Kenneth Anger, and David Lynch', in Hortense J. Spillers (ed.), *Comparative American Identities: Race, Sex and Nationality in the Modern Text* (Essays from the English Institute) (New York & London, 1991), 141–56, p. 141.
8. 'A Small Boy', p. 147.
9. Fred Kaplan, *Henry James: The Imagination of a Genius* (New York: Morrow, 1992), p. 303. Hereafter cited in the text.

tails.[1] In his account of the climax, Kaplan states that in the financial and social crisis which afflicts the Moreens at the end, 'Reluctantly, they now agree, at their son's urging, that Morgan can leave with [Pemberton]' (303).[2] But it is, importantly, neither altogether 'reluctantly', nor 'at their son's urging' that, as the story puts it, Mrs Moreen 'look[s] to [Pemberton] to carry a little further the influence he had so fortunately acquired with the boy—to induce his young charge to follow him into some modest retreat' [169]. Mrs Moreen's move—an active request made of Pemberton, not a passive agreement—is the culmination of a series of financially motivated insistences by her on the intimacy between Pemberton and Morgan, first to get him to stay on and tutor Morgan for nothing, and now to get both of them off the roll of expenses; though she is also anxious that Morgan should not work out how hollow the facade of the family respectability is.

Kaplan goes on from the Moreens' offer of Morgan to Pemberton:

> Ecstatically happy, [Morgan] looks up at Pemberton's face in expectation of a moment of mutual joy. To his dismay, he sees instead hesitation, anxiety, and fear. Morgan's already weak heart breaks. Pemberton pays the ultimate penalty for his moment of homosexual panic. (303–4)

This is tendentious—in the Sedgwickian sense of filling a Jamesian gap with a strong interpretation. The passage in the story reads:

> Morgan had turned away from his father—he stood looking at Pemberton with a light in his face. His sense of shame for their common humiliated state had dropped; the case had another side—the thing was to clutch at *that*. He had a moment of boyish joy, scarcely mitigated by the reflexion that with this unexpected consecration of his hope—too sudden and too violent; the turn taken was away from a *good* boy's book—the "escape" was left on their hands. The boyish joy was there an instant, and Pemberton was almost scared at the rush of gratitude and affection that broke through his first abasement. When he stammered "My dear fellow, what do you say to *that*?" how could one not say something enthusiastic? But there was

---

1. George Monteiro, 'The *Atlantic Monthly*'s Rejection of "The Pupil": An Exchange of Letters Between Henry James and Horace Scudder', *American Literary Realism, 1870–1910*, 23 (1990), 75–83, p. 78.
2. Kaplan's account of the plot doesn't inspire confidence: 'From Venice, having heard that Morgan has become ill with a weak heart, Pemberton joins the Moreens in Paris for the ostensible purpose of tutoring Morgan for his Oxford examinations.' In fact, Pemberton is in England, tutoring another, more 'opulent youth'; he has to cross the Channel to get to Paris. 'The ostensible purpose of tutoring Morgan for his Oxford examinations' is also skewed: Pemberton crosses to Paris simply in response to Mrs Moreen's cable announcing mendaciously, 'Morgan dreadfully ill'; and it is not Morgan (who is only fifteen) but 'the opulent youth, who was to be taken in hand for Balliol' (p. 499).

more need for courage at something else that immediately followed and that made the lad sit down quickly on the nearest
chair. He had turned quite livid and had raised his hand to his
left side. [170]

Kaplan makes no mention of the humiliation Morgan feels, I'll just
note, what the first texts call the 'tears of bitter shame' he has wept,[3]
when a moment before this he enters the hotel and sees the family
cases piled in the hall ready for their ignominious expulsion [169].
But the crucial question arises about Kaplan's great leap: 'To his
dismay, he sees instead hesitation, anxiety, and fear'. As we have
just seen there *is* no such vision by Morgan of Pemberton
described[4]—which is why I call it a great leap—yet it contrasts with
his earlier errors, in that it makes a stimulating, imaginative suggestion, picking up on Pemberton's being 'almost scared'.

What Kaplan does, then, perhaps seeing an analogy with Winterbourne's treatment of Daisy Miller or the governess's fatal behaviour toward Miles at the end of 'The Turn of the Screw', is to
make Morgan's look at Pemberton causally responsible for his
death; he dies of a *broken* heart. The framework he offers us to
understand this is that of 'homosexual panic', the concept rein-
vented from psychology and given wide currency by Eve Sedgwick.
That is to say, in Kaplan's reading, Pemberton has desired Morgan
homoerotically throughout—only to discover that, when the possibility of commitment, and thus self-identification as homosexual,
arises, he does not have the courage to meet the boy's responsive
passion. Presumably Morgan's 'stammer' is then taken to denote a
terror at the uncertainty he has already discerned in Pemberton's
face. If we accept this reading, incidentally, it's Morgan, not Pemberton, who 'pays the ultimate penalty for [Pemberton's] moment
of homosexual panic'. At any rate, Kaplan's implication is that James
consciously intends Pemberton's response in this way.

---

3. *Longman's Magazine*, XVII (March–April 1891), p. 631, p. 630; *The Lesson of the Master:
   The Marriages; The Pupil; Brooksmith; The Solution; Sir Edmund Orme* (New York &
   London, 1892), p. 177. Revising for the New York Edition, James replaces Morgan's
   'tears of bitter shame' three pages before the end with 'tears of a new and untasted
   bitterness' (NYE XI, p. 575), carrying the intensity of 'shame' forward to figure more
   dramatically in the very paragraph of Morgan's death, where 'His blush' (1892, p. 178)
   becomes 'His sense of shame for their common humiliated state' (NYE XI, p. 576).
4. Kaplan's suggestion may derive from Terence Martin, or more likely from Leon Edel's
   biography, where however Edel espouses not a homosexual reading but one in which
   James dramatizes his own shame at his family through Morgan: 'Pemberton had had a
   fantasy, into which Morgan had entered, that the two might some day go off to lead a
   life together. But when they are left alone Morgan, expecting to find Pemberton enthusiastic, sees him wavering—and his life becomes a void. Betrayed by his parents, frightened by the glimpse of vacillation in the beloved tutor, not old enough to tolerate
   disillusion, he feels himself suddenly alone. The panic is too much for his weak heart'
   (*Henry James: A Life* [New York: Harper & Row, 1985], pp. 430–31). They are not 'left
   alone' at the end—the Moreens are present throughout; and we can't know quite *what*
   Morgan 'feels'; but this is more helpfully inward with the story.

Where Kaplan's suggestion locates the 'homosexual panic' at the level of the action in the story, attributing it to a character, Pemberton, Helen Hoy, in an ebullient article called 'Homotextual Duplicity in Henry James's "The Pupil" ', attributes homosexual panic to James himself. Hoy bases her argument on the idea that James creates what she calls a 'homotext' by encoding homosexual relations here and elsewhere through various displacements, mostly of gender but here of age (making Morgan too young to be a sexual partner). Hoy's metafictional interest, tracing a plot in James's construction of the story, has a thinning effect, it should be said, on the action *within* the narrative: 'Superficially, the text . . . explores . . . the growing unmasking of Moreen family pretensions'; 'The narrative ostensibly insists . . . '; the story is treated as 'a cover story' and correspondingly simplified.[5] Towards the end of the tale, according to Hoy, the homoerotic subtext begins to break out and unbalance the action. As *James* sees the possibility of homoerotic fulfilment approaching *he* represses it by killing off Morgan; Hoy's idea is apparently that James has deliberately flirted with 'coming out', while always keeping Morgan's weak heart up his sleeve so he can play it when the chips are down. (The characters are not real enough in Hoy's reading for the question of homosexual panic on *Pemberton*'s part at the last really to arise.)

I have left to last in this enumeration of readers probably the story's first reader of all, after James and perhaps a typist. Horace Scudder, the editor of the *Atlantic Monthly*, unexpectedly rejected 'The Pupil' on grounds that have long been mysterious. The exchange of letters between Scudder and James has recently been published. The main burden of the rejection:

> Frankly, my reluctant judgment insists upon regarding the story as lacking in interest, in precision and in effectiveness. . . . The situation seems to me too delicate to permit quick handling, and with such a family to exploit I should suppose a volume would be necessary. At any rate I find the structure of the story so weak for carrying the sentiment that I am afraid other readers will be equally dissatisfied, and say hastily—'vague'—'unformed'.[6]

Scudder's silence here on the homoerotic question is hardly evidence one way or the other. *If* Scudder detects a homoerotic subtext

5. Hoy, "Homotextual Duplicity," 36, 37.
6. George Monteiro, 'The *Atlantic Monthly*'s Rejection of "The Pupil": An Exchange of Letters Between Henry James and Horace Scudder', p. 79. Monteiro suggests that between Scudder's rejection of it and its first publication in *Longman's Magazine* James revised it; on the odd ground—considering Matthiessen's judgement, for instance—that 'Surely no reader of "The Pupil" has ever called the finished product, that is to say, the story as James published it, either "vague" or "unformed" ' (p. 83).

he probably won't say so to James, and some may argue that the rather nebulous phrasing of his objection suggests some more special awkwardness than that of rejecting work by an established contributor. But in any case, even if we took Scudder as detecting a homoerotic subtext, he might still be mistaken, as might any number of subsequent readers getting the same impression. Questions of literary interpretation can only be answered by evidence and argument, not by votes or polls. However, an informed reading by a contemporary has interest and the evidential value of showing one response that was possible at the historical moment.

I want now to sketch some other considerations about the story and make some final observations. About the various kinds of homosexual or homoerotic readings I have been describing, which I willingly concede do not exhaust the range of possibilities, 'a skeptic may be forgiven', in William Shuter's words, 'for preserving a state of suspended judgment'. The real test, perhaps, would be a 'fuller', less polemical, account of 'The Pupil' in which a homoerotic reading came into serious and interesting tension with the complex balance of other more explicit strains in the story, about duty and sacrifice, money and honour, education and experience.

There can be no doubt that the story is centrally concerned with a relation of love between people of the same sex. When in the revised version of the story Morgan speaks sadly but stoically of his bad luck with his family, 'Pemberton held him fast, hands on his shoulders—he had never loved him so'.[7] How, though, we might ask, is our sense of the story enriched if we see Pemberton's relation to Morgan as really erotic and his frightened state at the end as 'homosexual panic'? In Kaplan's version of this reading, at least, the story becomes punitive (Pemberton 'pays the ultimate penalty', and so on) and it seems less potentially tragic. Too elaborate an interest in the boundary between heterosexual and homosexual, the grinding centrality of that axis, can elide, or usurp the interest of, other kinds of interpretation than the sexual.

Pemberton *has* some other compelling reasons for being frightened at the end: he knows of Morgan's weak heart and his extreme sensitivity about the fragile family honour, now so suddenly and publicly degraded; and, penniless again, he has no money with which he and Morgan *could* go off together. Even if Morgan does die from the shock of seeing the impossibility of escape registered on Pemberton's face—which we can hardly be sure of—blame does not necessarily attach to Pemberton for that, especially given Mor-

---

7. NYE XI, p. 561. The first versions read: 'Pemberton held him, his hands on his shoulders' (*Longman's Magazine*, p. 622; *The Lesson of the Master & c*, p. 166) [162].

gan's precocious perspicuity. James's handling of the money plot, whereby Pemberton is here paralysed and unable to help Morgan, is not necessarily a smokescreen for a truer homoerotic meaning. The first sentence of the whole story has Pemberton unable to 'speak of money to a person who spoke only of feelings' (NYE XI, 511) [133]; and a similar inhibition may hang over the critic wishing to attribute importance to financial constraints in the plotting of a story but faced with a critical community at large for whom 'feelings' and the sexual have such primacy that money questions are vulgarly undiscussable. Critical blindness to the evoked determinants of fictional situations has its own possibilities of 'repressive blankness'.

I want to return here to Eve Sedgwick's interest in shame for a hint about 'The Pupil'. She speaks of the 'terrifying powerlessness of gender-dissonant or otherwise stigmatized childhood'. I would like to pick up her sense of shame as making identity, and as contagious—both effects we may see in the story—only I think Morgan's shame is at being 'otherwise stigmatized' than through gender-dissonance. Morgan's shame centres on his dishonest family, which financially and morally exploits those who feel affection for him *through* their affection. Part of the point of the story's title, I think, is that Pemberton, the tutor, is progressively revealed as the true 'pupil' in the story, learning what the Moreens are like through Morgan's intelligence and correspondingly infected with this shame.

The context of James's other writings at this period, perhaps under the influence of French Naturalism and slightly later Ibsen, suggests a preoccupation with questions of inheritance, with agonized young protagonists struggling to defend compromised family honour.[8] Tony Tanner, quoting the remark made to the small James in *A Small Boy and Others* that 'I should think you'd be too proud—!',[9] has suggested that *pride* becomes a crucial motive in James's idea of renunciation. Here Morgan shows in his anguished scorn of his own family 'the small fine passion of his pride' (NYE XI, 552) [156]. He is 'a little gentleman', cultivating 'a private ideal', cursed like Hyacinth Robinson in *The Princess Casamassima* with a mixed inheritance. Morgan may then be read as one of James's 'poor sensitive gentlemen' of the 1890s, like the over-

8. Laura Wing in 'A London Life' (1888) and Adela Chart in 'The Marriages' (1892) disastrously strive to prevent what they see as family disgrace; Owen Wingrave, in the 1892 story of the same name, dies as mysteriously as Morgan of the conflict between his inextricable connection with his family and his espousal of higher, more idealistic values.
9. Henry James, *Autobiography*, ed. F. W. Dupee (New York, 1956), p. 130. Adrian Poole points out that near the end of *What Maisie Knew*, which appears in the same volume of the New York Edition, Mrs Wix rebukes Maisie with ' "I should think you'd be too proud to ask!" ' (p. 352).

initiated butler Brooksmith or the disablingly artistic writer Ray
Limbert in 'The Next Time', doomed in a crude world to martyrdom
for high values he cannot disown but cannot reconcile with his
situation. Morgan's precocious intelligence, a precursor of Maisie's,
expands at such a rate *through* his shame, his sensitized discovery
of nuances and codes and deceptions. And this shame is linked to
his sense of an honourable family tradition, valued only by himself,
being first compromised and then extinguished. His attempt to escape his family doom by fleeing with Pemberton, the one person
with whom he has been able to share his perceptions,[1] is itself at
least to some extent infected with this doom: Mrs Moreen, mani-
pulatively, is from the start *pushing* Pemberton towards Morgan,
and friendship between Pemberton and Morgan, fostered to allow
the Moreens to get Pemberton to work for nothing, keeps Morgan
handily out of the family's way while they scheme for worldly advantage, and postpones (as Mrs Moreen *hopes*—wrongly) Morgan's
discovery of their demoralization and social abjectness. Morgan
feels all the shame for a family otherwise lacking any 'throb of
shame' (NYE XI, 554) [157]; and both his first serious illness and
his death seem direct responses to his perception of his mother's
impudent exploitation of Pemberton's affection for him. The climax
of the story is primarily the climax of *this* interest in 'his sense of
shame for their common humiliated state', which is complexly
worked enough in itself not merely to be a superficial 'cover story'
for a 'real' subtext.

I shall end with a reflection on Scudder's response to the story. His
rejection found 'The situation . . . too delicate to permit quick handling, and with such a family to exploit I should suppose a volume
would be necessary. At any rate I find the structure of the story so
weak for carrying the sentiment that I am afraid other readers will
be equally dissatisfied, and say hastily—"vague"—"unformed".' One
might call this the insensitive reading of a busy editor under growing pressure to find material which would appeal to a mass public;
but James's letter to Scudder enclosing the story had emphasized
how he had 'tried to make [it] as short as possible' and 'boiled it
down repeatedly', and one might also suggest that James's struggles
with length, as with those novels in which he misplaced his middles
and had to accelerate the movement towards his conclusion, may
have led him partly to lose contact with what it is possible for a
reader to understand and to feel. The final pages are charged with

---

1. So that like Isabel and Ralph 'looking at the truth together' towards the end of *The
Portrait of a Lady*, Morgan and Pemberton 'look at the facts and keep nothing back'
(NYE XI, 551) [156].

emotional demands, on the reader as well as on Pemberton, and we have already remarked the ambiguous silence about Pemberton's response to Morgan's final appeal and whether the response is what causes his death (a silence Kaplan confidently talks away). We too, as readers, may feel called on for a response the structure has not enabled us wholeheartedly to supply: Morgan's heart condition, for instance, is too convenient a 'given', and Pemberton forgoes only a relatively lucrative tutorship out of his attachment to Morgan, having no emotional ties outside the Moreen circle that would call for a sharper sacrifice. In a sense, then, perhaps Scudder is right; it may be that James's conception is too ambitious for the length, that our unease and Scudder's dissatisfaction correspond (at a very high level of achievement) to a failure of technique, that the impulses do not quite vividly fuse in the acute tragic balance we sometimes call 'inevitability'.

The 'vagueness' of which both Scudder and Matthiessen complain, I finally suggest, may further correspond more to an ethical than to a psychosexual reticence on James's part. Just before criticizing 'The Pupil', Matthiessen remarks suggestively that 'James occupies a curious border line between the older psychologists like Hawthorne or George Eliot, whose concerns were primarily religious and ethical, and the post-Freudians'.[2] Pemberton is early in the tale described as having at Yale 'richly supposed himself to be reacting against a Puritan strain' (NYE XI, 519) [137], and it may be that his conduct *vis-à-vis* Morgan can best be understood as manifesting a deeply ingrained, but helplessly unworldly, sense of moral duty. Henry James Sr's insistence on ethical intensity and hatred of what he paradoxically called 'flagrant morality' might jointly account for James's diffidence about the high-minded impulse at the heart of his story, which its action may celebrate but also shows grievously defeated. Such an awkwardness in the story, rooted in the peculiar history and moral traditions of the James family, might in turn account—as in T. S. Eliot's reading of *Hamlet*—for the sense of a missing 'objective correlative', in Eve Sedgwick's term a 'residue'—giving a cue to the psychoanalytic procedures of 'Queer Theory' and their unearthing of psychosexually loaded repressions and 'homosexual panic'.

2. F. O. Matthiessen, *Henry James: The Major Phase* (New York: Oxford University Press, 1944), p. 93.

JULIE RIVKIN

[Revision and "The Middle Years"]†

If the Preface to *The Golden Bowl* evokes the unstable relation
between writer and reader, James's tale "The Middle Years" makes
the logical connection between the practice of revision and the role
of the reader its very subject. Published in 1893, over a decade
before James wrote the Preface to *The Golden Bowl*, "The Middle
Years" anticipates James's situation in preparing the New York Edition not by treating revision as a specific project undertaken at a
certain point in a literary career but instead by seeing it as intrinsic
to the activity of writing itself. The tale characterizes revision as the
hallmark of literary authority, but it also treats revision as a source
of authorial vulnerability; in fact, the heightened role of the reader
in this tale derives directly from the needs created by revision. However, reading proves to be no escape from the vulnerabilities of revision; both are situated within an economy of textual consumption
that makes evident the fears as well as the hopes that James only
hints at in the Preface to *The Golden Bowl*.

The tale's cast of four—an ailing writer, a doctor who is also an
admiring reader, a patient who rivals the writer for the doctor's
attention, and the patient's paid companion—enact a drama that
reveals James's intense ambivalence toward both the revision and
the reception of literary texts. The tale's protagonist is Ralph Dencombe, a writer whose failing health is a particular anguish because
he feels himself only now on the verge of writing his own best work.
Dencombe finds consolation if not a cure in the ministrations of
Doctor Hugh, a young medical man whose professional devotion to
the writer follows from his personal admiration for Dencombe's literary genius. But Dencombe must compete for Doctor Hugh's attention with another patient whose claim on the doctor is as urgent
as his own and who constitutes a threat to any fantasy of the ideal
reader. In the figure of the Countess—and her companion Miss
Vernham—the tale reveals the author's nightmare of an unsym-
pathetic reception from the reading public, a nightmare that cannot
be fully separated from its companion dream of the ideal reader

---

† From "Doctoring the Text: Henry James and Revision," in *Henry James's New York
Edition*, ed. David McWirter (Palo Alto: Stanford University Press, 1995),
pp. 142–63. Copyright © 1995 The Board of Trustees of the Leland Stanford Jr. University. The author's original references to volume 16 of the New York Edition of *The
Novels and Tales of Henry James* (New York: Scribner & Sons, 1907–1910) appear in
parentheses within the text. References to corresponding passages in this Norton Critical
Edition appear in brackets.

Doctor Hugh. Doctor Hugh may represent the authorial relief derived from a fantasy of relinquishing authority to a benign reader, a reader who can, in the words of James's Preface, "dream again in my company and in the interest of his own larger absorption of my sense," but the Countess and her companion reveal the fears attendant on that same relinquishing of control. If the tale seems to muffle the Countess and celebrate the doctor-reader, it does not entirely succeed in quieting the anxieties she represents. What readers tend to remember in reading "The Middle Years" is the celebration of art—vulnerable yet somehow triumphant—with which the tale closes. But the tale is actually more ambivalent than its conclusion indicates, and therefore the narrative middle—and the full cast of four rather than the celebrated twosome—are crucial to an interpretation of James's allegory of revision and reading.

Dencombe, the writer whose health fades just as he feels himself coming into possession of his own literary powers, sees the source of his mastery in the source of his fallibility; because of his dedication to revision, the work that he is able to complete is meager to the very degree that his time has been filled with so many reworkings. If Dencombe's obsessive revising expresses his sense that the work could always be improved by some supplementary attention from the "master," the tale also explores another supplementary practice that can take the place of revision. Reading becomes the necessary supplement to writing, and the tale raises the possibility that the literary text might find its completion not in the marginal penciling of the ailing author but in the admiring responses of the devoted reader.

The writing practices of the tale's protagonist—which is to say practices of revision—initially establish an oppositional relationship between writing and reading. As "a passionate corrector, a fingerer of style," Dencombe finds it difficult to reveal his less than perfect text—and thereby give up some portion of his authority—to a reading public: "The last thing he ever arrived at was a form final for himself. His ideal would have been to publish secretly, and then, on the published text, treat himself to the terrified revise, sacrificing always a first edition and beginning for posterity and even for the collectors, poor dears, with a second" (90) [219]. An appropriate emblem of supplementarity, this imaginary text without a first edition is seen as particularly a problem for those who fetishize "originality," the collectors. Theoretically, of course, the habit of revision that leads Dencombe to favor a second over a first edition would lead him to favor a third over a second; in other words, the process of revision is potentially endless. Dencombe's difficulty in arriving at a "form final for himself" can be described as his unwillingness to cease being an author, to relinquish his text to a reading public.

The first effect of his writing practice is to prolong his authority, extending his authorial control over his text at the very moment that he would otherwise release it for publication. Yet his recognition in this tale is that the practice that extends his authority paradoxically restricts it; having spent so long revising each of his works, he has not the time to produce enough of them. In his late years he has only arrived at his "Middle Years"; thus, his present lament that his creative life has been cut short can also be viewed as an effect of revision:

> His development had been abnormally slow, almost grotesquely gradual. He had been hindered and retarded by experience, he had for long periods only groped his way. It had taken too much of his life to produce too little of his art. The art had come, but it had come after everything else. At such a rate a first existence was too short—long enough only to collect material; so that to fructify, to use the material, one should have a second age, an extension. (82) [214]

The textual economy of revision is in fact the existential economy that governs his life's work. Just as Dencombe finds that a first economy necessitates a second, here he finds that a "first existence" demands "a second age, an extension."

As if to counter this sense of restricted resources and potentially infinite labors, Dencombe finds his attention drawn toward a scene that seems both to extend his future as a novelist and to bring revision to an end. What engages Dencombe's attention is not the work already complete, the novel in its packet from the publisher, but a novel as yet unwritten, a story being performed on the beach below him. A trio of figures—a gentleman with two ladies—immediately begins to generate a story: "Where moreover was the virtue of an approved novelist if one couldn't establish a relation between such figures? the clever theory for instance that the young man was the son of the opulent matron and that the humble dependent, the daughter of a clergyman or an officer, nourished a secret passion for him" (79) [212]. As Dencombe develops this hypothetical drama out of the lives before him, ignoring the published text at hand, he notices a curious reversal: the young man he observes is, in exact contrast to Dencombe, engaged in reading a book while "the romance of life [stands] neglected at his side" (ibid.). The inverse symmetry is striking, even before the book is identified as the one in Dencombe's lap. What the contrast highlights is the paired displacements of reading by writing and of writing by reading. For Dencombe, drawn to images that mark his extended career as a writer, this substitution of the completed text for the text as yet unwritten, of the act of reading for the act of authorship, has a surprising appeal. Just as the book's cover appears "alluringly red" (78) [212], the book's reader is "an object of envy to an observer from whose connexion with literature all such artlessness had faded" (ibid.). The effect, then, of Dencombe's turn toward future "material" and further composition is a return to the book at hand. Presumably the same color as the book Dencombe possesses, it appears "alluringly red" because it is "alluringly read."

Reading replaces writing and completes it; with reading, revision finally comes to an end. The figure who seemed to provide Dencombe with material for future texts provides him instead with a desire to read what he has already written. To his surprise, when he turns to his own novel his reading produces something entirely unexpected: he experiences "a strange alienation" (80) [212]. "He had forgotten what his book was about" (ibid.). This forgetting he attributes to "the assault of his old ailment," and it thereby anticipates a greater loss: "He couldn't have chanted to himself a single sentence, couldn't have turned with curiosity or confidence to any particular page. His subject had already gone from him, leaving scarce a superstition behind. He uttered a low moan as he breathed the chill of this dark void, so desperately it seemed to represent the completion of a sinister process" (ibid.). He forgets what he has written because the book has figuratively passed into the hands of a reader and is out of his authorial control and beyond his revisionary power. The end of revision—appropriately, given its existential parallel—is death.

But this "strange alienation" from his own work also has another effect; if it figures his death as an author it also signals his birth as a reader. Becoming other to himself provides gains as well as losses. If he had turned to his completed text simply for refuge, what he now discovers in it gives back more than he can remember having put into it. "Everything came back to him, but came back with a wonder, came back above all with a high and magnificent beauty" (81) [213]. Reading feels like a wondrous seduction; he finds himself "drawn down, as by a siren's hand" into the "dim underworld of fiction" (ibid.). This self-division or self-doubling occasioned by reading can feel like a death—the death of a singular authority with the power to revise endlessly—but it can also mark the escape from death, the extension of the life of the writer in the life of the reader. Even the images double one another: the "chill of the dark void" is transformed into "the dim underworld of fiction."

What Dencombe experiences in his own act of reading—this "othering" of himself—is reenacted in less solipsistic terms with the tale's other reader, Doctor Hugh. From the episode of the matched book that marks his first encounter with the older man, Doctor Hugh doubles Dencombe, intimating another form of extension from the one Dencombe had originally envisioned—the prolonged life of the single author. Indeed, Doctor Hugh's own multiple roles—potential character, reader, doctor, even surrogate family—suggest a variety of ways in which he might act as supplement and extension to the ailing author.

The contrast between a fatally depleting economy associated with authorship as opposed to a potentially renewing economy associated with reading emerges again in the first scene between the two men. The distinction between the two economies is emphasized by the structure of the scene, since it takes as its point of departure Dencombe's pretense of being merely another reader and as its conclusion the revelation of his identity as the author of *The Middle Years*. The two men are initially drawn to one another as two readers of the same book; in fact, Doctor Hugh leaves his copy of the book beside Dencombe as a pledge of his intention to return. Moreover, Dencombe's identity as the book's author first emerges because of the difference between the two men's copies. When Doctor Hugh mistakenly picks up Dencombe's copy of *The Middle Years* instead of his own and discovers that their texts are different, Dencombe both literally and figuratively reveals his hand through precisely the signs of his most characteristic writing practice—revision. Doctor Hugh notes the small penciled changes in Dencombe's text with reproach and then wonder; the man before him is neither reader nor reviewer but the author in person. There is a noticeable mirroring in their physical responses to this recognition: as Doctor Hugh guesses Dencombe's identity the doctor "change[s] color" (90) [219], a response that is doubled and intensified in this response of Dencombe himself: "Through a blur of ebbing consciousness [he] saw Doctor Hugh's mystified eyes. He only had time to feel he was about to be ill again—that emotion, excitement, fatigue, the heat of the sun, the solicitation of the air, had combined to play him a trick, before, stretching out a hand to his visitor with a plaintive cry, he lost his senses altogether" (91) [219]. Dencombe loses consciousness at the moment his reader Doctor Hugh discovers his authorial secret—revision. His loss of consciousness indicates the anxiety reading represents, an anxiety revision attempts to waylay. Doctor Hugh discovers Dencombe's weakness, his lack of a sense of completion and his fear of what it means to have his art pass out of his control and into the arena of consumption.

If Dencombe loses consciousness in revealing his identity to Doctor Hugh, he regains it with a generous reassurance from the young doctor: "You'll be all right again—I know all about you now" (92) [219]. Doctor Hugh's equation of Dencombe's recovery with his own knowledge suggests his own intuitive sense of himself as Dencombe's extension. As their earlier mirrored responses to the revelation intimate, the two men supplement one another in needs and talents. Not only is Doctor Hugh Dencombe's ideal reader, but his medical expertise seems precisely designed for Dencombe's rescue. Moreover, Doctor Hugh is eager to offer his own professional services in recompense for the tremendous literary gifts he has received from Dencombe. "I want to do something for you," the young man proclaims. "I want to do everything. You've done a tremendous lot for me" (ibid.). Even his practice of reading is the ideal counterpart to Dencombe's practice of writing: if Dencombe's "signature" is his penciled revision, Doctor Hugh distinguishes the works of his admired author by describing them as "the only ones he could read a second time" (86) [217]. Doctor Hugh too is a "revisionary" reader, one who returns to the text repeatedly—not as in Dencombe's case out of feeling of doubt regarding the writer's authority but for converse reasons—out of a feeling of respect for a complete and unrevisable authority. Indeed, Doctor Hugh reminds us, through this interdependence of writing and reading, that revision restores and extends as well as exhausts vitality and value. With his declaration to Dencombe—"You *shall* live!" (96) [222]—Doctor Hugh insists on the restorative side of this revisionary economy, his faith that he can use his life as doctor-reader to allow Dencombe to write again.

But this benign vision of relations between admired author and admiring reader does not tell the whole story, for Doctor Hugh does not come alone. When Dencombe makes himself dependent on the ministrations of the young doctor, he also renders himself subject to the women who accompany—and indeed employ—Doctor Hugh. Moreover, if Doctor Hugh represents the restorative possibilities associated with reading, the two women represent the dangers, dangers most associated with the author's lack of control. This loss of control can be traced in the spatial repositioning of these four figures; if at the tale's outset, the solitary author sat above the trio, looking down and exercising his control in his ability to imagine "combinations," he later finds himself on their level and "combined" with them in relations he never would have chosen. When Doctor Hugh climbs to Dencombe's level on the cliff, he not only brings the reader to the same level as the writer but brings what had been the author's material—those two less than cooperative women—up to the ground occupied by the author. This spatial change figures the change in relations that accompanies a turn to the readerly economy; the master mind who controls the world through observation must submit his body and his text to the same conditions that assail his characters. Reading submits the textual body to the attentions of another—an acknowledgment that the author is not capable of doing everything to doctor the text. But he ends up relinquishing his body to a treatment he never would have chosen, at the hands not of the devoted specialist but instead of the competing women.

Dencombe's resistance to the Countess and Miss Vernham is expressed in part as a critique of the terms according to which the older woman exercises a hold over Doctor Hugh, terms that are implicit in the Countess's personal history. The Countess is "the daughter of a celebrated baritone, whose taste *minus* his talent she had inherited" and also "the widow of a French nobleman and mistress of all that remained of the handsome fortune, the fruit of her father's earnings, that had constituted her dower" (88) [218]. The story told by the Countess's fortune is that the male artist is the origin of wealth, both literal and figurative. Moreover, "the fruit" of those artistic earnings goes to furnish a dowry, the form of payment that seals a woman's claim on a man and grants it institutional legitimacy. The death of men—both father and husband—releases that fortune to a woman who has no power to create one herself, since she has "taste without . . . talent." The fortune allows her to make "terms" with a new man—Doctor Hugh—that render his attention legitimate, while leaving another artist—Dencombe—without the resources that would allow him to continue his creative career. The Countess is, in other words, not only a consumer of art but a consumer of artists, with her parasitical mode of survival on her father's fortune and husband's title. Her relations with Doctor Hugh and Dencombe repeat and extend her earlier relations with the father and husband from whom she inherited her resources.

The Countess's physical condition becomes the emblem of her identity as a consumer. Her excessive size, grand fortune, and ill health seem of a piece; she is the appetitive self carried to a precarious extreme. One of her first remarks to Doctor Hugh emphasizes this association with physical appetite: "I find myself horribly hungry. At what time did you order luncheon?" Doctor Hugh's response—"I ordered nothing to-day—I'm going to make you diet" (83) [215]—suggests the best treatment for the Countess's disorder is a restriction of her appetites. If Dencombe's ill health can be seen as an excess of revisionary production, the Countess's can be seen as excess of absorption or consumption; she is a monstrous bloated parody of the reader as consumer, the one who inherits the artistic fortune and whom the law thereby favors to make legitimate claims, but who performs no labor and creates no value herself. Her power to purchase, like her appetite for food and her taste for art, becomes just another symptom of her unbridled consumption; moreover, her most extravagant purchase, the medical attention of Doctor Hugh, is so important to her that she cannot live without it: "She paid so much for his fidelity that she must have it all: she

refused him the right to other sympathies, charged him with scheming to make her die alone" (97–98) [223].

Recognizing that the Countess's legal claim on Doctor Hugh is
ultimately a financial one, Dencombe displays metaphoric resources
that surpass the Countess's. Further, unlike the Countess, he is no
mere inheritor of wealth created by another; he is instead the
source of treasure himself:

> [Dencombe] found another strain of eloquence to plead the
> cause of a certain splendid "last manner," the very citadel, as
> it would prove, of his reputation, the stronghold into which his
> real treasure would be gathered. . . . Even for himself he was
> inspired as he told what his treasure would consist of; the pre-
> cious metals he would dig from the mine, the jewels rare,
> strings of pearls, he would hang between the columns of his
> temple. (98–99) [223]

Dencombe's choice of figures not only makes creative genius the
source of all value, the mine from which all treasure comes, but it
also makes that creative genius a distinctly male possession. Dencombe's metaphor—"jewels rare . . . hang[ing] between the columns of his temple"—has become a cultural commonplace, the all
too familiar "family jewels." He resists the older woman's claim on
the young man—legitimate yet parasitical—with a display of his
resources that leaves the young man "pant[ing] for the combinations to come" (99) [224]. The effect is a promise that supplants
Doctor Hugh's commitment to the Countess: he "renewed to Dencombe his guarantee that his profession would hold itself responsible for such a life" (ibid.).

The resolution of the tale is to give Doctor Hugh the choice of
these two models of artistic creation and consumption—he gets to
choose which economy to endorse, which inheritance to claim.
Neither patient can survive without him, but he selects the idealized
relation between author and reader embodied in Dencombe. When
Dencombe discovers that the Countess has died and left the young
man "never a penny"—presumably the fortune will go to Miss
Vernham—Doctor Hugh interprets his choice: "I chose to accept,
whatever they might be, the consequences of my infatuation. . . .
The fortune be hanged! It's your own fault if I can't get your things
out of my head" (104–105) [227].

Dencombe's displacement of the Countess—and of Miss Vernham—is central to any account of the tale's allegory of revision.
Dencombe now has what the Countess attempted to contract for
—"the whole of [Doctor Hugh's] attention"—but more importantly,
Dencombe has also taken the place of a younger woman the doctor
might have wed. This alternative union depends for its value on the

renounced legacy of the Countess (which gives Dencombe the measure of how much Doctor Hugh cares) and for its representation on the displaced relationship with Miss Vernham. The language here—Doctor Hugh's "infatuation," his declarations in a voice that has "the ring of a marriage-bell"—derives from the heterosexual union with which such a story might have closed (105) [227]. Whatever contractual power the Countess once exerted over Doctor Hugh, that power has been displaced in this image of a wedding of male writer and male reader. It is an image not simply of love but of matching and legal sanction. That is, Dencombe finds in his ideal reader Doctor Hugh such a mirroring and confirmation of his authority that he is finally cured of the need to revise.

The medium of Doctor Hugh's cure is the tightly echoing dialogue with which the tale concludes, the responses of the reader seconding, confirming, and thereby completing the writer's words. What is often excerpted from this dialogue is Dencombe's passionate definition of the writer's activity; it is an account of art as fraught with doubt, as nothing more in fact than the need to revise: "A second chance—*that's* the delusion. There never was to be but one. We work in the dark—we do what we can—we give what we have. Our doubt is our passion and our passion is our task. The rest is the madness of art" (105) [227]. But this definition is transformed by its context in the dialogue of voices; the presence of the ideal reader assures Dencombe that revision is in fact unnecessary. The danger of the consuming women is removed, and instead Dencombe hears the voice of a reader so like himself that he need no longer fear his words going astray, his texts being misunderstood. The doubt that drove his revisionary practice is turned, in this repetition, into the very stuff of his accomplishment, the confirmation of his fully achieved authority.

> "If you've doubted, if you've despaired, you've always 'done' it," his visitor subtly argued.
> "We've done something or other," Dencombe conceded.
> "Something or other is everything. It's the feasible. It's *you*!"
> "Comforter!" poor Dencombe ironically sighed.
> "But it's true," insisted his friend.
> "It's true. It's frustration that doesn't count."
> "Frustration's only life," said Doctor Hugh.
> "Yes, it's what passes." Poor Dencombe was barely audible, but he had marked with the words the virtual end of his first and only chance. (106) [227–228]

It is hard to distinguish the source from the echo, the author from his reader, in that Dencombe repeats Doctor Hugh's phrases as often as Doctor Hugh does Dencombe's. This echoing dialogue between Dencombe and Doctor Hugh relieves Dencombe of the very anxiety that constituted his art as revisionary; Dencombe is saved here from the potential danger of reading, of a deviation from the author's sense that would undermine his authority. Instead, what Doctor Hugh returns to Dencombe is a sense of the same, an assurance of a unified and single meaning shared by author and reader. As a supplement, Doctor Hugh completes Dencombe's deficiency, ministering to both his bodily life and his text. Dencombe need no longer doctor himself. Not surprisingly, this exchange is able to provide for Dencombe's *The Middle Years* what it does for James's "The Middle Years"—closure, an end to the interminable need to revise.

The strangely similar male voices that conclude the tale must, however, be heard against the female voices they silence. The tale is haunted not just by the prospective death of the author but by the excluded figures of the textual consumer embodied in the Countess and Miss Vernham. In the figure of the Countess, the supplement appears in its debased and dangerous form; it is the excessive appetitive body, the avaricious purchaser, the threatening female sexual other. It is also the cause that makes interminable revision necessary, thus depleting the author's life and his creative possibilities. Now the Countess is dead, Doctor Hugh announces, and her final words have been to curse him and divest him of an inheritance. But although Dencombe might seem to have succeeded at getting Doctor Hugh alone, and although Doctor Hugh may provide Dencombe with the idealized image of the reader as authorial echo, as repetition without danger of deviation, still the very necessity of such absolute assurance testifies to the danger against which it operates. There would be no need for so singular a model of authority, purged entirely of the artistic doubt and the need to revise, if there were no ghosts at the margins, no haunting possibilities of a different kind of textual reception. What the tale cannot help but reveal is the author's lack of control in its other ghost, the Countess. Present at the end only in her lost legacy, she shows that textual effects are no ethereal echo that reverberate exclusively to the author's controlling voice but excesses and fallibilities beyond the anticipation of even the most foresightful of authors, the most doctored of texts.

JOYCE CAROL OATES

The Madness of Art: Henry James's "The Middle Years"†

This strange, parable-like tale of 1893, written in James's fiftieth year, belongs to that species of fiction by James that suggests dream or myth; fiction on the brink of dissolving into abstraction. It can hardly be read in "realistic" terms except as the dreamily fractured landscapes of Cézanne can be read against the "real" landscapes of Aix-en-Provence that evoked them.

Clearly, "The Middle Years" is a confession of the artist's anxiety over the worth of his art and the terrifying aloneness to which the demands of his art have brought him. James's own lament over the "essential loneliness of my life," in a letter of 1900, echoes here: "This aloneness—what is it still but the deepest thing about one? Deeper, about *me*, at any rate, than anything else; deeper than my 'genius,' deeper than my 'discipline,' deeper than my pride, deeper, above all, than the deep counterminings of art." The novelist-protagonist of "The Middle Years" yearns for a second chance at his art; yet more passionately for an audience, the "sympathy of the community" of which I've spoken. Not commercial success and a wide readership so much as someone who will understand, somebody to *care*.

The setting is Bournemouth "as a health resort" [211]. The time is an April day of softness and brightness. Poor Dencombe, as James speaks of him, mysteriously ill, fatigued by a brief walk from his hotel to a sea cliff bench, sits and opens, with no eagerness, a copy of his new, just-published novel *The Middle Years*. Dencombe is a writer of difficult, exquisite texts, never commercially successful, prone to an eloquent melancholy. "The infinite of life was gone . . ." he thinks, contemplating the sea, "It was the abyss of human illusion that was the real, the tideless deep" [211]. Exhausted, burnt-out, Dencombe awaits redemption passively, like so many of James's male, middle-aged artists or "sensitive" men; unless perhaps it is already too late? He dare not speculate into the future, out of a terror of what he might envision. "It was indeed general views that were terrible; short ones . . . were the remedy" [216].

Henry James presents as mordant comedy the predicament of a distinctly Jamesian novelist so exhausted by the effort of his art—

† Reprinted from *New Literary History* 27.2 (1996): 259–62. Copyright © The University of Virginia. Reprinted by permission of the Johns Hopkins University Press. References to this Norton Critical Edition appear in brackets.

"It had taken too much of his life to produce too little" [214]—that, confronted with his latest and perhaps last novel, not only is he incapable of feeling the mildest tinge of enthusiasm for it, but he seems to have forgotten it entirely. "Utter blankness" [213] has intervened. Not a single page, not a single sentence comes to him. Yet, as he reads, sitting on his bench above the sea cliff, he finds that *The Middle Years* is, even by the harsh measure of its author's judgment, "extraordinarily good" [213]. Note the powerful, even mystical language in which James describes this awakening of the author by way of becoming his own reader: "He dived once more into his story and was drawn down, as by a siren's hand, to where, in the dim underworld of fiction, the great glazed tank of art, strange silent subjects float" [213]. This analogue of fiction with the boundless and unchartable imagination at the point at which it is identical with the unconscious might strike the casual reader of Henry James as radically antithetical to the "Jamesian style"—the "Jamesian" mode of a finely calibrated and inexhaustibly contemplated fiction. It suggests, on the contrary, the tremendous pressure of the unconscious; its unknowability. The processes of art yield, and in a way are lost in, the product of the artist's effort—the aesthetic object. We can infer the mysterious potency of the former by the evidence of the latter, but this is a mere inference, a glimmering of something vast, rich, deep, unchartable. Excited by the discovery that his novel is so much finer than he'd expected, Dencombe wonders if he might have a second life, after all. "Ah for another go, ah for a better chance!" [214]

As if this murmured wish were a command, Dencombe is immediately met by the young, attractive, vibrantly alive Doctor Hugh—first glimpsed, in fact, with a book in hand from which he is reading aloud to two female companions; by chance, Doctor Hugh has Dencombe's very novel, with its "alluringly red" [212] cover. This is the artist's "aesthetic object" glorified and the fantastical "Doctor Hugh"—his very name an echo of "you"—is the artist's yearned-for audience: Dencombe's "greatest admirer in the new generation."

James's usually tactful scrim of admiration for women is here abruptly jettisoned: Doctor Hugh's patient-patroness, the Countess, is a large, indeed obese lady who wears a hat shaped like a mushroom; her companion is a young woman with vitreous eyes, like a figure in a play or a novel, "some sinister governess or tragic old maid" [215]. (In other tales of James's of this general period, "The Wheel of Time," for instance, and the renowned "The Beast in the Jungle," it is women who are deep, brooding, and faithful; women who sacrifice themselves at the altar of masculine self-absorption. *Intensities of fidelity*, in James's words, are identified with the feminine.) "The Middle Years" is, among other things, a gently homo-erotic fantasy; the passionate bond is between men—the mysteriously moribund elder and the life-giving, ardent younger. How touching is Dencombe in his plea to Doctor Hugh, in this almost comical Jamesian circumlocution, "I want to what they call 'live'" [222].

Only in fantasy, hardly in realistic fiction of the type and quality, for instance, of James's great novels *The Wings of the Dove* and *The Golden Bowl,* could such a denouement occur: by a melodramatic complication of plot the handsome young doctor is forced to choose between the wealthy neurasthenic Countess and poor Dencombe, and chooses Dencombe.

> ". . . I gave her up for *you.* I had to choose . . ."
> "You chose to let a fortune go?"
> "I chose to accept, whatever they might be, the conse-quences of my infatuation," smiled Doctor Hugh . . . "The fortune be hanged! It's your own fault if I can't get your things out of my mind" [227].

On his death bed, Dencombe is tempted to think that the entire experience has been a delusion, but Doctor Hugh assures him it has not—"Not your glory." Dencombe responds rhapsodically, "It *is* glory—to have been tested, to have had our little quality and cast our little spell. The thing is to have made somebody care." Doctor Hugh insists that Dencombe's life has been a success, "putting into his young voice the ring of a marriage bell" [227]. In this brief tale in which James includes so few metaphors and rhetorical flights of the kind characteristic of his mature style, this unexpected simile strikes the ear as deliberate, pointed: *the ring of a marriage bell.*

The buried theme of "The Middle Years" is this strange marriage of artist and "greatest admirer"; if we consider it in mythic terms, we might hypothesize a ritual of the [bloodless] sacrifice of the moribund elder; and the passing of potency to the younger. The "aesthetic object" is a literal prop in this ritual, the printed book *The Middle Years* with its "alluringly red" cover, a symbolic repre-sentation, perhaps, of male sexual potency, the very gift of life. In this homoerotic/mythic vision, the female is bypassed entirely; all physicality banished, or denied. Doctor Hugh is, not very plausibly, a physician of a purely disembodied sort; he may touch poor Den-combe's life, but he does not touch poor Dencombe's body, even to examine him. He is a physician in a higher, spiritual sense, the artist's personal redeemer, come at the end of Dencombe's life to assure him that, yes, contrary to Dencombe's fears, he *has* had glory, he *has* fulfilled his destiny. "The Middle Years" is as allegor-ical as a tale by Hawthorne or Melville; its minimal outwardly "realistic" details hardly disguise its deeper, abstract purpose, that of providing the mythic rite to assure the artist's "immortality" in the newer, younger generation. The entire dreamlike story reads like one of those extended passages in Henry James's journal in which the writer plumbs the depths of his own soul. Its moment of epiphany would seem, in the surpassing beauty of its language, to have generated the diaphanous fiction that surrounds it. In Dencombe's words: "A second chance—*that's* the delusion. There never was to be but one. We work in the dark—we do what we can—we give what we have. Our doubt is our passion, and our passion is our task. The rest is the madness of art" [227].

How significant that even the great artist's redemption can only be by way of his communion with a real, palpable, emotionally engaged audience; a reaching-out to, a touching of this "new generation"—the mysterious "Doctor Hugh"—*you*.

JOHN CARLOS ROWE

[Gender, Sexuality and Work in *In the Cage*]†

* * *

What Maisie Knew and *In the Cage* were two of the first works James dictated, and as several scholars have pointed out, there are remarkable similarities between James's practices of dictation and the scenes of telegraphy in *In the Cage*.[1] As Kaplan notes, James had experienced problems of rheumatism in his right wrist for more than a year when he decided in 1897 to employ a "secretary, William MacAlpine, to take dictation," and James "practiced the new skill during the spring of 1897 with some delight."[2] James's third and last secretary, Theodora Bosanquet, describes James's response to dictation as considerably more enthusiastic. " 'It all seems,' he once explained, 'to be so much more effectively and unceasingly *pulled* out of me in speech than in writing.' "[3] Both Mary Weld, his second typist, and Bosanquet took dictation directly on the Remington typewriter to which James grew so accustomed that "the click of the Remington machine acted as a positive spur. He found

---

† From "Spectral Mechanics: Gender, Sexuality and Work in *In the Cage*," *The Other Henry James*. Copyright © 1998, Duke University Press. All rights reserved. Reprinted with permission. References to this Norton Critical Edition appear in brackets following the author's original citations.
1. Henry James, "In the Cage," *The Novels and Tales of Henry James*, vol. 11 (New York: Charles Scribner's Sons, 1909). Hereafter cited within the text.
2. Fred Kaplan, *Henry James: The Imagination of Genius* (New York: William Morrow, 1992), p. 423.
3. Theodora Bosanquet, *Henry James at Work* (London: Hogarth Press, 1924), p. 248.

it more difficult to compose to the music of any other make."[4] But when he began dictating, "he experimented with two procedures. Sometimes MacAlpine, an expert stenographer, made longhand copies of the dictation; other times MacAlpine typed his words as he spoke them directly on the new Remington machine he had bought. He soon preferred the latter."[5]

In *Bodies and Machines*, Mark Seltzer stresses that James wanted the practice of "dictation to the machine" to be "absolutely identical with the act of writing" as James put the matter. Both Bosanquet and Mary Weld stressed James's desire that each be simply "part of the machinery." Seltzer concludes that this was James's psychic defense against a new system of communication that threatened the essential mastery and authority he, like other writers, had spent a career developing: "Reducing technologies of writing to the 'only' material and the material to the 'illusory,' James thus insists on the transparency of writing in general and on its disembodiment (such that, for instance, the difference of bodily motions—the difference of walking up and down—makes no difference)."[6]

Yet MacAlpine's first efforts were taken down in stenographer's symbols, then transcribed at the end of the day on the new Remington. It is imaginable that James experienced some of the same ignorance contemplating MacAlpine's stenography as Maisie experiences with the coded adult conversation that swirls about her. It was quite reasonable of James to have preferred the method of direct dictation to the Remington, as any writer without knowledge of stenography would prefer the greater control over the ongoing dictation afforded by an always available transcript to the greater speed afforded by shorthand transcription. There is yet another reason, however, why James may have chosen direct dictation over MacAlpine's stenography. Bosanquet observes: "The business of acting as a medium between the spoken and the typewritten word was at first as alarming as it was fascinating," but she was merely playing the amanuensis.[7] How much more "alarming and fascinating" must it have been to both James and MacAlpine to have worked together in a scene of communication in which the speech of James was transformed into written symbols legible only to MacAlpine, who until the end of the day, when he would type out a readable copy, would have virtual possession of the great writer's thoughts?

In *The Turn of the Screw*, the absent uncle maintains his authority by granting the governess the illusion that when she speaks

---

4. Ibid.
5. Kaplan, *Imagination of Genius*, pp. 423–24.
6. Mark Seltzer, *Bodies and Machines* (New York: Routledge, 1992), p. 195.
7. Bosanquet, *Henry James at Work*, p. 247.

and writes, her word is law.[8] James's dictation to MacAlpine reverses the traditional ways in which ideological control is effected through language; in this case, the author of a discourse, not the reader, must depend crucially on an other, in this case a hired technician, for the proper transcription and delivery of his words and his work. It is precisely the situation of *In the Cage*, with the difference that the Remington's click is replaced by the sounder's centralizing "tick" (the machine itself remaining invisible) and the stenographer's shorthand replaced by the Morse code into which the senders' messages must be translated.[9] James's own desire for a "typist without a mind" parallels that of the aristocrats in the novella, who hope for telegraphists who will simply translate and transmit their messages without interference. But interference is the constant threat posed by this new, decidedly public mode of communication that has pushed an archaic writing into the grubby corner of Cocker's store. (Writing, we should note parenthetically, has been doubly affected, both marginalized and yet made public in the service it renders the telegraph.) In a similar fashion, Maisie often serves to deliver messages between warring parents and stepparents, often misinterpreting both the original message and its reception. Maisie's childish mediation and the telegraphist's interpretations at the sounder serve as wild cards in the process of social communication.

James's own writing style is affected by the telegraphic mode, or at least by what James imagines is the paratactic mode both of telegrams and of the coded clicks by which they are transmitted. There are several marvelous conversations that are perfectly "telegraphic," especially at the end of chapter 18, when the telegraphist makes a pact not to "give up" Captain Everard and he blusters, "See here—see here," and the conversation with Mrs. Jordan in her flat in Maida Vale in the final three chapters (25–27), which I will discuss in more detail later in this chapter. A certain amount of James's imitation of a telegraphic style is part of his overall intention, but there is also a degree to which the telegraphic mode threatens to undermine James's customary control of discourse, especially the wonderfully complex and nuanced sentences that have become the hallmarks of his modernism. No two styles could be more opposite than the modernist long sentence with its implication

---

8. In referring to *The Turn of the Screw* throughout this chapter, I have in mind my own interpretation of the legal implications of the narrative in *The Theoretical Dimensions of Henry James* (Madison: University of Wisconsin Press, 1984), pp. 119–46.

9. The telegraphic sounder inspires imaginative associations for the telegraphist, as if James wants to evoke ironically the traditionally constitutive powers of literary writing. Thinking of Captain Everard, for example, the telegraphist imagines: "She could almost hear him, through the tick of the sounder, scatter with his stick, in his impatience, the fallen leaves of October" (*Cage*, 463).

of connotative complexity and the short and economical style of the telegram. Yet they are two styles that typify modernity.

James mediates between these opposing styles of modernity in a very interesting fashion in *In the Cage*. In general, he incorporates telegraphic messages into his narrative, and he then embeds them in a connotatively complex narrative. At one level, then, James defends his own style against the encroachments of modern technology (and its new modes of communication) by appropriating both the technology and its style.[1] For all their centrality to the plot and James's response to modernization in general, surprisingly little has been said about the telegraphic messages, except by Ralf Norrman and Janet Gabler-Hover.[2] The melodramatic plot turns on three telegrams included in the text, one of which (the second of the three) was sent by Lady Bradeen, corrected at the time by the telegraphist, apparently intercepted by Lady Bradeen's husband (or his representative), and concerning whose contents the putative lover of Lady Bradeen, Captain Everard, urgently inquires of the telegraphist, whose infatuation with him has encouraged her earlier to offer: "I'd do anything for you" (443) [268]. This telegram apparently finalizes arrangements for a romantic meeting between Lady Bradeen and Captain Everard, who have used different signatures and disguised identities throughout the narrative. The text of the telegram is important: "Miss Dolman, Parade Lodge, Parade Terrace, Dover. Let him instantly know right one, Hôtel de France, Ostend. Make it seven nine four nine six one. Wire me alternative Burfield's" (425) [259].

The dominant rhetorical mode of the telegram is *parataxis*, the practice of placing related clauses, words, and phrases in series without the use of connecting words. The paratactic mode has recently been used to characterize the dominant rhetoric of postmodern culture.[3] Beyond mere economy of expression, such parataxis in telegrams depersonalizes and even disguises the message, re-

---

1. The technique is typical of the high modernists. Extravagant metaphorization of otherwise functional technology, such as Hart Crane's representation of airplanes as "easters of speeding light" in *The Bridge*, were typical of several movements of modernism, especially symbolism and futurism.

2. Ralf Norrman, "The Intercepted Telegraph Plot in Henry James' *In the Cage*," *Notes and Queries* 24 (October 1977): n.s., p. 425–27, and Janet Gabler-Hover in "The Ethics of Determinism in Henry James's *In the Cage*," *The Henry James Review* 13, no. 3 (fall 1992): pp. 253–75.

3. N. Katherine Hayles, "The Paratactic Style of Postmodern Culture," *American Literary History* 2, no. 3 (fall 1990): p. 398: "Parataxis does not necessarily mean that there is no relation between the terms put into juxtaposition. Rather, the relation, unspecified except for proximity, is polysemous and unstable. Lacking a coordinating structure, it is subject to appropriation, interpretation, and reinscription into different modalities. This aspect of parataxis makes it into a cultural seismograph, extraordinarily sensitive to rifts, tremors, and realignments in bodies of discourse, as well as in bodies constituted through discourse and cultural practices."

sponding to the new public conditions of discourse required by the telegraph. Since the 1840s, the publicity with which the telegraph was associated had been cause of both grand optimism on the part of technophiles and apocalyptic warnings from confirmed Luddites. On January 3, 1845, for example, John Tawell, "dressed as a Quaker in a great brown coat reaching nearly to his feet, was arrested at a lodging house in London after murdering his mistress at Slough. The transmission of his description by telegraph to Paddington was largely responsible for his rapid arrest," and the newspapers celebrated the telegraph with the headline: "The cords that hung John Tawell."[4] The military advantages of the telegraph had been demonstrated in the U.S. Civil War, and the abuse of the telegraphic style was infamously recorded in Bismarck's infamous revision of the exchange between Kaiser Wilhelm I and the French ambassador Comte Vincente Benedetti in the Ems Dispatch of July 1870, which precipitated the Franco-Prussian War. As the police made more extensive use of telegraph networks following the celebrity of the Tawell arrest, they both increased their powers of surveillance and prompted public anxiety about the misuses of the telegraph by "the 'dangerous classes,' 'assassins and burglars'" who might use "the telegraph to decoy people from their homes. *The Detective*, a new weekly journal of 1858, urged companies to date stamp their telegrams only at the place where they were actually received, for telegrams written in London were dated 'Aberdeen' or 'Brighton' to deceive recipients."[5] In addition to the several ways James's fiction addresses and contributes to the modern arts of surveillance analyzed so well by Michel Foucault, we should add this connection between his writing and telegraphy.[6]

The potential for surveillance built into the telegraph system frightens Lady Bradeen and Captain Everard, prompting them to communicate in code. Certainly the numbers in the telegram constitute some sort of cipher code, undoubtedly suggested to James by the fact that the Morse code is itself a cipher code.[7] Honorific or purely decorative as the good captain's military title undoubtedly is, it nonetheless gives some warrant for his use of a system of coding developed primarily for military secrecy. As Ralf Norrman points out, in an essay otherwise notable for his pathological effort

4. Kieve, *Electric Telegraph* (London: Newton Abbot, David and Charles, 1973), p. 39.
5. Ibid., p. 245.
6. The best application of Foucault to this aspect of Henry James's writings is Mark Seltzer, *Henry James and the Art of Power* (Ithaca, N.Y.: Cornell University Press, 1984).
7. Shawn Rosenheim, *The Cryptographic Imagination: Secret Writing from Edgar Poe to the Internet* (Baltimore, Md.: Johns Hopkins University Press, 1997), p. 88: "Because the telegraph depends on Morse's code for its utility, there exists a natural affinity between telegraphy and cryptography."

to prove how the telegraphist "is wrong about everything," the crucial part of the telegram consists of "the series of numbers," since this is the information that the telegraphist remembers and apparently satisfies the anxious Captain Everard, who is himself transformed scenically by James into his own version of a telegraphic sender, but now of the luminous sort: "He shone at them all like a tall lighthouse, embracing even, for sympathy, the blinking young men. 'By all the powers—it's wrong!' " (484) [290]. He is delighted, even as the "blinking young men" act as naval signals to his lighthouse, because the numbers remembered by the telegraphist and jotted on the back of his card—"He fairly glared at it. 'Seven, nine, four—' 'Nine, six, one'—she obligingly completed the number"—are wrong, and we remember with the telegraphist, "If it's wrong it's all right," which she quotes to the still uncomprehending signal corps of young male clerks after the captain has fled "without another look, without a word of thanks, without time for anything or anybody," like some embodied telegram darting through the wire.[8]

* * *

In what we may take as either an interesting coincidence or significant historical fact for James in his use of telegraphy in the novella, Morse was both a distinguished painter and inspired inventor, suggesting either art's potential complicity in modern systems of surveillance and control or a potential link between the aesthetic and technological imaginations. Connecting Morse's interests in the telegraph and painting, Paul Staiti concludes that Morse's technological and artistic abilities were complementary:

> The greatest material evidence for abstract congruency in Morse's imaginings in art and machine technology exist in small but revealing moments when Morse was on the cusp between his two careers. For instance, he did some of his most imaginative work on the telegraph between 1835 and 1837, at precisely the same time and in the same building in which he painted his most imaginative pictures, *Allegorical Landscape of New York University* and *The Muse*. He drew faces rotating on gears, superimposed a troubled character on a design for the Atlantic cable, and wrote the word "signalization" on a sketch of macabre heads. There is a curiously Duchamp-like appearance to the receiver for his telegraph of 1837, built out of a canvas-stretcher, in the open space of which he invented

8. *In the Cage* is an interesting anticipation of postmodern narratives in many different respects, especially in its subtle insistence on the subordination of nature and the body to the technologies of urban modernity. The determination of people's identities by urban spaces and technologies and the virtual complete containment of any sort of "nature" (physical or human) shapes the prevailing atmosphere of *In the Cage*.

—metaphorically "pictured"—the electromagnetic recording device.[9]

Staiti's late-twentieth-century view of the inherent compatibility of art and technology—an opinion shared by many classical aestheticians—is not, however, James's prevailing outlook in *In the Cage* or in his cautious responses to modern inventions such as the telegraph, typewriter, bicycle, and automobile. Always interested in new technologies, James nonetheless responds to them, especially at this time in his life and art, in a defensive manner, as if they were direct competitors with the novel's ability to represent life, consciousness, social relations, and reality.

James preferred the term "amanuensis," rather than "secretary," to describe the job done by MacAlpine, Weld, and Bosanquet, and we often think of it as simply his pedantic word. But the telegraphist and the amanuensis (from *manu*, "hand," and *ensis*, "relating to") are more than just technicians. They command a technology whose mere operation exceeds the author's. Scribes were hired in ancient times for precisely their competencies in a relatively unfamiliar technology of communication, a fact generally reflected in their social positions in ancient Egypt and Greece. Rosenheim points out that although cryptography is an ancient art of secreting messages, it developed rapidly into a host of different techniques with the introduction of the telegraph, which "expanded the cryptograph's imaginative possibilities, particularly regarding its users' predilection for subversive histories and conspiracies."[1] In short, the telegraph rapidly became a medium of communicative *power*. In his references to those who transcribed his dictation as "amanuenses," James reflects both his recognition of the special, potentially *secret* power they might have wielded over his art, just as he went to considerable lengths to establish his own aesthetic superiority to the new, threatening technologies.

James's fictional technician is a working-class woman, whose poverty, alcoholic mother at home, and modest prospects of marriage to the grocer Mr. Mudge signify a class whose access to power has traditionally been foreclosed. This may be James's way of entertaining the power of modern technology without letting it actually exceed *his* artistic and imaginative controls. In the drawings by Morse to which Staiti refers, the artist and inventor come together in casual doodles in which technological and aesthetic images easily occupy the same space. For Henry James and other aesthetic moderns, machines and artworks are in more contestatory, troubled re-

9. Paul J. Staiti, *Samuel F. B. Morse* (Cambridge: Cambridge University Press, 1989), pp. 225–26.
1. Rosenheim, *Cryptographic Imagination*, p. 95.

lations. Ralf Norrman is unfortunately right most of the time in claiming that the telegraphist is wrong most of the time, but this does not mean that James's novella simply repeats the usual message of his earlier work: "The rich are different from you and me; they have all the power." Without understanding the significance, Norrman points out how frightened Lady Bradeen is when she comes to Cocker's store for the second and last time to send her infamous and apparently incorrect telegram:

> Lady Bradeen next discovers that a word is wrong and must be altered. The telegraphist, overcome with the desire to show that she "knows," takes a jump and gives the "right" word. " 'Isn't it Cooper's?' It was as if she had boldly leaped—cleared the top of the cage and alighted on her interlocutress. 'Cooper's?'—the stare was heightened by a blush. Yes, she had made Juno blush. This was all the greater reason for going on. 'I mean instead of Burfield's.' " At this her ladyship becomes quite helpless, "not a bit haughty nor outraged. She was only mystified and scared. 'Oh you know—?' "[2]

From this Norrman concludes that Lady Bradeen "is just aghast at the little spying, meddling telegraphist."[3] He is right to identify both the fear in Lady Bradeen's response and the ambiguity of her "you know?"—that is, "You know—[the right word]" or "You know— [about my affair with Captain Everard. . . . You spy into my private life and meddle in my business]."

In this scene, the telegraphist has assumed a psyche, a face made possible for Lady Bradeen by the challenge she has offered to the customary expectation of the merely efficient servant—pouring tea, delivering cards on a silver tray, silently placing sealed postal deliveries on the hall table. Lady Bradeen is accessible now in the very essence of the power that represents and maintains her class—the power of a special discourse banned from those who have not learned to drop their "aitches" (on which James comments in this narrative and *What Maisie Knew*). They are now translators and transcoders of the secrets of power, and on this new class of technicians, the ruling class increasingly must rely.

If she is "wrong about everything," as Norrman insists, it is only because the telegraphist has been reading the wrong books. Her "ha'penny stories" are the stuff of the governess's world in *Turn of the Screw*; it is little wonder that the telegraphist should end up hating upper-class women and falling in love with upper-class men. She ought to be reading a code and cipher book, a treatise on the

2. Norrman, "Telegraph Plot," p. 426.
3. Ibid.

future of the telegraph system, opportunities for women in Marconi's new Wireless Telegraph and Signal Co., formed as a private corporation in July 1897, the very time James was writing his novella, while Marconi was completing tests on the new wireless telegraph in England.[4] After all, the "telegraph industry was a new area of female employment," which advertised the "light work," despite the long hours ("generally a nine or ten-hour day, six days a week"), and the skills involved.[5] For technophiles and liberal progressives, the telegraph industry was an opportunity for working-class women to improve their positions from unskilled laborers to skilled technicians.

I do not wish to take social effects for their causes; technological innovation tends to be the consequence of new social needs. The telegraph responds to the demands of industrial, urban, densely populated societies in which market forces drive values (from wages to ethics) and the privacy of the individual is increasingly a lost illusion. The telegraph responds to a world in which the old boundaries between public and private, the industrial economy and household economics, and "society" in the senses of the nation and culture have broken down. The secret world of the ruling class is increasingly open to view. The uncle can command the governess "never [to] trouble him . . . neither appeal nor complain nor write about anything" with some expectation that the class divisions of his world will support this taboo.[6] Servants such as Quint and Jessel are presumed to carry their secrets to their graves, however much they might embody the corruption of their masters. But the private world of the Bradeens, Captain Everard, and Lord Rye is full of traffic from the outside world. Not only are their messages open to the view of the counter clerks and telegraphists at Cocker's Grocery, but Mrs. Jordan arranges the flowers for their patties, in place of the invisible and discreet servants of the previous generation; the telegraphist thinks of her as "a friend who had invented a new career for women—that of being in and out of people's houses to look after the flowers" (371) [231]. In earlier times, the servants gathered flowers from the vast gardens of the country estate; now Mrs. Jordan can imagine expanding her business to include the telegraphist, to whom she proposes taking over the accounts of all the "bachelors." Still dazzled by the upper classes, dreaming of a "match" out of a "ha'penny" romance, neither Mrs. Jordan nor the telegraphist understands what James makes explicit—the new pow-

4. Kieve, *Electric Telegraph*, pp. 243–44.
5. Ibid., p. 85.
6. Henry James, *The Turn of the Screw*, the New York Edition, vol. 12, p. 156.

ers of the working classes to understand and perhaps even seize what James had always understood as the primary mode of social production: discourse.

Jennifer Wicke points out that "the realm of language is not privileged, not exempt, and certainly not related to political economy in merely metaphorical ways" to encourage scholars of James to pay more attention to how textual questions are related to modes of socioeconomic production in his works and times.[7] Bauer and Lakritz have shown us how Taylorism rationalizes, systematizes, and mechanizes both the telegraphist's work and sexuality to the point where both she and the words she counts fail any longer to "count" in the sense of social significance or intellectual meaning.[8] While noting the material conditions of production in the late Victorian period, we must also remember that the telegraphist's "cage" differs importantly from the smoke-stack factories and the sweatshops where women and children had wasted their vision, minds, and lives in the earlier phases of industrialism. Shawn Rosenheim points out how "Morse's telegraph represented a watershed for mass culture" not only because it enabled news media—and thus national authority—to operate with such speed but also because "the Newtonian unities of being are replaced by the prosthetic extension of the self over a network of wires."[9] The telegraphist's work represents fundamental changes in the epistemology and ontology of modern experience, as well as in practical aspects of everyday life.

Just who owns the words and the flowers is less definite in this changing urban world than it was for the children, the governess, and Mrs. Grose at Bly. The telegraphist understands dimly what James knows with perfect clarity—that in this new age the values come not from accumulated possessions, not from hoarded wealth, but from the combinations and arrangements compatible with this exchange economy: "Combinations of flowers and greenstuff forsooth! What *she* could handle freely, she said to herself, was combinations of men and women" (373) [232]. For someone who counts words every day in terms of their monetary value, she knows well enough that textual combinations are the new sources of value. At one point, prompted by Mrs. Jordan's bragging about her ability to arrange a "thousand tulips" for her clients, the telegraphist reflects: "A thousand tulips at a shilling clearly took one further than a thousand words at a penny" (396) [244]. But the narrative sug-

---

7. Jennifer Wicke, "Henry James's Second Wave," *The Henry James Review* 10, no. 2 (spring 1989): pp. 150–51.
8. Dale Bauer and Andrew Lakritz, "Language, Class, and Sexuality in Henry James's *In the Cage*," *New Orleans Review* 14 (1987): p. 64.
9. Rosenheim, *Cryptographic Imagination*, p. 91.

gests that there are other ways for words to be worth vastly more than the coppers she counts out at Cocker's.

In Regents Park with Captain Everard, she surprises, puzzles, and probably frightens him with her combination of independence, frankness, and familiarity. Above all, she disturbs him, like some uncanny ghost of his own worry, with her claim to knowledge. Whatever she thinks she knows and however wrong it may be, she nonetheless has touched the one region in which the ruling class is vulnerable—its control and command of language. It is when she says, "Yes, I know," that "She immediately felt him surprised and even a little puzzled at her frank assent; but for herself the trouble she had taken could only, in these fleeting minutes . . . be all there like a little hoard of gold in her lap" (437) [265]. From the first chapter of *In the Cage* to the last, the telegraphist fitfully experiences the glimmers of a class consciousness that she mistakes most often for her own genius or for the love she imagines draws her to Captain Everard. Whatever class consciousness emerges, however, will not be of the traditional Marxian sort, nothing like what James had already ridiculed in Hyacinth's decorative labors in *The Princess Casamassima*. For James, such awareness must be integrally connected to the new productive value of language in the emerging economies of information and communication.

* * *

Beyond the veneer of conventional class and gender distinctions, James offers us peeks at an extraordinary diversity of new class and gender possibilities. Once again, the technology of the telegraph has not *caused* these new possibilities, not all of which are emancipatory, but it has some coincidence with the socioeconomic conditions informing such alternatives. Perhaps the most obvious example of such an alternative is Mr. Mudge, who is dismissed by critics almost as summarily as Napoleon was reputed to have defeated the English with the judgment, "A nation of shopkeepers." To be sure, Mr. Mudge's courtship of the telegraphist appears only slightly more agreeable to her than the counter clerk's idiotic passion, and Mudge's values seem to be utterly commercial. Nothing is valuable unless it pays a material return, and everything in their relationship is as managed as a Taylorized factory. Worst of all, perhaps, Mudge defends the class hierarchies in the manner of a classic petit bourgeois and what survivors of the Reagan-Bush years recognize as the tiresome rhetoric of "trickle-down" economics (410) [252]. What benefits the upper classes is likely to be good for the shopkeeper's business, as far as Mr. Mudge is concerned. Selling tomatoes or telegrams is the same business to him: "Above all it hurt him somewhere . . . to see anything *but* money made out of his betters" (410) [252].

Yet he does differ from caricatures of the Victorian bourgeois patriarch. When the telegraphist candidly tells him, "I went out the other night and sat in the Park with a gentleman," Mudge does not go to pieces as does the jealous husband in Trollope's *He Knew He Was Right* (1869) (456) [275]. When she challenges his masculinity by telling him, "You're awfully inferior" to Captain Everard, Mudge can say with both humor and pride in her, "Well, my dear, you're not inferior to anybody. You've got a cheek!" (458) [276]. And when she tells him she hasn't seen "the gentleman" since, Mudge can judge him with little consideration for his own inferiority: "Oh what a cad!" (460) [277]. Showing no regard for "his honor," Mudge expresses a quiet "confidence in her" that "only gave her ease and space, as she felt, for telling him the whole truth that no one knew" (456) [275]. In what other fiction of the late Victorian period do we find a man giving a woman psychic space while she tells him of her meeting with another man?

Let me not overdo this idealization of Mr. Mudge, with his concern for order, his pocket full of chocolate creams, and his acceptance of upper-class rule as if it were a law of nature. Yet as the only male character with a name escaping the phallic aggressiveness of Buckton, Drake, and Everard, Mudge better approaches understanding of the telegraphist than any other character, including Mrs. Jordan. What he offers may be his petty ambitions, a move from fashionable Mayfair to the dreary suburb of Chalk Farm, and "savings" of "three shillings" a week on lodgings. Chalk Farm is the suburb where swells such as Captain Everard gamble at the races, but it is also the neighborhood of "clerks and railroad men and electrical workers."[1] What Mudge offers her is a community of other workers, especially those in the newer communications and transportation industries.[2] Of all the people she knows, Mr. Mudge is the only one who gives her mother any recognition, and he does so in an exchange that shows he is not without imagination: "The little home . . . had been visited, in further talk she had had with him at Bournemouth, from garret to cellar, and they had especially lingered, with their respectively darkened brows, before the niche into which it was to be broached to her mother that she must find means to fit" (473–74) [284].

Hardly a revolutionary, Mr. Mudge nonetheless represents a dif-

---

1. John Kimmey, *Henry James and London: The City in His Fiction*, American University Studies, series 4, vol. 121 (New York: Peter Lang, 1991), p. 117.
2. Jeffrey Kieve, *Electric Telegraph*, p. 35, points out that the telegraph lines were first laid out along the railroad lines and that the first major telegraphic system was developed in the 1840s and 1850s by the Great Western Railroad Company.

ferent role for men in his times, reflecting perhaps necessary adjustments to the frank, independent, often bold behavior of the telegraphist. Perhaps James hesitates before Mr. Mudge in his usual caricature of the petit bourgeoisie. It may also be that what James treats with some wry affection in this characterization is, on closer examination, something like the regard Anthony Trollope accords his new bourgeois heroes such as Johnny Eames in *The Small House at Allington* (1864) or Phineas Phinn in the Palliser novels or others in a long list of good-natured, not particularly dashing, often clumsy, but steady and true young men. In Trollope's fiction, such heroes usually endure to win the women who have first declined their offers of marriage for the sake of some one finer. We should recognize this as a strategy of class and gender legitimation that works by demonizing an illusory aristocracy, so we must be cautious in identifying too readily with Mr. Mudge. The suburban Chalk Farm where he will settle with the telegraphist and her mother may turn out, after all, to be either a neighborhood of like-minded workers or an urban ghetto of exploited victims.

Suffice it to say that Mrs. Jordan is not Olive Chancellor or Henrietta Stackpole;[3] James has changed the caricature of the professional woman to render her with some seriousness. Mr. Mudge is not, as the name at first suggests, simply the blot on the otherwise finely written page of Mayfair. Among his other noms de plume for his telegrams, Captain Everard once selects "Mudge," and the accident is not lost on us. Whereas the captain can only expose his lack of imagination, his imitation of the rake, when the telegraphist engages him in Regents Park—"See here—see here!"—Mr. Mudge offers a community, a place for her alcoholic mother, a two-career family, and occasional holidays with "sundries," like those chocolate creams.

I am suggesting that some aspects of Judith Butler's postmodern understanding of gender as a function of discourse are already present in James's text, even though these features are not entirely under his control. New representations of gender establish new relations of gender, and both are often enough the consequence of new working and living conditions. All these gender relations have been shaped even more determinately than in previous Jamesian works by the conditions of their discursive production, although these are by no means separable from the material conditions of production.[4] Throughout *In the Cage*, James makes it clear that telegraphic communication depends on the cooperative labor of sender, technician, and receiver—a triad that drastically changes

3. Feminist characters in *The Bostonians* and *The Portrait of a Lady*, respectively [Editors].
4. Wicke, "Henry James's Second Wave," p. 150.

the transactional, intersubjective model for writing and speech. Few if any of the characters understand this change, which is as radical as the conflation of public and private spheres performed in telegraphy, and the telegraphist herself remains convinced to the very end that "people didn't understand her" (372) [232], "the immensity of her difference," "not different only at one point, . . . different all round" (403) [248]. But such difference belongs not to the telegraphist alone, "the betrothed of Mr. Mudge," but to the relations of a complex, changing social reality. It is a new social reality in which customary gender roles are "mudged," and I turn in this regard to two final examples: the telegraphist as "mother" and the dubious Mr. Drake.

I have already discussed how the sounder aurally dominates Cocker's Grocery and Post-Telegraph, even though it is invisible in its cage within the cage (within the shop). It is like some postmodern fetus ticking away at the center of the new object relations that determine subjects' identities: "She had made out even from the cage that it was a charming golden day: a patch of hazy autumn sunlight lay across the sanded floor and also, higher up, quickened into brightness a row of ruddy bottled syrups" (461) [277]. This may be the ironic negativity of a new, denaturalized world, but the positive side comes from the slippage of older names from their proper referents to a wider range of possible significations. Taking care of her alcoholic mother by working at Cocker's and by worrying in the meantime just where her mother manages to get her bottles, the telegraphist is already "mothering." And it is when Captain Everard arrives at Cocker's the most desperate for help that he appears to her "quite, now, as she said to herself, like a frightened child coming to its mother" (476–77) [286]. Even in her indulgence of the self-important fancies of her friend Mrs. Jordan, the telegraphist displays qualities of tenderness and care that are too often attributed by patriarchy to the mother and would thus seem inappropriate for the care shown by a woman ten years younger for an older, often deluded woman. There is also the diverse imagery of vaginal, womblike, maternal spaces throughout the text, beginning with the "cage" itself (derived as the word is from its Latin root, *cavea*, meaning "hollow or enclosed space") to the presumably pseudonymous Miss Dolman to whom telegrams are routed by Lady Bradeen and Captain Everard. A dolman is a Hussar's fur-lined coat, combining thus the captain's military and amorous exploits in a manner not unlike the uncle's "trophies of the hunt" in his London house in *The Turn of the Screw*.[5]

5. For a psychoanalytic approach to maternal imagery in *In the Cage*, see William Veeder, "Toxic Mothers, Cultural Criticism: *In the Cage* and Elsewhere," *The Henry James Review* 14 (Fall 1993): 264–72.

In the customary Jamesian narrative of feminine limitation, the young woman is incapable of becoming either Artist or Mother, especially those characters who pursue careers of their own. On one level, *In the Cage* follows just that rhetoric, so that the promise of the telegraphist's marriage to Mr. Mudge is merely a repetition of the pathetic genealogy of working-class families of which the alcoholic mother will remind the young couple. On another level, which I have characterized as one of "hints" and "peeks," as if James is not quite comfortable with its meanings, mothering is unmoored from its customary domesticity and its conflict with work and the public sphere. . . . The telegraphic sounder need not be merely a grotesque image of the automated mother of the new technology; it might also suggest how the proper transmission of generational value resides less in persons (and their fragile bodies) than in the means of communication. This, too, is often enough James's theme, even argument, as he thunders about the "historical consciousness" that can be achieved only through a proper interpretation of the semiotically dense texture of everyday reality. But now he offers an alternative to those otherwise barred from access to such means of communication.

In her extraordinary reading of "The Beast in the Jungle," Eve Sedgwick shows how Marcher refuses the homosexual plot of his story and becomes the "irredeemably self-ignorant man who embodies and enforces heterosexual compulsion" as he turns away from the "beast" and what it signifies.[6] Sedgwick reads Marcher's encounter in the cemetery with the male stranger—the stranger who is capable of mourning—as Marcher's reenactment of "a classic trajectory of male entitlement":

> Marcher begins with the possibility of *desire for* the man. . . . Deflecting that desire under a fear of profanation, he then replaces it with envy, with an *identification with* the man in that man's (baffled) desire for some other, presumably female dead object. . . . The loss by which a man *so bleeds and yet lives* is . . . supposed to be the castratory one of the phallus figured as mother, the inevitability of whose sacrifice ushers sons into the status of fathers and into the control (read both ways) of the Law.[7]

All of this presumes that the "woman" remains unchanged, the "figure" of "mother" as the one *without* the phallus, the image of the possibility of being unmanned and thus the motive for repression, not only of the castration feared in the Freudian family-

6. Eve Kosofsky Sedgwick, *Epistemology of the Closet* (Berkeley: University of California Press, 1990), p. 210 [512].
7. Ibid., p. 211 [512–513].

romance but also of a fundamental lack of authority that provokes the entire cycle of masculine desire in the first place. Yet the telegraphist in *In the Cage* is not merely a negative image, the convenient "female, dead object" used (fetishized) for a masculine narrative. The "mother" is no longer just the medium of masculine transmission of genealogical authority from father to son. At a certain level, the telegraphist assumes the phallus of a newly empowered "mother," especially as she assumes *maternal* functions outside the conventional and literal roles of mother reserved for a young, affianced, working-class girl. As mother to Captain Everard, to her own mother, to Mr. Mudge, and even to her friend Mrs. Jordan, the telegraphist escapes the strict division of private and public, as well as the presumed naturalness of the mother's relation to her own child. "Mothering" has been refigured by association with the powers of communication, and the degree to which the telegraphist dons those powers is some measure of an authority that no longer is precisely that of mother or father, but of some authority for transmission that exceeds their outmoded and gender-specific roles. Such a redefinition of motherhood can encompass masculine agency, such as Sir Claude's in *What Maisie Knew* when he claims: "I think I've produced life," meaning thereby something radically different from phallic possession.[8]

Finally, there is Mr. Drake, whose introduction by Mrs. Jordan in the last three chapters (25–27) as her affianced seems merely a clumsy deus ex machina. Despite—or perhaps because of—his very masculine name, Mr. Drake is the occasion for what I shall term James's *rhetorical cross-dressing*. The novella concludes with a conversation between Mrs. Jordan and the telegraphist that is hilarious in its double entendres involving the "gentleman" Drake. The misunderstandings revolve overtly around Mrs. Jordan's habit of exaggerating her involvement with the aristocracy, so that we assume along with the telegraphist that Mr. Drake is the equal of Lord Rye, Lord and Lady Bradeen, and Captain Everard. The bathos appears to be in his revelation as simply the butler, but we do not know this until a certain rhetorical banter has accomplished a very different effect.

> "I think you must have heard me speak of Mr. Drake?" Mrs. Jordan had never looked so queer, nor her smile so suggestive of a large benevolent bite.
> ". . . Oh yes; isn't he a friend of Lord Rye?"
> "A great and trusted friend. Almost—I may say—a loved friend."

8. Henry James, "What Maisie Knew," *The Novels and Tales of Henry James*, vol. 11 (New York: Charles Scribner's Sons, 1909), p. 354.

Mrs. Jordan's "almost" had such an oddity that her companion was moved, rather flippantly perhaps, to take it up. "Don't people as good as love their friends when they 'trust' them?" (491) [293]

If James has allowed mothering to slip somewhat from its conventional referents of mother and biological child, he is here more daringly causing love to drift from the amours of men and women (those "ha'penny stories") to the trust and care between people of whatever gender.

The rhetoric is explicitly homoerotic in these passages and for that very reason seems to emphasize James's more general point about affection and care that transcend traditional boundaries of masculine and feminine identities. In chapter 4,[9] I argued that James disguises homosexual desire in stories from the first half of the 1890s, such as "The Middle Years" and "The Death of the Lion," in part by demonizing lesbian sexuality (and thereby creating an apparent moral "choice" between male and female same-sex relations) and in part by sublimating sexual desire as *textual* passion. Although I argue that gender transgressions can be liberating in *What Maisie Knew*, they can also cause a child such as Maisie considerable anxiety and insecurity as she struggles to find her adolescent identity. In the final chapters of *In the Cage*, however, there seems to be little of this anxiety and much more of a certain delight in the comedy of gender and sexual varieties. If *In the Cage* represents a change in James's thinking, it is by no means consistently played out in James's writings from 1898 to the end of his life. *The Turn of the Screw* is strong evidence that James has not yet changed his mind completely. Even if we do not read *The Turn of the Screw* as an allegory of homosexual desire, enacted either in the imagined relations between Peter Quint and Miles or Miss Jessel and Flora, we must still read it as a narrative that focuses on forms of human possessiveness and control that are both perverse and sexual in their workings. *The Turn of the Screw* is organized as a tragedy, and the dark hints of sexuality's dangerous consequences encompass frequent hints of homosexuality as the horizon of such sinfulness.

The tone of *In the Cage* differs utterly from either the rhetorical dodges of the stories from the first half of the 1890s or the tragic and distinctly erotic gloom of *The Turn of the Screw*; it even seems to resolve the anxious play with gender instability at work in *What Maisie Knew*. As the conversation about Mr. Drake and Lord Rye's friendship increasingly becomes explicitly analogous to the telegraphist's friendship with Mrs. Jordan, the homoerotic rhetoric increases in frequency and explicitness: "Mr. Drake has rendered his

9. Chapter 4 of *The Other Henry James*, John Carlos Rowe.

lordship for several years services that his lordship has highly appreciated and that make it all the more—a—unexpected that they should, perhaps a little suddenly, separate." Still confused about the real identity of Mr. Drake as the butler, the telegraphist can only echo, " 'Separate?' Our young lady was mystified, . . . and she already saw that she had put the saddle on the wrong horse" (491–92) [293–294]. The rhetoric of the conversation between Mrs. Jordan and the telegraphist is a Jamesian tour de force, operating as it does simultaneously on the following registers: confusion of "gentleman" as either aristocrat or servant; confusion of Mr. Drake's sexual preference as either straight or gay; and confusion of what amounts to a ménage à quatre of Drake, Lord Rye, Lady Bradeen, and Mrs. Jordan with the confused relations of the telegraphist, Captain Everard, Lady Bradeen, and Mrs. Jordan.

All of this is further entangled with the sheer plot function played by Mr. Drake in providing information about the fates of Lord and Lady Bradeen and Captain Everard following the scene of the undelivered telegram. For this purpose, Mr. Drake must leave Lord Rye for the "service" of Lady Bradeen, at which point the telegraphist, still uncertain just who Mr. Drake is (servant, lover, fiancé, gentleman) can only wonder, with the help of Mrs. Jordan, about how "immensely surrounded" Lady Bradeen will be with male admirers (494) [295]. And when Mrs. Jordan tries to clarify what she has meant by Mr. Drake "going to Lady Bradeen" (493) [294], she only seems to confuse things:

> "He's 'going,' you say, to her?"
> At this Mrs. Jordan really faltered. "She has engaged him."
> "Engaged him?" . . .
> "In the same capacity as Lord Rye."
> "And was Lord Rye engaged?" (495) [295]

The rhetorical effect of this cross-dressing lasts only a moment, and at the beginning of the next chapter, the telegraphist begins to see that "Mr. Drake then verily *was* a person who opened the door!" (496) [296]. (It is fair, however, to add parenthetically that it is James opening the door to our repressed fears of homoeroticism.)

As Mrs. Jordan brags that she and Mr. Drake, like the telegraphist and Mr. Mudge, "shall have our own" house "too," she explains just what caused the breakup of Lord Rye and Mr. Drake:

> "For, don't you know? he makes it a condition that he sleeps out."
> "A condition?"—the girl felt out of it.
> "For any new position. It was on that he parted with Lord Rye. His lordship can't meet it. So Mr. Drake has given him up."

"And all for you?"—our young woman put it as cheerfully as possible.

"For me and Lady Bradeen." (500) [298]

These are just bits and pieces from a sustained banter of confused gender and class roles that stretches across three chapters at the very end of the novella. Desperate to find solid ground amid this shifting rhetoric, the telegraphist clings to the "one" (Captain Everard, presumably) she knows in Lady Bradeen's set by answering Mrs. Jordan's question, "He's a gentleman?" with "Yes, he's not a lady" (494) [295].

Neither Mrs. Jordan nor the telegraphist has intended such confusions of gender, sexuality, and class, but they have been produced nonetheless by the new circumstances of work, communication, and social relations. One of the venerable biographical anecdotes about the contemporary reception of *In the Cage* is André Raffalovich " 'once teasing' James 'to know what the Olympian young man in *In the Cage* had done wrong. He swore he did not know, he would rather not know.' "[1] Marc André Raffalovich (1864–1934) was the author of *L'Affaire d'Oscar Wilde* (1895) and *Uranisme et Unisexualité*, published in 1896, the year before James would write *In the Cage*, "in which he argued that homosexuality . . . and heterosexuality are two equally legitimate manifestations of human sexuality, rejected the current view that homosexuality was a disease, and advocated a life of chastity, supported by friendship, as the Christian ideal!"[2]

In his biographical account of James's "passionate friendships" with contemporaries such as Morton Fullerton, Howard Sturgis, and Hendrik Andersen, Fred Kaplan shows that what James most desired from male companions in his middle and later years was companionship. Without ignoring or diminishing James's capacity for sexual passion, however repressed or evaded, Kaplan understands that what James most desired was someone with whom he might talk, walk, bicycle, garden, and, perhaps above all *work*. When Sturgis "made his first visit early in 1900," James "read to him each evening from his work-in-progress, *The Ambassadors*. Sturgis was at work on a new novel, the details of which he shared with his host, who urged him on."[3]

At the furthest reach of the melodrama of *In the Cage*, the te-

---

1. Morton Dauwen Zabel, introduction to *In the Cage and Other Tales* (New York: W. W. Norton, 1958), p. 9; the anecdote was first told in Forrest Reid's *Private Road* (London: Faber and Faber, 1940), then quoted in Simon Nowell-Smith's *The Legend of the Master* (New York: Charles Scribner's Sons, 1948).

2. David Hilliard, as quoted in Richard Dellamora, *Masculine Desire: The Sexual Politics of Victorian Aestheticism* (Chapel Hill: University of North Carolina Press, 1990), pp. 148–49.

3. Kaplan, *Imagination of Genius*, p. 455.

legraphist may forget her dreary life in fantasies of the passionate loves, diabolical murders, and coded messages of the rich and famous. In the sad realism of late Victorian urban London, she is as trapped by her dead-end job as she will be by the hapless Mudge and the squall of children they will visit on the Malthusian nightmare of London. Mudge's chocolate creams will give way to silent screams.

But in the Jamesian text, the possibilities of the new workplace, the developing service industries, and the emancipatory potential of the new century begin to make a difference. To be sure, it is a difference of which the telegraphist herself is at best dimly aware, trapped as she must remain to the end in her stubborn insistence that no one understands her, that she is "different" from the other workers, especially those men whispering and insinuating as she tries to count the words and sell the stamps. Perhaps it is only possible for such changes in gender, class, and identity itself to be registered first in the textual space where a certain liberty has always been possible, where the constraints of convention, of consciousness, even of the unconscious, need not be taken as final. Certainly James found it safer to entertain the idea that the slippage of gender boundaries that he recognizes in this novella might accompany, for better or worse, the changing social and economic boundaries of the new age. He identifies far more consciously with the telegraphist, even down to her trip to Bournemouth, which recalls his first trip to the southern coast of England that would become his home until the very end at Lamb House, Rye. Whether he knows how much he shares the anxiety of Lady Bradeen, Captain Everard, and the others once in charge of the symbolic discourse of culture is difficult to determine from the surface of a novella with such depths. Sounding those depths, we find James's own unconscious betrayed, not only regarding his ambivalence about his own sexual preference, but also regarding his status as the master, the figure who had devoted his life to "coded" texts, not so much to prevent detection as to encourage, even provoke, it. In that, there is a great difference, all the difference, I would say, to distinguish Henry James from less worthy authorities.

EVE KOSOFSKY SEDGWICK

["The Beast in the Closet"]†

There has so far seemed no reason, or little reason, why what I have been calling "male homosexual panic" could not just as descriptively have been called "male heterosexual panic"—or, simply, "male sexual panic." Although I began with a structural and historicizing narrative that emphasized the pre- and proscriptively defining importance of men's bonds with men, potentially including genital bonds, the books I have discussed have not, for the most part, seemed to center emotionally or thematically on such bonds. In fact, it is, explicitly, a male panic in the face of *hetero*sexuality that many of these books most describe. And no assumption could be more homophobic than the automatic association of same-sex object choice with a fear of heterosexuality or of the other sex. It is all very well to insist, as I have done, that homosexual panic is necessarily a problem only, but endemically, of nonhomosexual-identified men; nevertheless the lack in these books of an embodied male-homosexual thematics, however inevitable, has had a dissolutive effect on the structure and texture of such an argument. Part, although only part, of the reason for that lack was historical: it was only close to the end of the nineteenth century that a cross-class homosexual role and a consistent, ideologically full thematic discourse of male homosexuality became entirely visible, in developments that were publicly dramatized in—though far from confined to—the Wilde trials.

In "The Beast in the Jungle," written at the threshold of the new century, the possibility of an embodied male-homosexual thematics has, I would like to argue, a precisely liminal presence. It is present as a—as a very particular, historicized—thematics of absence, and specifically of the absence of speech. The first (in some ways the only) thing we learn about John Marcher is that he has a "secret" (358) [308], a destiny, a something unknown in his future. " 'You said,' " May Bartram reminds him, " 'you had from your earliest time, as the deepest thing within you, the sense of being kept for something rare and strange, possibly prodigious and terrible, that

---

† From *Epistemology of the Closet* (Berkeley, CA: University of California Press, 1990), pp. 200–212. Copyright © 1990 The Regents of the University of California. Reprinted with permission from Eve Kosofsky Sedgwick. References to this Norton Critical Edition appear in brackets following the author's original citations, which refer to "The Beast in the Jungle," in volume 11 of *The Complete Tales of Henry James*, ed. Leon Edel (London: Rupert Hart-Davis, 1964).

was sooner or later to happen' " (359) [309]. I would argue that to the extent that Marcher's secret has *a* content, that content is homosexual.

Of course the extent to which Marcher's secret has anything that could be called a content is, not only dubious, but in the climactic last scene actively denied. "He had been the man of his time, *the* man, to whom nothing on earth was to have happened" (401) [339]. The denial that the secret has a content—the assertion that its content is precisely a lack—is a stylish and "satisfyingly" Jamesian formal gesture. The apparent gap of meaning that it points to is, however, far from being a genuinely empty one; it is no sooner asserted as a gap than filled to a plenitude with the most orthodox of ethical enforcements. To point rhetorically to the emptiness of the secret, "the nothing that is," is, in fact, oddly, *the same gesture* as the attribution to it of a compulsory content about heterosexuality—of the content specifically, "He should have desired her":

> *She* was what he had missed. . . . The fate he had been marked for he had met with a vengeance—he had emptied the cup to the lees; he had been the man of his time, *the* man, to whom nothing on earth was to have happened. That was the rare stroke—that was his visitation. . . . This the companion of his vigil had at a given moment made out, and she had then offered him the chance to baffle his doom. One's doom, however, was never baffled, and on the day she told him his own had come down she had seen him but stupidly stare at the escape she offered him.
>
> The escape would have been to love her; then, *then* he would have lived. (401) [338–39]

The supposedly "empty" meaning of Marcher's unspeakable doom is thus necessarily, specifically heterosexual; it refers to the perfectly specific absence of a prescribed heterosexual desire. If critics, eager to help James moralize this ending, persist in claiming to be able to translate freely and without residue from that (absent) heterosexual desire to an abstraction of all possibilities of human love, there are, I think, good reasons for trying to slow them down. The totalizing, insidiously symmetrical view that the "nothing" that is Marcher's unspeakable fate is necessarily a mirror image of the "everything" he could and should have had is, specifically, in an *oblique* relation to a very different history of meanings for assertions of the erotic negative.

Let us attempt, then, a different strategy for its recovery. A more frankly "full" meaning for that unspeakable fate might come from the centuries-long historical chain of substantive uses of space-clearing negatives to void and at the same time to underline the possibility of male same-sex genitality. The rhetorical name for this figure is preterition. Unspeakable, Unmentionable, *nefandam libidinem*, "that sin which should be neither named nor committed,"[1] the "detestable and abominable sin, amongst Christians not to be named,"

> Whose vice in special, if I would declare,
> It were enough for to perturb the air,

"things fearful to name," "the obscene sound of the unbeseeming words,"

> A sin so odious that the fame of it
> Will fright the damned in the darksome pit,[2]

"the love that dare not speak its name"[3]—such *were* the speakable nonmedical terms, in Christian tradition, for the homosexual possibility for men. The marginality of these terms' semantic and ontological status as substantive nouns reflected and shaped the exiguousness—but also the potentially enabling secrecy—of that "possibility." And the newly specifying, reifying medical and penal public discourse of the male homosexual role, in the years around the Wilde trials, far from retiring or obsolescing these preteritive names, seems instead to have packed them more firmly and distinctively with homosexual meaning.[4]

John Marcher's "secret," "his singularity" (366) [314], "the thing she knew, which grew to be at last, with the consecration of the years, never mentioned between them save as 'the real truth' about him" (366) [314], "the abyss" (375) [320], "his queer consciousness" (378) [323], "the great vagueness" (379) [323], "the secret of the gods" (379) [323], "what ignominy or what monstrosity" (379) [323], "dreadful things . . . I couldn't name" (381) [325]: the ways the story refers to Marcher's secret fate have the same quasi-nominative, quasi-obliterative structure.

1. Quoted in John Boswell, *Christianity, Social Tolerance, and Homosexuality: Gay People in Western Europe from the Beginning of the Christian Era to the Fourteenth Century* (Chicago: University of Chicago Press, 1980), p. 349 (from a legal document dated 533) and p. 380 (from a 1227 letter from Pope Honorius III).
2. Quoted in Alan Bray, *Homosexuality in Renaissance England* (London: Gay Men's Press, 1982)—the first two from p. 61 (from Edward Coke's *Institutes* and Sir David Lindsay's *Works*), the next two from p. 62 (from William Bradford's *Plimouth Plantation* and Guillaume Du Bartas's *Divine Weeks*), and the last from p. 22, also from Du Bartas.
3. Lord Alfred Douglas, "Two Loves," *The Chameleon* 1 (1894): 28.
4. For a striking anecdotal example of the mechanism of this, see Beverley Nichols, *Father Figure* (New York: Simon & Schuster, 1972), pp. 92–99.

There are, as well, some "fuller," though still highly equivocal, lexical pointers to a homosexual meaning: "The rest of the world of course thought him *queer*, but she, she only, knew how, and above all why, queer; which was precisely what enabled her to dispose the concealing veil in the right folds. She took his *gaiety* from him—since it had to pass with them for gaiety—as she took everything else. . . . She traced his unhappy *perversion* through reaches of its course into which he could scarce follow it" (367; emphasis added) [314–315]. Still, it is mostly in the reifying grammar of periphrasis and preterition—"such a cataclysm" (360) [310], "the great affair" (360) [310], "the catastrophe" (361) [310], "his predicament" (364) [312], "their real truth" (368) [315], "his inevitable topic" (371) [317], "all that they had thought, first and last" (372) [318], "horrors" (382) [325], something "more monstrous than all the monstrosities we've named" (383) [326], "all the loss and all the shame that are thinkable" (384) [326]—that a homosexual meaning becomes, to the degree that it does become, legible. "I don't focus it. I can't name it. I only know I'm exposed" (372) [318].

I am convinced, however, that part of the point of the story is that the reifying effect of periphrasis and preterition on this particular meaning is, if anything, *more* damaging than (though not separable from) its obliterative effect. To have succeeded—which was not to be taken for granted—in cracking the centuries-old code by which the-articulated-denial-of-articulability always had the possibility of meaning two things, of meaning either (heterosexual) "nothing" or "homosexual meaning," would also always have been to assume one's place in a discourse in which there was *a* homosexual meaning, in which all homosexual meaning meant a single thing. To crack a code and enjoy the reassuring exhilarations of knowingness is to buy into the specific formula "We Know What That Means." (I assume it is this mechanism that makes even critics who think about the male-erotic pathways of James's personal desires appear to be so untroubled about leaving them out of accounts of his writing.[5] As if this form of desire were the most calculable, the simplest to add or subtract or allow for in moving between life and art!) But if . . . men's accession to heterosexual entitlement

---

5. Exceptions that I know of include Georges-Michel Sarotte's discussion of James in *Like a Brother, Like a Lover: Male Homosexuality in the American Novel and Theater from Herman Melville to James Baldwin* trans. Richard Miller (New York: Doubleday / Anchor, 1978); Richard Hall, "Henry James: Interpreting an Obsessive Memory," *Journal of Homosexuality* 8, no. 3/4 (Spring–Summer 1983): 83–97; Robert K. Martin, "The 'High Felicity' of Comradeship: A New Reading of *Roderick Hudson*," *American Literary Realism* 11 (Spring 1978): 100–108; and Michael Moon, "Sexuality and Visual Terrorism in *The Wings of the Dove*," *Criticism* 28 (Fall 1986): 427–43.

has, for these modern centuries, always been on the ground of a cultivated and compulsory denial of the *un*knowability, of the arbitrariness and self-contradictoriness, of homo/heterosexual definition, then the fearful or triumphant interpretive formula "We Know What That Means" seems to take on an odd centrality. First, it is a lie. But, second, it is the particular lie that animates and perpetuates the mechanism of homophobic male self-ignorance and violence and manipulability.

It is worth, accordingly, trying to discriminate the possible plurality of meanings behind the unspeakables of "The Beast in the Jungle." To point, as I argue that the narrative itself points and as we have so far pointed, simply to *a* possibility of "homosexual meaning" is to say worse than nothing: it is to pretend to say one thing. But even on the surface of the story, the secret, "*the* thing," "the thing she knew," is discriminated, first of all discriminated temporally. There are at least two secrets: Marcher feels that he knows, but has never told anyone but May Bartram, (secret number one) that he is reserved for some very particular, uniquely rending fate in the future, whose nature is (secret number two) unknown to himself. Over the temporal extent of the story, both the balance, between the two characters, of cognitive mastery over the secrets' meanings, and the temporal placement, between future and past, of the second secret, shift; it is possible, in addition, that the actual content (if any) of the secrets changes with these temporal and cognitive changes, if time and intersubjectivity are of the essence of the secrets.

Let me, then, baldly spell out my hypothesis of what a series of "full"—that is, homosexually tinged—meanings for the Unspeakable might look like for this story, differing both over time and according to character.

For John Marcher, let us hypothesize, the future secret—the secret of his hidden fate—importantly includes, though it is not necessarily limited to, the possibility of something homosexual. *For Marcher*, the presence or possibility of a homosexual meaning attached to the inner, the future, secret has exactly the reifying, totalizing, and blinding effect we described earlier in regard to the phenomenon of the Unspeakable. Whatever (Marcher feels) may be to be discovered along those lines, it is, in the view of his panic, *one* thing, and the worst thing, "the superstition of the Beast" (394) [333]. His readiness to organize the whole course of his life around the preparation for it—the defense against it—remakes his life monolithically in the image of *its* monolith of, in his view, the inseparability of homosexual desire, yielding, discovery, scandal, shame, annihilation. Finally, he has "but one desire left": that *it* be "decently proportional to the posture he had kept, all his life, in the threatened presence of it" (379) [323].

This is how it happens that the outer secret, the secret of having a secret, functions, in Marcher's life, precisely as *the closet*. It is not a closet in which there is a homosexual man, for Marcher is not a homosexual man. Instead, it is the closet of, simply, the homosexual secret—the closet of imagining *a* homosexual secret. Yet it is unmistakable that Marcher lives as one who is *in the closet*. His angle on daily existence and intercourse is that of the closeted person,

> the secret of the difference between the forms he went through—those of his little office under government, those of caring for his modest patrimony, for his library, for his garden in the country, for the people in London whose invitations he accepted and repaid—and the detachment that reigned beneath them and that made of all behaviour, all that could in the least be called behaviour, a long act of dissimulation. What it had come to was that he wore a mask painted with the social simper, out of the eye-holes of which there looked eyes of an expression not in the least matching the other features. This the stupid world, even after years, had never more than half-discovered. (367–368) [315]

Whatever the content of the inner secret, too, it is one whose protection requires, for him, a playacting of heterosexuality that is conscious of being only window dressing. "You help me," he tells May Bartram, "to pass for a man like another" (375) [320]. And "what saves us, you know," she explains, "is that we answer so completely to so usual an appearance: that of the man and woman whose friendship has become such a daily habit—or almost—as to be at last indispensable" (368–369) [316]. Oddly, they not only appear to be but are such a man and woman. The element of deceiving the world, of window dressing, comes into their relationship *only* because of the compulsion he feels to invest it with the legitimating stamp of visible, institutionalized genitality: "The real form it should have taken on the basis that stood out large was the form of their marrying. But the devil in this was that the very basis itself put marrying out of the question. His conviction, his apprehension, his obsession, in short, wasn't a privilege he could invite a woman to share; and that consequence of it was precisely what was the matter with him" (365) [313].

Because of the terrified stultification of his fantasy about the inner or future secret, Marcher has, until the story's very last scene, an essentially static relation to and sense of both these secrets. Even the discovery that the outer secret is already shared with someone else, and the admission of May Bartram to the community it creates, "the dim day constituted by their discretions and privacies" (363) [312], does nothing to his closet but furnish it: camouflage it to the eyes of outsiders, and soften its inner cushioning for his own comfort. In fact the admission of May Bartram importantly *consolidates and fortifies* the closet for John Marcher.

In my hypothesis, however, May Bartram's view of Marcher's secrets is different from his and more fluid. I want to suggest that, while it is true that she feels desire for him, her involvement with him occurs originally on the ground of her understanding that he is imprisoned by homosexual panic; and her own interest in his closet is not at all in helping him fortify it but in helping him dissolve it.

In this reading, May Bartram from the first sees, correctly, that the possibility of Marcher's achieving a genuine ability to attend to a woman—sexually or in any other way—depends as an absolute precondition on the dispersion of his totalizing, basilisk fascination with and terror of homosexual possibility. It is only through his coming out of the closet—whether as *a homosexual man* or as a man with a less exclusively defined sexuality that nevertheless admits the possibility of desires for other men—that Marcher could even begin to perceive the attention of a woman as anything other than a terrifying demand or a devaluing complicity. The truth of this is already evident at the beginning of the story, in the surmises with which Marcher first meets May Bartram's allusion to something (he cannot remember what) he said to her years before: "The great thing was that he saw in this no vulgar reminder of any 'sweet' speech. The vanity of women had long memories, but she was making no claim on him of a compliment or a mistake. With another woman, a totally different one, he might have feared the recall possibly even of some imbecile 'offer' " (356) [307]. The alternative to this, however, in his eyes, is a different kind of "sweetness," that of a willingly shared confinement: "her knowledge . . . began, even if rather strangely, to taste sweet to him" (358) [308]. "Somehow the whole question was a new luxury to him—that is from the moment she was in possession. If she didn't take the sarcastic view she clearly took the sympathetic, and that was what he had had, in all the long time, from no one whomsoever. What he felt was that he couldn't at present have begun to tell her, and yet could profit perhaps exquisitely by the accident of having done so of old" (358) [308]. So begins the imprisonment of May Bartram in John Marcher's closet—an imprisonment that, the story makes explicit, is founded on his inability to perceive or value her as a person beyond her complicity in his view of his own predicament.

The conventional view of the story, emphasizing May Bartram's

interest in liberating, unmediatedly, Marcher's heterosexual possibilities, would see her as unsuccessful in doing so until too late
—until the true revelation that comes only after her death. If what
needs to be liberated is in the first place Marcher's potential for
homosexual desire, however, the trajectory of the story must be seen
as far bleaker. I hypothesize that what May Bartram would have
liked for Marcher, the narrative she wished to nurture for him,
would have been a progress from a vexed and gaping self-ignorance
around his homosexual possibilities to a self-knowledge of them that
would have freed him to find and enjoy a sexuality of whatever sort
emerged. What she sees happen to Marcher, instead, is the "progress" that the culture more insistently enforces: the progress from
a vexed and gaping self-ignorance around his homosexual possibilities to a completed and rationalized and wholly concealed and accepted one. The moment of Marcher's full incorporation of his
erotic self-ignorance is the moment at which the imperatives of the
culture cease to enforce him, and he becomes instead the enforcer
of the culture.

Section 4 of the story marks the moment at which May Bartram
realizes that, far from helping dissolve Marcher's closet, she has
instead and irremediably been permitting him to reinforce it. It is
in this section and the next, too, that it becomes explicit in the
story that Marcher's fate, what was to have happened to him and
did happen, involves a change in him from being the suffering object of a Law or judgment (of a doom in the original sense of the
word) to being the embodiment of that Law.

If the transition I am describing is, in certain respects, familiarly
oedipal, the structuring metaphor behind its description here seems
to be peculiarly alimentative. The question that haunts Marcher in
these sections is whether what he has thought of as the secret of
his future may not be, after all, in the past; and the question of
passing, of who is passing through what or what is passing through
whom, of what residue remains to *be* passed, is the form in which
he compulsively poses his riddle. Is the beast eating him, or is he
eating the beast? "It hasn't passed you by," May Bartram tells him.
"It has done its office. It has made you its own" (389) [330]. "It's
past. It's behind," she finally tells him, to which he replies, "*Nothing*, for me, is past; nothing *will* pass till I pass myself, which I pray
my stars may be as soon as possible. Say, however, . . . that I've
eaten my cake, as you contend, to the last crumb—how can the
thing I've never felt at all be the thing I was marked out to feel?"
(391) [332]. What May Bartram sees and Marcher does not is that
the process of incorporating—of embodying—the Law of masculine
self-ignorance is the one that has the least in the world to do with

feeling.[6] To gape at and, rebelliously, be forced to swallow the Law is to feel; but to have it finally stick to one's ribs, become however incongruously a part of one's own organism, is then to perfect at the same moment a new hard-won insentience of it and an assumption of (or subsumption by) an identification with it. May Bartram answers Marcher's question, "You take your 'feelings' for granted. You were to suffer your fate. That was not necessarily to know it" (391) [332]. Marcher's fate is to cease to suffer fate and instead to become it. May Bartram's fate, with the "slow fine shudder" that climaxes her ultimate appeal to Marcher, is herself to swallow this huge, bitter bolus with which *she* can have *no* deep identification, and to die of it—of what is, to her, knowledge, not power. "So on her lips would the law itself have sounded" (389) [330]. Or, tasted.

To end a reading of May Bartram with her death, to end with her silenced forever in that ultimate closet, "her" tomb that represents (to Marcher) *his fate*, * * * leaves us in danger of figuring May Bartram, or more generally the woman in heterosexuality, as only the exact, heroic supplement to the murderous enforcements of male homophobic/homosocial self-ignorance. "The Fox," Emily Dickinson wrote, "fits the Hound."[7] It would be only too easy to describe May Bartram as the fox that most irreducibly fits this particular hound. She seems the woman (don't we all know them?) who has not only the most delicate nose for but the most potent attraction toward men who are at crises of homosexual panic . . . —Though, for that matter, won't most women admit that an arousing nimbus, an excessively refluent and dangerous maelstrom of

6. A fascinating passage in James's *Notebooks* (New York: Oxford University Press, 1947), p. 318, written in 1905 in California, shows how in James a greater self-knowledge and a greater acceptance and *specificity* of homosexual desire transform this half-conscious enforcing rhetoric of anality, numbness, and silence into a much richer, pregnant address to James's male muse, an invocation of fisting-as-*écriture*:

> I sit here, after long weeks, at any rate, in front of my arrears, with an inward accumulation of material of which I feel the wealth, and as to which I can only invoke my familiar demon of patience, who always comes, doesn't he?, when I call. He is here with me in front of this cool green Pacific—he sits close and I feel his soft breath, which cools and steadies and inspires, on my cheek. Everything sinks in: nothing is lost; everything abides and fertilizes and renews its golden promise, making me think with closed eyes of deep and grateful longing when, in the full summer days of L[amb] H[ouse], my long dusty adventure over, I shall be able to [plunge] my hand, my arm, *in*, deep and far, and up to the shoulder—into the heavy bag of remembrance—of suggestion—of imagination—of art—and fish out every little figure and felicity, every little fact and fancy that can be to my purpose. These things are all packed away, now, thicker than I can penetrate, deeper than I can fathom, and there let them rest for the present, in their sacred cool darkness, till I shall let in upon them the mild still light of dear old L[amb] H[ouse]—in which they will begin to gleam and glitter and take form like the gold and jewels of a mine.

7. *Collected Poems of Emily Dickinson*, ed. Thomas H. Johnson (Boston: Little, Brown, 1960), p. 406.

eroticism, somehow attends men in general at such moments, even otherwise boring men?

If one is to avoid * * * describing May Bartram in terms that reduce her perfectly to the residueless sacrifice John Marcher makes to his Beast, it might be by inquiring into the difference of the paths of her own desire. What does she want, not for him, but for herself, from their relationship? What does she actually get? To speak less equivocally from my own eros and experience, there is a particular relation to truth and authority that a mapping of male homosexual panic offers to a woman in the emotional vicinity. The fact that male heterosexual entitlement in (at least modern Anglo-American) culture depends on a perfected but always friable self-ignorance in men as to the significance of their desire for other men means that it is always open to women to know something that it is much more dangerous for any nonhomosexual-identified man to know. The ground of May Bartram and John Marcher's relationship is from the first that she has the advantage of him, cognitively: she remembers, as he does not, where and when and with whom they have met before, and most of all she remembers his "secret" from a decade ago while he forgets having told it to her. This differential of knowledge affords her a "slight irony," an "advantage" (353) [305]—but one that he can at the same time use to his own profit as "the buried treasure of her knowledge," "this little hoard" (363) [312]. As their relationship continues, the sense of power and of a marked, rather free-floating irony about May Bartram becomes stronger and stronger, even in proportion to Marcher's accelerating progress toward self-ignorance and toward a blindly selfish expropriation of her emotional labor. Both the care and the creativity of her investment in him, the imaginative reach of her fostering his homosexual potential as a route back to his truer perception of herself, are forms of gender-political resilience in her as well as of love. They are forms of excitement, too, of real though insufficient power, and of pleasure.

In the last scene of "The Beast in the Jungle" John Marcher becomes, in this reading, not the finally self-knowing man who is capable of heterosexual love, but the irredeemably self-ignorant man who embodies and enforces heterosexual compulsion. In this reading, that is to say, May Bartram's prophecy to Marcher that "You'll never know now" (390) [331] is a true one.

Importantly for the homosexual plot, too, the final scene is also the only one in the entire story that reveals or tests the affective quality of Marcher's perception of another man. "The shock of the face" (399) [337]: this is, in the last scene, the beginning of what Marcher ultimately considers "the most extraordinary thing that had happened to him" (400) [338]. At the beginning of Marcher's con-

frontation with this male figure at the cemetery, the erotic possibilities of the connection between the men appear to be all open.
The man, whose "mute assault" Marcher feels "so deep down that
he winced at the steady thrust," is mourning profoundly over "a
grave apparently fresh," but (perhaps only to Marcher's closet-
sharpened suspicions?) a slightest potential of Whitmanian cruisi-
ness seems at first to tinge the air, as well:

> His pace was slow, so that—and all the more as there was a
> kind of hunger in his look—the two men were for a minute
> directly confronted. Marcher knew him at once for one of the
> deeply stricken . . . nothing lived but the deep ravage of the
> features he showed. He *showed* them—that was the point; he
> was moved, as he passed, by some impulse that was either a
> signal for sympathy or, more possibly, a challenge to an op-
> posed sorrow. He might already have been aware of our friend.
> . . . What Marcher was at all events conscious of was in the
> first place that the image of scarred passion presented to him
> was conscious too—of something that profaned the air; and in
> the second that, roused, startled, shocked, he was yet the next
> moment looking after it, as it went, with envy. (400–401)
> [337–38]

The path traveled by Marcher's desire in this brief and cryptic
nonencounter reenacts a classic trajectory of male entitlement.
Marcher begins with the possibility of *desire for* the man, in response to the man's open "hunger" ("which," afterward, "still flared
for him like a smoky torch" (401) [338]). Deflecting that desire
under a fear of profanation, he then replaces it with envy, with an
identification with the man in that man's (baffled) desire for some
other, presumably female, dead object. "The stranger passed, but
the raw glare of his grief remained, making our friend wonder in
pity what wrong, what injury not to be
healed. What had the man *had*, to make him by the loss of it so
bleed and yet live?" (401) [338].

What had the man *had*? The loss by which a man *so bleeds and
yet lives* is, is it not, supposed to be the castratory one of the phallus
figured as mother, the inevitability of whose sacrifice ushers sons
into the status of fathers and into the control (read both ways) of
the Law. What is strikingly open in the ending of "The Beast in the
Jungle" is how central to that process is man's desire for man—and
the denial of that desire. The imperative that there *be* a male figure
to take this place is the clearer in that, at an earlier climactic moment, in a female "shock of the face," May Bartram has presented
to Marcher her own face, in a conscious revelation that was far
more clearly of desire:

It had become suddenly, from her movement and attitude, beautiful and vivid to him that she had something more to give him; her wasted face delicately shone with it—it glittered almost as with the white lustre of silver in her expression. She was right, incontestably, for what he saw in her face was the truth, and strangely, without consequence, while their talk of it as dreadful was still in the air, she appeared to present it as inordinately soft. This, prompting bewilderment, made him but gape the more gratefully for her revelation, so that they continued for some minutes silent, her face shining at him, her contact imponderably pressing, and his stare all kind but all expectant. The end, none the less, was that what he had expected failed to come to him. (386) [328]

To the shock of the female face Marcher is not phobic but simply numb. It is only by turning his desire for the male face into an envious identification with male loss that Marcher finally comes into *any* relation to a woman—and then it is a relation through one dead woman (the other man's) to another dead woman of his own. That is to say, it is the relation of *compulsory* heterosexuality.

When Lytton Strachey's claim to be a conscientious objector was being examined, he was asked what he would do if a German were to try to rape his sister. "I should," he is said to have replied, "try and interpose my own body."[8] Not the joky gay self-knowledge but the heterosexual, self-ignorant acting out of just this fantasy ends "The Beast in the Jungle." To face the gaze of the Beast would have been, for Marcher, to dissolve it.[9] To face the "kind of hunger in the look" of the grieving man—to explore at all into the sharper lambencies of that encounter—would have been to dissolve the closet, to recreate its hypostatized compulsions as desires. Marcher, instead, to the very end, turns his back—recreating a double scenario of homosexual compulsion and heterosexual compulsion. "He saw the Jungle of his life and saw the lurking Beast; then, while he looked, perceived it, as by a stir of the air, rise, huge and hideous, for the leap that was to settle him. His eyes darkened—it was close; and, instinctively turning, in his hallucination, to avoid it, he flung himself, face down, on the tomb" (402) [339].

8. Lytton Strachey, quoted in Michael Holroyd, *Lytton Strachey: A Critical Biography* (London: W. H. Heinemann, 1968), 2: 179.
9. Ruth Bernard Yeazell makes clear the oddity of having Marcher turn his back on the Beast that is supposed, at this late moment, to represent his self-recognition (in *Language and Knowledge in the Late Novels of Henry James* [Chicago: University of Chicago Press, 1976], pp. 37–38).

KENNETH W. WARREN

["The Jolly Corner"]†

James's lengthy short story, which appeared first in the *English Review* and was quickly revised for the New York Edition of James's work, relates the experiences of fifty-six-year-old Spencer Brydon, whose return to New York after a lengthy absence mirrors James's own. His return, like his creator's, confronts him with a homeland he no longer knows, and which challenges him to give forth his impressions. But rather than have his protagonist focus on giving an account of the confusing changes in his homeland, James has Brydon admit that his "thoughts would still be almost altogether about something that concerns only myself." Recognizing, perhaps, that the subject of *The American Scene* was not so much America but himself, James, through Brydon, allows that subject to center his tale so that the focus becomes "what he might have been, how he might have led his life, and 'turned out,' if he had not so, at the outset, given [New York] up." Fueling these speculations for Brydon is his discovery, while supervising the conversion of one of his houses into apartment units, that despite having opted for an aesthetic life three decades ago, he has "a capacity for business and a sense for construction" (435, 448, 438) [341, 348, 343]. This belated discovery becomes so powerful as a possible missed opportunity that Brydon's desire to envision himself as he might have been takes palpable shape. The story finds Brydon, in the house of his birth, the house on the "jolly corner," stalking this alter ego, a figure his friend Alice Staverton claims has appeared in a dream.

James's story exhibits the various oppositions discussed earlier— for example, the "dollars" of New York are counterpointed by an incalculable aesthetic experience, represented by Miss Staverton. Though residing in New York throughout Brydon's absence, Alice nonetheless embodies for Brydon "*their* common, their quite faraway and antediluvian social period and order" (439) [343–44]. The quiet of private life she is able to preserve is played off New York's "public concussions"; and Brydon, who has been away "worshipping strange gods" (450) [350] now speculates about what he would have become had he offered a sacrifice at some domestic shrine. Brydon's

† From *Black and White Strangers: Race and American Literary Realism* (Chicago: The University of Chicago Press, 1993), pp. 124–30. Copyright © 1993 The University of Chicago Press. Reprinted with permission from Kenneth W. Warren. References to this Norton Critical Edition appear in brackets following the author's original citations, which refer to "The Jolly Corner" in the New York Edition of *The Novels and Tales of Henry James*, vol. 17 (New York: Charles Scribner & Sons, 1907–10).

private speculations share, in many respects, the depth and dimension of the copious travel narrative James had already composed. This being said, however, what is also intrinsic to "The Jolly Corner" is its patent absurdity and ridiculousness. Investing his search for his alter ego with all the emotional edge of a big-game hunt, Brydon must nonetheless admit that "he might, for a spectator, have figured some solemn simpleton playing at hide-and-seek" (459) [355]. His "jungle," the servants' rooms; his prey, the fearful imaginings of his Irish housekeeper—Brydon's drama could be played out on some comic stage. In fact, when after "a calculated absence of three nights" from his stalkings he feels himself being followed, he adopts a strategy of turning around abruptly to see if his alter ego might betray itself:

> He wheeled about, retracing his steps, as if he might so catch in his face at least the stirred air of some other quick revolution. It was indeed true that his fully dislocalised thought of these manoeuveres recalled to him Pantaloon, at the Christmas farce, buffeted and tricked from behind by ubiquitous Harlequin; but it left intact the influence of the conditions themselves each time he was re-exposed to them, so that in fact this association, had he suffered it to become constant, would on a certain side have but ministered to his intenser gravity. (460) [355]

Similar to the American stage of the period where high drama and farce cohabited in a way that did not appear incongruous, Brydon's reflections on his antics do not entirely banish the farcical interpretation. On the contrary, inasmuch as his more serious interpretation of his action persists despite the absurd overtones, Brydon remains convinced of the gravity of his quest.

As a youthful devotee of American theater, James had ample experience counterbalancing seriousness and farce as part of his aesthetic. "Young Henry was taken to all the leading New York theatres of the mid-century—Burton's, the Broadway, and the National, Wallack's Lyceum, Niblo's Gardens and Barnum's 'Lecture Room' attached to the Great American Museum."[1] Harlequinades were a staple of the stage—farces and burlesques, which often featured blackface characters. At one point "Negro specialties were featured on almost every playbill"[2] as afterpieces, and Christmas traditions included visits to minstrel shows like "Harlequin Jim Crow" and

---

1. Leon Edel, "Henry James: The Dramatic Years," in *The Complete Plays of Henry James* (Philadelphia: Lippincott, 1949), p. 23.
2. Carl Wittke, *Tambo and Bones: A History of the American Minstrel Stage* (Westport, Conn.: Greenwood Press, 1968), p. 37. On the ubiquity of minstrel performances on the American stage, see also George C. D. Odell, vol. 4 of *Annals of the New York Stage* (New York: Columbia University Press, 1931).

"The Magic Mustard Pot."[3] In *A Small Boy and Others* James specifically recalls attending in London "a Christmas production pre-
luding to the immemorial harlequinade," an experience that had
been presaged by his many visits to Niblo's Gardens in New York,
where, like other New York theaters, minstrel afterpieces were regularly staged, and where, James recalled, "we had . . . harlequin
and columbine, albeit of less pure a tradition."[4] In addition, James's
Autobiography indicates that the figure of the harlequin provided
him an apt metaphor for presenting the elder Henry James's attitudes towards his sons' search for a vocation. James's father's willingness to tolerate meanderings and changes of mind struck his son
as a "happy harlequinade."[5]

In alluding to harlequins (whose traditional costume includes
black and white mask and clothing) in "The Jolly Corner," which is
staged appropriately on the "black-and-white squares" of the floor
of Brydon's ancestral home, James casts the aesthetic/commercial
dichotomy on which the story turns in a slightly different light than
is commonly assumed. Brydon's facility at handling his business
concerns and the renovation of his other house lead Alice Staverton
to conjecture that "if he had but stayed at home he would have
anticipated the inventor of the sky scraper. If he had but stayed at
home he would have discovered his genius in time really to start
some new variety of awful architectural hare and run it till it burrowed in a gold-mine" (440–41) [344]. Brydon's alter ego's lack of
taste and his pursuit of money would have been figured in his designing of architectural grotesques. But the surprise and shock that
attend Brydon's confrontation with the figure he confronts downstairs indicate that what he finds is not what he expects. The face
he sees "was unknown, inconceivable, awful, disconnected from any
possibility" (474) [365]. What he finds is "a black stranger" with
white hands on which two fingers are missing.

Brydon is convinced of and appalled by the lack of identity between himself and the black stranger—"Such an identity fitted his
at *no* point" (477) [365]—and the shock leads to what he asserts
is his death: "Yes—I can only have died." As to the lack of identity
between Spencer and the phantom he confronts, however, Alice
Staverton, asserts the opposite. Not only is the stranger in some

3. See Harry Reynolds, *Minstrel Memories: The Story of Burnt Cork Minstrelsy in Great
   Britain from 1836 to 1937* (London: Alston Rivers, Ltd., 1928), pp. 77–78. On the
   Christmas tradition of minstrelsy, see the excerpt from the diary entry of Charles DeLong
   in Alexander Saxton, *The Rise and Fall of the White Republic: Class Politics and Mass
   Culture in Nineteenth-Century America* (New York: Verso, 1990), p. 172. Also particu-
   larly helpful here is Gates's discussion of black harlequin in *Figures in Black* (New York:
   Oxford University Press, 1987), pp. 51–53.
4. James, *A Small Boy and Others*, in *Autobiography*, ed. Frederick W. Dupee (New York:
   Criterion Books, 1956), pp. 181, 98.
5. Ibid., p. 302.

way Spencer, but according to Alice, Spencer himself had, on the morning of the latter's adventure, appeared to her as "a black stranger" (484) [368]—a figure perhaps in blackface. But instead of precipitating a death, whether figurative or literal, this figure performs the office of a cupid, bringing together Alice and Spencer so that the story ends with a mutual declaration of love.

Spencer's alter ego does correspond to Brydon's expectations in terms of wealth (Brydon surmises that his alter ego has a "million a year"), cementing again the connection between black figures on the one hand and public vulgarity and commercial interests on the other. Perhaps undergirding this story is not so much a contrast between aesthetics and business but the unsettling territory in which the two meet. Not only is Brydon's European freedom, as Alice astutely notes, made possible by the income derived from his American rents, but James in invoking images from the popular theater also seems to point up another disturbing possibility. The aesthetic alternative for a figure like Brydon or James would not have been to construct monstrous but impressive skyscrapers but to become a participant in the production of " 'intellectual' pabulum" to fulfill the democratic demand—a demand so great that "the journalist, the novelist, the dramatist, the genealogist, the historian, are pressed as well, for dear life, into the service."[6] Among the available options was participation on the minstrel stage. As Alexander Saxton points out, "typical purveyors of minstrelsy, then, were northern and urban; they were neither New Englanders nor Southerners (although their parents may have been); and if of rural or small town origin, were most likely to have come from upper New York State." Like James they were "eager to break into the exclusive and inhospitable precincts of big city theater."[7]

James clearly associated writing for the theater with the "thought of fabulous fortunes," worldly success, and aesthetic disfigurement—his plays were, in his words, "mutilated" and "massacred," not unlike the maimed figure Brydon meets in "The Jolly Corner." Writing for the theater was a form of devil worship, "a most unholy trade." And though James's major theatrical debacle, the production of *Guy Domville*, took place on the British stage, his desire for success as a dramatist was quite possibly a species of "the strong American impulse that he no doubt possessed . . . to elbow one's way to achievement by solid worldly enterprise!"[8] In a possible pun on *Guy Domville*, Spencer describes his unfitness to play his alter ego's role by saying that he couldn't have worn his monocle in the

6. Henry James, *Autobiography*, p. 458.
7. Saxton, *The Rise and Fall of the White Republic*, p. 168.
8. Edel, "The Dramatic Years," pp. 51, 52.

stranger's environment: "I couldn't have sported mine 'downtown.' They'd have guyed me there" (485) [369]. Moreover, inasmuch as minstrelsy continued to appear on the British stage through the turn of the century, the market in which James would have imagined himself a competitor would have featured blackface performers as well.

The remedy for James's problem was not a purge of the theater so to speak, but a habit of critical distinction. As we saw earlier, James's recollections of his childhood visits to the theater stressed his growth as a young critic, as someone who could make the proper distinctions. In "The Jolly Corner," where the possibility of seeing Spencer Brydon as a ridiculous figure, where the possibility of "guying" him is openly acknowledged, Alice Staverton, whose "imagination would still do him justice," provides the necessary discerning audience. * * * She can appreciate both the black stranger and Brydon's difference from him; she can accept and appreciate both.

The point here, however, is not so much that "The Jolly Corner" is directly about James's thwarted theatrical desires. Rather I want to stress that over the course of the 1880s, 1890s, and through the turn of the century, popular representations of black/white racial difference exert a constant pressure on the work of an author like James such that in thinking through the possibility of aesthetic redemption it seemed almost necessary to distance oneself from black strangers. By masking Brydon's other self in black, "The Jolly Corner," like black minstrelsy, simultaneously acknowledged the power of, while establishing the means of control over, the Other.

The pity and acceptance that Alice Staverton feels towards the black stranger dissipate in her relief that Brydon and not the stranger is the figure whose head rests on her lap. After having asserted an identity between Spencer and the black stranger, she recants and assures Brydon in the story's final sentence that "he isn't—no, he isn't—*you*!" (485) [369]—thus distancing Brydon and herself from the vulgarities of a New York in which the house on the jolly corner will seemingly function as an ironic oasis.

Alice Staverton's assurance to Brydon that he is not a part of the ravaged life that surrounds them is an assurance that many realists, confronted with the unsettling social changes brought about by immigration, economic upheaval, conservative backlash against progressive reform, as well as their own attacks on convention and tradition, could not themselves feel. Americans at the close of the nineteenth century found themselves in what Lawrence Levine calls "a universe of strangers," strangers who "spilled over into the public spaces that characterized nineteenth-century America and that included theaters, music halls, opera houses, museums, parks, fairs, and the rich public cultural life that took place daily on the streets of American cities." For elites like James, culture, in the sense of high culture, became a place of refuge, a place of "retreat."[9] Despite the fact that African-American access to these places, and to "culture" itself was often limited by statutory, economic, and even aesthetic factors, the black presence was never entirely absent. As attested to by the minstrel echoes in "The Jolly Corner," in the American context, "culture" could never be a comfortable refuge. Writers like Henry James were always confronting and seeking to contain their own participation in and complicity with the aspects of their society they deplored. It is within these efforts to define and distinguish among the values of American cultural life that it becomes possible to trace the racial dimensions of the American literary imagination.

---

9. Lawrence W. Levine, *Highbrow/Lowbrow: The Emergence of Cultural Hierarchy in America* (Cambridge, Mass.: Harvard University Press, 1988), p. 177.

Selected Bibliography

• indicates items included or excerpted in this Norton Critical Edition.

CHECKLISTS

Beebe, Maurice, and William T. Stafford. "Criticism of Henry James: A Selected Checklist." *Modern Fiction Studies* 12 (Spring 1966): 117–77.

Bradbury, Nicola. *An Annotated Bibliography of Henry James.* New York: St. Martin's Press, 1987.

Budd, John. *Henry James: A Bibliography of Criticism, 1975–1981.* Westport, Conn.: Greenwood Press, 1983.

Fogel, Daniel Mark, ed. *A Companion to Henry James Studies.* Westport, Conn.: Greenwood Press, 1993.

Funston, Judith E. *Henry James: A Reference Guide, 1975–1987.* Boston: G. K. Hall, 1991.

Ricks, Beatrice. *Henry James: A Bibliography of Secondary Works.* Metuchen, N.J.: Scarecrow Press, 1975.

Stafford, William T. *A Name, Title, and Place Index to the Critical Writings of Henry James.* Englewood, Colo.: Microcard Editions, 1975.

BOOKS

Anesko, Michael. *"Friction with the Market": Henry James and the Profession of Authorship.* New York: Oxford UP, 1986.

Bayley, John. *The Short Story: Henry James to Elizabeth Bowen.* New York: St. Martin's Press, 1988.

Beach, Joseph Warren. *The Method of Henry James.* Rev. ed. Philadelphia: A. Saifer, 1954.

• Bell, Millicent. *Meaning in Henry James.* Cambridge: Harvard UP, 1991.

Blair, Sara. *Henry James and the Writing of Race and Nation.* Cambridge, Eng.: Cambridge UP, 1996.

Brooks, Van Wyck. *The Pilgrimage of Henry James.* New York: Dutton, 1925.

Budd, Lou, and Edwin H. Cady, eds. *On Henry James.* Durham, N.C.: Duke UP, 1990.

Buelens, Gert, ed. *Enacting History in Henry James: Narrative, Power, and Ethics.* New York: Cambridge UP, 1997.

Cameron, Sharon. *Thinking in Henry James.* Chicago: U of Chicago P, 1989.

Chatman, Seymour. *The Later Style of Henry James.* New York: Oxford UP, 1972.

Dewey, Joseph, and Brooke Horvath, eds. *"The Finer Thread, the Tighter Weave": Essays on the Short Fiction of Henry James.* West Lafayette, Ind.: Purdue UP, 2001.

Edel, Leon. *Henry James.* 5 vols. Philadelphia: Lippincott, 1953–72.

Freedman, Jonathan L. *Professions of Taste: Henry James, British Aestheticism and Commodity Culture.* Palo Alto, Calif.: Stanford UP, 1990.

———, ed. *The Cambridge Companion to Henry James.* New York: Cambridge UP, 1998.

Gale, Robert L. *The Caught Imagination: Figurative Language in the Fiction of Henry James.* Chapel Hill: U of North Carolina P, 1964.

Habegger, Alfred. *Henry James and the "Woman Business."* New York: Cambridge UP, 1989.

Hocks, Richard A. *Henry James and Pragmatist Thought: A Study of the Relationship between the Philosophy of William James and the Literary Art of Henry James.* Chapel Hill: U of North Carolina P, 1974.

• ———. *Henry James, A Study of the Short Fiction*. Boston: Twayne, 1990.

Holland, Laurence B. *The Expense of Vision: Essays on the Craft of Henry James*. Princeton: Princeton UP, 1964.

Horne, Philip. *Henry James and Revision: The New York Edition*. New York: Oxford UP, 1990.

Jolly, Roslyn. *Henry James: History, Narrative, Fiction*. New York: Oxford UP, 1993.

Kaplan, Fred. *Henry James: The Imagination of Genius, A Biography*. New York: Morrow, 1992.

Krook, Dorothea. *The Ordeal of Consciousness in Henry James*. New York: Cambridge UP, 1962.

Matthiessen, F. O. *Henry James: The Major Phase*. New York: Oxford UP, 1944.

———. *The James Family*. New York: Knopf, 1947.

Pearson, John H. *The Prefaces of Henry James: Framing the Modern Reader*. University Park: Pennsylvania State UP, 1997.

Pippin, Robert B. *Henry James and Modern Moral Life*. New York: Cambridge UP, 2000.

Poirier, Richard. *The Comic Sense of Henry James*. New York: Oxford UP, 1960.

Posnock, Ross. *The Trial of Curiosity: Henry James, William James, and the Challenge of Modernity*. New York: Oxford UP, 1991.

Przbylowicz, Donna. *Desire and Repression: The Dialectic of Self and Other in the Late Works of Henry James*. Tuscaloosa: U of Alabama P, 1986.

• Rowe, John Carlos. *The Other Henry James*. Durham, N.C.: Duke UP, 1998.

———. *The Theoretical Dimension of Henry James*. Madison: U of Wisconsin P, 1984.

Salmon, Richard. *Henry James and the Culture of Publicity*. New York: Cambridge UP, 1997.

• Sedgwick, Eve Kosofsky. *Epistemology of the Closet*. Berkeley: U of California P, 1990.

Seltzer, Mark. *Henry James and the Art of Power*. Ithaca, N.Y.: Cornell UP, 1984.

Stevens, Hugh. *Henry James and Sexuality*. New York: Cambridge UP, 1998.

Tanner, Tony. *Henry James: The Writer and His Work*. Amherst: U of Massachusetts P, 1985.

Tintner, Adeline R. *The Cosmopolitan World of Henry James: An Intertextual Study*. Baton Rouge: Louisiana State UP, 1991.

———. *The Twentieth-Century World of Henry James: Changes in His Work after 1900*. Baton Rouge: Louisiana State UP, 2000.

Walker, Pierre A., ed. *Henry James on Culture: Collected Essays on Politics and the American Social Scene*. Lincoln: U of Nebraska P, 1999.

• Warren, Kenneth W. *Black and White Strangers: Race and American Literary Realism*. Chicago: U of Chicago P, 1993.

Wegelin, Christof. *The Image of Europe in Henry James*. Dallas: Southern Methodist UP, 1958.

Winner, Viola Hopkins. *Henry James and the Visual Arts*. Charlottesville: U of Virginia P, 1970.

Yeazell, Ruth Bernard. *Language and Knowledge in the Late Novels of Henry James*. Chicago: U of Chicago P, 1976.

ARTICLES

A short list of articles on the tales of Henry James must be so selective as to seem almost arbitrary. Readers are encouraged to explore the checklists mentioned above as well as back issues of the electronically available *Henry James Review* for a wealth of scholarship and bibliographic information not included here.

Bazargan, Susan. "Representation and Ideology in 'The Real Thing.' " *The Henry James Review* 12 (Spring 1991): 133–37.

Bell, Barbara Currier. "Beyond Irony in Henry James: 'The Aspern Papers.' " *Studies in the Novel* 13 (Fall 1981): 282–93.

Bell, Millicent. " 'The Aspern Papers': The Unvisitable Past." *The Henry James Review* 10 (Spring 1989): 120–27.

Blackmur, R. P. "Introduction" to *The Art of the Novel: Critical Prefaces by Henry James*. New York: Charles Scribner's Sons, 1934.

Brown, Ellen. "Revising Henry James: Reading the Spaces of 'The Aspern Papers.' "
  American Literature 63 (June 1991): 263–78.
Buelens, Gert. "In Possession of a Secret: Rhythms of Mastery and Surrender in 'The
  Beast in the Jungle.' " *The Henry James Review* 19 (Winter 1998): 17–35.
Carton, Evan. "The Anxiety of Effluence: Criticism, Currency, and 'The Aspern
  Papers.' " *The Henry James Review* 10 (Spring 1989): 116–20.
Clasby, Nancy. "Realism and the Archetypes: 'Daisy Miller.' " *Spring: A Journal of
  Archetype and Culture* 60 (Fall 1996): 31–44.
Deakin, Motley. "Two Studies of 'Daisy Miller.' " *The Henry James Review* 5 (Fall
  1983): 2–28.
Edel, Leon, "The Architecture of Henry James's 'The New York Edition.' " *New En-
  gland Quarterly* 24 (June 1951): 169–78.
Gabler-Hover, Janet. "The Ethics of Determinism in Henry James's 'In the Cage.' "
  The Henry James Review 13 (Fall 1992): 253–75.
Gargano, James W. " 'The Aspern Papers': The Untold Story." *Studies in Short Fiction*
  10 (1973): 1–10.
Hagberg, Garry L. "Dencombe's Final Moments: A Microcosm of Jamesian Philoso-
  phy." *The Henry James Review* 18 (Fall 1997): 223–33.
• Horne, Philip. "Henry James, The Master, and the 'Queer Affair' in 'The Pupil.' " In
  N. H. Reeve, ed., *Henry James: The Shorter Fiction, Reassessments*. New York: Mac-
  millan, 1997. 118–33.
Hoy, Helen. "Homotextual Duplicity in Henry James's 'The Pupil.' " *The Henry James
  Review* 14 (Winter 1993): 34–42.
Lackey, Kris. "Art and Class in 'The Real Thing.' " *Studies in Short Fiction* 26 (Spring
  1989): 190–92.
Lukacs, Paul. "Unambiguous Ambiguity: The International Theme of "Daisy Miller.' "
  Studies in American Fiction 16 (Fall 1988): 209–16.
Martin, Terence. "James's 'The Pupil': The Art of Seeing Through." *Modern Fiction
  Studies* 4 (Winter 1958–59): 335–45.
Mellard, James M. "Modal Counterpoint in James's 'The Aspern Papers.' " *Papers on
  Language and Literature* 4 (1968): 299–307.
Menke, Richard. "Telegraphic Realism: Henry James's 'In the Cage.' " *Publication of
  the Modern Language Association* 115 (October 2000): 975–90.
Monteiro, George. "The Atlantic Monthly's Rejection of 'The Pupil': An Exchange of
  Letters between Henry James and Horace Scudder." *American Literary Realism* 23
  (Fall 1990): 75–83.
• Moon, Michael. "A Small Boy and Others: Sexual Disorientation in Henry James,
  Kenneth Anger, and David Lynch." In Hortense J. Spillers, ed., *Comparative Amer-
  ican Identities: Race, Sex, and Nationality in the Modern Text*. New York: Routledge,
  1991. 148–52.
Moshe, Ron. "A Reading of 'The Real Thing.' " *Yale French Studies* 58 (1979): 190–
  212.
Nixon, Nicola. "The Reading Gaol of Henry James's 'In the Cage.' " *English Literary
  History* 66 (Spring 1999): 179–201.
• Oates, Joyce Carol. "The Madness of Art: Henry James's 'The Middle Years.' " *New
  Literary History* 27 (Spring 1996): 259–62.
Person, Leland S. Jr. "Eroticism and Creativity in 'The Aspern Papers.' " *Literature
  and Psychology* 32 (Spring 1986): 20–31.
———. "James's Homo-Aesthetics: Deploying Desire in the Tales of Writers and
  Artists." *The Henry James Review* 14 (Spring 1993): 188–203.
Reesman, Jeanne Campbell. " 'The Deepest Depths of the Artificial': Attacking
  Women and Reality in 'The Aspern Papers.' " *The Henry James Review* 19 (Spring
  1998): 148–65.
• Rivkin, Julie. "Doctoring the Text: Henry James and Revision." In David McWhirter,
  ed., *Henry James's New York Edition: The Construction of Authorship*. Stanford UP,
  1995. 152–62.
———. "Speaking with the Dead: Ethics and Representation in 'The Aspern Papers.' "
  The Henry James Review 10 (Spring 1989): 135–41.
Savoy, Eric. " 'In the Cage' and the Queer Effects of Gay History." *Novel: A Forum
  on Fiction* 28 (Spring 1995): 284–307.
Scharnhorst, Gary. "James, 'The Aspern Papers,' and the Ethics of Literary Biogra-
  phy." *Modern Fiction Studies* 36 (Summer 1990): 211–17.
Scheiber, Andrew J. "Embedded Narratives of Science and Culture in James's 'Daisy
  Miller.' " *College Literature* 21 (June 1994): 75–88.
Tambling, Jeremy. "Henry James's American Byron." *The Henry James Review* 20
  (Winter 1999): 43–50.

Thurschwell, Pamela. "Henry James and Theodora Bosanquet: On the Typewriter, 'In the Cage,' at the Ouija Board." *Textual Practice* 13 (Spring 1999): 5–23.

Tompkins, Jane P. " 'The Beast in the Jungle': An Analysis of James's Late Style." *Modern Fiction Studies* 16 (1970): 185–91.

• Veeder, William. "The Aspern Portrait," *The Henry James Review* 20 (Winter 1999): 22–42.

———. "Toxic Mothers, Cultural Criticism: 'In the Cage' and Elsewhere." *The Henry James Review* 14 (Fall 1993): 264–72.

Wardley, Lynn. "Reassembling 'Daisy Miller.' " *American Literary History* 3 (Summer 1991): 232–54.

Wegelin, Christof. "Art and Life in James's 'The Middle Years.' " *Modern Fiction Studies* 33 (Winter 1987): 639–46.

———. "Henry James and the Aristocracy." *Northwest Review* 1 (Spring 1958): 5–14.

Whitsitt, Sam. "A Lesson in Reading: Henry James's 'The Real Thing.' " *The Henry James Review* 16 (Fall 1995): 304–14.

Wilkinson, Myler. "Henry James and the Ethical Moment." *The Henry James Review* 11 (Fall 1990): 153–75.

Winner, Viola Hopkins. "Pictorialism in Henry James's Theory of the Novel." *Criticism* 9 (Winter 1967): 1–21.

Zwinger, Lynda. "Henry James Returned." *Arizona Quarterly* 53 (Winter 1997): 1–6.